Fate &
Fortune

Books by Fern Michaels

Sweet Vengeance
Holly and Ivy
Fancy Dancer
No Safe Secret
Wishes for Christmas
About Face
Perfect Match
A Family Affair
Forget Me Not
The Blossom Sisters
Balancing Act
Tuesday's Child
Betrayal
Southern Comfort
To Taste the Wine
Sins of the Flesh
Sins of Omission
Return to Sender
Mr. and Miss Anonymous
Up Close and Personal
Fool Me Once
Picture Perfect
The Future Scrolls
Kentucky Sunrise
Kentucky Heat
Kentucky Rich
Plain Jane
Charming Lily
What You Wish For
The Guest List
Listen to Your Heart
Celebration
Yesterday
Finders Keepers
Annie's Rainbow

Sara's Song
Vegas Sunrise
Vegas Heat
Vegas Rich
Whitefire
Wish List
Dear Emily
Christmas at Timberwoods
Fate & Fortune

The Sisterhood Novels

Need to Know
Crash and Burn
Point Blank
In Plain Sight
Eyes Only
Kiss and Tell
Blindsided
Gotcha!
Home Free
Déjà Vu
Cross Roads
Game Over
Deadly Deals
Vanishing Act
Razor Sharp
Under the Radar
Final Justice
Collateral Damage
Fast Track
Hokus Pokus
Hide and Seek
Free Fall
Lethal Justice
Sweet Revenge

Books by Fern Michaels (*cont.*)

The Jury
Vendetta
Payback
Weekend Warriors

The Men of the
Sisterhood Novels
Truth or Dare
High Stakes
Fast and Loose
Double Down

The Godmothers Series
Getaway (E-Novella
  Exclusive)
Spirited Away
(E-Novella Exclusive)
Hideaway (E-Novella
  Exclusive)
Classified
Breaking News
Deadline
Late Edition
Exclusive
The Scoop

E-Book Exclusives
Desperate Measures
Seasons of Her Life
To Have and to Hold
Serendipity
Captive Innocence

Captive Embraces
Captive Passions
Captive Secrets
Captive Splendors
Cinders to Satin
For All Their Lives
Texas Heat
Texas Rich
Texas Fury
Texas Sunrise

Anthologies
Mistletoe Magic
Winter Wishes
The Most Wonderful Time
When the Snow Falls
Secret Santa
A Winter Wonderland
I'll Be Home for
  Christmas
Making Spirits Bright
Holiday Magic
Snow Angels
Silver Bells
Comfort and Joy
Sugar and Spice
Let It Snow
A Gift of Joy
Five Golden Rings
Deck the Halls
Jingle All the Way

Published by Kensington Publishing Corporation

FERN MICHAELS

Fate & Fortune

ZEBRA BOOKS
KENSINGTON PUBLISHING CORP.
http://www.kensingtonbooks.com

ZEBRA BOOKS are published by

Kensington Publishing Corp.
119 West 40th Street
New York, NY 10018

Compilation copyright © 2018 by Kensington Publishing Corporation
Vixen in Velvet copyright © 1976 by Roberta Anderson & Mary Kuczkir
Whitefire copyright © 1978 by First Draft, Inc.; copyright © 2011 by MRK
Productions
Vixen in Velvet was originally published in September 1976 by Ballantine
Books, a division of Random House, Inc.

Fern Michaels is a registered trademark of KAP 5, Inc.

All Kensington titles, imprints, and distributed lines are available at special quantity discounts for bulk purchases for sales promotion, premiums, fundraising, educational, or institutional use. For details, write or phone the office of the Kensington Sales Manager: Attn.: Sales Department. Kensington Publishing Corp., 119 West 40th Street, New York, NY 10018. Phone: 1-800-221-2647.

Zebra and the Z logo Reg. U.S. Pat. & TM Off.

First Zebra Books Mass-Market Paperback Printing: June 2018
ISBN-13: 978-1-4201-1155-2
ISBN-10: 1-4201-1155-8

eISBN-13: 978-1-4201-4853-4
eISBN-10: 1-4201-4853-2

10 9 8 7 6 5 4 3 2 1

Printed in the United States of America

Contents

To
Tom Carpini—with Scarblade's thanks

Vixen in Velvet

Chapter One

A myriad of golds and oranges was fast fading into the gray that precedes nightfall. With the setting sun, the warm summer air was taking on the chill of early autumn. Dusk was growing deeper as the ornate coach drew to a halt long enough for the liveried footman to jump down from his seat next to the driver and light the pewter-sconced lanterns alongside the doors.

Lord Nelson Rawlings, distracted from his thoughts, sat uneasily in the plush interior and gazed into the pool of yellow light the lanterns spilled onto the hard, rutted road.

When the coach started again, Lord Rawlings tried in vain to settle himself comfortably in his jouncing seat.

"These roads are a horror," he complained to his three companions. "If we aren't killed before we get home it won't be any fault of the driver. I daresay he has yet to miss one rut in this—" He stumbled over the curses which caught in his throat in deference to his wife and daughter and completed his statement in a garbled voice, "—road!"

"Yes, Nelson, you must speak to the driver, this trip is unbearable! Every bone in my body aches," Lady Rawlings said in a soft, high, childlike voice.

"We have but two hours to ride and we'll be home, my dear," the lord assured his wife in soothing tones. "We must be brave and put up with these inconvenient conditions. After all, we did enjoy the summer at our country home. Now it's time to realize the hardships of travel."

"You're right, Nelson," Lady Lydia Rawlings concurred, her small delicate face lighting up at the thought that soon they would be home in their London quarters.

Once more, Lord Rawlings leaned back on the heavily padded seat and closed his eyes. His stomach was punishing him cruelly for the greasy lunch he had bolted down. Way-station food! he complained silently, as the dull ache was fast becoming more insistent, cramping his innards into tight fists. He fumbled in his vest coat for his mints and withdrew a plain, shell box which held the small, white cubes.

"Stomach troubling you, dear?" Lady Lydia asked with concern.

"Nothing to worry about," Lord Rawlings grumbled as he deftly hid the box within the palm of his hand. He didn't want Lady Lydia to notice that his gold pill box had been replaced by one so inferior. Lord Rawlings emitted a sigh, and replaced the case in his vest coat. It seemed to him he had spent the entire summer concealing small items of value within the folds of his coat and driving to the money lenders and pawnbrokers to exact the pittance of cash the items would bring. Under no circumstances did Lord Rawlings want his treasured wife to know the hard straits which the family now faced.

What was he to do? Since he had lost favor with the Crown and his rental lands had been seized, he had been sinking deeper and deeper into debt. Rawlings knew that once he was again in London the creditors would be after him with a vengeance. There was nowhere to turn. He had exhausted every possibility before leaving the city.

He shook his head and opened his eyes and let them

come to rest on the beautiful face of his daughter Victoria, who was seated across from him. His heart smiled as he gazed on her. A bonnet covered her golden hair but for a few wisps which escaped at her high forehead. Green eyes flecked with gold enhanced her pink and white complexion. Heavy, dark lashes fringed those strikingly colored eyes and concealed them from his view.

There was no other way, he debated with himself; he would have to sacrifice his daughter to Lord Fowler-Greene. As Rawlings thought of that portly gentleman who was older than himself, his stomach issued a sharp stab. He had wrestled with the problem throughout the summer. Victoria was twenty-two years old, much beyond the age when most girls married. Yet, he argued, this was the eighteenth century—modern times! It was foolish to consider as spirited a girl as Victoria an old maid, a spinster past her prime.

Still, he was getting on in years himself, he would be fifty-nine next birthday, and he wanted to see Victoria settled nicely. In case something should happen to him, he needn't worry what would become of Lady Lydia. Victoria would see to her mother's comforts and Victoria's husband would see to Lady Lydia's bills. And what person was more able than the wealthy Lord Fowler-Greene?

Although the general consensus held that Fowler-Greene was an overaged fop, Lord Rawlings had long ago decided that the guise of dandy covered a keen intelligence and a dedication to duty that very few were ever able to discern.

The lofty Lord Fowler-Greene had long had his eye on Victoria, and upon hearing of Lord Rawlings' difficulties, had more or less offered to help the latter out of his enigmatical problems, provided of course, that Lord Fowler-Greene would win a place in the Rawlings family, preferably as a son-in-law. All Lord Nelson had to do was convince his daughter that Lord Fowler-Greene would make a most suitable husband.

After the first encounter with Victoria concerning Lord Fowler-Greene, in which she unleashed an incredible verbal attack on him, the girl had not said another word on the subject. But Lord Rawlings was not one to be fooled into letting down his defenses. If he knew anything of anyone, it was his own daughter, and he knew the worst was yet to come on the subject of this marriage.

She was a wild one, he would give her that. Lady Lydia had long ago thrown up her hands in despair at their daughter's brazenness and unruly tongue. Nelson, too, had oft chosen to look the other way, but he also knew that if his circumstances were to come to her notice, she loved him enough to do anything for him, even marry a man she could hold no affection for. But he did not want it that way. He would have Victoria's cooperation because she thought it best for herself, because he would convince her she needed a strong man. He would rather have her wild and screaming, kicking at the idea, than have her quiet and complacent, silently suffering.

He took another look at his beloved daughter as she rested her head against the back of the seat. Her expression was sweet in repose, like an angel. Lord Rawlings shuddered again as he thought of how her remarkable eyes could freeze someone in his tracks one moment and, then, flash and change to so beguiling an expression that a person wished to stay in her presence indefinitely.

"Are you taking a chill, dear?" Lady Lydia asked solicitously.

Shaken from his reverie, Lord Rawlings answered, "No!" more abruptly than he intended. More than likely his conscience was guilty over the slight matter of selling his daughter into bondage. Still, there was no other way, and he must provide for Lydia. Sweet Lydia. His gaze rested on his wife's face as he ached to reach out and touch her. The same golden hair as her daughter's, paler now, peeked out from under her bonnet. Chapeau, he corrected himself. Lydia always referred to her hats as chapeau. His eyes raked over her slim body as he thought she'd not gained an ounce since their wedding.

Lady Lydia, too, had married for convenience, yet Lord Rawlings believed that she had come to love him. Not as much, surely, as he loved her, but enough to make him secure, enough to care about him and worry about his welfare. Dear, sweet Lydia. Her loyalty was much to be admired, even in the face of her only child marrying a man who was so much her senior. She had stated simply to Victoria, "If your father wishes it, darling, then it must be so." He imagined that when she and Victoria were alone, Lydia had spoken to Victoria of her own arranged marriage and tried to show the girl how well things worked out after all.

"Granger," Victoria called softly to her cousin, the fourth member of their party, who was seated next to her father. "Are you asleep?"

"No, Tori. Damned if I can sleep with this carriage jostling about." Granger cast an eye on his uncle, Lord Rawlings, and apologized. "Sorry, sir."

Lord Rawlings muttered something under his breath and turned his head toward the window. Granger gave his cousin a bold wink. Tori, as she was known to her family, laughed lightly as she glanced toward her father. Granger was always blaspheming, much to Lord Rawlings' annoyance, and Granger was constantly apologizing for it.

"Granger, please tell us of the highwaymen. The stories you tell are always so exciting, and we could all do with a bit of amusement. How do you know so much about highwaymen?" As an afterthought Tori added, "Gentleman that you are."

Granger Lapid glanced at his uncle warily. Why did Tori insist on upsetting the applecart by reminding Lord Rawlings of his knowledge of the nefarious characters that plagued the roads of England? The little minx, he thought, she likes nothing better than the bit of excitement that occurs whenever my presence is made known to Uncle Nelson.

Tori cast her green eyes on her cousin and did not fail to note his discomfiture. A smile played over her full lips and she lowered her heavy lashes to conceal her amusement. Poor Granger, she thought, so cowed by Father. Perhaps if he did not have to rely upon Father for his keep he would demonstrate more backbone. As she watched him it seemed as though she could see through his thin, wiry body directly to the spine which she was sure was absent from his anatomy. Granger nervously ruffled his light-brown hair, and a pinched expression played about his thin features.

"Go ahead, amuse the child," growled Rawlings. "If she hasn't the sense to see you've no knowledge of anything, much less the deeds and secrets of those scoundrels who plague our roads, then she hasn't the sense to be affected by your tall tales."

Granger looked questioningly at Tori, and she could see the hurt her father's statement had caused him. She was sorry she was the instigator. Tori was well aware that Granger indeed knew criminals and highwaymen. But she could never defend him to Lord Rawlings; to do so would be to admit that Granger visited those dark cellars and disreputable inns those felonious scoundrels frequented. Granger, not having the heart for a rogue's way of life, nevertheless sought his thrills by association with thieves and through those acqaintances, however remote, gained for himself some measure of importance.

"My dear Tori," Granger said in a nasal tone which he knew irritated her, "everyone knows about the highwaymen. They are a passel of thieving rogues. There is one in particular, Scarblade. They say he has a black heart, and," he added ominously, "he does not care whether he robs women or men. He shows no favoritism."

"How absolutely delightful. I should dearly love to be robbed by Scarblade." Her eyes lit up and took on a sparkle that set Granger's nerves on edge. He knew his cousin well.

She would go out of her way to be robbed if it were possible.

"Tori, you are impossible," Granger said sourly. "I, for one, don't want to be robbed. First of all, I have not even a farthing to my name." For an example he turned out the satin lining from his trousers' pockets for her to see. "What do you think Scarblade would do when I tell him I have nothing to give?"

"Why he would probably slit your throat. I do so hope it doesn't happen today," she said, fingering the fine yellow muslin of her skirt. "Blood does spurt so." Granger paled perceptibly as he looked at the laughing eyes of his cousin. "Please don't worry, Granger; if it happens I will throw myself at the mercy of this Scarblade and plead for your life. I'll tell him I'll do anything to save you. Besides, if I absolutely must, I can defend myself." She added, pouting her full, pretty mouth, "It's not been so long since you taught me to throw a knife. I am quite an accurate marksman, if you remember."

Granger blanched and nervously glanced at his uncle. He had been accused so frequently of teaching Tori unladylike behavior that he had almost forgotten it was Tori, not he, who led the way in social transgressions.

"It will make no difference, my dear cousin, this man wants only money and jewels. He doesn't care what he does to get them. A man's blood on his hands would not concern him. But I will tell you this: If we can get through the next few miles without being accosted, then we'll make it home safely. This section of the road is Scarblade's lair."

Lord Rawlings groaned aloud and Granger began to tell him that what he had spoken was the truth when he realized his uncle's disinterest. Granger knew when he was being ignored and allowed the matter to pass. What he did not know was that Lord Rawlings was thinking that if they should be robbed, his last shilling would be taken and he would be even more beset by financial worries.

Tori noted her father's attitude and prodded Granger further. "Do you really think this is his lair? And that we'll be robbed and our throats cut?" she asked softly, in an effort not to disturb Lord Rawlings.

Lady Lydia gasped, "Cut your hair? I won't hear of it! Did you hear the child, Nelson? She wants to cut her hair! My dear," she said, not waiting for a reply from her husband, "only madwomen and criminals have their hair cut. I won't have it! Do you hear? I never heard of such a thing! Foolish girl, what will you think of next? I knew it was a mistake to let you play in the kitchens when you were a child. I forbid it, Tori! Now let the matter rest. I want to hear no more of it!"

Resigned, Tori nodded her head. She knew from past experience it did no good to explain that her dear mother had misunderstood. Lady Lydia's hearing had been getting worse of late. Tori and her father pretended there was nothing the matter, for vanity's sake. But now, Tori wondered, what *would* she look like with her hair cut?

"What does Scarblade look like, Granger?"

"He's handsome, all right, at least that's what the ladies say. A scar on his left cheek in the shape of an S that flames brightly with the heat of passion. S for seduction," Granger smirked. "I've heard in town that one or two wealthy ladies have actually made arrangements for him to rob them a second time. A slip of the tongue, a casual mention, next they know they've found themselves in his clutches once again."

"Imagine that," Tori mused, "making arrangements to be robbed. Tell me more."

"He's said to have coal-black eyes. He rides a magnificent chestnut stallion that makes him ten feet tall. That's all I can tell you, Tori." Warily, Granger eyed the dusty windows and prayed silently that Scarblade was somewhere else this day.

"Oh," Tori breathed, enraptured by the tale, "I would like to meet this man."

"Victoria!" Lord Rawlings shouted, shocked at the words coming from his daughter, though why he was stunned was beyond him. She had been doing much as she pleased since she had learned to walk. It would be just like the girl to make an appointment to be robbed by this uncouth fellow. "I want no further talk of this nonsense!"

Tori always remained calm under her father's furious gaze and sudden shouts. She knew his bluff, she had cut her teeth on his outrages. Inwardly, Tori believed he had a kind heart, even to where Granger was concerned. Besides, she mused, the poor old darling really was frightened by Granger's story. She stifled a smile as she noticed Lord Rawlings fumble in his waistcoat for his purse.

Suddenly a shout from the top of the coach and the quickening of speed made the occupants fall over in helter-skelter positions.

"What is it? What's happened?" Lady Lydia quivered.

"I think we're about to be robbed," Tori laughed, as the pounding of hooves could be heard coming from behind the coach and thundering closer.

Chapter Two

As the yellow light from the side lanterns swayed back and forth, Tori could see the decidedly green cast to her cousin's pale face. She couldn't help but prod the barb again.

"Don't look so sick," she hissed. "Haven't I already promised you I would do everything possible to save your throat?"

Granger shot her back a venomous look and sneered through clenched teeth. "Hold your tongue, Tori. You shall be lucky if your own life is spared."

Lord Rawlings said in a whisper, "Hold! The pair of you! For if the robber spares your lives, I promise you I shan't!"

Lady Lydia, whimpering to herself in fright, came around long enough to side with her husband. "Tori, now is not the time for your ill jokes! Hush!"

Peering out the window, Tori could see that the coach had finally stopped in a thickly wooded glade. She heard scuffling atop the coach as the footmen were forced from their seats. A wave of fear washed over her, and in her ears a roaring sound echoed, making it hard for her to hear exactly what was happening outside.

Abruptly, the coach door opened and an authoritative voice boomed over the roar in her head, commanding the passengers to come forth.

Tori grasped her mother's hand, and with the help of one of the highwaymen they stepped down. Lord Rawlings and Granger were close behind.

Three men in rough clothing stood in a semicircle, while a giant of a man sat astride a huge chestnut. All wore soiled cloths, with eyeholes, tied around their heads, covering half their faces.

Tori tried to see the rider of the stallion in the deepening light, knowing she had the advantage because the coach lanterns were to her back and the thieves were bathed in yellow light.

"Your money and your jewels!" the rider demanded imperiously.

"Why should I give you my jewels?" Tori asked. "Who are you that you hide behind a mask and dare not show your face? I refuse to part with the emerald ring that I carry in my pocket!" she said brashly.

"Oh, no!" Granger muttered. Standing as close to Tori as he was, he could feel the quivering of her body. The vixen, Granger thought angrily, she's enjoying every moment of this. The little fool will see us killed!

"I think you will be more than glad to hand over your valuables," the man astride the chestnut replied in a dangerous tone.

"You sound very sure of yourself. Masked bandit, I have no intention of handing anything over to you, much less my ring! And you dare not molest a lady!"

Lord Rawlings stepped forward and grasped his daughter's arm, pulling her back from the point to which she had advanced during her last speech. "Forgive her, sir," he addressed the horseman, "'tis but my addlepated daughter. She's not the sense she was born with. An embarrassment to my wife and myself." He tapped his head near his temple and nodded despairingly. "We're just returning from the country where she was staying. The doctor said she would be better, but now I'm afraid all this excitement has only brought her back to her former, invalid state."

"Father!"

"Calm yourself, child, else you'll find yourself back at the house in the country," he hissed through clenched teeth as he grasped Tori's arm cruelly. Lady Lydia, unable to control herself any longer, began a fit of weeping, and Lord Rawlings left her to herself, feeling it would serve to convince the robbers of the sad state of their daughter.

Tori, resigned to being quiet for the moment, took to studying the three men who surrounded her and her family. They wore incongruous hats; brushed beavers and silk toppers, quite incompatible with their shoddy, rusty black suits, and no doubt supplied by their past victims. One of the three smiled at her lewdly, showing broken, rotted teeth. Tori felt disappointed. Granger had always said the highwaymen were handsome, but these were no more than street beggars. Feeling repulsed by the robber's lecherous smile, Tori retreated backward a step. Granger came close behind her and whispered, "What do you think you're doing? You don't even have an emerald ring! You'll kill us all yet, Tori!"

"Silence!" the lead horseman thundered. "I will repeat myself once more only: Your money and your jewels."

"Pay no heed to my daughter," Lord Rawlings protested in a commanding tone. "She is but a child and I can assure you, she owns no such ring. None of us have any monies or jewels. My wife wears only her wedding band, surely you would not deprive her of that small trinket?"

"If what you say is true, no. But such cannot be the case. You are persons of some quality and I see by the coach that you bear a seal of Parliament. Up to now I have been patient, but it is wearing thin. I am known to give only one warning, then the result you will bear alone. Now, hand to my men your money and jewels!"

"Nelson, why does he keep calling us fools?" Lady Lydia whimpered.

"Hush, dear. All will be well," Lord Rawlings comforted.

"And if we do not, will you slit our throats, Masked Bandit?" Tori demanded. "Will you draw and quarter us? Will you drag my mother and myself off to your lair and make slaves of us? Take me!" she cried dramatically, "for I will never part with my precious ring. It was given to me by my betrothed."

"Tori, for God's sake, keep still!" Granger hissed.

"Come here!" the rider demanded.

Brazenly, Tori walked to within a foot of the huge stallion and looked up into the face of the highwayman.

"Is it true? Would you become my slave rather than part with your betrothal ring?"

Tori nodded, suddenly at a loss for words. She had never seen such black eyes. He was a handsome brute, even with his face half covered. When he spoke to her, he punctuated his statement with a smile and Tori saw that his teeth were white and strong and, more, they all seemed accounted for, no gaping holes in this smile. He sat on the horse with an ease that made him and the magnificent beast seem as one. A lover of horseflesh, Tori found herself distractedly trying to keep her hand from feeling the hot, quivering animal.

"Beware of your answer," the horseman shouted. "One word from you and your family could be dead in seconds. Think carefully!"

His shouts had startled the chestnut, and the bandit felt the beast begin to rear up in fear. Tori, too, saw the horse move and she reached her hand out to touch its muzzle. Her gesture had the required effect, the stallion calmed. Its rider found himself awed by the girl's knowledge of horses and admired the stance she took in the face of danger.

"No!" Tori exclaimed softly. Suddenly, she started to tremble, shaking in her shoes. She had gone too far. She could read murder in the black eyes. "Let my family go. They mean you no harm. We have no money with us. My cousin is destitute. We are returning from our summer home and our luggage and personal belongings have gone before us in a flatwagon. I beg of you, let my family go!"

"You plead prettily for your family. Is this true what you say? Don't lie to me, for I can seek you out within an hour's time and have you all murdered in your beds."

"It is the truth," Tori said meekly.

"I will spare them if you give me the ring."

"I can't do that. It's from my betrothed."

"You must love this man very much to be willing to die for his ring."

"With all my heart," Tori said quietly.

Suddenly, without a moment's warning, a long arm reached down and grasped Tori under the shoulders. Feeling herself being lifted from the ground, she struggled, but the man's grip was firm.

He lifted her in one swoop onto the saddle before him. So quick was his action, Tori found herself caught between excitement and fear. Turning her head to face him, she determined to brave out her predicament. From somewhere she could hear her father making noises demanding her release, but his words became indistinct. Looking into dark, brooding eyes, Tori gazed at the deep curling scar that ran across the highwayman's cheekbone. It stood out sharply in the dim evening light. The girl fought an almost uncontrollable urge to reach up and caress the snakelike indentation. As the man's jaw tightened the scar moved to form a letter S. Tori's thoughts choked her as she remembered Granger's smirk and his words, "S for seduction!"

Forcing her gaze away from the fascinating line, Tori found herself locked in a stare with the highwayman. In his night-dark orbs there was an excitement, a passion! Her heaving breaths knotted in her throat.

The fast-fading light of late evening threw Tori in shadow.

Scarblade peered beneath the brim of her bonnet but could not see her face. He could only discern a loveliness there and a voluptuousness of figure as a ray of light from the lanterns on the carriage slashed across her rising bosom. He noted her scent, the feel of her weight against his thighs, and the slim fragility of her ribs encased within the silkiness of her gown.

Tori sensed his appraisal of her and her senses reeled as she became aware of his masculine scent mixed with the pungent smell of horse sweat. Feeling the rippling muscles beneath her, she noted a stirring tautness in his loins. Her breath came in choking rasps. She felt his fingers pressing into her ribs, drawing her imperceptibly closer. Then, just as she sensed he would kiss her, she became frightened of her own soaring emotions. Drawing away from him, she cut the air between them with a sharp retort. "Don't tell me you're that facetious sort of highwayman who warrants laughter in the ladies' bedchambers. That most low and ridiculous form of scoundrel known as a 'kissing bandit'!"

The highwayman froze, struck by her words, angered that she had sensed his intentions. "I give you your choice: You will hand over the ring or I will take it from you."

Tori could feel his breath upon her cheek and was aware of the oddly disconcerted emotions he stirred in her by his nearness. Slowly, Tori searched the pocket of her gown, her fingers grasped the small ring and withdrew it. She felt the wild beating of his heart as she leaned against her accoster. Her own fluttered madly within her breast and she felt herself being gently lowered to the ground. Half falling, she quickly regained her balance and stood tall.

"If you must have it, then it is yours." She tossed the ring into the air and watched as it was deftly snatched by Scarblade.

"That's enough, child; quickly now, come here to us," Lord Rawlings sputtered.

"Yes, please, dear," Lady Lydia entreated, a tinge of hysteria edging her voice.

"You hear your parents," Granger hissed, "now come here to us!"

Heedless of the frantic words of her family, Tori was only aware of the eyes of the highwayman upon her and their thinly veiled desire.

"I think, sir," she said haughtily, "we shall meet again one day. I am allowing you to safeguard the ring for me— one never knows in these times what dangerous men are lurking about on the highways. I trust you will guard it well!"

The bandit's jet eyes bore through her, and to her terror she discerned the scar on his cheek had deepened in color.

Chapter Three

Hidden in a woody glade, the bandit Scarblade quieted his nervous chestnut and watched the Rawlings' ornate coach rumble by. He took no pleasure in these robberies and found it hard to believe that he, Marcus Chancelor, would land himself in this unlikely position.

Like the pages of a calendar flipping backwards, his memory brought him to a point in time less than a year ago, and there before him were the reasons behind his banditry.

Evening fell silently on his sprawling, two-storied white clapboard home, wrapping the Carolina countryside in tender arms. He paced the spacious half-beamed room impatiently, stopping now and again to peer out the mullioned windows into the darkness, anticipating the sight of the horse-drawn cart. Marcus's long, easy strides were unhindered by the provincial furnishings that graced the room.

Carver, a manservant, entered the informal sitting room with a questioning look in his watery eyes. "Excuse me, sir, but your father isn't home yet?"

Marcus turned abruptly to face the elderly Carver. "No,

dammit, and if you come in here once more asking for him, I swear I'll skin your hide!"

Carver watched his young master, a sullen expression drawing the corners of his wide mouth downward.

"Yes, sir."

"Sorry, Carver," Marcus apologized. "If it weren't for the damn Indians, I wouldn't be so jumpy. Samuel's not as young as he thinks he is, and he might take on more than he can handle. You know how the Indians in the North Carolina area are plaguing the colonists with frequent raids and war parties."

"I know, sir. They just love to torment us." Carver mumbled to himself.

In two easy strides Marcus reached the desk in the corner of the room. He toyed nervously with the familiar rolls of blueprints, his ears pricked for the sound of approaching horses. He picked up the heavy parchments and opened them as he had on many occasions, studying the white lines etched in the thin coating of blue wax. These were the plans for the house that was in progress on the other side of the rise, closer to the river. The house his mother had dreamed of and which his father, Samuel, had promised to build for her. Now it was to be a shrine to her memory, she being dead these twenty-four years. Samuel was determined to see the house built just as she had dreamed, before he was called to rest beside her for all eternity.

Carefully, Marcus rolled the parchment and replaced it on the desk. Sorrowfully, he doubted his father would ever realize his ambition. Materials were expensive when one had to purchase them on the black market, and the constant threat of Indians made progress slow. Twice now they had burned the strong cedar beams to the ground, and Samuel, refusing to admit defeat, had sighed wearily, cursed soundly, and had begun over again.

Marcus punched the fist of one hand into the palm of the other, the soft buckskin of his shirt tightening across the bunching muscles of his back. "Blast and damn!" he swore just before he heard the anticipated sound of hooves on the path to the cabin. He raced to the window, his moccasins soundless on the rough wooden floor.

Carver hurried to the door as fast as his big, thick calloused feet would carry him. "I heard them. I know I did. Now don't you go teasing an old man."

Marcus paid no attention to the wiry man and pushed ahead of him, putting Carver at a distinct disadvantage as he tried to stretch his knobby old frame to see out in the darkness over Marcus's tall bulk.

Samuel Chancelor and Myles Lampton slowly climbed out of the flat black wagon, the ancient boards of the vehicle squeaking in protest at each man's portliness. Marcus stepped out of the lighted house to greet his father and the old man's lifelong friend. One look at Marcus's worried face and Samuel hurried to explain their absence to his son. In a voice which matched his son's deep timbre, Samuel told Marcus of an emergency meeting of the Chancelor's Valley Association.

Marcus, not satisfied with his father's excuse, berated the old gentleman. "But why did you and Myles leave so suddenly? Surely there was time enough to send me word in the lower acres. I would have gone with you."

"Now, son. Don't go fretting again. There'll be time for that later. Right now I want you to hear what Myles and I have to say."

Marcus settled back in the small provincial chair—his size and bulk incompatible with the furniture's delicacy. He studied Myles Lampton, measuring his face for a clue as to what they were referring to, knowing the man's countenance was more open and readable than Samuel's. Seeing no sign there, Marcus instead turned his concentration to Samuel.

"We were at a meeting of tradesmen and farmers," Samuel began, "and some of those rapscallions we're forced to deal with. Those bandits have boosted their prices again and they know we're at their mercy." Samuel was referring to the black-market traders who were the mainstay of Chancelor's Valley.

"Naturally we once again were forced to agree to their prices."

Myles broke into the conversation. "Yes, Marc, they only offered us half of what our tobacco is worth and demanded five times the worth for what they've smuggled."

"Marcus can imagine what went on, Myles," Samuel said impatiently. "Get to the point. Can't you see he is near jumping out of his skin to know?"

"All right. Here it is, Marcus: The Chancelor's Valley Association has decided to send you to England to plead our case directly to the King."

"I won't go!" Marcus stormed, his voice booming. "I'm needed here with you! What can I do that our *'honorable statesmen'* have not done?" he demanded sarcastically.

"You've every right to feel that way," Samuel soothed. "We all believe we're being sold down the river by our House of Lords, and our colonial governors." That's why someone from Chancelor's Valley must go and plead our case. Someone who is educated, well spoken, and authoritative. You were educated in England, hence you're the logical choice."

Marcus looked at his father and knew that Sam would never suggest the plan to him if he weren't convinced it was the best for all concerned. The unselfishness of his father struck him once again. It would be as difficult for Samuel to send his son across the ocean as it would be for Marcus to leave. Samuel had not displayed the best of health lately, and Marcus felt the old man had not much time left. Well, he wanted that time, he demanded it. He wouldn't leave Samuel alone here with Carver, with himself months and an ocean away.

"There are others as suited for the 'honor' as I," Marcus insisted.

"It's all arranged," Samuel broke in, his face an older replica of his son's, displaying the same authority. He did not fail to see the faint, barely discernible scar on Marcus's cheek turn a deep crimson. In anger the scar twisted like a slithering snake, wrested into the shape of an S by the tightening of his jaw. While he was still a student, a trip to Paris and a dalliance with the young and beautiful wife of a dragoon had precipitated a duel with rapiers which had left Marcus's left cheek inscribed.

Samuel had never been able to induce Marcus to speak of it, but he knew from witnesses that Marc had allowed himself to be cut rather than kill the French army officer, whose sense of honor demanded he fight to the death.

Samuel looked at Marcus with clinical interest; the scar did not detract from his handsome features. On the contrary, it made him a dashing rogue, a man to be reckoned with.

"You'll travel to Boston," said Samuel, "and there you'll meet Jason Elias. He is captain of his own ship and a trusted friend. He has guaranteed you passage and, above all, any assistance he can give you." Samuel's face wore the closed look Marcus knew so well. The look stated that, in Samuel's mind, the decision had been reached and there would be no need for further argument. Marcus felt a swollen, hard lump in his chest and knew his arguments would be fruitless.

"Think about it, son, that's all I ask. Think about it!"

"Marcus, your father's right. Think about it," Myles added, his round, heavy face flushed from brandy. "Chancelor's Valley seems to be lacking in eligible young ladies suited to your taste. In England you'll have the flower of womanhood to choose from—that would be to your liking, I think. A gentle mixture of business and pleasure, eh, Marc?"

Myles Lampton was taken aback by the scowl on Marcus's face, and he glanced at Samuel, who was evidently amused by his son's reaction.

"You'll get nowhere with that statement, Myles. Marcus's view of women is disdainful, to say the least. What is it you call them? Grasping, greedy, and willing to ride the back of any man to attain their ends?"

The white heat of anger rose to Marcus's features. "I have yet to find evidence to the contrary. Women are a breed unto themselves. Grasping and greedy, true, but that is a trait common to men as well as women. What I find so abominable is the conspiracy to be found between them and others of their sex. From birth they are raised and schooled in the talents to snare a man into marriage and use him to supply all those things which they feel are their due. And all the while they wink and smile at one another, bragging of what they suppose is their ingenuous charm in twisting a man, a mere mortal, around their little fingers. It would not occur to a woman to be sincere and forthright, not when flattery and trickery will profit her."

Samuel sighed heavily, the image of grandchildren at his knee fading into oblivion. "I think, Myles, that Marcus has been too long in male society."

"But Sam, what of that bit of scandal concerning Marcus and the attractive wife of the wealthy shipbuilder that filtered down to the valley last winter?"

"All true, Myles," Samuel answered, enjoying Marcus's discomfort. "Marcus may deride women for their faults, but that does not hinder him from enjoying their charms. I've almost given up hope for grandchildren. It seems as though I'm destined to die a lonely old man with an embittered, bachelor son for my only company."

"Don't make me laugh, Sam," Marcus smiled, calling his father by his Christian name as he had been wont to do since he was a boy. "I can only promise you this; if I should ever find a woman who contradicts all I've said about her sex and who offers a great personal sacrifice for the betterment of another, I would snatch her up and carry her to the valley immediately."

Myles looked sympathetically at his friend Samuel. "It would seem, Samuel, that your visions of grandchildren are indeed futile."

"Marcus has yet to learn, Myles, that life has its way of turning the oddest corners. Marcus has not yet met the young woman who will make him eat his words. I can only hope that when he does it will not be too late. Who knows, you may be correct, Myles. Marcus just may meet the young woman to suit him in England," Samuel said pointedly in his son's direction, settling once and for all the question of Marcus's pleading their case with the King.

Not caring to hear any more, Marcus rose from the chair and walked out into the clear, crisp night.

Moments later, Myles Lampton joined him, puffing on a long-stemmed pipe, exhaling fragrant clouds of smoke. "Marc, Sam would never ask this of you if he didn't think the situation warranted your going. Here we are, well over a hundred families striving to make a living off this new land. The Indians have raided and plundered our granaries and burned our fields, and still we remain. And why? Because the people here in Chancelor's Valley have the courage to stand up for their rights. We are a community peopled with political refugees. Men who have spoken out against the corruption of our governors. So, in retribution, we are virtual prisoners. The King has placed an embargo on our products, a blockade on our port. He's forbidden any trade with us from our neighbors. Marc," Myles said vehemently, "we are being starved out of existence. I know it pains you to leave Samuel . . . if I'm any judge, he's on the decline. But when he asked you to think about it, I believe he was telling you to give a thought to how he would feel if Chancelor's Valley, a community named for Sam himself, were to be driven out of existence. That would kill him more quickly than any ailment on the face of this earth. Sam himself suggested you as the man for the job. The others would have come to the same conclusion sooner or later, but the fact is, Sam wants you to do this, indeed, *needs* you to do this . . . for him."

The sun burned its way through the thin morning fog so typical of England at the start of summer.

Marcus left the dining hall of the House of Lords with the sound of those revered gentlemen's jeers in his ears. He had failed, miserably. He could feel his soul retreat into a small, dark corner of his heart. What was he to do? How could he return to North Carolina and tell his father that the King had refused his audience? For two weeks he had hounded the King's secretary to no avail. Then, thinking himself to have a better chance if someone from the House of Lords would plead his cause, he had tried persistently for an audience with one of these gentlemen. Here, too, he had failed. Finally, in desperation, he tricked and bribed his way into an early luncheon, and there, with his heart on his sleeve, Marcus told the lords of the plight of his people. Their answer was to have him thrown out on his ear.

A hackney driver called to him begging a fare. Marcus waved him on, preferring to walk back to his lodgings. His heart was heavy, his pride wounded. He wanted to smash out at something, someone. He heard the sound of his name being called, and he turned to see a footman running down the wide, cobblestoned street after him, waving a piece of paper in his hand. Marcus stopped and waited for the footman to catch up with him.

"Mr. Chancelor! Mr. Chancelor," the footman cried breathlessly, "wait, please, sir!" Marcus stood in his tracks until the footman reached him and handed him the piece of paper. "'Tis from Lord Fowler-Greene, sir, he expects a reply."

With trembling hands, Marcus opened the paper. There,

in a broad, scratchy hand, was an invitation to come to the Lord's home and discuss his problem further. "I promise you nothing," the note stated, "but perhaps we can come to some kind of agreement beneficial to both of us."

"Tell Lord Fowler-Greene I shall gladly come to his home at the appointed hour."

Still trembling with anticipation, Marcus bounded into the road to hail down the first hackney that came his way. This hope was too good to keep to himself. He had to get back to his rooms and share the news with Josh.

Josh will be as hopeful as I, Marcus thought exultantly. He could almost see the great blond giant dancing with glee and he could imagine him reaching for the brandy and proclaiming a toast.

Josh was Marcus's closest friend. Although the man was reaching his fiftieth year, they had much in common. A love of the outdoors, hunting, fishing, and a good long talk by a fire on a cold night.

Samuel had helped Josh out of a serious difficulty when both were just young men. After that, Josh had devoted himself first to Samuel, then later to Marcus. When Marcus had arrived in Boston to take Captain Elias's ship to England Josh had been there to meet him. The burly man would have it no other way than to accompany Marcus and be of any assistance he could.

Marcus knew this cost Josh dearly. The man's health was not what it should be, and the warm climate of North Carolina would have been more conducive to his recovery.

Marcus and Josh rode in the hired trap to Lord Fowler-Greene's home. The ride seemed interminably long, and both men clenched their fists tightly in expectation. "This could be the opportunity we've waited for, Josh," Marcus said stiffly. "Pray God, the man has a heart and decides to help us."

"Aye! Marcus, me lad, but how can he refuse when the need is so great?"

The trap pulled into a long, tree-lined drive and stopped before a tall brick structure. "The lord does well for himself, Marcus," Josh said in a husky whisper.

A manservant in formal livery pulled open the door, and Marcus and Josh announced themselves. The servant admitted them, curling his lips with disapproval at Josh's rough appearance. "My Lord is expecting you, Mr. Chancelor. I will announce you."

Shortly, the manservant came back into the foyer and asked them to follow him into the library.

Lord Fowler-Greene, a man at least a decade past his prime, stood in the center of a room lined with deep bookshelves and lighted with several chandeliers. Josh was plainly impressed with his opulent surroundings, and his eyes darted from one corner to the other, drinking in the elegant furnishings.

Lord Fowler-Greene offered the men some port. Marcus watched his labored movements, noting the lord's obesity hindered him as he trod across the Persian rug to pull the bell cord to summon his butler. "I understand you have a serious problem in your colony—North Carolina, is it?"

"Yes, sir," Marcus answered, looking grim. "I had hoped you could intervene with the King on our behalf."

"Precisely," the lord expostulated, "although intervening with the King was not exactly what I had in mind."

"I don't understand, sir," Marcus said, a puzzled look on his handsome face.

In a lighter tone the lord said, "'Tis a shame the King refuses to be a willing patron to your needs, but perhaps you would find it amenable to allow the King to be your . . . shall we say . . . not-so-willing ally?"

Still puzzled, Marcus remained quiet in order to allow the lord to explain this statement. "'Tis a known fact, Mr. Chancelor, that our roads are traveled by people of wealth as they gad about from one place to the other. I hear tales of some of our country's most beautiful ladies wearing the most ostentatious of jewels as they traverse from here to there. Would it not be a shame if these ladies, the wives of the very lords who had you . . . er, removed from the House of Lords this day, were to be relieved of those cumbersome jewels," quickly adding, "to be returned to them, of course, for a trifling finder's fee. In this way it could almost be said that the lords are contributing to relieve the plight of your colony."

Josh, immediately grasping Lord Fowler-Greene's words, said pointedly to Marcus, "Look sharp now, Marcus, me lad, the Lord is making some good sense!"

"Of course, Mr. Chancelor, the risks would be entirely yours. Perhaps I could find my way to notify you of a great shipment of this year's taxes which are being collected now, at this very moment, from the whole of England. Of course, you understand this is only half a year's taxes. I'm afraid you missed the last shipment."

Fowler-Greene's plan intrigued Marcus. Adventure and danger had always appealed to him, but to have this suggested by a member of the House of Lords! And what of the law? Marcus held a deep and abiding respect for rule and regulation. Could he intentionally defy the face of justice? The image of hunger-sunken faces of the people of Chancelor's Valley swam before him. Starvation induced by the purposeful misrepresentation of the same edicts he was having doubts about violating.

"I think, Lord Fowler-Greene, your meaning is clear to me. But I am obliged to ask you why? Why should you turn against those of your own class, your friends, and propose they should be subjected to robbery?"

Lord Fowler-Greene grasped the back of a high Duxbury chair fiercely; the knuckles of his bejeweled hands shone white. Looking at Marcus with a gaze so concentrated it seemed to bore through the younger man, he said in a voice edged with anger, "Because of a vision I have. A vision of the colonies peopled with a society that works and strives for an ideal—founded on trust and certain inherent freedoms . . ." Lord Fowler-Greene stopped in midsentence, glowering at the amused look on Marcus's face.

"It would appear, Lord Fowler-Greene, that you have made the acquaintance of Mr. Benjamin Franklin when he was envoy to England last summer."

"Yes, how astute of you." The lord visibly relaxed. "And I find I agree with him. England owes something to the colonies, and much as I try, I don't seem to be able to convince the House of Lords or the Crown of this fact. During this past decade or so, business and trade have prospered here in England because of the colonies. The results upon our own society have been small as yet, but I don't think them negligible. Newfound trade and wealth for the Crown without the rewards due to those who have made it possible rankles me and now I see my chance finally to offer tangible aid."

Marcus looked squarely at the man before him, mentally questioning the general impression the lord created, that of a bigoted old fool.

"I can see by your expression, Mr. Chancelor, that you are amazed that, contrary to all rumors, I have some faculty of mind. In spite of my love for luxury and certain other . . . er, idiosyncrasies, I do have the glory of England at heart. But I know that England's glory can only be enhanced by the success of the colonies, and hence, it is America's betterment which I seek."

The butler entered the room bearing a silver tray with a decanter of port and three long-stemmed glasses.

"Shall we drink to your success, Mr. Chancelor? Perhaps you would be wise to assume a pseudonym for your . . . er, ventures. Say, something with a bit more style, which will appeal to the lower orders. You might consider the title of Scarblade. It has a certain flair, don't you think?"

Chapter Four

"My God, Tori. What got into you? We could have been killed! Your father's right, you need to be horsewhipped!" Granger went on and on, seeming to enjoy the luxury of railing at her. It wasn't often he could best Tori in argument, but since they had driven away from the highwayman she seemed not to be listening to anyone. Her indifference pricked him and leaning closer, willing to engage her in argument, he said again, "You should be whipped!"

"Clip? What kind of clip?" chirped Lady Lydia's puzzled voice. "Clip? Victoria, I won't hear another word about cutting your hair! Nelson, speak to the girl! Do something!" Lady Lydia cried in her soprano voice as her fingers plucked at her reticule nervously. Worry pinched her delicate, pretty features. "You must attend to her marriage, Nelson, she needs a strong hand. On the morrow you'll attend to the matter, for I'll not have another night's sleep otherwise!" This last Lady Lydia said in a lowered voice meant for her husband's ears alone.

Lord Rawlings patted her small hand comfortingly. "The matter will be attended to, my dear. Rest, Lydia, soon we will be home." He cast a wary eye in the direction of his daughter, who was engrossed in a heated conversation with Granger on the merits of Scarblade. Once again, he let his hand travel to his waistcoat pocket to feel the slim purse. He heaved a weary sigh of relief now that the decision to wed his daughter was made.

"Granger, I swear I would have protected your life, truly, I would. You must learn to manage your allowance more carefully. Always keep a few farthings in your pocket. This way you won't tempt a highwayman to slice your gullet. Dear Granger, what am I to do with you? I shan't always be around to protect you." Tori teased unmercifully, smiling with pleasure at the perspiration which bathed his face.

"Wha . . . what? Victoria," Granger sputtered, "I envy the man that marries you."

"You do? Why?"

"Because if he has just one small part of a working brain, he will whip you three times a day and four on the Sabbath. You, dear cousin, are headed for one mighty dreadful time."

"Granger, in this day and age, there is not a man alive who would beat his wife," Tori said loftily.

"Cousin, when the man that marries you gets to know you, he will regret his bargain immediately. He will return you to your parents posthaste, and demand to be rid of you!"

"Granger, dearheart, the man who marries me shall love me for all time. I shall make his life exciting and full of meaning. I shall bear him rosy-cheeked children." As an afterthought, she added, "When I am ready, that is."

"I can see it before my eyes," Granger snorted. "You'll have a ring through his nose in a day's time."

"You see, Granger, when you put your devious mind to work, you truly understand," Tori said happily.

Granger ignored Tori's words and looked deeply into her sparkling green eyes. Seeing Granger's intent, she lowered her thick, dark lashes.

Too late, Tori, Granger thought. I know you too well. Something happened back there and you're frightened.

That's why all this inane babble. It's to draw my attention from the fear in your eyes. You're not half as brave as you would have everyone think, dear cousin. But there was something else glittering in those catlike orbs. And I don't think I miss my guess when I think it was something akin to . . . lust?

Tori heard Granger's snicker and she shot him a staggering look. "Ah, I think we are home!" she announced, her discomfiture disguised by her forced gaiety.

"Yes, my dear, we're home," Lord Rawlings said, happy as Tori to have neared the familiar surroundings. He glanced lovingly at his daughter. Soon, all his worries would be over. She really was too trying for a man reaching sixty. As he thought this last, he brightened. Why, if she's too much for me, and I am almost fifty-nine, she surely will be too much, much too much, for that old badger Fowler-Greene. I give him a year with her before he's burned out. His smile broadened. My dear Tori will make a handsome widow, a handsome, *rich* widow. He beamed as he speculated on this saving thought.

"Granger," Tori whispered, "come to my sitting room later. There is something I wish to discuss with you."

"What is it, Tori? I'm sorely tired this evening."

"We will discuss it later. Now don't forget!"

"How could I forget? You will nag me unmercifully if I don't do your bidding. But I warn you, Tori, I shall not help you in any more of your dastardly schemes."

"Well, if you prefer to live the life of a pauper, so be it. I happen to be in a position to help you line your pockets—somewhat, that is."

Granger's eyes took on a curious gleam, as they always did at the mention of money. Tori, looking at him in the dim light of the coach, knew he would do her bidding.

"Come, Mother, I'll help you. I know that you must be as weary as I this night. All that terrible excitement! What is this country coming to?" she said, her voice raised so Lady

Lydia would hear. "Imagine being accosted this night!" She shook her head for her mother's benefit.

"Your father is going to arrange a marriage for you, Tori, so that should put your mind at rest. Soon you will be someone else's prob . . . worry," she corrected.

"What do you mean, Mother?" Tori asked fearfully, a knot of panic clutching her stomach.

"Your marriage is to be arranged for only a fortnight from now. Is that not happy news?"

"Mother, I'm not ready for marriage," Tori wailed. "I thought we had this all out at our summer home. I can't believe you agree with Father in wanting to pack me off to Lord Fowler-Greene. I'm not ready!"

"My dear, there is nothing to it! Soon as you've become accustomed to the ways of the marriage bed, believe me, you shall be most happy. Your dear father assures me that you'll be happy. It's what you need, dear girl. If you're happy, then your father and I will be happy. We'll have a great feast. If I'm well enough tomorrow, I'll undertake to arrange all of the details. We must have a suitable gown for you."

"But, Mother . . ."

"Hush, child, let me think. I know that you're overcome. Don't try to thank me now, or your father; we're only too glad to attend to the details."

"But, Mother . . ."

"Not one more word! I'm sorely tired," Lady Lydia sighed as she walked on shaky legs up the marble steps to her bedchamber.

"Ahhk!" Tori squawked indignantly to herself. "I'll not marry unless I'm in love, and I certainly shall not marry some fat old man with hoards of money. It would be just my misfortune that he'll snore and snort all night and in the morning he'll belch and scratch. All I need is enough money to line Granger's pockets. If I have to, I'll join Scarblade's men and secure my money the way highwaymen do!"

"Tori, I wish to discuss a matter of some importance with you after the evening meal," Lord Rawlings commanded as he saw a familiar belligerent expression cross Tori's face.

"Very well, Father. I shall oblige you as a good daughter should," Tori said, suddenly meek.

Lord Rawlings did not miss the submissive tone. Suddenly his own stomach knotted in panic. He could feel in his bones that she was up to some form of trickery. Never in all of her twenty-two years had she agreed to anything, no matter how small, without some form of obstinacy. This time, though, he'd tie her and lock her in her bedchamber if she didn't agree. With this resolved and the happy thought that his daughter could not best him this time, he followed his wife.

Tori cast a loving eye in Granger's direction. He paled. Tori never looked lovingly at anyone, only at her reflection in a mirror. She winked roguishly as she mounted the steps. "Don't forget, Granger. Later, in my sitting room," Tori whispered. A thrill of apprehension shot through him.

Chapter Five

Tori flung herself on the high bed and stared up at the sculptured ceiling. She had to come up with some kind of plan to thwart her father! She would not marry that odious Lord Sidney Fowler-Greene, monies or no. Father would just have to come up with another way to see himself through the difficulties she knew he was having. He hadn't been as sly as he had thought when he would creep out of their summer home with some article of value beneath his frock coat. He had underestimated her perceptive eye. He can lower himself to the station of a scullion, as far as I care! Let him beg or, better, steal or, still better, crawl on his belly to curry favor with the Crown. He could not barter his own flesh and blood. She knew it was a lost argument. She also knew her father well. If necessary he would lock her in her chamber till the marriage vows were said. Granger was her only hope. He would have to help her. Granger would do anything for a price, as long as it didn't involve putting his head in a noose. Soon her father would have to oust him. There would be no money to keep him to say nothing of his handsome allowance. She giggled at the thought of Granger at the mercy of the elements, not to mention the highwaymen. He would not last two days on his own. What could she offer to entice him to help her. Quickly, she climbed from the bed and opened her jewel box. She looked in dismay at the paltry baubles that rested in the velvet depths. The lot wasn't worth ten sovereigns. Oh, why hadn't she pleaded with her father like the other girls did to acquire jewels. She pounced on her reticule and counted out the small hoard of money. Perhaps Granger would be satisfied with the meager sum. She would have to beg, plead, cry, and if all else failed, threaten. She knew a few secrets about Granger that he would not want bandied about, especially to Lord Rawlings.

Dinner was a dismal affair. Everything was cold, the meat, the eggs, the bread. Tori had no appetite and Lady Lydia soon retired, pleading a headache. Lord Rawlings escorted Tori into the library.

A fire had been laid in the hearth to ward off the chill of the rooms unused throughout the summer. Lord Rawlings pointed to a high-backed leather chair by the low fire and requested Tori to seat herself.

"There is a matter we must discuss. Please, my dear, listen to me with an open mind. As you well know, I have lost favor with the Crown. What you do not know is that without the rentals from those properties which have been removed from my title, we are in grave financial straits. I have barely enough to see us through the next several months. After that," he said, piteously eying Tori for a reaction, "it will be debtors' prison for me. Now I know," he said, raising a hand to forestall an objection Tori might be inclined to make, "that you do not want that to happen. Therefore, my dear, I had to arrange the marriage for you with Lord Fowler-Greene. You must put these romantic notions out of your mind. 'Tis a cruel world we live in and you are of an age when marriage is imperative. Why, in a few years we won't have an opportunity to marry you off. You don't want to see your dear mother languish and die for mourning me, locked away in Newgate, do you?"

At Tori's meek denial, he continued. "The purse that Lord Fowler-Greene has offered for your hand will take care of all my debts and leave your mother comfortable till I regain favor with the Crown, if ever." He added sorrowfully, "You will agree, won't you, Tori?"

"But, Father, couldn't we sell Mother's jewels? Perhaps I could take a post as a governess somewhere?"

"My dear, much as it pains me to say this, I fear I must. However, not a word of this to your mother. The jewels have been gone these many months. What remains in their place are trinkets made to look like the real ones. All that remains is the wedding necklace I gave your dear mother. I had not the heart to sell it!"

"The ruby and diamond necklace that is to come to me on Mother's death? Is that what you mean, Father?"

"Yes," he nodded wearily. "Your mother prizes it highly. That is why she keeps it beside her bed at all times."

"What you mean, Father, is that you could not get your hands on it," Tori said spiritedly. "Otherwise, you would have sold it also. Is that not a fact?" she asked brazenly.

Lord Rawlings flinched at his daughter's hard tone, or was it at the truth of the statement?

"Will you agree to the arrangement? Will you, Tori?"

Tori nodded affirmatively. She would agree to anything at that moment. She needed time to think and to plan. The whole night was before her.

"I want you to give me your word that there will be no trickery, Tori, else I will lock you in your bedchamber. Your word, Victoria," he said imperiously, "your word as a Christian."

"Father, let me remind you that I am not a child and do not wish to be treated as such. No, I will not give you my word. You will have to accept me as I am. You will arrange the marriage. I won't stop you. Let us leave it at that. Now if you will excuse me, I wish to bid Mother goodnight."

The little whelp, she's up to something, Lord Rawlings thought. I'll have the footman watch out for her. It is too late in the day for her to mix things. He poured himself a glass of port and sat back contemplating his soon-to-be-found wealth and the marriage of his daughter. All his worries would be over. Soon he would have grandchildren to bounce on his knee. Thinking of the age of Lord Sidney Fowler-Greene, he amended, "Well, children aren't all there is to a marriage. Besides, if they were to be as troublesome as Tori, it might be best not to have any."

Tori mounted the steps slowly, her heart beating quickly. She entered Lady Lydia's room and quietly walked over to the huge bed where her mother lay in a half-doze.

"Mother, may I have another peek at your wedding necklace?"

"Mmm. Yes," the childlike voice answered sleepily.

Tori bent and picked up the small leather bag that held the diamond and ruby necklace. She held it near the flickering flame of the bedside light, removed the gems, and held them so their luster sparkled and gleamed.

"Mother, is it not your plan to present me this necklace at some future date?"

"Hmmm."

"Then, perhaps you'll not mind too much if I take possession of it now, to do with as I please. Can you hear me, Mother? I'm going to take the necklace. It's all right, is it not? Somehow I feel it fitting that I should have the necklace since my own marriage is to be arranged."

"Yes, yes," came the sleepy reply.

"Oh, thank you," Tori exclaimed as she placed a resounding kiss on Lady Lydia's pale cheek. "You've saved my life!"

"That's nice, dear." Lady Lydia snuggled down further into the warm bed and turned her face deeper into the pillow.

Tori crept out of the room, feeling guilty for tricking her unsuspecting mother.

Back in her own suite of rooms, Tori sat on a small settee by the idle fireplace. The double glassed doors leading onto the balcony were open, allowing the gentle breezes of late September to waft into her room, bringing with them the fresh scent of fallen leaves rotting in the damp.

She placed the sparkling necklace on the delicate end table before her, putting her too few jewels beside it. With this as an added incentive, Granger was sure to help her. She never for a moment considered his refusal. Granger would do anything for money. So near poverty was he, Tori had no doubt of this. Poor Granger, ensconced in his mother's sister's household, dependent on Lord Rawlings' goodwill and generosity.

When Granger was fifteen, he had lost both mother and father in a shipwreck off the coast of Spain. Sir Lapid, Granger's father, had been a successful privateer and shipbuilder, dabbling in imports and exports. Pirates and heavy embargoes had put his livelihood in jeopardy, and Sir Lapid risked all he had on a venture in North Africa. Granger had stayed in England to complete his schooling and await his parents' return. Lady Sylvia, Granger's mother, had begged her husband to allow her to accompany him on his newest ship. After much cajoling and pouting, Sir Lapid had finally agreed. Then an ill-fated storm off the coast of Gibraltar had robbed Granger of both mother and father and, not the least, his inheritance. All Sir Lapid owned was tied up in the venture, and when the estate was settled and the debts paid, Granger was left with a small yearly allowance, barely enough to keep body and soul together.

Since that time, Lord Rawlings had taken the responsibility of his wife's nephew. If the truth were to be told, Lord

Rawlings was fond of Granger. If only the boy were not so irresponsible and shiftless, Lord Rawlings had told himself and his wife countless times, he would not find Granger so irritating. And what did the boy think to gain by regaling his innocent cousin Tori with tales of misadventure? Lord Rawlings blamed most of Tori's high-spirited ways on poor Granger.

Tori had just replaced the ruby necklace in its leather pouch and her own jewels in her pocket when a tentative rapping sounded on her door.

"Come in, Granger," she called cheerfully.

Warily, Granger entered, his eyes raking the room for some hidden message.

"Pray, cousin, sit here by me." Tori patted the cushion. "I'll not bite you. Come, come, don't be shy." She measured his mood. "We've been cousins and known each other too long to stand on ceremony. Pray, sit, Granger."

Still wary, Granger sat on the edge of the settee as if poised for flight. "Come on, cousin, let's get this over with. I told you before that I'm sorely tired."

"Dearest Granger, if that is to be the case, then I must tell you my little predicament immediately. I find myself in a very precarious predicament. I'm sure you know of my father's plans for me to wed Lord Fowler-Greene." Granger nodded. "Are you also aware that after his debts are paid there will be precious little left for my father and my mother?"

Granger looked puzzled, not liking the course of the conversation.

"That, Granger, means you'll have to find other lodgings and look elsewhere for an allowance. My parents will close this house and take up residence at the summer house. There, they'll live modestly and quietly. And Granger, there'll be no room for you," Tori stated ominously.

"But . . . but . . ."

"I'm truly sorry, but that is the way of it. I sorely wish there was some way I could help you."

"Oh, but there is, dear cousin." Granger smiled meaningfully, his emphasis on the "dear." "When you have wed Lord Fowler-Greene you will invite me to stay with you."

"Granger!" Tori said, shocked, "I cannot do it! Why, Lord Fowler-Greene will want me all to himself. After all, he is buying a wife, not all her poor relatives. Think, cousin, how will it look? Surely you jest!"

Granger examined the sincerity of Tori's expression. "You're right, Tori, I was jesting." The glumness of Granger's face almost gave Tori up to her secret laughter. Poor boy, so worried was he for his future he could not see past his nose to her tricks.

"But, Tori, what am I to do? Turn into a beggar?"

"Better yet, why don't you join Scarblade's men? They could use a member who has some breeding. I feel so sorry for you, Granger."

"Don't waste your sympathies on me, Tori; I still have my wits to live by. But you, poor cousin, you'll have naught but a pretty face and a fashionable figure with which to secure your future. And once Lord Fowler-Greene learns of your temper and lack of breeding in the wifely arts, you can be sure you'll be kept at home, away from polite society, where your spirit will not embarrass him."

"Embarrass him? What are you speaking of, Granger? How could I embarrass Lord Fowler-Greene? He should be ecstatic that I should consent to this marriage!"

Granger smiled wickedly; his recriminations against Tori always carried weight. He knew which road led to her sorest parts, the one that led directly to her pride. "But of course if you're a good girl and only speak with the ladies and never smile in a gentleman's direction, Lord Fowler-Greene will have naught to complain of. So you see, Tori, once again you are mistress of your own destiny."

"Granger," Tori exclaimed hotly, "if you do not drop this, this . . . I demand you speak the King's English! What do you mean I'll be kept at home? You know I cannot live a life of solitude. Speak now, Granger, explain yourself!"

Granger sat for a moment arranging the lace at his sleeves, pretending Tori's excited statements were unheard. At last, unable to withstand the sheer willfulness of her stare and the pitiful picture she made sitting there with her future at stake, actually fearful of his next words, Granger's core of cruelty rejoiced in satisfaction. How often Tori had placed him in just this situation, how many times she had threatened to do something which would see Granger cast out on his ear, left to fend for himself. But then, she was his cousin and he loved her only slightly less than he loved himself. No matter how great was his enjoyment of this verbal sparring in which Tori ranked among the most witty, he must now make his move to put an end to her anxiety over his statement.

"Odds fish, cousin, what I am about to tell you is the honest truth, I swear on my sainted mother's watery grave." Tori sighed audibly and settled back in her seat. "Of course, this is only taproom talk, but you know as well as I that there is no smoke without fire."

"Yes, Granger, now get on with what you have to tell me. I fear I cannot abide your philosophizing this night."

Granger sneered slightly in annoyance at Tori's disinterest in his sage impressions. "All right then, if you would have me come straight to the point, here it is. Lord Fowler-Greene has been a bachelor these many years, his first wife succumbing to a fever almost thirty years ago. Lady Fowler-Greene was a woman of quality and title. A bit long in the tooth when she married, true, but nevertheless, her wit and charm won for your betrothed the titles and manor which he now holds. One cannot say it was a love match, but the good lord fawned and doted on her. Who would not, seeing the great advantages one could gain by association with her?"

"To the point, Granger, to the point!" Tori said impatiently.

"It is this, Tori. Lord Fowler-Greene has been heard to say time and time over that never would he bed a woman who could not match his wife for manners and culture. The poor gentleman has never been known to avail himself of the wenches who would fall at his feet for the recompense he could well afford. Rumor has it that he has been celibate these many years since the demise of his dear wife."

"Hrmmmph! And why would anyone, be she wench or lady, seek to *faire l'amour* with that obese, sweating, scratching . . ."

"Tut, tut, Tori! Have you forgotten, you speak of your intended?"

"Oooh, Granger!" Tori raged, "I believe you are actually enjoying my predicament!"

"No, Tori. I know better than that! Our fortunes have been too closely linked these past years. I know that whatever is best for you is also best for me."

"On that you can depend. Were it not for me, Father would never have increased your allowance to much above that of a schoolboy's. I have not yet decided on a plan to gracefully withdraw from this engagement but when I do, Granger, I will depend on you to assist me."

"Your imperious tone irritates me, cousin. Do not be too sure of me. For once it might bring me pleasure to see you brought down."

Tori swallowed her rage. At all costs she would deny Granger the satisfaction of seeing her cowed. She gathered her poise and smiled sweetly. "As I said, you will assist me. Think, Granger, soon it will be cold and wintry. I can see you trouncing down the road, cold, hungry, destitute, begging for a crust of bread. Just when you think you cannot go one step farther, the highwaymen will be upon you. Oh, Granger, what they will do to your poor person. I can see it as if it has happened already. I will cry openly over your poor frozen body. The tears will freeze upon my cheeks. I shall pray for you, dear cousin," Tori mocked sadly. "Alas, it appears only the women in this family have any kind of stamina. Poor, poor Granger."

Granger trembled at her softly spoken words. He, himself, could picture the scene she had painted.

Tori reached out a slim white hand and offered him three gold sovereigns and her meager jewels. "You jest, cousin. This paltry sum would not keep me but a month."

"'Tis all I have!" she protested.

Granger looked Tori in the eye. "Lazy I may be, but a fool, never! Let us see the rest of the booty."

Grudgingly, Tori withdrew the small leather pouch from her pocket and threw it on his lap. She watched the greedy leer spread over Granger's face.

"That is more like it! You snitched this, didn't you?" he said suddenly. "You never owned anything like this in your life. Where did you get it? Never mind, I have no wish to know. This way, when I turn it into cash I'll not see your poor mother's face before me." Deftly Granger tossed the brillant necklace into the air and caught it.

Suddenly Tori snatched the necklace and stuffed it into her pocket. "Not so fast, cousin, you only get this," she said, patting her pocket, "when you agree to help me in whatever course I decide to take. A promise, Granger, your word as a gentleman!"

"Develop your scheme, Tori; you can rely on me for my assistance," he said, eying the pocket.

Later that evening, a weary Tori climbed into bed and pushed aside all thought of her predicament concerning Lord Fowler-Greene. Instead she clung to the memory of strong arms pressing her closer and black eyes caressing her.

Morning brought no solution to Tori's problem. Tori rose hollow-eyed and exhausted, feeling as though she had never slept. Dressing hurriedly in a pale-green morning gown which matched her eyes, she trudged tiredly down the stairs. She breakfasted in silence, picking at her food and glancing out the high, wide windows.

"Tori, you're not listening to me!" Lady Lydia's high, clear voice complained.

"Yes I am, Mother. I heard you. I fear I had a bad night. You are going to have a dinner party tomorrow evening, and, yes, it is quite all right with me."

"Your betrothed will be here, Tori," Lady Lydia chattered brightly. "The footman, just this past hour, has left with the invitation from your father. I am sure Lord Fowler-Greene will accept with haste. Do you not agree?"

"Yes, Mother," Tori said wanly.

Lady Lydia looked at her daughter with something akin to fear. The child looked ill. 'Tis the thought of the coming marriage. Lady Lydia brightened as she remembered how nervous she had been at a similar time in her life. That's all it is, she consoled herself. The child is just nervous. Immediately the lady felt better; after all, the child was bound to marry *someday*, and it might as well be now when she would still look lovely in a wedding gown. There are too many brides I've seen who were too long in the tooth. They never should have had formal weddings. Posh and tother to all that business about doing it for their mothers. The dear ladies should be grateful enough to see their daughters marry, let alone quibble over the grandeur of large ceremonies.

Her attention came back to Tori, who was picking at her food. "I hope, dear, that you will wear the green silk, it brings out the color of your eyes. We do so want to leave a good impression with Lord Fowler-Greene, don't we?"

"Yes, Mother." Tori pushed a thick slice of ham from side to side on her plate as her stomach heaved. She thought of her eager bridegroom and her years of association with him. Tori had had occasion to meet Lord Sidney Fowler-Greene numerous times since her childhood. She moaned inwardly as she remembered his fat, white, eternally damp hand which never lost an opportunity to tweak her chin or pat her cheek. His distasteful teasing, instructing her to hurry and grow up so he could make her his bride. Thank God, he had restrained himself when she had become a young lady. Only then was she saved from being pulled onto his lap and pressed against his enormous belly to suffer his foul breath on her face.

The years had not improved the lord. If anything, they had been most unkind. Where his face had once been round and plump, it now had fallen into folds of flesh that quivered at his every word. His nose resembled a lump of bread dough molded into a swollen ball and pressed into the middle of his face. His mouth was overgenerous, overmoist; a hint of what in his youth must have been sensual still remained, but now it was disfigured by years of imbibing and discolored by too frequent use of Indian snuff. The thought of coming into intimate contact with that mouth caused Tori to gag. Abruptly, she stood up and asked to be excused. Without waiting for an answer, she clamped a white hand over her mouth and ran from the room.

Startled by her daughter's abrupt action, Lady Lydia looked askance at the fleeing figure. "Nelson," she cried, "where are you? I must speak with you!" Her cry went unanswered. Lady Lydia's thoughts began to run together. She must be mistaken. It was probably due to her restless night's sleep. She dreamed that Tori had asked for the marriage necklace. Tori, who had no use for jewels!

Chapter Six

"If I need you, Annie, I'll ring for you!" Tori snapped. "I'm perfectly capable of dressing myself this evening. My head is pounding and I wish to be alone!" The little maid scuttered away. She had never seen her mistress in such a bad humor. She should be happy, what with her wedding so close.

Tori dressed in a state of dejection. Bovine, pompous old man, she fumed inwardly. I don't love him and I could never learn to love him. I don't want to marry him. I don't want to marry anyone! Silent tears splashed her cheeks and then a glimmer of an idea came to her. Granger says my good lord will only wed and bed a lady of quality, a woman of taste and manners. Why, it's a point of honor with him! Ooh, wouldn't I like to see society laugh in his face. Perhaps if I'm miserable and rude to him this evening he will change his mind and think I'm not good enough for him. "Would that it were so easy, Tori girl." She knew her father would never demand this marriage of her if it were not for the money involved. No, any overt action on her part to discourage Lord Fowler-Greene would not be taken well by Lord Rawlings, not well at all. Any attempt made in those

directions would have to be subtle, very subtle indeed for
Lord Rawlings not to catch on. Tori brightened. Perhaps,
she thought, if Lord Fowler-Greene were to become, let us
say, disenchanted with me, and he himself were to break the
engagement, it might be just possible his embarrassment
would incline him to pay Lord Rawlings the purse at any
rate.

"If only it were so," Tori wished aloud as she looked at
her reflection in her small mirror. "I have it!" she exclaimed.
Hurriedly, she applied bright vermillion to her cheeks and
lips and smiled at her reflection. "That should set Lord
Fowler-Greene on his ear." Defiantly, she tossed her head
and set a few stray curls to dancing. She sniffed and gathered up the hem of her skirt and left the room.

Lord Nelson eyed the color on his daughter's face and
squirmed in his chair. If he were to make an issue of the
matter, he knew full well that Tori would run off to her bedchamber and refuse to return. He could picture himself
dragging her as she kicked and fought all the way down the
stairs to meet her intended.

Lady Lydia looked at her beautiful daughter and smiled.
I wonder if she has the fever? she mused. It was probably
the excitement of meeting Lord Fowler-Greene again.

"I'm so glad you've chosen that particular gown to wear
this special evening, dear," Lady Lydia said, nodding her
approval at a peach-colored silk tied with soft blue ribbons.
"I've always said it gives your skin the color of spun
honey." Actually Lady Lydia was perturbed over the fact
that Tori had not worn the green silk as she had promised,
but Lady Lydia used good judgment in refraining from
making a point of it. She, too, could imagine Tori using the
mere comment as an excuse to argue and be absent from
this important dinner.

Suddenly, there was a sound of carriage wheels and the
bustle of footmen heading for the front door. "Ah, it appears
our guest and Lady Helen have arrived." Lord Nelson cast a

stern eye in his daughter's direction, and rose to greet his guests.

Tori fought the urge to stick out her tongue at her father's retreating back. She would do it later, she promised herself. As she reclined languidly on the small sofa next to her mother, she worked her face into a semblance of a smile. Granger would have described it as a grimace.

At the first sound of footsteps at the doorway, Tori jumped to her feet in deference to the ages of the entering guests. Lady Helen, Lord Fowler-Greene's widowed sister, preceded her brother into the room. She was a gaunt, tight-lipped woman, the direct opposite in appearance of her brother.

"Darling!" Lady Helen gushed, coming forth to embrace Tori as she scrutinized the girl's high color. Her narrow, black eyes flicked in disapproval while syrupy phrases dripped from her pinched lips. "How wonderful it will be to have you in the family, Victoria dear. I've long been lonely for a companion and Sidney must see to it that you spend considerable time with me at my home in Sussex. The country air is so invigorating."

Tori smiled politely and groaned inwardly. Why had she never thought of it? Of course Lady Helen would expect her sister-in-law to sit with her and embroider and read the French classics. As if Lord Sidney would not be enough to bear, now this too!

Lord Fowler-Greene approached, limping slightly from a recent attack of the gout. "Victoria, beloved!" he exclaimed, reaching for her hand. "You are more beautiful than ever." He kissed Tori's unwilling hand, then turned it and bestowed another kiss on the inside of her wrist, leaving a trail of saliva. His plump, hot hands clamped her shoulders and Tori could feel her flesh crawl as he pecked her on each cheek.

"Dear Victoria," Lord Sidney said unctuously, "I'm so happy to be here in the capacity of your betrothed. In fact I am deliriously happy at the thought of our coming marriage. I see that you are, too," he said, noticing the high color in Tori's cheeks. "And you, dear friend," Lord Fowler-Greene said, extending his hand in Lord Rawlings' direction, "we have been good friends and now we shall be more, much more."

Lord Rawlings smiled and allowed Lord Fowler-Greene to pound him on the back. He felt a little displaced, a bit more than chagrined that soon, very soon, the slathering Lord Fowler-Greene would be his son-in-law. And if he didn't miss his guess, the pompous ass would take to calling him "Father." A taste of bile rose in Lord Rawlings' throat and the bitterness made his lip curl.

"How good to see you smile, my good man," Lord Fowler-Greene boomed. "I know if it were myself about to lose my beautiful daughter, I would find little to smile about."

Then, turning to Lady Lydia, he said in a quite serious tone, "My good lady, I want to assure you that I will dote on your daughter day and night."

Lady Lydia smiled sweetly and then suddenly brightened perceptibly. "A moat!" she cried, thinking she had at last understood. "Lord Sidney, I did not know your house had a moat! Tori, is it not enchanting? A moat! Fancy that!" Lady Lydia tittered at the romantic thought. "Then you two shall be safe and secure against the elements, not to mention outlaws. Delightful!"

Granger, just entering the room, heard Lady Lydia's last remark. He choked slightly and had to be pounded on the back by Lord Nelson.

Dinner was announced and Lord Fowler-Greene led Tori by the arm, surreptitiously pinching her smooth skin. Outraged, Tori hissed quietly, "Do not be so familiar, sir. We are not married . . . yet!"

"Hrmmmph. Yes, yes. Quite. There are some ladies who like that sort of attention," Lord Fowler-Greene whispered.

"I can see you are not one of them and I am grateful. I, myself, believe a lady should never accept advances from men; however, since I am your intended, I'm sure you'll forgive my little, shall we say. *faux pas.*" Seeing the vicious look on Tori's face, he added hastily, "I shall save my fondlings for the bedchamber," then smiled lewdly.

Tori pretended not to hear this last statement, so angry with herself was she for missing her chance to give Lord Fowler-Greene food for thought. I should have pretended to like it! she scolded herself. If what Granger says about the old fool is true, I just missed my chance, but I promise I'll not miss another. I'll have the old fool thinking I can hardly wait to jump into bed with him. Perhaps my eagerness will put him off me. Ugh! I must do something! His breath smells like a bucket of slops. As she entered the dining room, she stepped over to her seat and awaited the entrance of the others.

Granger entered, Lady Helen on his arm. Tori misinterpreted his pained look as one of sympathy for himself. Actually, Granger's sympathies were totally with Tori.

Dinner was dismal. Granger appeared to be the only one enjoying the roast mutton. He, in fact, had his dish refilled twice. Lady Lydia kept glancing at Tori from beneath lowered lids, a frown on her still pretty face.

Lady Helen was engaged in expounding the merits of a new remedy for the dropsy which she had been using on her cook. Tori appeared to be interested for courtesy's sake, but the whole while her head was pounding unmercifully.

Lord Fowler-Greene was speaking to Lord Rawlings and his voice began to get louder and louder. Even Lady Helen, used as she was to her brother's volume, stopped speaking to listen.

"No, Nelson. You don't see it the way I do and I don't expect you ever will," Lord Fowler-Greene was saying in his great voice.

"I don't expect I ever could see it your way!" Lord Rawlings raised his voice a note above that of Lord Fowler-Greene.

"I don't do things under the cover as is your way. I thought the man should be given at least the consideration of a hearing and said so!"

Lord Fowler-Greene used the old statesman's tactic and lowered his voice. Immediately, all attention was on him, waiting expectantly for his next words. "You see, old friend," with a special emphasis on "friend," "you must think of the whole situation logically. You must view it in its entirety. If you would help this Marcus Chancelor, you must not incense those who would be inclined to oppose him. This you have already done·by your blatant support of the man."

"Blatant?" Lord Rawlings shouted. "What am I, a crude pigkeeper, or a Member of Parliament? Sidney, you weren't there when this all happened. Now you must hear the tale from my side." Lord Fowler-Greene settled himself back in his chair and rested his eyes on Lord Rawlings, flattering his friend with his total attention.

Lord Rawlings started, in a much softer tone of voice. "We were at lunch, the other members and myself. From somewhere entered a tall, good-looking young fellow. He was well dressed, very much the gentleman. Then he began to speak. Imagine everyone's shock when this apparent gentleman addressed us in that impossible slur that is spoken in the colonies. Then, what does he do, but after he has our shocked attention, he falls back into the purest-class English, like ours, Sidney, you know? One would think he was born and bred right here in London in sight of Whitehall. But I am drifting from the point. He addressed us and said his name was Marcus Chancelor, from Chancelor's Valley in the Carolinas. He told us of the hardships his people have had to suffer because of our blockade and those renegade Indians. All they have left is a bit of seed with which to plant the next harvest. It seems that Chancelor's Valley is inhabited by those who have spoken out against the government. Chancelor made it clear that they weren't speaking out against the King. Indeed, the people are steadfast royalists. Instead they were speaking out against the corrupt governors there in the colonies who line their pockets by the sweat of the workingman's brow. Since they are to be considered outcasts, the only possible means they have of supporting themselves is to deal in the black market which in the long run is a side enterprise of the very governors who condemn them. This Marcus Chancelor was not asking for any assistance other than to have the King lift the blockade which was suggested by these governors."

"I've heard all that, Nelson," Lord Fowler-Greene commiserated. "What I'd like to know is just exactly how you found yourself in your embarrassing predicament."

"Found myself? Placed is more likely!" Lord Rawlings protested. "I took up the young man's case with several of my colleagues. They seemed very interested. Then all of a sudden, temper seemed to change against me; indeed, the ill wind was blowing so strongly it was all I could do to remain standing on the floor of the House. I've strong suspicions that the governors this Chancelor was speaking of have friends who better their own interests by assuring those of the governors. Next I knew, I was named an offensive subject to the King, and my holdings had been stripped from me."

"Now were you wise, you could have helped Marcus Chancelor, for a price of course, for if his community could afford the outrageous prices foisted on them by the black market, surely they would have been relieved to pay you a trifling sum, just in gratitude, you understand. So, instead of working behind the scenes, you made an issue of it, found yourself opposed, and stuck with it anyway. Now you find yourself with nothing and also no way to help this Chancelor fellow whose cause you've championed." Lord Fowler-Greene noted the interested and dismayed expressions as he glanced around the table. "Odds fish! Is this the first you all are hearing of my good friend's problems?"

Chapter Seven

It was less than a week before the wedding. Lady Lydia sat chatting with Mrs. Carey as the seamstress fitted the dress. The long white satin of Tori's wedding gown sparkled and shone in the few rays of the sun that filtered through the huge leaded windows of her bedchamber.

"As I feared, Lady Rawlings, the child gets thinner each time I come, and then I have to restitch the seams. I fear she'll waste away to nothing. As one of experience, having fitted more brides than I can remember, either Miss Rawlings is overcome with excitement or she is unhappy with the match," Mrs. Carey sputtered, her mouth full of pins.

Lady Lydia, herself, had the same thoughts. But she knew for certain which way Tori's emotions lay. When Lady Lydia had tried speaking to her husband of the matter, he had said it was just one of Tori's tricks. Still, she didn't like the look in the girl's eyes. Lady Lydia had never seen defeat in Tori; this was unlike her. A mother doesn't know how to help her child at times like these, Lady Lydia complained to herself. What is a mother to do? If there was only something she could say to make the ordeal easier for her child. The lady sighed deeply as she leaned forward to feel the smooth satin fabric which hung on Tori's too sparse frame.

Tori roused herself from a half-dream and glanced at her mother and the seamstress. Noticing the gleaming satin as though for the first time, a look of loathing came across her face. It was noticed by the two women. Dutifully, Tori stood complacently as the seamstress turned her this way and that, pinning here, altering there. Where the gown had once clung to her curved figure it now hung limp. Lady Lydia frowned at the appearance of her daughter. Mrs. Carey sighed audibly. The seams must be taken in again, she would be up all night sewing. And for what? They would have to carry the girl to the ceremony on a litter or she missed her guess. And then who would see the lovely gown that she had stitched for over a fortnight? "A waste," Mrs. Carey muttered to herself. "A pure waste!"

All the while she measured and pinned, Tori stood, bemoaning the fates which had brought her to this crisis in her life. Tori willed her mind to dwell on happier moments. Her first ball, the morning rides through the countryside with the wind whipping her golden hair back from her eyes. The freedom she had felt and enjoyed. Sitting in the kitchen with Cook and the maids and mimicking their melodious cockney accent to their screams of laughter and approval at her adroitness. Granger and the sometimes vile tricks she played on him, only to take her turn and become the object of his practical jokes. Girlhood seemed to be rushing away from her, leaving behind only memories of those carefree days.

Lady Lydia became so disconcerted by Tori's silence, she could bear it no longer and made a feeble excuse to escape the maudlin atmosphere of the bedchamber. When she had left, Mrs. Carey too was feeling the heavy pall of silence and she strove to divert the girl's attention.

"You look so familiar to me, Miss Rawlings. I believe I've mentioned it before. At the time I could not remember who you resemble. But I have thought and thought and at last, late last night while I was stitching the hem of this gown, I finally remembered. There's a girl at the Owl's Eye Inn. Oh, I don't suppose you know of the place; believe me, were it not for a marvelous little shop nearby, I myself would never venture into that notorious district."

Seeing the disinterested expression Tori offered her, Mrs. Carey curbed her verbal wanderings. "As I was saying, Miss Rawlings, I've thought and thought these past days and finally it came to me. The serving wench at the Owl's Eye Inn is the dead image of you, Miss Rawlings. Don't take offense where none is intended, but I dare say she could pass for you in a bright light."

Tori squirmed as Mrs. Carey adjusted a pleat and again stood quietly listening with half an ear.

"She's the same hair as yourself, or it would be if it were done up proper. But I don't imagine the eyes are the likes of yours. I declare I've never seen eyes the likes of yours in all my born days!"

"Who is she?" Tori asked politely.

Mrs. Carey, so startled by Tori's sudden interest, gagged on one of her pins. "Why, I just told you, she's a serving wench at the inn. I don't know anything about her."

"And she works at which inn?" Tori asked, a brightness returning to her eyes.

"Why, like I told you, Miss Rawlings, the Owl's Eye Inn, in Chelsea. And a beautiful girl she is. 'Tis a shame she's not quality folk like yourself."

Tori began to fidget. "Mrs. Carey, have you seen my cousin Granger?"

"Yes, miss. He was downstairs when I arrived, if I'm not mistaken. Hold still, miss. I'm almost finished. There, that does it, little lady. The gown will be finished in time for the wedding. Though dreading it I am that I'll have to lose sleep again to alter the gown."

Tori wiggled from the gown and hastily dressed herself.

She almost stumbled, and Mrs. Carey had to come to her aid. God! She'd no idea she was so weak. She must have something to eat. She must regain her strength! There was no time to lose.

"Mrs. Carey, when you return downstairs, tell the cook to send me a heaping plateful of food. Any kind, it doesn't matter. And please have someone send my cousin Granger to me, immediately!"

"Yes, miss," Mrs. Carey managed to utter, so startled was she by the abrupt change in the girl. Still, the old woman remembered her own wedding to her Charlie. Hadn't she acted much the same way, excited one minute and composed the next? Yes, Mrs. Carey thought to herself, everything would work out. Especially now, since she wouldn't have to take in the seams on the bridal gown again. If Miss Rawlings continued to show this renewed spirit, surely she would put on the needed five pounds she required to fill out the gown.

Chapter Eight

"Aaaow, miss! That glad I am to see ye yer old self again." The maid, Annie, smiled as she watched Tori tear the leg from a succulent squab.

"Mmm . . ." Tori mumbled as she chewed excitedly. Laying the fowl aside, she ripped at a chunk of cheese and washed it down with a huge mug of milk. "I forgot how good food could taste," she said as she picked up the squab again. "You may leave now, Annie. You can return the tray to the kitchen in the morning. I won't need you the rest of the night. I'm due for a good long night's rest."

"That you are, miss. 'Ave a good night. That 'appy am I to see ye more like yer old self. I'm sure yer intended will be overjoyed t' 'ear about yer improved health."

"Mmm . . . yes," Tori said, her eyes bright. "I'm sure he will. Most happy. The lecherous old fool," she added under her breath.

As Annie was leaving, Granger appeared outside the open door.

"Granger! Come in, come in." As the door closed behind Annie, Tori cried excitedly, "I cannot believe my good fortune. I simply cannot believe it!"

"Tell me now. Has Lord Fowler-Greene met with an unfortunate accident?"

"Oh, hush!" Tori scolded, suddenly remembering her annoyance with Granger. "Where have you been? I've been waiting the better part of an hour for you to come to me. Didn't you receive my message?"

"Ah, Tori. I see by the return of your sweet nature that your health has returned. When I saw the maid carrying your tray, I thought there was an army quartered here. I see you have regained your appetite. To what do we all owe this remarkable recovery?"

Tori chose to ignore his sarcasm. "Granger, I cannot believe my good fortune. The gods are smiling in my favor. Listen to what I have to tell you. You will become as excited as I." Quickly, Tori recited the tale Mrs. Carey had told her of the serving girl at the Owl's Eye Inn. "Is it not fate, Granger? Aren't you happy for me?"

"Oh, I'm happy," Granger said, squirming in his chair. "Now that I know there are two of you in this world I fear I shall have to take up your father's offer of wedding Lady Helen."

"Dear Granger, he didn't! Did he—to a sixty-year-old sheep dog!" Tori laughed mirthfully. "Is it to be a double wedding? How much is your purse? What are you worth on the marriage market? Surely not as much as me. Let me look at you," Tori giggled as she eyed Granger's virile, young body. "I fear," she said sadly, "Lady Helen wouldn't know what to do with you. Pray, Granger, do you not agree?" She laughed aloud at her cousin's obvious discomfort.

"Many's the seed you've sown," Tori continued teasing. "Perhaps it is time to settle down and grow old. 'Tis a shame? Lady Helen is *well* past the childbearing age. There will be no lusty sons for you, dear Granger."

"Hah! And that old cuckold that you are to wed. What makes you think he'll even be able to bed you?"

"I have no intention of marrying and bedding that rooster. I have a plan, Granger. And if you have half the brains you were born with you will leave with me. For a man as versatile as yourself, there must be many ways of making a suitable living, or if that fails, marrying a wealthy woman."

Granger nodded morosely. He could not picture himself lying next to a shaggy sheep dog. Sheep dogs were fine creatures, in fact he actually liked them, but not in his bed! Now if Lady Helen was ripe and succulent like a fresh picked peach, he would have snatched at Lord Rawlings' offer. Still, one could not have everything. But on the other hand, what did he have? Just the promise of a ruby necklace if he helped Tori in whatever scheme she could devise.

"Let's get on with it, Tori. What exactly do you have in mind?"

"It is this, Granger. As soon as everyone is asleep, we will go to the Owl's Eye Inn and see this girl who looks so much like me. I shall offer her the chance to change places with me."

All of a sudden, Granger burst out into a roaring laugh. "Tori, do you realize what type of scoundrels custom the Owl's Eye Inn? No, I think not. In all likelihood, this wench is a slattern, a doxy. Can you just imagine that pompous ass's face when he discovers he has bedded a tavern wench? And after all these many years of boasts. Why he'll not be able to show his face in London!"

"That is what makes this so ideal, Granger. Lord Fowler-Greene will not want any publicity concerning the trick played on him. He wouldn't dare to openly accuse my father of participating in this sham, and in all likelihood he will be more than glad to forget the purse he will have paid for the honor of my hand. Don't you see, Granger, it's perfect. The most father has to lose is an old friend. Mind, I said an old friend, not a good one."

"Speaking of your father, Tori, what do you think this will do to him? He does have his code of honor, you know."

Tori snapped her fingers. "Why, dear cousin, it shall be as honorable for me to save myself from this impossible marriage as it was for Father to stretch out his hand and accept the purse. There is a word for what he has attempted to do, you know. It is called slavery. And me! His own child! I'd rather die first than marry someone named Sidney!"

"You just may at that! When Lord Fowler-Greene discovers the ruse, what then? We have already agreed he would want no publicity, true. But surely you don't think he will ignore the whole thing. No, I fear not, cousin." Granger rubbed his hand gently across his lace-cravated neck. "And that long neck of yours is so beautiful, Tori. It will be a shame to see it broken. Our Sidney does have his ways and means, you know. And think of the sympathy that will accrue to him when London hears of the fatal accident suffered by his young wife. Surely the King will see fit to bestow another land grant on the grieving widower."

Tori blanched slightly at Granger's softly spoken words. "It is no more than he deserves. I have no compassion for him."

"You have it wrong, cousin. It is you who will merit the pity. I hear you brought a healthy purse. That lecherous old fool, as you call him, willingly offered to double the purse, and your father accepted. That is how eager he is to bed you."

Tori's eyes glittered, showing more yellow than green, as they always did when she was incensed. "The man I bed will be something to behold, Granger, I promise you. No dirty old man for me! I'm young and healthy. I want a man who can set my pulses racing, not some fat, unwashed old fool who thinks the measure of a lady is her indignation at a hint of physical contact. I'll have the full experience of love or I shall never marry!"

Chapter Nine

Granger rapped softly on Tori's door a little past ten in the evening. The door swung open and his cousin stood there, excitement evident on her lovely face. "Come. Hurry. Aren't you ready yet? My neck isn't as long and pretty as yours, and I wouldn't look well at the end of a rope. For surely that is what will happen if Uncle Nelson finds I've helped you."

Tori shot him a vicious look and picked up a purple velvet cloak lined in white ermine to wrap around her slim body. "Have you arranged for the trap?"

"All is ready, and I must add that you owe me ten guineas with which I had to bribe the stableboy."

"Ten? You'll get two and not a farthing more. Don't try and make your fortune from me, you fox."

As Granger watched her arrange the cloak he said, "I see you dress for the occasion. Don't you think you'll be conspicuous? It is not Whitehall to which we go, you know," he hissed sarcastically.

"I may be robbed this evening, and I so want to be well dressed," Tori whispered. "It pays to always look one's best. Granger, you are so *gauche*. Really, I must wash my hands of you. All these years and I have tried, but Mother was right, you cannot make a brass urn from a lead one."

"Hand over the necklace, Tori," Granger scoffed. "I want it now. It is not that I don't trust you, but just in the event we are robbed I don't want you to offer it to some nefarious highwayman just for a thrill. Now hand it over."

Tori gave him the gleaming jewels. "You're so greedy, Granger! It sickens me," she said, wrinkling her nose and baring her white teeth.

Granger accepted the gems, his eyes as bright as the jewels. Deftly he slid them into his right boot. That they caused him pain was no matter. He would limp to hell if he had to. "And if we are accosted, and if you open that foolhardy mouth of yours, I'll shove my boot in it. Mark my words, Tori, I've had enough of your tricks. I want your word or we stay home."

Tori sniffed. "Very well, Granger. If you do not trust me, I give my word to you."

"Oh, it is not you I don't trust, it is that mouth of yours. It seems at times as though it has a mind of its own." He looked at her suspiciously. "You're probably some kind of witch."

"Shut up, Granger," Tori ordered. She, too, had often wondered if there were something wrong with her. But, she thought objectively, witches are ugly, so that took care of that little matter.

Granger and Tori sat in the Owl's Eye Inn. There was no sign of the girl whom she resembled.

As they sat there sipping a raw wine, Tori noted her surroundings. The interior of the inn was coarse and dirty. The rough, wooden benches on which they sat had sharp splinters projecting from the edges. The tallow candles, which were the only source of light, threw their yellow rays on the sawdust floor, and a rank smell of filth and spoiled food rose to pinch her nostrils.

"Tori, for God's sake, stop looking around as though you're quite impressed with the place. As it is, when the innkeeper noticed your dress he tripled the bill. I've only enough money to cover another glass of port at these prices."

"Be still, Granger. I've not had your advantages. I've been kept away from the seamier side of life. I'm enjoying myself, Here, look at those men on the other side of the room. Have you ever seen such wicked-looking characters?"

"Yes, I have. Those two men who rode with Scarblade had much the same look about them."

"What look is that, Granger?"

"Hungry! Now if you don't stop staring at them, I'll find myself in the position of defending your honor."

"They wouldn't dare!"

"Oh, wouldn't they! Look here, Tori. The only women that frequent a place like this are known doxies or the sluttish mistresses of the men you affectionately call highwaymen. Now turn around, Tori, for I don't feel like getting my throat slit on your account."

"Granger, what is this preoccupation with your throat? I worry about you, dear cousin. Perhaps a physician in Harley Street could put your mind at rest. I strongly suggest it."

As Tori teased Granger and watched for his reaction, she noticed his eyes lift and an expression of disbelief cross his face. She turned to note the object of his fascination and she, too, was aghast. There, under the flickering light of the sconce, stood a tall, slim blond girl with skin the color of spun honey and a prettiness of feature which Tori had, till now, thought her own.

"She does resemble me," Tori whispered in awe.

"Resemble you! Why, she even has that stubborn set of

chin! I'd say she could be a relative if I didn't know better. She looks a bit older than yourself, wouldn't you say? Now what are you doing?" Granger said crossly.

"Shhh! Do you think I want to give it all away? 'Tis better she doesn't see me till the last moment. If seeing me affects her the same as seeing her affected me, she'll run frightened. And as far as being a relative, it may be quite possible. Father did not live the life of a celibate until he married Mother, of that I'm sure!"

"Tori, have you no delicacy?" Granger admonished in mock horror. "So now what do we do? If you're not going to reveal yourself to the girl, we have made a wasted trip."

"Oh, I'll reveal myself to her, but not here in front of all these witnesses. Do you think I want to be blackmailed for the rest of my life? And if I don't miss my guess, these shady characters in here don't miss their chance to turn a dishonest penny."

Granger scratched his head. "You surprise me, cousin. I would have thought you never had a serious thought in your head. But when are we going to approach her?"

"We'll wait till she leaves and then follow her. Now what you can do for me is go up to the tap table and inquire of the innkeeper about the girl. Find out as much as you can about her. It will help, I'm sure of it."

"Don't you think it will seem strange that I'm in the company of a lovely young lady and here I am inquiring of another?"

"Granger, I'm sure you are quite used to being considered strange. Go on now!"

It wasn't until he had crossed halfway to the tap table that he realized the pointed jibe behind Tori's words. He turned abruptly and looked at his cousin, who was sitting at the table sipping the crude wine with a look of innocence about her.

* * *

Granger returned with the information Tori wanted to hear. The girl lived alone and had no known family. The proprietor called her Dolly Flowers and Granger admitted as delicately as he could that the innkeeper would "speak" to Dolly if the gentleman so chose.

"Oh, Granger, how wonderful!"

"Eh! Wonderful, you call it? What, that the girl is a slut and for a price she'd bed any man willing to pay? Maybe I wasn't clear, Tori: the man would have sold me the night with Dolly!"

"Granger, don't be so stuffy with me. I'm not an ignorant schoolgirl you know. I've read about places like this and girls like that. Don't look so horrified!"

"Don't misunderstand, cousin. The fact that Dolly is an honest businesswoman—well, a businesswoman at any rate, does not offend me. Heaven knows, it would be a lonely life for a bachelor like myself were it not for the likes of her. What shocks me is that you think it wonderful that a pretty girl like that engages in the 'oldest profession.'"

"Don't be stupid, Granger. If she were a girl of virtue how could we expect her to join in our plans? After all, it is crucial that she actually bed Lord Fowler-Greene, else we would not have an advantage over him. What would be the use? The only club we carry is his fear of it being exposed that he has gone against his word of these many years to bed only a lady of quality. And as far as Dolly blackmailing us, she would not do it, not when she has much more to gain by beleaguering dear Sidney."

"Ah, that is where your plan fails, dear cousin. Lord Fowler-Greene is a man of many moods. If she ever threatened to open her mouth, he would have her throat slit."

"There is your preoccupation with throats again! Don't be silly, Granger. Lord Fowler-Greene would never do that. Dolly will be protected simply because we know of the scheme. Lord Fowler-Greene would never take the risk of harming Dolly when he does not know for sure how many of us were involved in it. So you see, it is all bundled nicely. Lord Fowler-Greene gets the surprise of his life, my father gets the purse, you have the necklace and I—I, dear Granger—have my freedom."

"Not yet you don't. We still have to convince Dolly. Now drink up."

Tori stood with her back to the side of the inn. The malodorous refuse and slops which were dumped there caused Tori to wrinkle her nose. Granger paced back and forth beneath the single lamp that lighted their dank surroundings, checking his silver pocket watch.

"What's keeping that girl?" he muttered, limping slightly because of the necklace still in his boot. "I don't much care for waiting around here. God only knows who we'll meet!"

A few moments later a side door opened and closed softly. Dolly emerged, humming to herself. Granger approached the girl, startling her so that she almost lost her footing as she picked her way through the offal. Tori emerged from the shadows and fell in behind Granger. They walked single file down the street and crossed over to a dark alley. Suddenly, the girl stopped short.

"Aaaow, ye na be followin' me, are ye? Listen, Oi've na a ha'penny ta me naime, so get on wi' ye. Wha' are ye wantin' wi' me, anyway? Surely na a turn in th' 'ay, eh sir?" she said, eying the dark form of Tori.

"Ask her, Granger," Tori hissed. "I can't wait a moment longer!"

Granger cleared his throat. "Miss Flowers, I am Granger Lapid, and this," he said, pointing toward Tori, "is Miss Rawlings. We have a proposition to place before you," he said courteously. "I wonder if we might have a moment of your time?"

"'Ere now," Dolly said sternly, "Oi don' loike these queer

threesomes. Oi'm a good girl, Oi am. Oi don' care fer some o' th' games ye gentry loike ta play!"

"No, no," Granger protested, "you misunderstand, It's not that way at all."

"Ooh, in tha' case, sir," Dolly brightened, "la, guvnor, ye can 'ave all me toime. Oi'm na averse ta th' charms o' a gentleman the loikes o' yersel'. Ye can 'ave all me toime." Taking a close look at Granger, she added to Tori, "'E's quite pretty, 'e is. Wouldn' ye say, miss?"

"I agree," Tori smirked. "He is pretty."

A look of consternation crossed Dolly's face. "'Ere now, 'ow did ye know me naime?"

Granger sputtered and confessed, "The innkeeper told me."

"Oh, Oi see. Well, whazzit ye wan' o' me?"

Granger struck a match and Tori removed the hood of her ermine cloak. Dolly gasped. "It's me double! Saints preserve us," she muttered, crossing herself.

"Miss Flowers, I want you to change places with me," Tori blurted. "I want you to go through a marriage in my place."

"Yer na serious. Na ye are! Oi can see by yer face, ye are!"

"I am most serious, Miss Flowers. And I assure you I'm not crazy if that's what you're thinking. If you do this for me, you'll be richer than you ever dreamed. Please do this for me," Tori begged, tears stinging her eyes.

"An' jes' who izzit Oi'll be marryin'?" Dolly asked.

"What difference does that make?" Tori answered hotly, afraid of revealing too much of the plan. "Will you do it?"

"Jes' a minute, miss . . . Rawlings, izzit? If Oi marry this . . . person in yer name, it's na a legal marriage. It's sor' o' proxy. So where's all this money cum from?"

"Well, let's just say," Granger interjected, "marriage to

you would be a bit of an embarrassment to the old boy. He'll pay you well to keep your mouth shut!"

"Ah, yeh, bu' 'old on 'ere. There's too many toimes Oi've 'eard o' people gettin' their necks broke 'cuz they've threatened ta tell some secret. Tha' blackmail, ye know."

"He'd be afraid to do anything to you, he'd worry that we'd know what he'd done. Besides, he's not that sort of man, is he, Tori?"

"Oh, no, indeed not, he's a kindly old gentleman," she lied.

"Well, if 'e's so koindly, whyn' ye marry 'im yersel'?"

"I would," Tori said pathetically, "but my heart belongs to another. Anyway," Tori added so hotly that Dolly was taken aback, "what my reasons are, are none of your business. I'm offering you a chance to make your fortune, are you going to accept or not?"

"As Oi said afore, who izzit Oi'd be marryin'? Wha's wrong wi' th' man? Does 'e 'ave only one leg? Wha' are 'is failin's? Oi've a righ' ta know! Oi'm a young girl, Oi am!"

Suddenly Tori smiled. "I see. You need have no fear, Miss Flowers. While your bridegroom is up in his years he is most active in this province. Of course, I cannot speak from experience, but knowing his pinching fingers as I do, I am almost sure he'll warm your bed on your wedding night."

"An' wha' o' yersel'? When Oi taikes yer place wha' becomes o' ye?"

"Why, of course, Dolly, I shall take your place."

"Oooh, Oi'd loike ta see tha', Oi would," Dolly laughed.

"An' would ye now? 'Ere luv, lemme tell ya a thin' er two. When yer dealin' wi' th' loikes o' Tori Rawlings yer dealin' wi' th' experts!"

"Aaaaaow! Did ye 'ear 'er now?" Dolly poked Granger in the ribs. "Who'd 'ave though' she could speak th' cockney?"

"Oi learned it from th' kitchen maid," Tori said imperiously.

Granger and Dolly laughed heartily. "Well, it's been noice knowin' ye an' 'earin' o' yer plan, but Oi'm afraid Oi can' include mesel'." Seeing no reaction on Tori's face, she hastened to add, "At leas' fer th' toime bein', tha' is. Oi'll 'ave ta sleep on it."

"There's no time!" Tori wailed, "the wedding is the day after tomorrow. You must give me your decision!"

"Oi'll give yer me decision tomorrow, bu' Miss Rawlings, Oi migh' arrive at a quicker decision if Oi 'ad a noice warm cloak the loikes o' yers. Jus' so's Oi could get a good nigh's sleep."

Tori snatched the ties and wiggled out of the cloak. "Take it, it's yours. A prewedding gift from me to you."

"Aaaaow!" Dolly exclaimed, rubbing the soft fur of the lining. "Cum by in th' mornin'. Oi'll give me moind then. Oi lodge at th' Rooster's Crown," Dolly said as she tucked the cloak tightly about her shoulders and turned on her heels.

Chapter Ten

Tori and Granger rode within the plush interior of the trap. She was silent, casting furtive glances toward Granger. Finally, unable to stand his silence any longer, she all but shouted, "Well, what do you think? Will she do it?"

Granger nodded gloomily. "I don't see how you hope to get away with it even if she does agree. And you gave her your cloak. She might just as well take off with it, and then where will you be?"

"But I asked you if you thought she would agree—what is it, Granger, will she or won't she?"

"Who knows what a woman thinks and does? Look at you," he said, jabbing a finger in her direction. "If anyone ever told me I would be a party to something like this, I'd give that person a wide berth. You had better start to think how you're going to arrange all this, that is, if she chooses to go along with it." Granger squirmed in his seat.

As they approached the house, Tori turned to Granger. "Best tell the driver to slow the horses. We don't want to awaken anyone. How would you explain the late hour and that you have me in your company?"

"I would tell them the truth," Granger said uneasily as he

peered at the darkened house. "I'll just tell them it was all your idea. Who do you think they would believe, especially with your past history of trickery?" he added sourly.

Once in her chamber, Tori ripped the clothes from her body and threw herself on the high bed. The girl had to agree, she just had to! There was no other way out! Tori pounded her fist into the plump pillow and almost wept. Time was so short.

Tori knew she would never sleep this night. Rising from the bed, she moved over to the washstand and bathed her face in the icy water. Donning a fresh nightgown, she paced the floor, then hurried to the windows and peered out through the leaded panes. Soon it would be dawn of the day before her wedding. How could her parents do this to her? She was their only child! To sell her like a calf at auction and have no remorse was beyond all her understanding.

Quietly, she slipped out of her door and headed for Granger's room. She expected him to be sleeping soundly.

"You know, Tori, you sound like a bull elephant," he said nastily when she tipped over a vase in the darkness. "I expected you hours ago, what kept you?"

"Oh, Granger," Tori said as she threw herself into his arms, "you couldn't sleep, either. Truly, you're the best cousin I ever had!"

"Be truthful, Tori, I'm the only cousin you have," he answered dryly, but his answering embrace comforted her and reassured her that he was with her through the thick or thin of it.

"Are you ready, Granger? You have to go back and get Dolly's answer. I don't think I can bear another moment of the suspense. Granger, you must promise her anything, anything. Just see to it that she agrees!"

"Yes, Your Majesty." Just as Tori was about to speak

again Granger hushed her with a motion of his arm. "And yes, I'll not forget what you explained to me. If she agrees, she is to come here tomorrow dressed in a hood and veil. She is to say that she carries a parcel from Lord Fowler-Greene and she must deliver it to you personally. When she is in your chamber, the switch will be made. Correct?"

Tori rushed over to him and helped him into his cape. He picked up a long glowing taper to light his way down the stairs.

"Granger, I implore you, ride carefully. Don't fall off the horse. Look out for bandits and, above all, don't eat anything! You know that when you eat and your nerves are jangling you cannot move for hours. And I do not have the mettle to wait for hours. Go now," she added brightly.

"I have a better idea, Tori," Granger said hotly. "Why don't you go yourself? This way you'll save yourself all this worry."

"And deprive you of another glimpse of the ravishing Dolly? Granger, you above all should know that I've not a mean bone in my body."

Granger snorted in disgust. "You wouldn't give any woman the benefit of a compliment, save our friend Dolly Flowers. Now I wonder why that could be. Perhaps it is because of the resemblance you bear to each other?"

Granger left the room without a backward glance. He brightened considerably at the thought of the beautiful Dolly, and surely if he made good time he would make her lodgings before the full light of day. He brightened still more when he recalled how Dolly remarked on his handsomeness. He rode faster.

Leaving his horse at a nearby livery stable to protect the poor nag from thieves, he made his way the few short blocks to Dolly's lodgings on swift feet. There was no way to tell which room off the long dark hall was Dolly's. Carefully and quietly, Granger opened first one door and then another. Some of the rooms were empty and others were oc-

cupied by sleeping forms snoring loudly in protest against
the penetrating dampness.

After the fifth try he saw the white ermine cloak in the
first faint rays of dawn that managed to creep through the
filth-caked windows. He walked quietly over to the narrow
cot and eyed it as though taking measurements. Dolly slept
with her face pressed into the lining of the cloak. Her closed
lids displayed her long lashes. A lock of flaxen hair, so like
Tori's, curved sweetly on her cheek. In sleep her face bore a
mask of innocence that time and a hard life would never
steal. Clearing his throat nervously, Granger shook Dolly's
shoulder and demanded in a hoarse whisper, "Have you decided?"

Dolly opened sleepy eyes and smiled up at Granger.
"Oh, it's ye. Oi wuz 'avin' mesel' a luvly dream." Through
slitted eyes she peered up at him. "Did Oi tell ye las' nigh'
tha' Oi think y'ere pretty?" As if to emphasize her words,
she wiggled seductively on the narrow cot. Then she
stretched luxuriously. "O' course, luv, Oi made me decision
las' nigh'."

She smiled again as she rubbed the fur. The cloak slid
away from one shoulder revealing a creamy expanse of
flesh that looked softer than the ermine. Granger drew in his
breath and Dolly smiled.

"Cum 'ere, luv, an' si' by me. Tell me more o' thi' plan."

Granger, never one to dally in the presence of a lady,
quickly sat on the edge of the cot and watched as the cloak
slid even farther while the wiggling Dolly tried to make
room for him.

Dolly made a half-move to restore the cloak, but
Granger put out his hand to stop her. When next Dolly
touched the cloak it was to remove it entirely.

"Oi do thank ye, Granger," Dolly said with enthusiasm
as she watched Granger fasten his waistcoat. He looked

puzzled. "Why dearie, this day is th' end o' me carefree youth," she exclaimed. "Tomorrow Oi'll be a married laidy!"

"I must say, Dolly, that when Lord Fowler-Greene discovers what a gem you are, he'll be cock o' the walk!"

"Providin' 'e can still walk, tha' is." Dolly laughed uproariously.

Chapter Eleven

Dolly shed her clothes, careful of her elaborate hairdo. Granger had explained that it was imperative she visit Tori's hairdresser and have her flaxen hair styled to match his cousin's. Feeling the chill of the room, she hurried and wrapped the ermine cloak around her nude body. Delighting in the feel of the silky fur against her skin, she padded her way across the room to peer into the cracked looking glass. As she studied her image a knock sounded on the door.

"Why, it mus' be th' Blade," she thought. "'E's th' only gent Oi've ever 'ad who takes th' trouble ta knock." For a second she hesitated. What would he say when he saw her? Dolly stepped to the center of the room and assumed a graceful position, allowing the cloak to slip seductively.

"Cum in, Scarblade," she called. Scarblade's tall frame entered the room; his coal-black eyes flickered around the bare, dim surroundings. "Ow, Scarblade," Dolly said petulantly, "ye know it maikes me 'air stand on end when ye do tha'!"

"Do what?" he barked, his eyes taking her in for the first time.

"Ye, when ye rake yer eyes aroun' loike tha'. As if ye expected th' King's men ta jump out o' th' shadows an' grab ye."

"One can never tell, Dolly."

"Aye, but ta think Oi'd 'ide an enemy o' yers 'ere and let ye walk inta a trap. It's very little ye think o' me!"

"Ah, Dolly, don't carry on so. And tell me, what have you done to yourself?" His generous mouth broke into a wide grin. "Are you planning to attend a masked ball?" His dark eyes narrowed to slits and the light danced off them like quicksilver.

"Aye, ye say tha', milord," Dolly said haughtily. "An' do Oi offend ye?"

"Where did you get that cloak?" Scarblade said, ignoring her question.

"It's none o' yer business, Oi'm sure."

"I'm making it my business! Now answer me. Where did you get it?" He took two long strides and had her by the arm.

"Ah! Take yer 'ands off me, Scarblade. Ye don' own me, ye know. 'Tiz true we 'ad many a good roll on tha' cot o' moine, but Oi'm a laidy from this day on. Stop pawin' me loike this!"

"Don't you like it?" Scarblade asked roughly, as he pulled her closer to him. Dolly could feel his heart pounding within his massive chest and she discerned a tightening of his body as he held her against him. "I can remember days, Dolly, love, when your passion equaled mine." His lips were in her hair and Dolly regained herself enough to remember her new coiffure. She pulled away from him and the effort left her breathless.

"Well, dearie, those days is gone and Oi don' loike it any longer!"

"I can see you've become a grand lady since last I've seen you. What are you up to, Dolly? Who did you steal that cloak from?"

"Oi didn' steal it! It wuz given ta me. By a gent, Oi migh'

add!" she said sweetly as she caressed the velvet. "An why are ye so concerned abou' wha' Oi wear? Ye never were before! Oi'm weary o' ye, Scarblade. They say yer th' busiest 'ighwayman in all England, an' yet 'ave ye ever given me more'n a few shillin's ta pay me ren' or get me shoes fixed? Naw, never!" Her voice rose to a decibel below a screech. "An' who're ye savin' all tha' gold fer, tell me tha', Scarblade? Jus' tell me! Ye fer sartin don' spend it on yersel'!" she said, eying his plain, black frock coat and cotton hose. Her eyes darted over his tightly fitting dove-gray trousers and she fought back the memory of his strong, muscular legs as they had forced hers apart.

"Dolly," he said smoothly, fighting to control his laughter, "one word of advice. If you want others to think you a lady you must keep your composure."

Dolly shrugged elaborately, and the cloak slipped again to reveal a creamy shoulder and the sloping curve of her white breast. Scarblade drew in his breath, his desire mounting. With a smile, Dolly drew the cloak more snugly about her.

"If it's gifts you want, Dolly, you'd better stay with the er . . . gentleman acquaintance you've made, for you'll not receive gifts from me," he said quietly as the twinges of desire bloomed to an ache. "You never asked for anything before this. I thought our passion was a mutual thing. Come on now, Dolly, take the pins out of your hair and come to me."

"Ye'll no' be gettin' any luv from me this nigh', Scarblade," Dolly said as she peered at her reflection in the cracked glass. Even as she said it she could feel the hunger for him growing within her.

"I'll give you a few shillings to have your hair done in the morning if that's what's wrong," he said quietly, coaxingly.

Quickly Dolly glanced over her shoulder, puzzled by the softness in his tone. But then she thought of sitting a whole morning having her hair dressed and felt revolted by the memory. Besides, she thought craftily, this is me chance ta make me a fortune. Oi'll not lose it fer a roll on th' cot, no matter 'ow sweet!

"No, thanks," she said regally, noting the effect on Scar- blade when he closed his eyes to slits and glared at her. "Now, if ye don' moind, Oi wish . . . Oi wish ta . . . be alone." Her voice shook slightly with indecision. "Oi've other fish ta fry, Scarblade, an' ye'll no' stop me!"

He laughed, a deep booming sound, starting from within his broad chest. "So, Dolly, it seems you're more a lady than I gave you credit for. You share the same qualities as the more high-born of your sex, namely greed." He stepped over to the narrow cot and sat down, casually placing an elbow on his knee.

Dolly watched him, steeling herself for his wrath. In- stead, she was rewarded for her silence with still another in- solent laugh. "Come here, Dolly. You know you want to," he said quietly, outstretching his muscular arms to her. For an instant Dolly was undecided, remembering how warm and safe his arms could make her feel.

"An' wha'll ye give me? Eh?" she asked huskily, desire for him deepening her voice.

"Anything you wish. What shall it be?" he asked, mea- suring her through narrowed eyes that burned through her.

"A gold guinea!"

"A gold guinea it shall be." He reached into the purse hung from his belt, retrieved a golden coin, and hurled it to- ward her.

Dolly skittered across the floor in an effort to capture the coin, disbelief stamped on her face. "'Tiz abou' toime ye've cum across wi' sumpin fer me, it is. A girl 'as ta watch 'ersel' an' make 'er own way in this world, she does."

Picking up the gold coin and dropping it into the pocket of her cloak, Dolly stood and looked at the man who lounged upon her cot. She gasped when the full force of his gaze came to rest on her. His mouth was drawn into a tight line, and she saw the scar on his cheek color with anger. His dark, heavy brows netted together and the black eyes beneath them burned into her, shaming her.

Dolly affected a pleasant smile. "Oi wuz jus' teasin' ye. Oi never wanted yer money. Oi jus' wanted ta see wha' ye'd do . . ."

Scarblade turned his head and rose from the bed, gathered up the frock coat that he had so carelessly tossed upon the solitary chair, and walked out.

Tori, clad only in her petticoat, paced her room on the morning of her wedding day. She kept an open watch on the delicate ormolu clock and drew no comfort from the slowly moving hands. Granger knocked on her door and whispered, "Is she here yet?"

Tori leaned against the oak doorframe. "No, Granger, do you think she's changed her mind? What if something happened to her? Perhaps you should start out to look for her."

"Be sensible, Tori. Where on earth could I tell your father I was going, dressed in all this finery? Don't dither so, she'll be here. I promise you."

"But Granger, I have but an hour left!" Tori said, panic making her voice shrill.

"Don't forget she has to walk from her lodgings," Granger reminded her. Then he whispered, "Wait a minute, here comes your maid and there's someone behind her."

"Pray that it is her," Tori cried.

"There is a servant here for you, Miss Victoria. She's sent from Lord Fowler-Greene. Seems that he's sent you a present and she is instructed to place it in your hands herself. I'll wait and show her out," Annie added curiously.

"That won't be necessary. You'd better see if Mother can use some help. Granger will see her out. Hurry now!" Tori pleaded. Annie left the room reluctantly, glancing over her shoulder at the wrapped parcel the servant clutched in her hands.

Quickly, Tori closed the door and threw the heavy bolt. "What the devil took you so long to get here?" she demanded of Dolly. "I'm so glad you could come!" she added sarcastically.

"Me pleasure, miss," Dolly cooed, ignoring the caustic tone of Tori's voice. Dolly looked around the handsome room and marveled at the costly hangings.

"Hurry, Dolly! Hurry! There's not much time. Take off all your clothes. I hope you had a bath this morning!"

Dolly bristled at this questioning of her personal hygiene.

"Soon you'll be rich," Tori said as she feverishly ripped off her petticoats and handed them to Dolly. "Everything has to be right from the skin out."

"Oi can see, a real laidy," Dolly smiled as she fingered the rich, embroidered lace on the petticoats.

"Never mind the lace. You'll have time enough to look at it. Just put them on, hurry! My mother will be here soon and there are several things I must tell you. Quickly now!"

Fifteen minutes later Dolly was resplendent in Tori's wedding gown. "Now the veil, Dolly." Tori placed the heavy seeded-pearl crown on Dolly's head and threw the net over her face. Then she finished dressing in Dolly's worn gown and fastened a soiled apron around her waist. "Ugh! How can you go about in these rags?"

"Well, miss, when ye've got no' a crown ta yer name ta buy soap or a crumb o' food ta fill yer belly, th' state o' yer clothes is th' las' thin' ta worry about!" Dolly shot at Tori.

Tori said, "You must keep your mouth shut from now till tomorrow morning. Whatever you do, don't lift the veil in my parents' presence. If you can manage to smile and act sweet and agreeable to Lord Fowler-Greene till he gets you to the bedchamber, then you can let your other er . . . accomplishments take over. If you just play coy with the lord you should do fine. I think it only fair to warn you, though, he loves to pinch."

"Oh 'e does, does 'e? Well Oi'll soon cure 'im o' tha'!" Dolly giggled.

Tori joined in the laughter. "Listen to me now, Dolly, I shall take your place at your lodgings till Granger comes for me. When the lord finds out he's been duped, you're on your own. You will have to outthink and outsmart him. Do you think you can carry it off?"

Dolly nodded. "It's no' me brain Oi'll be usin', miss. But yes, Oi think Oi can carry it off. Coo, imagine, Oi'll be a real laidy. Me old mum should only see me in this getup. Oi'm no' a virgin, ye know," she said, eying the white gown and frowning.

Tori smiled. "Somehow I didn't think you were."

"Do ye think th' old boy'll notice?" Dolly asked anxiously.

"It's up to you to see that he doesn't," Tori snapped.

"Luv, however in th' world do ye think Oi can manage tha'?"

"I'm the wrong one to ask for advice."

"Oi can see tha'," Dolly scoffed.

"I must go now, Dolly." Impulsively Tori hugged the white-clad Dolly and whispered, "The best of luck to you, Dolly. And thank you from the bottom of my heart." With a jaunty salute Tori left the room, headed for the back stairway, and fled down to the kitchen regions. Once out in the open road, she paused a moment and looked back at her home. She felt a small tug at her heart and blinked back the tears. "I had to do it," she said to herself as she trudged into town to Dolly's lodgings. She would have to get herself settled and wait for Granger.

* * *

Lady Lydia opened the door to tell Tori that the judge was waiting. "I am so happy that you're ready. You look lovely, my dear," she said happily. "Your father will be so pleased. I think he thought this day would never come. And your intended!" She rolled her saucer-shaped, bright blue eyes. "He's beside himself! I don't think he yet believes his good fortune in winning you."

Dolly bobbed her head, saying nothing.

Both women left the room and started down the steep stairwell.

Lord Rawlings looked lovingly at Dolly. So it was true. She was actually going to go through with the wedding. He could hardly contain himself at his good fortune. He patted his waistcoat and felt the key to the strong box. Still, something niggled at him. The wedding wasn't over with yet. Once the "I do's" were said then he could breathe easy.

"Victoria, you have been a good and faithful daughter. I love you dearly, as does your mother. I want to say that I know you will be very happy." When he received no response to this declaration his stomach turned over. I knew it, he muttered to himself; she won't go through with it. At the time she is supposed to say "I do", she'll say "I won't!" He clasped Dolly's hands in his own and whispered fiercely, "All I can say to you, Victoria, is that you'd better say 'I do.' Do you understand? If you bollix this up, I'll have you whipped, which isn't such a terrible thing. I should have had it done before. You are much too strong-willed. This wedding is to go off as planned. Do you understand, Victoria?"

A slow smile spread over Dolly's lips. The whole family was crackers. She had every intention of getting married. In fact, wild horses couldn't drag her from here. Catching a glimpse of her intended, she blanched slightly. So wha', she chided herself. 'E migh' be a dear old duck. 'E's probably starvin' fer affection. If there's one thin' Dolly's an expert at, tha's it. Oi'll jus' luv 'im ta death, she giggled to herself.

Chapter Twelve

Dolly bade the wedding guests, drunk on wine and food, a silent farewell. Once in the darkened coach she lifted her veil and immediately was engulfed in a clenching embrace which she returned just as ardently as it was given. There ensued much giggling and laughter for the balance of the trip. There was a small yelp of pain from Lord Fowler-Greene as he had his ear bitten soundly, but playfully.

"You little vixen," he laughed. For reply Dolly nibbled daintly on his other ear. Lord Fowler-Greene groaned in delight. He used his pearl-handled walking stick to pound on the front of the coach. "Faster, driver," he roared. When the horses picked up speed, Lord Fowler-Greene was thrown off balance and landed on the floor with Dolly on top of him. Dolly kissed him passionately, all the while tweaking his ear. Kissing his lips, his chin, and his neck, she whispered softly in his ear. While the words were not distinguishable, Lord Fowler-Greene whispered, "More."

* * *

Dolly turned her head from left to right and back again in an effort to take in her new surroundings as she was led through the darkened foyer and up the ornate staircase to his bedchamber. When she hesitated to admire a view from the gallery, Lord Fowler-Greene prodded her forward with an intimate pinch on the back of the thigh.

She smiled and playfully twitched the fold of skin beneath his chin. Lord Fowler-Greene blushed and pinched her again in an effort to disguise his embarrassment. He'd not had excessive experience with women, not even when his wife was alive. And to have his advances met with a friendly welcome was indeed a novel treat.

"Hurry, hurry," he breathed. "This way."

Dolly laughed and pleased him with a quickening of her step.

In his haste to reach the door, the lord tripped on the edge of her gown. Dolly quickly reached out a supporting arm and prevented him from falling. She gathered him closely to her, murmuring soft, winsome phrases. Lord Fowler-Greene found himself with his face tightly pressed against Dolly's soft, yielding breasts. The aroma of Tori's cologne wafted to his nostrils and set his mind reeling. Oh, give me strength, he prayed fervently, I hope I have the strength.

He regained his footing and opened the door. Glancing into the room, he saw to his pleasure that all was in readiness as he had requested.

Dolly stepped across the threshold and drew in her breath in a silent "oh" of wonder. Her eyes traveled from the giant bed, set on a dais and hung with heavy red velvet draperies, to the accent tables laden with fresh-cut roses. The rug beneath her feet was thick and soft and the candle glow illuminated the gold leaf pattern on the red damask wall covering. Everywhere she looked there was another bowl of fresh-cut roses. Where such flowers could be found in the late fall of the year staggered her imagination.

Lord Fowler-Greene stepped lightly over to Dolly and helped her to remove her white, ermine-lined cloak.

Dolly bent her head to facilitate its removal and Lord Fowler-Greene succumbed to the urge to plant a kiss on the nape of her neck. Dolly leaned back and pressed against him and he held her for a moment. Turning slowly, she allowed him to embrace her and feel the warmth of her body. Dolly smiled secretly when he whispered in her ear, "I promise to go slowly, my dear, but you're so lovely . . . forgive me." He pressed his mouth to hers and she took the initiative. Slowly her lips parted, allowing him to search out the warm, moist recesses of her mouth.

Dolly remembered who she was supposed to be, and fearing to give over the game, drew back from him, a shocked expression on her face.

"Now, now, darling, I see I have much to teach you. 'Tis perfectly normal, a natural thing. Don't be frightened. 'Tis only because I love you so much." He panted as he pushed her toward the bed.

They fell together, the lord on top of her, squeezing the breath from her body with his immense weight. Oh, Dolly thought to herself, this'll never do.

"Milord," she gasped. "I'm only a small girl, forgive me." She pushed him from her onto the mattress. Extricating herself, she slid from the bed and whispered, "One little moment, milord," carefully trying to hide her cockney accent.

Slowly and deliberately, she unfastened her gown and let it fall to the floor. Gracefully, she stepped out from its wide skirt and removed her slippers, all the while looking into the mesmerized eyes of Lord Fowler-Greene.

Free of the encumbrance of her gown, Dolly hopped onto the bed beside him, cooing soft words of endearment. Sportingly, she began to undress him. First the buttons on his waistcoat, then his cravat. Lord Fowler-Greene allowed her to undress him, helping her with subtle movements, much like a child being aided by its nursemaid.

When at last all restricting garments were removed, Dolly sweetly told him he would have no need for his jewelry as she was afraid he would inadvertently scratch her. She removed his heavy rings, testing their size on her slim fingers and weighing their bulk before plunking them down on the bedside table. Lord Fowler-Greene reached out his arms and pulled her toward him, and she deftly escaped his embrace.

She stood up quickly, looking down at the wide neck of Lord Fowler-Greene's blouse that revealed his white, hairless belly. The sight of it reminded her of the mackerels she used to split when she worked at the fish market, and she almost hesitated, thinking, A girl does 'ave 'er standards. Then her eyes traveled to the bedside table on which rested his huge, jeweled rings and a new determination was wrought in her.

Before she could change her mind, she began to undo the laces of her camisole. Lord Fowler-Greene watched her, lust dancing in his eyes. A primeval bellow rose in his throat as he divested himself of his few remaining garments.

Dolly watched him through slitted eyes as she busied herself with ribbons and laces in an effort to free herself of her many petticoats.

Lord Fowler-Greene settled back against the velvet throw and dazedly watched the tableau she presented. The whiteness of her body stood out in relief against the deep reds of the room. The flickering candles threw lacy, dappled patterns on her lissome form. As she raised her hands to free her long flaxen hair of its pins, her uplifted arms displayed the clean, flowing lines of her breasts.

Lord Fowler-Greene's breath caught in his throat as she turned to him and stretched her arms out, reaching for him.

* * *

Lord Fowler-Greene lay next to Dolly, a quizzical expression in his eyes. Sensing his gaze upon her, Dolly lifted her lids and smiled at him. "Who are you?" he asked bluntly. "Surely you're not Victoria."

"Wha' makes ye think not, milord?"

"Victoria Rawlings has the eyes of a cat. Yours, child, are a willow gray. I ask you again, who are you?"

"When did ye first perceive th' difference, milord?" Dolly asked haltingly, fear in her eyes.

"Oh, no, be not afraid, child. I wouldn't hurt you. I love you," he said simply.

"Ye do?"

"Yes," he breathed. "I know goodness when I see it. But tell me, how did you come to be in this marriage bed? Where is Miss Rawlings?"

Hesitatingly, Dolly told him of the deception.

"That old fox Lord Rawlings is behind all this. He sought to embarrass me and still keep the purse, a double purse! I can see him now, laughing at me. And what recourse would I have? If I create a stir he puts me in the position of being the laughingstock of London. This way, he thinks to keep his daughter and my money besides." Anger welled up in him as he thought of the trick played. His impulse was to thrash Dolly and send her packing. His gaze lingered on her as she lay on his bed, her face pinched in concentration to read his intentions, her eyes tear-filled. The coverlet had slipped from her and disclosed a shapely thigh. Something instinctive tore through his chest and engulfed him. He opened his arms for her and she came to him, pressing herself against him. He held her gently, smoothing the silky skin of her back. Love flooded through him, a sensation he had never known. He could do worse, much worse. As he held her he murmured against her hair, "Methinks, dear child, I made the better of the bargain."

Dolly pressed closer, reaching out behind the lord to the bedside table. Picking up one of the heavy jewels she had so carelessly placed there, she buried her face in her husband's shoulder, smiling wickedly.

Tori trudged wearily into town and headed directly for the Rooster's Crown, stopping from time to time to remove pebbles from her shoes. She looked gloomily at her road-torn slippers and wondered how long they would last.

Quietly, she opened the door of the rooming house and started down the dark passageway. Dolly had said the fifth door. Cautiously, she opened it and peered inside. She gasped. This was where she was to stay? A small, narrow and lumpy cot was to be her bed. There was a crooked chest that served as a wardrobe, with a cracked mirror hanging above it. As if drawn by magic, Tori looked around for other comforts. There were none. Not even a rag rug. The only consolation was that there seemed to be no bugs, and sparsely furnished as the tiny room was, it was clean.

Tori opened the chest. There wasn't much, another tattered gown such as she had on, a frayed petticoat, and a pair of woolen stockings. There was a chill in the room and Tori wrapped her arms around herself as she closed the lid. Looking at the cot and the two skimpy blankets, she muttered aloud, "I'll freeze!" Tori looked around again and bent over to peer under the bed. The ermine-lined cloak! Where was it? That's what the little slut was carrying in the package; she hadn't even left the cloak! Tori grimaced. Dolly had a brain, she did. She didn't leave anything to chance. A girl after her own heart. Tori suddenly giggled, flinging herself down onto the cot to rest her aching feet from the long, unaccustomed walk.

Huddled there, Tori looked up as the door opened.

"Oi though' Oi would foind ye 'ere lazin' 'roun'. Get up, me girl an' 'and over th' ren'. Oi waited too long as 'tis. No 'one more day'! Cough it up, me girl!"

"Wha' . . . what?"

"Th' ren'!" the blowsy woman yelled. "Where izzit?"

Panic gripped Tori, "I . . . I don't have it," she whimpered.

"Oi though' as much. Well, ye won' get it lazing 'roun' 'ere. Get yer backside over ta th' inn an' clean an' scrub. An' tell Jake ta pay ye yer wages t'night an' ye best brin' th' coppers straigh' ta me. Otherwise," she added ominously, "ye'll be spendin' yer winter in Newgate!"

"Newgate? You can't mean that!" Tori said vociferously.

"Oh, an' don' Oi? Do ye think ye can stay 'ere an' no' pay me rent? Oi wan' wha's me due, do ye 'ear? An' th' way Oi sees, a month's lodgin's ye owe me!" The slattern moved closer, threateningly. Tori could see the cruel lines in her face and smell the rank odor of spilled ale and decayed teeth.

"But I can't go to work at the inn. I'm waiting . . . I'm waiting. Besides, I . . . I don't feel well. But I'll get it for you as soon as I'm better."

"Wha's all this 'orse dung, when ye're better? Didn' Oi see a gen'leman cum in 'ere las' eve? An do ye 'spec' me ta believe 'e didn' leave ye naught? Hah!" she shouted raucously. "Do ye now?"

Tori bristled at the onslaught against her character and then she remembered it was Dolly the landlady was speaking of. She also remembered Dolly's cockney accent. "Well 'e didn' leave me anythin'! An' when Oi'm better Oi'll 'ave th' money fer ye!"

The fat slattern moved closer for a better look at Tori. Picking up the candle from the rickety table, she lit it with a flint. Holding the candle higher, she peered through nearsighted eyes, squinting at the girl. Fear gripped Tori's innards and she involuntarily drew back on the cot. Undoubtedly, the landlady knew Dolly quite well, and Tori wasn't at all sure that the difference between the two girls' appearance would go unnoticed if one were looking for it. Tori averted her eyes, allowing the landlady to think the candleglow was irritating to them.

"Aye! Ye do look a little peaked at tha', Dolly. Oi can' place me finger on it but ye do look feverish. Poor lass . . ." Just as Tori was sure she was gaining the slattern's sympathy, a look of horror came into the watery, brown eyes of the landlady. "Look 'ere, ye've no' gone an' gotten yersel' ridden wi' plague, 'ave ye?"

At the mere mention of the word, the woman withdrew a few steps. If there was anything she feared more than the pox, it was the plague. Almost indiscernibly, she wiped her hand on her filthy apron, and then remembering the candle in her hand, dropped it back onto the table as though it had suddenly become too hot for her to touch. She spit on her hands and rubbed them again.

"Now look 'ere! Oi'll no' 'ave yer sickness in me 'ouse, Oi'll no'! Oi runs a decent 'ouse 'ere an' Oi'll no' 'ave th' loikes o' ye callin' in th' 'ealth authorities an' closin' me down. Now out wi' it! Do ye 'ave th' plague? Wha's wrong wi' ye?"

Tori immediately saw she had the edge so far as the landlady was concerned. "No, Oi don' 'ave th' plague. Oi'm simply no' mesel' t'day. Mayhaps Oi'll be feelin' mesel' by mornin'." And Granger had better get himself here by that time, she thought sourly. I'll not have his tales of drinking to excess at my wedding.

"'Ere, wha's th' meanin' o' usin' tha' uppity talk wi' me? 'Mayhaps Oi'll be mesel' in th' mornin','" the landlady mimicked. Then she shouted, "'Ave some respec' ta who yer talkin' ta, miss, or Oi'll 'ave ye thrown out on yer ear this minute!"

Tori bristled, about to rebuke the slattern. Then suddenly, she took another tack. "Why, missus, ye talk so much o' th' plague mayhaps yer th' one 'avin' th' vision, ye know, a 'eavenly warnin'. Oi should be careful or 'twill be yersel'." Tori allowed a veil of horror to slowly descend over her face and then she feigned an enlightened expression. "Why, missus, Oi 'ear tha' a weakness o' th' eyes is one o' th' first warnin's an' then an achin' o' th' 'ead an' then a shortness o' temper. An' lastly, th' wretched black spots tha' mark its victims. 'Ow 'ave ye been feelin' lately? Oi mus' say ye don' seem ta be yer usual composed sel'."

A dawning of understanding fell over the puffed and gray face of the landlady. Tori thought the small, oblique, brown eyes would pop from her head. A heavy, hamlike paw was clutched to her thick neck as Tori continued her charade. "Also, they tell o' a dryness o' th' mouth among other thin's."

"An' 'ow do ye know so much abou' th' plague?" the proprietress said in a raspy voice. She was clearly stunned by the similarity of symptoms.

"Why, missus, at one toime Oi worked in th' 'ouse o' a family doctor," Tori lied, "an' along wi' learnin' th' symptoms o' th' plauge Oi also learned somethin' o' th' cures."

"Hah! There be no cure fer th' plauge!"

"Oh, but there is, if catched ear'y."

"Please, be a good child an' tell me wha' ye know o' th' cure. Fer Oi'll tell ye a secret, Oi've got a friend whose 'ealth concerns me. She's no' been 'ersel' o' late an' Oi'm dearly worried fer 'er."

Tori stifled a grin at the landlady's try at deception. "Well, a good strong, 'ot posset made from barley an' goose fat always wuz th' doctor's favorite remedy, an' lots o' rest. Why, 'e would make 'is patients lie abed fer weeks! 'E believed contact wi' other people at a toime when th' ebb o' life wuz so low would worsen th' disease an' mayhaps catch other sickness."

"Oh, yes. Oi can see where 'e could well believe tha'," the landlady said in a weak voice as she retreated another three steps away from Tori. "Well, it'll never be said th' Mrs. Coombs wuz a fool an' never took good advice when it wuz 'anded ta 'er. Oi'll jus' go tell me friend ta lie down.

'Ow long did th' doctor say ta rest? 'Ow much goose grease should be in th' posset?"

Tori breathed a sigh of relief as the slattern backed out of the room and hurried down the hall to her own quarters. Worrying about her own health would keep Mrs. Coombs busy enough to let Tori stay here until Granger would come and get her.

Then the reality of the situation hit her. Oh, why hadn't Dolly told her the rent was due? And food! Where was she to get food?

Tori slept that night fitfully, fighting the cold and hunger that tormented her. There she sat all the next day, dreading the return of Mrs. Coombs and anxiously awaiting the arrival of Granger. Her night was spent the same as the one before, and added to her tortures was the smell of food cooking, wafting from somewhere down the alley and seeping through the crack in the window. Tori expostulated with every oath she knew and cursed Granger with a vengeance. Worse than the hunger and the cold was the anxiety over what could have happened to keep him from coming for her. Lastly, she berated herself for not having had the forethought to bring a little money.

All sorts of situations crept into her unwilling mind in the long hours she spent in the draughty room. Was Dolly discovered? Did Lord Fowler-Greene kill her? Was Granger a victim of some unforeseen accident? No imagining was too wild, no prediction too dire. In her cold and weakened state every horror played itself to the fullest, until Tori was a shaking heap among the few rags which covered her cot of despair.

Finally, Tori could stand the hunger no longer. She had to come to grips with her condition. "Oi think, me girl," she scolded herself, imitating Mrs. Coombs, "ye'll 'ave ta work fer yer keep!" Tori's stomach commenced to rumble at the thought of food. Then remembering the greasy slop that was served at the inn, she shivered.

What had started out as a happy lark, had turned into something dark and gloomy, not to mention possibly disastrous. "Why, I could starve or worse yet, freeze to death. What am I going to do?" she wailed to the small, mean-looking room.

Full of self-pity, Tori let her mind wander to the wedding reception with its copious food and drink. Her thoughts kept going to the ermine-lined cloak. Blast the girl! Dolly was probably right this minute stuffing her mouth full of meat and sweets and was comfortable and warm. Then she thought of Lord Fowler-Greene and shuddered again. "Never!" she shouted. Well, she would have to move her backside as the landlady said, and get over to the Owl's Eye Inn. Even if she had to work all day, she would make enough to satisfy her hunger.

Her face a mirror of dejection, Tori trekked around the building to the servants' entrance of the Owl's Eye Inn. Hesitantly, she opened the door and entered. She was rewarded with a smart cuff to the side of her head. Stunned, Tori blinked back the tears.

"Ye be late, Dolly. Oi' don' plan ta warn ye again. Oi'll be dockin' ye a copper this nigh'. If it 'appens again, Oi'll be gettin' rid o' ye. There be others tha' wan' me generosity."

"Generosity?" Tori squealed; then she remembered her place. Lowering her furious eyes, she nodded meekly.

"Well, don' stand there. Get ta work! Sweep an' mop these floors, then take out th' slop an' get ta th' kitchen. To-day'll be busy. There be a weddin' over ta' th' Jocelyns'. Some o' th' guests will be stoppin' fer some ale. Now git a move on afore Oi cuff ye again."

Tori scuttled away to the far corner of the room where she spied a broom. She held it clumsily, never having used one before. Still, she had seen the servants wield one and it looked easy enough. Gingerly she moved it back and forth across the floor. The dirt slithered here and yon.

"Th' slop pails, lass," the cook bellowed. "Get a move on afore 'is 'ighness takes 'is boot ta ye. Stop th' dreamin'. 'Tiz a poor pastime these days. 'Tiz only 'ard work tha'll give ye th' coppers ta fill yer belly."

"Oi'm 'ungry," Tori said pitifully.

The cook, eyes aghast, couldn't believe her ears. "'Ungry! Why ye know ye don' get no food till th' inn closes an' tha's almos' twelve 'ours from now. Wha' in God's name 'as gotten inta ye, Dolly? An' t'day it's only cabbage an' bread, 'is 'ighness said ta take ye down a peg fer th' sloppy work ye been doin' this mornin'."

"Oi detest cabbage," Tori said belligerently. "Dry bread!"

"Oi, but ye'll eat it when ye're 'ungry!" Tori yelped as she saw the cook upraise her hand to swat the sassy girl. Mollified by Tori's reaction, the cook headed back to the kitchen with Tori in her wake.

"Get after the slop pails, lass. Why ye be followin' me?" Tori looked blank. "Oi swear," the cook continued, "yer wits be addled this day. Get over ta' th' lodgin's an' get those pails!"

Tori walked on dragging feet over to the inn's lodgings and down the hall. As she grasped the handle of the chamber pot, her stomach somersaulted; she dumped the contents into the pail. God, how could she ever do this? Setting the pail down, she leaned against the wall and gagged and tried to stem the flow of tears. She had to do it! If Dolly could do it then so could she! Gritting her teeth, she picked up the pail and opened the door. She repeated her task with each of the other six rooms and walked around the side of the building looking for the pit which emptied into the middens. Staggering near to the edge, she near vomited from the stench.

Unable to go one step farther she leaned against the outside wall and gasped for breath. Her legs felt like jelly, her arms seemed as if they had been pulled from their sockets, her stomach muscles were drawn into a tight knot, and her neck felt like someone had tied a garrote around it. Again tears threatened to overflow.

She had to sleep. She needed rest. And she was so hungry. Tori knew if she stopped now she would never be able to move.

With a mighty heave she flung herself from the dank-smelling wall and stood upright on her trembling, quaking legs.

Back in the inn she spotted her tormentor in the process of emptying a tankard of ale. "There be guests in th' dinin' 'all. Take th' orders an' serve th' food. An' be quick abou' it. We don' need any yellin', bawlin' customers."

Brushing the hair from her face, Tori entered the dining hall. She glanced around at the customers—all men who eyed her lecherously.

"Cum 'ere, Dolly, me girl, an' give me a kiss," one bearded giant roared.

Tori paled at the request and walked hesitantly over to the man. "Sir," she asked quietly, "wha'll ye 'ave fer dinner?"

"Sir, izzit?" the man roared. "Ye be a tease, Dolly, me luv, cum 'ere an' give me a kiss."

Tori's step faltered as the man reached a long arm and brought her onto his lap. He gave her a smacking kiss on the mouth and set her upright. Tori gasped.

"Now ye can get me my meat an' potatoes," he laughed.

So this was the kind of game they played at the inn. Dolly was a plaything of sorts. She worked like a mule and then had to suffer these indignities! Through clenched teeth, Tori told the cook the customer's order. She carried it in shaking hands and placed it before the bearded man. She smiled tremulously.

"Ye'll 'ave ta move faster, Dolly, me luv," a man shouted. "Oi canno' fill me belly on pretty smiles." Tori hastened to obey.

As Tori stood waiting behind the kitchen doors she watched the cook dish out generous portions of lamb and cabbage. The rough language and the boots of the men rattled her, and for the hundredth time that day she pitied Dolly for the long, hard years she had worked in the inn.

The cook pushed a tray of food at her and glanced curiously into her face. "'Ere, Dolly, lass, wha's eatin' ye? Ye know if ye let them bullies get ye down they'll stomp on ye! 'Ere, 'ere, where's tha' ole spunk o' yers? Get out there, Dolly, and give them wha' fer."

So, Dolly was spunky, was she? And none too gentle with the clientele's feelings, too? Well, perhaps that was the way Dolly found to help her get through one long day after another. Taking a deep breath, Tori stepped out into the dining hall and delivered the tray. As she was bending over the table, she felt a hand reach up under her skirts and pinch the back of her thigh. Almost spilling a tankard of ale, she swung around and, not caring who was the recipient, slapped the reddened face of the man nearest her.

Shocked at what she'd done, Tori prepared herself to do battle. Instead she was complimented and cheered by laughing jeers directed at the man whose face she'd slapped.

"Tha' be more loike our old Dolly," a voice called from the far side of the room. "Brew and vinegar, Oi always says, eh men?"

When her tasks were finally finished, she looked at the cook in hope of food for herself.

The cook took a piece of boiled cabbage the size of an apple and a chunk of dry bread and handed it to Tori. Looking at the unappetizing meal, she shook her head. Her stomach turned and the bile rose to her throat.

Shaking her head, Tori walked into the taproom for her wages. Weary to the bone, she didn't see the booted foot of the bearded giant till it was too late. He caught her as she fell and started to paw her before the others. Tears gathered in Tori's eyes as she fought off the man with all her remaining strength.

"Cum on, Dolly, it'll be fun an' games. Stop th' blubberin'." Even though the tone was kindly, Tori was in no mood for the jeering and jesting at her expense. Seeing the tears, the man let her go. She walked over to the proprietor and waited patiently for her day's wages. He doled them out and held back several of the coppers. Tori looked at the meager coins and wondered if it would be enough to pay the rent. Eyes smarting, she turned to leave when someone grabbed her from behind and swung her into the air. Tori screamed in fright as the man tossed her to a companion. They tossed her back and forth and roared with laughter at her screams. Unnoticed in the mêlée the door opened and a cold, hard voice rang out, booming over the commotion.

"Leave the girl!"

Tori, crying openly, looked up at the tall man with the piercing black eyes. Someone hissed!

"Are you all right Dolly?" the brusk voice demanded. Tori nodded affirmatively. "Come with me. I'll take you to your room to be sure you get there safely," he said, raking the occupants of the taproom with a threatening, pointed stare.

"Watch out, Dolly. Wha' makes ye think Scarblade's th' one ta make ye safe?" a voice jeered, only to be cut off by a black look.

The innkeeper called nastily, "An' don' return on th' morrow! Oi'll be havin' a new lass 'ere. One tha' can do th' work an' no' weep an' wail all th' day. It wuz only a l'il jest th' men were 'avin'."

Tori cast a frightened look at the innkeeper. "But . . ."

"Ye got yer wages, now take yersel' off!"

Tori was barely cognizant of the events of the past few moments. She was only aware of her gratitude to this tall dark stranger who had saved her from the rough handling she had suffered. Suddenly she realized the identity of her rescuer!

Chapter Thirteen

Once he opened the door of her room he looked at her and waited for her to speak. Tori, in a quandary, did not know if the man and Dolly were friends, or what to say. He solved the problem for her. Looking into the room, he let his eyes rake it from top to bottom. He saw no sign of the ermine-lined cloak. Also, Dolly herself seemed different somehow.

"Dolly, where's the cloak?" he asked coldly, making his voice light.

"What?" Tori managed to answer.

"The ermine-lined cloak that you said a gentleman gave you. Where is it?"

"Oh." Tori's thoughts raced. "Oi . . . Oi returned it ta th' gent since it seemed ta upset ye," she said, quietly. Evidently it was the correct response to his question, for the man looked pleased.

"So, you had a change of heart, is that it?" Tori nodded and watched him carefully. "You stole it, didn't you?" the man demanded. "No gentleman gave it to you. You just wanted to trick me into giving you something of equal value. Am I right?"

Not knowing what the correct answer should be, Tori merely nodded. "I thought as much!" Scarblade smiled, apparently pleased to have his convictions made valid. "Come here now and take those blasted pins from your hair," he said in a deep-timbred voice. "I'm in a mood for loving this night."

Tori blinked. Did he mean . . . could he mean . . . ? Her mind raced, frantically searching for some diversion to occupy him while she tried to think of a way to make her escape.

"And none of your wiles, my lass. I've come to claim the gold guinea or what it was meant to pay for." His eyes swept over her mockingly, dangerously. Tori knew this was not a man to cross.

"What's it to be, Dolly? The money or the goods? You'll not get off as easily as you did last night."

What did he mean? Had Dolly rejected his advances? No, somehow Tori could not believe that was so. Dolly had an eye and an inborn appreciation for the male sex. It wouldn't be like Dolly to have refused this handsome rake anything!

A movement of his hand revealed he carried a bottle of wine. "Surely ye'll invite me ta 'ave a sip wi' ye," Tori said coaxingly.

"Of course, I brought it especially for you, knowing your taste for the grape. Get your cup, Dolly. We'll have a little celebration."

"Celebration?"

"Aye! To mark the settling of the differences of last evening. Go on now," he said as he worked with the cork in the bottle.

She moved across the room. "Ye know Oi've not much cause fer celebratin' now, wi' losin' me only means o' livelihood this evenin'," she said, falling back into Dolly's native cockney.

He gave a grunt as he pulled the cork from the bottle,

then gave a raucous shout of laughter and seemed beside himself with the humor he found in her words.

"Your only means of livelihood! Ah, Dolly love, now you've no reason to play the grand duchess with me. This is the Blade, remember? You'll make do somehow, I'll count on that. A lovely young girl like yourself and so . . . agreeable! Dolly love, an agreeable female always finds her way in the world. Besides, where's that hoard of coins you're so fond of reminding me of? Last I knew, you had a king's ransom in gold sovereigns. Now you wouldn't be trying to connive me out of my hard-earned cash, would you?"

So, Tori thought enraged, it seems Dolly carried more than an ermine cape in the bundle she kept clutched so close to her heart. The bawd! Leaving me without a ha'penny and the rent due . . . and Granger! When I get my hands on his neck . . .

But more immediate problems flooded her mind. What was she to do with Scarblade? He truly believed she was Dolly and what he expected of her brought a hot flush of color to her cheeks. In a rush, the emotions she experienced while sitting atop the giant chestnut welled through her with all their vividness.

His dark, heavy-browed eyes with their hidden depths of excitement and a thinly veiled passion looked into hers. Again she felt herself struggling to keep her breath from knotting in her throat as she had that September day when she had met the infamous Scarblade for the first time. But to meet him again . . . and in this manner!

"Drink up, Dolly, is my wine not good enough for your ladyship?" he mocked. He approached her and Tori felt her knees weaken. If he touched her she knew full well what effect it would have on her awakened passions. She hedged, retreated a step, put the cracked cup up to her lips, and took a hearty swallow, choking on the raw brew. Scarblade put the bottle to his mouth and partook deeply of its contents. When he finished he put the bottle down and gazed at her with heavy-lidded eyes. His white teeth flashed during a quick smile and he called softly to her, "Dolly love, will you take the pins from your hair now?" Tori noticed the scar on his cheek become more pronounced, and this, more than his burning looks, terrified her. "S for seduction" echoed through her thoughts.

He spoke so intimately. Couldn't he see she wasn't Dolly? Surely once a man slept with a woman he wouldn't be so easily fooled. Dolly and Tori were very close in looks and build, but there were definite differences. The eyes for example—how could he fail to notice Tori's tear-bright, cat-green eyes, so different from Dolly's, which were a soft, willow gray? It occurred to Tori that as far as Scarblade was concerned, there was no discernible difference between women. He could enjoy them, use them, and possibly profit by them—and never take real notice of their dissimilarities.

Tori struggled to gain control of her shaking knees. Then in a brazen retort to his demand that she let down her hair, she removed a pin, gathered a curl, and returned the pin to hold it more securely.

Scarblade's eyes narrowed. In one step he was against her, holding her fast to his lean, hard body. His lips were hot and wine-scented as they pressed against hers. She could feel her lips part beneath his as she struggled to free herself, as if fighting for her life. Scarblade held her closer, enveloping her within the strong fold of his arms.

Weakened by conflicting emotions, Tori ceased her struggles. Scarblade's answer was a renewed ardor as he pressed long, passionate kisses to her lips. She felt his hands in her hair, on her breasts, on the small of her back, and reaching lower.

Tori felt her sensibilities leave her and in their place, from deep within, came an answering response. As though of their own volition, her arms sought the rippling muscles of his back, the narrowness of his waist. Her thighs pressed against his, feeling their strength through her skirts. He was no longer kissing her and she was aware that his breath came in sharp rasps that matched her own. Low groans of pleasure escaped his lips as he began to trail them along her neck and then down to the cleft between her breasts Tori clung to him, welcoming him, pressing herself closer, and she was aware of his tumescence. Violently she struggled to free herself from him. What was wrong with her to acquiesce to his salacious, lustful advances? Had playing the role of Dolly become so ingrained in this short time that she was actually falling prey to that girl's loose morals?

Tori lashed out blindly, feeling the broken nails of her hand gouge and rake at his chest and neck. Fury inflamed her cheeks, and shame and humiliation at what she had almost allowed to happen brought hot, stinging tears of frustration to her eyes.

"You devil!" she shouted. "Keep your hands off me." She lashed out again with a clawlike hand aimed at the ebony eyes that burned through her, too furious to remember to feign Dolly's accent.

Scarblade sidestepped her flailing arm, caught it cruelly by the wrist, and pulled her against him, holding her there in an iron grip.

All the weariness of the past few days overcame her. Dry, wracking sobs of approaching hysteria caught in her throat. She was the vanquished and he the victor. Let him do with her what he would, then just leave her to sleep, perhaps to die.

Closely pressed one against the other, they held each other; Tori's lips were burning and bruised, and from time to time an involuntary trembling took hold of her.

Through the light material of her bodice he could feel the provocation of her breasts, and was aware that she could feel him swell with desire.

Feeling his lips part from hers, Tori opened her eyes and the flaming S on his cheek seemed to hypnotize her with its denotation of sexual arousal. He could read the desire in her

eyes and his caresses on her breasts became more active.
Again Tori surrendered herself, near to a faint, as though all
energy within her was anticipating a most unsuspected
pleasure.

The sound of shrieking laughter filled her brain and she
felt the 'Blade move away from her. Slowly, her sensibilities returned, as though she were pulling herself from a
dream. When Tori turned she was startled to see Mrs. Coombs
filling the open doorway with her bulk.

The hag was watching Scarblade and taking note of the
murderous expression on his face; her laughter died in her
throat. Retrieving her composure to a degree, Mrs. Coombs
made her excuse for her abrupt entrance. "It's me rent," she
said harshly, defying Scarblade to dispute her right to be
there. "Oi've cum fer it an' Oi wants it now!" Hanks of
greasy hair hung over her bloated, swollen face, and she
tossed her head with a jerking motion. "Well," she demanded, "do ye 'ave it er no'?"

Scarblade put his hand into a pocket, withdrew some
coins, and tossed them to her. "Here!" he said in a deep
voice that rankled with suppressed fury, "this should more
than satisfy you."

Mrs. Coombs scurried to capture the scattered coins,
near losing her balance in her haste. When she had picked
up the last coin she turned to Tori with hate-filled eyes that
bore into the girl's being. "An' Oi'll thank ye ta take yer
leave o' me 'ouse. Oi'll no' 'ave th' loikes o' ye scandalizin'
me 'ouse. An' be quick abou' it or Oi'll 'ave th' watch on
ye, an' it'll be more than jus' back rent Oi'll be 'avin' ye
picked up fer. Oi'll tell 'em 'ow ye tried ta kill me, Oi will!"

Tori's obvious confusion was well marked by Mrs.
Coombs. "An' Oi suppose ye'll deny ye tried ta kill me.
Barley an' goose grease posset, indeed! Oi near passed me
innards inta th' chamber pot, Oi did. Now out, Oi tell ye!
This 'ere's a respectable 'ouse . . ."

Scarblade had heard enough. This old harridan was going too far. The intensity of his passion was replaced with a scornful dislike bordering close on hatred. "You have your money, Mrs. Coombs, more than enough. Certainly more than this poor room is worth."

Mrs. Coombs drew herself to full height, and although Tori could see the faint twitching of her many-tiered chin, the landlady spoke with authority. "Out she goes, ye hear? Now!" came the sneering final edict.

Tori opened the small chest which served as a wardrobe, withdrew the meager items, and rolled them into a small bundle. Her step faltered as she walked past Scarblade and out the door. Where could she go? How would Granger find her?

There was a strange look on Scarblade's face as he watched her trudge down the filth-strewn alley. She was really going! This wasn't like Dolly! In fact, she had been acting strange these past two days. Normally she would have fought back and the landlady would be cowed by the tumult of Dolly's fury, terrified of her threats to have the old harridan's neck stretched by some of her rapscallion friends. He had seen her do it in the past. And then the business of the cloak! If she had been pressed for coins she could have sold the cloak and then had enough money for the rent. It didn't make sense! He watched the girl as she trudged down the road. She almost looked ill; where would she go?

The moon came from behind the clouds and lit up the narrow street. She would no doubt sleep in some alley and be at the mercy of any slum ruffian.

Scarblade turned to the slovenly Mrs. Coombs and sent her flying down the hall to escape his murderous glare. Moments later, he mounted his huge chestnut and started down the road after Dolly. He wanted that girl as never before. He tried to fight the feelings that raced to the surface. She seemed different tonight. She had fought him like a tiger and struggled against him. On other nights, she had come to him willingly and lain in his arms. She had been soft and warm, yielding to him in her passion. This was a new twist. Suddenly, his arms ached to hold her again, to feel her flesh pressing against him as a few moments ago, exciting him as never before. He had been pleasantly surprised by the strength she displayed. He had enjoyed her resistance almost as much as her response.

Quickening the pace of his horse, he rode abreast of Dolly and pulled up on the reins. "Come here," he said, "I'll help you." Tori kept on walking, neither looking up nor to the side of her. Tired, she knew that if she stopped even for a second she would not be able to continue. When the highwayman was done with her, had his way, he would leave her to rot. She must walk!

Scarblade scooped her up with a mighty arm and settled her across his lap. Tori, taken off guard, went limp and almost slid out of his arms. She was reminded again of another time when she sat next to him and knew the wild beating of his heart. She felt oddly at peace and didn't want ever to move from his hard embrace. She raised her head and looked with soft, glowing eyes at the man who held her. Scarblade met the adoring gaze and drew in his breath. He bent to kiss her and pulled her closer, holding her securely, and the chestnut made its way through the quiet city streets. The only sound Tori was aware of was the horses' clapping hooves and her own wildly beating heart.

Minutes later, partly due to the slow plodding of the horse and partly to a feeling of security, Tori's eyes closed and she slept.

From time to time Scarblade looked at the dozing girl with the strange smile on her face.

They rode that way for close to two hours, the tall man with the carbon-black eyes and the sleeping girl.

Scarblade rode into the clearing of a vast wooded area where he was met with a soft query.

"All's well," the Blade spoke softly. "I didn't think I

would be so late this night. I had a spot of trouble, as you can see."

"It be Dolly, guvner," said the deep, musical voice.

"Aye. She has been evicted and found herself homeless. And," the Blade said quietly, "she has been near beaten. Make a pallet for the lass and take her gently, Josh."

The burly, blond man lifted the sleeping girl from the Blade's arms. "Lord, I don't remember Dolly being this beautiful," he said, looking down at her.

"It's strange you should say that, Josh. I myself was thinking much the same thing."

The big man kicked his own pallet near a tree and spread the cover with his foot. Gently he lay the sleeping girl down and stood back to observe her. Having an eye for beauty, he grinned. Marcus was going to find he was about to have a few problems when the men spotted her.

Josh walked over to the fire where Marcus sat hunched with a cup of ale in his hands. "I fear there will be trouble if the girl stays," Josh said quietly, but with an ominous tone.

Marcus nodded soberly. "I know. But what was I to do, Josh? I couldn't let her walk the streets and fend for herself. She has not a copper to her name and only those rags she wears. If you had been in my place what would you have done?"

Josh nodded. "Much the same, me lad."

Marcus shrugged. "I think we best wait till morning and see how the lass responds. I'll give her a purse so she can start over somewhere. Is the watch yours this night, Josh?" At the other's nod, Marcus admonished him to keep a sharp eye on the girl and to wake him if she stirred.

Marcus peered up at the star-filled night and felt the cold air wrap itself around his body. He would have to find winter quarters soon. And the girl, what of the girl? She certainly could not last long out in the elements. Why did he keep calling her the girl? Her name was Dolly and many's the time her name came easily to his lips. Why not now?

Somehow it did not seem like Dolly. Oh, she looked like her and she wore her clothes, but her manner was different. This girl was soft and warm and she had melting eyes when they weren't breathing fire. He shrugged. It was Dolly, who else could it be?

Finally he slept, a fitful sleep. A beautiful girl kept telling him to guard her ring while a girl in rags pleaded with him to hold her close. Marcus wakened as dawn broke. His eyes went immediately to the slumbering girl and to Josh. Josh nodded. All was well.

Marcus rose wearily to his feet and walked over to the pail. He dunked his whole head in the ice-encrusted water. Droplets glinted off his dark, wavy mane as he toweled himself and strode to the fire. Josh handed him a steaming cup of coffee, and a brooding look masked his features as he sipped it.

"There is something I think best you know," Josh said hesitantly. Marcus raised thick brows. "'Tis the brothers, John and Charles. They were arguing last eve about things being divided more equally. They mean to make trouble. I heard Charles brag about the price on your head. He said they could turn you in and collect the reward. Then they could keep up with their plundering and keep all the spoils. And there wouldn't be anyone to share the loaf. I see no problem with Richard and Ned. They're good and loyal men, if you care for their ilk."

"Charles said that, did he?" Marcus asked thoughtfully.

"There's going to be trouble, Marc," Josh said soberly as he glanced about to see that no one was within listening distance when he used Scarblade's Christian name. It was an agreement between them that Marcus would only reveal his true identity to his band of men when all were aboard ship and safely bound for America. "I can feel it in my bones. And I think," he added ominously, "it's going to happen when we do the job you outlined."

Marcus nodded his agreement. "No doubt you're right,

Josh. I'll just have to stay ahead of them all the way. If I have to, I'll dispose of them. I'll need your help, Josh. I want you to keep an eye on the pair of them."

Josh was seized with a violent fit of coughing. As he groped for a handkerchief, Marcus felt saddened at the condition of his friend. "We have to get you out of this torturous climate, Josh. Once in the warm air of the Carolinas your recovery will be rapid. This cold, damp air does no one's bones any good," he said as he rubbed his forearms briskly.

Josh nodded weakly, the spasm over. "I long to see all my friends there," he sighed. "While I don't approve of all of this plundering, I can see that it's the only way to save the colony. I just pray that God sees fit to spare me to make the trip back, Marc," he said sadly. "Each day I feel myself grow weaker; there's no sense trying to fool myself—nor you, either."

Marcus frowned. He, too, noticed the change in the big man's condition. Josh had been strong and robust, but he now had the appearance of a man who was wasting. While his ruddy complexion still had a rosy hue, it was an unnatural color. The color of fever. Still, the bearded man was held in awe by the other men. He towered by a good head over the others. His arms were like corded saplings and his hands like huge hams. He could fell a tree in record time and then haul it away single-handedly. His golden crop of hair and thatch of beard were the envy of all the men. He had gray eyes, soft as a morning dove, that sized the worth of a man in a moment's time. For this Marcus was thankful. His own judgment had not been too trustworthy of late. While Marcus had the wits and the ingenuity to carry out the daring robberies, he depended on the brawn and the muscle of Josh. That and the common sense he showed when needed.

"Did you carry out the task I assigned to you?" Marcus asked suddenly. He had to shake himself out of this melancholy and get down to business. Time was short and every day counted. He must have his work finished when the ship sailed.

"Aye, Marcus, me lad. I delivered the full cask of sovereigns to the ship. Cap'n Elias has his instructions. He'll not part with one sovereign unless it is to you in person. The money is well guarded. I paid him well, Marc. And the offer of a new home in the Carolinas was like a piece of cake for the man and his family. He just awaits your decision on the sailing day. Have no fear. He is trustworthy. And that speaks for his crew as well."

"We need more, Josh. That pitiful cask is but enough for a year on the black market. Then what? Time is short for us now, and traffic on the roadways is light." A wave of rage welled up in Marcus, constricting the muscles around his heart. "Damn the King!" he swore viciously. "If he would only lift the blockade, cancel the embargo, he would save himself the trouble of putting a price on our heads and allow his soldiers better use of their time than searching the highways and the byways for the likes of us. And if we do get caught . . . hundreds of people will have lost everything—their land, their hopes, the promise of their children's future."

"If we can carry off the plan you have in mind we will be set for life. Do you think it will work, Marc?" Josh asked anxiously.

"If everyone does his job right I don't see how it can fail. It will be the most daring robbery in the history of England. And my conscience doesn't bother me a whit!" Marcus laughed.

"Imagine the look on the King's face when he finds out the covey of wagons bearing the taxes have been robbed. And it will all be in gold sovereigns. Only a short time to go and we can be on our way." Josh sighed. "I cannot wait to see America again. I've had enough of this land."

"The guard will be heavy," Marcus warned. "I wish I

knew what to expect. And what kind of weapons they'll have."

"Have no fear, Marc. Before it is time to ride, I myself will pay a visit to the Wild Boar Inn. With a little gentle persuasion one can find out what color undergarments the King wears." He roared at his small joke and convulsed in a fit of coughing. This time, the handkerchief came away red, Marcus noticed out of the corner of his eye. As Josh tried to hide the telltale signs, Marcus felt a hard knot in the pit of his stomach. He could not, he would not, lose Josh! They had been friends for a lifetime. If he had to, he would blow life into the man's chest to keep him alive.

"And the girl, Marc. What's to be done?"

Marcus shrugged. "I see by the look on your face that there is doubt of her. Is it that you think she is a spy for the Crown?" he teased the burly, blond giant.

Josh nodded wearily, doubt lining his ruddy face.

"But Josh, you're not serious. You don't know the circumstances—" Quickly he told him the story and watched the big man's face.

"It would sound like a bit of playacting to me, Marc. This business with the cloak, that's what worries me. The Dolly we both know would never have returned something that valuable. I think it is a trap. And another thing," he said, wagging a huge finger, "she has the looks of Dolly and the hair. But the hands, Marcus, me lad. Did you see her hands? Lily-white and not used to work. Aye! Blistered and red, true, but all the same, the hands of a lady. Dolly had the hands of a workingman. Strong, useful, calloused."

"No, I didn't notice, Josh. You see why you are invaluable to me?" Quietly Marcus rose, walked over to the sleeping girl, and looked down at her hands. What Josh said was true. Her hands were grimy and some of the tapered nails were broken, yet Josh was right. They were not Dolly's hands. He looked carefully at her and felt again the odd sensation of recognition. Who was she?

He squinted his eyes and frowned. Now he had not one, but two problems. John and Charles and this wench calling herself Dolly. He walked back to the fires and accepted another mug of coffee from Josh. "You're right, Josh. I was a fool to bring her here."

"Don't feel badly, Marc," Josh laughed. "Just be careful and watch your step. That's my advice to you."

Marcus grimaced. "I'll watch my step and everyone else's, too," he grumbled sullenly.

"What are you going to do with her, me lad?"

"I don't know just yet, Josh. We'll just have to take it one day at a time. I can just see all our hard planning thrown in the air if she's a spy. We need that tax money, Josh; otherwise the whole trip was for nothing. Just a temporary reprieve. Our people will starve in a matter of months. We can't let anything happen. See," he said, directing a looming, portentous glance in Tori's direction. "She's wakening, Josh."

Tori raised herself on one elbow and opened her eyes. Where was she? Memory flooded her being, bringing with it a sharp rebuke. Lord, how she ached! Would she be able to move? Her muscles were sore and cramped. Her head throbbed viciously. She sighed and looked around. Her heart skipped a beat as her eyes locked with those of the highwayman who sat near the fire.

In the early-morning light the final difference between Dolly and this girl was evident. Her eyes were bright with fever. What had he been thinking of not to have noticed them last night?

Tori tried to struggle to her feet only to fall to her knees. Both Scarblade and Josh watched. Josh had to hold Marcus's arm or he would have gone to her side.

Marcus relaxed. He watched the girl gain her feet and stand wavering in the cold air. She looked around the campsite and spotted the pail of water. Tori tottered to the rough plank that held the pail and wrapped her arms around the ancient tree. She swayed dizzily. Marcus jumped to his feet. Josh missed his coattails by a mere inch. Just as Tori started to fall, Marcus caught her.

"Best take it slow, Dolly, my girl," the Blade laughed. "It would appear to my men that you have taken to sipping or nipping, whatever the case may be." Tori frowned at his words. Her head felt thick and full of cotton. Rubbing her hands over her forehead she felt uneasy at the warmness of her skin.

"Take your hands off me," she croaked in a hoarse whisper. "Leave me be. When I want your help, I'll ask for it." Again she swayed precariously.

"Then hurry and ask for it, for in another minute you will fall to the ground," Marcus snapped.

Tori fought an angry retort as she felt herself falling. "Help me," she pleaded, her eyes bright. Marcus caught her as she sunk to the ground and she knew no more.

Taking in the scene, Josh ambled over and felt the girl's hot forehead. "She is feverish, and look at her cheeks. Just what we need," he grumbled, "a sick girl on our hands. A sick girl who just might be a spy for the Crown," he emphasized.

Marcus nodded impatiently as he lowered the girl to the pallet. "Fetch more blankets, Josh, and make some kind of a poultice for her fever." As Josh made off to do his bidding, he saw Marcus carefully pull the rough blankets up to the girl's chin. Josh smiled to himself. He, too, could well remember the feel of a girl in his arms.

Tori opened her eyes and gazed into the sloe-black eyes of Marcus. "Am I sick?" she quavered. Marcus nodded. Tori closed her eyes as though there were lead weights tied to the lids. She felt that to open them would take all the strength she possessed. Something deep in her mind told her this man would take care of her and let nothing happen to her. She drifted off into a feverish sleep. Tori felt gentle hands place something on her head and neck. A feeling of sudden warmth engulfed her as piles of blankets were heaped on her.

"The fever is high, Marcus," Josh said irritably. "She should have a physician look at her."

Marcus shook his head. "Just do the best you can, Josh. That's all for now. We can't risk moving her, and you well know that no physician can be brought here."

"But, Marc, she should be indoors. This cold, damp air will have her chest congested in no time. She has to be raised off the ground."

"Perhaps if we fashion a makeshift tent of some blankets and raise the pallet she will fare better."

There was much grumbling on the part of the men, but they hastened to obey Marcus's orders. Anyone who had ever seen Scarblade's temper once vowed never to be the one to raise it a second time.

Soon the improvised quarters were arranged and Tori raised on her narrow pallet well off the ground. Josh appointed himself her nurse and ministered to her like a guardian angel. He knew in his heart that this girl had some manner of hold on his friend, Marcus, whether Marcus admitted it or not.

Chapter Fourteen

"It's time! There should be good pickings tonight, men," Scarblade shouted, enthusiasm lightening his voice. "The wedding that was held yesterday will see the guests leaving today. Yesterday there was but a mere handful that took their leave. If we ride quickly and carefully we should be able to overtake close to a dozen before the night is over. Mount up, men, and follow the roads I've mapped out. Josh is staying behind with the girl. Remember my warning. There is to be no killing and no abuse." The men shouted their agreement and galloped out of the clearing while Marcus rode over to the makeshift tent and inquired of Josh.

"She's the same. She mutters but it's nothing important that she speaks. Ride safely, good friend, and take care!" Marcus turned and spurred the beast he rode.

Again Josh touched the girl. She appeared to be worse. If possible, her cheeks were more flushed. There was nothing else to do but wait.

All through the day Josh sat at her side and swabbed her head and arms. From time to time Tori opened her feverish eyes and saw a gigantic man with a golden beard watching her. She mumbled occasionally in her delirium. He tried in vain to catch the snatches of words but they made no sense to him. She spoke of "darling Granger, dear Granger"! Josh shook his large head like an angry bear and patted the girl's hand. "Sleep now," he said softly.

Josh kept up with the herb-soaked cloths, and several hours later, when he checked her again, she appeared to be awake and talking coherently.

"How sick am I?" she questioned hoarsely.

"Well, lass, a few hours ago I wouldn't have given a ha'pence for your chances, your fever was that high. But now," he smiled, "I think it has broken and that you will be well in a few days' time. How do you feel?" he asked.

"Weak," Tori whispered. "My bones ache and my head throbs like a drum. Where am I?"

"With Scarblade and his men, lass. I am Josh. Surely you remember me?"

Tori looked puzzled; then memory returned in snatches. She nodded weakly. She must not give herself away.

"Tell me, Dolly. How is it you are in this position, sick and such?"

"I had not the money for the rent. The old hag threw me out and Scarblade helped me," Tori whispered, her strength almost gone. Her eyes closed and she slept. But this time it was a healthy sleep. Gone was the flush from her face, and her brow was cool to the touch.

Josh dragged his weary bones to the fire and helped himself to some rabbit stew. He washed it down with ale and immediately had an attack of coughing. The blood was coming up in greater quantities these days. He had hoped to hide it from Marcus but the younger man had seen it this morning. He would have to make sure that nothing happened to himself till after the tax robbery. Marcus needed him, as did the colonists in that far-off place, North Carolina. God would give him the strength. He laughed at the irony of the situation, praying to God to let him live so he could help rob the King. "But to feed starving people," he defended himself. If there was a God, He would see to it that the task was carried out.

For hours Josh sat by the fire, feeding it from time to time so that the flames crackled and danced. He spread a mound of blankets near the fire and lay down. He dozed and woke as the embers sputtered and sizzled. It was but an hour to dawn when the sound of hoofbeats could be heard coming across the clearing. Josh stirred himself and placed the tall coffeepot on the flame.

There was much laughing and joking as the men tied their horses and came near the fire. Josh poured the steaming brew and watched silently as the men drank. Marcus was the last to arrive. His eyes questioned Josh but he spoke not a word.

"The fever is down and the lass will be as right as rain in a few days' time. How did the night go?"

"Almost a king's ransom," Charles laughed loudly. "We made a pretty penny this night. All the fine ladies had their best jewels with them."

Josh watched silently as the men dumped their booty on the dirty rag in front of the fire.

"At least two hundred sovereigns," John laughed. "Right, Scarblade?"

Marcus let his eyes rake the pile of gleaming jewels. Tomorrow they would have to be redeemed for sovereigns. After dividing with the men he would have about one hundred sovereigns to give to Captain Elias to add to the cask he held for him. He sighed. It still wasn't enough. But there was no question of withholding the men's shares. He must be fair to them.

"Listen to me, men. I have warned you before many times. Don't spend any of the guineas or the sovereigns as yet. Bide your time and wait."

There followed a chorus of grumbling, but it was good-natured for the most part. They knew Marcus was right. All but Charles.

"Ah, Scarblade," he sneered. "Wha's th' good o' 'avin' th' money if we can' use it? Oi, messel', wan' ta do a bit o' wenchin' an' Oi need money an' this is as good a toime as any ta say tha' John an' me ain't satisfied wi' th' way th' division on th' spoils go. Oi wants more! Oi takes as many risks as ye an' th' others. Ye get 'alf a share an' th' other 'alf is ta share among th' four o' us. 'Tiz 'ardly fair, Scarblade. Own up ta th' fact!"

Marcus had never liked the looks of Charles Smythe, and he liked his brother John even less. Were it not for the fact that they came highly recommended, he never would have engaged these two unlikely fellows.

Charles and John, of a like height, six feet tall at least, were both slim and light-haired. While John was the less attractive of the pair, being dirtier and more malicious-looking, both shared the same quickness and furtiveness of eye. Marcus, when he looked at them, was reminded of two half-starved, mangy dogs, scurrying to a far corner with a much-prized bone, all the while casting nervous, watchful glances to see no one came near to deprive them of their booty.

Now Marcus was incensed because of their ever-encroaching greed. Ned and Richard, on the other hand, had endeared themselves to Marcus. Poor, beggarly street urchins, who in manhood had become petty thieves and pickpockets, they now rode with Marcus for the promise of a better life in Chancelor's Valley. Still, Marcus was leary of Charles's and John's influence upon them. They were not far removed from the street urchins they once were.

Marcus's anger toward Charles burst forth. "You agreed when we set out on the venture. I warned you then that I was not in this to make money for myself. It is for the colonists in America. Your share is your own. To a man you agreed. I also offered you land and a home in America for those of you who want to return with me. Ned and Richard are wise enough to accept my offer for a better life. You would be wise to consider it also. What more can I offer you?" Marcus said coldly, his raven-black eyes narrowed.

"An even split," Charles barked, his mouth slanted in a sneer.

"There's no way that the money will be split evenly. If you don't like it you're free to ride out of here. No one will be the wiser," Marcus growled threateningly.

"Ride out, izzit?" sneered Charles, "wi' th' biggest robbery yet ta take place? If we left ye'd 'ave all th' tax money fer those people o' yers. No, Scarblade, we'll stick ta ye loike a mustard plaster till after th' tax robbery. Then we'll decide."

"Then it'll be too late," Marcus said through clenched teeth. "For I sail the day after. Or were you thinking of turning me in, Charles, and collecting the reward and the rest of my share? Speak up, man, or I'll tie you to the nearest tree."

"No, 'Blade, Oi wuz jus' 'avin' a bit o' fun wi' ye. Ye be righ', tiz a fair arraingemen'. Oi gave me word an' it's good. Oi speak fer me brother John as well." Marcus didn't believe a word of the man's talk. He knew him too well. He shot a knowing look at Josh, who didn't believe him either.

Tori fingered the rough material of the breeches she wore. At last her fondest dream had come true: to wear breeches. Yet, now that she had her way she suddenly longed for her own beautiful gowns. She didn't fancy looking like a boy after all!

Tori watched Scarblade mount his steed with great ease; she longed to do the same. She would miss the men when she left. While they hadn't been exactly welcoming, they had treated her kindly. But now it was time to leave. She was feeling better after her bout of illness. If Scarblade would let her have a horse, she could be on her way by first light of day. If not, then she would have to walk. Where would she go? She'd have to try to find Granger. Having made her decision, Tori approached Scarblade hesitantly.

Almost shyly, she raised her eyes, for the man inspired fear within her still, and flashes of that night in Dolly's room flooded and ebbed within her. The man's powers had thrilled her and yet filled her with dread. That he was a man to be reckoned with Tori was convinced; she had only to see the effect his commands had upon his men to know this. She had witnessed his anger. Feet planted firmly apart, S-shaped scar blazing on his handsome face, black eyes scornful in his ominous rebuke of the unfortunate object of his wrath. Now Tori herself risked being the recipient of Scarblade's anger and she trembled slightly with dread.

"Scarblade, it's toime Oi left," she said softly as he swung around at her slight movement.

"Leave? Where will you go?" he asked, his eyes cold, his mouth tight.

Tori shrugged. "Oi'll find a place fer mesel'. I can' stay longer wi' ye. Oi truly appreciate yer kindness while Oi wuz sick. Propriety makes it necessary tha' Oi leave."

Scarblade smiled wickedly. "Propriety, is it?"

Disconcerted, Tori realized her mistake. Dolly wouldn't care about propriety, let alone know the word. "'Tiz a word Oi 'eard from a friend o' moine. Don' it sound nice when it rolls off yer tongue?"

"I'm afraid your wishes count for naught, my lady," Scarblade said coldly as he dismounted from his steed.

"Wha' d'ye mean?" Tori asked fearfully.

"Just what I said, dear lady," Scarblade said, his face all cold indifference.

Alarm caused Tori's eyes to grow wide. Panic settled over her like a pall. "Wha' kind o' man are ye, anyway?" she demanded. "If Oi choose ta put off yer advances, why don' ye take it loike a man instead o' some churlish lout? Ta keep me 'ere till Oi weaken will never 'appen, so let me leave an' Oi'll no' bother ye again."

"Dolly, my love," Scarblade chuckled, "it is Dolly, is it not?"

So that's it, Tori thought. Her mind raced. "Wha's in a name?" she inquired softly, her heart pumping madly.

"In your case, quite a lot, dear lady," Scarblade mocked. "For example, if you were really Dolly, the men would respect you for the life you lead, which is hard-working and fair. A day's work for a day's wages. A little frolic on the side and everyone is happy. Now for the other example, let us say that you were a lady of quality, and a spy for the Crown. That," he said coldly, "makes a new story. Why, the men would be most upset! I would find it hard to interfere if they decided to have their way with you. They would rape you, to a man. They could use a garrote on you, they could shoot you down like the spy you are. I see by the tears that are welling up in your eyes that you are about to deny the truth."

Tori fought them back. "So my name is not Dolly. That does not make me a spy for the Crown. For personal reasons I took Dolly's name, but I assure you that I am no spy. And if you think to frighten me with the tales you have just spun for my benefit, think again. I can ride as well as any man here. I can also outthink any one of you. To die is not so terrible, if what one believes in is worth dying for, is that not so, Scarblade?"

He measured the girl before him. Why did she make him feel like a schoolboy? He felt like hunching over and scuffing his feet in unison.

"I want to warn you, my lady. I have no control over the men. You will stay. There is to be no mention of your leaving, now or later. When it is time for you to make your departure I will give you notice, not a second before. Is that understood? For your sake I will try and keep the men in line and away from you."

"So you can have me to yourself?" Tori demanded. "The spoils to the victor?" Tori was instantly contrite for her unfair words. If anything, Scarblade had drawn a wide berth around her.

As she faced the truth behind her anger her face flushed a deep crimson and she knew her ire stemmed from Scarblade's obvious indifference. Almost insulting, when one considered the wild moment they had shared in Dolly's room.

Marcus narrowed his eyes and brought his face within inches of Tori's. "I shall be the victor, make no mistake. As to the spoils, I think not. You are too skinny for my taste. I prefer more flesh on my women. And I prefer to have them come to me. They appreciate me more." Marcus laughed mockingly as he reached out a long muscular arm to jostle her shoulder.

"You, you insufferable . . . lout," Tori spat. "Don't touch me unless I give you permission!" she shouted angrily. "I am not some piece of merchandise to be pawed and passed from hand to hand! And furthermore, I will not give you my word that I'll not try to leave here. I will leave! You cannot keep me a prisoner here for your own nefarious pleasures. I won't have it! Do you hear?" Tori shouted as she stamped her foot in the dust. "I'll kill the first man who comes near me!" she said as she pummeled his chest with her small fists, eyes glittering angrily.

Marcus looked down at the shining, golden head as she pounded his chest. Suddenly he smiled as he grasped her arms; she was a handful, there was no doubt about that. He marveled at the soft feel of her through the thin material of the shirt she wore. Her cheeks flushed and her eyes sparkled. Marcus looked into the angry eyes and felt a sharp longing come to the surface. Slowly he brought his face closer. Tori, reading the intent in his eyes, struggled to escape the strong hand which held her. She was unable to move; his lips touched hers and she continued to struggle, aware of her resolve slipping away. Tori felt warm all over, her blood coursed, she felt dizzy and light-headed. Unexpectedly, she found herself on her knees, her arms upstretched, reaching.

Tori looked up into his somber, licorice eyes. What she saw there made her silent.

Awareness dawned on her of the picture she made there, kneeling in subjugation before this dark-haired, sun-bronzed giant with her arms supplicating his favors.

Tori hated him with every fiber of her being. What kind of devil was this who could rankle her to an hysterical fit of scratching one moment and then dissolve her sensibilities to those of a wanton.

And he, with booted feet spread firmly apart, the cut of his trousers clinging to the tense, steely muscles of his thighs. The wind-tousled dark head was cocked majestically, his expression uncaring and aloof. Only his hands, which were clenching and unclenching on his hips, revealed something of his embroiled emotions.

Suddenly he lifted his piercing gaze from her, his attention caught by something in front of him. Turning slowly, Tori came face to face with the sneering men who now stood in a semicircle behind her.

Lust distorted their faces. She looked to Josh for assistance. There was only kindness and pity in his eyes. Tori blinked as he bent to help her to her feet.

"Back to your tent, lass, before there's trouble," he cautioned. Tori stumbled and hastened to obey. The laughter that followed her undignified retreat stung her to the quick.

Chapter Fifteen

Curling herself into a tight ball in the corner of the tent, Tori pulled her legs up to her chin and closed her eyes, hiding her shame. Where was Granger? What had happened to him? Why hadn't he come to Dolly's room? What was to become of her if she stayed here? She had to find some way to leave! With Scarblade and Josh she felt reasonably safe, but she didn't trust the men. Ned and Richard were all right, she supposed, they seemed engrossed in the job they had set out to do, and seemed to respect her rights as an individual. But Charles and John made her very uncomfortable with their leers and blatant remarks about her morals. It was no secret that they thought they were entitled to her favors for a price.

Tori decided she would wait till Josh had the night watch. Several times she had lain awake and seen that when it was his turn he would doze and drop his guard. Tori knew he was ill, very ill, and she wished there were something she could do for him. Josh had tended her so gently when she had the fever, and she knew him to be kind, a gentle man in spite of the fact that he was in complete sympathy with Scarblade.

Someone approached, then stopped outside her tent. Tori

listened as the men spoke together. "It's too risky to let Josh go with us tonight, Scarblade," Richard said quietly. Marcus respected Richard's and his friend Ned's opinions. They were tough and serious boys in their early twenties. Marcus felt he could rely on them because both wanted to better themselves. Whenever Marcus sat about the campfire talking of North Carolina, a wistful look would shine in their eyes.

"If he has a fit of coughing it would be our undoing." Richard continued speaking of Josh. "It's best that he stays and guards the girl and sees to the camp."

Marcus grumbled his agreement. Richard asked, "Have you given any thought to finding out who the lass is, Scarblade? We know to a man that she isn't Dolly. So who is she and why is she here? Are you holding her for a ransom? A little money in our pockets isn't hard to take. And she doesn't belong here, 'Blade. She's too soft for this kind of life; there's something about her, as though she's a real lady. But she's got a lot of spunk, I'll give her that."

"I'll decide what to do with her later," Marcus said loudly; "right now there's business to be decided."

"Ha!" jeered Charles, who had approached Scarblade and Richard and had heard the tail end of their conversation. "Now's th' toime th' decision's ta be made! If ye don' wan' ta 'old 'er fer ransom then let's 'ave a bit o' wenchin'. 'Tiz always yer decision, Scarblade. There wuz nothin' said in th' beginnin' abou' any wenches joinin' us. Ye made th' rules an' we all followed 'em. Th' wench is somethin' else. Ye denied me an even split so Oi'd 'ave some money in me pocket fer a bit o' wenchin' on th' town an' now ye mean ta deprive me an' th' men o' this 'eaven-sen' opportunity!"

There were loud mutterings from the rest of the men; they sounded to be in accord with Charles. Marcus cast an ominous glance in Josh's direction. The big man had his hand on the pistol which rested at his hip. From the look of things it would be two against the group.

"I said I'd decide later; there's business to be settled now," Marcus shouted angrily.

"Th' business can wait! Th' wench is ta be decided now!" Charles sneered ominously. The men behind him muttered their agreement.

Tori crouched in her tent, eyes wide, heart beating fast, waiting for the decision that was to come.

Josh stood tall and appeared to be coiled to spring; Marcus, his attitude contrary to the blazing scar on his cheek, casually rocked back and forth on his heels.

"If that's the way it is, then listen to me," Marcus spoke clearly and loudly. Tori could imagine the picture of night-dark eyes flashing bolts of lightning, mouth drawn tight over strong white teeth, that pose of authority so natural to him, the wind ruffling his dark hair about his pantherlike head.

"The wench is a spy sent by the Crown. Now do you still want to use her and whatever else you have in your minds? Or do you want her where we can watch her and have her sent back with our good tidings after the tax robbery in the condition she arrived? In the end, if I let you have your way you'll have to kill her. There'll be no other way out for any of us. She can recognize everyone. She can point all of us out and as for myself, I much prefer to do my dancing on the ground, not on the long end of a rope on Tyburn Hill."

Josh spoke, "Scarblade's right, lads. I don't want to hang for a wench."

There was much grumbling on the part of the men, but it appeared that Scarblade had won. Tori, a quivering mass of nerves, sat huddled in the tent and found herself giving thanks to the tall highwayman.

Charles left the small circle of men and advanced on the tent; entering, he seized the startled Tori by the arm and dragged her into the clearing. "She's mine!" he said as he held her in front of him. "Raise yer weapon, Josh, an' ye'll kill 'er. We deserve 'er, we've ridden long an' 'ard fer ye,

Scarblade, an' we deserve a bit o' frolic. Wha's it ta ye? An'
all this blather tha' ye speak, dancin' on th' end of a rope, indeed," he scoffed. "Once we're on th' ship an' she's on th'
wharf, wha' could th' King do then? Or perhaps we could
brin' 'er along ta pass th' toime on a long sea voyage!"
Charles's hands tightened painfully, biting into her arms
abusively.

"Speak for yourself, Charles," Richard said, "I want no
part of it."

Ned chimed in with Richard, "I don't want to force a
woman to bed with me, count me out!"

Tori looked from Ned to Richard and breathed a sigh of
relief. At least they refused to go along with Charles. But
would they stand against him if Charles won out? Tori felt a
knot of fear grow within her. Would Scarblade let Charles
have her? Would he care so little? Charles waited for Scarblade's reply but Tori knew he meant to have her . . . regardless!

She jerked her arms free of Charles's grasp. "Take your
hands off me. I have nowhere to go," Tori hissed; "where
could I run?" She stood tall and resolute and let her eyes go
from Scarblade to Josh. Scarblade's eyes were cold and unreadable; if he thought she would beg he was mistaken. She
had never begged in her life! Her heart beat rapidly, her
breath came in heaves.

Scarblade watched a tiny smile play about the girl's
mouth; she appeared unafraid and there was an alien glint in
her eyes. He had to make a decision and he looked meaningfully at the girl, willing her to speak.

Reading the request in his eyes, Tori turned and faced the
men. She drew herself up to full height and resought and
found Scarblade's eyes. It was to him she spoke, her tone
soft and feminine but each word encased in a sheath of
steely assertiveness. She had their attention.

"Your men may have their way with me as you will. But,
you were right, they would have to kill me when they're

through. For I promise you," she said softly, " any man who touches me will be dealt with by me! I'll follow you to the ends of the earth if necessary! I'll wreak upon you a vengeance the likes of which you have never seen. When I have found you, and I will, I shall remove your ears with a dull knife; take one eye from its socket with my own fingers, remove your teeth one by one, and make a soup from these things. You will eat and retch on your own flesh! Then I'll use this same dull knife and without a second thought, I'll carve your manhood from your body! I shall sit on a tall horse and listen to your screams and laugh." She uttered a silvery tinkle of a laugh and Josh shuddered. He believed every word she said.

"Now which of you wants the first honor?" Tori asked softly, almost conversationally. Charles and John slowly backed away from her, hesitation and doubt evident on their faces. Charles moved closer to Tori as Josh came to stand beside her. Tori waited while Charles was still some distance from her; there was no mistaking the lust in his eyes even at that distance. Before Josh knew how it happened, Tori had the knife from his belt in her hand. She moved back several paces and looked with loathing at Charles. Letting a smile of satisfaction spread over her face, she saw Charles's step falter. Tori tested the weight of the blade in her hand and turned it so that she grasped its point. She hefted the blade experimentally as Charles advanced slowly toward her.

Scarblade drew in his breath as Tori raised her arm, the tip of the knife held secure. She drew back her arm and flexed her wrist. "Another step and your manhood is gone," she said quietly.

Charles stopped, a grimace on his face. "'Ave no fear, little laidy, Oi've no thought o' ye this day. Bes' we ferget th' whole thin'." He watched anxiously as Tori continued to hold the knife by the tip.

With a fast and fluid motion she hefted and threw the

weapon. It sailed through the air like a silver-tipped bird and found its mark in a daisy which had somehow escaped the ravages of the encroaching winter. Tori narrowed her eyes and looked where the knife rested. Satisfied, she walked to her tent and lowered the blanket that served as a door. Sitting down on the pallet, she succumbed to a fit of trembling. "Thank you, Granger, for helping me," she repeated over and over. "Thank you, God, for guiding the knife to where I aimed it!"

Tori was shaken from her show of bravado. Granger had taught her to throw a knife when they were children. But today her small skill had exceeded her greatest expectations.

Outside, Scarblade bent to pick up the knife. He looked at Charles. "Dead center, she hardly disturbed the petals." Charles's face was white; he felt played for the fool, humiliated.

Scarblade looked with concern at Charles's face. "This is the end of the matter, let the girl be! I've a feeling you're no match for her."

"Then she is a spy! Where else could she learn ta throw a knife loike tha'? It's a certainty it's no' th' accomplishmen' o' a laidy! She's a gypsy, Oi tells ye!"

Scarblade turned to Josh, who leaned against a tree, his huge arms folded across his chest. Scarblade grinned as he asked, "Did you see that, Josh?"

Josh joined him in his laughter, "A lass after me own heart. 'Tis a shame she's promised to another."

"What?" Marcus asked in a sharp tone.

"'Tis true, Marc. In her delirium she kept speaking of 'darlin' Granger' and then just calling his name over and over," Josh said slyly.

Marcus did not fail to glean Josh's meaning. Calling for her lover, was she? Little bawd, dreaming of another while tempting him with her full, moist mouth.

Shooting Josh a reproachful look, Marcus stalked off in the opposite direction from Tori's tent. He was certain that if he should come across the girl he would take that long, white neck of hers and squeeze it till it snapped.

Why didn't he just let the men have their way with her? He'd like to see her taken down from her high horse . . . and yet . . . and yet . . .

The oval perfection of her face haunted him; her features were like Dolly's as was the color of her hair, but there the similarity ended. This girl's features were more refined. The delicate winged arch of her brows, the clotted-cream complexion, that petulant upper lip, so inviting to kiss, so tempting for a man to take it in his teeth and bite it!

A dull ache from the pit of his guts began to spread within him, warming him. He remembered her as she looked a short while ago. Down on her knees, her outstretched arms beckoning him, her round, high breasts heaving beneath the thin fabric of her blouse. It would have been so easy, so fitting to seize her and carry her off and satiate himself with her beauty. Scarblade stomped off into the woods, a glare looming in his black eyes.

Chapter Sixteen

"Are you ready to leave . . . Dolly?" Scarblade asked mockingly.

"I thought I told you that I would not be a party to any robbing or banditry," Tori spat, throwing back her head in defiance.

"Either you ride or I'll tie you to yonder tree and let the wolves take a choice morsel or two from your lovely frame. Make up your mind, for I'm rapidly losing patience!"

Tori looked imploringly at Josh. He shrugged his huge shoulders in resignation, but Tori thought she saw a glimmer of amusement on the giant's florid face.

"No!" Tori screeched, stomping her foot in the dirt. "I won't do it, you cannot make me do something which is against my will!" she added rebelliously.

"And I," Scarblade shouted derisively, "have very large hands, the better to whip you with if necessary. Now move!"

"I refuse," Tori answered haughtily. No sooner were the words out of her mouth than Scarblade was off his horse and standing next to her. His mocking eyes infuriated her to the point where she could no longer hold her tongue.

"Do you think for one minute I'll mount that horse and ride from this clearing to hold up some coach and steal from innocent people? Well, Scarblade, gentleman of gentlemen, I bid you think again. For you will have to give me a pistol—and I promise you I will use it. I," she said with contempt, "aim low, very low."

"Is that your final word?" Scarblade smiled.

Tori, taken off guard by the disarming smile, stammered, "Yes."

"Then you leave me no other choice but to seek out this friend of yours—you do have a friend named Granger, do you not?" Tori could only stare blankly. "We shall seek him out on the morrow and string him from the nearest tree. The decision is yours; I give you five seconds!"

Two seconds later came the soft reply. "You . . . . you despicable creature, you loathesome vermin, you . . . you . . . you odious highwayman!"

Tori mounted the horse he held by the reins. "Don't touch me," she screeched, "you . . . insufferable desperado." Jerking the reins in her fury, the horse reared on its hind legs. Deliberately, she yanked the reins to curry in the beast and in her doing so the horse nearly pawed Marcus as he hastened to get out of the way.

"So, you're fleet of foot also. You have many accomplishments, Scarblade," Tori said mockingly.

There was horror in Scarblade's face. "You'd have let that horse come down on me," he said in awe, his eyes turning into glinting carbon.

"My mistake, kind sir, you were too fast for me. Yes, I would have let him come down on you and not shed a tear."

Furiously, Scarblade mounted the chestnut. That a mere slip of a girl could best him, and before his men! He wondered if she knew how to shoot a pistol. Probably, he thought sourly, if she knew how to throw a knife. What else can she do that I don't know about? he wondered. The fine hairs on the back of his neck itched. She was probably this minute casting some kind of spell on him. That was it, she was a witch!

"Wipe that silly smile off your face, Josh, or I'll wipe it off for you," Scarblade sniffed.

"Aye, lad, I was just thinking of a wild pig caught in a net."

Scarblade shot him a venomous look. Josh continued to smile. He knew the girl could have reined in the horse in a second's time. She had the situation well under control. From his position in line he had seen the smile on her face and the wicked wink she had bestowed on him. Yes, Marcus had met his match in this one.

"The girl goes with me. I don't trust the others with her. We separate at the fork in the road. Let us pray it is a good night; Lord Starling only invites the richest people to his intimate dinner parties."

"Aye, lad, we have the right of it. We separate in twos and meet back here at the fork."

The small party rode quietly in single file. When they reached the fork in the road they separated and Scarblade and Tori rode abreast. Scarblade handed her the pistol and Tori almost dropped it.

"It's heavy."

"Does that mean you don't know how to shoot? Somehow, I thought you would be an excellent shot. You seem to know how to do everything else," he said snidely.

Tori refused to be baited. She capitulated. "Remember the daisy? Well, I could shoot the petals one after the other and leave no mark on the next. Does that answer your question?"

She smiled in satisfaction, her eyes frosty. Never, until this day, had she held a pistol. In fact, this was the closest she had ever come to one. The lie had been worth it from the look on the highwayman's face. Truly, it appeared he

had believed her when she said she would shoot very low.
Suddenly she laughed, a silvery, tinkling sound.

Scarblade gritted his teeth at the sound, and once more
the fine hairs on his neck prickled.

"This is the road to the Starlings' estate. Soon they'll be
arriving. We'll just wait here in this rutted lane, you'll remain quiet and let me approach the coach. Just stay in the
back of me and keep your eyes alert. If necessary, let the
passengers see the pistol. I warn you, keep that tongue of
yours still!"

"Yes milord. If I were not astride this beast, I'd be giving
you a deep curtsey," she jeered.

"'Twould not surprise me if that tongue of yours was
forked."

"Why milord, see for yourself," Tori said prettily, then
stuck out her tongue and wiggled it, laughing mirthfully at
the expression on his face.

Scarblade closed his eyes wearily. Somewhere he had
gone wrong. Everything had been fine till he had brought
the girl to his camp. Now everything was at sixes and sev-
ens. She had to be a witch! What kind of woman was she?
Where had she been born and raised? He shook his head in
defeat.

"Quiet now, I hear the beat of the horses' hooves. We'll
let the coach get past us, then I'll ride to the head so the
driver can see me and pull in. You stay behind the coach,
and no tricks. Just remember, your darling Granger hanging
from a tree."

Tori wrinkled her nose and curled her lip. "Just remember Granger and the rope," she mimed him softly. "The
things I do for you, Granger," she muttered under her breath
as she affixed a black mask such as Scarblade wore over her
face.

The ornate coach thundered by the small lane. Scarblade
gave a start and headed out; she followed and rode behind
the coach. She saw the team being reined in and pulled her

mount to a halt. She sat quietly behind Scarblade as the door of the coach opened and four people emerged.

"Your money and your jewels! Best hurry, my fine friends, for it has the look of rain or snow," came the request.

Pistol in hand, Tori's eyes fell on his tall figure. I should shoot his leg off, she thought viciously.

One of the ladies, seeing Tori's lissome form astride the horse, exclaimed "It's only a boy!" The others took up her cry and seemed surprised. No doubt, the thought of a mere boy earmarked for a life of crime would upset these quality folk.

Well, I'll just teach this Scarblade a lesson, Tori thought viciously. Force me to do this against my will, will he? Well, we'll just see about that! For one fleeting moment Granger's face flashed before her eyes. She blinked, the vision was gone.

Tori inched her horse closer to the carriage so she could better observe the passengers and at the same time be almost abreast of Scarblade.

"Oh, my lady," she spoke pitifully, "you have noticed that I resemble a boy? 'Tis sad, is it not, to think of a mere boy taking to the open road with a band of outlaws?" The bewigged and powdered ladies shook their heads in agreement.

"What would you think if I told you that not only does this . . . this desperado use mere boys, but girls as well?" With a flourish she removed her cap and a mass of golden curls tumbled over her shoulders. There was shock and outrage written on the ladies' faces. The men were indignant, Scarblade was furious! Tori grinned impishly; she bowed low in the saddle, waving her arm in a wide salute. Pulling on the reins, she made the horse daintily step backward.

"You hellcat!" Scarblade hissed. "I'll tend to you in a moment."

"Throw your money and jewels in a pile by that rock," he said, pointing. "Be quick about it or I fear you'll all have a good case of frostbite if your coach should leave without you." Scarblade raised his eyes and pointed to a small trunk with a curving lid. "And throw down that trunk from the luggage rack. Be quick about it!"

A lady raised a cry of protest. "No, please, my best gowns!"

Scarblade silenced her outrage with a penetrating look from beneath lowered lids. He smiled approvingly at the woman, causing her to blush under his insolent gaze. "Milady," he said in a deep, intimate voice, "a beauty such as yours needs no artificial heightening."

The lady in question turned to her companions with a simper of delight on her lips. One of the gentlemen, most likely the woman's husband, sent her a stinging jab to the ribs.

Scarblade smiled and Tori did not fail to notice it. She yearned to rake nails across his handsome face.

With a quick movement he slapped the lead horse of the team and the coach lumbered down the corded road. "Be quick now, for you have a small journey ahead of you, on foot. Without a driver the horses will not travel far, and I'm certain you'll catch up with them soon."

The party from the coach started down the road, and the halted coach was within sight. Scarblade and Tori watched them hastily climb into the vehicle. The driver lashed at the team and they sped down the road.

Scarblade motioned to Tori to gather up the spoils.

"Do it yourself, I'm not your lackey."

Infuriated beyond words, Scarblade wanted to wring her neck. "Do as I say," he thundered, "immediately!"

"No!" Tori held the reins and backed up slowly, the pistol held tightly in her hand. "Come one step nearer and I'll shoot," she added dramatically.

Scarblade sat and measured the girl. He knew she would shoot. The question was, would she shoot to kill, to wound, or to warn?

"Damn your soul," he roared, knowing all the while that if he dismounted she would be gone in a flash.

Tori, sensing his thoughts, laughed. "It would seem, Master Scarblade, that we have here what is known as a stalemate. Would you not agree?" She leaned over the horse's mane, the pistol held loosely, the golden hair tumbling over her shoulders.

Scarblade drew in his breath. She was beautiful with the moonlight behind her making a nimbus about her golden tresses. Silently, Scarblade returned the pistol to his belt, straightened in the saddle, and spoke coldly. "You may leave now. You're on your own; you're free to ride out of here."

"You're lying through your teeth," Tori spat. "You won't let me go!"

"You're free to leave," Marcus repeated.

"You're trying to trick me," Tori said suspiciously.

"You think that only because you have a narrow, suspicious mind," Scarblade said coldly. "What are you waiting for? Ride!"

"Your word that I will not be stopped."

He nodded curtly.

Tori saw the handsome man astride the huge beast and tried to read his thoughts. It had to be a trick, but still, she couldn't be sure. She would have to try. Brushing the golden tendrils from her face she once more looked deep into the eyes of the highwayman; then, before she could think twice, Tori shoved the pistol into the waistband of her trousers and spurred the horse. She dug heels into its flanks over and over again, and rode as if the devils of hell were on her heels. She glanced behind her, her hair flying wildly in the wind. She was right, Scarblade was after her!

She should have known all he wanted was the pistol out of her hand. He knew that she could not ride and brandish the gun, let alone fire it. Again she dug her heels into the horse and risked a glance behind her. He was gaining on her. She whimpered as she lowered her head to keep the biting wind from stinging her eyes. Suddenly, with no warning, she felt herself being lifted from the saddle and sailing through the air.

"Let me go!" she screamed. "Don't you dare touch me! Put me down!" she ordered. "You gave me your word! Let me go!"

"Gladly," came the reply. She felt herself falling through the air, and landed awkwardly in a drift of snow.

"How dare you . . . you . . ."

"The words you are no doubt looking for are odious, insufferable, despicable, loathsome, and vermin. I think that covers it," the man laughed.

"How dare you laugh at me?"

"Why not?" Scarblade asked, unperturbed.

"Because . . . because . . ." The S-shaped scar on his cheek deepened in color and Tori was torn between excitement and dread. "Damn you!" Tori spat.

"Tsk, tsk," the bandit said, mockingly clucking his tongue, "such language, and you a fine lady and all."

"Shut up," Tori snarled.

"The fun is over," he said emotionlessly. "Come over here; we'll have to ride double."

"I'm not riding double with you, Scarblade; get that through your head. I'll stay here and freeze."

Scarblade slid from the saddle and stalked over to the girl. He looked down at her and held out his hand. She made no move to accept his offer. He grasped her thin wrist and pulled her to her feet.

"Take your hands off me," she spat as she struggled to free herself. He grasped her other wrist and held her prisoner. She lashed out with her foot, giving him a forceful blow to his shin.

"If you want to fight, I'll give you a fight, you hell-cat." He locked his leg around both of hers, forcing her to lean against his hard-muscled body.

Tori, caught by surprise, leaned for a moment against his

broad chest. She could feel the wild beating of his heart, or was it hers? Weakened by his nearness, she allowed him to hold her firmly as he looked down into her eyes. The aching desire for her fast became a turbulent squall.

Scarblade observed her soft mouth and her wide, gold-green eyes. He longed to kiss them and her downy cheeks. He wanted to smother this lovely girl with passion, to feel her respond to him as she had that night in Dolly's room.

Tori, caught in his unrelenting embrace, her heart beating like that of a small creature caught in a net, suddenly went limp. Her eyes were misty and her lips parted as she looked into the depths of his smoky orbs. She felt lost in them and could not have moved if her life depended on it. Warm lips met and her head reeled. She brought up her hands and gently held his face and . . . felt so warm, so safe, so wanted.

Scarblade pulled away from her, a mocking, infuriating smile on his lips. Tori felt tremor after tremor of humiliation shoot through her. The man was of the devil's own making, her mind roared. To stir her this way and have her yielding to him, only to be cast away and to read the glow of victory in those jeering ebony eyes. There had been fire and passion in that brief kiss—was the man, who found it so easy to put her aside; made of steel?

Chapter Seventeen

Tori sat inside her tent reviewing in her mind how she had been thrust into a den of thieves. It had occurred to her once or twice before that it was her own deviousness that had put her in this predicament. But not caring for the implications of the truth, Tori ignored the facts and bemoaned the fates. Sitting there quietly, she heard Scarblade approach Josh and say in a low tone, "Josh, the time has come for Marcus Chancelor's visit to England to end. I'll go into London this evening and take care of that little matter."

"Have you decided how you're going to go about it?" Josh asked hoarsely. He had lost a good deal of his strength in the past few days.

"Not quite," Scarblade answered, "but I think the more people who know this is to be Marcus's last evening in town, the better. I'll go to the lodgings and dress myself in something more suitable for an evening visiting a playhouse and some of the more respectable inns."

Tori pricked up her ears. Somehow the name Marcus Chancelor seemed familiar to her although she couldn't place it. She could no longer hear what Scarblade was saying to Josh, for the men had moved away from her tent. Her eyes sparkled and her heavy heart lifted. To go to London and a playhouse and possibly even Covent Garden. Her mind boggled at the idea; it seemed ages since she had worn a dress and sat in refined company.

Peeking out from under the flap of the tent, Tori saw she was quite alone. She didn't try to fool herself into thinking she could escape, for surely she would be detected, but it was only a few steps to where sat the trunk that Scarblade had taken from the last robbery.

Quickly, she crept out of the tent and grasped the heavy ornate handle on the side of the small trunk. In less than a moment she had the luggage inside the tent. She struggled with the straps that secured the lid, silently praying the clothes inside would fit her. Self-recrimination stung her when she remembered Scarblade bringing the trunk to her and telling her to make use of the contents. Winter was upon them, he had said, qualifying his concern for her by adding that they hadn't time to care for a sick woman. How foolish she had been to rebuke his gift, however ungraciously offered.

When at last she opened the straps she lifted the lid excitedly. Please make them fit me, she prayed. Beneath the thin, blue paper which covered the contents lay two gowns, one of blue and the other of iridescent green. Beneath the gowns were slippers, chemises, shawls, ribbons, and assorted toiletries.

Holding the blue gown to herself, she saw it was slightly large, but a few pins here and a ribbon there, and it would be better than she could have hoped for.

Hastily, she placed the blue silk next to the shimmering green. There was really no choice. The second matched her eyes perfectly.

As Tori rummaged through the trunk to find more ribbons, Scarblade stepped under the flap and stood watching her, an amused expression lighting his features.

"I thought you wouldn't have the trunk if it were lined with gold?"

Her first inclination was to spit a stinging retort; then, thinking better of the idea, she turned to him and smiled her sweetest smile.

"But that was before I had an occasion to wear these gowns. Now that we're going to Covent Garden this evening, you'll have to agree I must look my best."

"We're going . . . where?" Scarblade asked incredulously.

"Why to the playhouse, of course. You don't want me to look shoddy, do you?"

"See here, I've no intention of bringing you to London with me! Wherever did you get such a daft idea?"

"But I heard you telling Josh you're going to London to see Master Chancelor."

"You can just get that idea right out of your head. I must hand it to you, you're an accomplished young lady in the areas of knife-throwing, horseback riding, and . . . ahem . . . eavesdropping. Not to mention lying, stealing, and . . ."

"Save your breath. I've no desire to be embarrassed by your effusive praise," Tori answered lightly, flashing him a bright smile.

"Why, you little minx!" Scarblade exclaimed, making a threatening motion toward her.

Tori screeched loudly as she tore from the tent, Scarblade close on her heels.

"Here, now," Josh shouted as he suddenly stood in front of the breathless Tori. "What's doing here?"

"This little . . . our 'guest' fancies herself accompanying me to London."

"Hmmm . . . that mightn't be such a bad notion. Master Chancelor might prefer to have a lovely lady on his arm when he makes his farewell to London society. Besides, a beautiful woman always attracts considerable attention, and

I assume Master Chancelor wants his farewell to London to be noted."

Marcus took his friend's words well, considering Josh's good advice of the past. "Very well, then. Josh makes good sense. But I want your word you'll not make a scene or try to escape. If you do, I'm not above killing you." Marcus's eyes measured her, awaiting her promise. "And it will not be as last time you made a promise to me. This time you'll keep it or suffer the consequences." The raven-colored eyes turned to stone, causing Tori to suffer an involuntary shiver.

"I swear to you," she said earnestly, "I'll not try to escape, nor will I make a scene. But I do need some time away from this camp and from Charles."

"Aye! The lass speaks the truth. I've seen him watching her. If you take her with you, 'twill give me a good night's rest. So weary am I of protecting her from the devil."

Tori threw Josh an appreciative smile. "I'll be with you as quick as I can," she said to Scarblade. "An hour at the most."

"An hour! Surely you can get your things together more quickly than that? Besides," he added, "I'll say the lady could use a bath. Get your things together now. I'm sure Master Chancelor will allow you to use his rooms to make yourself presentable for the opera."

Tori couldn't believe her luck. Going to the opera and a bath! She was ready in short order, her gown and accessories bundled in a roll strapped to the back of her saddle.

On the ride into the city, Scarblade was sullenly silent, wondering how he had gotten himself into the situation of taking the girl with him. What a fool he had been to listen to Josh and believe the girl's promises. Who would watch her and keep her from escaping when he paid his visit to Lord Fowler-Greene?

When they approached the outskirts of the city, Marcus rode beside her, his thigh occasionally brushing hers. He seemed poised, as if to grab her should she be so bold as to try an escape.

"Don't you think people will find it rather strange to see you riding so . . . shall we say, intimately with another of your own sex?"

He drew away from her as though his thigh had touched fire. He had completely forgotten she was dressed in breeches and that a cap covered her long golden hair—to all the world she appeared like a young man.

Within the hour they had ridden to a wide, tree-lined street facing a small, triangular park. "Master Chancelor has rooms in the end house," the highwayman said, so suddenly she was startled.

Then it all came back to her in a rush. She was sitting in the dining room at home having dinner with her parents, Granger, Lady Helen, and Lord Fowler-Greene. That was where she had heard the name. Lord Fowler-Greene was telling them about a gentleman from America who came and pleaded with the House of Lords to convince the King to help his colony. The details were vague after all this time, but she remembered her father had been favorably impressed, in fact, so favorably impressed that Lord Rawlings had pleaded the man's case and because of that lost favor with the Crown.

"So," she said aloud, "I've this Marcus Chancelor to thank for my present predicament!"

Scarblade led the horses around the back of the house where a stableboy came out to meet them.

"See that they're fed and rubbed down," he ordered, tossing the boy a coin. Then he turned to Tori and led her back to the house, entering the three-story structure by the back door.

"I think you'll find all you'll need in Master Chancelor's rooms. I believe there is a housemaid who will help you ready yourself for the evening. I'll arrange to have a bath drawn for you immediately. While you're bathing I'll take the opportunity to see to a matter of business." He spoke so softly, so kindly, Tori almost forgot the conditions under which she was visiting Marcus Chancelor's rooms. Certainly, anyone hearing him speak to her thus would find it hard to believe he wished himself rid of her.

Scarblade walked up the flight of stairs and opened the door with a key. She found it surprising that a gentleman like Marcus Chancelor would give a highwayman access to his living quarters. With a start she suddenly realized she hadn't contemplated the implications of Lord Rawlings' upstanding Master Chancelor consorting with a rogue like Scarblade. Perhaps Lord Fowler-Greene was correct in saying Lord Rawlings was foolish to defend the stranger to the House of Lords.

Tori had never been in rooms which were let to respectable boarders and she found herself pleasantly surprised that they should be so clean and well kept. They were furnished simply and yet stylishly, seeming to reflect quality more than obvious wealth. They were certainly better than Dolly's quarters!

She went to the window that faced the street and looked down into the park across the way. It was empty of people, owing no doubt to the snow, but she could imagine that in fair weather it would be buzzing with activity.

"Planning your escape?" came a deep voice from behind her.

"Indeed not, at least not until I've had my bath!" She turned to face him and was startled by the presence of a stranger in the room. It was a full moment until she realized she was looking into a mirror and the strange young man she saw was none other than herself.

Marcus watched her and realized the reason for her amazement. "Why, with your appreciation for men, surely you approve of your appearance?"

Tori faced him with more than her usual grace and femininity, as if trying to compensate for the boyish figure she cut. "Sir, I'll not argue with you while I'm so unfortunately at a disadvantage. After my bath and toilet I'm sure you'll find I have the edge."

With a churlish grin Scarblade thought, the knights had their armor, the Indians their war paint, and women their own particular battle garb.

A shy knock sounded on the door and he bid the person to enter. The housemaid stood there, dressed in her blue-and-white-striped muslin apron and snowy white mobcap. "The water for the bath, sirs," she meekly volunteered, stepping over to a screen that hid the gleaming copper tub. Three footmen entered the room and hastened over to the bath and poured in great pails of steaming water which they conveyed on a wheeled cart. When the bath was full, they left, pulling their forelocks in salute to Scarblade. When the maid attempted to leave he stopped her. "You'll be attending the young lady to her bath."

The young maid looked around the room inquisitively, then looked back with a question in her eyes. "This young lady, Emmy. Take off your cap."

Tori pulled the cap from her head, her golden hair falling almost to her waist. A slight gasp escaped the maid's lips, but so well trained was she that she asked no questions.

"The lady and myself have had a long, hard ride, and in this murderous snow. The lady felt it best to don the warmer clothing of a young man."

Another glance from the bright, intelligent eyes of Emmy told Tori that Scarblade's story seemed plausible enough to her. As a housemaid she had seen many strange things, and a lady dressed as a boy did not head the list.

"I have faith the lady will have no further use for the costume, Emmy," Scarblade said congenially, "so I'll wait outside the door, and when she disrobes you can hand me her clothes." He produced the bundle that included Tori's gown and handed it to Emmy. "Have the laundry maids press these and make them presentable."

"Aye, sir," Emmy answered. And if she were puzzled by the strange request to relieve Tori of her clothing, she said nothing.

Once Tori was submerged in the hot water of her bath, she cleared her mind of all her worries. She had resented Scarblade leaving her without a stitch to wear, but she saw he had come to a solution to his problem of her trying to escape. Now he could go about his business without fear. Where could she go for help if she were stark naked? Certainly Emmy would be of no assistance.

Emmy returned with the iridescent green gown and its voluminous petticoats freshly pressed. In the maid's absence, Tori had washed her hair, and now she requested Emmy to pour fresh water over her head so she could rinse it free of the soap. The water in the pail had cooled and Tori shrieked with surprise.

The two girls found themselves laughing in delight, and from there the conversation went easily. Tori listened to Emmy as she spoke of the young man she hoped to marry. "I suppose, miss, that you and Master Chancelor are planning to marry. I saw the gleam in his eye when he looked at you," she giggled. "I wish me Jimmy would look at me tha' way."

"Oh, no, Emmy we're not . . ." Tori stopped in midsentence, a look of astonishment on her clean, scrubbed face. "Who did you say, Emmy?"

"Why, Master Chancelor! If I may say so, the kitchen maid and laundry maids are all agog over 'im. Oooh, I wish me Jimmy had some o' his looks, I do. Just t'other day I wuz saying to me mum . . ."

Tori withdrew into her own thoughts, trying to set the pieces right in her mind. Could it be? Was Emmy correct? Tori knew the girl had no reason to lie to her, and certainly she wasn't stupid. Scarblade was Marcus Chancelor, the man responsible for her predicament! She laughed aloud, seeing the humor in her situation. Marcus Chancelor, because of him her father had lost favor with the Crown. Because of him she had been forced into that impossible match with Lord Fowler-Greene. Because of Marcus Chancelor she had sought out Dolly and arranged to play out the deception on Lord Fowler-Greene. And now, because of Marcus Chancelor, she was being held a prisoner in a camp of highwaymen!

Her laughter bordered on hysteria and Emmy became alarmed. "Oh, miss, what's wrong? What can I do for ye?"

Regaining her control, Tori said sharply, "Hurry, Emmy, get me the towels. I must make myself ready for Master Chancelor when he arrives. I want to 'surprise' him!"

Emmy hurried to do the lady's bidding. The miss was certainly upset about something! And Emmy hadn't liked the way she had said the word 'surprise'!"

As Tori dried her hair she sat on the chair near the window looking out at the falling dusk. When the footmen came to empty the copper tub, Emmy had shielded Tori from their view with the screen.

"I hope I didn't upset your ladyship by anything I said," Emmy said apologetically.

"Not at all, Emmy. If anything, you've put my mind at ease about a number of things."

"Well, I wouldn't like to think Master Chancelor would be displeased by your . . . er, surprise, him being such a nice gentleman and all."

"Have no worry, Emmy, the surprise I plan for Master Marcus Chancelor will certainly please him. You see, I plan to be at my best this evening. I shall dazzle him with my charms, entertain him with my wit, and flatter him with my attention. Why I daresay the man will be beside himself with pleasure!" Tori smiled wickedly to herself.

Behind the screen Emmy shrugged her shoulders in bewilderment. Somehow she was terribly glad she and her Jimmy were not of the gentry. Being quality folk must complicate one's life.

* * *

Marcus dismounted and tied his great chestnut to the hitching post outside Lord Fowler-Greene's home. He took the steps up to the door two at a time, his heels making a clicking sound on the recently shoveled porch. As Marcus was about to touch the ornate brass knocker, Lord Fowler-Greene's manservant pulled open the door.

"Milord, Lord Fowler-Greene awaits you, he's in the library."

Marcus wasted no time in getting to the library. He threw open the room's heavy oak doors to find Lord Fowler-Greene sitting in what Marcus supposed was his favorite chair, leafing through an old, dusty volume from the shelves. Immediately upon seeing Marcus, the lord rose and approached him, extending his hand in welcome. "Marcus, this is indeed an unexpected surprise."

Marcus smiled and returned the hearty handshake. "I came to tell you I'll soon be leaving England. I want to thank you on behalf of Chancelor's Valley for all you've done for us."

"'Twas hardly enough; the pleasure was mine, I assure you." In truth the lord had taken a great liking to Marcus and was exceedingly sympathetic to the needs in the colonies. Marcus brought Lord Fowler-Greene up to date on his activities, omitting any mention of the girl he kept prisoner.

They shook hands, and Marcus, sending him one last salute, left the library, closing the doors behind him.

He was eager to get back to his rooms. He knew the girl well enough not to give her too much leeway. He heard a sound behind him and turned, stunned to see Dolly tripping lightly down the stairs.

"Scarblade, Scarblade!" she cried, hurrying toward him to throw herself into his arms. "Ain't it wonderful? Imagine me here in this place! The gods have surely been kind to yer old friend Dolly."

"Dolly," Marcus asked incredulously, "is it really you?"

"Aye. Look at me, have ye ever seen me looking so grand? Did you know I'm now Lady Fowler-Greene? Can you imagine?" Marcus noticed Dolly's speech seemed a bit stilted, but he also noticed that her diction had certainly improved from the heavy cockney.

"Are you now Lady Fowler-Greene? I'd heard the lord had married, and a love match at that, but I'd not heard he'd fallen for a serving wench from the Owl's Eye Inn. I'd no idea the lord even frequented a hole such as that."

"Shhh!" Dolly cautioned. "I'm being kept under wraps, at least until I've learned the manners of a lady and can speak like one, too. Oh, 'Blade, 'tis long hard days Oi—I—" she corrected herself, "I put in learning how to act the lady with Lady Helen as my teacher." Her lip curled when she mentioned her sister-in-law.

"But how did you come to find yourself married to a lord?"

"You'll think me daft," Dolly laughed. "Come into the breakfast room and I'll tell you all about it."

Tori, looking resplendent in her gown, was standing before the mirror when Marcus strode into the room. He stopped for a moment as he caught sight of her. The wide, low cut of her neckline revealed her smooth, white shoulders and accentuated the curving fullness of her bosom and long slim throat. The color of the dress turned her freshly washed hair, which was artfully arranged atop her head, to a paler shade of gold. Emmy, experienced housemaid that she was, had deftly used a curling iron to produce thick, glossy ringlets over Tori's left ear.

Marcus found himself bewitched by the amazing difference in Tori's appearance. Tori shivered under his scrutiny. Gallantly he reached to the bed for a rich velvet cloak and deftly draped it about her shoulders. Nuzzling her ear, he said in a low, throaty tone, "What a bewitching bandit you make, Dolly, a vixen in velvet."

"Don't you approve, milord?" Tori asked, a ripple of delight singing through her. Her thoughts were becoming muddled. Must he stand so close?

"Oh yes, madam. I approve heartily!"

"Good! I most want to please you!" she answered waspishly, her sarcastic tone bringing some semblance of composure to her.

Seeing her fully dressed, Marcus was disconcerted. His business with Lord Fowler-Greene had taken longer than expected. He hadn't thought to tell Emmy not to bring in the lady's clothes until he returned. "You had your opportunity to escape, why didn't you?"

"I promised, milord," Tori replied sweetly. For the moment she was shaken. What was wrong with her? She hadn't even thought of escaping! It wasn't her promise that kept her here, she realized; it was her determination to 'surprise' Marcus Chancelor. Fool! she rebuked herself, too besotted with your scheme to take advantage of an ideal opportunity!

Coming further into the room, Marcus spied the copper tub refilled with steaming water. Angrily, he realized he didn't know what to do with the girl while he himself bathed.

Seeing his glance at the bath, Tori guessed what was on his mind. "We can set the screen up around the tub, milord, and I can sit in the far corner of the room whilst you bathe."

"I assure you, Dolly—" he said the name mockingly— "it wasn't my modesty I was thinking of; in fact, I may decide you should scrub my back!" Marcus cast her a distrustful look. What would prevent her from running out of the room while he was so conveniently indisposed?

"I promise I'll not try to run away," Tori sputtered, a little worried that he might actually be uncourtly enough to strip and bathe in front of her. "Haven't I already had my golden opportunity?" she argued, then insisted, "I didn't take advantage of it, did I? I've given my word as a lady, and I mean to keep it."

In actual fact, Tori played the idea over in her mind, mulling the possibilities of a successful escape. But all the while carbon-black eyes swam before her and she admitted the horrible truth to herself that she did not want to be free of this Marcus Chancelor. She would rather ride the roads with a band of thieves than deny herself ever seeing Scarblade again, ever feeling his strong arms about her and his lips pressed hard against hers.

Quickly turning away from him to hide the blush suffusing her face, she sat meekly in a far corner of the room while Marcus hurriedly bathed and dressed. When he stepped out from behind the screen, Tori was pleasantly surprised by the handsomeness of his appearance. The dark stubble of beard was cleanly removed, as were the dirty garments he had worn. Here before her stood a gentleman dressed in fine evening wear. The black of his coat was set off by the blue brocade of his waistcoat and the pristine whiteness of his cravat.

Her eyes raked over him and she saw him smiling strangely at her, the scar on his cheek giving him a rakish look.

Quickly she hid her admiration and busied herself with her ribbons. Marcus came and stood close behind her, putting his hands lightly on her waist. "You're lovely, really." Inhaling deeply of her womanly scent, he kissed her warmly on the shoulder.

Tori turned to face him. "How kind of you to say so, milord. And may I say you also cut a fine figure. It would seem we are quite a stunning pair," she teased, "I being the better, of course."

The shared laughter eased the strain between them, and after seeing to a few details, they left for an evening at the opera.

Marcus had hired a coach for the evening. Once settled within, Tori braved a question. "When am I to meet your friend, Master Chancelor?"

He did not honor her with an answer, if indeed he had one. He merely sat across from her, his knees occasionally touching hers with the rocking of the carriage, and stared at her.

Knowing when to give over, Tori sat silently for the remainder of the trip to the inn where they were to have dinner.

Sitting in a secluded corner of the dining room, Tori looked across at Marcus with a penetrating gaze that made him uncomfortable. He would not forget the impact their arrival had on the other patrons. Several gentlemen seated in a group had turned and stared pointedly at Tori when she entered. A low murmur of conversation swept the room, and soon it was apparent the gentlemen were very envious of Marcus's position as Tori's escort. The ladies present also turned to appraise the charms of this woman who could create a stir among their men.

Tori had also noticed the stir their arrival had created. She swelled with pride at being the envy of the other ladies who had to content themselves with pasty-looking, nondescript suitors and spouses. She knew they would have gladly traded places with her to be in the company of a handsome, rugged, well-dressed gentleman with licorice-black eyes.

Marcus gave his order to the servant and turned his full attention on Tori. "Have you ever been to the opera . . . Dolly? It seems odd to call you by that name; it's certain you are anything but a tavern wench, much as you would have me believe otherwise."

Tori looked up at him through her long, thick lashes, noting the effect this wile had on him. "I think, since we are to be friends, we must know each other's true names, Marcus Chancelor. I am Victoria Rawlings. My close friends and family call me Tori."

He raised an eyebrow. "So . . . Miss Rawlings, is it?"

Now that he knew the elegant Miss Rawlings was no spy, the following day's tasks would be much easier. And that witch Dolly . . . Lady Fowler-Greene. The two of them, Miss Rawlings and Dolly . . . birds of a feather. Still, he tried to control the shock he felt at her words. He had not expected that she would learn his identity. "I might have expected Emmy would mention my name. Yes, it's true, my name is Marcus Chancelor." Before she could utter the question which came to her lips, Marcus leaned forward and told her the reason for assuming a pseudonym. When he had completed his story, he was touched by the sparkle of tears he noted in Tori's eyes.

"So now you know the reason for my robbing and plundering, as you so aptly refer to it. But Tori," he cautioned, the sound of her name on his lips giving her an unexpected thrill, "you must always refer to me as Scarblade, at least in front of the men at camp. Not even they know my true identity. It's much safer for the plan; the less they know the better the chances of getting the money back to North Carolina. Only Josh, who has known me since I was a boy, knows the truth."

Tori agreed, although why she could not say. She should be furious with Marcus Chancelor. Were it not for him, she reasoned, she would not find herself in her present circumstances. But something had touched her, his face when he had spoken of this far-off colony had lifted and brightened. His voice had filled with a tenderness and yearning. No, Tori wouldn't give him away, if for nothing else than to protect him from that animal Charles. Somehow Tori felt Charles might someday be Marcus's undoing. Josh seemed to believe in Marcus's cause, and that was sound enough reason for her.

After a delicious dinner, Tori and Marcus again climbed into their hired coach and rode the short distance to Covent Garden. The immense ornate doors of that famous theater stood open welcomingly. Tori had visited the Garden on nu-

merous occasions with her parents and Granger, but this
night seemed special. Now she was on the arm of a most attractive gentleman and she shone brightly under the envious
glances they received.

Once or twice Tori saw recognition in the eyes of an acquaintance. At first she thought one of them might approach
her till she remembered that to all concerned she was now
the wife of Lord Fowler-Greene and under no circumstances
would anyone call attention to the fact that the lord was
being cuckolded for a gentleman so much younger and far
more handsome.

Seated in a private box, Tori and Marcus listened to the
ethereal strains of the music. With the lights low and the
players on stage, Marcus observed his companion. She certainly was a many-faceted girl, he found himself thinking,
at home here in the most popular theater in England as well
as upon a horse or throwing a knife. He could not help but
admire her vitality, her onward rush to meet life and enjoy it
to its fullest. The candlelight played soft shadows on her
face and shoulders, and he once again tasted the freshness
of her skin beneath his lips. Although she was composed
and sophisticated at the moment, he, perceived a hint of the
wildcat beneath the surface and found it fascinating.

After the opera, Marcus suggested they partake of a
brandy at a nearby tavern. When she looked at him questioningly, he mentioned it was a very fashionable place to
go after a performance at the Garden, and many of the society matrons went there.

"I'd really rather not, Marcus. The long ride into the city
and the interminable cold has gotten the better of me, I'm
afraid. Couldn't we just go back to your rooms and have a
brandy there? I noticed a server on the table by the window."

Marcus smiled, the first genuine smile she had ever received from her, and Tori found herself breathless under his warm gaze. "I'm so glad you suggested we return home. I'm not very comfortable in places of fashion. I much prefer quiet and intimacy."

Tori glowed when he called his rooms "home," and wondered how it would feel if it were *their* home. All the way back Marcus and Tori sat looking out the grimy windows of the trap, marveling at how the snow could make a wonderland from the dirty city streets.

Once back in the flat, Marcus poured brandy into little tumblers. He handed her the burnished liquid and made a toast, "Farewell, Scarblade and Dolly, good cheer Tori and Marcus." Tori drank deeply, stirred by the quiet depth of his voice and the poignancy of the toast.

"I'm afraid you'll not get much sleep tonight, Tori; we must be back at camp by the morrow. But, why don't you try to get some rest? I'll wake you when it's time to leave."

Tori eyed the wide bed longingly; how long had it been since she had tucked herself under a real feather quilt? Her eyes felt heavy and she stifled a yawn. "Go on, Tori," he urged. "I'll just make myself comfortable here on the chair."

Tori smiled her agreement and stepped behind the screen in the far corner of the room to remove her gown. As she was taking down the minute hooks which fastened the gown's back, she wondered how it was that it seemed so natural to be preparing for bed with Marcus in her room. When she stepped out of her garments, she realized for the first time that she had no nightdress to wear and the billowing petticoats which had stiffened the skirt of the green silk certainly were far from suitable.

It was then that she spied one of Marcus's dress shirts hanging from the corner of the screen. A bit self-consciously, she donned the fine lawn blouse, aware of the fact that it didn't even come down to her knees.

Peeking out from behind the screen with the intention of

instructing Marcus to close his eyes while she jumped into the high poster bed, she saw that he had slid down in the chair, feet outstretched, and had fallen asleep.

He looked so young, almost boyish, as he lounged there, the lines of worry gone from between his heavy, dark brows. Quietly, she stepped over to the mirror to remove the pins from her coiffure. Picking up a heavy brush from the dresser top, she stroked it through her hair, the shimmering, golden locks cascading to her waist. Pulling the brush through the last stubborn snarl, she caught a glimpse of Marcus's reflection and realized he was watching her. The image of his face as he studied her was disconcerting, and she turned her attention to removing the last few snarls, conscious all the while that his eyes were upon her.

Marcus, used to dozing lightly due to long nights on watch at the camp, had awakened to find the light from the nearby candle outlining Tori's slim woman's body through the gossamer thinness of his lawn shirt. As she lifted her arms to her head the shirt shortened to reveal lean, rounded haunches and betrayed the darker crease that separated her buttocks from her thighs.

A cascade of golden waves fell to below her waist, drawing his attention to honey-colored, lissome, smooth legs ending in neat, delicately shaped ankles. A smile played about his lips as he noticed the tightening of the muscles in her legs as she stretched herself on tiptoe to view the unrelenting snarl that defied her brush.

Tori replaced the brush on the dresser and turned to find herself locked in a warm embrace. His mouth came crashing down on hers, his arms surrounded her, pressing her closer, tighter, hurting her.

She clung to him, more for support than out of passion, the pressure of his lips forcing hers to part. Instinctively she began to draw away . . . but he would not let her.

The scar deepened in color, as if burning his cheek. Marcus lifted his mouth from hers and they stared into each other's eyes. His dark gaze smouldered, penetrating into her wide, yellow-green eyes. Her face filled with wonderment and she slid into his embrace and kissed him, soaring with the glory of her passion.

He tightened his arms around her and returned her kisses with tender touches of his tongue. His hands strayed to her breasts and she welcomed his advances. Her heart pounding violently, thighs pressed against his, she became aware of his arousal.

Tori was melting, dissolving, becoming a part of him, kissing him with more and more abandon. Overcome by the passion and desire she felt for him, Tori caressed him with infinite tenderness and let the tide of her own desire carry her.

Marcus looked down into Tori's humid eyes with a questioning tenderness. With an answering look from her, he lifted her into his arms and carried her across the room to his bed.

Chapter Eighteen

"There's no other way, Josh! The girl comes with us!" Marcus's voice was unyielding, a tone he had never used with his old friend.

"She's got you bewitched, Marc. Leave her behind. I don't understand you." The giant's worried, pale-blue eyes penetrated Marcus's anger.

"I'm sorry, Josh," Marcus was contrite, "there isn't anything I wouldn't do for you, but I cannot go along with you on this. We all ride together, and that means the girl. You know as well as I do what's at stake. We can't afford any mishaps now—sailing time is too close—they already postponed the tax delivery, and I think that was due to the last robbery we committed. There's been a leak somewhere."

Marcus lifted his eyes in earnest to his old friend. "We are now well behind on the sailing. I can't afford any more delay. In four months it will be planting time, and I feel that the lives of all the people in the valley hang on my head. It's a grim business, Josh."

The bandit's eyes became hard and cold. "The snows are already here, what then? There's no place for us to winter, we have to make haste!" In a somber tone he stated again, simply, "The girl rides with us."

Josh saw the hard set of Marcus's face and knew he had lost. It was the first time Marcus had not paid heed to his advice. "Oh, the gods be with us, Marcus. Who's to tell her, you or me?"

"I leave you the honor, Josh." Marcus had no wish to gaze into those melting eyes. He needed time to keep his senses alert. Whenever he came near her he remembered the feel of her in his arms, her soft, moist mouth beneath his.

Josh nodded morosely. "First, I best ride on to the Boare Inn and see what I can smell out."

Marcus asked, "Are you well enough, Josh? You must keep your strength for what's at hand."

"Aye, I'm well enough," Josh answered, heaving himself to his feet. "If I ride now I should be back by sundown. Watch Charles, Marc. He had his eye on the girl and he means to have her one way or the other."

Marcus let his eyes go to the sleeping Charles and his brother John. Marcus, too, had seen the way Charles looked at the girl, and it rankled him more now than ever. If Charles dared to touch her he'd find himself at the business end of Scarblade's knife!

Still, Marcus could not set Tori free; too much was at stake, and he found himself reluctant to part with her. Somehow she had penetrated his reserve, inched herself beneath his skin, and he was aware of the void her leaving would create in his life.

Josh mounted his sorrel and rode quietly out of the clearing. Once on the road, he flicked the reins and the animal broke into a fast gallop, bearing the weight of Josh's huge frame with ease.

The day crawled by. The men took turns chipping wood and keeping the fire roaring. By late afternoon the skies clouded over and there was a sharp drop in the temperature.

The men gathered around the fire and talked in low tones. "I think we should build a ring of fires," Marcus spoke. "If it snows—and I think it will—we're in for a spot of trouble. Let's heave to, lads, and get at the wood. No stinting now, put your backs into it. If I don't miss my guess the snow will start by nightfall."

The men muttered and grumbled but fell to the work. They had no wish to have the blood freeze in their veins.

Tori sat huddled by the fire, shivering; the thin rags she wore were no help from the cold. She wrapped a moth-eaten blanket close about her and drew her legs up to her chin. She felt hot tears sting her eyes. She longed for her bed and a warm cover over her, but most of all she wished to be far away from Marcus Chancelor—Scarblade!

Earlier in the day, Tori had watched Scarblade bending to the task of chopping wood for the fires. His leather tunic strained over the bunching muscles in his back, the knotted tendons in his forearms glistening with a veil of sweat as he brought up the axe and swung it down with a force that bit into the frozen wood and split it with a shattering crack. The power in his muscled torso and legs gave her a thrill of re-membered intimacy.

Softly, she approached him, driven by the need to touch him, to feel once again the hardness of his body against hers. The shabby cloak slipped from her shoulders, the wind tum-bled her hair about her head. She reached out and touched his arm, and startled by her coming upon him so quietly, he turned toward her. His ebony eyes took in her full, parted lips, lids half closed over the yellow-green eyes.

Abruptly, he pushed her away from him with such a vio-lence her teeth rattled. His eyes avoided hers; the pain of re-jection pricked her eyelids. In a gruff voice he commanded her to go to her tent.

Humiliation prevented her from coming forth with an oath. Not remembering how she had fled his accusing eyes, she lay there in her darkened tent forcing back the tears. He had used her and she, God forgive her, had helped him, enjoyed it, loved it! And now he was through with her as though she were some cheap doxy.

Oh, how I hate him! she cried silently, I hate him! But realizing the truth for what it was, "God help me, I love him, I love him!"

Now, when she thought of him, the name Marcus came to her lips. But she had sworn to think of him and refer to him as only Scarblade. This was a promise she had no intention of breaking. Foolish and fast of tongue she might be, but she had no stomach for being responsible for the lives of those people in North Carolina.

Tori knew she was to ride with the men; she had heard Marcus and Josh talking. Suddenly, for the first time in days, she felt warm. Looking around, she saw the fires flare up. There were eight of them spread in a wide circle, and she could still hear the sharp ring of the men's axes as they continued to chop wood. There must be enough to last the night.

Marcus carried the bedrolls and deposited them inside the circle. Her breath came in quick gasps as he sought for and found her eyes on him.

"The least you could have done, Scarblade, in your plundering, was to steal me a fur wrap. I'm freezing," she said petulantly. "Do you care?" she cried. "If I wake up frozen, I'll be on your conscience," she spat. "That is, if you have one! What kind of man are you? Be honest!"

Marcus stood still, his eyes glowing like coals in his bitter face. "What do you know about honesty? You used the name of another and have the effrontery to sit there and tell me what I should and should not do. But for my intervention you would be six feet under the hard, cold ground."

Tori was undaunted. "I can take care of myself, Scarblade. I didn't ask you to interfere in my behalf. I didn't ask to be brought here! In fact, I tried to leave."

"So you could go straight to the sheriff's men and turn us in. Did you expect to collect the reward?"

"Yes!" Tori snarled. "I would betray you in a moment if I believed I could get away with it. I owe you naught! You're keeping me against my will." She jumped up from the ground, her eyes blazing. Oh, God, when will I learn to keep my mouth shut? she thought. Why do I seek to hurt him? I only blacken myself in his eyes. "Scarblade, give me a horse and I give you my word I'll ride out of here and you'll hear no more of me. I won't go to the sheriff, my word," she pleaded. He had to agree, he had to set her free, to be away from him, to put him out of her mind if she could.

Scarblade snorted as he stretched out his hand as if to grab her. Tori, sensing his intention, backed off, stumbling slightly. "Don't lay a hand on me, Scarblade!"

"I wouldn't think of it, Dolly," he mocked. "Actually I had no intention of touching you. I merely put out a hand to feel the snow. It's started," he said as he raised his eyes.

"So it has," Tori said quietly, knowing the hardship the weather would bring to his task.

Scarblade and the other men joined Tori in the center of the ring of fires, enjoying the blazing warmth. The hours crawled by, and Tori dozed off several times only to be awakened by the surging chill in her extremities. Her feet were colder than the snow that continued to fall in great fluffy flakes, and she was certain she could sense the beginnings of chilblains on her fingers.

Scarblade often left the warmth of the ring to walk out to the edge of the encampment, no doubt to listen for the approach of Josh. It had been too many hours since he had left to attend to his mission, and it was clear that Scarblade was sorely worried. Tori, too, was apprehensive about Josh's safety. His condition had worsened due to the cold and lack of substantial food.

Darkness had long since fallen and Scarblade could wait

no longer for Josh. Arousing the grumbling men with the toe of his boot, he commanded them to ready their horses to make a search for his friend.

"Wha' o' th' girl?" John asked. "Are ye goin' ta take 'er wi' ye?"

Scarblade turned and noted the expression of worry in Tori's face. "What of it, Dolly?" he asked, his concern masking the challenge in his eyes. "Will you wait here for Josh's return, for it would seem he met with a mishap along the way. He'd never be so long in returning if something hadn't happened, and if I don't miss my guess, he became too ill to continue his journey. He just might need the tender touch of a woman when we bring him back. What say you, can you be trusted?"

Tori saw the silent pleading in Marcus's eyes and felt the sharp stab of concern for Josh. "Yes, I'll be here waiting. He saw me through my illness, and I'll not run off and leave him to the rough hands of you and your men. Go and find him, Scarblade, and bring him to me."

Marcus, relieved at hearing her promise, flashed a smile. "We'll not be long, for there are only two ways to travel to where he was going." Without further words, Marcus hurried off to mount his chestnut and to begin the search.

At their leaving, Tori began the chore of stoking the fires and warming her own blankets and bedroll in expectation of Josh's arrival. He would need a warm bed and hot soup, she thought, as she began warming a kettle of beef broth. So busy at her task was she that she failed to hear the stealthy sounds of someone stalking her. An arm shot out from behind her and knocked her to the ground. She struggled in vain against the wiry strength that held her fast, forcing her over onto her back and fumbling with the wide belt she wore. Shaking the masses of hair from her eyes, she saw her attacker—Charles!

Numbly, Tori protested against the wild cruelty in his

eyes, and when she struggled to gain leverage to fight him off he sent her a stinging blow to the head. Blackness threatened to engulf her and a dizziness upset her equilibrium.

Terrified, Tori gathered all her strength and frantically tried to put him off her. If she could only get to her feet she might be able to hide from him in this blinding snowstorm.

But it was not to be. Charles held her fast with the weight of his body and tore her clothes from her in a frenzy. Her shoes had come off in her struggles, and Charles had torn the shawl and thin cambric shirt from her shoulders, leaving her reddened flesh exposed to the ravages of his lips. Having no patience for her camisole, he ripped it from her while one arm was pressed against her throat, leaving Tori to gasp for air.

Shifting his weight and imprisoning her legs beneath his own, he fumbled with her belt buckle again, this time succeeding in loosening it and tearing down her trousers. His greedy, lascivious eyes shone with triumph as he proceeded to undo his own trousers.

Tori swore and cursed, words she had not known she knew. She was fighting, struggling to gain a grasp on her attacker, aiming with clawlike hands for those horrible glittering eyes.

A sound behind her and Charles ceased his attack, a fearful, terrified expression like that of a trapped animal on his face.

Slowly, he backed off her, his fear so great that Tori imagined she could smell it. Pulling herself away from Charles, she looked off to where he was staring. Scarblade!

"So, Charles! It wasn't until we were well off in the opposite direction that I remembered I had left the girl here alone and unprotected. It would appear that I was correct in my concern for her!"

"Oi wuz jus' 'avin' a bit o' fun, Scarblade. Oi didn' mean no 'arm, Oi didn'. She loikes it, Oi tells ye, don' ye, Dolly, tell 'im 'ow ye loikes it!"

Charles's face was a study in terror as he begged her for aid. Seeing he was whipping a dead horse, he changed his tune. "Go on, tell 'im," he demanded. "Tell 'im 'ow this ain't th' firs' toime, 'ow there's been plenty o' toimes afore this. An' tell 'im 'ow ye loikes it rough! Won' ye tell 'im now!"

For an answer, Tori spat, her face wrought into lines of disgust and hate. Scarblade pounced on Charles, bringing a heavy fist into his face. Tori watched, mesmerized by the violence of the scuffle. Charles didn't have a chance, Scarblade was too big, too strong.

The deep-ridged scar glowed with malevolent portent as Scarblade grabbed Charles's tunic with both hands. Quickly, viciously, Scarblade drew back his right arm, his knuckles white and stark against the eerie fire's glow. There was a lightninglike blow to Charles's terror-drawn mouth, and Tori stepped backwards as the rotted stumps of Charles's teeth splintered and shattered beneath Scarblade's force.

As Scarblade whipped his hand back for a second blow droplets of crimson rained upon the flames. Tori was revolted by the sound of the spitting and hissing as the blood boiled in the fire.

Panting from the exertion of the fight, Scarblade turned to Tori, concern written in his eyes. She sat there, numb with horror and trembling with cold. She did not seem to notice Marcus as he adjusted her clothing into a more reputable state, moving her arms and legs as needed, as though she were a wooden doll.

"Tori, Tori," he called to her softly, trying desperately to break through her daze. Slowly she turned to face him, great tears falling from her wide, staring eyes. Choking sobs escaped her parted lips, deepening to wracking heaves.

Tenderly Marcus picked her up and carried her close to the fire and held her on his lap, stroking her head and whispering soft and tender words, trying to keep her from becoming hysterical. He realized how deeply affected she had been by Charles's cruelty. This was a woman who would give herself totally to a man she loved, willingly give the pleasures of her body, as he well knew. But by the same token, to be touched by someone she could not love was indeed a fate worse than death.

After a time Tori came around, her heavy, quaking sobs abating to a mild hiccoughing. "Will you be all right now?" Scarblade asked, his voice heavy with emotion. "I should have killed that bastard son of a . . ."

Tori put her cold hands to his lips and held them there. "I'm glad you didn't kill him, I wouldn't want you to have the blood of a man upon your hands for me. I promise you, I shall be fine."

Marcus could see that she spoke the truth. The color was returning to her cheeks and her lips had lost their whiteness. But her eyes were still blazing and widely staring.

"Marcus, I want you to go and look for Josh, he needs you more than I do right now. I promise you, I'll be fine." Her eyes strayed to the place where Charles had crept off, and she gave an involuntary shiver. Marcus knew it cost her much to think of Josh and be left alone.

Reading his thoughts, Tori said, "If you would leave me your pistol I'll be more careful that no one creeps up on me.

"You're a brave girl, Tori," Marcus said, his voice husky and his eyes dark and tender. Tori caught her breath and felt herself melt into his arms, but stopped herself just in time. No matter how grateful she was to Marcus for saving her from Charles's attack, she would not put herself in a position to be rejected and humiliated by Marcus still another time.

Chapter Nineteen

M arcus jumped to his feet when a sound of rushing horses entered the encampment.

It was John and Richard, leading Josh's horse with the huge man tied to the saddle. There were icicles encrusted onto his eyebrows, and Tori was sure the man's eyes were frozen shut.

Marcus grasped the big man around the shoulders as Richard held his feet. "Get him wrapped in blankets and I'll get coffee and broth into him," Tori said. "If he has a coughing spell now . . ." She didn't finish the sentence. Marcus knew what she was about to say.

Carefully he lowered Josh to the ground and quickly wrapped him in blankets which Tori had warmed by the fire.

An hour later, due to Tori's careful ministering, Josh felt his strength returning. "I feel better already, darlin'," Josh said, attempting a smile. "Let me get my breath and I'll tell you what I found out at the inn. You'll be much surprised."

The thin, swirling snow continued to fall in heavy, wet flakes. The wind howled ominously as the flames crackled.

"It will be a bastard of a storm," Scarblade said, looking thoughtfully at Josh.

"Aye, so it will," Josh murmured drowsily. "But it'll be to your advantage, Scarblade. Wait till you hear what I have to tell you."

"When you're rested, Josh. There's no hurry. There's nowhere to go this night. I want to stoke the fires and get the logs inside the circle before the snow gets too heavy. You will see to Josh, won't you . . . Dolly?" he asked in his old mocking tone.

Tori's eyes filled with tears as she looked at Josh's still form, and for an answer to his question she raised her glistening eyes to Marcus.

Josh dozed from time to time and Tori kept herself busy changing the hot rocks and pulling the worn blankets up around his neck. Soon the men had a stack of logs near each of the burning fires. They came stomping cold feet to stand next to Josh and silently wish his speedy recovery.

Some time after Tori had made Josh as comfortable as possible, she was aware that Charles had crept from the frozen woods close to a warming fire. His brother John was tending the wounds he had suffered from Marcus's battering fists. The brothers cast menacing looks in Marcus's direction, and John, being the bolder for not having met Marcus in open confrontation, was intoning whispers to Richard, who had obligingly melted snow to bathe Charles's face. Richard and John engaged in a brief difference of opinion, Richard no doubt defending his leader Scarblade.

Spitting into the fire and scowling at John, Richard rose to his feet and moved to another of the crackling fires to join Ned.

Tori experienced a sense of shame to be fought over like some bitch in heat, and she quickly reviewed her past actions, wondering if somehow she had given justification for Charles's attitude. Instinctively, she knew he was not finished with her and that Scarblade too had not yet felt the strength of his revenge.

Later Tori ladled out the hot broth to the men, John taking a bowl to Charles, and refilled their cups with strong coffee. Marcus observed the four small rabbits on the stick as they roasted. It would have to be enough.

The skimpy meal over, the men retired to the fires, wrapping themselves in blankets and huddling together. The snow had now turned to blinding swirls as the wind howled. "The wolves will be out soon," Scarblade said to Tori. She raised her startled eyes to meet his. "They won't come near the fires," he said reassuringly. "I've seen them make a ring outside a fire, though."

Tori shuddered. There was no hint of mockery in his tone and she believed him. Tales of the wolves Tori had heard came spiraling back to her in full horror.

The firelight dealt kindly with Josh's features, and he appeared less ravaged. Tori admired this kind, wise man. It wasn't really anything he said or did, it was the man himself. He most truly believed in what he was doing. She had caught snatches of his conversations with Marcus about the people in America. "My people," Josh had said. His and Marcus's people. Tori knew their people were starving.

When Marcus had spoken of the small children going hungry her stomach had heaved as she remembered the elaborate banquet that must have been served at the wedding feast. Half the food would have been wasted. To think that small children were starving made her want to cry. With this heavy thought she dozed off.

Suddenly Tori was awakened by some strange sound. Peering out past the fires into the darkness, Tori found herself staring at diminutive winking lights. It was a full moment before she realized they were the eyes of animals reflecting the blazing fires. Low, whining, grumbling sounds filtered by the falling snow and howling wind fell on her ears. Her flesh crawled and she shivered with fear. The wolves, she thought, terrified. Then, remembering Marcus saying they would never go beyond the outer fires, she calmed. Odd, she thought, how much I trust him.

Leaning over Josh at dawn's first, feeble light, Tori cradled the great leonine head to her bosom and removed the sweat-soaked rags from beneath it. The cold was making them stiff with frost and they cracked in her fingers as she exchanged them for dry ones.

"Pray tell, lass, why do I find myself in this compromising position? What will the men think?"

Tori flushed a bright crimson and her eyes sparkled. "Ah, Josh, by your tone I can tell you're feeling better. I'm so glad," she said sincerely. "What do I care about what the men think? They think the same thoughts regardless. They're a pack of jackals, the lot of them. How you and Scarblade ever became mixed with them is beyond me. Lay still, Josh, I'll get you some hot coffee."

"Scarblade! Come here!" Josh called, and when Marcus was near, said, "I best be telling you the news I picked up at the Boare Inn yesterday. I'll be speaking softly, so listen carefully."

"Do you want me to leave?" Tori asked hesitantly.

"There's no place to go, lass," Josh said as he looked at the swirling snow. "Stay. You might as well hear now as later." Marcus agreed, and Tori settled herself next to Josh and sipped her coffee.

"While at the Boare I heard the men talking about the taxes being collected. Did ye know, Marcus, that this year they were doubled?"

"Doubled?" Marcus exclaimed in surprise. "Why?"

"It seems our good King George III has left boyhood behind him. It's amazing how the price of wenching doubles and triples in those advanced years."

"I see," Marcus laughed. "So we shall find ourselves that much richer. Good!"

"A little after the noon hour two of the sheriff's men who collected the taxes stopped for some ale. I listened quite openly. They didn't seem afraid to speak. Right cocky they were. One of the men, evidently not used to drinking ale, got in his cups sooner than the other and they began to argue about the delivery. The sober one kept saying they prayed for snow so that their route would be disguised." Marcus looked perplexed.

"I couldn't figure it out at first myself," Josh laughed. "Seems they know if it snows no one will be able to keep up with the wagons. They say the wagons are to be drawn by a team of six horses, the King's own horses. I tell you, Marcus, me lad, I found it hard not to laugh in their faces. The wagons, carrying heavy loads, will have to move slowly. We'll have all the speed on our side." He craned his neck. "And they won't be able to see us for the swirling snow. In minutes we'll be covered with snow ourselves, and we'll blend in with the landscape. The wagons, on the other hand, will leave deep ruts. What d'you think?"

Marcus shrugged. "How much of an armed guard is there? Do you think they're expecting any trouble?"

Josh answered, "Aye. They've one man to ride point. John can overtake him at the bend by Cutters' farm. There's to be the driver and an armed guard waiting atop the coach. Crack shots, both of them!" Josh added gloomily. "There's to be four wagons in all. That makes a total of twelve men and the one riding point. There're only six of us, counting the girl, seven."

"And the route, Josh? Which is it? Is it the one we marked on the map?"

"Aye, one and the same. And I know the route and lanes like the back of me hand. There's not a place for a one of them to sidetrack us."

"What of a trap? Could there be more of the King's men waiting to ambush us anywhere along the way?"

"I think not. If so, the men were not told of it. They couldn't wait to tell how carefully this route had been set up. No, they would have bragged of it. I think you have the inside track. 'Tis a daring deed we do, and if caught . . ." He drew his fingers across his neck in a slicing gesture.

"There's no other way, Josh. Let's have no second thoughts now. What time are the coaches to leave?"

"Right now! Dawn! That gives us three hours till they hit Cutters' farm. We have to make our move then and be quick about it. From there it's another hour's ride in normal weather to the wharf. We load the casks, and that's the end of it. But it may take two, three hours if this weather keeps up. Best be prepared!"

Marcus sat hunched against the weather, his face cold and unreadable. Josh and Tori sat silently watching him.

"It sounds too easy, Josh. I feel there is a trap somewhere."

"Ye be wrong, Marc. In this weather how could there be? Ye can't see your hand in front of your face."

"If there is a trap, we'll just have to take over the wagons and assume the positions of the guards. I have an idea swimming around in my head," Marc said, glancing at Tori. "But we'll only use it if necessary."

Tori, noticing Marcus's look at her, shuddered with fear— was she to be the decoy?

Chapter Twenty

The snow swirled and spat above the dancing, roaring fire. Tori sat huddled by the blaze and watched the emotions flicker across Marcus's face. He looked terribly worried.

He rose to his feet and walked over to replenish the smaller fires and to stir the men.

"I feel a bit like a newborn babe," Josh said with a wan smile. "Or else I'm developing sea legs in anticipation of our journey." He pulled his cloak close around him and rubbed his hands together. Tori stood shivering and tried to wrap the thin blanket securely around her sparse frame. Finally, with much tugging and struggling, she had it wrapped to her satisfaction. Her thoughts went to the ermine-lined cloak, and for a second she could almost feel its warmth and the softness caress her body.

Marcus led the horses to the outer circle of the fires and directed the men to tie ropes securely from one saddle to the next. They would have to ride in a straight line so as not to get lost in the snow. It was blinding. It would be almost impossible to keep one's eyes open. He felt a momentary twinge as he watched Josh and the girl mount the horses.

Josh's great sorrel snorted and pawed the ground. Josh would ride the lead, as he said his horse could make the trip blindfolded. Marcus hoped he was right, this had to go off as planned, time was so short.

Tori cast a backward glance at the small ring of fires. For a second she felt a pang at leaving the clearing. I must be mad, she thought to herself. I'm on my way home! Still, somehow she felt an aching loss.

For close to two hours the small band headed into the wind and the heavy snow. Josh rode with his head hunched in his cloak. Everyone followed blindly. Suddenly the sorrel halted and Josh called back to Marcus, "'Tis the fork. If there is to be a trap, it will be over the rise. What is it to be, Scarblade?"

"Keep going," Marcus shouted to be heard over the wind. "If they're camped there, they'll have to have some kind of fire."

"You'll see the smoke and smell it," Josh called back, "the winds will carry it to us."

"Keep going!" was the command Josh shouted as he prodded the sorrel gently. The snow was getting deeper by the hour. Progress was almost at a crawl.

The small party rode silently, each busy with his own thoughts. Tori let her mind wander to happier days when she was a child and had nothing to occupy her mind but flights of fancy.

Marcus prayed silently that Josh would be fit enough to make it to the ship alive and well.

Josh had thoughts only of trying to fight down the ache in his chest. Warm climates and sunshine loomed so far away on the horizon that he felt he would never see them again. "I will," he said determinedly. "I have to!"

Charles rode behind the hunched figure of Tori. Soon as they made camp this night, he would satisfy his want of her once and for all. Josh would be too sick by then to interfere.

He would kill Scarblade if he had to. He shrugged deeper into the cloak and felt warm at the thought.

John and Ned and Richard had no thoughts other than how to spend the gold they were to have as their share.

The sorrel came to a stop and reared on its hind legs. He pawed the ground and snorted fearlessly. Marcus slid from the chestnut he rode and trudged to Josh.

"You were right, Scarblade. There's a camp over there, beyond the hill. How many, lad?"

"Probably a dozen. They know we ride only six. They probably figure that two to one of us. The odds are not good, Josh. I have a plan."

Quickly he told Josh, who shook his head vehemently. "They'll kill her. They wouldn't be feeble-minded now! What would a lone girl be doing out here in such a storm? Use your head!"

Marcus shook his head stubbornly. "I am using my head. It's the only way. She has to be the bait! She's a fair-looking lass. Their first thoughts will be to have a little fun. 'Tis too cold for anything else. When she has them all around her we'll just have to make the best of it, and from what I've seen, she'll manage. There's no other way, Josh. You know that. We can't have come this far to lose now."

"What if the girl wasn't here?" Josh asked stubbornly. "What then?"

"There's no time to worry about what might have been. This is now, Josh, we must act now! I'll get the girl."

Back hunched against the wind, Marcus sought Tori. His heart thudded dully within him, the cords in his throat constricted into tight knots. Harshly, he accused himself. He was a man used to enjoying a woman's charms and not suffering a moment's conscience. But Tori was different, she wasn't a woman to be used and cast carelessly aside. She was the kind of woman a man marries. And I'm not a marrying man, he rebuked himself, remembering the conversation he had had with Myles Lampton and Samuel before he

left for England. To find a woman who contradicts all I've
said about her sex. One to offer a great sacrifice for another.
To snatch her up and carry her off to the valley.

With these thoughts, Marcus trudged back to Tori and,
quickly and in cold tones, outlined his plan. To his surprise,
she accepted readily. "Can you do it?" His ebony eyes bore
into hers and a shadow of regret dimmed their brightness.
He hated having to entreat her to do this, but he knew no
other solution.

Tori recognized the shadow in his eyes for what it was
and lowered her gaze, not daring to probe deeper into those
night-dark mirrors, not daring to listen to her heart which
was beating a tattoo of *He cares! I know he cares for me!*
Lips trembling and choking back tears, Tori nodded her
agreement.

What difference did it make what she did? Sometime
within the last hour she had become convinced that she
would never get home alive. If she could in some way help
the people of Chancelor's Valley, she would.

Marcus untied the rope tethering her horse and led her to
the front of the line. "There is one thing I must tell you,
Tori." He hesitated for a second.

Tori looked across at the man who sat next to her astride
his own steed. She saw the look of hopelessness that was
beginning to cloud the handsome looks of the notorious
Scarblade. "They may shoot me down," he said.

She held in her tears. "I knew that the moment you explained the situation to me. I pray that you succeed in your
mission. And if it is not too forward of me, would you perhaps do me one last favor?"

Marcus swallowed back a lump in his throat and nodded.

"Take care of Josh and see that he gets to that ship of
yours." Before Marcus could reply Tori had spurred the
horse and was off, leaving Marcus squinting into the driving snow that concealed her as effectively as the damask
curtains surrounding a marriage bed.

Anger coursed through him with such a red-hot fire that he gasped. To have to be put in such a position that he sent a mere girl out to do a man's job and probably to be killed. He couldn't think of that. There were hundreds of lives that depended on him. Other young girls and small children. He could not let her color his thinking. Josh sighed mightily as he brought his steed abreast of Marcus.

"Don't think, Marcus! You were right! There was no other way." He could not resist adding, "You were wrong, Marc, only about the girl. Too long you have carried the worries of that young colony on your shoulders; and while they are broad, there is always someone willing to help. The girl has proved that!" He motioned with his hand and the men dismounted, their pistols drawn. Slowly they crept forward in the deep snow.

A shot rang out, splitting the frozen silence with a crack. Josh forcibly restrained Marcus while Charles whispered quietly to the men.

"Easy does it, lads. Not a sound now. We form a half-circle. Fire quick and fast. There will be no second chance."

Vehemently clutching Charles's arm Marcus whispered, "No killing."

"'Tis too late for that, Scarblade!" Charles muttered through his swollen, broken mouth that bore the mark of the brutal beating he had received the day before. "It's either kill or be killed!" The other men nodded.

Marcus knew he was outnumbered. He tried again. "Then try to wound only, I want no killing on my soul."

"'Tis your soul ye be worryin' about, izzit, Scarblade? I'm not!"

Josh crawled back to the small half-circle of men. "There be eight of them, Scarblade, and the girl is sitting by the fire. What do you think? I swear she has them bewitched." Suddenly he chuckled at the expression on his friend's face.

Within minutes it was over. Charles, with the stealth of a cat, had two heads together and gave them a vicious crack.

Josh had one man's neck in the crook of his arm. Ned, Richard, and John stood silently with drawn pistols. The five remaining royal guards surrendered and laid down their weapons.

Scarblade, heaving a sigh, thanked God there had been no killing. "Quickly now, bind them and leave them by the fire," he ordered John. "Before we go have one of the men replenish the fire and bind them loosely enough so they can free themselves after a time."

Scarblade looked into the cold, hostile eyes of Victoria Rawlings and felt a strange emotion rise up in his chest. The gold-green eyes appeared sleepy and feline in the firelight. She lowered her eyes and struggled to her feet.

Well done, Tori, she said to herself. What had she expected? A pretty "thank you," perhaps? Perhaps just one kind word. She waited. There was some strange look on the man's face, a look she could not fathom.

Josh shouted to be heard over the roaring flames and the driving snow. "This man," he said, jabbing a huge hand at a trussed form by the fire, "says that if we ride south we should overtake the wagons in an hour's time." He lowered his voice so that only Marcus could hear. "Then we would be at best another two hours' ride from the ship."

"If it is south, then we ride north," Scarblade said suddenly. "I had a feeling they would change the route. Persuade him, Josh, gently that is, for the truth."

"'Tis the truth," Josh roared. "A smashed nose and a few missing teeth were all it took to convince him. We ride south. It'll still be only an hour's ride. 'Tis an uphill grade and the wagons will be heavy."

"Change horses with these men; ours are worn and we have many more hours of travel." Scarblade's voice boomed, and the small band of men hurried to obey their leader.

Josh shook his head and patted his sorrel lovingly and said the horse could ride for days. He would never leave her behind. "'Tis the only thing I've left," he stated simply.

In the confusion of leading the string of horses to be

changed no one noticed Tori as she struggled, her left arm hanging limply as she tried to mount the beast assigned her. She gritted her teeth and gave a great lunge and sat slumped over, breathing heavily, eyes glazed with pain.

Tori had followed Marcus's plan to the letter. She had trudged through the snow toward the guards' encampment, brazenly allowing the twigs and roots which lay beneath the snow to crack under her weight. Marcus had instructed her not to come upon the King's men suddenly—she was to give them some warning of her approach. But Marcus had not known the condition of the guards. He could not have known that they were frozen with the cold and starved from lack of provisions and frightened for their lives, owing to their solemn responsibility for the tax shipment.

Tori hadn't even heard the report of the pistol. She was only aware of the young, half-starved, terror-stricken face of the guardsman, who in his panic, had shot blindly into the brush. When the small platoon of soldiers came to their senses they flushed the underbrush and found Tori. Roughly, they pulled her to her feet and dragged her close to the fire, where they forced her to sit. They began an interrogation and were waiting for her answer when Marcus and his men broke into their camp.

Carefully, she placed her hand inside the worn blanket she used as a cape, and it came away red and sticky, as she had known it would. She felt faintly sick and a little dizzy. Again she gritted her teeth, thinking, hoping, it was only a flesh wound.

Again the small band rode into the driving snow. Tori felt her arm going numb and gratefully admitted the absence of all feeling was better than the pain.

The string of horses plodded onward. From time to time the snow would let up and one rider would be able to see the rider in front of him. Then the swirling snow would come faster, blinding the men and the lone girl. The cold crept into their bones, locking their joints as they sat huddled on the slow-moving horses.

Tori sat her beast and suffered moments when she had to fight mightily to keep from slipping to the ground. She swayed dizzily as a violent gust of wind almost knocked her from the horse. Her breath seemed to freeze in the very air. The horse halted, and she sat silently and waited, cold and frozen, praying no one would ask her to dismount.

Josh sat slumped in the saddle. Marcus slid from his horse and plowed through the knee-deep snow. "What is it, Josh?"

"The wagons are ahead of us, at a dead stop. See the ruts? Methinks one of the wagons has a broken hub. I've been watching the tracks and I can see the way it weaves. The only thing I'm not sure of is which wagon it is; if it's the middle one then it will be all right. 'Tis hard to tell, but I know from the way their tracks freshen that they're at a standstill."

Marcus, eyes narrowed in the driving snow, said, "Then we'll have to go on foot."

"I don't know, Marc; I'm frozen fair. If it comes to a fight the men will be no better than I. We may come out second best," Josh murmured.

"Aye, Josh, but on the other hand, those men are just as cold as we are. Their arms will bend just as uselessly as ours. We'll do the best we can; we'll creep up and take the last wagon and work from there. Silence is the keyword. Let the girl stay on her horse."

The men trudged in a tight group to the stalled wagons. Scarblade waved his arm to the men as a signal to follow, then drew his pistol. "We have surprise on our side; by now they are no doubt sure that there will be no trouble. Easy now."

For a man of his height and bulk he crept with phenomenal grace through the deep snow. The men followed in his tracks.

"Look, Josh," Scarblade whispered. "The canvas canopy is frozen over. They can't see outside. Just pray that the hatch at the rear is not frozen shut. That will give us the most trouble. If it is, then I'll have to shoot off the latch. You'd better be there with drawn pistols and," he added ominously, "be prepared to use them if necessary."

The men crouched low in the deep snow and advanced slowly to the wagons. Josh, in the lead, was the first to approach the door. Crouched low, he peered at the latch. He bent closer; the ice was encrusted over the whole frame. Cautiously, he tried the handle: it didn't move. He crouched silently and thought for a moment. There was no sound from the coach. He held one large hand up in warning and suddenly gave the lock a vicious crack and at the same time grasped the handle. The King's men inside, sitting near frozen all in a huddle in a vain attempt to keep warm, were taken by surprise.

Josh had the pistol aimed at the men in a second. There was no time for the men to try for their own pistols.

Marcus, entering the coach behind Josh, dragged the men from their positions and shoved them into the snow toward Charles and the men.

"Bind them well, but leave enough slack so they can free themselves later. Quietly now," he whispered. "A sound from you and you'll get a bullet for your reward." The men looked with glazed eyes into the cold, hostile ones of the man with the blazing scar on his cheek.

One of the King's guards was heard to gasp in fear, "Scarblade!"

Once the guard was bound and securely locked within the coach, Scarblade's men advanced on the next coach. It lurched in a sickly way to the side. It was the one with the first wagon. The guards were in a near stupor. They offered no resistance. "They'll be dead in another few hours," Josh cautioned to the men. "So will the others. You cannot last in this bitter cold with nothing to warm your bones. Tying them will make no difference. There's no fight in any of them. There's nothing we can do for them. They have taken an oath to stay with the convoy and cannot leave; either way is death to them. Otherwise they would have untied the team and tried to make it to shelter on their own.

"Once the monies are gone from the coaches they can then safely untie the team and leave if they want. But," he admonished, "they have neither the strength nor the will to do it. They will lie there and die. 'Tis not our fault, Scarblade."

The third wagon held only three men, all dead. They advanced to the first and Josh drew his pistol and shot off the lock. The door swung drunkenly and he looked inside. The men lay on top of each other for warmth, their bodies covered with the fine snow that had seeped in around the canvas hood. Marcus prodded a still form on top. It rolled to the side and lay still. "He's dead. So are the others," he said as he nudged each in turn. " 'Tis a sad business. They gave their lives for the Crown. You have to admire them for that."

"Try telling that to their families when their bellies are empty," Josh almost snarled. "What will the Crown do for them then? They'll starve just like your colonists!"

"Charles," Marcus called suddenly, "untie the men from the first carriage and offer them the use of the horses. We have to do that much for them. If they reach the authorities the game will be up. But I think they will choose to stay and die. The disgrace alone would make the rest of their lives a living hell."

"All right, Scarblade," Josh spoke. "What is it we do now? How do we transport the monies to the ship?"

"We have to use the first wagon, we could never get the others free of the snow. With a mighty effort this one may be pulled free. I'll drive it with Ned. The rest of you will have to load your saddlebags and carry what you can on horseback. We take as much as we can. The rest we have to leave behind.

"I think the bulk of it may be fitted into the wagon. They only used the four wagons for protection, not so much for the weight. Let's see to it," Scarblade called. "The faster we work, the warmer we'll get. Soon we'll be sweating and then we can be on our way." Suddenly he looked upward. "The snow is letting up! Look!"

"Right you are, lad," Josh laughed. "'Twill be easier if we can see what we are about. Let's go, lads. What do you think?" he asked, looking at Marcus. "Should we take the pouches out of the casks? 'Twill make a lighter load, and we have to use the pouches when we ride the horses."

"The lighter the load the better. Pray, Josh, that we make it. This snow is mighty deep and the horses are cold and tired."

"Aye, lad. We all best pray," Josh said soberly. "And while you see to it, I want to check the girl," he added as he turned the huge sorrel around. He looked with pity at the near frozen girl in the saddle. "We'll be moving again, lass. Do you think you can make it?"

Tori nodded wearily. She had to fight to open her eyes. "It's stopped snowing!" she said in amazement. "Were you successful, Josh? How did it go?" she asked anxiously.

"The men in the wagons are all dead or near dead."

"Then why is it we're still alive, Josh? We've been riding as many hours as the coaches."

"Ye be wrong, lass. The convoy must have started last night sometime to have gotten this far. Don't forget we did not start out till midmorning this day. Must have been all the praying I did," Josh joked.

Tori, unable to make her mouth move, just nodded. God, she was so cold, so tired, and so very hungry.

Josh looked with concern at the weary girl in the saddle. "We will stop at the first station we come to. There will be one in a short ride. Do ye think ye can last, lass?"

Tori forced her jaw muscles to work and said through

clenched teeth, "I'll be all right, Josh. Shall I move up to the coaches?"

"Move the horse, lass, and shake your arms to keep the blood moving."

Tori almost laughed aloud. Move her arms! The wound must have started to bleed again; she could feel a warm stickiness inside her sleeve. "Yes," she murmured, "I'll move my arms. Gently she prodded the horse and sat numbly and cold in the saddle as the huge beast plowed through the high snow. Once by the wagons, she reined in the animal and sat watching as the men loaded the casks into the lead wagons.

Tori looked at the high snow and then at Marcus Chancelor. Feeling the girl's eyes on him, he looked up, his arms full, and almost faltered at her appearance. She looked near death's door.

"Are you all right?" he asked, concern on his face. "I wish there was room in the wagon for you, but the casks will be stacked to the very top."

Tori heaved a sigh. She could never have dismounted. She clenched her teeth and made a tight fist with her hand. Please God, she murmured silently, just help me. Let me get through the next hour and then you can let me die.

Chapter Twenty-One

"There be the inn, lads," Josh called. "We made it," he cried happily.

Marcus reined in the team and climbed down. "Let us settle in the inn before I make my way to the ship. I must warm my bones and get some food in my belly or I won't be going anywhere. We best watch our words now and be careful," Marcus admonished the men. "Bring the saddlebags into the inn and the men can have their share before I leave."

Tori sat rigid while the men dismounted. She knew she could not do it on her own. She felt strong arms lift her free of the saddle. Josh held her gently but, even so, the grip he had on her arm almost made her cry out. The color drained from her face. She swayed and would have fallen except for his hold.

"'Twill be all right, lass. Just a few more minutes and ye'll be warm and cozy. And all the food you want. Lean on me, lass." The big man half carried her, half dragged her into the warmth of the inn.

Tori looked around as the heat struck her like a blow. The huge room was empty except for a burly man. He watched silently and suspiciously as Josh led the girl to the fire and laid her down gently. "Soon ye'll be warm," he said with a smile. "I have to help the men now. Rest."

Rest! With this throbbing arm? The pain was starting up again. She looked up and saw the innkeeper. There was something wrong with him. Narrowing her eyes, she saw he had a pistol ready. Seeing his intent, horror gripped her. God in heaven, to have come so far to have a miserable innkeeper ruin it all! Pulling herself to a sitting position, she knocked her shoulder against the fire tongs.

"You can do it, you can do whatever you must!" Who had said that to her? Granger? He was always telling her she could do the impossible things he outlined for her. All right, Granger. I'll do it! she thought as she gritted her teeth. The innkeeper, his eyes on the open doorway, paid the girl no heed. Tori clutched the heavy instrument in her good hand and tried to get to her feet. She managed to get herself up, but her head was spinning.

From where she stood she had a clear view of the door. She knew that the first person through it would get a bullet in his heart. She hefted the tongs with her good arm and mentally weighed her chances and those of the person entering the room. She drew her eyes from the door to the innkeeper, then back to the door, and almost fainted.

Marcus and John were carrying a cask between them. God in Heaven! She swayed and swung in the direction of the innkeeper. Marcus, seeing her about to fall, dropped his end of the chest and pushed John out of the way as he raced for Tori. He saw John fall to the floor, the innkeeper lifting his hand to his head and crashing down in a heap.

Marcus reached Tori just as she herself slid to the floor. Josh roared as Charles pushed him out of the way. "Oi seen it! Ye killed me brother!" he cried hoarsely. "Ye pushed 'im inta th' line o' fire ta take th' ball. Oi seen it! Oi seen it!" he kept repeating over and over.

"Ye've lost yer wits, man," Josh bellowed. "The cold has

numbed yer brain. Be still till we get the right of it. What happened, Scarblade?"

Marcus, his mind in a turmoil, could only stare at the still form he held in his arms. "She tried to save us, Josh. The shot went wild and John got it. Look by the man, there's the tongs she threw. See with your own eyes."

"That's the way of it, Charles. Be still now. These wild ravings will not help John."

Charles pushed Josh out of the way. "Oi seen 'im," he said stubbornly.

"Aye! I did push him, but it was because I saw the girl about to fall," Marcus explained. "I feared she would hit her head on the hearth. It's the truth, Charles. The man shot wildly when the girl threw the tongs to save your brother and me!"

"Take the bodies into the kitchens," Josh said to Richard and Ned, who had come running into the room. "We can't give them a decent burial in this heavy snow. Cover them," he added kindly.

"Oi need no 'elp, Scarblade," Charles said sullenly "Oi can take care o' me own, an' some others," he added softly to himself.

Josh's eyes questioned Marcus. "I don't know the why of it, Josh. Who knows what that man was thinking. We did him no harm, and from the looks of this place there's nothing to steal," Marcus said, lowering his eyes to the slight, inert form in his arms.

"She saved my life, Josh. But for her the ball that rests in John would be in me. Help me make her comfortable, then see if you can find something warm and dry to wrap her in. She doesn't look well."

"Aye lad, I was thinking the same thing myself." Soon he lumbered back to the fire, his arms full of quilts and blankets. "They be good and clean. No vermin in any of them," he said, smiling reassuringly at Marcus. Gently they lay Tori by the fire and tried to unwrap the blanket that she had wound about her.

"'Tiz stuck to her arm, somehow," Josh said as he gave the wet blanket a tug. "Mother of God," he roared to Richard, who had come to stand by the fire. With the cloak soaked and the knife in readiness, Josh cut the caked cloth from her arm. Staring at him was a large, angry, swelling, bleeding wound. Josh gulped in sympathy. "The pain must have been unbearable," he said softly to Marcus. "We must staunch the flow of blood. Already she has lost more than can be good for her. I don't mean to be sounding cruel, Marcus, but you best be on your way. I can take care of the girl. Like you said, time is short and you're burning it. She's weak, but once the bleeding is stopped and we get something warm into her, she'll be on the mend. My word, Scarblade, she'll be fine."

Slowly Marcus rose to his feet, his eyes on Tori. His head whirled, his thoughts followed a maze. Why did this have to happen? Pain shot through him and clouded his eyes. Slowly he nodded. "Take good care of her, Josh. There is much I have to speak to her about."

With Richard's help, Tori's wound was cleaned and a dressing applied. She was swathed in blankets and laid by the fire. Josh ordered the men to find food. "Hot food and no slop," he roared.

Tori laid next to the blazing fire, dozing fitfully at first, eventually drifting off into a deep, dreamless sleep. "I tell you, Josh, there'll be trouble. Charles has gone for the sheriff. When he sneaked out, I have no way of knowing; 'twas John's death that set him in a fury!"

"'Twas an accident, not Scarblade's doing." Josh defended the highwayman.

"Aye, Josh, we know. Still, if the authorities come here— what then? How do we explain John's body and that of the innkeeper?"

"I've been thinking, lads, we have to hide both the bodies. I hate to ask you, and I would do it myself, but with this chest of mine I fear another stint in that cold air would finish me off. Ye'll have to dig out to the storehouse and wrap the bodies and put them under the piled snow. 'Tiz the best we can do for the moment. When and if the authorities come I'll pretend that I'm the innkeeper. And ye'll be my help and the lass will be me ailing sister. It may work. If not," he shrugged elaborately, "best put the pouches alongside the bodies."

Hours later, their grisly task completed, Ned and Richard sat hunched by the fire. Josh stood with his back to the men, his heavy face a mixture of worry and fear. "Scarblade should have been back by now. 'Tis almost six hours. He would have been riding alone and making better time on the return trip. 'Tis worried I am," he said, rubbing his jaw.

Ned and Richard nodded, their own faces creased with worry.

"Tell me now, the two of you. Did ye make a decision as to whether ye'll sail with the ship on the morrow?"

"Aye, Josh, we sail with ye," Ned said quietly.

"Good lads. I was hoping that would be your decision. What do ye think, lads? About Scarblade, I mean."

Richard frowned. "He should have been back hours ago. I suspect that Charles had his finger, if not his whole hand, in the pie somewhere."

Josh nodded worriedly. "The only thing that will be safe will be the money. Scarblade was right in not telling anyone where the ship is docked or its name. But Scarblade could have been waylaid coming back by either Charles or the authorities—or both, for that matter! I think," Josh said, rubbing his large hands together, "that Charles will not make mention of the money at all but try to get Scarblade strung up for what he thinks is murder. The Blade will have a hard time trying to prove he had no part in the shooting."

Hours passed, with Ned and Richard finally giving up

their frantic pacing. They now slept in a corner of the room. The door was thrust open, and four burly men entered the inn, pistols drawn.

"Easy does it, lads, what's the meaning of this intrusion? What we have is yours, there's no reason for drawn pistols. Step lively, men," he roared to Ned and Richard. "Get these gentlemen some food and ale!"

"'Tis not food or ale we be lookin' for, 'tis the band of Scarblade!"

"Why do ye come to my humble inn? There be no henchmen here, as you can see," Josh said, waving his arms around the room. He affected the speech of the intruders, making himself seem one of them. "What makes ye think they would be here? Nary a soul has set foot in this inn since the snows come yesterday. Sit yourselves down, men, and let's talk."

"'Tis not talking we want," said one of the men, brandishing a pistol.

"Aye lads, I can see tha'. Well then, search if ye want. Whatever it is ye'll not be findin' it here. 'Tis nothing here that don't belong."

"Search the inn," the man with the pistol ordered. "Every inch of it, miss nothing!"

"Ye look like a man with a keen mind," Josh smiled, "tell me what's the trouble and why are ye here?"

"'Tis a wild tale we heard this day," the man said, slightly mollified by Josh's tone. "'Twas a man named Charles Smythe," he said, "claiming that Scarblade's men and Scarblade killed his brother, and the innkeeper, too."

"Scarblade, is it?" Josh roared with laughter. "And why would he be making use of my humble inn? And I'm the innkeeper, as you can see. Methinks this man Charles was havin' a bit o' sport wi' ye. 'Tis a shame makin' ye ride in this foul weather for a jest. I hope ye find him and string him high," Josh said virtuously.

The three men came back. "There's nothing, sir, no sign. I think tha' scoundrel was makin' sport wi' us."

The first man nodded slightly. "Then," he said, fixing his eyes on Josh, "ye'll be tellin' me yer name as innkeeper."

Josh roared with laughter. It was lucky he had seen the small wooden sign in the taproom that proclaimed one Andrew Simpson was the innkeeper. "'Tis Andrew Simpson, lad. Tha' me name, the same one me old mum stuck on me the day I crawled from 'er belly."

"And who is the lass by the fire?"

"'Tis only me sister, dim-witted at that," he said, tapping his forehead. "'Tis only Nellie. Look smart, lass!"

Tori gasped. Dim-witted! A sharp retort came to her lips, but she bit her tongue and the pain brought tears to her eyes. She then let the eyes roll back in her head and made a small mewing sound.

"'Tis worse than most I've seen," the stranger said in sympathy. "They should be locked away someplace or shot."

"Aye," Josh laughed. "She fair saps the strength of even me. I've been thinkin' of late she gets worse. There be days she just muses and rolls her eyes. I tell you it makes me fair sick. Still, she is me own sister."

On cue, Tori rolled her eyes again and made the same catlike noises. She worked the saliva in her mouth with her tongue and let it trickle from her mouth.

"'Tis sickening," the man said righteously.

"Pay her no heed, man. Sit with your back to the fire if she offends you."

Josh ordered Richard and Ned to fetch some food and ale, then sat down at the rough table, his eyes alert. The man was no fool and for the moment he was satisfied, but what about after? He had to convince him and get him out of the inn.

"'Tis some blizzard we had yesterday," Josh said conversationally.

"Aye," the man agreed. "There's armed guards crawling the area from here to the fork down by the Cutters' farm," he said, watching Josh carefully.

Josh looked properly blank. "Why?" he asked bluntly.

The man's eyes narrowed as he looked at Josh. "I guess there's no harm in telling you; sooner or later the men will be here for some food and ale. The convoy of wagons with the tax money did not reach its destination."

"What?" Josh barked, a look of shock on his face.

Satisfied that the shock was genuine, the man, who said his name was Simon, continued. "They say that Scarblade and his men robbed it."

"In that blizzard?" Josh asked, his voice incredulous.

"Aye, that be about the right of it, man."

"More likely, the wagons got stuck in the heavy snow," Josh scoffed.

"Not that convoy. They had the best horses to be had, and those were special wagons. A blizzard wouldn't have stopped them. No, they were probably held up by the high-wayman."

"If what ye say is true, man, I wouldn't give ye a hair for the life o' that madman, Scarblade."

"Have no fear, the man has been caught."

"What?" Josh barked, a look of shock on his face. "They actually caught the scoundrel . . . Scarblade?" he asked, his voice shaking.

"'Tis true he was empty-handed and denied the knowledge of the robbery. But they have him for the other crimes. 'Tis just a matter of time before we have knowledge of the tax money."

"If what you say is true, what did he do with the gold if he was empty-handed?"

"Who knows? Probably passed it to some accomplice."

"I still can't believe it," Josh said incredulously. "They captured Scarblade, did you hear, men?" Ned and Richard nodded, their faces unreadable.

"Did they hang him?" Josh asked him, his voice suddenly cold.

"Not yet, but they will," Simon laughed.

"And you say he had no money on him. Perhaps he didn't rob the tax convoy?"

"'Tis no matter at this time." Simon smiled wickedly. "He'll hang for the other robberies. Well," he said, wiping his plate clean, "we'll be thanking you for the food and the ale. Best be getting on the road. If ye see or hear of anyone looking like Scarblade's henchmen, notify the authorities. And," he said, looking in Tori's direction, "best see about the dimwit."

As soon as the men left, Josh slammed the heavy bolt on the door and looked around the bare room. He resembled a stallion held at bay.

"You heard, lads. We best be making plans right quick, too."

Tori struggled to her feet. "What can we do, Josh? They'll hang him!" she almost wept.

"Not yet, they haven't. And until that day we have hope."

"We'll stay with you, Josh," Ned said softly. "We'll be back."

Josh once again slammed the bolt. He looked at Tori and frowned, saying nothing.

"Where will they have taken him? Do you have any idea?"

Josh shook his head. "Wherever it is he has no hope of escaping. Someplace where only the most trusted can get to see him."

"Like who, Josh? What do you mean, 'the most trusted.'"

"For instance, Lord Whimsey, Lord Starling, and Lord Barclane, probably Lord Fowler-Greene."

"Who?" Tori gasped. "Lord Fowler-Greene, did you say?" Tori's eyes held shock and disbelief at the name. "Are you saying that they are the only men who would have access to Marcus?"

"'Tis safe to assume so, lass. Why do ye ask?"

"Oh, no," Tori wailed, "oh, no!" She lowered her shaking body to the rough plank bench and looked at Josh with tear-filled eyes. "Of all the people in this whole world!"

Chapter Twenty-Two

Aloud, insistent knock on the door startled them both. Tori glanced at Josh with a question in her eyes. "It's dim-witted ye be, lass, remember that," he said as he went to throw open the bolt.

A man entered, his hat low over his eyes and the collar of his cloak turned up against the cold. He stomped his feet and rubbed his hands briskly. "I seek shelter and food," he stated in a breathless voice. "I've been riding for days and am fair near to death for hunger." Slowly he removed his hat and threw the cloak to the floor.

Tori gasped, "Granger! Is that you, Granger? Merciful God," she said, rushing over to him and throwing her good arm around him. Abruptly she pulled back. "Damn your very soul, Granger, why didn't you come for me to Dolly's? Where have you been?" she demanded of him.

"Tori, is it really you? Do my eyes deceive me? Tell me it's you!"

Josh stood to the side, eying the tableau. So this was Granger! "Darling" Granger of the girl's delirium. He snorted in disgust. A poor specimen of a man if he ever saw one! Tori must be dim-witted!

"'Tis I, Granger. Oh, Granger, what has happened? How are my parents? Come sit, you look ill. Are you ill?"

"Well, if I'm not I will be if you don't shut up, Tori. That mouth of yours never stops! My head throbs," he said pitifully, "and I'm so hungry I could chew this tankard."

"Josh, fetch me some food. Granger is hungry," Tori commanded.

"Is he now?" Josh smirked. And that's not all he is, Josh thought, wrinkling his nose. He wondered when this dandy had last had a bath. Tori must have wondered the same, for she blurted, "You smell, Granger!"

"You'd smell too if you'd slept with a herd of goats," Granger snapped defensively. "Fearing a stranger, no one would give me a place to roost. Being penniless, a goat herd was the only place I could find to keep warm!"

"Oh, Granger, you didn't?" she said with a tinkling laugh.

"I had too much to drink at your wedding," Granger admitted shamefaced. "I went off with Lord Fowler-Greene's sister, Lady Helen, and I might add, when I had tired of her she held me a virtual prisoner!" Granger shivered slightly, remembering those few days in Lady Helen's service. "Then, when I had more time to think of what Lord Fowler-Greene would do when he discovered Dolly in your place, I . . . I was afraid of what he might do. You know, Tori," Granger admonished hotly, "you never gave one little thought to me in your little plan! You were off safely somewhere and I was left holding the bag!"

"Safely somewhere! Why, you ungrateful . . . lily-livered . . . stupid . . . safe!" Tori shrieked. "Let me tell you something, you . . ." Tori stopped in midspeech, noting the glitter in Granger's eyes. The glitter became a gleam and they both broke out in rollicking laughter. "You tease!"

Abating his laughter, Granger went on with his story. "I set out at last to find you at Dolly's rooms. When I didn't, I struck out on my own, following my ever erroneous instincts. One evening shortly afterward, I was accosted and left penniless, which is to say near to death in this uncaring world. When I appealed to your father he told me this was the perfect time for me to begin to fend for myself. I was on my way to throw myself on the mercies of an old school chum. Then I happened here."

Josh came back into the room and plunked down a heavy plate piled high with food. Granger tore at the meat like a starving man. Over his head Josh looked questioningly at Tori.

"He's the answer to our prayers," she said with a glance toward Granger. At Josh's doubtful look she hastened to explain. Quickly, while Granger devoured his food, Tori told the story of her near-wedding and the deception, and the following events. Josh now looked at Granger with a glimmer of an idea. "Let me finish our story, Josh," Tori said, "then we can tell him what he must do for us."

"Whatever it is, the answer is no!" Granger said between mouthfuls. "I wouldn't be sitting here now if it weren't for you, Tori. And I wouldn't be smelling like a herd of goats, either!"

"Tell me of my parents, are they well?" she asked to divert his attention. Swallowing a great mouthful of food, Granger threw Tori a considering look. Noting his reaction to her question, she pressed further: "Tell me, Granger, are they well?"

"For a moment I forgot you didn't know," Granger said softly. "They sailed for America a month past. It appeared due to some mysterious influence; your father regained favor with the Crown and was offered the opportunity to take the mayoralty of a new settlement in America."

"They have really gone, gone to America?" Tears rolled down Tori's cheeks at the thought of never seeing her parents again. "Did you tell them, Granger? Do they know of the deception I played?"

"No, Tori. I think Lord Fowler-Greene was the mysteri-

ous source that helped your father gain favor. They left with
the thought that you were all married and happy," Granger
said quietly. "But they didn't know you're with child," he
said, grinning.

"What?" Tori gasped.

Granger nodded. "Our mutual friend Dolly has been instrumental in making Lord Fowler-Greene very happy."

Marcus awoke hearing a steady drip-drip somewhere
close to his head. At first he had no recollection of where he
was or how he came to be here in this dark, stinking hole.
Slowly, the past came back to him, each memory flashing
through the cold facts of reality.

On examination, he accepted the fact that there was not
much to remember. He had been discovered, pursued, and
captured, and thrown into this stinking dungeon somewhere
in the bowels of Newgate.

He could feel the oozing slime on the stone walls and the
scratches cut into the mortar between the stone blocks. He
pushed back thoughts of the hair-raising stories of men gone
mad, left to rot here in the dungeons. He wondered what
human hand had etched those scratches, clawed in desperation into the imprisoning walls.

His cell was furnished with a long plank along the back
wall. It was here he had found himself when he awakened
from resting his weary bones. There were no windows or
portals to the outside; and the only air he breathed filtered
through the bars in the door. The stench was sickening—
rotting flesh, decayed food, bad water, sewage, and human
offal assaulted his nostrils.

A light scraping sound caught his attention and he
sought out its source. A young rat crept out from a crevice
in the wall. It scurried by in panic, as though it, too, desperately sought release from this wretched hole. It ran from
one side to the other attempting to climb its way free, but

the walls were so slimy the animal could not get a grip. Finally, as though dreading the thought and resigning itself, it scurried back through the crack from which it came.

Marcus sat on the edge of the plank, despair weighing down upon his broad chest.

An echo of tinkling laughter struck a chord in his reverie, and the image of yellow-green eyes danced before him. He lay down on the thin plank, the splinters of the chewed wood biting into him.

He laughed, at first shortly then more rollickingly. How ironic! He thought back to the quiet evening in Chancelor's Valley when his father first announced that Marcus was to go to England to beseech the King. It was then that he first promised that if he should find a woman who offered a great personal sacrifice he would snatch her up and carry her back.

And hadn't Tori done just that? Offered her life by going among the King's guard where she was shot and, further, knocked the innkeeper with the fire tongs, thereby committing a murder to save him? Beauty, compassion, spirit, and courage, and now that he had at last found the woman he wanted, he was powerless to claim her. Instead of snatching her off to Chancelor's Valley he would rot in the stinking bowels of Newgate and the next bit of sky he saw would be from the long end of a rope on Tyburn Hill.

Tori watched Granger sitting nonchalantly on the rough bench opposite her. "You'll help us, won't you, Granger?"

He nodded wearily. He had searched these many days for Tori. Now that he had found her he almost wished he hadn't. He should have known that she would be in trouble. "It's a wild tale you spin, cousin. Unfortunately, I believe every word of it. Nothing else would make sense, knowing you. You actually participated in the tax robbery? I'll wager the whole scheme was your idea, wasn't it?" he asked suspiciously.

"Say anything, think anything, I don't care. I'm that happy to see you. Are you warm enough?" she asked solicitously. "You are? Good! Get his cloak, Josh, he must ride now! This minute! You'll go to Lord Fowler-Greene."

Granger nodded from time to time as he listened to her instructions. Josh, too, added what he thought should be said and done. "Get back as soon as ye can, lad. We'll do what we can from here."

After Granger's departure, Tori and Josh sat at a table, each busy with private thoughts, Josh moving only to replenish the fire. Tori sat huddled, her mind in a turmoil. What would become of her, she wondered. With her parents gone to America and Granger, at best, good for nothing, how could the two of them survive?

"Why not come to America with us, lass? 'Tis the least we can do for ye."

"America," Tori gasped. "What would I do in America?"

"Well, for one, your folks are there. You could go to them and start a new life."

"Are you sure it would be all right?"

"Aye, lass. I'll personally make sure 'tis all right."

"And Granger, could he come, too?"

"Aye," Josh agreed sourly, "providing he takes a bath!"

"I'll personally see to it," Tori laughed. "Won't Mother and Father be surprised when we both walk in." She giggled at the thought of Lord Nelson's face when he laid his eyes on Granger.

With the gelding, his last personal possession, Granger plowed his way through the deep snow. As he lurched in the saddle he thought of the coming conversation with Lord Fowler-Greene. Would he help Tori? Would he help Tori's bandit?

Probably, Granger snorted, since the lord was so in love with love he would no doubt agree to anything.

Startled, Granger looked up at a commanding voice which ordered him to halt. Cold, numb, weary, Granger waited for the onslaught of questions.

"Have ye seen any men on horseback riding this way?" the voice shouted.

"Not a soul have I seen these many hours," Granger lied.

"Where are ye headin', man?"

"To the home of Lord Fowler-Greene. What seems to be the trouble?" Granger asked fearfully.

"'Tis none of yer concern. Ride on, man." With this command the snow-covered figure herded his men in the opposite direction.

Granger heaved a sigh of relief and spurred his gelding forward. The next posse might head for the Boare Inn, and with the way his and Tori's fortune had been running of late, one of the men would know that Josh was not the innkeeper. Suddenly a vision of Tori swinging from a rope in a gentle breeze appeared before him. He gulped and again spurred the horse. He was almost there.

Every bone in his body ached for attention. A warm bath, some wine, and a soft woman. Ah . . . since these pleasures were to be denied him, temporarily at least, he continued to ride to the estate of Lord Fowler-Greene.

The gelding approached the wide, corded road that had been cleared of snow and wound to the fine house nestled in a grove of trees. Granger blinked at the beauty of the surroundings. The trees were covered with the gleaming snow and ice. He rode under their boughs, thinking it was like an arched shelter for a bride. He could almost see himself and the lord's sister Lady Helen, walking under these same bowed branches not so long ago. His stomach turned and he banished the thought from his mind.

Dismounting proved to be more of an ordeal than Granger had anticipated. His foot caught in the stirrup and he fell to the ground. Cursing under his breath, he lay for a moment on the drive. His foot free, he grasped the stirrup and regained his posture. Clapping his hands together to restore their circulation, he mounted the stone steps on shaky legs. He pulled the bell and listened to the deep sound of the gong.

The heavy door opened and a small woman peered out at him. "What can I be doin' for ye?" she questioned.

"Granger Lapid to see Lord Fowler-Greene," he said imperiously, not forgetting how to deal with insolent servants.

Cowed by his commanding tone, she softened her approach. "Aye, come in and warm yerself. I'll announce ye."

Granger stood by the roaring fire and held out his frozen hands to the welcoming warmth. Praying silently, he looked around the huge room. Wealth! Ah, to have such a lovely home and no pecuniary worries. Perhaps one day he, too, would have such a room.

Shaken from his silent prayers, Granger looked up at the sound of heavy footsteps entering the room. "Ah, Lord Fowler-Greene, how are you this fine day? And how is Lady Fowler-Greene?" As an afterthought, he then asked after the health of Lady Helen.

"Fine, just fine," boomed the lord. "And yourself, Granger? How are you bearing up under this storm we have just witnessed?"

"Fine, fine," Granger mimed him. "My Lord, I've come here on a matter of extreme urgency and to implore your aid."

Lord Fowler-Greene looked puzzled. Suddenly, his expression changed to fear: someone had found out about Dolly. "What?" he almost shuddered.

"It is the highwayman, Scarblade. He's been captured."

"Are you sure, man? How have you come by this knowledge?"

"From Josh, the Blade's first-in-command." Quickly, breathlessly, Granger recounted the story that Josh and Tori had told him.

Lord Fowler-Greene rubbed his jowls thoughtfully. "And

what is it you want from me, Granger? How can I help? I've no connection with this highwayman!"

"My Lord, Josh feels that you would know where they have taken the Blade."

"Did I not make myself clear? I had no idea they captured him? Perhaps Lord Whimsey would know," Fowler-Greene said thoughtfully. "And if I find out where the man is, what then?"

"We need your help, Your Lordship."

"You're asking me to go against the Crown. My boy, what makes you think I would be a party to such an escapade?"

"'Tis not my idea, your Lordship. It was Josh's. He seems to think you would help." Granger could read the indecision on the man's face. Would he help?

"You know what would happen if I were found to be aiding Scarblade?"

"Aye," Granger said sadly, "how well I know."

Lord Fowler-Greene paced the floor. He nibbled on his knuckles and watched Granger through slitted eyes, quickly considering the alternatives. To deny help for Chancelor he risked a greater chance to be discovered in his friendship with the man. On the other side, he might show his hand in trying to help. Still, the risks were greater were he to refuse his services.

"Very well, I shall send a rider to Lord Whimsey with a note. That's as far as I'll go. The rest will be yours to do on your own. I warn you now, the man will be under a heavy guard. And I doubt if you can bribe the guards." He shook his head. "'Tis a fool's errand you come on, Granger. I fear there is no chance to save Scarblade."

"My Lord, when one is in these . . . circumstances . . ." Granger said delicately, "would one be permitted a visitor? Say a dear sister?"

"'Tis happened before; depends on the time and the place. It would be worth a try."

"And the chances of a bribe, you say it won't work?"

Lord Fowler-Greene shook his head. "'Twould be worth the man's life to accept a bribe, and so it would have to be a large one. Gold, hard gold, I'd say would be best."

"I hesitate to ask this of you, Your Lordship, but we are desperate? There anything that you could contribute?"

"You go too far, man," the lord said heatedly. "You ask me to contribute when Scarblade has stolen a year's taxes from the Crown? The man is far richer than I!"

As the two men waited for a response from Lord Whimsey, they sat silently lost in their own thoughts. Lord Fowler-Greene rang the bellpull and a maid appeared presently. "Fetch some wine and perhaps some honey cakes. My guest looks in the need of some refreshment. Tell me, Granger, what do you hear from your dear cousin, Victoria?"

Granger gulped. He was in no mood for cat-and-mouse games. He blurted out Tori's story, omitting nothing. Lord Fowler-Greene nodded sadly. "I helped all I could," he said softly. "I pleaded Lord Rawlings' case as best I could. Seems I was a little too hasty. What will become of the child now? And you, Granger, what will become of you?"

"My Lord, do not concern yourself with the likes of my cousin or myself. Somehow, we will manage."

"Have you given any thought to sailing on the ship with your . . . er . . . friends to America?"

Granger looked stunned at the question. He shook his head.

"I will pay your way, the both of you, if it is what you desire. 'Tis the least I can do for the happiness you have found for me. Aye, Granger," he said, noting the disbelief on the man's face, "I have found such happiness! I never thought it possible to love one as much as I love Dolly. But," he said, holding up a plump finger, "I would rest easier if all the perpetrators of that little deception were somewhere far away. A place like America," he said smiling.

Granger smiled knowingly, conveying his agreement.

"I would even be willing to throw in a handsome purse to make sure that it is a happy occasion. One that you want, of course."

Granger was quick to note the lord's eagerness in having himself and Tori a long distance from England. "My good Lord, you are too generous. But I'm afraid Tori would not think of leaving her lover, Scarblade, behind. Even if it were only to place flowers on the poor man's grave."

The havoc that Tori could wreak on the lord's plans for Dolly's social debut rankled Lord Fowler-Greene. If he wanted Granger and Tori where they could do no embarrassment to him it was clear he would have to do all he could to help Scarblade and see that the American was safely escorted out of England.

Granger soon held a heavy leather pouch in his hand. "'Tis a most generous thing you do, milord. I'll never be able to repay you."

"My dear boy, I've been rewarded enough!" The lord spoke lovingly of his wife and the happy event that would transpire in the summer. "A son, I hope," he laughed, "to carry on the name. 'Tis wonderful, beyond belief!" Granger listened to his happy talk with half an ear. So it ended happily; whoever would have thought that Tori would have been an instrument of happiness. He still found it hard to believe.

The sound of the closing door jarred the lord from his happy thoughts. "'Tis your answer, Granger." He accepted the stiff paper from the rider and dismissed him. He weighed the letter for a moment. "Are you sure that this is what you want? From this moment on, there will be no turning back for you." When Granger did not respond, Lord Fowler-Greene broke the seal and said quietly, "Very well." His face blanched; he looked at Granger with worried eyes. "'Tis the dungeons of Newgate!"

Chapter Twenty-Three

Tori gazed at Granger with tear-filled eyes. "The dungeons. We'll never get him out." She looked imploringly at Josh. "What are we to do?"

The big man was at a loss for words. "I wish I knew, lass."

Granger, noting the anxiety on both faces, quickly told them of Lord Fowler-Greene's thought.

"You'll be able to pay him a visit as his sister, and you, Josh, as a friar. I took the liberty of procuring a friar's robe from the village monastery. It might be short in the hem for a man of your height, Josh, but I'm sure it will do, though to what end, I have no idea." His heart was heavy in his chest as he watched tears well in Tori's eyes.

"What do you think, Josh? Should we leave now? Is it worth a try?"

"We have nothing to lose, lass. Bundle warm, for it will be a good ride."

"Here then is the letter from Lord Fowler-Greene granting you permission to visit the prisoner."

"Thank you, Granger," Tori whispered, and within minutes she and Josh were dressed to leave, Tori wearing the iridescent green gown she had worn to the opera with Marcus. When they left Scarblade's encampment, Tori had packed all her belongings into her saddlebag. Could it have been only a few days ago she had sat next to Marcus listening to the ethereal strains of music?

They rode silently, and when they reined in their horses they were before the tall gray-walled prison. Tori wailed, "It looks so like death!"

"Aye, lass. It is a house of death. You understand they will hang Marcus? There's no pretending, lass; it's a fact."

Tori nodded solemnly as she followed Josh up the worn stone steps. They entered a dim, dark hall and waited for one of the jailors to come to them.

The man who approached them sported a huge circle of keys and limped heavily on one leg. He was a coarse, burly man with a shock of matted, sandy-brown hair. One side of his face was distorted by a long scar pulling down his upper lip. Just seeing his cruel, ugly expression sent a chill of horror through Tori's body.

Josh presented the sealed letter from Lord Fowler-Greene and stood with a bowed head, correct for a holy friar.

"Ye be in toime, th' thievin' bandit is ta be 'ung as soon as them orders can be signed. Owin' ta th' snow, it migh' be longer'n we 'ope fer. An' ye be good, Friar, pray fer 'is damned soul." The jailor laughed raucously, muttering something about what a sight it would be to see the great Scarblade getting his comeuppance on Tyburn Hill.

They walked for what seemed an interminable time, down one rancid, filth-infested corridor after another; down stairs so steep and dark, Tori reached frantically for Josh's supporting arm. The deeper into Newgate they went, the worse the smell, and Tori fought the retches that threatened to choke her. Finally, the jailor stopped and withdrew a large key ring. The clanking of the metal against the bars seemed to echo and thunder in Tori's ears.

"Highwayman!" roared the voice of the jailor, "there be

a friar and yer sister ta visit ya. Look smart now!" He withdrew a safe distance and waited, his pistol held loosely in
one hand, the ring of metal keys in the other.

Tori, eyes for naught except the tall figure that stood by
the bars, his hands clenched, looked into raven-black orbs
and felt herself sway with remembered feelings. She could
not bring herself to speak.

"Marcus, lad, what is it we're to do? What can we do to
get ye out of here?" Josh whispered.

"There is no way, good friend. This is the end of the road
for me. Have you followed my instructions?" he asked
Josh, all the while keeping his eyes on Tori, drinking in her
beauty and remembering the feel of her in his arms.

"There has to be a way," Tori said suddenly as she raced
to the bars and grasped Marcus's hands. "I won't let them
hang you, I won't!" she cried as the tears fell down her
cheeks. "I love you, Marcus," she whispered, "I love you!"

Marcus stamped the sight of Tori on his memory. "You'd
best go now," he said, his voice cracking with emotion. "I
don't want you to see me this way." Looking at Josh, he
said commandingly, "Promise you'll not allow her to be on
Tyburn Hill! Take her away from here! Away from me!"

Tori's head throbbed dully. How could he do this to her?
Cast her away as though she meant nothing to him, as
though there had never been anything between them. To
deny her this one last comfort, a kind word, a kiss, a hint
that she meant something more than just a woman who had
warmed his bed one night. A conquest, nothing more, and
once conquered to be done with, not even leaving her the
comfort of dignity.

Tori had blurted out her deepest emotions to a prisoner in
the mouldering, foul-smelling dungeons of Newgate and he
wanted none of her. She heard the echo of her words. "I love
you," she had cried, and he ordered her taken away.

Staggering beneath the blow of his command, Tori shrank
back into the shadows, despising herself for her weakness,

then exulting in her strength. She loved him, this man called Scarblade, and she knew she would love him in spite of his indifference to her until the day she died.

Josh's voice broke through to her. "We can try bribing the jailor, Marcus. Surely somewhere, someplace, there must be something that could be used as a bribe. I know ye won't permit us to touch the tax money, lad, but perhaps . . ."

Suddenly, Marcus's eyes lighted. "There is one thing. I don't know if it would work. Once, not long ago, a young lady entrusted something to my care. Actually, I pilfered it from her in one of the robberies. A valuable ring. She said I was to guard it, the little minx, and one day return it to her. Perhaps it could be used," he said, a faint ray of hope in his eyes.

"Aye, lad. Where is this ring you speak of?"

"In my saddlebag atop one of the spare horses, wrapped in a pouch. Try, Josh. There's nothing to lose!"

Tori almost fainted. She knew what he spoke of, that stupid glass trinket he had taken from her. Did he really think it valuable? She cursed the day Granger had given it to her. Only a piece of glass. Looking deeper into the black eyes, she saw there a faint ray of hope. She could not take it from him; there had to be some other way. Her mind raced as she noted the jailor lumbering toward them.

Josh followed her eyes. "'Tis time to leave, lad. I'll see to the task you gave me."

Tori looked longingly at Marcus, her heart in her eyes, a smile on her lips. She wanted to say something, but his glance at her was forbidding and the words died in her throat.

"If I do not see you, Tori . . ."

"But I shall see you, Marcus, I promise you."

On the way out of the dungeons, Josh asked the jailor the question bothering Tori. "Tomorrow, may we return?"

"I see no 'arm in this," the jailor laughed, eying Tori lewdly, "as long as ye 'ave that letter of admission."

Outside in the cold, bracing air, Tori gasped deep breaths. So disheartened was she, she had not the heart to tell Josh of the glass ring. He would know soon enough when they got back to the inn and removed it from Marcus's saddlebag. What would he say then? That this was the end? What else could it mean? A glass ring was not the answer! She doubted seriously if the jailor could be bribed at all.

Having no other safe accommodations to go to, the dejected trio returned to Marcus Chancelor's rooms. Huddled before the blazing fire, Tori sat next to Josh while he fingered the fake jewel. She told him the story haltingly. Granger tried to comfort her, to no avail.

"Then 'tis truly the end; for the gold is already aboard ship and cannot be touched. Cap'n Elias would sooner part with his head than go against Marcus's own orders and part with a shilling of the booty," Josh said pitifully. "After all he has done there is naught to be done to free him."

"Not so quick, my friend," Tori interrupted; "there may be a way. Listen to me carefully. Did I not do a good job of convincing the sheriff's men that I was a dimwit?" At Josh's nod, she continued, "Then why can't I play the harlot? What else in the world would distract the jailor? If you had seen him look at me you'd know what I speak of."

"My God, Tori," Granger gasped, but Tori ignored his outburst.

"What do you think, Josh? Will it work?"

Hope sprang into the big man's eyes. Till the meaning of her words penetrated his brain. Still, the hope remained, glowing feebly.

"Lass, Marcus would have none of it. Ye cannot sell yourself to get his freedom. He'd never forgive himself."

"Just answer one question, is there any other way? Is there, Josh?" Her voice became shrill as she saw Josh shake his head. "It's my body and I'll use it as I see fit! Are you telling me that if I go through with my plan that Marcus will turn against me? Is that what you're trying to spare me? Well, save your breath! He is already done with me, he ordered you to take me away, he can't bear the sight of me."

Josh shrugged his shoulders dejectedly.

"The decision is mine, regardless of the outcome," Tori said quietly. "Besides, Marcus has made it very clear what he thinks of me, and I've nothing to lose. If he dies, Josh, I die, too!"

"Tori," Granger asked hesitantly, "are you sure this is what you want? That this is the only way? I'll do whatever you ask if you're sure in your heart that this is what you want." He looked into her beautiful eyes and did not need to wait for an answer.

Tori sat before the fire, her arms clasped about her drawn-up knees. From time to time she glanced at Josh and winced inwardly at the expression on his face. There was no other way! Hour after hour passed, and dawn slowly crept upon the sullen trio.

Josh stirred himself and stoked the fire which had burned almost to the embers. "We must all have something to eat before we set out." The effort of talking brought on a fit of coughing. It was Granger who helped the weakened giant to a seat, his eyes full of concern as he noted the condition of the handkerchief Josh held near his mouth. The spasm lasted longer than the others, and Josh looked weak and drained. He forced a smile for Granger's benefit. "Don't worry, lad, I can do me part. You make me a promise, though," he gasped weakly. "If I fall behind you're to leave me. Your promise, lad, swear."

Granger murmured his agreement.

Tori nibbled on a cold piece of meat and washed it down with warm ale. She coughed and sputtered; she couldn't eat. Not now! Not ever!

Granger paced the room while Josh rested. "Look!" he exclaimed, "it's snowing again!"

"No," Tori wailed, "not again!" She looked at Josh and her heart lurched. Good God, he had never looked this bad; perhaps Granger could take his place.

Josh answered her unspoken question: "The weather will help us just as it did the day of the robbery. Get dressed, we leave in ten minutes."

"This robe will have to suffice, Granger. 'Tis the best I can do. Since all we friars are in poor straits it'll pass muster. Here," Josh said, "slip this pistol into your boot like me and be careful. They'll search us this day." He slipped a knife similarly into his own boot with shaking fingers.

Tori watched the trembling hand and placed her hand on his shoulder. "Josh, would it not be better if you stayed behind or went ahead to the ship? Granger and I can do what has to be done. If we're killed it'll make little difference. Please, Josh, return to the ship; you may stand a chance that way."

"'Tis good of ye to think of me, lass, but I'll be having none of it. Me days are numbered as ye know. I must be a party in this, for Marcus is me friend. I couldn't go to me Maker without at least trying to save him."

Tears welled in Tori's eyes. "All right, Josh, I'm ready."

The cold made Tori gasp, and her arm throbbed as the bitter wind seeped in under her cloak. She ignored the pain; her thoughts of Josh and the coming task she must perform occupied her mind. Could she do it? Of course, she could do anything she had to. Are you prepared to die? Tori questioned herself. If I must, came her quiet reply.

Cold, numb, weary, the small party dismounted and climbed the snow-packed steps. The jailor looked at them with suspicious eyes. Tori took the initiative with a slight wave of her hand to Josh and Granger.

"Sir," she said boldly, extending the missive written by Lord Fowler-Greene. She watched the jailor covertly, her gold-green eyes lackluster. She extended her arm in what she hoped was a languid gesture and patted the jailor's filthy cheek.

"It's fortunate that you're indoors in this weather. When I leave here I fear I may get lost in the storm. The good friars are headed in another direction," she cooed softly, the cat's eyes half closed as she watched his reaction. He was only too happy to talk.

"If'n Oi'm any judge a worse storm than th' other day. It's brewin', Oi tells ye. Lucky Oi am tha' Oi've comfortable quarters ta go ta. A fire, a bed wi' a little ale an' some meat an' cheese. Wha' more can a man ask?" He leered at Tori.

"Why, sir, you left something out—a woman to warm that bed of yours."

"There be no women in th' dungeons an' Oi've no jurisdiction over th' ones on th' debtors' side," the jailor smirked.

Josh was the first to proceed, then Granger, the jailor, and finally, Tori. She suddenly clutched the keeper's ragged arm and asked anxiously, "Are you the one that'll hang my brother?"

The jailor laughed. His foul breath reached Tori's nostrils, and she fought a retch. "No' Oi, th' 'angman does th' job. Bu' Oi plan ta watch," he laughed gleefully. "Oi loikes ta 'ear th' snap o' th' neck!"

Tori blanched but didn't falter. "Well, I shall not be here to hear it," she sighed. "I shall be lost in the snowstorm. Remember to look for my body in the spring," she laughed.

As they continued down the labyrinth of passageways, the air became more stagnant and mephitic. Tori could hear Granger gulp and Josh plodded ahead, his mind on other things. Tori stepped lightly, her flimsy slippers soaked from the numerous scummy puddles she had trod in.

The jailor walked abreast of her, glancing at her now and again, his murky eyes appraising her knowingly.

Tori fought the urge to draw away from his foul-smelling body but had only to see Marcus's face flash before her to make her stay close to the ugly, wretched jailor.

As a tendril of moss hanging from overhead touched Tori's cheek she cried out and moved closer to the jailor.

Taken by surprise, he was quick to take advantage of her movement. He laughed as he caught her, and she lurched against him. Tori felt a large hand cup her breast and heard his in-drawn breath. Boldly, she looked into his murky eyes, not objecting to his advances, feeling his hand tighten as she stood shivering in the cold. The jailor opened his mouth to smile, and she saw stubs of rotted teeth and a white, coated tongue. The sight was so repulsive she closed her eyes and willed herself to stay close to him.

The jailor, taking this as a sign of acquiescence, slipped his hand inside her gown, his rough, scaly hands scratching the soft skin of her breast.

"Not here," she whispered. "Later. I must see my brother first." He was reluctant to let her move from his side and grasped her breast tighter. His fingers found her nipple and he ground it between his fingers. Tori's eyes teared with the pain, and with one quick movement she was free and leaning against the wall. "Wait here, I must see my brother; then if you want for the rest of the day I'll stay with you," she said, turning from his ugly face.

The jailor, overcome with the promise, slouched against the wall; he watched Tori move to the heavily barred cell. His breath came in short gasps as he anticipated the outcome of the day. There were still a good many hours till he would have to take the next watch, and then, he thought hotly, he had the rest of the night.

His hands were on fire; never had he felt flesh so smooth and warm. He longed to cover that soft breast with his mouth while his hands did other things. It had been a long time since he had had a woman. He would have to make up for lost time today. The lust in his loins couldn't be fought any longer; his body was an inferno.

Tori glanced at Josh, who refused to meet her eyes. Granger was busy talking to two watchmen who stood outside the barred door. Both, Tori noticed, had pistols in their belts. Marcus's cell was within sight now.

The jailor's hoarse voice called, and Tori looked at Granger. "I'll not be long, Friar, perhaps five minutes," she croaked meaningfully. The jailor advanced on her, not waiting for her return.

She looked in horror at his glazed eyes and his drooling mouth and clenched her teeth as she saw him lay down the key ring and the pistol on the sweating stone floor. His torch rested precariously against the wall and he appeared a specter in the dim orange glow. Pray God that Granger's hand would not slip and there would be no outcry. She worked her face into what passed for a smile and advanced toward the jailor. Impatient with her slow progress, he reached out an arm and roughly pulled her to him.

Her body taut as a spring, she fell against him. One of his knees parted her legs. Hot hands fumbled at the wide neck of her gown while his wet mouth assaulted hers.

Abruptly, one of his arms dropped and she tried to grasp it and put him away from her. Surely he would not take her here with the others! She was aware of him lifting her skirts and his hot breath scorched her face. He was like a rutting pig! His other hand dropped and she was free for a second; only his legs pinned her against the wall, his knees holding the voluminous skirt to her thighs. Then she was thrown against the wall, and the last she knew was a loud *whack* mingled with the outraged roar of some wounded animal.

Marcus had seen Josh and a young man approach his cell, but his attention was drawn to a chalk-faced, bloodless-lipped Tori as she spoke to "Friar" Josh. What was going on here? Why did Josh look so constrained? What was Tori doing here?

He had heard a harsh voice that he recognized as the jailor's and dimly realized he was calling Tori.

From where Marcus's cell was located he could barely make out the jailor leaning the torch against the sweating wall and saw Tori walking slowly toward him.

Rage exploding within him, Marcus witnessed the attack

the jailor was making upon Tori . . . his Tori! And she was allowing it!

Anguish squeezed his heart, burst his lungs, and escaped his throat in the roar of some primeval animal losing its mate to an ancient enemy.

Seeing Tori's collapse onto the slimy, stone floor, Josh bellowed oaths mingled with threats, advanced on the grotesque jailor, his hand fumbling inside his boot for the pistol. He failed to see the man's upraised arm and the knife that was held tightly in it.

Stone-faced, Marcus watched as Josh's life's blood seeped out, spreading through the rough, dark-brown monk's cloth.

"Get the girl out of here," Marcus barked, repressed sorrow tightening his jaw, his scar burning dully on his whitened cheek. White-lipped anger hoarsened his voice. "Get Tori out of here!" he called to Granger, who was bending above her, attempting to lift her into his arms. "Now! Get her away before she sees . . . !"

Even as Marcus spoke the words, Tori's lids fluttered open. Bewilderment furrowed her brow as she looked upon the passageways filled with guards. Then her eyes fell to the form beside her. "Josh . . ."

Granger pulled her to her feet. "Don't look Tori, there's nothing we can do for him now."

"No . . . no . . . it can't be . . . it mustn't . . ." Granger lifted her into his arms, but she fought him; she had to get to Josh, her friend, Marcus's friend. . . . Arms outstretched, agony inscribed on her features, she reached to his still form, refusing to believe he was gone.

Granger dragged her away, but for one moment her eyes locked with Marcus's. She saw her own anguish mirrored in his dead-dull black eyes. Tori stirred dizzily, she felt herself being carried. She looked up into Granger's troubled face. Slowly, the realization washed over her that their plan had failed . . . failed miserably! Then her thoughts sank into merciful blackness.

Chapter Twenty-Four

The interior of the Owl's Eye Inn was lit with a dim yellow glow from greasy, soot-blackened hurricane lamps, their tallow candles smoking off an acrid odor. Granger sat in a corner of the taproom nursing a mug of mulled wine, inconspicuous among the shuffle of men and a few doxies vying for the men's favors and trade. Every time the tarnished bell above the door sounded he quickly glanced up, his eyes searching for the one person he hoped to find this night.

A few days after the fiasco of trying to rescue Scarblade from Newgate, Ned and Richard had brought word to Granger that Charles was known to have been carousing drunkenly and boasting that he had been one of Scarblade's men. Ned also informed Granger that Charles's natural meanness and brutal behavior had not won him any friends among the riffraff that inhabited the neighborhood. Granger had come to the Owl's Eye to see just how far Charles's bragging had gone and how damaging his boasts were to Scarblade.

At the sound of the bell, Granger looked up to see a tall thin man enter, his face still swollen and bruised from a fairly recent beating. Granger sat quietly listening for any hints of the man's identity.

A group of men who had been drinking at the bar saw the tall man and pointedly took up their tankards and moved to a table across from Granger. They muttered beneath their breaths and looked accusingly at the man they had made room for at the bar.

One's words fell on Granger's ears. "'E's a mean coot, 'e is, an' badly used, Oi'll gran' ye, but 'tiz no excuse fer wha' 'e done ta tha' poor whore!"

"Whazzit 'e's done?" the second asked.

"As Oi 'ears it when poor Sally put 'im off 'er 'e took offense an' beat th' poor lass ta death. Thems th' know it wuz 'im fer sure won' do nothin' abou' it becuz we don' loike th' authorities interferin' in our business. Bu' 'twuz 'im, all righ'."

Charles, aware of the hostile glances of the men in the taproom, swore profusely, yelling into the room that if any there among them felt man enough to take him on he was ready for all comers. No one made a move toward him and yet Charles was not satisfied. "Why are ye all lookin' at me tha' way? Tha' little whore is out o' th' way o' trouble now, th' thievin' little tart. Refusin' me th' way she did. A man 'as 'is rights, 'e 'as!" Charles then turned his attention to the tankard the innkeep had set before him, giving the men a view of his back.

Granger shuddered to think that this man had tried to force himself on Tori. Granger wouldn't like to tangle with the man himself, and was more than glad that Scarblade had left the mark of his fists upon the man's ugly face.

Charles again turned to face the center of the tap room. "An' th' gold! All tha' gold an' me wi' na a tuppence ta me pockets."

He was speaking of the tax robbery, Granger was sure of it. And now Scarblade was to lose his life for it and the colony would still suffer. What a shame that Lord Fowler-

Greene prevented Captain Elias from sailing to North Carolina with the booty. Scarblade would hang for naught.

Sounds of a scuffle brought Granger from his thoughts. Charles had thrown his tankard at the innkeeper, accusing the man of serving him spoiled ale. The looks of hatred the others laid on the man were enough to make a sane man crawl, but still none of them moved to put an arm on Charles and toss him out. Granger was reminded of the words he had heard a few moments ago, and though he knew they feared Charles and hated him, he also knew they wouldn't call the patrols, for many of them also had a price on their heads and none of them would want the law poking around.

Charles drunkenly mumbled, his words becoming clearer and louder. "Me own brother wuz murdered, do ye 'ear?" He leered a malevolent toothless grin to the room. "An' the dirty bastard'll 'ang fer it, Oi made sure o' tha', Oi did."

Failing to attract attention from this statement, he became more heated in his response. "An' any among ye who thinks tha' th' barstard wuz Scarblade wha' wuz th' brains behind those robberies, let me tell ye a few truths. Oi, Charles Smythe, wuz th' brains an' me brother John me righ' 'and man. An' if anyone deserves th' fame fer bein' Scarblade, 'tiz me!"

A glimmer of an idea was born in Granger's mind as he listened to the despicable man boast. Perhaps . . . he thought to himself, the Newgate jailors have the wrong man after all. Picking himself up and draining his tankard, Granger walked on unsteady feet to the bar. Placing himself next to Charles, he pretended to be the worse for wear due to the wine. When next Charles turned to bemoan the fates that had taken his brother, Granger paid him his sympathies.

Charles, hearing the first friendly voice directed at him in weeks, quickly offered to buy Granger a refill of mulled wine and proceeded to bend his ear with stories of injustices which had been inflicted upon him. Granger kept a sorrowful expression on his face and punctuated Charles's statements in all the correct places with a "tsk-tsk . . ."

Throughout the course of this one-sided conversation, Granger managed enough praise to bolster the man's spirits and led him on to making crowing boasts about himself.

"So, as anyone can see, Oi wuz th' leader o' tha' pack, Oi wuz. It wuz me who gave th' orders an' saw ta it tha' they wuz follered out."

Granger took the lead and said, "If you were the leader then who's that miserable soul who's pacing off a cell in Newgate?"

Charles, sensing he had the reluctant attention of all within earshot, raised his voice to a roar, "Tha's th' rot wha' killed me brother! Bu' 'e wuz jus' a flunky, Oi'm Scarblade, Oi am! Oi'm th' one wi' th' 'ead on me shoulders no' tha' pig-lovin' dog! Oi'm Scarblade!"

Unable to contend with Charles's boasts a moment longer, the crowd in the taproom began to sneer and mock. "Scarblade indeed!" One voice was heard above the others! "An' Oi'll be supposin' th' it's you wha' 'as captured th' 'earts o' all th' laidies that ye robbed. Scarblade, indeed!— why a poor workin' girl loike Sally wouldn' bed ye fer thrice th' price!"

Enraged, Charles turned in a fury upon those who had dared to ridicule him. "Oi'm Scarblade, if'n Oi says so. An' who're ye ta talk ta me tha' way? Ye petty thieves an' pimps"—he pointed a gnarled, filthy finger at one of the men—"an' ye, Stevie Nespoint, Oi suppose ye doubt who Oi am, too? There's no doubtin' who ye are, an' wouldn' th' watch patrol luv ta know tha' who they're lookin' fer in a little matter o' purse snatchin' is sittin' righ' 'ere! An' ye," he roared, pointing his finger at another, "what abou' tha' little matter o' settin' fire ta th' roomin' 'ouse so's ye wouldn' 'ave to pay yer rent wha' wuz due? No record, no rent, right? There's bounty fer mos' o' ye, an' those tha' ain' bein' sought wuz at one toime er another. 'Ow would ye loike me ta put th' bulldogs on ye, th' lot o' ye? Tha' would teach ye no' ta mock th' man tha' calls 'imself Scarblade!"

The silence that followed his outrage was stifling, brewing, ominous. Granger knew that Charles was too drunk to know the harm he had done himself.

"Oi'll have another ale," he growled at the innkeeper.

"There'll be no further service for ye here, Sir Scarblade," the innkeeper said jeeringly, removing the tankard that Charles had been drinking from and throwing it into the garbage that was stacked at one end of the bar.

Charles lunged across the bar, grabbing for the innkeeper's neck. The keeper, a heavy, robust man, moved adroitly and avoided contact. "Throw him out!" he boomed at three men who had seated themselves near the door.

Kicking and struggling, Charles was lifted off his feet and removed from the taproom. Sounds of a scuffle came through the open door, and Granger pressed through the throng of people in time to see Charles beaten and thrown into the road beneath the hooves of a horse tethered at the rail.

The startled, nervous animal reared up on its hind legs, bringing down its sharp hooves on Charles. Again and again the horse tried frantically to escape the body which lay beneath him. Charles, uttering a last bloodchilling scream, took the full force of the blows about his head and shoulders. Someone unleashed the terrified animal, and it raced headlong down the street.

Tori sat inside the open trap, the only means of conveyance she had been able to hire on this mid-December day, the day they would hang Scarblade on Tyburn Hill. It had been three days since she had seen Granger or Josh and indeed she hadn't sought them out. Tori had removed herself from their company and retired to the boardinghouse, in fact the very room that had been Marcus's. Seeking to find some small measure of comfort from being in the same room that she and Marcus had shared on that one night of love, a night she would remember always, she had been overjoyed to find it had not been let to anyone else.

The trap made its way over the rutted, muddy roads to Tyburn Hill. Disinterestedly, Tori brushed at the muddy spots which had splashed up onto her green woolsey skirt. Again she found herself grateful to Dolly, who had thought to send on to her the trunks of clothing and personal belongings that her parents had conveyed to the Fowler-Greene house before their departure for America. Tori received them gladly, not being able to bear wearing the green silk gown she had worn to the opera with Marcus to witness his final debasement on the gallows.

The driver did not think it at all strange that this lovely, well-dressed young lady should direct him to Tyburn Hill. He laughed to himself: If taproom gossip was correct, most of society's matrons would be there to shed a tear for the passing of a most gallant and attractive highwayman.

Tori arrived late, and because the rows of carriages flanking the gallows themselves were already full, the driver of her hack grudgingly contented himself with a place well to the rear of the field.

A young boy selling hot-cross buns ran up to the trap in hopes of a sale. The driver bought one and jerked his thumb toward Tori. "Get away from me customer," he scolded the boy; "can't yer see this mus' be her first 'anging? She's as white and pinched lookin' as me auld mum's apron."

Disgust and nausea surged in Tori as she gaped at the spectacle before her. Children hawked leaflets purporting to contain the last words of the condemned man. Hags sold "relics"—cloth and locks of hair—from past hangings.

Peasant and gentry alike thronged about. Bawds vied for marks and pickpockets had a field day. Youths pitched pennies, old men sold potions and remedies, housewives enticed people to buy their wares of ribbons, laces, smoked meats, fish, and hot breads. Justice, if Scarblade's hanging could be called just, would be meted out in the tawdry, tinselly surroundings of a circus.

Lifting her eyes to the far-off gallows, Tori stared hypnotized by the swaying length of knotted rope which the slightest wind tossed to and fro.

As she watched, several men came from beneath the wooden structure and mounted the stairs. Vainly, her eyes strained across the distance in an effort to see Marcus. One of the men was dressed in black, and he, she supposed, was the executioner. She could not see Marcus, and suddenly she realized she did not want to see him! It was better to remember him the way he was, not this way: stripped of all dignity; denied human compassion, to die without solemnity, the sacrifice at a pagan orgy!

In a voice that quivered with emotion, she ordered the hackney to take her back to the boardinghouse.

"Aaow, miss, it jest be gettin' good! Oi wouldn't want ta miss the 'angin! Hang on fer a minute, it wouldn't be long."

"Now, I tell you!" she screamed in panic, "take me out of here now!" Noting the hackney's continued insolence, Tori commanded him more firmly, her voice holding the practiced note of nobility instructing a servant. The driver's ears perked up, but still he hesitated.

Hysteria mounted within her, choking off all reason. Fiercely, Tori pounded him with clenched fists, pummeling his head and shoulders, forcing him from his seat. With a mighty shove she sent the man flying from his perch to the trodden mud below. Grasping up the reins which were looped over the seat and taking up the whip, she forced the startled horse to veer to the left, taking her out and away from the ghoulish scene at the gallows. Tori had the trap turned about and the whip was held in suspension above the animal's flanks when she heard it!

The crowd had become hushed with anticipation and it came to her ears as plainly as though she were within three feet of it. The clank, the clap, the split, the gasp of the crowd, the sudden thudding yawn of the gallow's trap door, penetrated her being like a shot from a pistol. Her spine stiffened, her head snapped back, and she thought she should be dead. She wished she were dead! But she wasn't. Frantically, mercilessly, she lashed out at the poor beast's flanks, compelling him to make swift her escape from Tyburn Hill!

The pounding became louder, someone was calling her name. "Tori, Tori, open the door! I know you're in there. Tori, open the door!"

Slowly, painfully, she pulled herself away from the webs of a tearful, exhausted sleep. "Go away, I don't want to see anyone," she called back in a toneless voice she did not recognize as her own.

"Tori, I must see you; let me in, it's Granger," he insisted, still pounding.

Reluctantly, woodenly, she climbed from the bed and unlocked the door. Granger burst in, deep concern for her in his eyes. "He's free! Your Marcus is free!"

At first she couldn't comprehend the meaning of his words. Then their significance dawned upon her. Relief engulfed her, making her dizzy and light-headed. Clarity of thought returning, Tori pounced on her cousin with disbelief. "But I was there, on Tyburn Hill! I saw the executioner. Granger, I heard the gallows' trap door! What are you saying?"

"No, no, Tori, Marcus is alive. They hung someone else today, a man who murdered his mistress or something like that. The courts hastened the man's hanging by a week; they couldn't take a chance on disappointing the mob! Marcus is alive and free, I tell you!"

Realizing the shock she suffered, Granger gently led Tori back to the bed and sat down beside her, slowly telling her the sequence of events which led to Marcus's release.

When Granger reported to Lord Fowler-Greene the circumstances surrounding Charles Smythe's death, the lord pounced on this information and put it to his use.

Convincing Captain Elias to go against Marcus's orders and part with the tax money, Lord Fowler-Greene brought the gold directly to the King, boldly declaring that Marcus himself was instrumental in securing the pilfered taxes. Scarblade was dead, having met his destiny beneath the hooves of a crazed horse, and Marcus Chancelor, the man from America who came to plead with the Crown to lift the embargoes and blockades on his colony, had himself, before his unjust apprehension, located the stolen tax monies and delivered them into Lord Fowler-Greene's hands.

The lord explained that he had not gone directly to the authorities with this information because he wanted to bear out the truth of Marcus Chancelor's innocence.

So it was true, remarkable but true. Tori's mind struggled to comprehend Granger's statements. "Where is he?" she asked her cousin.

"He's at Captain Elias's ship! I almost forgot to tell you the best part. The King lifted the embargoes and blockades and bestowed on Marcus a hefty reward which he says will get his colony through the next harvest quite nicely."

Tori's eyes widened. "You saw him, you spoke to him?"

"Yes, of course." The portent of his words as he watched her face stopped him in midsentence. It was all there for him to see, the pained, wounded expression in her eyes, the slight trembling of her lips.

Granger knew his cousin well, and could read her thoughts like a taproom sign. They said, *If he's alive and free why didn't he come to me? It's true then, he's done with me....*

Trying to ease her, Granger said gently. "He had arrangements to make, Tori, the reward, the legal documents lifting the embargo and blockade. He hasn't had an opportunity."

Before his eyes Tori's expression changed to one of hard, cold uncaring; her yellow-green eyes became icy and glittering.

"I'm sure I don't know what you're talking about, Granger. I'm afraid your little tale has tired me. If you would please leave now—" She gave a little yawn to communicate polite boredom.

Bewildered by her attitude, Granger allowed himself to be ushered out the door. He heard the *snick* of the lock and knew that any and all explanations he could make for Marcus would be useless. He had often said Tori had a mind like an iron trap, and she was giving evidence of this once again.

Once more alone in the room, Tori flung herself on the high poster bed and buried her face in the pillow. A myriad of emotions filled her mind. Putting aside her joy at Marcus's release, only one thought rose to the surface, and she choked on the inescapable truth: he did not want her! He had quit himself of her and was glad of it. His rejection of her had been real and she was the fool for trying to read some considerate motive into it. She had offered herself to him and he had tried her and found her lacking.

Shame burned her face as she pushed it deeper into the soft pillow, imagining it still carried the scent of him.

Early the next morning, Tori was dressed in her brightest, gayest traveling suit; her baggage was packed and waiting for the footman to bring it down to the coach she ordered.

Her intentions were to throw herself upon Lord Fowler-Greene's mercies, to entreat him to advance her enough money to book passage on a ship to her parents' new home in America.

There was nothing left for her here in England, and truth to be told, she was glad to leave.

Making the last of her things ready, she heard a light tapping sounding at the door. Supposing it was the footman, she bid him enter.

"Tori." The sound of her name dissipated the stillness of

the room, seeping into her consciousness and carrying with it the betrayal of longing and want.

Tori spun around to face him, her eyes bright and luminous with unshed tears. He looked dashing, slightly pale from his stay in Newgate, but, nevertheless, the most handsome man she had ever seen. The cut of his coat accentuated the breadth of his shoulders and the narrowness of his hips. His snowy-white cravat set off the darkness of his skin and the ebony of his eyes.

"You!" she hissed. "What do you want here? How did you know where to find me? Go away, Marcus, there's nothing for you here."

"Granger told me—" he began before she cut in on him.

"So, Granger, was it? And what did he tell you? That I was dying for the sight of you? That you had slighted his dear cousin and he begged you for amends? Get out, Marcus . . ."

In two long strides he was upon her, grasping her firmly by the arms and shaking her soundly. "Your cousin Granger warned me about you. He said you had a mouth that didn't stop! Not that I didn't know that myself, you little vixen! Now shut up, and for once in your life listen to me. I didn't come to you immediately after my release yesterday because . . . because . . . Tori," he asked, "do you know how long it takes to shed oneself of the vermin that's picked up in a hell-hole like Newgate? And then Lord Fowler-Greene had to fill me in on the story behind my release, Then, finally, came the King. Not even you, my hotheaded little darling, outranks the King!"

His grip on her arms became painful as he shook her again and growled at her through clenched teeth. "When the King commands an audience poor commoners like me obey! Then I had to see to the loading of the stores which are a gift to Chancelor's Valley from the Crown. We sail today in an hour's time, so it had to be seen to immediately."

He released her with a backward thrust, sending her reeling across the room, stumbling against and falling upon the bed. "All the while we were loading, Granger told me of the scheme you and Josh and he cooked up to spring me out of Newgate! I thought that filthy ape was raping you, Tori. I had no idea it was all part of some crazy scheme to free me."

His face darkened as he thought of that day of doom that had cost Josh his life. She read the pain on his features, and the pain became hers. She, too, missed Josh and would grieve for him. But the sad memory must not stop her; this time he had gone too far. Who did he think he was, what did he think of her? Some child who must be rewarded for her good intentions?

"So!" she shrieked; "Granger has told you of our combined efforts to help you, and now you feel you must be properly grateful! Oh, I knew it, I knew it!"

"Grateful? For what? For almost being a helpless witness to that filthy dog of a jailor raping you? My God! I wanted to kill that pig for touching you! If I could have gotten my hands on him I *would* be swinging from the gallows." He approached her, stalking her, and she shrank from him.

"God, Tori, they told me if I didn't stop raving they were going to confine me to Bedlam! And you think I'm grateful? For your driving me near out of my mind?"

That disastrous day in the dungeons of Newgate flooded back to her. The stench of the dungeons—Josh's death—the roar . . . that blood-chilling, wounded animal roar. That had been Marcus yelling his helplessness to defend her.

"You're my woman, Tori," he said, his voice husky. "I should have known it long ago. Your beauty and courage intrigued me from the first time we met. And now, I realize you have the spirit and compassion that I've been searching for. Tori, my bewitching vixen, I'll love you always with every fiber of my body and soul."

Cautiously, Tori lifted her eyes to meet his. Stunned by

the impact of his words and the meaning in his eyes, she remained still.

Silently, Marcus swooped down upon her and lifted her into his arms. His face was close to hers, his breath caressed her cheek, and when he spoke his tone was soft: "I need you. I want you." Kissing her, he lay Tori back on the bed and with a devilish grin whispered, "We still have an hour till the ship sails."

Whitefire

Chapter 1

Katerina Vaschenko led the last of the horses from the underground paddock and secured them for the night in their roomy stalls. She walked among the animals, counting silently as she patted and stroked the horses' flanks. "Mikhailo!" she shouted. "Where is Wildflower?"

Mikhailo Kornilo lumbered into the stable and eyed the young Cossack girl with fear in his eyes. "I thought she was with the other mares."

"Wildflower has been skittish these past days, so I allowed Stepan to work with her alone. He wouldn't be foolish enough to take her outside for air, would he?" she asked the wizened old man anxiously.

Mikhailo ran gnarled old hands through his sparse white hair and made his own quick count of the noble animals. "Stepan may be foolish, but not that foolish. He knows the mares are not to be taken outdoors until the last of the snows are gone and the temperature rises. No doubt he's walking her around the arena for exercise. The Kat will be happy with the price this particular foal will bring," he said confidently.

"Mikhailo, I checked the arena on my way here and it

was empty. Fetch my father and have the others make a search. The mare has to be found."

Her face a mask of concern, Katerina drew the sable cape closer about her slim shoulders and fastened the hood over her coppery hair. Stroking the muzzle of the closest mare, she crooned soft words to the quiet animal.

The sweet, pungent smell of the horses stayed with her as she made her way down the damp corridor to the stone stairway.

Quickly, before she could change her mind, she thrust open the heavy pine doors and ran outside. Biting snow lashed against her as she fought her way to the outdoor stables, instinctively skirting a deformed clump of brush.

The wind drove the breath from her body as Katerina flung herself against the stable doors. "Stepan, are you in there?" she shouted breathlessly. "Is Wildflower with you? Stepan, answer me!" she screamed as she shut the weighty panels behind her. Her only reply was a skittering noise to the left of her foot. One of the cats. In her heart she had known Wildflower and Stepan were not there even before she had come inside. God, what had the boy done with the horse?

Shivering, not with cold, but with a fear so deep her blood seemed to freeze in her veins, Katerina whimpered silently as she pushed open the door and trudged back to the House of the Kat. Of all the horses to be gone, why did it have to be Wildflower?

The moment she entered the house, harsh curses from the men met her ears. She had been right—her father was livid.

"I don't know how it happened, Father. Stepan was exercising the mare because she was skittish," she said to the man advancing on her, his dark eyes spewing fire. "I just came from the outdoor stable and the boy's not there."

"We have searched every inch of this house and Stepan and the mare are gone. If the mare managed to find her way outdoors, it will be the end of her and the foal she carries.

How could you have been so lax, Katerina, you know the mares are your responsibility."

"Father," she said, laying her hand gently on his shoulder, "don't be angry with me. I'll search them out and bring both of them home. As you said, the mares are my responsibility."

"The boy is not capable of making a decision concerning Wildflower, he has the mind of a ten-year-old child!" her father shouted furiously, his black eyes snapping.

"I only have one set of eyes, and there has never been cause to worry over Stepan's care of the mares before. There must be an explanation."

"I only agreed to allow the boy to help you because you said he could be trusted. I see now that I was wrong."

Katerina listened to her father's harsh tones and felt bewildered. He had never spoken to her in such a manner. Eyes downcast, she knew she had failed him. Her large amber eyes widened in shock and her body felt numb with the realization. "I'll bring them back."

"There's nothing you can do now. Don't act as foolish as the boy. Where will you go? Where will you look for them? You just returned from the outdoor stables, didn't you feel the wind and snow? Women!" He spat venomously.

Katerina stared into her father's eyes, her back stiffening at what she read. "And while you're blaming me, ask yourself where Mikhailo was," she defended herself. "Women are only as foolish as men allow them to be." The large eyes were pinpoints of flame, threatening to burst into a raging bonfire. Her cheeks were flushed with anger as she retied the hood of her cape securely. "Since the mares are my responsibility," she said coldly, "I'll find the boy and the horse and bring them both back."

"Fool! How long do you think you can survive in that blizzard? I tell you, it's too late!" he shouted, his broad chest constricting in fury.

"It's only too late when I see their dead bodies or . . .

when you see mine. And I have no intention of allowing that to happen."

"I forbid you to go out in the storm, Katerina. What horse did you plan on riding? Ah, I see by your expression that Bluefire is your choice. Another foolish mistake. You would endanger still another horse, is that it? Women!" He spat again.

"So I'm a foolish woman. At least I'll try, which is more than I can say for you and the other men. How do you know it's too late? How can you say the boy isn't secluded in some cave, safe, along with the mare?"

Katlof Vaschenko looked at the amber eyes and at the grim, angry set of her narrow jaw. He knew he couldn't stop his daughter, and he had no wish to see her lash out at him for trying. An unfamiliar feeling settled between his shoulders as he watched Katerina pull on heavy woolen gloves. His shoulders slumping, he made his way to the warm kitchen, where his ailing father waited. "I'll pray for your safety, little one," he whispered silently.

Katerina placed a heavy blanket over the gelding, Bluefire, and she was ready to go. Was the snow falling faster or was she so petrified she couldn't see straight? All that brave talk in front of her father was just that—brave talk. How could she live with the others and have them think she was unfit for her duties? She was her father's daughter, and so she had to prove herself time and time again. No Cossack was shown favoritism. Each stood on his merits. Each was proud of his heritage and would die to protect it. She was no different. She would find the mare or die trying.

Within moments Katerina was smothered by the stinging, rice-sized pellets and could not see the reins she held.

She worked the sable hood down over her forehead till it resembled a shroud. The grisly thought made her clench her teeth in frustration at her position.

I'll freeze, she thought as her hands sought for and found the horse's thick mane. Already the reins were crusted with ice and slipping out of her grasp. If only she weren't riding into the storm with the full force of the wind in her face, she might have a chance.

Hunching her shoulders, she rode with her face pressed into the horse's warm neck. From time to time, Katerina feebly called out for Stepan.

The slim figure astride the white gelding battled the elements for over an hour. She raised her head when she felt the snow and the wind slacken off. "Good boy," she said, thumping Bluefire on his side. "I knew you would get me into the forest. Easy, boy, slow and easy," Katerina said softly as she rubbed her snow-crusted hands over the horse's neck. "Just get us down the mountain and out to the steppe. That's where we'll find Stepan and Wildflower. You can do it," she continued to croon to the magnificent animal. Stepan just wanted to take the mare back to Volin to be with his family. He meant no harm, she reasoned.

Bluefire trod lightly, aware of the girl on his back, sensing her fear and agitation as he picked his way through the quickly building drifts.

It was so cold, so very cold. If she could just sleep. The thick, sooty lashes lowered, and she dozed, unaware of the huge overhanging fir branches that seemed to move with a will of their own as the horse made his way carefully down the mountain.

An inner voice needled Katerina's subconscious: you can't sleep, you have to stay awake. Suddenly, she was jolted in her saddle. She forced her eyes open and looked around. The snow was too deep for the horse to carry her. She would have to walk.

She slid from Bluefire's back, grasped the reins in her hands, and trudged alongside the gelding. She lurched to the right and then to the left. Forcing her mind to concentrate on walking, she counted—one, two, three, four. Over and over Katerina repeated the words till her throat was dry and harsh. Her legs were getting heavier and harder to move. Bluefire was having as much difficulty as she was; she could tell from the tightening of the reins that the gelding was tired. She had to stop or they would both die. No, they had to keep moving. If she stopped, she would sleep and never wake up.

Think about the men back at the House of the Kat, sitting in the warm kitchen, drinking vodka. Think about that, she told herself. Through clenched teeth, she muttered, "Do they care if I freeze to death? Do they care if Bluefire freezes, too? All any of them cares about is Wildflower and the foal she carries. Horses! That is all they care about. Men are bastards, all men are bastards!" she seethed.

The anger that raced through her like raging fire was all the impetus Katerina needed to make her pick up her feet and plod through the deep snow. Her mind and body gained a new will, a searing urgency to win, to prove she could do what the men did. She would find Stepan and Wildflower and bring them, safe and sound, to the House of the Kat. Just pray, she told herself, that Stepan left before the snow began and is safe in Volin. He is safe! She could feel it in her bones.

The gelding reared back on his hind legs, whinnying softly. Katerina raised her head and looked about, the low-limbed fir trees with their coverlets of sparkling crystals blinding her momentarily.

The steppe.

Bluefire waited placidly while Katerina made up her mind. The snow wasn't as heavy here as at home, and the falling flakes seemed to be abating. Sighing deeply, she rubbed her eyes, forcing them to stay open. She had to go on. The gelding would find his way across the steppe without any help from her.

One more day and she would be at the Cossack camp. It was twilight now, her favorite time of day. She would be in Volin tomorrow, and then she would see for herself that Stepan and Wildflower were safe.

Her spirits lifted at the thought, and Bluefire sensed her mood. His legs lifted a little higher and he snorted, mist billowing out of his mouth in the cold, bracing air.

"Good boy," Katerina purred into the horse's ear. "I knew you could do it," she said, remounting her horse.

She rode steadily, the blinding whiteness all around her. So vast, so endless—like time. No sound permeated the air save the horse's breaths as he carried the beautiful young woman forward.

Katerina shook her head to free it of the warm sable hood and reined in. "Stepan is right, this is where we belong. This great, endless plain is ours, our heritage. Not that godforsaken stone fortress in the Carpathians. This is home. This is where we belong. It belongs to every Cossack who lives and breathes. Stepan knew this, and that's why he brought Wildflower here."

The gelding whinnied softly and pawed the snow, a sign that he was anxious to be traveling again. Intent on her thoughts, Katerina failed to see a small spiral of bluish smoke to her left.

Katerina dug her heels into Bluefire's flanks, and the horse reared again and danced his way through the great whiteness toward Volin.

The small campfire blazed brightly as one of the men threw on some extra brush. Another added some grease from his saddlebag, and the fire hissed and spurted. The men laughed uproariously as still another of the men raised a jug of vodka to his lips and passed it around to the others. One man, however, stood aloof, observing the merrymaking men that rode with him. They were good soldiers, dedicated to their cause and what they believed in. They served him well, and he had no complaints. Someday soon, with the proper training, they would all take their place in the Khan's army and do whatever was expected of them. For days they had ridden into the vicious storm with no respite from the elements, their only food dry bread and moldy cheese. They deserved their carousing and the three freshly killed rabbits that turned on the spit.

Banyen Amur stared into the openness around him, his indigo eyes narrowed to ward off the harsh glare. He hated this plain, and he hated the Cossacks that could and did live on it.

He was cold and hungry, and he needed a woman. If he had his choice, he would take the woman first, for she would warm his blood and be food for his soul. His belly could wait for another time and another place.

He was tall and muscular, with a broad chest and a loose-limbed stride. His hair was the color of a raven's wing in bright sunlight, and while his forehead was broad, his nose was chiseled and sharp, adding character to his strong, square chin.

His men called him an arrogant son of a bitch, but admitted he was a fair and just man to serve under. Women jostled each other and swooned when he favored them with one of his rare smiles. One look out of the agate eyes and a woman turned to what he called mush, and brought a smile to his sensual mouth. He chose his women with cool, calculating deliberation, the dark eyes measuring the curve of their breasts and the length of their thighs. If the return look was coy or vapid, he would go to the next woman, until he found a match for his own measured look. He liked fire in his bed, not warmed-over mush. One day he would find a woman that suited him, and he would give her the supreme pleasure of bearing him a son. He would rebuild his estates and get married and keep his wife pregnant nine months out of every year. He would have a mistress in his house, and one in town for the awkward months. Women belonged in bedrooms and kitchens. What else could they do . . . He smiled to himself. Thoughts of love never entered his mind. Love was for fools and old men who didn't know what to do with their loins in their advancing years. He would never be caught in that trap. Women had their place so far as he was concerned, and he planned to keep it that way.

Men made fools of themselves over women. Men fought and died for women. Men lost empires because of women. The only thing he would give a woman was the honor of bearing his child and his name.

Banyen patted the black Arabian stallion fondly and slouched nonchalantly against the animal's hard belly. He straightened his shoulders and shrugged the sable burnoose he wore to a more comfortable position. The soft leather boots that caressed his sinewy legs were due to be changed to fur and warm socks for his feet. He might as well do it now so he could eat his portion of rabbit in comfort.

A small sound suddenly caught his ear, and immediately his hand went to his saber. A horse out here in this godforsaken emptiness! Who? What?

He looked at his men and motioned for silence. Weapons were drawn and the roasting rabbits forgotten as tired eyes became keen and alert. Banyen raised one finger to show that it was a lone rider who approached. "Where there is one, there could be more," he said softly to his men.

Katerina stared intently in the last rays of the evening light. A camp with a fire. Food! Which Cossack tribe was it camped in the middle of the plain, and why? An uneasy feeling settled over her as the horse trotted closer and closer. Her eyes widened at the garb on the tall figure standing near a horse and the campfire, surrounded by men. Mongols! What would they do? Would they let her pass? Would they believe her when she told them she had Mongol blood in her veins? Not likely. She looked like a Cossack. Her shoulders straightened imperceptibly as she advanced to the camp. Deftly she reined in Bluefire and watched the man who appeared to be the group's leader admiring her gelding.

Neither spoke. Katerina waited. Banyen waited. The

men waited. A worm of fear found its way into Katerina's stomach and worked its way up to her chest. She swallowed and looked at the tall man, who was staring at her with bold, arrogant, lustful eyes.

White teeth glistened in the dimness of twilight as Banyen smiled. "Prince Banyen at your service," he said, bowing low with a flourish. His tone was cool, mocking, as he walked over to her placid horse. Katerina dug her heels into Bluefire's flanks, and the gelding slowly backed away from the advancing Mongol.

Katerina nodded. "What are you doing here? This is Don Cossack land."

At the sound of the soft, melodious voice Banyen's face registered shock. A woman! "This is Cossack land?" Banyen mocked her words, straining to get a glimpse of her face. "As long as I'm standing on this land, it belongs to me—unless, of course, you would like to fight me for it. I see no Cossacks protecting it. You're a Cossack, aren't you? No one save a Cossack rides pure whites, especially a horse such as yours. Well," he said harshly, "will you challenge me for this ground I stand on?"

"You can stand here till you take root for all I care," Katerina snapped. "And, no, I have no wish to challenge you or your men. Others like the vicious Tereks will challenge you."

Banyen laughed, his head thrown back in merriment. "What others? There is no one on this godforsaken steppe except you, me, and my men," he said, bowing again. "Come here, let me see what you look like," he said, advancing. Nimbly, Bluefire again backed off a pace and then two more. "Please," Banyen said, holding up his hand, "allow me to extend an invitation to dinner—roast rabbit, newly caught. I insist," he said, lunging toward her. "Don't make the mistake of refusing my generous offer."

"I'm not hungry. Thank you for the invitation, but I must ride on."

"Perhaps the cold has affected your hearing. I said don't refuse my offer!"

The clear amber eyes narrowed. "And I told you I'm not hungry!" Katerina's foot came up and knocked his hand from her arm. Filled with panic, she lowered her head and grasped the gelding's mane as her heels dug into the horse, spurring it on.

A roar of outrage reached her ears as Bluefire raced through the snow. She knew in her heart she would be caught. The gelding was as tired as she was, but the Mongol prince and his stallion looked rested. Oh, God, what was she going to do? You were right, Father, you may yet find my frozen body, but it won't be because of Stepan and Wildflower. Damn him to hell! Who did he think he was, ordering her to share his dinner? Cossack rabbits that were needed for her own people. As she urged the horse to do his best, she turned her head, and momentarily the noble animal was thrown off stride. The stallion was gaining on her. "O God, I don't want to die!" she cried quietly to the shimmering stars.

As she dug her heels into Bluefire's flanks, she apologized to the galloping horse for the pain she was inflicting on him, then begged, "Please, please!"

Out of the corner of her eye she watched the stallion advance, the man's arm outflung to pull her from her seat. Katerina leaned precariously to the right and all but slipped from the animal beneath her. When she righted herself, she was pulled from Bluefire's back and literally flung through the air. She came to rest against the side of the skittery horse, as it was trying to stop.

"Let me go! Take your hands off me!" Katerina screeched.

"And if I do that, what will you do?" Banyen laughed, delighted with this unexpected challenge.

"Kill you, that's what I'll do! I'll scratch your face till it's nothing but a bloody pulp!"

The stallion stood quietly as master and girl spat epithets

at each other. "And what do you think I'll be doing while you're scratching my face to a bloody pulp?" Banyen laughed.

"Bleeding!" Katerina snarled.

"A she-cat."

Katerina tried to free herself from her awkward position, one arm pinned against the horse and the other flailing in the air. Each time the man jerked her closer to the horse, her feet left the ground and her arm twisted painfully in his vise-like grip. She bit into her full bottom lip and felt the salty taste of her own blood. Her mind raced as she tried to figure how she could get away from him. Suddenly she relaxed, her muscles loose and flexible. Banyen leaned over to grasp her other arm and draw her atop his horse. Her small fist shot out and made direct contact with his eye. Stunned, he relaxed his hold. Seizing her opportunity to escape, Katerina was off and running instantly, the snow spurting up from her heels. On and on she ran, with no sense of direction. Her breathing was harsh and ragged as the cold, bracing air was forced into her lungs. With her long legs, Katerina could usually outrun most of the youths in the village, but the heavy accumulation of snow was hampering her now and she wondered how much longer she could last. She was so tired. A razor-sharp pain ripped across her chest and Katerina doubled over, falling to her knees.

Banyen fought to control his own labored breathing. Straddling her, Banyen pinned Katerina's arms above her head, then leaned over and brought his mouth down on hers. She sank her teeth into his cheek, and felt the flesh tear when he tried to pull away from her. His head jerked upright as if a snake had bitten him. He felt blood trickle down his chin as he brought his hand up to his mouth. "Bitch!"

"Bastard!"

Banyen reached out a long arm and grasped her ankle as

she tried to get away. "Stupid Cossack woman, with your thick stockings and a man's boots," he said harshly.

"Smelly Mongol pig!" Katerina hissed.

"You belong with a farmer at the plow," Banyen said raggedly. "What kind of clothes are these?" he demanded, releasing one of her arms so he could finger the thick material of her dress. "Even peasants wear better than this."

Katerina brought up her knee, and Banyen was thrust backward by the force of her blow. Madly, she scrambled out of his way as he bent over, his muscular hands clutching his groin.

"I hope I kill you!" Katerina screamed as she got to her feet. "When they bury you, I'll sing a dirge about the way you died."

"Bitch!" Banyen said through the mist that threatened to choke off his vision.

"Bastard! Dirty, sneaky Mongol pig!" Katerina screamed as she plunged recklessly forward. Rough hands seized her and dragged her backward. The men from the campfire!

"Here she is, Banyen! Do you still want her after what she did to you," one of the leering men asked, "or will you be generous and allow the rest of us to have some sport with her?"

"Bring her here!"

The icy words sent a wave of fear down Katerina's spine. She was flung to the ground and pulled by her long cascading hair to his side.

"One more move out of you and you'll be the first bald-headed Cossack woman on these plains."

"I should kill you for what you just did to me," Banyen said harshly.

"I won't make it easy for you, so be prepared. How many times can you survive what I just did to you? I'll do it again and again, every chance I get. Let me go, you foul Mongol! I've been in stables that smelled better than you do!"

"And I've smelled and seen better whores than you!" Banyen retaliated.

"Then go find one and leave me alone! I'm warning you, I'll do what I said. Let me go!"

He nodded curtly to his men. "Throw her in one of the tents by herself for the night. Maybe that will cool her off," Banyen grunted. "She'll be lucky if she doesn't freeze to death. We can decide what to do with her in the morning."

Katerina woke as Bluefire nuzzled her cheek. She rose to her feet uncertainly and looked around, the inky night cloaking her body as a mother shields her child from harm. There was no sound in the velvety darkness except Bluefire's soft whickers.

Katerina's amber eyes lightened till they were the color of a ripe apricot. She was alive and that was all that mattered. Somewhere, somehow, she would meet the Mongol again and she would have the advantage. He would pay dearly. At least she knew what he looked like. He couldn't say the same. At the campfire, she had been far enough away from the flames, and the hood had cast her face into shadow. No one would know. It would be her secret, and she would die by her own hand before she let another Cossack know she had ever come out second best.

She grasped Bluefire's mane and climbed onto his back. Trembling, she urged the horse forward, her neck buried in his soft hair. Bluefire picked his way gently over the snow as the girl sobbed heartbrokenly.

It was the mute boy, Stepan, who first saw her and hurried to the road to lead the gelding to the summer stables. Shyly, his eyes full of love and trust, he helped Katerina dismount and led her shaking body to a stall at the end of the stable. He pointed to the alabaster mare, who was contentedly nibbling at some hay. His round head bobbed up and down happily as he kept pointing and grinning at the horse.

"She's safe, is that what you're trying to tell me?"

Stepan nodded, a smile on his face. The boy opened the stall and pointed to the horse's broad belly and then to her hooves. He rubbed the horse's snout fondly, and the mare rewarded him with a soft whinny of delight.

Katerina would chastise him later, for all the good it would do. For now, all she wanted was a hot bath and some clean clothing. God, would she ever feel warm again? Would she ever be the same again?

"Stepan, would you please build a fire in my father's house and boil some water for me?" The youth grinned and waved his hands in the air. "You already did that when you saw me riding across the steppe. Thank you. Stepan," she said wearily.

Tenderly, she patted the boy on his arm, her eyes full of tears. "Stay with Wildflower and give her some hay and a few oats and then bed her down for the night. Do the same for Bluefire." The boy smiled and entered the stall, careful to latch it behind him.

Katerina would have a week of living by herself, until the others came down from the Carpathians. In seven days one could school oneself to many things. She was well, and Wildflower was safe. That was all that mattered.

Chapter 2

The first scent of spring wafted in the air as the tenacious grip of winter held fast the last remnants of snow to the onion-domed towers of the Kremlin. As the snow began to ebb, the glory and magnificence of St. Basil's Cathedral, just outside the Kremlin, slowly emerged to the wonderment of all. The nine soaring, bulbous domes, each different in color and design, struck a note of exquisite beauty for all of Russia to behold. Czar Ivan Vasilovich was justly proud of his creation.

The Terem Palace, official residence of Czar Ivan IV, which stood within the walls of the Kremlin, stood with equal majesty. The Czar, like others before him, surrounded himself with the indigenous art of the Russian people. Everywhere the eye could see, the ornate frescoes, paintings, and motifs were embellished with gold overlay or blazoned with precious stones.

Princess Halya Zhuk's bearing was regal as she crossed the main floors of the palace, confident that her flaxen hair was arranged with care and precision to show off her delicate features to every advantage. As she began her ascent up the stone stairway to the Czar's living quarters, she smoothed the sea-green gown, which reflected the emerald depths of her eyes. In these quiet moments when she was alone, she never ceased drinking in the splendor of the decorative walls and ceilings. A sensitivity that lay deep within her, a sensitivity that she kept completely hidden, stirred in her breast as she weakened and completely enjoyed her surroundings.

Steps that once were filled with joy now became steps of anguish. Each encounter with Ivan was totally unpredictable. One minute he would be loving and forgiving, and a moment later, as though possessed, he would perform cruel and sadistic acts, terrorizing everyone in sight. She wondered fearfully what he would have in store for her today.

Halya stood a moment before the carved door to Ivan's receiving chamber, forcing herself to reach for the golden knob. She withdrew her hand and paused a second longer, finally deciding to knock.

A voice boomed imperiously, "Whoever it is may enter my chambers."

Composing herself, Halya answered, "It is Halya, Ivan. I came as quickly as I could when I received your summons."

"I need the gentleness of your touch and the softness of your lips to quell my surging blood. As usual, my day has been nothing but problems, problems, and more problems. If I don't do everything myself, nothing gets done," he said petulantly. "I summoned you for another reason, Halya, not to listen to me complain. Come into my chamber, where we can speak privately."

Halya's mind reeled with thoughts of what was to come. Months before, it had been a pleasure to be bedded by Ivan, for his body was hard and muscular, and his lovemaking was the same way, hard and demanding. In recent months, however, Ivan had neglected himself, so thoroughly he was now flabby. When he stood before her unclothed, the bulges and flabbiness were offensively apparent. She felt repulsed when her eyes noted the limp flesh that extended to his manhood. Her heart pounded with fright as she wondered what obscene acts he would ask her to perform to arouse him sexually.

"Halya, many times you have expressed the desire to become my fifth wife, or is it my sixth? If that is still your wish, then you must continue to please me. As you know, my true and first love is being Czar of Russia; second is my devotion to the Church. Third is deciding how I shall put to death a traitor. My last love, Halya, is a wild, uninhibited woman in my bed. That is the reason I have decided that one day soon you will be my wife. You are an excellent whore, and the thought of marrying you delights me. I'll notify you when I decide to make it official," he said, leering at her, his eyes glazed with lust.

Anger rose in Halya at his words, but she said nothing. In her heart she knew her true test was about to begin. Could she play at passion and desire and arouse his sagging member? Her mind raced: she would pretend, she would entice, she would seduce a young soldier; and then, as suddenly as she had thought it, she negated the idea. No, her imaginary lover must be a king, an emperor, or someone else of great stature. She would perform for a Khan and be a captured woman who was brought before him to delight and heighten his desire. Failing, she would die. Ivan's voice broke through her thoughts, making her aware of what she had to do.

"It's time to begin, Halya. I'll set the stage for you, and you will do exactly as I say. When you are performing well, and my blood begins to pound, you will not hear my voice. When that happens you will know I am pleased and your lustful acts are engulfing me. I am now ready," he said, lying back against a mound of pillows.

Halya fought a welling retch as she watched him lick at the saliva that drooled from the corners of his mouth.

"You will of course undress; however, as you dance

around the room I want you to drop your clothing, piece by piece, on top of me, as I lie here in bed. For every garment you drop you will remove an article of clothing from me. Before you start to perform I think we should have an audience. I will summon two passionate men from my private guard and watch them squirm in ecstasy as they watch you. A magnificent idea, why didn't I think of it sooner?" Ivan cried happily as he rang for his boyar.

"Fetch me two virile men from the Oprichnina. Bring me the two who boast and fornicate the most. You will have no trouble finding them, word travels fast among men of their conquests," he ordered the boyar, who stood at attention, a stunned look on his face.

The boyar scurried from the room to do Ivan's bidding. He could barely contain himself at the thought that soon he would have another lunatic escapade of the Czar's to recount to the other boyars.

"Halya, my love, have you given any thought to your dance of seduction?" Not waiting for a reply, he continued, "My blood boils at the thought of how the young bucks will react to my mistress swaying naked before them. You *will* be naked, won't you, Halya?" he asked hesitantly.

Halya nodded. Oh God, oh God, Ivan was insane and she was crazy to do as he asked. Everything would have been different with Kostya.

"Your men, as you requested," the boyar said quietly as he thrust open the door, admitting two handsome soldiers from the Oprichnina.

The Czar lolled on the bed, spittle dribbling from his mouth as he addressed the two men. "Princess Halya is going to dance, and I wished a small audience to join me so her talents can be fully appreciated. You are to stand near the door in a stance so: your feet slightly apart, body erect, and hands clasped behind your backs. You are not to utter a sound."

The soldiers nodded, puzzled looks on their faces.

"Begin, Halya," Ivan said, reclining again against the overstuffed cushions.

Her body trembling, Halya moved to the center of the floor, trying to sort out her thoughts. She felt humiliated and embarrassed at the way the men stared at her. Still, she supposed it was better than being put to death by Ivan for refusing to do his bidding. She risked a second glance in their direction and found herself wondering how they would look without their handsome uniforms. Their imagined nudity made her remember Ivan as he was when she first saw him. Now, beside the flabbiness, his aquiline nose seemed more obnoxious. His black hair, which had once blended into a comely mustache and beard, had turned into wisps of straggly, unkempt hair. The clear bright eyes were glazed, and his sensual mouth was slack and unappealing. But she was also reminded of another person, whom she had loved with all her heart and soul . . . Quickly she forced the memory from her mind to concentrate on her job—surely he was dead.

Halya turned to Ivan and pouted coyly. "My Czar, would it be possible to summon a balalaika player to sit outside the door and play for me?"

"Very well, but no more delays, Halya," he grumbled, the spittle from his mouth dribbling down his chin and onto his neck.

With the first sounds of the melodious notes Halya began to dance, her movements slow and sensual as she responded to the music. Her slim body lent itself to wantonness as she brought into play the proud high-tipped breasts and rounded haunches. As she swirled and swayed to the rhythm, her tiny feet barely touching the floor, her hands caressed her body, lingering in a display of blatant sexuality.

Perspiration beaded the faces of the soldiers as their eyes filled with unabashed desire. Sensing their craving, Halya

threw herself into a frenzy of immoral gestures and moves
that she knew would delight Ivan.

Her fingers tore at the buttons of her gown as abandon
rose like a tidal wave throughout her body. Dropping her
dress at her feet, she cupped her breasts, still hidden beneath her camisole. Slowly, inch by inch, she removed
Ivan's gold caftan, delighting in his moans of mounting
passion as her hands touched his naked flesh. His eyes were
wild; his tongue dangled from his gaping mouth.

She whirled away from the Czar, working with slow deliberation at the ribbons of her camisole. She knew both
Ivan and the soldiers were waiting for her to divest herself
of the garment, waiting in pain for the first glimpse of her
bare skin. She glided out of reach, her tight haunches moving to the rhythm of the balalaika as her body began to un-
dulate provocatively. Sensuously she moved her fingers to
the tiny ribbons, undoing each one with a wicked smile on
her face.

The Czar rolled over on the bed, his eyes glazed as he
stared first at Halya and then at the two soldiers. He cackled
gleefully at the sight of the well-fitted black trousers
bulging with the swollen manhood trapped within. As he
watched, the swelling pushed forward, fighting to escape to
freedom. He jumped up and down on the bed, pointing a
sticklike finger at the two men, his laughter insane and
shrill.

Halya continued dancing, her fingers untying the last
bow. As she leaned toward Ivan, her breasts spilled from the
dainty embroidered camisole. A knowing smile played
about her mouth as she heard low groans coming from the
direction of the doorway. She, too, now noticed the growing, aroused manhood bursting at the confines of their
trousers.

She ripped away the undergarment with a flourish, freeing her taut, full breasts for all to see. Cupping them, their
rosy crests pointed and erect, she swayed ever closer until

she was directly in front of the soldiers. Her movements taunting, she flaunted her body without restraint. Moan after moan followed her as she danced back to Ivan. Slowly she extended a long, shapely leg from between the open front of her lace petticoat. Languidly she thrust it out and withdrew the stocking from thigh to toe. Twirling it in the air, Halya swept past the soldiers, her naked breasts heaving as she allowed the stocking to brush across their agonized faces. At Ivan's bedside, she dropped the silk and reached down to remove his slippers.

The soldiers continued to watch, their faces full of incredulous shock. Before them lay the Czar, completely stripped of clothes. The princess was still dressed in her petticoat and one sheer stocking. How much more were they to endure?

Moving over to a chair closer to where the soldiers stood, Halya lifted her leg, reached to the top of the limb, and, again slowly, removed the remaining stocking. She caressed her body, her fingers sliding over her breasts and arms, down to her flat stomach, and finally once again cupping her breasts.

Her eyes were fixed on the soldiers as she worked at her petticoat, dropping it from her satiny waist. Halya turned at the sound of a deep groan, knowing she had driven the men beyond human control.

Ivan, in a state of tightly checked arousal and anticipation of what was to come, made no comment when the soldiers ran from the room, their trousers wet and stained.

Halya danced as if passion had become the driver and ruler of her undulating body. Gliding gracefully to the bedside once more, her pear-shaped orbs hard and firm, she motioned for Ivan to touch her. Salivating, he clutched at her breasts, her thighs and legs, as low animal-like noises escaped his mouth.

Perspiration dripping from his face, Ivan felt blood soar

through his veins as the pain in his loins became unbearable. He reached for Halya, clutching at her golden hair, moaning wildly as he brought his mouth crashing down upon hers.

"Ivan, take me! Please! Take me!"

Ivan mounted her, hoping against hope that all his soaring blood would erect his manhood. When it failed to do so, he rolled from her body, tears streaming down his sunken cheeks.

Exhausted, Halya lay next to Ivan, who, unfulfilled, nibbled at her still-erect nipples. Halya lay quietly, indifferent to his touch, wishing she were with the one man who could have fulfilled her.

Determined to overcome his impotence, Ivan continued to nibble at Halya's swollen breasts. His hands traveled down her body, searching out the coveted moist, warm place between her slim thighs.

Halya's body became alive, responding once again to his tender caresses.

"Try, Ivan," Halya pleaded as she parted her legs, welcoming him to her. Silently she reprimanded herself for the charade she was acting. Halya tried desperately to convince herself she might one day love Ivan and forget Kostya.

In desperation, Ivan strained every part of his being to produce the taut muscles necessary to satisfy her. At Halya's scream of despair, Ivan fell back in resignation, ignoring the princess, totally absorbed in his own despair.

Halya lay back on the bed, her eyes closed to prevent the threatened tears from spilling down her cheeks. Was this going to be her life from now on? God, help me, she prayed silently.

Though it was early when Halya woke, her eyes searched every corner of the room for Ivan. When she was satisfied that he was not there, she slid from the bed and quickly dressed to return to her own quarters. She needed a warm bath to help her forget the previous hours.

Halya placed her hand on the doorknob, but was unexpectedly thrown off balance with the Czar's entrance into the room.

"I want to commend you on your . . . your performance last. evening. You were exquisite! I do try to please you, Halya, I think you know that," he said, his voice a soothing melody.

"Yes, Ivan, I know you try, and I understand you have many tragedies in your life," she said quietly. As soon as the words left her mouth, she realized her mistake. "Ivan, I . . . I'm sorry—"

Obscene expletives flew from the Czar's mouth. His aging, aristocratic face turned purple with rage. "You were told never to refer to my past!" he screamed at the top of his lungs. "You are here for one purpose and one purpose only—to brighten my life and make me happy. Get down on your knees and beg me to forgive you!"

Halya did as ordered, tears streaming down her cheeks. "Please, I beg of you, forgive me," she pleaded.

"Very well, I forgive you, this time," he said, his rage forgotten. "Come near me, let me hold you for a moment." Halya nestled nervously in his arms. "Let me kiss the lips that drove me to the heights of desire last evening."

Suddenly he thrust her from his arms and looked directly into her green eyes. "I have something to tell you, something that will make you happy."

Moving to the edge of the bed, Ivan motioned Halya to sit beside him. The stale scent of the past hours lingered in the air as he clasped her soft hands in his tight grip. "I am so pleased with you that I have decided to make you my next wife. You soothe me and at the same time you excite me." Gently, he cupped her chin in his hand and stared deeply into her eyes. "Does my offer make you happy, Halya?"

Her stomach lurched at his words. Forcing a smile, the princess spoke enthusiastically for his benefit. "Yes, Ivan, it makes me most happy." Halya knew she would do anything that would enable her to sit beside him on the throne of Russia, even if it meant acting out the sexual fantasies he demanded. Her eyes closed momentarily when she realized that, as Ivan's Czarina, her name would become as famous as his, and perhaps her one true love from childhood would seek her out when her whereabouts became known—unless he was dead, as she feared.

"Now I must tell you of my other plans," he said coolly, his mood changing once again. "I have a mission to be filled and I need a man with knowledge of horses, an equerry. Soon the Don Cossacks will be bringing their herds to the steppe and readying them for sale. Each year in the spring I send an emissary to pick the best of the Cosars for my Oprichniks. This year I have decided my equerry will be your brother, Yuri. Even now he is beginning his preparations for the journey, and tomorrow he will leave for Volin."

"Volin! My brother! What are you telling me?" Halya asked fearfully. "Ivan, my brother is too young to be sent on a mission. He just passed his eighteenth birthday and only trained in the Kadets for a year. Just this past month, he entered the Zemsky Sobor, and you know he has another year to complete his apprenticeship for the assembly," she said tearfully, her eyes wide and full of apprehension.

"I am aware of his apprenticeship, and I considered it carefully before I reached my final decision."

"But, Ivan, he's just a boy," Halya continued to plead.

"Enough! I will say the following to you and then the discussion is closed. When I was three, I became Czar; when I was sixteen, I was married; and at twenty I led my armies in two battles. Don't speak to me of an eighteen-year-old being a boy. He's a man, and if he isn't one now he will be when he returns. I chose him because of his knowledge of horses, the same knowledge you yourself possess. You were the one who informed me of your family's equestrian background. You told me once that you and your brother could ride a horse before you could walk a straight line. So you see, Halya, he is the man for my mission. The matter is ended."

Her anger in check, Halya rose from the bed and quickly strode toward the door. As she walked on lagging feet back to her bedchamber, her mind raced. Why was the Czar sending Yuri to Volin? Certainly not for the reason he stated.

Once inside her room with her bath prepared, Halya slid into the warm wetness and allowed the water to calm her shattered nerves. How unfair it is, she thought sadly. Yuri is still a boy, and when he's gone I'll have no one except Ivan. Her full lower lip trembled and tears gathered in her moss-green eyes at what she considered her unjust life. Was it only three years ago that she had been brought to the palace to become Ivan's fourth wife? It seemed like an eternity ago that the missive reached her parents in Moldavia informing them that Czar Ivan wished the Princess Halya to be presented to him with the intention of making her his wife. "God help me," she moaned softly as her mind reeled back in time.

Within days after the message was received, her trunks and Yuri's were packed and they were sent by coach to Moscow, she to become Ivan's wife and Yuri to become a Kadet.

The driver of the three-horse sleigh had carefully reined in the animals as he maneuvered the sleigh through the maze of streets lined with log houses that encompassed the Wooden City, so named because of its principal building material.

"Has anyone told you of Kitai Gorod?" the driver asked, amused at the pair as they stared in awe at their surroundings.

"We're new to Moscow," Halya had said hesitantly. "What is Kitai Gorod?"

"It is the third city within Moscow and so called because the people who live here fill their kitais with earth, piling the one on top of the other against the walls to stave off attacks from invaders."

"I want to see the palaces where the nobles and the Czar live!" Yuri had cried out in boyish excitement.

"First we have to travel through Red Square. Once we travel through Spassky Gate we will be in the Kremlin. To your left is Czar Ivan's home, the Terem Palace. To your right are the chasovnyas, the private chapels of the influential citizens of Moscow. The structure you see being worked on is St. Basil's, the Czar ordered it built to commemorate his victory over the Tatars. Your tour is over. Wait on the stairwell and servants will take you to the Czar."

Was it only three years ago when she and Yuri stood on the stairwell waiting for Ivan's servants?

Yuri had succeeded in becoming a soldier. But instead of becoming the Czar's wife, she had become his mistress.

Aware once more of her surroundings, Halya stepped from her bath into the robe her maid held out for her.

"Fetch my clothes and dress my hair, quickly now, for I have little patience this day. I want to spend as much time with my brother as possible," she explained to the fearful servant.

The girl, near tears, worked in quiet desperation, knowing the princess would show no mercy when it came to anyone save the Czar and her brother.

The maid stood back respectfully, hoping for a quiet word of approval.

"It took you long enough," Halya said furiously. "If you're finished, why do you stand there? Leave me!"

When the door had closed behind the trembling girl, Halya examined herself in the mirror, pleased with her appearance except for the hateful expression on her face.

Studying herself, she realized her callous behavior toward the maid was meant for Ivan. God, how she detested him for what he was doing to her brother. Forcing a smile to her lips, however, she flounced from the room to console Yuri and wish him a safe and speedy return.

Halya walked through the halls and archways and down the stairways that led from the Terem Palace to the building where men of the Zemsky Sobor were quartered.

Thrusting open the door of Yuri's room, she threw herself into his arms. "Yuri, tell me it isn't true, tell me you aren't going to Volin. Did you do something? Is the Czar banishing you? If you did something wrong, perhaps I can help you," she pleaded desperately.

"Halya, calm yourself. It is not a punishment. The trip to Volin could well be the greatest opportunity of my career. Don't you understand, Halya, the Czar chose me to represent him, his own emissary, to the Cossacks. I'm to have the privilege of handpicking the horses from the Cosars! It's an honor, Halya, and one I am proud of," he said excitedly, his handsome face beaming. "Be proud of me. Of all the men he could have chosen, he selected me." Enthusiasm burst from his whole being, culminating in his handsome face, his grin emphasizing the deep cleft in his chin.

Halya was shocked at his words. Indebted to the Czar for sending him on a mission that could be extremely dangerous! She must get through to him and make him understand how dangerous and unpredictable the Cossacks were.

"If I do all that is asked, this could be the beginning of a great career for me. Both of us should be pleased that the Czar chose me. Halya, do you see . . . ?"

"Yuri, stop it. He's using you. Ivan never does anything without some insane reason behind it. Why can't I make you see? There are older, more responsible men than you, and far more capable of handling this mission, and that is what concerns me. Why is he sending a boy to do a man's mission?"

"Are you saying you have no faith in me?" Yuri asked angrily.

"It's Ivan I have no faith in. I know you will do well and I wish you well. It's just that I feel so protective toward you and I want nothing to go wrong. You're all I have and I don't want to lose you," she cried tearfully.

"You won't lose me, Halya. When my mission is completed I think we should ask permission to travel to Moldavia to see our parents. Would you like that?" he asked, hoping to divert her from her unhappy thoughts.

"Of course I would, and I'll look forward to it. Godspeed, Yuri."

"I leave at dawn, Halya, so let this be our temporary farewell. I want you to spend your time thinking about how happy our parents will be to see us. Promise me, Halya, that you will not worry about me, for if you do, then I will not be able to function with a clear head."

"You have my promise," his sister said, throwing her arms around Yuri and smothering him with wet kisses.

As she ran to her room she cried over and over, "If it's the last thing I do, if it takes my last breath, you'll pay dearly, Ivan, for what you're doing to my brother. Yuri is all I have and you're taking him away from me, just as I was taken from my one true love to be brought here to be your mistress."

Inside her room, with the door bolted, she threw herself on the bed and cried brokenheartedly. Later, when she dried her tears, her face was cool and composed. Looking in the mirror, Halya spoke slowly and distinctly. "If anything happens to Yuri, I will kill you without a second thought!"

Chapter 3

Katerina lay in the middle of the fluffy pedina and delighted in the warmth the goose-down quilt exuded. Warmth, precious warmth. "God, I thought I would never be warm again," she sighed. For now, she had the comfort of the soft quilt, her home, and the fire burning in the oven. She felt safe and protected with the devoted Prokopoviches, Stepan's parents. This was what she wanted, and what she needed, this secure feeling. Here in her own bed, the Mongol couldn't reach her. All he could do was invade her mind. In her bed, in her house, he couldn't reach out his long arms and touch her, nor threaten her as he had on the steppes.

She was fully awake, but she stayed beneath the pedina, unable to leave its warmth, as she remembered the last two days and that cold night. Katerina let her arms creep above the cover, and at the first touch of the chill air against her bare flesh, she quickly snuggled down into the depths of the soft comforter.

Her hazel eyes focused on a closed shutter where light was seeping through a crack. Her thoughts began to drift, and the Mongol again began to take them over. Katerina fought him, pushed him away as she had in the snow. "I won't allow you to . . . I won't let this happen. I'll think of other things, things that please me and make me happy. I'll think of the steppe when I was a little girl, and my father. My father and me . . ." It was working. For now, she was a five-year-old running through the high grass of the plain. She saw herself playing in the fields of flowers that grew there: pale blue, indigo, and lilac cornflowers, the yellow broom and the white meadowsweet. Millions of blossoms that turned the vast expanse into a shimmering, waving ocean of breathtaking color. In her mind, she became a bird taking wing, soaring to the heavens and looking down from the sky, reveling in what God had created.

Not until she was full grown and seated upon her horse was she able to see the great distances the grasslands covered. Every Cossack on the steppe knew the flower stalks grew taller than any child and the high grasses could swallow up a man on his horse so he became invisible to the naked eye.

As a child, Katerina loved playing in the fields. Vague images of her mother looking for her as she hid came floating back. Hard as she tried, she could not see her mother's face. If only she were alive. But she had been killed by invading Poles soon after Katerina's fifth birthday. They had cut down her mother and older brother as if they were sheaves of wheat. If they were alive, they would be with her in the mountains and she would be . . . safe. Just the thought of that word, and the Mongol wove his way vividly into her mind. Katerina shook her head fitfully to clear his hateful face from her tortured mind. Her eyes drifted to the wooden icon hanging on the rough plank wall. She prayed silently, the familiar words giving her some small measure of comfort.

You must get up, an inner voice whispered. You've got to keep busy. You must work so there is no time to think. And when your body cries out for rest, then you will sleep. In sleep, you'll be able to forget.

Quickly, before she could change her mind, Katerina slipped from the cozy bed and dressed hurriedly. She splashed water on her face from the wooden bowl that Stepan had placed near the hearth and felt ready to confront whatever the day would bring. Woolen underclothing, a wide-sleeved Cossack blouse, snug-fitting trousers, and fleece-lined boots would keep her warm, yet would not hamper her while she worked. Satisfied with her appearance, Katerina left the crackling fire and started the short walk to the Prokopoviches' house.

Stepan waited impatiently, his round blue eyes full of concern. Katerina was late. Breakfast, always served at the first sign of dawn, had been over two hours ago. His round, childish face puckered up in thought. Should he go after her and make sure she was all right?

He turned to his mother, who was standing near the oven, and waved his arms in agitation.

Olga Prokopovich placed the ladle she held in a heavy wooden bowl and looked fondly at her son. She shook her head, jostling a strand of dark hair loose from under her kokoshnik. "She's tired, Stepan. She's probably still sleeping." Olga laid her head in the crook of her arm and closed her eyes, demonstrating, so the boy would understand. She laid a plump hand on his muscular arm and looked up at Stepan with twinkling blue eyes. "Put the bowl and the cup on the table for Katerina," she said, hoping to take his mind off the time. Stepan nodded happily. Olga's glance met her husband's, and they smiled. How they loved this man-child. In their opinion he was as strong as any Cossack fighter. He was their son and they loved him unashamedly.

A cold draft of air swirled and eddied about as Katerina entered the room, stamping the snow from her boots. "I know I'm late, but Stepan's fire was so warm I couldn't bear to leave my bed," she said, as she tousled the boy's fair hair. She turned to Olga. "Today was my one day of luxury. From now on I'll be here on time for breakfast."

The older woman nodded and smiled as she looked into the girl's amber eyes. Where was the sparkle, where was the merriment that was always there? Out of the corner of her eye, she looked at Ostap to see if he, too, had noticed. Her husband was lighting his short Cossack pipe, the fragrant cloud of blue-gray smoke swirling around him. Only to Olga was his sharp gaze apparent.

His pipe going to his satisfaction, Ostap pulled on his sheepskin coat and buttoned it to the neck. "I'll leave you women to your talk"—he grinned—"and see to my other women. The ones that don't answer back and complain when there's no fresh-cut firewood."

Olga clasped his round, ruddy face in her plump hands and kissed him resoundingly. "Go then to your horses and see if they can keep you warm, and before dinnertime you'll be back and in our bed, looking for me to cuddle you." She laughed, her body shaking in delight.

Ostap grinned and winked at Katerina. His expression clearly stated, Women!

Olga ran her hands over her slate-gray kirtle and offered Katerina a cup of tea. Stepan set a bowl of steaming porridge in front of her and made a motion for his friend to eat.

She laughed. "After two days of nothing but black bread, this is going to taste like caviar."

"Each morning until your father and the others return you will breakfast with us," the old woman said matter-of-factly.

Katerina smiled. "I was hoping you would ask me."

When the simple meal was over, Katerina motioned for Stepan to sit next to her. "There is much that has to be done, and we're going to work long and hard to prepare for my father's return. We will both be so tired at the end of the day your mother will have to feed us with a spoon."

Stepan uttered a gurgling sound of approval as he held up Katerina's spoon for his mother to see. She nodded at Stepan, a wide smile on her pleasant face.

Katerina clasped the rosy-cheeked woman to her, to Stepan's delight. "Your cooking is delicious, and thoughts of your wonderful dinner will keep both of us hurrying throughout the day."

"Hot beet soup, roast lamb with dumplings, and a spiced honey cake baked especially for you."

Both women laughed as Stepan rolled his eyes and rubbed his stomach.

Without waiting any longer, the two young people headed for the barn, Stepan running slightly ahead. He turned once, motioning for Katerina to hurry, anxious for her to see the care and attention he had given Wildflower.

Inside the moist, sweet-smelling stable, Stepan placed Katerina's hand on the mare's belly and grinned.

Katerina laughed. "What do you think, Ostap, is the mare well?"

Ostap shrugged. "There are no signs of complications, and the mare is hale and hearty, thanks to my son's care."

Katerina nodded as she pulled a woolen cap over her hair. "We are going to walk around the village and see what has to be done in preparation for Father's return."

Ostap puffed on his pipe and motioned to them to hurry and close the door before the mare felt a draft.

Katerina spied her father's summer home, the largest in the village, as was proper for the hetman, and felt fear settle over her. Her large eyes raked the quietness around her. The village was no different from any other Cossack settlement; the huts, constructed of logs, were insulated with moss to conserve heat in the cold months, each boasting an oven made of baked clay, laid out in a circle surrounding the camp to prevent attack from wild marauders. Wearily she rubbed at her temples.

Inside one of the huts, Katerina forced her mind to the task at hand. She had to pay attention to Stepan and the work she had to do.

On the rough plank wall hung the only adornment, the

treasured icon that held a place of honor on a wall in every home. The Blessed Mother with Christ Child, painted on a smooth wooden plaque and trimmed in gilt, pleased Katerina as she gazed at it. She, like all the people of the Ukraine, had been taught at a very early age two values: love and protection of the steppe and reverence and preservation of their Eastern Orthodox religion. These were dearer than life itself.

Together, Katerina and Stepan cleaned the hut, sweeping and dusting with zeal. The spring move down from the mountains was almost at hand, and she wanted the home to be neat and refreshed for the Kat's arrival.

Their task finished, Katerina spoke. "I know your father has kept the fences in good order, but let's check them to be sure none of the posts have worked loose." They walked in companionable silence to the southeast corner of the village, where the animal compound stood empty, waiting to open its gates to the horses. Katerina's eyes darted about, looking for a fallen post or split rails. All appeared to be in good order, with the exception of a protruding nail here and there inviting the blows of a hammer.

They continued their inspection until reaching the massive barn. "In the next few weeks this area will be filled with wonderment. Mares will birth their foals, the foals will test their new legs, and, once tried, their wobbly legs will carry them eagerly to their mother's milk. There they will suckle until their bellies are full. All will be quiet again, until the mares and the foals, nestled in an atmosphere of love, talk to each other. The sound will be heard throughout the village. Then, in three years, the fillies and colts will be ready for market. In seven years those blotchy gray-white foals will be pure white Cosars," she whispered to Stepan, who nodded his head in agreement.

Katerina sought the compartments containing mountains of hay, wheat, and oats. The storage bins were filled to capacity. "We'll begin by laying straw on the floors of the stalls and fill all the feed and water troughs. When we finish here, we'll check the storehouse to see if we have enough smoked meats, and the root cellar to see how well the vegetables fared through the winter. The men will bring back the sheep and goats, and fresh meat will be in abundance, except for game and rabbit. If we complete our chores ahead of time, we'll go hunting. Would you like that, Stepan?"

The boy waved his arms wildly, a grin splitting his face.

"Roast goose for the first night back." Katerina laughed. "I have an idea, Stepan. With your mother and father's help we can carry all the tables and benches from the huts to the barn and prepare a feast for the men's return. A feast for all to enjoy before the hard work of spring begins. Start with the straw, Stepan, and I'll get the water."

The sun was high in the west and the shadows grew longer as they entered the storehouse. "We'll have to do this fast, Stepan, the light is fading." Quickly they checked the shelves and hooks in the storehouse. Seeing that the smoked meat was plentiful, they turned to the fragrant root cellar, which they found to be pregnant with foodstuffs. "No problem, Stepan, there's plenty of food until the next harvest. If you aren't too tired, we can check the toolshed now and get an early start in the morning."

Stepan nodded and pulled on her arm to show that he was willing to go with her.

Inside the shed the lantern cast eerie spectral shadows upon the rough walls as Katerina inspected the tools. "Your father has a system all his own," she said, laughing. "You see how all the tools on these three walls have been finished, sharpened to perfection. These," she said, pointing to the fourth wall, "are still to be done."

Katerina leaned against the wall as Stepan removed one tool and then another to test its sharpness. Wearily she let her thick lashes drop; she was tired, but not exhausted enough to sleep. She opened her eyes again as Stepan bent down to pick up a tool near her. Katerina's breath caught in

her throat for a second. If only she had had a weapon with . . .
would she have used it? Could she stick a knife in a man's ribs
or heart? Could she bludgeon to save herself? The Mongol's
face with his midnight-dark eyes swam before her. Could
she have killed him? A shudder ripped through her slender
body as Stepan reached up to take the lantern from where it
hung above her, a puzzled look on his face. "It's all right.
I'm just tired," she said, trying to reassure him. "I'll race
you back to the house. The first one there gets all of the
spiced honey cake." Stepan's eyes lit up as Katerina tore
ahead of him. He loped along behind, the lantern bobbing
freely in the air, the yellow light twinkling and winking in
the darkness.

The following days were grueling. Katerina worked with
Stepan at her side from dawn till dusk. She ate her dinner
quickly, took a hot bath, and fell into bed. When she slept,
her dreams were invaded by a dark-eyed man with hair the
color of night. He stalked her slowly, insidiously, through
the thick trees. She always woke just as she was about to be
captured, a hammer raised in her hand, her coppery hair wet
and matted, and a sheen of perspiration on her face. Could
she slay him when the time came? Finding no answer, she
would crawl from her bed and work nonstop throughout the
day, only to fall into bed and have the same bad dream.

"Volin," she said to Stepan one morning, "will shine like
a kopeck when we are finished. My father will be proud of
me." She still hadn't forgiven him for berating her the way
he had, but she knew she would the moment she saw him.
At that moment she would forgive him anything, because
beneath their arguments they deeply loved each other. Their
quarrels were usually caused by their similar temperament.

By the end of the week Katerina noticed the dried, yellow grass poking through the snow and pointed it out to
Stepan with the toe of her boot. He waved his arms and uttered a sound much like that of a new baby. It was the first
sign that winter was slipping away and spring would soon

cause the earth to give birth to its greenery. Once again the steppe would be covered with a rainbow of color, as animals and birds returned to sing the sounds of life.

"We have a few good hours of daylight left, Stepan. Come, we're going hunting." An hour after sunset, they returned with nine geese and seven rabbits. "Hardly a feast, but each will get a portion."

Stepan waved his arms and hands to show he agreed as they thrust out their bounty for Olga and Ostap to see.

That night as Katerina soaked in her bath, the steamy wetness relaxing her, she thought of the coming weeks. Soon the farming would begin and the fields would be seeded. Once the sowing was done, the buyers would begin to arrive and the bartering for the Cosars would start. It was exciting to watch the outsiders and her father trying to outsmart each other. She slid farther down into the tub and tried to remember what it was she had to do the following day. She wanted everything in order for her father's arrival. How could she have forgotten? She had to stack the wood, light the ovens, and lay the oblong lace cloth on each bread table, in a north-to-south direction, and place an unlit candle, a loaf of black bread, and a tiny dish of salt upon it. This was the Cossack custom for good health and good luck in the new year. When she finished she would walk to the end of the road and watch for her father. She missed him, Mikhailo, the horses, and the old man who sat by the fire waiting to die.

The bathwater was cooling; it was time to get out and snuggle into the warm bed. Lord, she was tired to the very bone. If only she could have one good night's sleep, one without the Mongol invading her dreams.

It was not to be. As soon as the dark lashes were stilled and her breathing was regular, a dark-eyed man on horseback raced after her as she spurred Bluefire onward. She thrashed about in the big bed, the quilt sliding onto the floor from her frantic movements. He was gaining; closer and closer he came, until he was abreast of her. His dark eyes were laughing and his white teeth gleamed in the early night. He wore a brown cape, which he threw to the ground as he reached out a long arm and dragged her from Bluefire's broad back. She fell to the ground, and from somewhere she felt her fingers touch a heavy wooden pallet. He stood over her, laughing, his stance arrogant, his face amused and mocking. She struggled to her knees, the mallet raised, ready to strike. A bloodcurdling scream ripped from her mouth as she tumbled from the high bed onto the softness of the quilt. She rubbed the back of her hand across her forehead, and was not surprised to see it come away wet.

Her heart beating madly, she gathered the covering around her and walked to the huge oven. Katerina secured the quilt around her and lay down on the felt-covered floor, her eyes wide and staring.

The following morning Katerina and Stepan worked diligently to finish their tasks, scurrying from hut to hut performing their specific duties.

Laughing and teasing each other, they walked to the end of the road. Suddenly Katerina commanded, "Sh-h-h, listen. Do you hear them?"

The boy tilted his head toward the open steppe. He motioned that he heard nothing.

"Listen again," she urged, "the hoofbeats are louder now, you should hear them." Again he turned his head, intent on listening, his face brightening and a broad grin emerging, acknowledging that he, too, heard.

As the horses thundered closer, Katerina stood directly in the middle of the road, her hands on her hips, her legs astride, waiting for her father. Moments later, Katlof came thundering down the road, majestic atop Snowfire, almost running her down. She didn't move a muscle. Her father brought the horse to an abrupt stop.

"So, you're alive after all!" he shouted, looking down at her fiercely.

"Yes, I'm alive, and so are Wildflower and Bluefire!"

Katlof dismounted and stood at the side of his horse, a stern look on his face. "Then come here, baryshna, and give your father a proper welcome home."

As Katerina ran toward him, the stern look dissolved, a broad smile crossing his face. As they embraced each other, her father said, "In my heart I knew you were alive. Why didn't you send word? Why didn't you return?"

"Because, Father, I haven't forgotten your scolding, and I hadn't forgiven you until this moment. I was angry with you so I thought I would let you spend a week agonizing and praying for me," she said coolly. "I thought it would do you good."

"Ha!" roared Katlof. "Spoken like a true Cossack," he said, as he gave her a hearty slap on her back. "A true Cossack, that's my Katerina!" he chuckled.

A Cossack rode up and led Snowfire away as Katlof and Katerina walked toward their summer dwelling together. "So, Daughter, tell your father what you have been doing this past week."

"You'll see." She laughed as she led him through the town toward their hut.

Before they entered, Katerina looked out across the endless plain and thought, the steppe and I have something in common—it goes on endlessly, as does my bad dream. She knew then she would never be free of the Mongol. A feeling of panic began to engulf her. She silently pleaded, God, dear God, help me! "Please!" she whispered as she closed the door behind her.

Again they embraced fondly. Katlof stepped back, staring down into her eyes. "I'm sorry for my tirade back in the fortress," he said gruffly. "How like your mother you are. You have the same fiery Mongol temper and the same gentle persuasiveness."

"Was she beautiful, Father?"

"You have only to look in the mirror to see the beauty of

your mother. Because of you, your mother is always with me," he said tenderly.

Katerina threw herself into his arms, burrowing her head into his broad chest.

His words, softly spoken, were barely audible. "How I love you, child, you're my life, my reason for being. Without you I would have nothing."

Tears welled in the amber eyes. "I'll never fail you again, Father."

Spring was everywhere. Most evident was the farmland, where the ground, now softened by the thaw, left the earth ready for the plow. Cossacks could be seen with plow straps draped around their shoulders as the Cosars that were fit only for farming pulled the primitive plows forward.

The village bustled with activity as each Cossack performed his tasks. There were farmers, hunters of game, lumberjacks, and the women who worked in the homes and helped in the field. The remaining Cossacks tended the famed Cosars.

Katerina and Katlof spent their days in the barn with the mares, watching the miracle of birth. The birthing made her feel clean and near to God as she watched the foals leave the shelter of their mothers' wombs, bringing a closeness between her and her father that was renewed every year at this time. As they watched, the attachment expressed between mother and foal engulfed them also. Katrina looked at her father with love-filled amber eyes as he enfolded her in the crook of his arm. She felt safe and secure, out of harm's way. Safe from the Mongol for the moment.

As the weeks passed, the steppe was again a playground for wild game and birds. The young fillies and colts frolicked and ran along with the wild inhabitants through the short grass and budding flowers. Katerina adored watching the horses when they were on the plain, running like the wind, testing their spindly legs, and at the same time strengthening them. When she could stand it no longer, she would leap on Bluefire's back and race along with the colts and fillies.

Each day as new foals were born, Katerina and Katlof were in attendance. "It looks like an especially good year for selling stock. Except for one or two sickly colts, we haven't lost one horse, and with the proper attention, the two sick fillies will be up and around again," Katlof said quietly.

"Father, let me nurse the two sick colts. You know how they respond to me; let me take care of them!" she begged.

"If you want to spend that much time with the animals, of course you may tend them. But as you know, it's a full-time task which must be done with much love and patience," he stressed.

"Just trust me," she said confidently.

"Very well, Katerina."

Every day and every night for weeks, Katerina hand-fed the colts and tended to their every need, sleeping in the barn at night to make sure nothing went awry. Almost a month to the day, they were up on their legs, kicking up their heels with the urge to run. Katerina led them from the barn to the open steppe, where they disappeared like the wind. She had done well; her father would be proud. She had the Kaṭ's touch. As she gazed after them, she noticed a streak of white flash by. It was Whitefire, prancing and running with his offspring. Busy with the ill horses, she had forgotten it was time for Whitefire to perform stud service. The stallion would stay in Volin for two months, and then Stepan would take him back to the Carpathians.

Leaving the barn, Katerina looked toward the compound and saw it filled to capacity with the mares selected for next year's supply of foals. This was Katlof's system, so long as his herd was plentiful and healthy, he divided the mares into thirds, each group going to stud once every three years.

As she watched the men release a mare to run with Whitefire, feelings of desire began to stir in her. It was spring, and the animals, birds, and horses were busy reproducing. She smiled as Whitefire chased a mare behind a small clump of trees. Soon thereafter, the stallion reappeared, reared up on his hind legs, and whinnied triumphantly. It was done: another mare carried the seed of the prized horse.

Strange feelings and emotions began to course through her as she watched the mares. But deep within her she felt a need for tenderness, for love. She wondered if she could love. Was love the same as lust? Underneath it all, was it just a matter of copulation? She couldn't and wouldn't believe that was all there was to it.

That night two lovers stole into the barn under cover of darkness, unaware of her gaze. How sweetly they embraced each other and how passionately they vowed their endearments in husky murmurings. As quickly as they had appeared, they were gone, leaving a wide-eyed Katerina staring after them.

Her heart fluttered in her chest at the thought of the young couple. She wanted desperately to be held, to be kissed tenderly and gently. She felt confused and afraid.

Forcing her mind to think of other things, she walked back to the hut to tell her father the colts were well and running in the fields, healthy young Cosars.

Excitement began to build in the village as each passing day brought the buyers one day closer. This year the thought of the buyers coming for the Cosars held no appeal for Katerina. Something was missing in her life, and she couldn't come to terms with the alien feeling. Throwing herself into her work, she toiled during the day and then rode Bluefire across the plains for hours to clear her head, and still the aching feeling stayed with her.

Someday, somewhere, she would find what she was looking for, and when she did, she would know it, she was sure of it. As always when the thought entered her mind, the Mongol was right behind, mocking her with his dark eyes. Then she would wonder . . . would she know, would she really know?

Chapter 4

Word spread quickly through the village—Czar Ivan's emissary would be arriving any day now. To Katlof, he was just another buyer, but his people were always impressed when the Czar's man came to Volin. They knew if it was not for the Cosars, a nobleman would never set foot in this part of the steppe.

Katerina was glad that she had managed to keep outward appearances normal during the past weeks, but inside she was depressed, lonely, and hurt. She hoped her father wasn't aware of her inner turmoil, and since he hadn't asked if anything was wrong, she knew she was playing her part well.

Maybe the arrival of the Czar's emissary would distract her from her thoughts for a few days. She wondered what the man would look like. Would he be any different from the grouchy, businesslike nobles that came before him, who selected the horses, settled on a price, and were gone?

When breakfast was over and the hut was in order, she dressed and headed for the barn. Tending the brood mares, Katerina heard a commotion outside the barn. "Yaschu, what's going on?"

"One of the riders just rode into the village with news of the emissary from Moscow."

"What news?"

"The rider said the Czar's buyer is on his way and should arrive within the hour."

Katerina felt a stir of anticipation, but paid it no mind and went back inside, content to care for the horses.

From outside the barn she heard someone shout, "They're here!" Putting aside her work, she left, looking for her father, and found him standing at the front of the village, waiting for the emissary. Two men approached quickly on horseback. Katerina walked to her home, deciding to wait and watch from there, knowing her father didn't like to be disturbed when he was conducting business.

Katerina's sharp eyes noticed that this buyer was younger than his predecessors. From his horse the emissary looked down at her father and said, "I'm looking for Katlof Vaschenko. Can you tell me where I might find him?"

At the sound of his deep, vibrant voice, Katerina felt her heart pound. She could see him clearly now, in his crimson jacket and black trousers. The shine from his leather boots winked in the bright sunlight as he moved to dismount the graceful brown Arabian. Respectfully, as the Kat identified himself, he removed the pointed black cap resting rakishly on his head. "Yuri Zhuk, emissary to Czar Ivan, and this man is Gregory Bohacky with whom I've been visiting," Yuri said, motioning to his comrade. "Gregory comes from Kiev and is a cousin of the Czar's. He also wishes to purchase pure whites. Gregory will observe the herd now and make his final selection during midsummer," for he must leave immediately.

Katerina drew in her breath as she watched Yuri dismount and walk toward her father. The Russian extended a long, muscular arm and handed Katlof a rolled piece of parchment to read. The Kat raked his eyes over the crackling paper and nodded slightly. He was proud of his rare ability to read, having learned it as a boy from a priest. It had stood him in good stead more than once and he had encouraged most of the Dons to become literate as well.

His voice carried to Katerina. "The Czar shall have one thousand horses by the end of spring, but only if he pays the price I ask. There will be no haggling and no bargaining. Do you have the money with you?"

"Czar Ivan said the money will be paid on delivery of the horses," came the low, husky reply.

"And the Kat says not one horse leaves until the money is paid . . . in advance," came the cold, firm reply.

"The Czar wishes me to remind you that the price is not what was originally agreed on. He wishes to know why the price has doubled."

"The price has doubled because I wish it. If there are more words between us, the price will triple."

Yuri Zhuk, emissary to Czar Ivan, looked at the leader of the Cossack village with smoldering eyes and knew he would pay whatever the amount was for the horses sired by Whitefire. "Agreed," Yuri said curtly. "I'll make my selection tomorrow at dawn, when the horses are at their best."

"The matter is settled then," the Kat said briskly. "The following day you will leave here with a signed contract for one thousand horses. This evening you will have supper in my house." With a curt nod of his head, the Cossack chief walked away, leaving Yuri to stare after him.

Oles, one of the young men from the tribe, told him in cool, jeering tones that he was to remain in the Kat's house until dinner.

Yuri's dark eyes were angry, and his jaw tightened at what he considered the Cossack's crude manners. He straightened his slim shoulders as he followed the Cossack. How sure they were; how confident they appeared. Here he stood, an emissary from Czar Ivan, and he was being treated with thinly disguised insolence and mocking superiority. Tales of Cossack fierceness were widespread, as were the tales of the Kat's horses. The Cossack, in Yuri's view, had no equal. Some people were born to royalty, like himself, while others were born to be a Cossack. Yuri knew instantly he would have given his life's blood to have been born a Cossack.

A wild whoop of laughter split the air. Yuri turned to watch as a group of young Cossacks mounted their horses and rode the length of the dusty road, their weapons thrust in front of them. It must be some sort of drill, he thought to himself. For an hour he watched as horses and riders cavorted on the sleek white horses, animal and rider one, each magnificent beast perfectly attuned to the man on his back.

Weapons drawn, the equestrians charged at each other with split second timing. A moment before impact, a rider would slide beneath his horse and come up, weapon flicking the air, from the horse's right flank. To Yuri's amazement, no weapon ever touched another, nobody was unseated during the drill. A pity these men did not fight for the Czar. They were a race, a people, an entity unto themselves. No soldier, no warrior, no matter how experienced, would wish to go to battle against a Cossack.

At a sound from behind, Yuri turned to see a girl with hair the color of burnished copper in the doorway of a hut. Her heavily fringed eyes shone like rich amber. Yuri's eyes widened appreciatively. Cossack women were more beautiful than he had imagined. Her tawny skin intrigued him, as did the doe eyes. Mongol blood must run in her veins, he told himself as he smiled at her and bowed graciously. "Yuri Zhuk, at your service."

Katerina inclined her head slightly, her breath quickening at his show of good manners. Not one of the young Cossacks would bow to her or show her respect in any way. This man looked at her with approval and liked what he saw.

The thick lashes fell over her high cheekbones as she advanced a step and stood looking up at him. "I am Katerina

Vaschenko. The Kat is my father. He asked that I show you around our village before supper, if it is agreeable to you," she said hastily.

"Only if you promise to tell me about the Cossacks." He grinned, showing even white teeth, his voice deep yet melodious.

Familiar with the company of the boisterous, fun-loving Cossack youths, who did nothing but taunt her, Katerina felt at a disadvantage with this tall, muscular man. Her cheeks flushed a bright crimson as she pictured what he would look like stripped to the waist. She shook her head to clear it, and forced herself to look into the Russian's eyes. Her tongue moistened her dry lips as she imagined his nude muscles moving in his powerful back as he hunched his shoulders to make himself more comfortable in her presence. She wanted to feel the wide, sensuous mouth on hers. Swallowing hard, she tried to force herself to ignore such wanton thoughts, but found herself mesmerized by his dark, smoldering eyes as they stared deeply into hers. What would his lean, hard body feel like next to hers? How would his hands feel on her flesh? Why was he looking at her like that? Surely he couldn't read her mind, or could he? Or was it that he was thinking the same thing? The moment she saw him ride into the village, she knew he was different. She had to do something, say something. How long was she going to stand and stare at him like some ignorant child? "If you'll come with me," she said, her voice soft and thick with emotion.

They walked from one end of the village to the other, each aware of the other, deliberately keeping a space between them. Katerina knew that if her arm so much as touched his, she would crumble and faint. She was petrified at this strange feeling that was taking hold of her.

At last she risked a sideward glance in his direction

when he turned to look at a small watering pond for the new colts. A sheaf of dark hair fell low on his wide forehead. His nose was straight and chiseled, his jaw lean and square, with a pronounced cleft in his chin. He didn't have the full cheeks of other Russians, and his skin was weathered but not rough like the Cossack youths'. He sported no beard or mustache, reflecting an individual who dared to defy fashion. Her heart thundered as she imagined his cheek next to hers before their lips met in a searing, passionate kiss.

Katerina stumbled and would have fallen if Yuri hadn't reached out a strong arm to grasp her and bring her closer till she was steady on her feet. Leaning against him, her breathing labored, she laid her head on his broad chest and listened to the furious pounding of his heart. She raised clear amber eyes and looked directly into his as the tip of her tongue again moistened her lips, his eyes pulling her into their depths. Katerina felt him stiffen as she brought her head up till her face was inches from his. I should do what the other girls do, flutter my eyelashes, smile, and tease him with my eyes, she thought. It was impossible, and Yuri wasn't one of those loutish young boys that . . .

Katerina felt her body forced back slowly till she was against the wall of the stable. Like a hungry child, she raised her mouth and waited for the feel of the Russian's lips. Her body was feverish, and she felt her breasts grow taut beneath the thin fabric of her sarafan. She strained toward him and felt a hard yet gentle hand slip beneath her bodice. Fire raced through her as she sought to fullfill her newly aroused hunger. She arched her back, and soft moans escaped her as she felt the hardness of his manhood against her thigh. Katerina felt herself soar as her breasts fought and strained against the fabric that held them prisoner. Her inner heat threatened to consume her until in the dim recesses of her mind, she heard her name being called. She tore her mouth from Yuri's, her eyes glazed and full of wanting. "I . . . I have . . . I have to . . . go back." Turning, she tripped and ran, her body welcoming the light breeze that wafted about her. "Oh, what did I do? How did I . . . I just saw him for the first time . . . oh, God! . . . I don't care," she cried as she raced indoors and slammed the door behind her, her hands clapped to her flaming cheeks.

Yuri, his chiseled features calm, watched as Katerina raced back to her father's house. The disturbing ache in his nether regions stayed with him. When it became a violent pain, he would do something about it. For now, it wasn't so uncomfortable that he couldn't live with it. The promise of exquisite release would soon be his.

The meal was silent. Katlof Vaschenko ate the thick cabbage soup without lifting his eyes from the bowl. When he finished, he wiped his mouth on the sleeve of the coarse tunic he wore. He leaned back and eyed the Russian with open suspicion. "There was no need for you to make the journey to this village. The Czar was aware of my demands and agreed to them at the time the mares were bred. When you return to your post to report to the Czar, you will deliver a message . . . from the Kat. No more visits. The horses will be delivered on schedule. For many years now, all of Russia has tried to steal our horses, tried to steal our breeding secrets. I'm the only one who knows the secret," he lied, "and I will carry it to my grave. The crossbreeding of the Cosars has been our livelihood for centuries and will never be divulged to anyone, and that includes the Czar. The stallions are not kept here on the steppe; after they impregnate the mares they are taken away. I'm telling you this so there won't be any need for you to creep among our people, as the last man did, to try to learn by deceit and trickery what isn't to be told. There aren't any stallions here except those that have been castrated," he lied. "Tales of your ferocious Czar have filtered here, and it would be wise if you tell him that the

Don as well as the Terek Cossacks are not happy with the tales of his mass murders of people and his lunatic ways. For now, his only thought is to have my Cosars. If it weren't for my horses, he wouldn't have a cavalry. Remind him of this matter when you return."

Yuri's dark eyes narrowed slightly as he watched the slovenly Kat lean back on the rough-hewn chair. The Kat's eyes were cold and unreadable. His body tipped precariously on the wooden chair as he eyed the Russian, daring him to dispute what he said. Yuri felt nauseated as the man's odor reached him. He smelled of stale horseflesh and his own dirty sweat, and the fumes of vodka were strong enough to set the room on fire. His coarse, homespun clothing and mud-crusted boots were those of a fighting Cossack. This fearless leader of men, this awesome breeder of horseflesh, was no different from his men. He looked the same, he dressed the same, and he smelled the same.

"I shall give your message to the Czar . . . exactly as stated," Yuri said coolly. "I would like to hear the story of the horses—that is, if you wouldn't mind telling me. There are many hours to get through till dawn, when I inspect them." What he didn't say was that he had no desire to sleep in the moldy-looking feather bed that was to be his. Besides, it was something to help while away the time till the old man was sodden, and then he could take the beautiful Katerina outside to some grassy spot and unleash his violent pain.

With supreme effort he managed to keep his eyes averted from the tawny-skinned Katerina during the meal. He felt the amber, catlike eyes on him, and knew the Kat was aware of it also. He would have to be careful. She was probably being saved for one of those smelly oafs in the horse pens. Yuri's mouth tightened as he visualized her soft, honeyed skin being caressed by some filthy, sweaty hand. He had to force himself to remain seated, his face schooled to show nothing of his thoughts: of one of those rancid, evil faces with the thick, slobbering lips salivating over her naked body.

He was saved from further thought when the Kat got off his seat, pulled aside a curtain, and brought forth a jug of vodka. He wiped his hand across his heavy beard as he plopped the jug on the table, with a dirty hand motioning that Yuri should take the first drink. There weren't any glasses. Yuri raised the heavy jug to his lips and drank deeply.

The older man's eyes registered shock when the young Russian set the jug down, precisely on the same spot he lifted it from. His eyes didn't water, and he wasn't coughing and sputtering.

Yuri grinned as he stared at the Cossack. "My guts aren't on fire. I've been drinking vodka since I was six years old. I admit this," he said, pointing to the jug, "has the kick of one of your stallions, but I've had worse."

The Kat laughed. "When the jug is finished and if you are still on your feet, then, and only then, will I tell you about my horses." He brought the jug to his lips and drank with deep gurgling sounds.

Yuri took his turn, to the amazement of Katerina, who was watching with wide, frightened eyes. Why was her father doing this? Why was he pretending to be this . . . this dirty, unkempt, uncultured man? He was up to something, and she would have to stay in the kitchen till she found out what it was. Surely he wouldn't kill the Russian, or would he? She had never seen him in this sort of a mood before.

Yuri drank and set the jug down, a patient look on his face.

The Kat took another long, gurgling drink and handed the jug to the young Russian. "Drink as I drink," he said harshly. "There's more where that came from. Half vodka and half blood runs in my veins. What runs in yours, Russian?"

"Russian blood," Yuri said curtly as he brought the jug to his lips.

"Fetch another jug, Katerina," her father said, never taking his eyes from the young man sitting across the table from him.

Katerina withdrew behind the curtain and brought out a jug, placing it on the table with a loud thump to show her disapproval. She looked at her father with contempt and at Yuri with suspicion. The Russian didn't have a chance. Her father would probably trick him into confessing an ulterior motive once Yuri could not think logically anymore. She walked from the room, disgust written in the straightness of her back and her firm, hard gait. And they said women were fools!

Katerina looked at the star-filled night and felt saddened. Spring was a time for lovers and she was alone. The coming months of summer would pass quickly and soon it would be time to take the mares back to the Carpathians and settle in for the long, cold winter. I survived after all; I managed to get through spring, and I can get through summer and winter the same way, she thought bitterly. The thoughts of the new colts and fillies that would be born did not help to dispel the gloom. What was her father up to? What did the Russian have in his mind? Why did she constantly think of the Mongol of the steppe? What was it about the young Russian that appealed to her? If only she knew what was in the soldier's mind. Whatever it was, he would be no match for her father.

Would Yuri seek her out after the drinking was over? Would he be able to handle himself, or would he be like the others when they drank vodka for hours on end? Would he want to make love to her as she wanted him to?

Katerina walked for what seemed like hours. When she returned to the hut, she wasn't surprised to see four jugs sitting on the table and her father talking freely of the horses.

She let her eyes wander toward Yuri and then to her father. She closed the door behind her as she gave Yuri one last, lingering look, which he did not return.

Katerina settled herself on a bench outside the door and listened as her father disclosed how he came to be called the Kat.

Quarts of vodka let words tumble freely from the Kat's mouth. "I'll tell you about my beautiful horses," he said, slurring his words. "Do you know how long it takes and how difficult it is to breed pure whites? Do you know how many generations it has taken to breed this horse with that horse and end with stallions like Whitefire and his son, Snowfire?"

Yuri drew in his breath and leaned his elbows on the simple plank table, his eyes keen, his ears alert. "Tell me," he said quietly.

The Kat laughed. "First more vodka. I'll drink and then you drink." He reached for the jug in the center of the table. Both men drank heartily, but it was Yuri who replaced the earthen bottle in the same spot it had been taken from. His hand was steady, although his head reeled. "Go on about the horses," he urged.

"It began long ago with the Przhevalski horse and . . . and another horse. Would you like to know what we did?" he baited the young Russian.

"Of course, but only if you want to tell me," Yuri replied nonchalantly.

"Do you wonder how I got to be named the Kat?" Yuri nodded. "My father, his father, and his father before him had a knack for handling stallions. One day my great-great-grandfather was sent to the barn to watch the horses. He was but a lad, and his father told him he couldn't leave until he understood the animals. My great-great-grandfather sat on a stool and watched the horses eat and he watched them sleep. He talked to them as his father talked to them. The story goes that he stayed in the barn for two days and two nights and still he didn't understand what his father expected of him.

"With nothing to occupy his time, save watching and talking to the horses, he noticed a cat wander through the stalls, gently rubbing against the horses' legs and purring softly and contentedly. The stallions quieted immediately, as did the rest of the horses. They lowered their heads to the ground while the cat purred and nuzzled their noses. My great-great-grandfather learned from the cat how to touch and how to speak to them."

"An amazing story," Yuri said quietly.

"And now you wish to know the secret, eh, my young friend," the Kat said drunkenly. He slapped the Russian on the arm and started to speak. "The secret is . . . is . . ." He stopped. "I'll tell it to you this way," the shrewd Cossack went on. "There is an old Arab proverb that says: the fleetest of horses is the chestnut, the most enduring the bay, the most spirited the black, the most blessed the one with the white forehead. That is the secret, my young friend."

"Is it!" breathed a puzzled Yuri, who dared not ask one question.

"You fool, did you think for one moment that I was so drunk I would tell you our secret? Better men than you, my friend, have tried and died for their efforts. Fool!" He pushed the liquor toward the Russian. "Have a drink."

Yuri rose from the table and walked to the door. As his hand touched the latch, the Cossack thundered, "I said have another drink!"

Yuri turned, his eyes full of hate. "I don't drink with liars," he said softly as he left the room, the latch clicking softly behind him.

The Kat picked up the jug and sent it crashing against the wall. "Fool! Better men than you have tried and died for their efforts, just as you will!" he shouted over and over, until his eyes grew heavy. Finally he lowered his head onto his folded arms and slept.

* * *

Katerina sensed Yuri approaching. Drawing in her breath, she turned to meet him and rushed into his arms, welcoming him with her whole being. "I've been waiting," she said simply.

"I know," he said huskily. "I'm here now." He pulled her into his arms in a hard embrace before she could utter another word. His lips crushed hers, driving the breath from her body as she pressed willingly against him. Yuri's arms tightened around her. His long muscular legs, next to hers, drove her back till she rested against the gnarled old tree where she had been sitting. His hands caressed her back, her breasts, the flatness of her stomach. He lifted his mouth from hers and looked deeply into her eyes in the bright moonlight. "You're so beautiful," he said hungrily as his mouth opened her lips, demanding more and still more from her straining body. She felt his hands inside the looseness of her sarafan, her breasts becoming alive under his touch. His strong hands caressed the warm, bare flesh till she moaned in delight.

Suddenly they were on the ground, the grass soft and cool. Fumbling, with shaking hands, she removed her clothing while Yuri did the same. When their nude bodies met, low moans escaped them both as his lips crushed hers, his body pressed hers, demanding more.

Crying softly with desire, she lay beside him as Yuri explored her body, which was pliant to his every demand. Her senses soared and whirled about her as she opened her mouth to his gently exploring tongue, her taut breasts boring into his hard, muscular chest. She moved invitingly beneath him, striving to make them one, always one.

Unable to bear the exquisite torture, she parted her thighs, and he entered her, gently at first and then with deep plunges, her pain a momentary thing as she was caught up in the passion of the pressure within her. Wave after wave of passion engulfed her as Yuri's violent pain was released to meet hers in the cascade of their emotions.

They lay quietly, each content to feel the other's nearness, neither speaking. From time to time Katerina reached out to touch his arm to make sure she wasn't dreaming.

As she nestled herself in the comforting hold of his arm, she said quietly, "I'll miss you when you return to Moscow."

"I'll return for you at summer's end. Promise that you will wait for me."

He wanted her, but was it for now or would it be for always? "I'll wait for you," she said huskily.

Yuri raised himself on one elbow. "I've bedded many women, but none like you. I think I loved you the moment I saw you standing in the house, waiting for me. I'll love you forever, for all eternity."

"Where will we go, what will we do?" Katerina asked quietly.

"Don't concern yourself, I'll take care of you. I have many plans to make. When I return, all will be in readiness. Would you like to live in Kiev with a houseful of servants, and have fine clothes and fine food?"

"Oh, yes," she murmured happily. There was no need for her to tell him that in the mountains during the winter months they lived a life of royalty, in the tradition of the Vaschenkos. No need to reveal that her father was not what he seemed. Later she would tell him. Later she would let him know everything. For now, this was her time—hers and Yuri's.

They slept, their naked flesh entwined on the grassy copse, far from the house.

Yuri's selection of the horses was slow and thorough. Katerina sat, unobserved, willing the tedious process to be over. Unable to keep her shining eyes off the muscular

Russian, she followed his every move. All she could think of was the velvety night and how it felt to have Yuri's arms embrace her.

She watched as the tall Russian shook his head over something, his jaw tight and angry. Even from where she sat, she could hear his harsh complaint to her father.

"The agreement was two hundred horses from the stallion Whitefire and the mare Wildflower, not one hundred and fifty, not one hundred, but two hundred. Two hundred pure whites. The other eight hundred were to salve your ego. Do you take me for a fool?" he demanded angrily. "The purpose of this agreement was for the whites." Angrily he waved a long arm at the black and russet horses that roamed the pens. "What good are they in the snow? The Czar wants only the whites. You agreed, you gave your word. If you wish to renege on the agreement, then I must cancel the bargain we made. Two hundred pure whites or nothing," he said adamantly.

The Kat grinned at the determined look on the Russian's face. "It never hurts to barter. You shall have your two hundred whites—one hundred and twenty-five mares and seventy-five castrated stallions." When the Russian flinched, the Kat roared with laughter. "Does the word bother you, my friend, or is it the act itself? Never mind, it isn't important what you feel. When we return from the Carpathians in April, the horses will be taken to Moscow.

"Oles," he called loudly, "take the Russian to the pasture so he can inspect the mares." His eyes told the Cossack to watch and let nothing go unnoticed.

Yuri correctly interpreted the look and smiled to himself.

He could feel Katerina's eyes on him while he made his selection, nodding as each horse was examined. He could do worse. With a little finery she would be acceptable at court, he mused as he finished his chore.

Katerina, who had been standing next to her father during the counting, looked at him with wide eyes. He knew!

Why didn't he say something? What would he do? She watched the Cossack hetman turn and stride away, a look of fury on his bearded face.

How to get through the rest of the day? A walk, a ride on her horse, Bluefire? A nap under the gnarled old tree where she had made love with Yuri?

When the inky black night had closed around her and the birds slept, she settled herself under the leafy tree to wait for Yuri. She felt confused. She wanted him, felt a need for him, and would willingly go with him, yet he wasn't the man she wanted to spend her life with. His eyes didn't return unspoken words. Perhaps there was no such man. Now that her father knew, she felt fear for what he would do to the Russian and terror of what he would do to her. Once he knew she was no longer a virgin, he would lose face with his fellow Cossacks. It would make no difference that he was the hetman. A Cossack girl married a Cossack man, not a Russian or a Mongol. Now, why had she thought of the Mongol? Why did he creep into her mind? She had to stop thinking about that day on the steppe. That time was over. What did Yuri mean when he said he would return for her? Did he mean to marry her or did he mean they would live together without a wedding ceremony? Men didn't marry women who weren't virgins.

Yuri came to her quietly, his footsteps hushed, his breathing soft. His arms reached for her and held her close. He crushed his face into her wealth of coppery hair and groaned softly. "I've been waiting all day for this moment," he said tenderly. "My body might have been choosing horses, but my mind and my thoughts were on you," he said huskily.

They settled themselves beneath the old tree, Katerina's head on his chest, her breathing tortured as she sought for and found his lips. Hungrily, he crushed her lips to his with a low growl of passion. The kiss was deep, savage in its intensity. They paused only long enough to shed their clothing, their bodies meeting just as passionately, entwining as his hungry mouth once more sought hers. Unable to contain herself, Katerina enticed him by straining against him till he entered her almost brutally. A sheen of perspiration flashed on his muscular torso as he sought for and conquered her, again and again.

Spent, they lay in each other's arms, talking softly. From time to time Yuri kissed her gently as his hand caressed her firm breasts. "When we're together, I shall keep you a prisoner in your chambers." He smiled down at her. Katerina snuggled closer to him, saying nothing. "Spend every waking hour thinking of me," he teased. "When will you speak to your father?" he asked quietly, a sense of urgency in his voice.

"After you leave. I can tell you now that he'll be furious. A Cossack girl belongs with a man of her own kind."

"Girls have a way of twisting their fathers around to their way of thinking. I've seen my sister do it many times," he said with amusement.

Katerina didn't want to discuss her father's reaction. "What do you think of the steppe, and how did you like doing business with the Kat?"

"He is a shrewd businessman. For a while he thought he could outwit me with the whites. I would have canceled the bargain which was made. The Czar agreed to the additional eight hundred horses for the sake of two hundred whites. What good is a black or russet in winter combat? I asked your father for four hundred whites in the autumn of next year, but he wouldn't agree. I don't know what I'm going to do when I return to Moscow and report that he wouldn't agree to next year's shipment. The Czar will be outraged. One stallion out of Whitefire is all I would need to breed my own horses. Think about it, Katerina. We could go to Kiev and breed the horses as your father does here on the steppe. One stallion, that's all we would need."

"No, darling, that is not all you would need. There's more to it than you think," she said, nibbling on his ear.

"The breeding of the pure whites is a science . . . a . . . Never mind, it is not for me to say."

"Perhaps, if we were to marry, your father would give us a stallion as a wedding gift," Yuri teased lightly as he ran his hand over her thigh. "I haven't seen the stallions, where are they kept?" he said, crushing his lips to hers. "Tell me, darling, so that when I go back to the Czar I can tell him I've seen the magnificent beasts." Her senses were reeling, her body was full of desire, but still something managed to worm its way into her subconscious. "Whitefire and Wildflower are here under guard," she whispered.

Yuri clasped her head in his two hands and drew her to him. "Where is Whitefire?" he questioned.

"Only my father . . ." She felt herself being lifted from the ground as a deep roar of outrage thundered in the quiet night. She saw a heavy pouch sail through the air and land at Yuri's side.

"There will be no horses for the Czar. I'll leave it to you to make a suitable explanation. You have but minutes to ride from this village. One moment longer than I deem necessary and every Cossack in this village will be on your trail. Get dressed, Katerina," Katlof said coldly, "you betrayed us—the Cossack heritage. And for what? For the lust of this Russian. Fool!" He spat angrily. "He holds your naked body to his and questions you about our secret, and for the pleasure of his body you betray us. Don't deny it. I heard him ask you and I heard you answer him." His eyes full of hate, he stood back and spat on her.

Yuri was on his feet instantly, his eyes full of murder as he lunged at the Cossack chief. They tussled on the ground, and within minutes the Russian was pinned beneath the hetman's powerful hands.

"I said minutes and I meant minutes! If you wish to waste them fighting with me, that's your business, but you've been warned."

"Father, you are—" Crack! Katerina stumbled backward,

her hand clasped to her cheek. Again she tried. "You're mista—" This time she landed on the ground, sprawling awkwardly next to Yuri, who was struggling to his feet.

"She told me nothing. It's true that I asked, but she divulged nothing," Yuri said harshly. "She's telling you the truth."

"All Russians are known for their lies," the Kat said coldly. "My daughter is my affair, not yours. Never yours," he said vehemently.

His face full of rage, Yuri looked at the Cossack a moment and then at Katerina. "I meant what I said. I'll be back for you at the end of summer. If you choose to go with me, I'll keep the promise I made to you. If you choose to stay with this . . . this . . . barbarian, then I will understand."

"Take me with you," Katerina pleaded tearfully.

"It isn't possible now. I said I'll return and I will. You must trust me."

"I'll count the days myself," the Kat sneered. He looked down at his tearful daughter and said coldly, "He got what he wanted and he won't be back. We'll count the days together."

Yuri, now fully clothed, jumped upon his horse and rode from the camp. Some distance out, he shouted, "Remember what I said, I'll return!"

The ride back to the village was unbearable. Katerina dared not look back to catch one last glimpse of Yuri, and she didn't dare look at her father. They rode to Volin in deafening silence.

Before retiring, Katlof informed Katerina in as few words as possible that in the morning she would stand trial before the council. Katlof knew what the outcome would be if she was found guilty, but he had to put his feelings aside and allow the justice of the Cossacks to prevail.

A Cossack escorted Katerina into the hall and down to the semicircular table where the men sat. She stood solemnly before her father and the council. Katlof's eyes bored into her as he stood, magnificent in his full-dress Cossack uniform. The somber panel, six men on the left and six men on the right of the hetman, wearing ankle-length caftans, boots, and black sheepskin hats, sat and waited. Her father stared at her with loathing as he spoke. "Katerina Vaschenko, you stand accused of breaking the tribal law of chastity, and the tribal law of silence regarding the secret bloodline of the Cosars. Do you have anything to say before we pronounce your sentence?"

"Yes, Fa . . . yes, my hetman, I'm not guilty."

Katlof lost control of himself for a moment. "Not guilty! You, who betrayed your heritage! You, who lay in the arms of a Russian emissary who asked questions that you eagerly answered! You, who in your wild lust betrayed God Himself!"

Within moments she was reduced to jelly, her amber eyes pleading for understanding.

"Papa!" she screamed. "That's not true! I didn't tell the secret! It's true that I lusted after the Russian and it's true I lay in his arms, but I didn't tell the secret. When Yuri gets to Moscow, the only report he can give the Czar is that he made love to me. Why . . . why won't you believe me?"

She looked at each member of the council and knew that they believed her father. She had been accused, tried, and found guilty by all. The council offered no resistance to Katlof's feelings or his judgments.

"I have spoken with the men of the council and all are agreed: you are guilty. Step forward to hear your sentence, Katerina. It is the judgment of the council that since you broke the law of silence, you will not speak to anyone and no one will be permitted to speak to you. You may stay in Volin and in our hut, and may continue to work with the Cosars. This is your punishment, and from this moment until the Feast of Christmas, silence will be your bedfellow."

Katerina turned and walked proudly away and proclaimed,

"I am a Cossack through and through and would never, never, even under the penalty of death, reveal any of our secrets. I have never lied to you, my father. What I say is the truth. If you wish to carry out this sentence because I lay with the Russian, then do so, but it is the only thing I'm guilty of. The mating secret of Whitefire is safe; I didn't divulge it. Be fair and just in your sentencing, Father. Sentence me for what I did, not what you think I did!" she cried brokenly.

Katlof's expression was cold and indifferent. "No more words! Go in silence!" he shouted harshly.

Dejected and alone, Katerina walked from the hall and headed to the barn and the mares. At least she still had the animals; they still loved her.

Spring gave way to summer, and the days passed quickly for the villagers, who were busy with the horses and farms. The grasslands sang with activity. Horses could be seen everywhere on the plains, under watchful eyes. The steppe, now dressed in a myriad of full color, was dazzling to the eye. The tall, swaying stalks of wheat, barley, and oats created the illusion of shimmering gold, while the broad stripes of green-leafed and multicolored vegetables painted a dazzling mosaic. This was what Katerina loved about the steppe. It was a place to be proud of, a place in which to feel deeply about the land and her people. When she was not in the barn tending the horses, she rode or walked through this wonderland of color. With no one to talk with, the time to summer's end was agonizing. Occasionally, when no one was looking, Stepan would slip a note to Katerina, telling her he adored her and was her friend forever. It helped ease the days and her tormented mind. During the day, without someone to talk to, to distract her thoughts, her mind was constantly invaded by Yuri and his promise to come for her. In the darkest hours of the night the Mongol continued to pursue her.

Chapter 5

Katerina looked around the enclosure that held the alabaster mares and smiled slightly. This was the time of day she liked best: the hour before twilight, which cloaked the bustling Don Cossack village of Volin with its velvety mantle of darkness.

The sweet, pungent smell of horseflesh permeated the air as Katerina leaned into the pen. The fillies and colts trotted to the rail fence, vying for the slim girl's attention. A long-legged colt nuzzled her delicate outstretched hand, looking for an apple. Katerina laughed softly as the young animal's mother gently nosed him away from the fence. Secure in the knowledge that her offspring was taken care of, the mare swished her tail and tried to pry open Katerina's hand. "Very well, you may have the apple, but only because you're so exquisitely beautiful," she crooned, opening her fingers. The mare took the fruit and held it gently in her mouth as she trotted away in search of the colt.

Katerina settled herself on a trough and tried to shake the uneasiness that had settled between her shoulders. Whatever it was that was disturbing her was having its effect on the mares, for they, too, were skittish, and clustered to-

gether in small groups. Perhaps a wild animal has worked
its way into the pen, she thought nervously. Any other day,
any other time, she would have been able to shake off this
peculiar feeling, which was becoming more pronounced.
The horses gathered closer still, whinnying softly and pawing nervously at the ground, their thick, lush tails swinging
furiously.

Did they sense that tomorrow at the first rays of the sun
they would start the journey to their winter quarters? That
had to be the reason. What other could there be, she ratio-
nalized uneasily.

The catlike hazel eyes narrowed as Katerina strained to
look deeper into the enclosure to see if anything, save the
mares, moved. "Anything on four legs, that is," she said
quietly to herself. Her voice was a thick, rich purr. The
horses became quiet and began to separate. She leaned back
again, her eyes scanning the quiet village. This past month
her father had avoided her as if she carried some dread disease. There were no more quiet evening talks, no more ca-
maraderie between her father and herself. He was distant
and cold. Somehow, before morning she had to make things
right between them, before they began the journey to the
House of the Kat. Things had to be settled between them
before they were quartered together for the winter in the
Carpathians.

She shook her head, and the copper-colored curls, free of
their pins, tumbled to her shoulders. She brushed them
away impatiently to clear her vision. Her body stiffened at
an unfamiliar sound, like that of a knife being scraped
against new leather. It made her think of her father's raspy
voice when he had sentenced her.

One of the mares kicked up her hind legs and began to
circle the pen, snorting and flicking her plumed tail. Papa
should be here, he had a sixth sense where the horses were
concerned. If something was wrong, he should be told. She
knew he was in the barns with the other men, readying the

wagons for tomorrow's journey. She postponed the moment when she would have to go to him and tell him something was wrong. How could she bear to see the hurt and the hostility in his eyes? How could she accept the fact that, in his heart, he thought she had betrayed him? She couldn't. She had tried, but her tongue became thick and refused to do her bidding. When she tried to explain, tried to convince him that he was wrong, she was not talking to her father but to the Kat, the head of the Don Cossack village. She wasn't answering to her father but to the chief of the Cossacks.

Katerina blinked, driving the hateful memory from her mind as one of the creamy mares again pranced nervously around the pen, snorting and scraping the dirt in a near frenzy. He should have killed me, she thought bitterly. Anything was better than being ostracized by her own people. With each passing day she felt as if she were dying slowly, inch by inch. Yuri, Yuri, she cried silently. Where are you; why haven't you come for me as you promised? You said you would return at the end of the summer and take me back to Moscow with you. You said you loved me. Is my father right, did you make love to me so I would tell you the secret of Whitefire? Was it true?

"No!" she screamed as she ran from the mares' pen down through the dusty road and out to the fields. She ran till there was no breath left in her body. Twice she fell, and twice she staggered to her feet and kept running. She flew from the eyes, from the horses, from the Kat and from her father. She had to keep running and never stop. When Yuri came, and he would come, they would be gone. Back to the Carpathians, where he would never be able to find her.

She fell to the ground and sobbed, great racking tears that shook her slender body. Finally, drying her face, she sat up and looked around. How long had she stayed here? How far had she come? What did it matter? What did anything matter now? There wasn't one person who cared what she did or where she went. Not anymore. She was alone. If she allowed her father to have his way, she would always be alone. Branded a traitor by every Cossack on the steppe, she could never again take her rightful place in the Don village.

Katerina looked at the minuscule stars overhead and knew she had stayed away too long. It was time to see her father and make one last effort to make him understand. There must be trust between us, she cried silently. Still she didn't move. Her eyes closed wearily as she lay back on the thick grass.

The tall reeds were still, their slender shafts straight and supple in the gentle night air. Nothing stirred, save the snake-like movements of the Terek Cossacks as they crawled on their bellies through the shoulder-high stalks. The moment the moon took cover behind approaching storm clouds, the Tereks infiltrated the grasses. Each man crawled with his knife clutched between his teeth. They made no sign, nor did they disturb the graceful lengths of greenery that hid them and kept their presence secret from the Don Cossacks. Each man bore a sense of pride as he crawled. This was the closest any man had ever come to the village of Volin, except for the horse traders and buyers. Gregory Bohacky was right, his timing was incredible. The lonely nights they had ridden to get to the outer perimeters of the village, and then sat sentinel, were finally going to be rewarded. After tonight the village would be no more; the Cosars would belong to the Tereks and then to the highest bidder, Czar Ivan.

Gregory lay still, barely inches from the fences that encircled the compound. Still shielded by the tall grasses, he could hear the men of Volin brawling and shouting boisterously as they consumed jug after jug of vodka. From the sound of the merrymaking, he wagered they had been drinking for days as they prepared for their departure to the Carpathians. He listened for Katlof and smirked when he heard him drunkenly address one of his men. He was the only man to worry about. If the hetman was sodden, the others would be in even worse condition. They would be able to wield a weapon, but not with any accuracy. Gregory knew in his gut that his men could cut down the entire village and be back in their own quarters within a short time.

He cast an anxious eye overhead to see if the threatening storm clouds would continue to give him cover. His long body relaxed in the grass as he pondered his next move.

To his left and standing sentry outside the wall surrounding the compound a guard argued vehemently with a Cossack youth. "Someone has to be alert. What you're doing is a disgrace to the village. All of you are so drunk you can barely stand. You're a disgrace to our forefathers."

"Bah, you talk like an old woman. This is a night for pleasure and celebrating. All the wagons are loaded, the horses have been readied for hours, and the houses will soon be closed for the winter. If the hetman says we can drink, then we can drink," the young man said drunkenly as he brought a bottle to his lips and drank greedily. "The Kat said to bring you this jug, but since you don't want it, I'll drink it myself." The youth laughed raucously as he toppled from the wall, alcohol spilling over his face.

The guard looked at him and felt only disgust. One of the horses whickered, and his head jerked upright. He knew that sound, he had been hearing it for hours. It didn't come from an animal, at least not one with four legs. Should he leave his post and report what he thought he knew? And to whom? he asked himself. The Kat was in no condition to hear what he said, let alone make a decision. One other guard stood at his post on the far side of the compound. Should he venture over there and ask him if he, too, had heard the noise and if he realized what it meant? An ominous feeling crept up his spine. No matter what, a Cossack never left his post. There it was again. The soft whicker and then an even softer one in reply. He peered into the velvety darkness and could see nothing. He looked down at the prone young Cossack and cursed long and loud.

A wild whoop was heard; the guard's hand automatically came up with his sword outstretched in front of him. He was cut down from behind before he could move. Everywhere wild shouts and curses filled the air as men struggled and fought. The Don Cossacks, in their drunken condition, were no match for the trim, hard-fighting Tereks with only one thought in mind: the Cosars!

Katlof reeled drunkenly toward the fire, where his sword rested among the others. His hand reached for his saber; just as his fingers closed over the hilt, he felt a blade strike him across the back between his shoulders. He dropped to his knees. As he cried out to his people, "Run! Hide!" blood gushed from his mouth.

Women and children fell beneath the savage onslaught, the Tereks merciless in their attack. Katlof watched in horror as a small child crawled away from his dead mother's arms toward the fire. He reached out a hand as a wild-eyed Terek scooped up the child and tossed him into the roaring inferno. He died with the child's agonized screams ringing in his ears. It was over in a matter of moments.

Gregory stood near the fire on top of one of the loaded wagons, his arm held high above his head in a show of victory. A wild cry rang out as the men reached to pull their leader to the ground. "Ready the horses and burn these wagons after you confiscate the supplies. We can use them ourselves. And don't forget the vodka, we'll do our own celebrating when we return to camp. We did what no Russian has been able to do!" he shouted arrogantly. "We now own the Cosars. Czar Ivan will be proud of us!" A lusty shout of approval rang through the blood-soaked night.

"Are they all dead?" one of Gregory's men shouted.

"Every last bitch and bastard!" came a hoarse shout in reply.

Gregory smiled to himself as the moon slid behind its hiding place, storm clouds moving on. With a wicked flourish of his sword and a wild cry of victory, Gregory spurred the horse beneath him, his men thundering behind him as they rode victoriously from Volin.

When Gregory Bohacky turned his head, those mounted behind glimpsed his heavily greased mustache. No one ever joked about the corkscrew curl at each end, as Gregory's mustache was his manhood, his pride and joy. Many words were spoken about it in jest behind his back, where he would never overhear, but nobody ever uttered a demeaning word to his face. To his face, only words of adoration or praise, if one valued one's head.

The pale moonlight silhouetted the hard outline of his profile as he looked over his shoulder. A sheepskin hat sat on top of his black, curly hair, which circled his chiseled face, emphasizing the small, shrewd blue eyes set upon high-boned cheeks that were separated by a large, aquiline nose. The one redeeming feature that made him attractive to women was his full, sensuous mouth and the voice within. His commands held an authoritative manner, leaving no doubt that he meant what he said. But when he wooed the lovelies of his choice, his resonant voice was a choir singing the Gregorian chants, compelling and hypnotizing, so soothing that surrender was a gift of thanks, gladly and freely given to him. Gregory Bohacky, a warrior among warriors, a man among men, was so respected by those under him that he inspired complete obedience.

Gregory twisted in the saddle, raising his hand upward, signaling his men to stop. "The hour grows late and soon our village will be in view. Our families will be asleep, but tonight when we arrive, the thunder of the Cosar hooves, along with our cries of joy, will awaken everyone. Tonight our mir will ring with joy, music, and dancing, and the vodka will flow like the Dnieper. Tonight we'll celebrate our victory and conquest, stopping only when we all fall unconscious. We have done what others only dreamed of doing—we captured the Cosars from the Don Cossacks!" A loud roar of approval boomed from the warriors, almost stampeding the horses.

"Keep those beauties calm and quiet, my brothers, we mustn't lose them now. As happy as I am, I'll behead any man who lets one horse escape!"

The threat of the Don Cossacks coming after them was as nonexistent as the lives of the people of Volin. Secure in this knowledge, the Tereks broke into a Cossack song of victory, their voices filling the night air with a melody of joy.

Gregory, at the water's edge of the Dnieper, reined in his horse and instructed his men, "As we cross the river, carefully lead the Cosars through the rocks, for lame horses are of no value to anyone. When we are once again on our island of Khortitsa, I'll personally check the animals, and someone will pay with his life if one lame Cosar is found."

Restraining his stallion, Gregory waited on the bank as the Cossacks led the horses through the shallow waters. He smiled to himself as he watched. Never had he seen his rough men handle anything or anyone as gently as they handled the Cosars; not even their women were afforded such tenderness. The mothers of the village would mock us forever if they witnessed this scene, he thought.

As they left the banks of the Dnieper behind, the faint outline of their huts came into view. Gregory felt a warm glow sweep over him; it was good to be home. Returning this time was that much sweeter, for he would be proclaimed a hero. The gutting of Volin and his victorious capture of the horses would have the mir celebrating for days, and the men would talk of his exploits for years after his death. Gregory Bohacky would be a folk hero in Russian history, and the Tereks would sing his praises across the vast, endless steppe of the Ukraine. He trembled as he envisioned his welcome from the moment his stallion's hoof first crossed the village entrance. The anticipation telegraphed itself to his legs as he dug his heels into the animal's flanks, driving him into a full canter. His men sensed his eagerness and rode rapidly behind him, the Cosars driven along with them.

A guard hidden from view called out, "Is that you, comrade Bohacky? If it is, show yourself."

Stepping forward into the light of a blazing campfire, Gregory answered, "Yes, comrade, it is Bohacky."

"What do you bring with you? I see many black objects in the distance," remarked the guard as he stepped from behind the high wooden wall that surrounded the camp.

"Those black objects you see in the darkness are white objects, and those white objects are the famous Cosar horses. The whole lot of them from the village of Volin!"

"You joke, Gregory! It can't be. The Cosars belong to the Don Cossacks. They would never let them go."

"They didn't let them go, comrade, we captured them!"

"But the Don Cossacks? I don't understand, you must be making jokes!"

"Comrade, I never make jokes. The Cosars now belong to the Tereks. The Don Cossacks of Volin are no more! We killed every last one of them. No one will come chasing after us for the horses; we saw to that!"

The guard shook his head in disbelief.

"Are our people asleep?" asked Gregory.

"All is quiet. With only four hours before dawn, the warm beds hold fast our people."

"Comrade, wake them from their sleep and tell, no, shout the good news! Tell them Gregory Bohacky has returned triumphant from Volin with the Cosars! Tonight we begin the celebration. Wake the women and have them prepare food for the victory feast. Wake everyone and tell them!"

"Yes, comrade!"

"Then why are you standing here looking at me? Wake

everyone. We'll drive the Cosars through the village to help you. Move, comrade!" he shouted.

The guard mounted his horse, galloping down the roads, shouting as he went, "Wake up, wake up, Gregory Bohacky has returned from Volin with the Cosars! Wake up, wake up! The Cosars are here! Tonight we celebrate!"

The commotion woke Yuri. He arose from his bed, opened the door, and listened.

"The Cosars are ours! Volin is no more!" shouted the men.

Yuri couldn't believe what he heard. His mind reeled as he tried to think. "Katerina, I must go to Katerina . . . she can't be . . . I must get dressed."

Within moments, he was outside his host's hut looking for a horse.

"Ah! Yuri, my friend, I see you have heard the good news," shouted Gregory above the din.

"I must have a horse!"

"A horse? You shall have one and anything else you may want this night," exclaimed Gregory happily, as he motioned to a Terek to bring a horse.

"Before I go—"

"Go where?"

"You must tell me what happened at Volin. What do they mean, Volin is no more?" Yuri asked hesitantly, afraid to hear the answer.

"I am a hero now comrade. You have shared the hut of a Terek legend this summer," Bohacky boasted.

Impatient, Yuri lost control. "I demand you tell me what happened at Volin!"

"I'll gladly tell you. We took the Dons, slaughtered all the people, and burned the village to the ground. The Tereks are proud Cossacks now."

"Proud? You slaughter a village and you're proud? What of Katerina? Did you kill her, too? You knew how I felt about her, how could you do this? She was all I had left. Your hospitality is no longer needed by me."

He jumped on the back of the waiting horse and disappeared into the night, the words of Gregory echoing in his head.

Still seated atop his stallion, Bohacky laughingly mocked Yuri's words and said, "Bah, women! Tonight's victory is all we'll ever need." He turned from the darkness and looked at his village and watched as shuttered windows flew open and candlelight peeped out at the night. Heads appeared in windows and hands rubbed away the sleep.

The Tereks quickly donned their tunics as the women scurried for their sarafans, and within minutes the men were out in the village circle, throwing wood on the campfire to brighten the area. Gregory ordered the women to prepare poppy cakes and kasha and sausage, and to ready a sheep and a goat for roasting on the spit. "Bring on the vodka, beer, and forty-year-old mead."

The handful of women in Khortitsa worked feverishly to cook the food for the carousing men, knowing that when they finished they would be allowed to return to their huts. Once inside, they would whisper among themselves of the night's events, not venturing outside until the men had fallen into a drunken stupor.

Khortitsa was a village of men. The women who were allowed to stay were middle-aged, forgotten and old before their time, forsaken by their husbands for the saber and life of the Cossack. Other tribes whispered about Khortitsa and its savage breed of Cossacks, the misfits of life: the killers, robbers, escaped prisoners, rapists, and political escapees. Khortitsa was a stewpot of vicious, cunning men. Cossacks who lived for the saber and the horse. There were no rules in the village. Rules were made for others, not for the Terek. Freedom was their motto, their life.

The few daughters born in the village were quickly sent

off to the Crimea for safety, the threat of rape and death hanging over them if they were allowed to stay, but when a male child was born a celebration was held which lasted for three days. When a boy reached eight, a saber was thrust into his hands and his training as a Cossack began in earnest. At the age of twelve, he was expected to perform as well as any man, and when he reached eighteen he was given his fighting outfit—wide trousers of pleats and folds, drawn in with a golden cord, boots of morocco leather, a Cossack coat of bright crimson cloth, and a sash, gaily patterned, into which went an embossed Turkish pistol and a saber. His hat was a black, gold-topped astrakhan cap. In his battle attire he was a Cossack to be feared, and his forging would come in the fires of his first battle.

Campfires burned brightly along the roads of the village as the men ate, celebrated, and drank. The guards watched enviously, knowing their turn would come to join the merrymaking when some of the men sobered. For now their only concern was the safety and well-being of the Cosars in the compound, under heavy guard. They could eat till they burst, but they couldn't drink.

That night, and for several nights thereafter, the Terek celebrated the capture of their golden treasure—the Cosar horses—every pound worth its weight in gold.

Yuri Zhuk lay in the thicket and knew he was dying. Never a religious man, he prayed, in his brief moments of lucidity, that his end would be quick and merciful. A wild fever raged through his body, and his dark eyes were glazed with a thin white film. The pain in his throat and neck was so intense, he began to pound the earth where he lay. He had heard of others that lived with no tongue, but he had no desire to be one of them. He blinked as pain shot up his arm. For a moment he had forgotten the loss of his fingers. Blood spurted from the severed stumps of his hands, and he wanted to cry out, but he didn't. Instead he rolled over and crushed his face into the welcoming dirt, the brush and twigs crackling with his movements. He wanted to savor this moment of clarity before he died. He wanted to remember how it was, and he wanted to remember Katerina's face. If God chooses to smile upon me, perhaps the pleasant thoughts will drive away the pain, he thought as his mind wandered back in time.

What a fool he had been. The moment he rode from the Cossack camp he should have known that they would come after him. How confident, how arrogant he had felt when he had ridden out onto the steppe at the end of spring. There had only been one thought in his mind: spend the summer cementing ties with Ivan's allies on the steppe, get back to Russia, make up some story for the Czar to explain his failure, and return for Katerina.

He knew he was being followed even now, months later, though he heard no sound. The fine hairs on the back of his neck prickled, and that was all the warning he needed. Making camp for the night at the first sign of dusk, he was certain that eyes watched him. Only once in the short time he waited for the Cossack did he have any feeling of panic. He had been trained well in the Czar's army before his advancement to his present position and he would give a good accounting of himself, of that he was certain.

The two Cossacks had ridden boldly into his camp as soon as darkness settled. The only light was the small, flickering campfire, which threw the two riders into ghastly, eerie shadows. Yuri had waited for what he knew was coming. Oles, the young Cossack from the village, had walked over to the fire and stood looking down at the Russian. From where he lay Yuri could see the wild gleam in his eye as he made a motion for his companion to dismount. When both men stood towering over him, Yuri rose to his feet, his saber held loosely in his hand. "What do you want here at this time of night?" he asked harshly.

Oles and his friend stared at the Russian, their faces cold, dark, and forbidding. Yuri felt a twinge of fright. One man he could handle, but two Cossacks was something he hadn't planned on. They would fight by their own rules, not the rules he had been trained under.

"The Kat ordered your death. We were selected to carry out the order. You crept into our camp and tried to steal our secrets and then ravaged the hetman's daughter. Your death is to be slow and painful. The secrets of our village will never find their way to Moscow and that lunatic Czar you serve under. We have finally succeeded in tracking you after all these weeks. Your tongue is to be removed and then your hands," Oles said coldly.

"Secrets be damned!" Yuri shouted. "It isn't Katerina that is making you do this. I didn't ravage her; she came to me of her own free will. I don't expect you to believe me, but she didn't tell me any secrets, and if she had, I wouldn't divulge them to the Czar. I love her and want to marry her. My plans are to return to Moscow and settle things, and then I am coming back for Katerina."

"You lie; all Russians lie. The Kat said you lie, and that is all we need to know. Even if you somehow managed to escape us and return to Moscow, you would be too late. We leave for the mountains on the last day of August. There is no way you could find your way into the Carpathians once the snows come. You were doomed from the moment you rode into our village."

So intent were the three men on their conversation that they heard nothing until a wild whoop split the soft, dark night. Yuri backed away from the flickering fire as a dozen men converged into the semidarkness with sabers drawn and evil smiles on their faces, Oles swiveled and immediately brought up his saber as he danced around the tiny fire. Iron clanked against iron as the three men fought for their lives. They were outnumbered, and Yuri watched as the valiant Cossacks lost their heads with wicked sweeps of the strangers' sabers. He threw down his saber and waited.

"Who are you?" he demanded.

"Your executioners." One of the men laughed. "Surround him," the leader ordered his men, "and lash him to the horse. Throw those heads into a sack so they can be returned to Gregory."

Katerina jumped to her feet; she had to get back to the village. Her father was right. Yuri had not come and summer was over. Had the Czar put him in prison when he failed to deliver his contract for the pure whites out of Whitefire? Had the Kat sent someone after Yuri and killed him? She would never know. Tomorrow they would go to the mountains, and that would end any remaining hopes.

Her eyes were wild as she looked around the grassy copse and lashed out at the gnarled old tree with her booted foot. Now she would never know if he had lied or not.

It would soon be dawn and time to start for the mountains, and still she hadn't talked with her father. No, there was no point in trying to talk to her father now.

It was a night made for lovers, but Katerina didn't notice the warm, scented air or the star-filled night as the moon crept from behind its hiding place, lighting up the steppe as she trudged along the grassy field. She welcomed the indigo darkness when the moon slipped behind the cloud. The inky blackness was her ally, her confidant.

Blinded with tears, she skirted a small outgrowth of shrubbery and raised her eyes when a high-pitched wail reached her ears. She wiped at her eyes, and for the first time was aware of the smoke on the road and around the pens. They were gone! All the horses were gone! Everyone was dead! All around the compounds and enclosures lay the lifeless bodies of the Cossacks. The buildings were burned and gutted, the stables nothing but smoldering ashes. "Father!" she screamed.

"He's over here."

Katerina whirled at the sound of the voice and ran to

where an old woman, leaning heavily on a cane, pointed. She dropped to her knees and gathered her father to her, crying openly. "Tell me what happened—who did this?"

"You know who did this!" the old woman shouted malevolently. "You are responsible!"

"No! No! I was over by the copse. I didn't know. I heard nothing, saw nothing. Who did this?"

"They're all dead! The horses are all gone. Soon I'll die like the others." The old crone cackled as she opened her shawl to show a large, gaping wound in her side. "They thought I was dead when they left."

"Who? Tell me, who did this?" Katerina screamed.

"Your own father said you were a traitor to our people. You ask me who did this? It was the Terek Cossacks that rode into this camp, but it was your Russian that made it possible. With the horses, they could do nothing. Even with the two stallions, Snowfire and Wildfire, they could not breed, but you told the Russian the secret and now it's over. Your heritage is gone! Your father lies dead! My husband and my three sons lie dead!" She coughed suddenly, and a bright stream of blood spurted from her dry, cracked lips. "Look around you, traitor, and see what your lusting ways have done. Bah!" she said, waving the stick she carried in the air. "He did not come for you as he promised. He will never come for you! Your father sent men after him when he left here. They were ordered to cut out his tongue and cut off his hands. Now he can never tell the secret."

"You lie! The children, the women, where are they?"

The old woman cackled insanely. "Dead. All of them. I am the only one left, and soon I will die and you will be the only one alive. What will you do? How will you live with this on your soul?"

How can this have happened? Katerina cried silently. "Where were our glorious fighters, where were all the glorious Cossacks?" she demanded bitterly of the woman. "Drunk with vodka water? Look at me!" she commanded the old woman. "They were drunk, weren't they? Once we started the trip to the mountains, there would be no vodka during the trip and none at my father's house. Speak the truth before you die, old woman!"

"They fought superbly," the woman said weakly. "There was none that did not rise to the battle. They died valiantly. And for what? To save the horses for you. For you, because you are your father's daughter." Suddenly she lashed out with her stout stick and brought it down on Katerina's arm. The pain was excruciating, but Katerina made no sound as she watched the old woman fall to the ground.

Katerina crawled over to the old woman and gently closed her eyes. "I didn't betray my father or my people," she whispered.

There was a chill in the early-morning air as she waited for the sun to come up. Only her eyes moved.

When the sun was high in the sky and the last drop of dew was scorched from the lush grass, she still sat. She stared at her father and at the others and did nothing. The pain in her arm was wild, and she welcomed it. It would keep her sane and remind her of what had happened.

She was hungry and thirsty, but still she didn't move. Food would lodge in her throat and choke her, water would make her vomit.

By sundown the pain in her arm was alive and fierce. Her lips were dry and parched from sitting in the open sun all day. Still she sat, her eyes going from body to body and then back to her father.

At dawn the following day, the stench of the dead bodies forced her to her feet. Hobbling to the water trough, she wet her lips with her hand and smeared water over her face, wiping it on the shoulder of her dress. She had to do something about the bodies. Carefully she explored her injured arm, feeling to see if any bones were broken. She could move it, but just barely. Another day and Mikhailo would know something was wrong when the caravan didn't arrive in the mountains. He would ride down on horseback to see if something was wrong. But the dead had to be taken care of. The bodies would have to go into a drainage pit; when Mikhailo came, he could cover it over and give the necessary eulogy. There was no other way. She bit into her full lower lip till the blood spurted. Her amber eyes went to the pit at the far side of the enclosure and back to the dead bodies. She would have to drag them one by one till they were all taken care of.

A grim look on her face, the cinnamon eyes narrowed against the bright sun, she started her grisly chore. Her arms felt as if they were being pulled from their sockets as she dragged body after body to the pit. Her legs gave out once and she collapsed, falling onto Olga's corpse. She screamed and quickly rolled over as a gurgling sound from the body split the quiet air around her. If there was one thing she could be thankful for it was that Stepan had returned to the mountains to alert Mikhailo of their coming.

This is my punishment for lying with a man, she said over and over to herself as she rose to drag another friend's body to the pit. I am guilty of nothing except lying with a man. I will pay the price because I want to live. "I'll drag everyone to the pit if it kills me," she said harshly as she bent to grasp a pair of feet in her hands.

Some time later, only her father's body remained. Katerina looked down at him, her face expressionless. How could she drag him through the road like a sack of flour? The same way you dragged the others, a voice inside her answered.

Savagely, she bent to grasp the big man under the armpits, her injured arm sending shooting pains down the side of her body. She clenched her teeth and began to pull him down the length of the road. Tears of pain and sorrow trailed down her cheeks as she cried over and over, "I did not betray our people! I harmed no one but myself." Over and over she repeated the words until she came to the pit. "I did nothing,

Father," she said quietly as she pushed his body in with the others. "Forgive me for what you thought I did. I forgive you," she cried brokenly as she collapsed at the edge of the cavernous hole.

Mikhailo, the horse trainer from the House of the Kat, found her a day later, feverish and muttering in delirium.

He looked around the devastated village and then at the girl. He shook his shaggy gray head as he picked her up gently and laid her down beneath the shade of a tree and sponged off her dirty face. From his saddlebags he lifted a goatskin and poured a trickle of vodka into her mouth, waiting for her to swallow. Her eyes opened, and at the sight of the old, weather-beaten face she sighed and slept. Mikhailo bound the injured arm in a splint and sat back, waiting for her to wake again.

Angry at what he did not understand, the old man made a small fire and boiled some water. Carefully he added herbs and waited for the water to boil again. When it cooled, he would give it to Katerina for her fever. More than that he could not do.

From time to time he would lay his hand on her brow and then spoon the herb tea into her mouth. She muttered and thrashed about, then would lie still, the dark lashes like smudges of soot on her pale cheeks.

She was sleeping peacefully, a natural sleep; the fever had broken. He walked around the village, hoping that some explanation would rear up at him. From the countless blood-crusted weapons that lay upon the bloody roads, it was evident that the village had been attacked. Who? Was it some nameless tribe? The horses and the mares were gone. Thank God Whitefire and Stepan were already in the mountains. He knew why, there was no point in asking himself that question. There wasn't a man, a Cossack, a soldier of a Czar, that wouldn't pay, and pay handsomely, for the Cosar horses. Men had killed and fought for the horses, and they would kill and fight again.

Mikhailo Kornilo was a small man by Cossack standards, but he was a fighter and had served his tribe well until the day a wild-eyed Tatar severed his leg at the knee with one flourish of his scimitar. Now he had grown stocky with food in his belly three times a day and vodka water at night. He shook his wooden peg leg and cursed all Tatars for what happened. His normally ruddy face was crimson with the expletives he spat out. His straggly gray-and-white beard was sparse as his hands now pulled and tugged at it in anger. His brown eyes traveled around the village and came to rest on the sleeping Katerina. He was her godfather. He remembered how he had dangled her on his knee when she was a baby. Too ugly to take a wife, he had devoted himself to Katlof and his family, and they, in turn, regarded him as one of their own. He gladly would have given his life for any of them, but now it was too late.

One day soon the elder Katmon would die. Already he was preparing for an elaborate funeral. Soon the old man would join Katlof and the other dead Cossacks, leaving only Katerina, Stepan, himself, and the other old people. His eyes lighted for a moment when he remembered that Whitefire was safe in the Carpathian Mountains. If one had to be thankful for small favors, this was the one to be thankful for. Katerina knew the secret. Katerina would rebuild, and he and Stepan would help her. It never entered his mind that the mares were gone, that without Wildflower, the stallion, Whitefire, was just another stallion. He tugged at the straggly beard as he limped back to the sleeping girl.

Three days later Katerina was on her feet, her eyes haunted, her mouth a grim, tight line. "What are we to do, Mikhailo? It will take us ten years to get any breeding stock. Twenty before we have a herd. I've been thinking while I lay here."

"You plan to go to your mother's people, is that what

you're going to tell me? I see it in your eyes. You intend to ask the Khan for help?"

"There is no other way, Mikhailo. I must get the horses. How can I live with this?" she said, waving her arm around what had been Volin. "I have to try. If I fail, then that is something else, but first I must make the effort. I didn't betray our people. You say you believe me. That's all I need to know. Somehow you will make it sound right when you tell Grandfather what happened."

"And the Russian?" It was a question that, up until now, Katerina had refused to think about. Now she would have to bring the matter into the open and discuss it with Mikhailo.

"I loved him. He loved me. Nothing you or anyone else says will ever convince me differently. I don't know what happened. I was told that Father sent two of the men after Yuri to slice out his tongue and cut off his hands so he couldn't divulge the secret. Father would never let him go back to Moscow thinking I gave him the secret. He's dead, Mikhailo. And my father killed him just as surely as if he wielded the weapon himself. I have to try to prove to myself that Yuri was not responsible for what happened. Every Cossack on the steppe will think me guilty, and this must not be allowed to happen. I don't know who or why the raid happened, but I will find out!"

"So you will journey to the Khanate of Sibir, and then what? You're a woman, what can you do?"

"As you know, the Khan is my mother's brother. He'll help me. Sit down, Mikhailo, for what I have to tell you will shock you off your feet."

The old man eyed her warily but sat down, his face full of dread.

"We all know that the Mongols' military strength has deteriorated to the point where they are no longer the fierce warriors they once were. I plan to ask the Khan for men from his prisons to take back with me to the House of the Kat. I will work with them through the winter months and make Cossacks out of them. In the spring we will ride out and seek that which belongs to me—the Cosar horses."

The old man shook his head. "Just like that, eh? The Khan will give you the prisoners, criminals of the worst sort, and you are going to train them to be fighting Cossacks! And then you will set out in search of your horses. You're a woman. What makes you think you can do this, and what makes you think you can make the Khan help you? A Cossack is born, you can't create a Cossack."

"Make no mistake, Mikhailo, as sure as the first wildflower blossoms on the frozen banks of the Dnieper River, a new breed of Cossacks will be born," she said savagely.

"I know in my bones the Khan won't help you," Mikhailo said.

"He'll help me," Katerina said coldly. "And the reason I know I will succeed is because I am my father's daughter. Yes, I'm a woman, but I'm also a Cossack. If it comes to money, I will give the Khan whatever he asks. I will do whatever he wants if he agrees to my plan."

"Criminals! The men are criminals! They'll kill you!" the old man said fearfully.

"Mikhailo, you don't for one second believe that a man, a Mongol, could kill me, do you? Where is the Cossack courage you forced me to cut my teeth on? Have you no faith in my ability? Where else can I get the men? Men that will fight for me? Our village is wiped out; our men are gone. You and I are all that are left, save Grandfather and the elders in the mountains. If you have a better solution I would be happy to hear it."

"I have no thoughts, Katerina. But criminals? How many do you plan to bring back with you?"

"As many as the Khan will give me."

"What if they kill you on the journey home?"

"Mikhailo, they will be shackled together. If I am not worried, then you should not be. It is the only way. I'll leave in the morning, and I'll have to take your horse. When you next see me I shall have my new Cossacks with me. Be gentle with Grandfather when you tell him. Make him understand, please, Mikhailo."

"How can I make him understand when I don't understand myself?" her godfather asked irritably. "Mongols are ugly sons of bitches."

"I hate to remind you, but Mongol blood runs in my veins. You know my mother was a Mongol. I never knew you thought I was ugly," she teased lightly.

"You are beautiful, but Mongols are ugly," the old man said sourly. "Sneaky! Don't turn your back on them or they stick a knife in you. Mark my words."

"Mikhailo, who is better, a Mongol or a Cossack?"

"A Cossack—what sort of question is that?"

"Then you have your answer. I want your promise that you will not worry about me."

"How long?" the old man asked curtly.

"A week's ride each way. Three days at the Mongol camp. I'll be in the mountains before the snows come. My word, Mikhailo, as a Cossack. You'll see me before the snows come. If I'm to get an early start, I must sleep now." She kissed the leathery cheek and lay down. She was asleep immediately.

The sun was coming up and the old man had not closed his eyes once. He watched the sleeping girl who was now a woman with fear in his eyes. She was right; she was her father's daughter. If there was a way to bring the Mongols back to the mountains, she would do it. Never had he seen such a look in anyone's eyes. Not even in Katlof's eyes, and he was the most awesome, the most fearsome of all the Cossacks.

From the time she was able to ride, Katerina had been trained with the others, purely out of indulgence by her famous father. It amused him to see her unseat one of the mighty Cossacks, and then he would sit and drink with her till the sun came up. He would praise her and tell her that she was as good a Cossack as any of his men. Proof of his sincerity was when he bestowed the gelding Bluefire on her when she reached sixteen.

Before it had been for sport, but now it was a matter of survival—Katerina's survival. She was so full of hate and vengeance she would do what she said, and she would win. He was sure of it. When she awoke he turned to her and said, "With your father's death your birthright demands that I now address you as the Kat. You have now been given a grave responsibility, Katerina."

"I knew I was the Kat the moment I walked into the village and saw my father's dead body. There is no need for you to remind me," Katerina said sharply.

Katerina eyed Mikhailo carefully as she swung herself onto the horse. "If I'm to ride all the way to the Khanate of Sibir, these clothes are best. They were all I could find among Stepan's outgrown clothing. A bit small but I'll manage," she said, patting at the skintight trousers that covered her slim haunches. "I'll need the boots for the Urals." The old man eyed her attire solemnly and nodded his shaggy head. He drew in his breath as he watched a button pop on the tight-fitting shirt, exposing a creamy expanse of flesh. He was an old man, what right did he have to voice an opinion of her clothing; and besides, he thought sourly, she wouldn't listen to anything he had to say. From this moment on she would listen to no one save herself. He shrugged his stocky shoulders as he watched her gather the reins in her strong, capable hands.

With one deft movement she had the tawny hair in a twirl and bunched on top of her head. "A safe journey to you, Mikhailo, and remember to be gentle with Grandfather." With a light wave of her hand she was off, the thick leather boots spurring the horse beneath her.

Mikhailo watched horse and rider as they rode with the wind. "And a safe journey to you, Kat," he muttered as he watched the young woman rein in the horse at the top of the rise. She looked back and then kicked the horse again. Would she return? Of course she would; she was her father's daughter, wasn't she? And when she did, she would have a Mongol army with her as she had promised. No, that wasn't right—she would have men, hardened criminals, that would be trained to become an army. A chill washed over him as he pictured her return to the Carpathians with her band of criminals. What in the name of God would Katmon say when he was told? Be gentle with him, the Kat had said. "Ha!" Mikhailo snorted. How does one tell a sick, dying old man that his granddaughter would be arriving with the first snows with a band of Mongol criminals? How was he to tell him that his son was dead; all the Cossacks slaughtered because of . . . This was no time to think of what had happened or what might happen when he returned to the House of the Kat. For now, he had better get these limbs moving if he expected to make the next village by sunset.

With a last look around the gutted village, Mikhailo squared his shoulders and started down the long, dusty road. By nightfall of the following day, he might be back in the mountains. That was all he would think about on his trek.

Katerina rode the gelding as though she were in training. Her slim body was hunched over, her head almost touching the horse's mane. There was no need to spur the russet horse, for he knew he was supposed to run at breakneck speed till the reins were tightened.

When the sun was high, Katerina slowed the obedient animal and let him nibble at the sea of green grass and drink from a bubbling stream. Shielding her eyes from the strong sunlight, she refused to let her mind think of anything except the horse that was eating serenely beneath her. Her eyes raked the quietness around her as she turned, first in one direction and then in another. She had seen no sign of life since starting to keep close to the high growth, off the main roads. Again she let her eyes rake the quiet surroundings. The feeling of eyes boring into her was so strong that she pulled a knife from her belt and moved stealthily into a pile of brush and crouched down. The horse, finished with his munching, reared his head and pawed the ground. So he, too, knows something is wrong, the Kat thought. An animal? A snake perhaps? Two-legged or four-legged? she mused to herself. A slight rustle to her left and she swiveled, the knife grasped firmly in her hand. Crouching lower, she moved from the thicket to open ground and waited, her breath quickening as the gelding paced anxiously. The amber eyes glittered as she crept toward a dense thicket and lashed out with her booted foot, her knife raised high, ready for a deep plunge.

The sight that met her eyes drove her backward, a look of horror on her face. She ran till she reached a tree, which she clasped with all her being to hold her upright. Breathing raggedly, she closed her eyes, tears streaming down her cheeks. Suddenly she struck out with the knife, gouging the tree, shredding the rich brown bark. Again and again she struck out, till the ripe yellow wood beneath the bark gleamed in the bright sunlight. The blade slipped from her hands, and she crumpled to the ground. Great sobs racked her body as she flailed at the hard dirt.

Yuri rolled over and felt himself retch. Thick red blood poured from the gaping hole in his face. He thrashed about in the thicket, praying he wouldn't choke to death. A sound alerted him, and he lay still. Were they coming after him again? He prayed. He tried to move his neck, thinking he could ease the pain, but the heady scent of the wildflowers near him nauseated him and he knew he was going to be sick again. Don't think about it, think of Katerina, he told himself. Think of her beautiful face; remember how soft she felt in your arms. Remember the feel of her lips on yours. Don't think of the barbaric Tereks and don't think of the hatred they have for Katlof and his Don Cossacks. Think only of Katerina. More blood spurted from his mouth as he opened his eyes and looked up at the bright, golden sunshine. My mind must be playing tricks, he thought as Katerina's face came into his field of vision. The end must be near, and God was rewarding him by allowing him the vision of the Cossack girl. A wild animal sound escaped from his wounded throat as in the last moments of lucidity he realized she was real. He had been blessed with staying miraculously alive until he saw her once more. It was this slender hope that had pulled him through nearly a week of pain and delirium. Disbelief and horror danced in her eyes before she turned and ran.

He must not allow her to think her people had done this to him. Somehow he must let her know that it was the Tereks who had severed his tongue and fingers and left him to die when he would not tell that which he had no knowledge of. If only he could communicate that he had suffered for her love. Even if he had known the secret, he would have carried it to his grave before revealing it. Perhaps she would be able to read these things in his eyes. He prayed again; his eyes closed tightly. When he opened them, she was standing over him, tears streaming down her cheeks.

It was Yuri, but only his dark eyes were recognizable. His face was a mass of dry, caked blood, and bloody stumps remained where his hands used to be. Deep gurgling, inhuman sounds escaped from him as his tortured eyes pleaded with her, begged her. She nodded slightly to show she understood. Her words were an agonized whisper: "Did my father's men do this?" Yuri feebly shook his head. When he closed his eyes, her knife found its mark.

Her eyes were cold and bitter as she covered his still body with the brush.

Viciously, she dug her heels into the horse's flanks and galloped across the grassy turf of the endless steppe.

For hours she raced the spirited horse. Her frenzied mood transferred itself to the animal beneath her. She barely noticed when she left the greenery of the wooded steppe and emerged onto the vast wasteland of the endless eastern plain, reaching as far as the eye could see. There was nothing before her but virgin ground until she reached the Urals. The hot, dry wind licked at her face as the scorching, relentless sun beat down upon the tormented woman. She had to get as far away as she could, as fast as she could. She would never look back, not now, not ever. All she knew was that she had one more score to settle. One more reason for going to the Khan.

If her father's men hadn't tracked Yuri, who had? Would Yuri lie to her when he was dying? Had she correctly interpreted the slight, infinitesimal shake of the head? Hot, scorching tears blinded her as she continued with her wild ride.

She felt the beast beneath her gradually slow as she wiped at her glistening eyes. A village. She drew in the reins slowly and let the horse have its head. The gelding entered the town at a fast trot and stopped with no instruction from Katerina. She remained seated.

A Cossack, who walked with a swaggering gait, came over. "Welcome," he said gruffly.

Katerina nodded. Her voice was emotionless as she told him of the raid and the slaughter of her people. The Cossack hetman's eyes widened as he looked at the beautiful woman dressed in a man's clothing. "How could this have happened to Vaschenko?"

Ashamedly, her eyes downcast, the words painfully forced out: "My father and his men were drunk. They never knew what happened." The Cossack shook his head sadly as she straightened up. "I'll be riding for many days, can you spare me provisions?"

The elderly Cossack nodded. He disappeared momentarily into a building, and when he reappeared he held a bulging sack in his hand.

Katerina reached down for the offered food and water,

and with a curt nod of thanks was off, riding as though the devil were at her heels.

Several of the men of the village approached the hetman and looked at him expectantly.

"Let her go. She is one of us. There is the fire of hell driving her. Never have I seen that look in anyone's face. Not even in the Kat's."

"Where is she going?" one of the men asked curiously.

The hetman shrugged. "To hell, to put out that raging inferno that is consuming her." Quietly, he speculatively watched as Katerina rode out into the desolation of the steppe. Where is she going? he wondered. Every Cossack needs a tribe. She has nothing, save an aged grandfather and more old men in that mountain fortress. Finding no answers, the hetman let his mind wander to the Terek Cossacks and wondered vaguely if they were responsible for her people's deaths. He knew in his heart that as she made her way across the steppe the other Cossacks would brand her a renegade. There was no place in the Cossack heritage for a rebel, especially one who was a woman.

Chapter 6

For three days Katerina rode across the parched steppe, stopping only to sleep and to water her horse. On the fourth day she crossed into the Ural Mountains. At the base of the range she stopped the gelding for a moment while she pondered her next move. If I go north where the ridge is narrow and treeless, I'll lose two days. Or I can cross through the southern section, which is laden with trees and much wider. From here, straight across this end, I could be through the mountains in four days. She frowned. It would be easier riding across the north ridge, and would probably take only a day to cross. I could lose four days getting to and from there, and I might ride into the first snow. She decided on a southerly trek; she would risk the steep terrain and thick forest. The Kat saw a pass directly ahead and decided she would ride her horse through the passes and walk the animal over the precipitous slopes. She dug her heels into the animal's flanks and headed for the pass.

She thanked God for the clothing she wore, and especially for the thick boots. Katerina admitted to herself that she was tiring and in need of more food; her sack was almost empty. The boiled potatoes were gone, and all that was left was a small bit of cheese and a chunk of black bread that was so hard she feared she would crack her teeth on it. The food would be gone by nightfall, and then she would have nothing, with four days of travel still to go. She cursed long and loudly to the animal beneath her. "I can live on my hate for as long as it takes me to reach the Khan," she muttered as she rode through the first pass. Moments later, she was confronted with the first steep ridge. She dismounted and walked the horse alongside her. Finding release from her tension by talking to the animal, she continued with her bitter tirade. "When I find him, and I will, I'll carve his heart from his body and hang it on a spear to dry. But first," she said viciously, "I'll cut his tongue from his throat and cut off his feet. Then I'll cut out his heart." Bile rose in her throat as she remembered the feel of the knife in her hands when she plunged it into the center of Yuri's heart. "There will be no pain in my heart when I retaliate for what was done to Yuri and my people. I'll feel only sweet blessed revenge!"

As she and the horse carefully edged their way up the side of the slope, her thoughts continued. Who was it who attacked Yuri? If only I could rid myself of this anger. Was it Father's men or renegade Cossacks? Poor Yuri, why did they have to be so cruel? When I first saw him he seemed so confident, so strong, but seeing him with Father made me realize there was a weakness about him. Was it because he was so young? Was it because he was unsure of himself in dealing with us Cossacks? Even when he made love to me, our union was strong and good together, but I felt something was missing. That elusive feeling must be what I'm yearning for. What is it? I said I would find it in the eyes of the man I want forever. It wasn't in Yuri's eyes. Perhaps that is what they call love? Is that what is missing when animal lust is not enough? The combination of lust and love together must drive one to the gates of heaven. Someday I'll have this feeling; I'll not settle for anything less.

Her thoughts were so intense, she failed to see a low branch hidden by the stygian darkness. She walked straight into it and fell, her feet going out from under her. Her head reeled as she tried to get up. Was it the fall, or was she weak from too little food? Whatever, she had to stop.

She tied the reins of the horse to a tree and lay down on the hard, rock-strewn ground. The pain of the stones beneath her was all she needed to remind her of where she was and where she was going.

Eventually she slept, the rocks digging into her soft flesh. When she awoke, she could barely move, the aching was so intense. She tried flexing her arms and massaging her thighs, trying to work out the shooting sensations that were so severe she had to gasp for breath. Through clenched teeth she muttered over and over, "I need this pain. If I'm to survive, then I must have this pain to make me remember."

Twice more she slipped and fell as she made her way down the mountain grade. The jagged edges of the rock and the scrubby outgrowth of brush tore at her thin shirt, leaving it hanging in tatters on her back.

For the next three days and nights she walked her horse up and down the steep ridges. Whenever a pass opened up, she rode the animal like the wind to make up for the time-consuming climbs. They stopped only to get water from the many streams that trickled through the range from the many rivers up north. Straight ahead should be the Ural River, she reasoned as she rode through the opening of the last pass. "The Ural River means the end of the mountains; it's all flat riding from here," she told the horse as they rested. "We'll pick a shallow spot in the river and be across in no time. After we skirt the town of Troitsk we should be on my uncle's doorstep." Reaching down, she patted the horse on the neck. "My faithful friend, you have brought me a long way; you have done your job well, and I'm grateful to you. When we get to my uncle's camp I'll make sure you are treated to plenty of feed and water."

She pushed on, and soon the Ural River was in sight. She did as she'd promised the horse and found a suitable place to ford. Weary, almost leaning completely forward on the horse, she spurred him onward. As they passed the town of Troitsk she found herself too weak to go on. She stopped the horse and sat leaning forward on the animal's mane. She looked and she listened.

Her eyes burned with lack of sleep and fatigue. Katerina dismounted and waited for the traveler who was approaching so he could make known his name. Barely able to stand erect, she found her vision blurring as the horseman reined in his mount and sat looking down at her in disbelief. She grasped the saddle to steady herself and tried to speak. She wet her parched lips and opened her mouth, but the words wouldn't come. Her head reeled, and she blinked, trying to bring the solitary figure into focus "I need . . ." and then she remembered nothing more.

The man dismounted, his eyes never leaving the woman on the ground. It could be a trick. What was a woman doing here in this godforsaken place? Who was she and what did she want? Why was she traveling alone? He stood a moment, his hands on slim, muscular hips, his indigo eyes speculative as he continued to gaze at the fallen girl. Impatiently he brushed at a sheaf of rich ebony hair that fell over his forehead as he dropped to his knees for a closer inspection. He frowned at the parched lips and at the dirty sunburned face. Strong, square teeth played with a full lower lip as he narrowed his eyes at the array of yellowish-purple bruises that peppered her arms and back. His mouth was a grim, tight white line as he felt his hands go to the thick, luxurious copper hair. How soft it felt. His sun-bronzed hand traced a gentle line around her soft mouth, and she stirred slightly, moaning softly.

A small dark bird fluttered among the branches of the solitary tree as Banyen Amur sat back on his haunches to wait for her to awaken. He was patient; waiting was nothing new to him. He decided that there was nothing wrong with her, save overexertion. She would awaken soon.

When Katerina woke, she was fully aware of where she was and of the man sitting watching her. She watched him for a second through her heavily fringed lashes and felt her heart begin to pound in her chest. She watched him a moment longer as his finger trailed over a jagged scar on his cheek. The pounding in her chest lessened as she remembered how he had come by the scar. The thick lashes parted slightly as she took in his appearance. His loose blouson shirt was deep indigo, almost the color of his eyes, and he wore it tucked into form-fitting black breeches. Soft leather boots rode high on his legs, making the muscles bulge with the softness of the richly polished leather. From her position on the ground she could see the questions in his eyes, the puzzled look on his hard, high-cast face. She lowered her gaze to his long, slender, sun-darkened hands, hands that would be capable of gentling a horse or stroking a woman's flesh. Don't think about that, she cautioned herself. Her eyes still narrowed, she watched him flex his shoulders, the muscles rippling and dancing across his chest. Yuri had been a boy compared to this man.

Katerina struggled to her knees and found herself within inches of him. She looked deeply, piercingly, and saw nothing but blankness. A small sigh escaped her as she was again struck by his sun-bronzed skin and the darkness of his hair. Swallowing hard, she fought to speak, hoping he would not recognize her voice. Why didn't he offer her a drink; was he going to make her ask for water? He was waiting; it was evident in the patient look on his chiseled features. He would want to know who she was and where she was going. This was Mongol territory. "I'm on my way to Sibir to see my uncle, the Khan. I have . . . traveled for . . . for many days. I must see . . . I must see him," she said in a halting voice.

"Why?" The one-word question was harsh and cold.

Katerina didn't like the sudden spark she saw flash in the agate eyes. "That's my . . . my affair."

"And now I'm making it my affair," the man said coolly, almost mockingly.

Katerina's body trembled as she tried to speak. "I must see . . . I must see him . . . I need his help. Please, you must take me to . . . take me to him." She would have fallen with the exertion of speaking except that he gathered her close and held her upright.

"Weak-kneed females, they're all alike," he muttered to himself as he slung her over her horse's back. He gazed at what instinct told him was a supple, pliant body beneath the thick clothing. One of these days he was going to find a woman to his liking, and then he would do the honorable thing and marry her. "I detest swooning, vapid women," he said to his horse as he gathered the reins in his lean, capable hands. So she would be jostled on the ride back to camp; it wouldn't harm her. It would be interesting to see if she really was the Khan's niece. Knowing the old fox as well as he did, he could almost see him bristle with rage when he, Banyen, dumped her in his presence.

As they rode toward the Khan's camp he wondered why this female wanted to see the Khan. It made him remember when he had first come to the Khan for help, after the Russians had wiped out his family and everything they had. What would I have done—for that matter, where would I have gone—if I didn't have Khan Afstar to turn to? Where would other roads have taken me? What would I be doing this very minute and where would I be if I hadn't come to Sibir? It isn't what I want to do with the rest of my life, and it isn't something I enjoy doing right now, but I have no other choice. Someday I'll conquer all that was lost to me, and I'll command my own camp, he thought bitterly. When I have my lands back again, I'll take a wife so I can have many sons to reign after me. It won't be a question of love, just a matter of choosing someone pleasing to my eye and pleasant to be with, when I choose to be with her, and someone who will be a good mother to my children. No man will intimidate my sons.

A noise behind him caused him to turn around.

"Damn you, get me off this horse," Katerina shouted to Banyen's back. "Untie me this moment. Wait till the Khan sees how you bring me into his camp. Untie me, you arrogant bastard!" She shouted to be heard over the horses' clattering hooves.

"In good time, all in good time," Banyen called over his shoulder, a wide grin splitting his face. "Didn't anyone ever tell you that all the good things in life come to those who are patient and quiet?"

Katerina clamped her lips tightly. He was right. All good things, like a knife between his ribs, would be worth waiting for. She seethed as she was jostled with the even gait of the horse.

She must be the Khan's niece; there was a certain resemblance that was reminiscent of the old fox. That and her strong language. She seemed to have the tongue of a viper. A match for the aging Khan. He wondered if she would be so feisty when he got her into his bed. It never occurred to him to doubt the inevitable. From the moment he set eyes on her he was relishing the feel of her naked body against his. A little on the scrawny side, but the Khan could fatten her up and then he would take his pleasure. Now what in all hell could she be traveling this terrain for, and what did she want with the Khan? He knew in his gut it would turn out to be something not to his liking.

From her undignified position on the horse, Banyen's muscular thigh and his booted foot were all she could see as she fought to keep her head from bobbing about. Her neck was stiff, and her stomach was beginning to feel queasy. "How much farther is it?" she shouted.

"I thought I told you to be quiet. When we arrive at the camp you'll be the first to know," Banyen called back.

"You insufferable—"

"Bastard." Banyen laughed. "I've been called worse."

"When I get off this horse, I'll—"

"Fall into my arms and kiss me with passion-filled lips."
Banyen laughed again.

Katerina smoldered with anger. Hot, searing anger. She
would kill him the first chance she got. Perhaps she could
ask the Khan to put the bastard out of his misery and save
her the trouble. Who was he? What did he have to do with
her uncle? Of all the people in the world, why did it have to
be him who found her? This was the second time he had humiliated her. There won't be a third time, she vowed silently.
His day was coming, as the Cossacks said, and when it came,
she would show him no mercy. She would be as mean and as
bad as he was that night on the steppe. And then she would
mock and ridicule him as he was doing to her now.

The amber eyes spewed fire as she was untied from the
horse. Her knees gave out, and she slumped to the ground.
She never knew where she got the strength, but she reached
out a slender arm and jerked with all her strength till the tall
figure lost his balance and sprawled on the ground. The
knife from her trousers was in her hand as she crouched
low, her teeth bared in a snarl. Her burnished hair was in
wild disarray, tumbling down and around her shoulders.
Her arms moved effortlessly as she flicked the air with the
slender blade. "I'll grant you it's not much in the way of a
weapon, but it can kill if the aim is true," she panted.
Banyen nodded, his dark eyes hooded as he got to his feet.
"You first, Mongol," Katerina said harshly, "and don't do
anything but walk. If the blade doesn't find its mark, it will
cripple you, which is just as well. Now move."

Banyen's eyes narrowed till they were mere slits, but he
moved. He knew he could take her if he wanted to. She was
tired, and she looked hungry; she wouldn't be able to put up
much of a battle. He told himself it amused him to do her
bidding. He recalled another time when he also had felt

amused, and he would carry the scar with him for the rest of his life. She might get one good swing at him and slice him where it counted most. For now he would do as she said. Let her think she had won . . . this time. There would be other times, and he would win then, as he always did.

Katerina squinted in the bright sunlight and was aware of her femininity for the first time since meeting the Mongol. She looked a mess; her clothing dirty and torn, her hair hanging down like a ruffian's. She knew her face was dirty, and for some reason that bothered her. She told herself she wanted to put her best effort forth for her uncle. It wasn't the Mongol; it couldn't be because of him. The other time he had ridiculed her and . . . What did he do, Katerina? she asked herself. *He left me to freeze in the tent.* She moved closer to the man in front of her and jabbed at his broad back with the tip of the knife. Bright-red droplets of blood seeped through the indigo shirt, turning into blackish streaks. "I told you to move; I didn't say crawl," she said viciously as she jabbed again and then danced away from his muscular form when he turned, his arm outstretched, to grab at her. "Oh, no," she spat. "It's my turn now. If I tell you to move again, I'll throw the knife, I won't just play with it. Now *walk.*"

Banyen's jaw tightened as he turned to do her bidding. Damnable woman, who did she think she was talking to? Maybe he should tell her who he was. He negated the idea, knowing she would snigger and certainly never would be impressed.

Banyen stopped and pointed with his arm. "The Khan's tent," he said, bowing low with a flourish.

Katerina couldn't believe her eyes. Never before had she seen anything like this. This flat wasteland, fit only for the sheep and goats that grazed on it, was like the steppe—it went on endlessly. The yurts that stood upon flatland created an illusion of a fantasyland to Katerina. No matter in which direction she looked, there stood row upon row of ten-foot-tall tents. To Katerina they looked like a forest of trees that had been chopped off on top. The dwellings were covered with felt pieces of all descriptions and sizes, each home reflecting the tastes of its owner. The grandest of all, of course, were the three yurts that belonged to her uncle. They were covered with a high-quality felt, thicker and heavier than the rest. They also were highly decorated on the outside. She wasn't sure whether she had been here before or not when she was a child; she couldn't remember. She thought it strange for men to live out in the open like this. The Cossacks lived out in the open, too, but they had their sturdy huts to go into at night. The yurts looked so fragile, so vulnerable. She realized that on land as flat as this, as on the steppe, someone could easily be seen approaching the camp. At least, she thought, the steppe has flowers, trees, and grass on it. Other than the small tufts of grass that the livestock fed on, this camp was nothing but desert wasteland. The heat in the dead of summer must be unbearable.

She took in all the sights as she carefully watched Banyen out of the corner of her eye. He reached forward to open the closed flap of the yurt for her, but she didn't move.

"You first, Mongol, and no tricks. I am who I say I am, remember that," Katerina said, brandishing the thin blade in his general direction.

Banyen grinned. "Do you want me to announce you or would you rather go in unannounced and have your head sliced from your shoulders? If I'm to announce you, then I should know your name. We strive for formality here in camp," he said, bowing low again.

"You missed your calling, whatever it was. You make an excellent buffoon," Katerina snapped. "Tell my uncle Katerina Vaschenko is here to see him."

Banyen entered the tent and strode over to the Khan, who reclined against a pile of elaborately embroidered cushions. "While riding patrol I came across a female bent on traveling here to the camp to see you. She's weak from hunger, and not too steady on her feet. But that doesn't seem to interfere with her tongue; it's like a viper. She already left me a memento," he said, turning for the Khan's inspection. "She says her name is Katerina Vaschenko."

The Khan rose awkwardly from his comfortable position in his nest of cushions. "Katerina!" His voice was full of shock. "And you say she is alone. Fetch her to me immediately, Banyen! Why did you make her stand outside like a beggar? Fetch her this moment," he said imperiously. Banyen's mouth tightened, but he lifted the flap from the tent and motioned to Katerina to enter.

At the sight of her uncle's dear face Katerina felt tears sting her eyes. She ran to him as she had when she was a child. When he gathered her close, the tears coursed down her cheeks. The Khan, embarrassed at her display of affection in front of Banyen, motioned to him to leave his tent.

"Tell me, child, what is it? What brings you here to my camp? Come, sit here with me and tell me what is troubling you."

Gulping back her sobs, Katerina wiped at her tear-filled eyes. "They're dead. They're all dead. Grandfather himself waits to go to his Maker. Only Mikhailo, Grandfather, and a few of the others are left in the mountains. All of the horses are gone. All of them."

"But I don't understand. Are you telling me all the Cossacks from the village are gone, dead?" he asked in an outraged voice.

Katerina nodded tremulously. "A raiding party. It happened the night before we were to leave for the mountains. I was away from the camp when it happened. When I got back they had all been killed and the horses were gone. I didn't know what to do. Mikhailo came down from the mountains when we didn't arrive on schedule and helped me bury the dead. I came here because I didn't know what else to do. Will you help me?"

"What can I do for you?" he asked quietly as the enormity of what she had said dawned on him. "You have only to ask, but I don't know what assistance I can offer. Do you want a patrol of my soldiers to help you find the marauders?"

"More than a patrol, Uncle, much more. Before I came here I discussed the matter with Mikhailo. In all truth, he was against my plan, but I managed to convince him it would work. I told him my uncle, the Khan, would help me. You must help me," she pleaded. "I have nowhere else to turn." Before she could lose her courage, Katerina continued, "I want the men from your stockades, all of them. I want to take them back to the mountains with me and train them to be Cossacks. Please, Uncle, don't look at me as if I'd lost my mind. It will work, I know it will. Give me the men that have no hope, the men who are destined for death. Those are the men I want. The more vicious, the more bloodthirsty, the better. I have to get the horses back. I can't do it alone. I'll work with them through the long winter, and in the spring we'll leave the mountains and we'll find the Cosars. It's the only way."

The Khan narrowed his oblique eyes as he listened to his niece plead with him. He loved her and would help in any way he could so long as he benefited in some way, he told himself. It had been a long time since he had seen hate such as hers. He asked himself where he had seen such a look. Of course—in Banyen's eyes the day he was brought to the camp. He rubbed his hands through his coarse black hair, making it stand out in tufts about his round head, as he continued to listen to her plead her cause. The coal black eyes were shrewd, watchful, and ever speculative. Short, stubby fingers stroked an undefined chin as he interjected a word from time to time.

"It will work, Uncle, I know it will," Katerina said vehemently.

"These men from the stockade are the dregs of the earth.

The first chance they get, they'll kill you. What chance will you, a woman, have against them?"

"I'm a Cossack, or did you forget, Uncle? If there's any killing to be done, it will be me who does it, not your prisoners. If you believe nothing else, believe that."

"Listen to me, little one, these men, these prisoners, are due to go to their death shortly. An offer such as you make will mean that they will leave no stone unturned to gain their freedom. Once you set out with them, that will be their only objective. Why do you think they will go with you and train through the long, cold winter and then fight for your cause? This is foolish woman-talk. It will never work."

"I'm telling you it will work. I'll take them, shackled in irons, through the Urals, across the steppe, and up to the mountains. The snows are due soon. Where could they go? There's nothing for them on the outside. They have a chance to regain their dignity and fight for something worthwhile. I'll even agree to pay them so afterward they can begin a new life. As you know, Uncle, the Cosars have bequeathed my family a fortune in gold. If I lived a thousand years I could never hope to spend the fortune that rests in the House of the Kat. I'll pay anything, do anything, to succeed. They have a choice—a new life with me or death at the hands of your men. Which do you think they'll accept?"

Katerina felt a lump settle in the pit of her stomach. She wasn't convincing him. "Very well, Uncle, what is it you wish to bargain for in return for your help?" she asked shrewdly.

The Khan laughed. "You know me well, little one. There is one small request you can grant me. A colt and a filly from Whitefire," he said slyly.

"You know it's forbidden, Uncle. However, I see you will accept nothing less. You drive a hard bargain, but one I'll accept, only because I'm desperate."

"Forbidden by whom? You just told me Volin was wiped out. You're the leader now, the decision is yours alone.

Let's be sure we both understand the bargain we're making," the Khan said, standing up, his scarlet shirt and shiny black trousers bright against the dimness of the yurt.

"I understand the bargain," Katerina said coolly. "You also have my word: when the first wildflower sprouts on the frozen banks of the Dnieper in the spring, a new breed of Cossack will be born," she said grimly, her amber eyes flashing.

The Khan looked deeply into her eyes and believed her implicitly. If anyone could do it, she could.

"Sit down, Katerina, we'll have some food and drink. There is much we must discuss." He clapped his pudgy hands, and an old serving woman entered the tent. His tone was husky and guttural when he gave his orders. The old hag looked at Katerina with suspicion as she scurried away to do the Khan's bidding.

Katerina settled herself on the pile of fox and mink furs. "I see that you surround yourself with all the trappings of wealth," she said, looking around at the brightly colored silken hangings. "And a wooden floor," she said snidely. "Not to mention a blanket of sable that stretches from one end of the yurt to the other." She noted that a small fire glowed in the center of the yurt, banked and ready to flare with a shovel of sheep dung.

The old Khan waved his pudgy arms around his yurt and smiled. "It befits my simple station in life. True, a little lavish compared to the other yurts, but . . . comfortable. The season has been excellent for trading the hides and wool from the sheep."

"Your treasury is . . . ample, is that what you're saying?"

"Very much so. I have no complaints. Now tell me, what does an old man like myself need with wealth? I like this simple life and the few little luxuries I allow myself. I'm content. Since you have just agreed to the filly and colt from Whitefire, my happiness is unsurpassed."

Katerina flinched. No matter what she promised, she

knew in her heart that she would find a way to get out of the bargain. There was no way he would get the offspring except over her dead body. She forced her face to blankness as she poked at the fire with iron tongs.

Her amber eyes were sleepy, catlike, and the Khan felt uneasy, a strange feeling creeping in and around his stomach. By now she should have been married, with babies sucking at her breasts. Indulgent fathers! he snorted to himself.

"Let us suppose that I agree to what you ask, and let us further agree that you are amenable to bestowing a colt and filly upon me for my generosity, what is your ultimate goal once you train my prisoners for whatever it is you have in mind?"

"I thought it was already agreed upon."

"Ah, Katerina, one should never assume anything until it is a fact—will you never learn? Your father did you no favors by allowing you to be trained with his men. No, it's not definite. Tell me, an old man who is in his failing years, what exactly are your plans? Spare me all the nonessentials. I'm also bearing in mind something Katlof once told me: a Cossack is born a Cossack, there is no in-between."

Katerina clenched her teeth, a bitter, cold look in her eyes. The light breeze that wafted through the tent opening caused the silken hangings to flutter and sway, creating slight rustling noises, a restful sound that was making her drowsy. "I need the men to get the Cosars back. I must have trained men who will serve under me and do as I command them. I'll raid and plunder every village from here to Moscow to get back what is mine. This is the only way I can do it. You must help me, I beg you on my mother's life! I can train the men. I'll make Cossacks out of them or die trying. Believe me, Uncle, I will succeed. If what my father told me was true, your own armies could stand some training. When we rode into your camp it was a sorry sight that greeted me.

How did your armies deteriorate so? How did you allow it to happen? Tell me, what's gone wrong?"

The Khan shrugged his ample shoulders as he settled himself more comfortably by the banked fire. "Men get tired of fighting and want to return to their families. They scatter and come back when they have no more use for their relatives. What you say is true. We've grown fat and complacent." He laughed, patting his ample girth. "For now, there is nothing to fight. Only a foolish man leads men to war for the sake of war. I am not a foolish man. In the ways of women, perhaps," he said, a roguish twinkle in his dark eyes. "Very well, I agree, but with one other condition. I'll send fifty of my best and youngest men along with Prince Banyen. If you are so determined to train the prisoners, then you can give my men some training also. Upon their return in the spring, they will train others. Do you agree to this stipulation?"

The amber eyes flashed warningly. "And this Prince Banyen, is he the man that brought me here?" The Khan nodded. "Tell me," she asked softly, "who is to be in charge of these men of yours? If I agree, then it must be me. I'll not take orders from that . . . that . . . insufferable, that arrogant . . . bastard. Those, Uncle, are my terms. Be sure that your prince understands this, for I have no liking for him and I would just as soon stick a knife through his ribs as look at him."

The Khan's eyes were outraged at her words. "What did he do to you? Tell me and I'll have him whipped. Did he . . . did he?"

"No, Uncle, he didn't. I have no liking for him, it's as simple as that. Before the end of winter one of us will kill the other. I plan to be alive when the snows melt, so be warned. It's my way or not at all. This is your golden opportunity, Uncle," she said in a low, rich voice, hoping to sway him to her way of thinking. "My visit here and my request will serve a twofold purpose. You can rebuild your

armies with my help, and you will be the only man in all of
Russia that can boast he has foals from Whitefire. A colt
that will grow to be a stallion, not a gelding. Think about it,
Uncle, before you decide."

"Banyen will be like a devil if I agree to your terms. He
has no love for women." He shook his head and laughed. "It
will do him good. Perhaps when the snow melts you will be
enamored of each other."

"Don't plan on it, Uncle. I've decided the man hasn't
been born yet that will be good enough for me, so put that
thought from your mind."

"Strange that you should say that." The Khan laughed
wickedly. "That's exactly what Banyen said. He said there
wasn't a woman in the world that was fitting to share his
name."

"Is that what he said?" Katerina snapped.

"As a matter of fact, those were my exact words,"
Banyen said, entering the tent. "Would you like me to repeat them for your benefit?" His expression mocked her as
she looked up at him.

Katerina laughed, a rich, full laugh that seemed to circle
the yurt and come to settle around him. The hackles on the
back of his neck seemed to rise and then fall against his
sun-darkened throat.

"Sit down, Banyen, join us in a light repast. I've just
committed you to a mission."

Katerina watched as the agate eyes turned the color of
deep indigo at the Khan's words. His muscular body stiffened, and the bronze hands were clenched into fists at his
sides. His mouth was grim and tight as he waited expectantly for the words he knew would not be to his liking.

"First, allow me to introduce you to my niece, Katerina
Vaschenko. She's come here to me for help, and I've agreed
to do as she asks in return for two very small favors. You
and fifty of our best and youngest men, along with prisoners
of her choosing from the stockade, will accompany her

back to the Carpathians, where you will all undergo exten-
sive Cossack training. In the spring you will return here
with our men, who will train the others. The prisoners will
remain in the Carpathians with my niece, who will then . . .
That isn't important," he said suddenly. "My niece will be
in charge, is that understood?"

"And if I refuse?" Banyen demanded curtly.

"You won't," the Khan said calmly. "You're too good a
soldier to disobey an order. If you do, you know the consequences. It's my command, Banyen, and one I won't repeat.
My dear," he said, as an afterthought, "allow me to present
Prince Banyen."

"Nobility and titles don't impress me," Katerina said
aloofly. "It's what's inside a man that counts, and you,
Prince Banyen, are sadly lacking. It will be interesting to
see how you fare in the mountains. Very interesting indeed."
She laughed again as she watched his dark hand reach up to
touch the scar on his cheek. His dark eyes were murderous
as he stalked from the tent, his back straight and stiff.

Katerina's voice was calm, yet the Khan sensed a tone of
danger in her softly spoken words. "Who is Prince Banyen?
How is it he commands this ragamuffin parcel of men you
call an army?"

The Khan sighed wearily. "Kindness, Katerina. Please,
kinder words when you speak of my army. We'll rise again
as we did before, for this is but a momentary relapse. I have
placed all my faith in Banyen to rebuild my army and make
them the noble fighters of yesteryear. Banyen's father was
the prince of a league, controlling many banners and baks.
Czar Ivan, in one of his mad rages, sent his soldiers out, and
the Khanate of Kazan was burned to the ground. As a boy,
he wandered until he came to Astrakhan, where he stayed
until the Khan surrendered, and then he ran away. For years
he lived with whoever would have him, until one day my
men found him wandering near the Urals, alone and dazed,
near death. They brought him here, and to this day I still

wonder how he survived. If Kazan flourished, one day Banyen would have been the next Khan, but his entire family was slaughtered and everything lost. He'll do as I say, because he owes me his life, and he needs my help to avenge his people. A brilliant strategist, he's not entirely without compassion. One day he may let you see that side of him. Now he's bitter and angry and has little patience, but that will change. What I'm saying is not to push him too far or you may rue the day you did. In open combat he has no equal, and on horseback the animal and man are one." He laughed. "And he devours women the way I consume food. Later, I don't wish to hear you say you weren't warned. Enough of this, where is that infernal crone with our meal?" he complained loudly, just as the old servant entered the yurt. Carefully she placed the platters of roast lamb and the decanter of wine near the fire, and slowly backed away.

Katerina drank deeply from the decanter and wiped her mouth with the back of her hand. She bit into a plump piece of lamb, and didn't stop till every morsel of meat was gone from the bone.

"Rest, little one. I have business outside the yurt. No one will bother you. Sleep," he said fondly as he laid a gentle hand on her coppery hair.

Katerina needed no further urging. She cradled her head on her arm and was asleep instantly on the sable carpet.

Khan Afstar stood with his hands posed on his ample hips, waiting for Banyen to walk toward him. He didn't like the arrogant gait nor the murderous look in the young prince's eyes. He schooled his own face to impassiveness as he looked around the camp at the multitude of tents that dotted the landscape. Far to the right of the giant compound, his entire army was garrisoned. Even from where he stood, shading his eyes from the brilliant sun, he could see that the yurts were sadly in need of repair. Men roamed about as if they had no destination in mind. Men should be busy or they grew fat and soft. What was Banyen thinking of to let them behave in so aimless a fashion? "What's the meaning of this?" he demanded, pointing toward the garrison.

"The men are tired. I gave them a few hours of respite to do as they wished. Not everything can be done in a matter of a few days. It was you yourself who told me this. I can't make staunch fighting men overnight from derelicts who have grown sodden with wine and rich, spicy food. If they drill too long, they collapse. All things in good time. When the time comes to storm Moscow, they'll be ready—you have my word."

"I see by the harsh look on your face you have no liking for my orders. I have my reasons, Banyen. This may be my one and only chance to ferret out the Whitefire secret. I want you to go with Katerina under the guise of commander of my men. What I want you to do is gain the secret. I don't care how you do it, just do it. I have the utmost faith in your abilities. Make yourself available to my niece. Woo her if necessary, but don't come back without the answer."

The scar on Banyen's cheek began to throb with the hard set of his jaw. "And that means another delay. Very well, I always repay my debts, and this is one that will be paid first. I am well aware that I owe you my life. For that I'll do your bidding . . . this time. But when I return from the Carpathians I'll take matters in my own hands. Perhaps you forget how you promised me the aid of your men if I took over the training of your armies. A twofold arrangement, you said. I'll never forget why I'm a paid soldier in this sorry excuse for an army. It would be simpler to just buy your army."

The Khan shook his head. "When will you young people learn that all things are gained by patience and timing? Revenge will be yours, but when I deem the moment is right, and that will be when we lead every Mongol in Sibir and the surrounding territories through the streets of Moscow. Vengeance will be that much sweeter, take my word for it."

"If it's the last thing I do before I die, I swear to you my sword will taste Ivan's blood."

The Khan motioned to Banyen to sit beside him on a tufted sheepskin pillow. "Sit with me, here under this canopy, so we can talk. The sun will go down soon, and the day will get cooler. It's a pleasant hour of the day to talk and have some wine. Besides, my young prince, I want to know more about your reasons for wanting Ivan's blood. When you first came to my camp you told me your family was slaughtered and all your father's territories taken away. I heard of the attack, but the details have never been told to me. Do you wish to speak about it now? I never urged you before because, as I just told you, I'm a man who selects his moments wisely, Banyen. You will see how it serves you and how much sweeter the fruits of victory. Now, angry one, tell me what happened to your people," the Khan urged Banyen.

"Why should you be interested?" Banyen questioned sarcastically. "You have my hide tied to a bargain, and I'm without a piece of gold. At one time I could have bought anything, including your so-called army. I don't understand your interest, since my story can be of no value to you."

"Allow me to be the judge. I'm interested for many reasons. I always make a point of being informed of all battles and attacks, it teaches me the ways of the enemy. As for my second reason, if you haven't realized it by now, then you shall. All Mongols are brothers, and when one Mongol gets killed it is a brother that is killed. I wish to retaliate for that injustice. Banyen, if you can put your anger aside for a moment, I'm interested in the attack on Kazan. I would imagine you were quite young when it happened—can you remember?"

Before Afstar could say another word, Banyen raged, "Can I remember? A stupid question! If you saw your mother and father slaughtered, would you forget it? Would you, even though you were only six years old? Spared because some distant Russian forefather let you be born with a different color of eyes than the others," he roared at the Khan.

"No, I wouldn't. Calm yourself, Banyen, tell me how it happened. Perhaps if you talk about it, it will ease the pain a bit. I'm not saying you should forget, or that you could. I'm only suggesting that if you talk about it, it might help."

"It won't help, as I have no wish to discuss it now. End it, Afstar."

"Your trouble lies within you. You are too full of hate and vengeance to think clearly. After a winter in the mountains with the girl, your mind might clear enough for you to realize that emotions must be put aside, for one to think and plan attacks with care," the Khan instructed the wrath-filled prince.

"Speaking of the mountains and my niece, have you mulled over which of the young men you'll take with you? I suggest you choose healthy young men, if there are any, for the winter is harsh in the Carpathians. If the snow starts while you're on your way, half the journey will be made through knee-deep snow."

"When do we leave?" Banyen asked coldly.

The Khan shrugged. "A day or two, perhaps three. My niece needs to regain her strength before she starts out on that arduous trek through the Urals. Patience, Banyen."

Soft gray twilight cast the high-domed yurts into an endless expanse of bubbles. To Banyen's narrowed eyes, it was home, the only home he had known since the loss of his family and estates. He hated the squalor, the undisciplined men in their slovenly clothing, and their rough, crude manners. How was he to make a marching army from such degradation? Perhaps if morale were higher, or some sort of incentive offered, he might have a better chance of succeeding. His chest constricted at what he imagined would hap-

pen with his first charge into battle. The men would drop
like flies or run with fear. They weren't soldiers, they were
inexperienced youngsters. He had to try—what else could
he do? He needed the Khan and the Khan's men. He
shrugged; there was no point in torturing himself with
thoughts such as these. His eyes traveled to the Khan's yurt
and the sleeping girl. He frowned. She reminded him of
someone. While he might agree to the Khan's terms, that
was all he'd agree to. Once in the mountains, he would do
as he damn well pleased. Never would he take orders from
a woman, even a beautiful woman. He would conquer her
first.

A vision of her crouched low, her teeth bared, the knife
thrust in front of her, made him draw in his breath. A formidable enemy, no doubt about that, but he was a man and she
a mere woman. He allowed his mind to drift, envisioning
her in a silk gown, her hair loose upon her bare shoulders.
Of course, he smirked, her eyes would be filled with desire
and her mouth would tremble for the feel of his lips. Perhaps this time the Khan was right, and patience was what
was needed. He could be as patient as the next man, but
when his patience was at an end, it would end.

Chapter 7

The dreary fall season took its toll on the Czar's patience as he grew bored with the endless array of dinners and affairs. Nothing pleased him, not even his personally selected harem of beauties, who tried to bewitch and tantalize him. "I need something different to entertain me, I grow weary with dinners and women," he wailed. "Does anyone have a new idea for their Czar, something to excite me?" he questioned his gathered nobles.

The room was silent. Suddenly a quivering voice at the rear of the room was heard: "My Czar, the Oprichniks have taken many traitors as prisoners. Perhaps we could have them entertain you, under your supervision, of course."

"Yes, a splendid idea. I will have them perform for me and my subjects. Who is it that speaks? I order him to step forward."

A young nobleman slowly made his way through the crowd toward Ivan. Trying to control his trembling limbs, he bowed graciously before the Czar. "I am the person you seek, Czar Ivan. I pray I have not offended you with my outburst," he said meekly.

"On the contrary, young man, stand before me and let me

look at you. You're close to the age of my eldest son, and I would have been proud of him had he made such a joyful suggestion." Ivan beamed. "On Saturday next we will have a mass execution at the Place of the Skulls in Red Square. I personally appoint you to announce this news to the people of Moscow. I want Red Square filled to capacity with my subjects. It is my wish that every citizen attend; if they refuse, they will join the traitors at the chopping block. Be off with you and prepare your announcements, for you have but a week. If the square is filled to my satisfaction, when we return to the palace I will have you dubbed a lord."

"Thank you, my Czar," the young man mumbled, making a low, sweeping bow. "I will not fail you, you have my word."

The days following the Czar's announcement were busy ones in the Kremlin. Ivan was everywhere, joyfully directing the workmen who labored day and night erecting intricate instruments of torture and execution: large pans for frying the victims, huge caldrons of water suspended over faggots, ropes that would cut a body in two when tightened, bear cages, iron claws, pincers, and the gallows.

The day of the executions arrived. When Ivan rode into the square, accompanied by his guards, he was appalled by the lack of spectators, and immediately called for his guards to produce the young nobleman. When the young man appeared before Ivan, fearing for his life, the Czar spoke. "You were instructed to fill this square to capacity and I can count the number of people on one hand. Where is everyone?" he roared.

"My Czar, I did as you directed and made known this day to every citizen. They were told to attend. However, if I may, my Czar—I have heard talk that the citizenry is fearful of your wrath. Forgive me, Czar Ivan."

"If what you say is true, then we must set the matter straight. Come, you will ride with me through the city while I tell the people they have naught to fear."

As they rode Ivan shouted to the populace in a loud ringing voice, "Good people, come! There is nothing to fear, no harm will touch you, I promise! My word as Czar Ivan!"

Assured by the Czar's words, the people straggled into Red Square.

As the citizenry began to move about, the Czar rose majestically and spoke: "All traitors to death!"

A thunderous roar of approval rose from the crowd, with cries of "Long live the Czar!" The young nobleman smiled contentedly.

Three hundred prisoners, their chains clanking behind them, were led into the square, the majority of them half dead from previous torturing. To win his people over, Ivan dramatically showed mercy to several of the traitors by freeing them, and granted a few others the right to exile.

For the most-hated enemies of the state, Ivan saved the greatest and most extreme torture. One boyar was hung by his feet and cut into pieces. A trusted treasurer was placed in iced water and then in boiling water repeatedly, until his skin peeled off him like an eel, while Ivan laughed in delight.

As the executions continued throughout the day, Ivan's eyes rolled in ecstasy over the pain and blood of the traitors. At sundown Ivan and his son rode to the home of a dead nobleman, where he ordered the man's widow tortured until she told where their family treasure was hidden. Throughout the long night Ivan and his son rode to the houses of the executed nobles and seized their treasure. Wearied from the ride, Ivan then ordered eighty widows of executed nobles drowned.

For days thereafter, to add to the disgrace of the traitors, Ivan allowed their mutilated bodies to lie rotting in the square. Hungry dogs feasted on their flesh as passing citizens spat contemptuously on them. Finally the Czar ordered his men to rid the square of the foul-smelling bodies.

In a remorseful mood, feeling sorrow for the souls of the

traitors, Ivan spent hours in church, praying for their souls, and donated large sums of money to the holy institution. Tiring of prayers, he then went to Alexandrov, where he took to his bed pleading exhaustion.

His days of penance over, Ivan returned in splendor to Moscow, dressed in his finest regal attire. Parading into Red Square with his guards forming columns on either side of him, he rode his stallion up the steps of Terem Palace, directly into the dining hall. Clapping his hands, he shouted, "Tonight I want a feast commemorating my return. Let the cooks prepare the finest in delicacies for my guests. Invite by my special request beggars, thieves, whores, and murderers. Bring them into the palace and have the servants dress them in finery. Inform the boyars they must give their finest clothing to these people, by my order. I want them dressed and seated an hour after dark, at which time we will dine." His announcement finished, Ivan rode his horse down the marble corridors to his bedchamber and dismounted, leaving the horse in the hallway.

That evening Ivan dined among the dregs of Moscow society. "For entertainment tonight I have a surprise for all my noble guests. I have summoned the wives of the boyars to dance for us. Ladies and gentlemen, please direct your attention to the middle of the hall," he cackled, pointing a bony finger in front of him.

Dressed in beautiful gauzy material in an array of colors, the boyars' wives minced their way around the hall, trying to cover their bodies with their hands and arms. The ladies, aware that the gauze hid nothing, only accentuating their breasts and thighs, danced with their eyes downcast as the male guests leered at them. Thoughts of tasting their delicious femininity was more than most of them could bear. They shouted obscene remarks to the women as they drank and ate like the lowlife they were. Ivan delighted in every minute of it. "These are my people!" he shouted.

With a wave of his hand he dismissed the dancing women, to groans of dismay. "Gentlemen, noblemen, please, I have more to dazzle your eyes. Allow me to present my witches and magicians to mystify you. They will perform feats never before seen by man. Bring on the witches and magicians," he commanded.

At the height of the magic show, his personal messenger darted into the hall. "My Czar, I beg your pardon, but I've come a long way and have news for you."

"You dare intrude during the performance!" Ivan bellowed. "Your news had better be worthy of this interruption. What is it? Tell me at once!"

The messenger rushed forward. "When I stopped in Kiev I was told to deliver this to you, my Czar."

Ivan's eyes scanned the parchment. A loud rancorous laugh echoed above the din as Ivan doubled over in mirth. "I can't believe that God is this good to me. This announcement is the prize that makes my evening complete. Ladies and nobles," he said, grinning sadistically, "let it be known to one and all that Yuri Zhuk, my noble emissary, is dead." He crushed the parchment as convulsions of laughter rocked him. "My emissary was found in a clump of bushes outside Volin, with his tongue and fingers missing. Delightful!" He drooled, his drunken eyes rolling in his twisted face. "Enough, enough of this, back to the witches. Where are my witches? Continue, I order you to continue!" he roared. "Tomorrow I must . . . no, not tomorrow, but soon, I must send for Halya and tell her this delightful news."

On Ivan's orders, everyone drank, feasted, and fornicated throughout the night. Czar Ivan was once again delighting in the affairs of state.

Chapter 8

Katerina woke once, shortly after midnight. She stirred restlessly and settled her bruised body more comfortably on the plush carpet. Within seconds she was asleep again, this time deeply and totally, a dark-haired man stalking her through snow. She moaned while she dreamed, as she slipped and fell time and again in her struggles to get away from the man bent on capturing her. As always, the moment his hands were within reach of her she woke, her body drenched with perspiration, her eyes wild and haunted, a scream on her lips. She lay back, exhausted, as tears welled in the luminous amber eyes and flowed down her satiny cheeks. One day soon it would be her turn. When that day came she would sleep again, as when she was a child, peacefully and happily. Slowly, as if they had a will of their own, the thick heavy lashes lowered, and she was again asleep, her cheek pressed into the richness of the carpet.

The Khan stood over his sleeping niece, willing her to wake. As if she sensed his presence, the doe eyes opened and she stared up at him, frowning, trying to remember where she was. Recognition of her uncle and the warm closeness of the yurt reminded her, and she struggled to her feet.

"If you have a change of clothing for me I would be grateful, and I would also like a bath if it's at all possible."

The Khan nodded as he tossed her a vivid striped cotton shirt. "The yurt next to this one has bathwater and a light breakfast waiting. When you've finished, join me and Prince Banyen by the open fire in the center of the compound."

The slim girl worked at her shoulders, trying to loosen the tension and the tightness that had settled over her in sleep. She rubbed at her arms and thighs, trying unsuccessfully to ease the stiffness in her muscles. Perhaps the bath will help, she told herself as she left the tent in search of food and the luxury of warm water.

Not wanting to waste time, she removed her filthy clothing and slid down into the oil-scented water with a thick wedge of goat cheese and a chunk of bread. This was indeed a wonder. Now where did the Khan get scented oil? She suppressed a wicked smile at what she imagined was his favorite pastime.

She ate the cheese ferociously and chewed at the bread as if she hadn't eaten in days. Later she would gorge herself at the noon meal. For now, she needed her wits about her for the coming hours she would spend with the Khan and Prince Banyen. Just the thought of his name and she trembled. The gold-tinted eyes darkened to newly minted copper as she reached for a length of toweling. She stepped from the round tub onto a deerskin. The moment her bare foot touched the fur she stumbled, and would have fallen if she hadn't reached out to grasp the rim of the tub. Don't think about him, she cautioned herself as she pulled on the trousers Stepan had outgrown. The brilliant shirt was tight and felt confining. Her breasts strained against the thin fabric as she tucked the end into the band of the trousers. She longed for a mirror to see the condition of her hair. Sighing, she gathered it into a knot and tied it back with a loose strand of hair from the side of her head. What did she care what she looked like? She was clean, and that was all that mattered.

When Katerina left the bathing yurt she shaded her eyes against the brilliant sun. She looked around to get her bearings and was surprised to see people moving about, their colorful garb dazzling in the shimmering light. They moved slowly, intent on what they were about. Children ran and played, laughing boisterously as they scampered over piled twigs and strewn rock piles. She was surprised when she received no more than a passing glance from the playful children and busy women. She frowned. Where were the men? Katerina squinted against the glare of the sun and saw that at the very outer perimeter of the compound men were drilling with weapons. Horses whickered softly as men climbed onto their backs to ready themselves for a charge. She was puzzled. If the Khan's wealth was as great as she had been led to believe, why was he bothering with this ragtag group of soldiers? Money could buy him a fit and ready army. He was up to something. And whatever it was, it had something to do with her, she knew it just as sure as she knew Prince Banyen had . . .

Skirting the playful children, Katerina picked her way among the yurts, avoiding the chattering women who were busy washing and cooking outdoors. She nodded slightly to the prince and touched her uncle fondly on the arm to show she was ready for whatever it was he had planned. Banyen's eyes raked her as she skipped along to keep up with his long-legged stride. She said nothing, knowing the Khan preferred that she remain quiet. So—he was taking her to the stockade to show her the prisoners. She was shocked but schooled her face to reveal nothing. Never had she seen or smelled such . . . such . . . Words failed her.

"Breathe through your mouth," Banyen suggested.

The stockade ran the entire width of the encampment. It consisted of poles hewn from the nearby forest. The poles, seven feet tall, were crisscrossed by rough-hewn planks.

Overhead, animal hides were laced tightly across the tops of the structure to ward off the hot, scorching sun and biting wind, and the snows of winter. Instinctively she knew that in the summer the bodies of the prisoners baked, burned, shriveled, and stank. In the winter they would shake with the cold and turn blue from frostbite. The lucky ones would survive; the rest would freeze and die.

The skin on the men was blistered from the heat, and full of sores. Many were sick and dying. She knew the older men would never live through the winter. Ringlets of dried blood formed clusters around their wrists and ankles where the shackles rubbed the skin.

"Do you wonder why so many prisoners are penned like animals in so small an area? The Khan can only spare a few men for guard duty. You can see it takes at least twenty men to surround and maintain a constant guard. They are relieved of duty three times a day, so sixty men a day are involved in guarding prisoners when they should be doing other things," Banyen said gruffly.

"Why don't you put them to work? Why are they standing so close together? I don't understand," Katerina asked softly.

"Is this what you want, Katerina?" the Khan asked. "Do you still wish my help? There is a tribal meeting I must attend. I'll join you at the noon meal. Be sure, little one, that you know what you are doing," he said, patting her arm.

"I see there are still many questions in your eyes," Banyen observed.

Outraged, Katerina took a deep breath. "I've seen animals treated better. This is . . . this is inhuman. How can one human being treat another in such a manner? They live and breathe as you and I do."

Banyen ignored her words. "As the prisoners die, we move in the outer poles. They are in no condition to attempt escape, not even the healthiest, believe me. If they were fortunate enough to escape, they would be killed instantly.

"It would not be advisable to see them when they are fed the watered-down mush. They fight and kill to get their ration, many times knocking their bowl over in a desperate attempt to get more. They kill to be chosen for work, and they kill for food. They think nothing of slipping their shackled arms around each other's necks and strangling one another for more food. We don't stop them, it's one less mouth to feed. It's called survival," Banyen said coldly. Women! Such outrage over suffering, and yet she recovers quickly enough, he thought. Women always wore two faces. Who was she really concerned for? Was it for his benefit, or did she truly feel sympathy for the prisoners? He admitted he didn't know, and he didn't give a damn.

"Yes, I know the meaning of the word," Katerina said curtly. She knew the Mongols hated to take prisoners, and when they did they were known to be very cruel, but she had never realized just how much so until now. "What did these men do? What crimes have they committed?"

Banyen stepped forward, and with the tip of his saber he pointed at a man and ordered him to speak to the lady. "Tell her why you're shackled and in the stockade."

"Murder."

"And you, what was your crime?"

"I stole horses."

"You?"

"I was caught raiding a village."

"You?"

"Murder."

"Murder."

"Is the punishment the same for all crimes?" Katerina demanded. "The punishment should befit the crime."

Banyen grinned. "We have one here who not only raped a woman, he also killed her. Kostya," he shouted, "step forward."

Katerina couldn't help herself. She stepped near the man

and said in a low voice, "Are you here because you raped a woman, or because you killed her? In your mind, what are you being punished for?"

He was tall and fair-haired, with the bluest eyes Katerina had ever seen. His golden beard glistened in the bright sun. His eyes appeared puzzled, but he answered readily enough. "I didn't rape the woman, she came to me willingly. Men have no need to rape, only animals and savages do that. Women are plentiful and willing to fall into a man's arms. While I slept she tried to steal my pouch of coins. I woke and we struggled. She fell and hit her head on a boulder and died. That is why I'm here."

"That's what he says. The girl's father tells another story," Banyen said coolly.

"He goes with me," Katerina said softly.

Deep murmurings came from the stockade at these strange goings-on. Who was the woman dressed in man's clothing? Why was she asking questions, and why did the prince look as if he wanted to commit murder? One man after another was called to step forward and state his crime. All spoke readily, their eyes questioning.

"You," Katerina said, pointing a finger at a broad-chested man with small round eyes. She watched the powerful play of muscles on his upper arms and chest as he shouldered his way to take his place near the front of the line. "What is your crime?"

"My family was dying from hunger. I waylaid a wagon full of grain and killed the men who were driving the wagon."

"What happened to your family?"

"They died from starvation. One babe in arms and two barely able to walk," he said simply.

"Your name."

"Rokal, mistress."

"He goes with me also," Katerina said quietly.

"It would appear that you have a soft heart for a sad tale," Banyen said mockingly.

"I have no heart," Katerina said coldly. "But I can judge a man's worth by the look in his eye. Remember that."

Banyen's eyes mocked her. "I'll remember."

The selection continued till the noon hour, when Banyen called a halt. "Enough for now. Tomorrow you can question the prisoners that are working today. I don't want you to come to me later and say you were cheated, that the best had the work detail."

"Tell me, what happens when the snows come and the weather is bad? Where are the prisoners taken then, to which yurt? I can't believe you leave them in the stockade."

Banyen's eyes darkened with rage. "They stay right where they are. Fir branches are tacked to the animal skins overhead and to the sides to prevent the wind from driving at them full force. They huddle together for warmth."

"That's inhuman. An animal is treated better than that," Katerina said viciously.

"They should have thought about the matter before they committed their crimes," Banyen said coolly. "I repeat, I didn't say I approve. It is the way of the league. Only the Khan can change the rules."

"It's wrong. The punishment should fit the crime. These men have nothing to look forward to but their death. It's inhuman." She spat.

"How generous you are with other people's lives. If you were slain, I wonder what would happen to your killer?"

Katerina's eyes darkened.

"Women rise again and again." Suddenly she stuck out her booted foot, catching Banyen behind the knee. He went down, his hands outstretched to break his fall. Katerina stood aside, her hands on her slim hips, laughing in delight. "The position becomes you, groveling in the dirt. It's where you belong." Turning, she walked slowly back to the yurt, her slim haunches swaying seductively before Banyen's murderous eyes.

Katerina's nerves were on edge; the days were passing too quickly. She knew she had to make fast work of her selection or she would get caught in the snow and ice when she went through the Urals. Still, she forced herself to make a slow, thorough appraisal of all the men. She couldn't afford any mistakes, now or later.

For three days she stood near the stockade, breathing heavily through her mouth as man after man stepped forward. She let her eyes measure his form, his muscular capability, and the tilt of his head. She listened with a keen ear to his crime and stared deeply into his face with eyes that were keener and sharper than her ears. She also watched Banyen, covertly. His agate eyes gave away his feelings. When they lightened she knew he approved of her choice; when they darkened to indigo she knew he didn't approve. For the past three hours his eyes had remained a deep, dark shade of blue, which not only amused her but delighted her. She watched carefully to see if any of the prisoners would reveal some feeling about the prince. Only Kostya, the first man she had chosen, revealed anything, and she was uncertain what name to put to his expression.

Banyen was impatient with her lengthy, time-consuming choice of men. He listened with half an ear as Katerina ordered one of the men to flex his arm as if in preparation for a weapon thrust. He saw her eyes narrow, and mentally calculate where the weapon would have landed. He fixed his sights on a point to the far left of the stockade, where Katerina's gaze also rested. She nodded. His impatience quickly turned to anger as she continued with her methodical system of choosing an army. "One would think you were choosing prize cattle for showing," he snapped.

"Not cattle. Human beings that are being treated like cattle."

Banyen ignored her words. "The noon hour approaches and the sun will be unbearable. Make fast work of the last or you'll be standing here alone."

Katerina swiveled till she was facing him. "Don't ever make the mistake you just did. Don't ever tell me what to do. Do you understand? You're here by sufferance. Remember that. You do what I tell you, not the other way around."

Banyen's eyes became mere slits as he noted an amused look in some of the prisoners' faces. Kostya eyed him strangely, as he always did, and the man named Rokal was grinning. He knew he should say something, do something, but he held back. Let her think she had him in her power. If it amused her to humiliate him in front of the prisoners, let her; his time would come.

"Is that something else I should remember? The list grows overly long," he said arrogantly.

"Whatever pleases you," Katerina snapped. "Remain quiet so I can finish with my selection."

"You have only to command and I will obey," Banyen ridiculed as he slouched against a gnarled tree trunk. Why was she so hostile to him? He'd done nothing to her, save sling her across the horse's back and bring her into camp. What was that strange look in her eye when she stared at him? He could feel the animosity every time she was near him. Was it just him or was it all men? What was the reason she disliked him so? He corrected his thoughts: "dislike" was too tame a word. Did she hate all men? Evidently not, he answered himself. There had been an approving look in her eye when she chose Kostya. Did she fear men? No, he answered himself again. If she feared men she wouldn't be standing where she was now, with the plans she had in mind. No, it was himself. Why?

His mouth tightened as he watched the swell of her breasts, the sway of her hips as she walked up and down in front of the men. He liked the look of her long legs in the tight-fitting trousers. Those legs, he knew, could be pliant or firm, whichever she chose. She could be soft and she could be hard. He didn't know how he knew, he just did. Katerina Vaschenko had passions that he would wager had never risen to the surface. He grinned. He was just the man to unleash them and bring them to a roaring, tumultuous conclusion. His eyes widened slightly at Kostya's look. He's thinking the same thing, Banyen fumed. Bastard!

An hour past noon Katerina finished her selection. She had her hundred and fifty men. She fixed a steely eye on Banyen and walked away from him. Tomorrow the prisoners would be readied for the trip back to the mountains. One more day and she would leave the camp. She turned as she heard footsteps behind her. "Women walk behind men," Banyen said through clenched teeth.

"If there was a man about, perhaps I would do as you . . . suggest. Seeing nothing more than a prince, I'll continue as I am. Furthermore," she said, turning, "I walk behind no man . . . or prince. Why don't you go about your . . . duties and leave me alone."

Damnable woman! He wanted to grab her by the long, shining hair and pull her to him till he felt her body grow soft with desire. Why in hell did she have this strange effect on him? What was there about her that intrigued and heightened his desire? He wanted her, but he had wanted other women, too. What made this one so different from the others?

A smile tugged at the corner of Katerina's mouth as she imagined the look of frustrated outrage that would be settling over his face. He wanted her, she saw it in his eyes every time he looked at her. "Good," she muttered to herself. Men filled with passion became reckless, foolhardy. Her eyes were merry as she shortened her stride and wiggled her hips seductively. "I hope his eyes fall from their sockets," she muttered through clenched teeth.

* * *

"Come with me, child, I want you to see the sun come up over the Khanate. It's a beautiful sight, and I wish us to view it together. There are several things I want to discuss with you."

They walked slowly, uncle and niece, through the compound, where everything was quiet and still. A new day will begin soon, Katerina thought. And what will it bring? she questioned herself.

The Khan pointed a pudgy finger to the east. "A new day, for both of us."

Katerina looked at the huge orange ball covered with what looked like gossamer wings and sighed deeply. "It's been a long time since I saw anything so beautiful," she said huskily. "You're right, Uncle, this is a new beginning."

"Child, tell me your reasoning as to why you didn't want the prisoners told of your plans. It would seem a little late to tell them on the morning they are to leave. Banyen does not approve, but then, of late Banyen approves of very little of life's goings-on. He's been here two years now, and I still don't know him. Your reason?"

Katerina shrugged. "Would it have made a difference? They have no choice. They go with me whether they like it or not. This way they have less time to worry on the matter. I expect no trouble from any of them. Your prince is the one that worries me," she said sharply. "I'm giving the men a chance to live, why would they reject the offer? Is there something you know that you aren't telling me?"

"No." He raised his round head and looked at the huge ball rising in the sky. "Another week and you'll be in the Urals, and that, my dear, is when your problems begin. You can't beat the snows. It's too late."

"There's no cause for worry, Uncle. I've gone through the snows before. Mikhailo knows I'm coming. He'll string the pass with bells, as he's always done. You must have faith in me; I'll succeed. Now tell me what else is bothering you. I see many questions in your eyes."

"Your assurance that you intend to give me the colt and the filly."

"But that was understood and I gave you my word," Katerina said glibly.

"What is this hostility you have for Prince Banyen? I want to understand what it is—"

"Don't press me, Uncle. I don't like his mocking eyes and his arrogance. I resent his manner in regard to women, myself in particular. Evenly matched, I know I could bring him to his knees, and I think he knows it also. Time will tell. I warned you when I first came here that I will not allow him to interfere with my plans. If I have to kill him I will." Her hazel eyes were pinpoints of flame as she gazed at her uncle. "If you think he can ferret out the secret of Whitefire, think again. Because we are flesh and blood means nothing when it comes to the horses. One wayward move on his part and he dies, is that understood, Uncle?"

The Khan cringed at her words. He shrugged. Banyen was a man and she was a woman. He knew in his heart which of them would win. "Understood," he said softly. "Look," he said, pointing his arm in the direction of the stockade. "Banyen is preparing the prisoners. By the noon hour all will be in readiness. The food sacks were made up last night, and the barrels of water are being loaded on the wagons now. Blankets and carpets will also be given you. Does it meet with your satisfaction?"

Katerina nodded assent. "It's time then for me to speak with the prisoners. If you don't mind, Uncle, I'd prefer to do it alone, but before I do that, there is one other question I want to ask you. This . . . army you have garrisoned here, is this the army you plan to use when you attack Moscow? I overheard you talking to one of your tribal elders about the high price you've been paying for soldiers. Where are these soldiers and how many of them are there? If you're buying an army, why is Prince Banyen working and training these men? What does it mean? If he's needed here with your men, why are you sending him to the Carpathians with me? No lies, Uncle, I want the truth from your lips."

"You are your father's daughter, there is no doubt of that. You pick at something as a dog picks at a bone. Leave me to my reasoning, whatever it may be. I've agreed to your demands, and other than my two small requests, I have not badgered you." Suddenly there was a ring of iron in the jovial voice. "Leave it, Katerina. Go, talk to your men, and then join me for breakfast in my yurt."

Katerina agreed and strode off, her back stiff and straight, her thoughts whirling. The old fox was clever, and sly. What was he up to? She would watch Banyen as carefully as he planned to watch her. Sooner or later he would give away his plans. Men were fools in that they thought women were stupid.

Her voice was sharp and clear when she spoke to the prisoners. She fixed her eyes on Kostya when she spoke, and was pleased to see the light of interest in his eyes. "You men have been specially chosen by me to travel to the Carpathian Mountains. With the Khan's permission, I'm giving you back your lives. I'm going to train you to be Cossacks through the long cold winter. I warn you now that there will be no escape from the House of the Kat. You will all remain in your chains until we get to the mountains. Once we are there, your irons will be removed and you will walk about as free soldiers. I ask that you give me your loyalty, and in turn I will feed you, clothe you, and pay you an adequate sum of money that will be yours to do with as you see fit. What you did in the past does not interest me. It's what you do in the mountains that concerns me. It won't be easy, I can tell you that now. I'll talk with you again when we get to the House of the Kat." Loud murmurings and buzzings followed her as she strode from the stockade. Her step was light, purposeful, as her stride lengthened. She could almost feel Banyen's glittering eyes boring into her back.

Perhaps it had been a mistake to let him see her hostility. Sooner or later he would begin to wonder why she felt as she did about him. Certainly her past actions were too strong to be laid to his tying her to a horse like a sack of flour. She would have to temper her tongue and be careful when she was around him.

Breakfast was a somber affair. Strong, bitter black coffee, pungent goat cheese, and round, flat bread spread with honey were offered to her by the Khan, whose face was a study in blankness. Katerina wondered if he was already regretting his bargain. She remained quiet, her thoughts on Banyen and the long trek back to the mountains. She suddenly felt uneasy. It wasn't the thought of taking the prisoners, shackled as they were, nor the fifty men from the Khan's army with her, it was Banyen. Her uneasiness increased with each mouthful of food she swallowed. Her eyes fell to the sable carpet, and automatically she withdrew her booted foot till it rested on the plank floor of the yurt.

Prince Banyen led first one prisoner and then another from the stockade. He himself saw to their manacles and brought each man toward the wagons with a terse order to remain quiet and be still. Low-voiced murmurs reached his ears as the men conversed and speculated in low whispers. It was Kostya who voiced the question aloud to one of the others.

"There's more to this venture than the woman told us. After she trains us to be Cossacks, what is it we're to do? That, my fellow prisoners, is the fly in the honey pot. Still, she's given us back our lives. How many of us do you think would survive the first cold spell and snowstorm in this stockade? For that we should offer thanks."

"She's a woman, and we number a hundred and fifty men," a prisoner named Dmitri said in a low whisper.

Rokal grinned, showing short, stubby teeth. "Look over your shoulder, my friend, and tell me what you see."

"There will be no chance for any of us to escape," Kostya said softly. "And why should we? The woman promised us food and money to do as she asked. I for one have no wish to die in the snows. Let us agree among ourselves that we will give this venture a chance."

"I vote with Kostya," Rokal said softly. One by one the others by the wagon agreed.

The man called Dmitri, his eyes nearly closed against the brightness of the day, watched as Banyen's men readied themselves for the trip. Kostya is right, he decided. Later, when the snows melted in the spring and he had good food in his belly, along with gold in his pocket, would be time enough to get free. For now he would agree. Beyond that, he would make no promises, to the woman or his fellow prisoners.

The sun beat down upon the tiny crystals of silica, heating them, making the temperature rise to a hot, uncomfortable degree. Everyone felt the effects of the heat, including the animals. The wagons stood like sentinels, waiting for the horses to be harnessed to them. The prisoners stood shackled together on the hot sand, waiting. The Mongol soldiers who comprised the guard were busy preparing their horses and wiping away the perspiration that ran freely down their bodies. The remainder of the soldiers fastened the last of the ropes, securing supplies and foodstuffs aboard two wagons. A caravan of ten wagons, two hundred men, Prince Banyen, and one woman waited, poised on the brink of success or failure.

The Khan, with Banyen and Katerina, watched the final preparations from under a canopy, escaping the onslaught of the hot sun. "Katerina, one would think from the feel of this heat that you should have the usual ride through the

Urals. Banyen and I know, however, that this is not the case. The Urals are tricky and treacherous this time of year. You feel the sleighs unnecessary trouble at this time, but I assure you, once into the Urals you'll thank me for my foresight. Word reached me several days ago that the northern ridge is deep in snow, and your only chance is the southern ridge, even if it is longer. You still might have a chance to bypass the worst of the accumulation. The men are almost finished, so if there is anything else you need tell me now," Afstar said, concerned for her well-being. He knew her journey would be a difficult one.

Katerina's heart pounded as she looked at the caravan, and a momentary panic gripped her. Was she capable of the task that lay before her? Could she handle two hundred men and Prince Banyen? Were Mikhailo and the Khan right? Could she accomplish what she intended? Then, as a Mongol soldier brought up her horse, the Cosars and Volin flashed before her. No matter what, nothing would ever stop her from avenging the demise of her people and returning the Cosars to their rightful home. The image she had of her father lying dead with the others, the huts burned to the ground, was all she ever needed as a source from which to draw her strength. Each time the scene flashed before her, unbounded power soared through her body, energizing her very being with unparalleled confidence. She knew she could do anything.

Reaching for the reins of the horse, she turned to her uncle. "I can't think of anything else that's needed, everything has been checked. If we've overlooked anything, it won't matter once we're on our way. I thank you, Uncle, for all you have done for me, and for all you have given me. Most of all, I wish to thank you for believing in me and what I must do. My mother would bless you many times over if she were here. She would be very proud of her brother." Putting her arms around the Khan, she embraced him tenderly and kissed him on the cheek. Once again she looked him in the eye, and said, "With all my heart, my people, who are no more, and I thank you."

Katerina mounted her horse, her seat relaxed, her cat eyes sleepy and lynx-like as she waited for Banyen's signal to start the small caravan. A patrol of twenty soldiers was to lead the way on horseback. The remainder of the soldiers would ride in the wagons behind the prisoners, Katerina would ride behind Banyen. "Are you ready?" she asked him.

Banyen's stallion stood before him, waiting. The prince reached out his hand to the Khan. "I'll not give speeches of thanks. I merely wish to say I'll be back in the spring. When I return, I wish to hear news of preparations for our attack. I need say no more. Farewell, my friend." He released his hand from the Khan's and leaped onto his horse.

Afstar looked up at both of them with worry in his eyes. "You embark on a difficult journey. You'll need all your strength and will. Katerina, you especially have a long journey, as yours doesn't end with the Urals. Good fortune to you both."

"We'll succeed, Uncle, never fear. There is much to do, and it will be done," she said, with such confidence that even Banyen almost believed her. "Give the command to move," Katerina ordered Banyen, "for we must make the Ural River by nightfall. Once again I bid you farewell, Uncle. Banyen will bring news of my progress to you in the spring." Katerina dug her heels deep into the horse's flanks, the animal responding immediately, with Banyen close behind.

He looked at Katerina's easy, relaxed position in the saddle and felt desire rise in him. The tight, confining shirt she wore was open at the throat, revealing a deep cleavage as her breasts rose and fell rhythmically with her steady breathing. He let his gaze linger on the slight spread of her thigh in the form-fitting trousers. Long and supple. His heart pounded in his chest when he thought how she would feel next to him, her flesh as naked as his.

Katerina felt his appraisal of her and stared pointedly into indigo eyes. She allowed a small smile to tug at her lips as she returned his bold look. She motioned him with her finger to come closer. Suspecting a trick, Banyen held his whip loosely in his hand, ready to strike out if necessary. Katerina leaned closer till she was barely inches from his sun-darkened face. "I know how to kill just as you do. I can do it quickly and silently and not shed a drop of blood, or I can arrange to have your blood flow like a river . . . Remember what I said, Mongol, this is no game we're playing. When this is over, there will not be a prize for the winner."

Dark eyes scoffed at her words, confusing Katerina, throwing her off balance. She had threatened to kill him and he accepted it lightly. Suddenly she felt vulnerable and weak beneath his gaze.

"Do my ears deceive me, are you threatening me? Never mind, I know a threat when I hear one. Answer one question for me, woman, why do you have such . . . an unreasonable dislike for me? I had to tie you to the horse when I brought you to camp. If I had set you upright, you would have fallen and possibly killed yourself. If you recall, you were in a greatly weakened condition. I see no resentment in your eyes for these . . . scum," he said, pointing to the prisoners, "nor do I see anything but fondness in your eyes for the Khan. I and I alone am the recipient of your dislike. Why?"

Katerina stared deeply into the indigo eyes for barely a moment, willing him to remember. She saw only blankness. "You really don't know, do you. A pity," she said, straightening her slim body on the horse. "One day possibly the answer will come to you. When it does," she said, wagging a finger playfully at him, "it will be too late."

Banyen's face filled with rage. What kind of riddle was that? Damn fool woman! Did she think he was a mind reader? Why couldn't she just tell him whatever it was? Oh no, beat the bush, go around it but never through it. He squared his broad shoulders, gave her a last scorching look, and rode to the front of the twenty-man patrol. With a brisk wave of his hand, the small caravan began to move.

The prince rode silently ahead of his men, his anger driving his thoughts back in time to the rage he had felt as a boy of six. He lay face down in the dirt, left for dead, as Ivan and his troops stormed Kazan.

Scared, every muscle in his body still, he dared to move his eyes. When the cannons had finished, and the village had been leveled, he watched the soldiers ride in and slaughter every last person, including his mother and father. He watched as Ivan and his men feasted on goats and sheep afterward, and for sport used the bodies of children for target practice. Banyen's anger turned to revenge as he thought of Ivan. The sound of a voice startled him.

Katerina turned in the saddle and waved to Afstar. "My promise, Uncle, when the first wildflower sprouts on the frozen banks of the Dnieper, a new breed of Cossack will be born!" With a last wave of her hand, she spurred the horse forward and raced to take her place behind Banyen.

The Khan patted his ample girth, a smile on his lips. He had lost count of the times he had seen the wildflowers poke through mounds of snow, only to darken and die within hours. His dark eyes became hooded as he recalled a lone sprout that had survived long after the others were nothing more than brown specks in the smooth, unblemished snow.

Chapter 9

Halya Zhuk paced her luxurious bedchamber, a furious look in her eyes. Something must have happened to Yuri, he was weeks overdue. Angrily she thrust out a satin-slippered foot and kicked at the dressing table. Bottles and jars teetered precariously as she continued to jab the table. It was Ivan's fault. Each time she questioned him he grew angry and hostile. And yesterday, in one of his insane rages, he had said Yuri was dead and it was no great loss. He acted as if he knew something he wasn't telling her. Yuri couldn't be dead, not her baby brother.

She flung herself on the high bed, scalding tears seeping into the rich brocade of the coverlet. If Yuri was dead then nothing mattered. She would go back to Moldavia to be with her aging parents, if they were still alive. And that's another thing, she thought as she sat up in the bed. How many times had she asked Ivan to send a messenger to her home to find out the condition of her parents? He promised, then did nothing. What if she returned only to find them dead? Another attack of weeping seized her. What should she do? "I don't want to become Czarina, not anymore. I just want to leave here and go where people are sane and normal. I don't want to sit next to him. He's ugly, fat, and disgusting." She hiccuped. "I can't bear to have his cold, flabby flesh next to mine, and I can't bear to . . . to . . . I hate him!" she cried passionately.

The week before, when Ivan had returned from Alexandrov, he had been stranger than ever. The great palace buzzed about his bizarre behavior. One of the boyars said Ivan ordered a sleigh with seventeen hundred gold plates to be driven to Alexandrov. Afterward, he immured himself in a ramshackle hut. On his return to Moscow he insisted on the right to judge and punish traitors, and also to form a state within a state, if the people wanted him to stay.

The Prince of Moscow, as he rendered himself, now paid homage to a Tatar called Simeon Bekbulatovich.

Halya had seen Ivan only once since his return, and had been shocked at his appearance. His clothes hung on his slovenly body, which reeked of wine and sweat. She gagged when he gathered her in his arms, murmuring insane things. In desperation, Halya filled him with liquor till he fell unconscious, then crept from the room, her ears burning with his decadent words. He was crazy, and she had to leave now, before he took it into his head to kill her.

Halya looked around her elegant room, and at the rows of elaborate gowns that had been sewn for her when Ivan claimed her for his next wife. Every jewel imaginable had been added to her coffers to enhance her beauty. Anything she fancied was given to her upon a simple request. Can I give up all this richness? she wondered, looking around at the magnificent tapestries that adorned the walls, and the thick, colorful carpets that covered the marble floor. The elaborately brocaded silken drapery on the high windows and bed were such as she had imagined existed only in fairy tales. Coffers for her rings, pendants, and bracelets rested on finely made tables. All the boxes were of solid gold and lined with rich, thick velvet. Sometimes, when Halya had nothing else to do, she amused herself by the hour playing with the gems, lining them up on the bed. They were hers for her willingness to do whatever Ivan asked. When she left she would take them with her—nothing else, just the gems. Jewels could buy anything and were an acceptable bribe when one was needed. They had been earned by the use of her body. Yes, they belonged to her, and she would never part with them.

Halya left the bed and stood on a small carved stool to peer out the small window. Dusk. She hated this time of day, for as night fell Ivan began to grow restless and make demands on her. His day at an end, and his belly satisfied, he would begin to think of the ache in his loins. A bellow would go up, heard all over the palace, and within minutes two of his trusted guards would be at her door, informing her that the Czar demanded her presence in his chambers. Please, not tonight! she prayed silently. Please, not tonight!

Her slender shoulders shook and heaved with her unchecked sobs as she stepped down from the easement. In her heart she knew there wouldn't be a reprieve for her this evening, as it had been over ten days since he had summoned her to his rooms. She didn't know which was worse, the acts she was forced to perform or the dread of anticipation.

Shortly after sunset, the moment she dreaded arrived. A knock sounded on her door. "The Czar desires your company this evening," a guard said imperiously.

The moment the door closed, Halya threw the bolt and tore through her room, plucking first at one gown and then another from the deep recesses of the wardrobe. Finally she settled on a sea-green silk, cut low over her breasts, adding a string of emeralds around her neck as she preened before the glass. She looked beautiful and Ivan would appreciate her, she was sure of it. Carefully, Halya arranged her hair into deep swirls, allowing one long curl to drape her shoulder. When she remembered how Ivan liked to wind his fingers around the curl and force her head down between his legs, she shuddered. Tossing the lock of hair over her shoulder, she gagged and swore never to do that again, never, never again! After tonight she would do as she saw fit, and would answer to no one. She would start a new life, but only after she had found out about Yuri.

Slowly she walked to Ivan's bedchamber. Inside the room, she found him completely nude, dancing obscenely in the center of a ring of naked women. She gasped at the sight, afraid to make a sound.

"Would you care to join us, Halya?" He drooled as his grotesque body was eagerly caressed by the laughing females.

"Perhaps another time, dear Ivan," she said hesitatingly. She prayed that he would not ask her to disrobe and perform humiliating acts in front of the other women.

"Yes, another time," he said threateningly. "I have other plans for you tonight." A sadistic sneer formed on his twisted mouth as his mad, glazed eyes rolled in his head. Halya trembled at his words.

With a vague wave of his bejeweled fingers, the women were gone. Gathering a robe around him, he picked up a rolled parchment from a nearby table. "I have news for you of your brother, Yuri." An evil grin quivered on his lips, the madness still lingering in his eyes. "I have word of the hero you call your brother, the boy I called a man. You were right—he was a boy. I must tell you the results of his journey."

Ivan played with Halya, watching her every expression, delighting in the intensity of her anticipation. "This message has been in my bedchamber for several days now . . . no, not several days, but two weeks . . . no, a month. Yes, that seems more like it. A month ago my personal courier brought this missive to me." Ivan waved the crackly parchment in her face, taunting her with its contents.

Desperately trying to control herself, Halya asked calmly, "Has my brother served you well, my Czar?"

A roar of mad laughter split the tense air, sending icy shivers down Halya's spine. "Oh, yes, my lovely one, he has served me well." Knowing this was the moment to inflict the most pain, Ivan seized it. "He served me so well that he died for me." The twisted mouth in his demented face spewed forth an evil, demonic laugh, wrought from the center of the earth.

Halya fell back in shock at the sight of Ivan's face and the sound that emanated from it. A moment later she lay faint on the floor.

The sight of her body, collapsed, threw the Czar into a dance of delight, and another heinous laugh gurgled out of his throat. Sitting down beside the princess, he stared at her unconscious form. A variety of noises and movements befell him, as though he were possessed by a demon.

Halya stirred. She sat up, supporting herself on one arm, and beheld the transformed face of Ivan before her. Controlling her instinct to run, she fought the urge to vomit. Never had she seen such madness as that which played on the face of Ivan. Trembling fearfully, she rose to her feet.

"Go to your room now and change for my banquet. Within minutes I want you at my side in the common hall. I want everyone to see my whore sitting next to me."

Halya flew from the room, relieved to be away from him. Running through the hallways, she sobbed uncontrollably as she thought of Yuri. Inside her chamber, she slammed the door and cried out with anguish, "Yuri, oh, Yuri! My brother dead! How? Why? Now I have no one!" she cried brokenheartedly, collapsing on her bed.

A knock at her door made her remember Ivan's order. "My princess, Ivan is calling for you, you must come!" her maid begged, running into the room.

"Quickly, help me change my gown," Halya said, motioning the girl to hurry. "Fetch me the black dress and slippers. Tonight is a sad night, and black fits my mood." She felt dead, drained of all emotion, detached. Ivan would not bother her this night. A numbness settled in her, freeing her from everything but thoughts of Yuri and her hatred of the Czar. Dressed, she walked down the long corridors to the hall, vowing Ivan would find his death at her hands.

When Halya's escorts seated her next to Ivan, she was stunned to see an unkempt, filthy man with a curled mustache sitting in the place of honor, on the Czar's left. Her eyes widened at this strange behavior. It could only mean that Ivan was up to some dastardly thing that would bring harm to someone. Dear God, she prayed, please don't let it be me. She forced a bright smile and spoke lovingly to Ivan, who looked at her as though he had never seen her before. Her stomach churned as she watched him pick at a stray thread on his elaborate crimson robe. The thread seemed to annoy him. Unexpectedly, he ordered one of the guards, standing behind his throne, to cut the sleeve from the robe immediately. The guard blinked, grasped a long-handled knife, and slit the rich fabric from shoulder to wrist. Ivan took the sleeve and tied it around the head of the man seated next to him. He laughed and sat back in his high gold throne, the saliva dribbling down his chin. The boyars sat mesmerized at his lack of manners and lowered their eyes to the gold plates in front of them. A few of the women smiled at his wicked display, immediately sobering at a well-placed kick under the table by a husband.

The man at Ivan's left felt embarrassed and confused, for he knew he was the object of ridicule, but he was powerless to do anything about it. He suffered in silence, the offensive sleeve of scarlet tied rakishly to his head. He reached down and picked up a piece of meat, intent on bringing it to his mouth.

Ivan slapped the meat from his hand and stared at him. "Were you born in a stable, sir? I eat first, to be sure the food isn't poisoned. After I have eaten, the boyars eat, and then you may, if there is anything left. I'm not ready to dine yet, so you'll have to wait until I give you permission. I may not sup at all this night. I see nothing on the table that pleases me," he said petulantly.

Halya watched nervously. No one ate, no one made a motion that could in any way be misconstrued by the Czar. When he said nothing tempted him, then nothing should tempt them. If there was one among them who was starving, he would starve. Halya looked at her own plate and closed her eyes. She knew if her life depended on it she couldn't eat.

Suddenly Ivan stood up and bowed before his guests. "I called you all here today for a reason," he announced. "I wish you to pay homage to this man," he said, pointing to his left. "He's here on a matter of business, business that could well mean that . . . Never mind, there's not one among you that can be trusted with such important news. Rise," he commanded, "and bow to my new envoy. Another day I'll tell you his name and where he comes from."

"From the look of him, he came from the nearest pig trough," came a low, muttered response.

"Who is it that dares to speak when I'm talking, and dares to make such an offensive remark to my newly appointed envoy? Speak, or all of your heads will be severed. On the count of one, the man responsible had better step forward. One!"

Four boyars immediately stood and pushed forward a rotund man who was trying to pull away, his hand reaching for his wife.

"Remove his head and place it in the middle of the floor," Ivan ordered. "I'm hungry now, I think I'll have some meat." He stretched his bare arm toward a heaping platter of lamb and withdrew a large chunk. His eyes focused on his bare arm, then moved to his new envoy's head and the sleeve that was tied around it. He ripped it from the envoy's head and stuck his arm into it. When the heavy silk slipped to his wrist in a bunch, he frowned and chewed on his meat. The envoy sat stunned, as did Halya, who feared her deep breathing would be the subject of Ivan's next attack.

The large room was silent as a guard walked slowly to the center of the hall, a large domed platter in his hands. Quickly he set the platter down and stood back to await further orders. Ivan continued to chew, his vision cut off by the assembled boyars at various tables. "Is it ready?" he called, stretching his neck.

"Yes, my Czar, it is ready," the man replied.

"Good. Remove the cover and let us feast our eyes. Did he bleed much?" he asked casually.

The guard knew the expected response by heart. "Like a pig, my Czar," he said, as he lifted the lid and exposed the severed head. Gasps rang out through the hall.

"You may leave," Ivan said imperiously.

The new envoy turned in his chair and closed his eyes. Halya clamped her teeth together and forced her hands to remain still in her lap. What would he do next?

Without warning, Ivan stood up and waved his arms, the fallen sleeve dangling over his long, thin fingers. "The dinner is over! Place your tax monies in the basket with your names and lot numbers. And no cheating," he said, wagging his finger playfully in the air. "Take the food away," he ordered the servants. "They don't deserve fine food served on my priceless plates. Send it all to my quarters and I'll feast by myself."

Halya sat, hardly daring to breathe, waiting for Ivan to leave the room. Not till she was sure he was far down the corridor did she move, and then she ran as if the hounds of hell were on her heels. Out of the corner of her eye she noticed that the slovenly dressed man with the curled mustache wore a deep, perplexed frown on his face. Who was he, and what was he doing here? What manner of envoy was he, dressed like a beggar with dirty, mud-caked boots and filthy, baggy trousers?

On and on she raced, till she came to her room. She skidded to a stop, almost losing her balance in her haste to enter and lock the door behind her. Quickly she slipped the cover from the thick, fluffy pillow and started to throw her jewels into it, helter-skelter. When the coffers were empty she tossed a few pieces of underclothing into the sack and tied the end into a stout knot. She then stripped off her gown and pulled out a pale lavender afternoon dress with simple lines and folds. In an instant she had it over her head and quickly grabbed a matching cape. She had all she needed; she was ready to leave.

Halya dropped to her knees at the side of her bed and bowed her head. With all her being she prayed for guidance and strength to do what she had to do.

While Halya prayed, Gregory Bohacky, the new envoy, exited the dining hall behind the grim-faced, muttering boyars. Carefully he avoided the severed head on the large gold platter. His stomach heaved as he made his way through the corridors in search of the room a guard said was to be his. He walked for what seemed a long time, till he came to familiar surroundings. A flash of scarlet and a loud bellow caused him to stop in his tracks.

"Enter, my envoy," Ivan called in lordly fashion. "We have much to discuss. Let's do it now so you can leave at dawn. Tell me, how did you like your first state dinner? Wasn't it interesting? I find if one takes control of the situation one doesn't get kicked from behind. Sit, and tell me of the Cosars and how we'll do business. I see by the look on your face you were not successful in gaining the secret. It's of no importance now, as long as you have the horses. The sum agreed upon was six chests of gold, I believe. Am I right?"

"No, Czar Ivan, you aren't right. The horses are worth their weight in gold. There is now a price on my head, as well as that of every man in my tribe. That, and that alone, has made the price double," he said bravely. "I had to slaughter the whole village of Volin to get those damnable animals, and I expect to be well paid! If not, there are other buyers. Don't be hasty and think you can kill me, for if you do, and I don't return when expected, the horses will be moved. It was arranged before I journeyed here. If you agree to do business, then the Cosars will be delivered on schedule. Half the money now and the other half on delivery, as agreed two years ago."

"That was two years ago, and this is today. My treasury is not as great now as it was then. We must renegotiate the terms."

"There will be no bargaining. I have stated my price and it is the only price I'll agree to. Take it or leave it."

"You drive a hard deal. To think that after I made you my special envoy you have the audacity to try to cheat me. I'll call my Oprichniks—yes, I'll call them and have you beheaded." He reached out and pulled a long velvet rope. The sound of a gong thundered in the room and into the outer corridors. A guard opened the door and waited expectantly. "Fetch your leader for me immediately," Ivan ordered.

Gregory felt fear gnawing into his chest as his breathing became strained. Ivan was insane, incapable of being reasonable. He had to leave and get away from this lunatic whose spittle was drooling down his chin. He thought quickly, and his eyes narrowed as he looked deeply into the insane stare of the Czar. "How would you like to see the stallion Whitefire? I rode him here myself so you could be the first and only man to claim he saw the famous stallion." He made his tone purposely light, almost cajoling, in the hopes of diverting Ivan from thoughts of his murder.

"Is what you say true?" Ivan asked excitedly. "But of course, my envoy, I wish to see the stallion. Where did you stable him?"

"If the Czar will stand on the balcony, I'll get the stallion and ride him beneath the window. You'll be able to boast what no man has ever boasted. If you like, I'll let you ride him," Gregory said enticingly.

"Yes, yes, that's what I want to do! A night ride on White-fire. How wonderful you are to suggest such a thing. I knew I made a wise choice when I appointed you my envoy," the gullible Czar said happily, forgetting the order he had given a minute ago. "Go, ready the stallion, and I'll change to suitable clothing. As we ride through Moscow, you shall go ahead of me and announce to one and all that I ride the stallion Whitefire. Agreed?"

Gregory nodded and immediately left the room, his throat dry and his head reeling with his near mishap. How much time did he have to ride away before the lunatic sent someone after him? Not long, he surmised. He vowed to ride like the wind.

Ivan set about changing his robes to clothing more befitting a ride through the streets at night. He carefully chose a tunic of lemon yellow, trimmed with black braid. He preened like a peacock in front of the mirror and then sat down to wait. What seemed like hours later, he called for one of his guards and ordered him to the stable to find Gregory and see what was causing the delay. When the guard returned a short while later, Ivan knew by the look on his face that Bohacky was gone. He cursed long and loud, to the discomfort of the guard, who feared for his life. In a rage-filled voice he ordered the guard out. "He shall pay with his life for his treachery!"

Irate, Ivan slammed the door and bolted it. His eyes full of madness and hate, he shouted to the guards outside, "No one nears my door tonight!"

Until dawn, unholy screams, low moans, and demonic laughter emanated from behind closed doors, ringing throughout the palace. Then all was silent.

Chapter 10

As the first day of their journey began, Katerina felt the need to assert her leadership of the caravan immediately or else her raw recruits would easily turn to a more powerful person to be their commander. While she and Banyen rode up ahead, Katerina turned to him, her eyes narrowed against the glare of the sun, and said, "I don't care for this arrangement. Have your guards change the position of the wagons so the food and supplies come first. They must be where we can see them at all times. Place two wagons of prisoners next, then a wagon of soldiers, the prisoners, the soldiers again, the last wagon of prisoners, and then the sleighs. Put six guards on horses in the rear, five spread out on each side of the caravan, and another four behind the supply and food wagons. I hope the two soldiers in charge of each wagon are trustworthy and know how to handle the wagons. Do you approve? Before you answer, let me tell you, whether you like it or not, that's the way it shall be!" she said with grim determination.

"Why do you bother to ask if you have no intention of changing anything?" he questioned, with a look of arrogance on his face.

"I owe you no explanations, I ask you out of courtesy, and to see if you agree with my methods," she retorted, just as arrogantly.

"The arrangement will do," he said sharply, not wanting her to know that he couldn't have planned it better. She does have a brilliant mind, he thought. But it belonged in the body of a man, not a woman. If she were a man, she would be someone to reckon with, a leader among men. With a mind such as hers, bolstered with such zeal, there would be no stopping such a person. Without realizing it, Banyen stopped his horse as the thought struck full force: there'll be no stopping her! His mouth hung open as he shook his head, his mind racing. I sit here and describe the qualities of a man among men, a leader among leaders—I sit here and describe a woman! He was thunderstruck. He muttered, "I can see my work is cut out for me. It should be an interesting winter."

"Banyen!" Katerina shouted at him. "Why did you stop? What's the matter? Is there a problem? Banyen, what is it?"

Her voice brought him to his senses. He spurred his stallion with a vengeance, the animal breaking into a gallop. In moments he was alongside Katerina. "There's nothing wrong, I just got caught up in determining the best way over the mountains," he lied. "We have four hours of light left, do you think we'll make the river before then?"

"When I rode from the Urals to Sibir it took about that long, but with the wagons, I don't know. If we reach the river after sunset, it won't be too bad, the land ahead is all flat. Our problems begin when we try getting those confounded wagons up and over the mountains. Why I ever let my uncle talk me into using them I'll never know. I still think horses would have been better. Even with shackles, the prisoners would have managed. If their leg irons were off, with enough chain between the wrist shackles, it would have worked. I think my uncle preferred to give me ten wagons rather than two hundred horses. Tell me, Banyen, does he even have that many horses?" she asked seriously.

"I never took an accurate count. A good source of strong men and fast horses is what he needs to rebuild his army and I have no doubt he'll find them. He is a shrewd man, and an excellent trader backed with a wealth of gold and jewels. When I return in the spring, I know Sibir will be greatly changed. Enough of this talk," he said suddenly, realizing there was much work to be done, "we have to get these wagons moving." He broke away from Katerina and rode down the length of the caravan, shouting at the drivers to keep the wagons going as fast as they could.

The Kat rode her horse to the side of the road and stopped. She sat and watched as the wagons rolled by, trying to determine the pace, trying to estimate how much time would be needed to get from one place to another. The sun was sinking lower in the sky; only two hours of light were left. Her first calculation had been right—they would make the Ural River an hour after sundown. Not too bad, she thought. It will take an hour and a half to eat and bed down, giving all but the guards a good night's sleep.

Banyen rode up to her, the men and wagons moving to his satisfaction.

The Kat turned to Banyen. "After we have eaten and all is secured, we must talk about getting the wagons over the mountains."

"Do you have any ideas? If so, will you handle it like the wagon arrangement? Ask my opinion when you've already made up your mind?" he baited her, with a sneer on his lips.

"I have several suggestions, but I would like to hear your opinion, what you think best," she said, controlling the anger in her voice. You sarcastic bastard, she thought. A man always has to act like a man, never like a human being, she told herself. Whacking her horse on the haunches with her hand, she sent him pounding ahead of the caravan, leaving Banyen behind. She rode the horse hard for a mile or two, trying to rid herself of the aggravation the Mongol stirred within her. Why did she let him get to her? The question kept returning. What would it be like to make love with him if he were tender and caring? No doubt he kept many women happy with his slim, muscular body, his good looks and willing mouth. Anger coursed through Katerina again. She had to stop thinking about him, there was a caravan to get through the mountains to the House of the Kat. A winter of training unruly prisoners, trying to make Cossacks out of them. This wasn't the time to act like a woman; she had to be the Kat first, last, and always, until her people had been avenged and the Cosars returned.

As fast as she rode away from the caravan, she returned. The river was now in sight, and they would soon be at its banks. The darkness brought to a close the first day of their journey. Katerina trotted by Banyen's side as they headed for the river, enjoying the warm night air, lavishing in it, knowing that, once into the mountains, heat would be a matter of clothing, not the season.

Once again she and Banyen rode the length of the wagons, making sure everything was in order. Satisfied, they ordered the men to make camp for the evening.

The banks of the Ural River glistened with the dancing flames of their bonfires. It reminded Katerina of fireflies dancing in the summer night. She watched as the soldiers made the prisoners line up in an orderly manner to receive their ration of food. If all else fails, Katerina thought, I'll have the satisfaction of knowing I freed men from inevitable death and have given them the right to live, eat, and sleep like normal human beings. I'll have given them an ample supply of food so that no man goes to sleep hungry, and blankets to protect them against the night air. Compared to the stockade, where conditions were hopeless, this camp and the comforts she could provide would bring no complaints.

The prisoners and guards ate as Katerina and Banyen

waited by the fire for their food. A middle-aged man from the Khan's camp served as the cook for the group, helped by a driver on the food wagon. The ration passed out was the same for all: one cold boiled potato, a chunk of black bread, a wedge of cheese, and a piece of marinated lamb. The only luxury in camp was two skinfuls of wine, a present from the Khan to Katerina. The cook handed them their food in shallow wooden bowls and left.

Banyen motioned to Katerina to move closer to the fire, where it was warmer. "The nights are cool and will be getting cooler," he said quietly.

Katerina took his suggestion and started to eat. Pulling a goatskin from behind her, she offered Banyen a drink. His nearness bothered her. The scent of his body hovered over and around her, his lean hardness stirring her as she watched him carefully. A long arm reached for the wineskin. Tapered fingers touched and quickly withdrew. Slowly she inched away from him, afraid of what might happen if she were to feel the length of his body against hers.

Banyen smiled knowingly, aware of her discomfort.

"Don't worry about the others watching us drink," she said, trying to ease the tension. "They sit far enough away. I don't wish to make them envious. Let's discuss how we'll take the wagons over the mountains."

"You know more about that than I do, you just came through the Urals. You could tell me how steep they are, and if the rocks and trees will be a problem," he said, as he chewed on a piece of lamb.

"The real difficulty is the inclines. Some mountains have gradual slopes loaded with rocks and trees, while the others are steep and clear. We must be prepared to deal with all the elements. If the snow starts, the wagons will surely slip and slide. Tomorrow we go through the first pass, and should reach the mountain ridge around noon. It's the largest and the steepest. It will probably take us two days to get to the top. Do you have any suggestions?" she asked Banyen, who had listened attentively.

"Yes, I suggest we cross the river first." He laughed.

"I thought we were going to be serious about this," Katerina fumed.

"I am serious," he went on. "I think we should cross the river first. Was there a shallow spot you rode through?"

"Where I crossed the water would be too deep for the wagons. My horse had to swim."

"In the morning I'll test a few spots, and pick one for the wagons to cross. If we unload them, with just one driver and a team of four horses, we should get them most of the way. We'll tie ropes on each wagon and put five men on each rope. With the horses and men pulling, we should be able to get the wagons up the mountain. If we find snow, God help us." He sighed, reached for the wineskin, and took a long drink.

Katerina finished the last of her food, put down the bowl, and watched Banyen drink. Full and warm, she longed for a good night's sleep. She asked Banyen for the wine and took a short sip. Afterward she moved to get up. His strong hand reached out to grasp her slender arm. "What is it? I'm tired and wish to sleep. A busy morning awaits us," she said harshly, pulling away from him.

The wine, the warmth, and the sight of Katerina's tawny hair glistening in the light of the fire aroused desire in him. "Katerina, we've a long journey, the fire is warm, and the nights are lonely sleeping by oneself. Join me here and we'll share the delights of the night together," he muttered, his voice mellowed from the wine and his deep, dark eyes heavy with sleep.

"You fool, you're full of drink. Sleep it off by yourself, for when I stay with a man, he'll be sober and full of passion, not half drunk and half asleep." She pushed him over with her foot and stalked off into the darkness to her bedroll.

Dawn found Katerina and the cook quickly moving from wagon to wagon with the allotted pieces of bread. Eager to get an early start, she had awakened the cook and told him to distribute the food and make quick work of it. When the task was finished, she walked to the fire, now glowing red embers, and looked down at Banyen. She nudged his torso with her foot. "Get up, we've got to get the men up and moving." Her words went unheard. Once again she poked him, on the other side, but this time a little harder. The pressure of her foot in his back finally roused him

"What's the matter?" Banyen muttered, sitting up and rubbing the sleep from his eyes. He looked up and saw Katerina standing over him, her hands on her hips.

"Tonight you'll be given one drink of wine and that's all. I have no time to wet-nurse a man who downs too much. There's much to be done, and you need a clear head to do it. Now, get up and get to the river and douse yourself with water. You were supposed to be up before everyone this morning, checking the river for a suitable crossing spot, and you lie there like a wounded animal. While you're there find the place for us to cross, if it isn't too much trouble," she ordered sarcastically.

Banyen stood up, called a soldier to roll up his blanket, looked Katerina square in the eyes with burning hatred, then stalked off toward his horse. There was no need for words; his expression said it all.

His head pounding with every step he took, Banyen made his way to the bank. The dark eyes closed slightly when he saw Kostya, stripped to the waist, dousing himself with the icy water. Gingerly he dropped to his knees and began to scoop small handfuls of water to his face. He flinched at the stinging coldness.

"Better to do it all at once," Kostya said helpfully. "One good dousing and the pain in your head will subside, and that tight feeling in your shoulders will lessen. Your mind will clear with the shock of the cold water."

"I had too much wine," Banyen mumbled as he continued to dabble the water on his face and neck.

"I noticed." Kostya grinned. "Here, let me help you," he said, drawing Banyen to his feet. "Stand fast now, and don't move." Quickly he thrust out his arm and grasped Banyen around the neck, at the same time wedging his knee in the small of his back. He jerked the prince backward and released him. "How does your upper back feel now?"

Banyen flexed his arms and shoulders, staring quizzically into bright blue eyes. His headache gone and his back normal, he spoke quietly. "Why did you do that?"

"You were suffering. I would be less than human if I didn't offer to help you. Today is a day when all of us will need every ounce of strength we have. How can you do your job if you aren't fit? I didn't do it for thanks. If you need my help again, you have only to ask me. There is no thought in my mind to escape, so rest easy. I made a bargain with the woman, and I'll stick by it."

Banyen nodded as he watched Kostya walk back to the camp. "Damnation!" he exclaimed. He believed every word the prisoner said, and was also freed from last night's overindulgence. His head was clear, and his back felt better than it had in months.

The camp was bustling. By the time Banyen got back, all was in readiness.

"I've found the place to cross, so let's be on our way, if it's convenient for you," he mocked Katerina.

She held out his piece of bread. "Here, take this, it will quell your fermenting stomach. You'll have to eat it as we ride."

Banyen rode to the head of the caravan with Katerina at his side, his head throbbing once again. When they were in position, he shouted back to the drivers to follow him.

They soon arrived at the fording site. After a quick inspection by Katerina, she nodded approval for the wagons to move. One by one, they labored through the water, creaking and groaning as they tilted and slid on the slippery moss-covered rocks. It took more time to cross than Katerina had anticipated; valuable time was lost again. She knew she couldn't beat the snow. Angrily she urged Banyen and the men to speed up their pace. Katerina was well aware that the men were in no hurry to go anywhere. They were out of the Khan's stockade, and that was all that mattered to them. They were free of that hellhole.

Two hours into the first pass, light snow began to fall. Katerina's heart sank. *If it starts this early into the Urals, once we leave the mountains the snow will be waiting on the steppe.*

"Banyen, we must keep moving at a faster pace if we are to make the first mountain by nightfall," she said harshly. "If you have a keen eye, you should have noticed the flurries. Light snow now means we're bound to reach heavier snow as we go along. We must keep these men moving, keep after them, they travel as if they have all the time in the world."

"You're overly concerned, I think," Banyen said. "We're moving right along, and if we push them they might get angry and rebel. Besides, to go much faster would be risky for the wagons."

"I just knew you wouldn't agree with me," she said with indignation. "I'll find a way to get these men to move more rapidly, there must be something that will bait them to hurry. I'll be back shortly, I'm going to ride up ahead to see how things look." A sharp kick in the horse's sides and she was off, cantering down the pass. "I can't let him make me angry," she muttered as she rode hard, trying to rid herself of the resentment she felt toward him.

"A rider coming in the distance," called one of Banyen's soldiers.

"Keep the wagons moving," Banyen ordered. "It's the girl returning."

Katerina brought her horse to Banyen's side. "The big

mountain is just ahead. From what I could see, the lower slope is still clear of snow, but there's no way of knowing what we'll reach a few hundred feet up. We must make our best time on these flats. While I rode I also came up with an idea to entice these men to work harder."

The moment the high mountain loomed before them the men began to grumble and groan. They knew immediately they were in for a hazardous climb.

Katerina ordered the men to form a line and proceed slowly up the mountain. "You prisoners will leave the wagons and travel by foot, climbing and descending. If a wagon gets stuck, or slips, you men will lend a hand any time it is needed. You will put your backs to pushing and pulling when necessary. Banyen, post a guard to watch over them, and at the first wrong move, cut down the troublemaker. This caravan will get through to the Carpathians, even if it means many of your bodies will be strewn along the way to prove I mean what I say!"

The wagons were emptied, and the trek up the mountain began.

Two hours before nightfall of the following day, the top ridge of the mountain was in sight. Suddenly a whirlwind of snow unleashed its millions of silent, devastating crystal flakes. It was man against the elements.

"If we push hard we can make the summit tonight. We should be able to make camp before the snow creates any problems. Hurry! Otherwise you'll taste your first uphill battle with snow, making everything twice as difficult. You made good time until now, and I'm proud of what you have accomplished," she said, her voice full of praise and encouragement for the men.

Banyen sat in his Mongol saddle and watched in amazement as Kostya and the other men put on a show of superhuman effort.

At nightfall the wagons lined the upper peak, while everyone made ready for their well-earned meal. The bonfires on the ridge cast a magic glow that encircled the mountain. The glowing fires of red-yellow reflected their dance onto the millions of tiny crystals that fell heavily from the heavy skies. Steam rose as the flakes hit the fires, creating the illusion that the breast of the mountain was heaving in its sleep.

The company ate, some quickly, the smarter ones slowly. Everyone was anxious to get to sleep, their bodies spent from the uphill climb.

Each fire was sheltered by a lean-to. The guards, who had built them, huddled beneath, keeping watch. The camp was quiet except for Banyen and Katerina, who sat conversing by the fire. Secure in their plans for the downhill trek, Katerina offered Banyen his one long drink of wine. When he finished, she bid him good night and crawled under her blanket next to the fire. The prince, in no mood for another scene, quietly made himself comfortable by the crackling flames. He watched the sleeping girl, somehow drawn to her in spite of her roughness. Why? Why did she intrigue him? Certainly she was beautiful, shapely, and desirable, but so were other women. What lay beneath the outer shell?

Many nights had been spent in the arms of welcoming, soft women, women eager to please him. Would Katerina ever be so willing? Why in the name of God did he desire a woman who dressed and thought like a man, yet, in her own way, was more of a woman than any who had lain with him?

Morning found everyone huddled beneath their blankets, covered by cold white snow. Katerina woke to find Banyen sitting by the fire, chewing his piece of bread.

"You're awake early," she said, startled to find him out of bed. "I see you're eating already. Is the cook also up?"

"Yes. But the men are still asleep. It's just you, me, and the cook. Now what do you think of the drunken Mongol?" he asked.

"I think you're doing what you are supposed to do. If

you want applause, you've come to the wrong place," she replied icily. "Get on with it, wake the men. I want those wagons going down the mountain as soon as possible."

When the men had finished eating, Banyen called for their attention. "Listen to me carefully. The wagons must go down the mountain in single file, one at a time, ten lengths apart. That way, if one slips the others will not be caught in the slide. We'll try the first wagon with the horses, no ropes, and see how it goes. If the wagon slips we'll have to use the ropes. They'll be tied to the back of each wagon, and we might need one or two up front. Several men will handle each rope, pulling back so we can ease each one down the slope. The unloaded wagon will go first. Bring it up here and harness the horses. Tie the ropes on now, for once it begins to slide it's too late. You prisoners, divide into groups to walk alongside the wagon, and be prepared to grab the ropes. Number one wagon, move!" he ordered the first team.

Slowly and carefully the wagon edged its way down the steep grade. The driver strained, leaning far back into the seat, the horses almost sitting on their haunches. Gingerly the animals descended in the ankle-deep snow. One by one they made their way, driver and team working together.

Katerina called for the food wagon to be brought forward. As it pulled up, she warned the drivers and the men on foot, "If this wagon goes careening down the mountain we'll eat snow all the way to the Carpathians, if we don't freeze first. I trust you all agree." The team prepared to go downward. "One moment, I've changed my mind." At the sound of Katerina's voice, the men stopped in their tracks. "I've decided to send a sleigh wagon down next. If the weight of the sleigh causes the wagon to slide, and the horses can't control it, we'll know how to handle the supply wagons. Bring that wagon around to the front," she ordered the drivers. Katerina could see the concerned look on the faces of the two drivers.

"Listen to me," she addressed the men on foot. "You

must hold the ropes immediately, so take your positions now. If the wagon goes out of control, release the ropes and save yourselves. You drivers, cut the horses free, then jump. I don't want any men or animals killed. We can manage without a wagon, but I need every one of you." With a wave of her hand, the wagon moved ahead.

Banyen and the others stood on the edge of the crest, watching the agonizing descent. The men strained at the ropes as the wagon, horses, and drivers eased slowly down the decline. Katerina turned to Banyen. "I wish my uncle had never given me these damn wagons. If we were on foot we'd be down near the bottom for all the time the first wagons are taking. I'm sorry I consented to this madness." She held her breath as a wagon slipped momentarily.

Suddenly the air was split with a loud, bloodcurdling "Yeow-ow-ow!" Those on the ridge watched in horror as the wagon gave way. The men holding the ropes tried desperately to let go, but they were caught and went cascading down the mountain. The drivers leaped from the wagon, forgetting to cut loose the horses. The animals and men struggled for their lives. The screams of both could be heard everywhere as the wagon reeled into a fir tree, splintering to pieces. The sleigh broke loose, tumbling down the slope. Three prisoners, still tangled in the ropes, were smashed against trees and rocks, until all that remained were broken, lifeless bodies.

Katerina turned her back on the tragic sight, kicking out at the rock next to her. "I knew it, I knew these damn Mongol wagons were a mistake. Now I've lost three men and four horses."

Kostya made his way down the slope behind Katerina. Working side by side, they freed the wounded who lay trapped beneath boards from the heavy wagon. Using all his power, Kostya freed one of the men, only to lose him to a dead horse that slid down the snow, dragging the man down with him.

Stunned at the tears that glistened in Kostya's eyes, Katerina laid her hand on his arm. "There was nothing you could do. There's no time to dwell on the matter, others need our help." Her own words were tortured, a look of agony covering her delicately boned face.

"Nor can you blame yourself for what happened," he replied. "Each of us must do the best we can." Bright blue eyes stared into Katerina's. "The men will not blame you for this. You have my word."

Katerina nodded but said nothing, her throat constricting at his words.

Diligently they worked together with the help of the other prisoners, binding wounds and helping them to safety. Perspiration dripped from Kostya's face as Banyen put his arm around him to lead him away. "It's finished. You have to rest, or you'll be no good to us the remainder of the journey. A few moments to sit and you'll be as good as new." He grinned into the blue eyes. "Call it an act of human nature, mine."

Banyen and Katerina agreed that it would be madness to send a second wagon down with the sleigh aboard. Four mounted soldiers were ordered to secure ropes to the sleigh and loop the ends to their saddles. That done, they started down the hazardous mountain. While the others watched breathlessly, the sleigh and soldiers made it safely to the bottom.

Katerina was beside herself as she realized that the day was passing and all they had accomplished was the descent. She had figured a day, but she had hoped for better time. Again she cursed the wagons.

The prince walked alongside her and tried to calm her. "Don't worry, we'll get these down shortly, and the worst of it will be over. Tomorrow, if a pass is ahead, we'll make up for lost time."

"Damn those wagons!" she hissed again. "Three men,

four horses, one wagon, and one sleigh, gone. Damn . . .
damn . . . damn! Are the last two ready to go?"

"Yes. We've added more ropes and more men to hold
them."

The extra hands and ropes proved effective. The last of
the wagons went safely down the mountain.

The Kat announced that they would make camp for the
night at the base of the mountain. Every man was hungry
and tired from the grueling day. As quickly as possible, the
fires were made and the food was prepared. The men ate,
the horses were bedded down, and soon the camp fell silent.
Neither Banyen nor Katerina was in the mood for conversation. They were spent, their only thought of rest.

The next week was a repetition of small ridges and long
passes. Up one mountain and down another.

Katerina was relieved when they finally approached the
pass that led out of the Urals. Quietly she checked with the
cook on their food supply, and found they could spare some
extra for each man. A small reward, she thought happily.

That night they camped at the mouth of the pass. "Men,
listen to me. You see the snow is with us every day, and it
will get worse. We've been through hard times, and we still
have a hazardous journey ahead. If the drivers of each
wagon can keep the horses at a lively pace, I promise all
fifty kopecks."

Wide grins and shouts of approval went up over the
camp. Katerina smirked to herself. Men would do anything
for money. The following morning would be their true test:
the crossing of the Kama River.

The Kat watched through half-closed eyes as she got to
her feet and took her place at the end of the line to await her
dinner portion. The meal over, the fires roaring brightly in
their efforts to reach the sky, she sat back and closed her
eyes. She was jarred from her light sleep by a shout from
the cook, who volunteered to play a tune for the men on his
balalaika. She listened while he played and sang songs of

the Russian people and their land. Tears burned her eyes at the haunting, beautiful words. When the cook finished his tune, he played another. This time he sang of the flowers and the sweet song of the nightingale. He stopped playing for a moment, reached out his hand to draw Katerina to her feet, and motioned her to act out the scenes as he played. Caught up in the moment, she agreed, and began to move her hands gently to the music as she had done before, as a child.

Banyen and the others watched, enthralled by her slow, rhythmic movements to the sound of the balalaika. She smiled, her small teeth pearl-white in the orange glow from the fire, her movements sure and relaxed. Banyen stared, never having seen her like this before. Suddenly he wanted to reach out and clasp her to him, to take her slender, swaying body in his arms. He wanted to feel the warmth of her beneath him while he released his aching loins into her. The welt on his cheek began to throb as he watched the men leering at her. He was sure they were all thinking the same thing, just as he knew he needed to take another breath to live. He hated it. The wound ached again, making his cheek twitch as he placed his index finger over it, trying to stop the pain. What was bothering him? Jealousy? He had never been jealous of a woman in his life. His dark eyes scanned the men around the campfire, and he knew he had to do something before . . .

Banyen stood up. "The hour grows late. The men need their sleep," he said curtly.

A loud groan of dismay circled the fire. It was the Kat who seconded Banyen's words and gathered up her bed-roll. "The prince is right. The cook will play for us another tune, and then we'll all dance. Tomorrow you'll thank Prince Banyen for his foresight." She unrolled her blanket, spread it by the fire, and lay down. The only sound heard throughout the camp was the crackling of the fires.

Banyen lay awake long after everyone else was asleep,

his mind refusing to let him rest. The vision of Katerina dancing left him only with the thought of conquering her so that his body would be appeased. He wanted to reach out, here and now, and take her. Blood coursed through him, keeping alive the fire in his loins. Wondering about the taste of her lips, he thought of the ways he would make love to her. He imagined how she would feel in his arms, the softness of her body and the firmness of her breasts against his chest. Rolling over onto his belly, he willed the ache to subside. The men looked asleep, but he wondered if they too tossed with an ache in their groin. Frustration gave way to exhaustion, and he slept.

As dawn broke through the darkness, the camp stirred. The men got up and ate. Some were already at work. Katerina and Banyen discussed the best way to cross the Kama River.

"I know the Kama is treacherous and deep but I think crossing over the ice would be the quickest and easiest way to get to the other side. I'll test the ice by walking on it, and if it holds me I'll go out on my horse," Katerina said.

"I disagree with you. I think we should find a shallow area," urged Banyen.

Katerina ignored his words as she tested the ice around the banks, satisfied with its thickness. Cautiously she edged out onto the ice-covered river. She walked a third of the way without hearing or seeing a crack. On her return she trod briskly, stopping now and then to jump up and down, testing the ice. At the bank of the river a soldier waited with her horse. Once again she ventured across the ice, this time a little farther. Satisfied, she turned the horse around and headed back.

"I have no doubts the ice will hold the wagons, no doubts at all. It's strong enough to hold anything."

"In the middle of the river the current moves deep and fast, and the ice doesn't get as thick as at the edges. I'm telling you, it won't hold."

"Line up the wagons and prepare to move. An empty wagon will go first, followed by the ones with food and supplies. After that, move the wagons with the men. If the ice should give way, it will happen before the men go out. Now move them onto the ice," Katerina said forcefully.

Cautiously the empty wagon crossed the river. Katerina turned to Banyen and gave him a satisfied smile. Next, the food wagon eased over the ice. Once past the center of the river, the other bank in sight, the cook heaved a sigh of relief. The supply wagon followed. As it crossed the middle of the river, hairline cracks, invisible to the eye, started to form.

"Next," called Katerina, ordering the wagons filled with the men to go. "Stay two wagon lengths behind each other. There is nothing to fear. You see how the ice holds. Remember, two lengths behind."

As the wagons began to move, the guards on horseback trotted along. When they reached the middle of the river, the ice began to rumble. "The ice is cracking!" the prisoners shouted in unison.

All eyes were on the frozen river, watching as a horse in the first team lost its footing and fell to one knee, dragging down three other animals. As they fell, a loud thundering crack ripped through the air. The first load of prisoners reached the bank just as the ice behind them cracked and split asunder. The river's mouth, wide open, swallowed the men, horses, and wagons into its mad, rushing, carnivorous depths.

The death cry of the men and horses clawed at everyone's ears. As men and animals struggled to get out of the icy water, their screams tore at Banyen and Katerina. The Kat headed for the shattered ice, shouting for the others to try to save the men.

Banyen rushed after her, shouting. "No! You'll only waste more lives. You can't save those in the water. When it's this cold they can only survive for a minute. Katerina, do you hear me? Only a minute. The men in the water are dead men. Let them go and save the others."

Katerina stopped in her tracks. He was right.

"Get that sleigh and the other wagons off the ice quickly! Back them off carefully!" Banyen shouted, his voice full of authority.

Banyen could see apathy overtaking Katerina. She stood on the bank, helpless, motionless. Her head dropped down on her chest in defeat. He quickly grabbed her arm and pushed her toward the rescue party. "Katerina, there's much to be done and we need everybody's help. Take the reins and lead the horses onto the bank," he ordered, trying to bring her back to her senses. "You had to let the men in the river go. I'm not coldhearted, but I've seen men drown in the rivers before in the winter. There's nothing anyone can do, they die quickly. They don't suffer. We have to help the living. Some of the men left hanging on the ice need a fire to dry their clothes and warm their bodies. The horses have to be dried, too. Then we must regroup and set up camp, for this day is lost."

She was totally to blame, and he wouldn't let her forget it, but now was not the time; he had to get her back to work. "Katerina, have your men start large fires. Do it!" he shouted, giving her a vicious shove. "The prisoners are looking at you, you're their leader, give them their orders."

Slowly she turned to the men and without emotion ordered them to make fires. Little by little she busied herself, until she gradually had worked off the lethargy.

Banyen was busy helping and directing. "You, guard, ride up the river and look for a shallow spot to get these four wagons across. When you find such a place, get back to me. I want to make camp on the other bank by nightfall."

Darkness found them camped along the opposite bank, huddled around the fires, feeling the cold more piercingly this night than any other.

Katerina was furious with herself. Another day lost and

it's my fault. By the time we reach Volin, the snow will be falling and knee-deep on the ground. Each day counts, each day makes the trip to the Carpathians more difficult. The wagons will slow our progress as they slip and slide in the snow. Perhaps there'll be some sleighs left in Volin and we can use them instead, she thought.

Banyen wanted to chastise her to her face, but he knew the wrong decision and the deaths of the men and horses were punishment enough. But when he could he would lash out at her, this Cossack girl, and teach her that stupid womanly pride had cost them time and lives. She would pay when the delay caught them in the heavy snows of the Carpathians.

Katerina called the cook and one other driver, and after supper that night they checked the remaining wagons and sleigh to make sure they weren't damaged. She shook her head as they walked, muttering, "Four men, one wagon, one sleigh, and four horses lost on the mountain. Now two more wagons, eight horses . . . a total of ten guards with their horses and thirty-five prisoners, all dead." The men walking with her heard her but said nothing. Everything looked in order. She prayed silently that the rest of the journey would be accomplished without the loss of more lives. From here to Volin the land was level, the glorious flat steppe. The only enemy left to fight would be the heavy accumulation of snow between Volin and the House of the Kat.

As they made their way back to camp she knew that within four days they would probably be near Volin.

Banyen and the men were asleep when they returned, exhausted from the tragic day. This was one day none of them would ever forget, not even the rough, hardened prisoners. She lay back by the fire, curling up to keep warm under her blanket. As her eyelids grew heavy, the thought of arriving in Volin comforted her. The thought of the steppe also made her feel a little better. She had cursed the flat, desolate plains during the winter for their endless snow and icy cold, and in the summer she had cursed them for their heat. This night Katerina found she loved the plains, their vast, barren emptiness. It would mean no hills, no rivers, no death. Straight ahead was Volin, waiting. The picture of home faded as her cinnamon eyes closed and the pain of the tragic day was lost in sleep.

Chapter 11

Katerina tried to force her eyes to remain open in the swirling storm, to no avail. It was up to her now, her and the lead horse. The Khan's soldiers and Banyen couldn't help her now. Their fate would be decided by the horse. She would have to trust to the animal's blind instinct in getting to the pass. If Mikhailo had had the foresight to bring extra horses and sleighs to Volin, then he would have strung the pass with bells in anticipation of the heavy snows and her late arrival. Somewhere out there in the vast, all-consuming whiteness was the pass that would take her to the House of the Kat. She closed her eyes, the driving blizzard coating her thick lashes. She whispered encouraging words to the horse, aware that the animal couldn't hear her in the blizzard that raged around them.

They rode for hours, the animals straining to pull their heavy burdens through the deep snow. Katerina sat huddled in the sleigh, her ermine cape and heavy fur rug pulled tightly around her. For the first time she felt the faint stirrings of panic. What if this mare that Mikhailo had brought missed the pass? She, Katerina Vaschenko, would be responsible for the deaths of all these men. How confident she had been! How glibly she had assured the Khan that she wouldn't have any trouble getting back to the Carpathians. And she wouldn't have, if it hadn't been for her stupidity on the Kama. She paid for that daily. The presence of the Mongol was her reminder of it all. She felt his closeness in the sleigh they shared and was surprised that he made no snide remarks concerning the snow and the fact that they were two days overdue. Was that why he was quiet and not baiting her with his testy remarks about her abilities?

She was numb with cold, all feeling gone from her legs and feet. Dear God, help me, she prayed silently. Don't let us freeze to death.

Through the loud winds she thought she heard the high, clear sound of a bell. Where did the sound come from? It couldn't be from the horses' harness; the bells were too tiny, and the sound would be lost in the force of the driving wind. Katerina sat upright, and felt Banyen also straighten from his slumped position next to her. She stared into the white void of nothingness. It was a bell! Thank you, Mikhailo, she sighed. When the horse heard the bell he would know he was near the pass and close to home and a pail of oats. Once through the pass, he could find his way back to the House of the Kat blindfolded.

Squirming deeper into the fur lap robe, Katerina let her tired body relax. The snow was needle-sharp as it stung her face and beat against the sleigh. She was so tired, so very tired. All she wanted to do was sleep, but she knew that if she allowed herself the luxury she would never wake. She felt Banyen stir, trying to make himself more comfortable. Think about Prince Banyen, her mind shrieked, that will keep you awake. Think how it will feel when you finally get your revenge.

Her mind wandered as the horse strained and heaved to pull the heavy sleigh. The driving, pelting snow and ice were Banyen's hands forcing her back, back, back, till she sprawled on the blanket. The force of the wind was his hot, searing breath as he leaned over her, closer, closer, always closer. The fir tree overhead with its swinging, dipping branches, which beat against the sides of the sleigh, was his body. The low-slung branch that reached out its tentacles to strike her full force across the side of her head was her shock of pain. She screamed as she lurched and fell against Banyen.

Banyen reached out an arm protectively to grasp her slim body. His eyes took in the fallen branch, and his hand felt warm stickiness on the side of her face. Damnation, this was all he needed. His hands explored her face, roughly at first, and then more gently as he felt the gash on her cheek. How smooth and satiny her skin felt beneath the ermine hood. The thick lashes fluttered against his hand as he brushed her hair from the wound. "A limb from one of the firs dropped on you," he said softly. "You were just stunned. Your animal has entered the pass, the bells are clear now, and the snow is not quite so thick." He gathered her close, his hands inside the ermine cape encircling her body. How vulnerable she feels, how cold, how defenseless, he thought as he brought her nearer to him, his own cape open so that their bodies met in warmth. "An old Mongol custom—two bodies together for heat will allow us to survive," he said huskily.

Katerina was too tired to resist, too weary to care, and she decided she liked the feel of him. For now, it was all that mattered. How gentle his hands were. For the first time in days she felt warm. She burrowed her head in his chest, her eyes sleepy and relaxed. She felt his hands cup her face gently as he lowered his face to hers. Katerina parted her lips as his full mouth settled possessively over hers. She felt light, soft nibbles against her lips. The pressure of his lips on hers was increasingly demanding, persuasive. Her breathing became his as he explored her moist mouth with his searching tongue. His hands on her body inside the fur cape were hypnotic, touching her intimately, spreading fire throughout her body. Her arms moved naturally to encircle his broad back, the black-tipped hood slipping from her head. She felt his hands cradle her head as her wealth of copper hair fell over their faces. His lips ground against hers hungrily as she eagerly gave him the sweetness of her mouth. She began to moan softly as his hands tantalized her with their gentle, sensuous caresses. The warm feel of his body and the rippling muscles beneath her hands so delighted her, she crushed her lips against his, demanding he return her ardor. Her heart pounded with exquisite torture as she heard him emit low animal groans of passion. His hard mouth was devouring her as his embrace became more urgent, more frantic. "I knew I could melt that cold, icy reserve of yours," Banyen panted heavily as his mouth came down against hers, crushing her, driving the breath from her body.

The sleigh lurched as the words penetrated Katerina's mind. Knew . . . he knew he could . . . ! "Damnable devil!" she screeched as she pushed with all her strength. Banyen was flung over the side of the sleigh into the swirling drifts. "Walk!" she screamed into the void. "If you try to get back in this sleigh I'll kill you!"

Tears trickled down her reddened cheeks as she straightened her clothing and drew the ermine cape over her head. Her chest heaved at his remembered nearness, the feel of him. How could she have let it happen? How could she have been such a fool? She was tired and weary, numb with cold, she defended herself. Her defenses were down, she had been vulnerable, but thank God she had come to her senses. It wouldn't happen again, she would make sure of that. For a brief moment the thought saddened her, and she quickly thrust it from her mind. There was no room in her life for men and passion. She had a mission to fulfill, and when she accomplished that . . .

Katerina wondered vaguely what time of day it was. Here in the pass, with the low-slung pine trees, it was too dark to tell if it was evening or late afternoon. It really doesn't matter, she told herself. It was just something to think about so that the damn Mongol wouldn't invade her thoughts again.

The sound of the bells was clear, more distinct. The worst of the storm must be nearing an end. The lead horse seemed to be going faster. Did it mean he was almost through the pass, or was the snow less deep? No, the storm was abating. She could see the horse's broad back in the flurry of whiteness. She could even see the bells strung across the evergreen trees. "Another hour," she shouted, "and you shall have the warmest blanket and the biggest pail of oats I can find!" The horse whickered in pleasure at her words. The matched blacks snorted and strained, their glossy hides snow-covered, making them look spectral in the dim light. Katerina had done it. She hadn't let the snow defeat her, or bury her beneath its blanket of coldness. Banyen had been wrong. He had said they would die and it would be her fault. Wrong again, Mongol!

Banyen seethed and smoldered with anger as he trudged through the knee-deep snow. He clutched at the second sleigh in line to keep from falling. He stumbled along as the sleigh half dragged him through the deep snow. His arms felt as if they were being pulled from their sockets. By God, he would kill her the first chance he got. Damn the Khan and his orders! But first he would torture her and taste her body, he promised himself.

The storm seemed to be letting up, and he noted that the sound of the bells was clearer, more distinct. It couldn't be much farther. He cursed Katerina and all Cossacks for their bloodthirsty ways. They were as bad as Czar Ivan. Thoughts of the Czar and how he planned to kill him kept Banyen going. Hatred could make a man endure and survive anything. Vengeance was a balm to the soul, food for the heart. He prayed that when the day arrived for him to

kill the Czar, Ivan would be lucid. There would be no pleasure in killing an insane man.

As he trudged forward, he forced his mind to think of
Ivan and the atrocities he had committed. The vision of his
parents' savage slaughter floated before his eyes. It was true
that he had been a child at the time of their death, but it was
a sight that would stay with him for the rest of his life. As he
grew older, the Czar and his activities had become an obsession with him. He would ferret out any and all tales of
the mad Czar and relish what he would do in retaliation.
How could a man, a Czar, cut the eyes and tongues from
people's heads and laugh? How could a man, a Czar, string
small children up by their feet so the swordsmen could
practice, using their bodies as targets?

Perhaps the Czar's insanity stemmed from his boyhood,
when, it was said, he was sequestered with a dimwitted
brother and a monk who tutored them. The story was told
that Ivan blamed the boyars for his parents' death, and when
he had himself crowned Czar he began waging his war
against those boyars whose power equaled his own.

Banyen's mind filled with hatred for the man he had sworn
to kill. It would be an act of goodness, for he would rid the
world of an insane, murderous madman, whose touch wreaked
havoc on all nations within his reach.

Just let him meet me face to face so I can drive my saber
through his heart. "God, grant me Ivan is sane when vengeance
is mine," he muttered as he slipped in the snow, his mind not
willing his feet to do his bidding. Regaining his position by
clutching the sleigh, he failed to see the huge walls of the
fortress looming in the distance. Each step was made with
hatred and vengeance, hatred for Ivan, and hatred for Afstar's niece. "God grant me the will, the strength to do what
has to be done," he muttered over and over as he continued
his trek.

*   *   *

The lead horse snorted to show they were approaching the huge fortress known as the House of the Kat.

Katerina sat up straight, her eyes searching the dimness around her. They were home! We made it through the snow! she thought happily. Soon she would look upon her aging grandfather for the first time since the raid on Volin. How would he look, and how would he feel? Would he blame her?

The heavy, monstrous doors swung open, and the crimson sleigh, followed by the others, entered the deep cavernous underground stable. The tinkling bells on the horses' harness sounded merry and cheerful in the dim, cold expanse.

Katerina clambered from the sleigh and wrapped her arms around Mikhailo and Stepan, who stood waiting with raised lanterns.

"So you thought I wouldn't make it! Thank you, Mikhailo, for stringing the bells."

The old man looked at the young woman with respect in his eyes. "I knew the snows would come early, my bones felt it. I was worried, and so was Stepan, who helped me."

When all the sleighs had been placed side by side, and the horses taken to their stalls, the heavy doors were closed against the swirling, biting snow.

Other lanterns were lit as Katerina, Mikhailo, and Stepan walked among the shackled prisoners. It was Katerina who spoke first, her eyes on Banyen. "Your shackles will be removed. Sleeping quarters have been provided and blankets await you. Food will be brought to you soon. You, Prince Banyen," she said coldly, "will remain with the men."

The thick ermine cape trailing behind her, Katerina entered the dank tunnel that led to the main part of the house, the eyes of all the men on her back. Kostya's eyes were heavy, almost sleepy-looking; Banyen's were narrowed and speculative. When he turned, he felt Kostya's gaze on him.

A grin tugged at Kostya's mouth as he held out his hands for the shackles to be removed.

Upstairs, the old man sitting near the fire warming his brittle bones, a yellow cat in his lap, looked up with rheumy, watery eyes at his grandchild. He watched as she tossed her fur cape on the table, her coppery hair tumbling over her shoulders, the golden-flecked eyes like tapered candle flames in the dim, shadowy room.

The blazing fire in the hearth drew her to the dancing, flickering light as a moth to light. She rubbed her long, slender fingers as she stared at her grandfather, wanting to throw her arms around him and tell him how sorry she was. There were so many things she wanted to say to the old man, but she remained silent, waiting for him to acknowledge her in some way, to show he didn't fault her for the slaughter in Volin.

Katmon's head trembled as he stared at the slim girl, willing her to speak to him. When she remained quiet, he spoke, his voice thin and reedy.

"You're not to blame, little one. What will be will be. Mikhailo told me of your trip to the Khanate. I applaud this action on your part. I pray in this frail old heart of mine that I'll be here to see if you succeed in the spring."

Katerina dropped to her knees. "Zedda, I was afraid to speak for fear I would see anger in your eyes, anger that I . . . I see no forgiveness in your eyes either, and that makes me happy, for I know truly in my heart that you don't think me guilty in any way." She laid her coppery head on her grandfather's bony knee and felt tears sting her eyes. How wasted he was since she last saw him. How weak. His voice trembled like that of a frightened child. She felt the gnarled hands stroke her hair with tenderness. "I'll make it come right, Zedda, you have my promise. I'll get our horses back, every last one of them. My word as a Cossack, Grandfather."

"I know that, my child. You're Katlof's daughter, and for that, and that alone, you'll succeed. Now you must eat and sleep. We'll talk more in the morning. Your room was read-ied by Stepan days ago, and a roaring fire has been going since then. Eat, Hanna made thick potato soup for your ar-rival. There is also fresh-baked bread and plenty of hot tea."

"Well then, I'd better do as you say or Hanna will give me no rest." Katerina sighed with amusement. "I believe that no matter how old I get, she will always nag me as though I were still a child." Katerina patted the elderly man fondly on his arm and sat down near the fire to dine. From time to time she watched the aging man as his transparent lids quivered and then closed over the faded eyes. How sad he must feel in his heart, she thought, to lose his only son to marauders. How unbearable to know all the horses are gone from Volin. The first time in their history, the Cosars were stolen by murderers and thieves.

She finished her simple meal and looked around for Mikhailo or one of the others. Of course they were all with the prisoners, helping to get them settled. Zedda would be all right alone, dozing by the fire. She added another log and tucked in the lap robe a little tighter around his stick-thin legs. She kissed him lightly on the forehead and left the warmth of the kitchen.

Katerina shed her rough clothing and donned a warm woolen nightdress. She climbed into the high feather bed and was surprised to feel the heated rocks at the foot, where her feet rested. Dear Stepan, he thought of everything. She lay back, sleepy and contented. She had done well. There was respect in Mikhailo's eyes, and the old man in the kitchen loved her. She knew her father couldn't have done any better than she in bringing the wagons through the mountains and down through the pass. Yes, she had done well!

When Katerina woke, she had no idea of the time. The fire still blazed brightly in the silent room. Sometime shortly before dawn, she wondered if Zedda would be awake. If not, she would kiss him lightly on the cheek and he would open his eyes as always when she ran to him with a bad dream.

He always made the villains in her nightmares disappear with a few carefully chosen words and a gentle smile. Perhaps his magic would work again even though she was grown.

Quickly she wrapped herself in the white-and-black fur and raced down the cold corridors till she came to the kitchen. Zedda was awake and staring into the flickering flames, his hand resting on the yellow cat's head. Turning his head at her entrance, he motioned her to sit next to him. "A bad dream, Katerina? Tell your Zedda all about it." He smiled.

"No nightmare this time, Zedda, I just couldn't sleep. I think I'm too tired, if that's possible. My stupidity on the ice torments me. Once I gave Father my promise that I would never fail again, but I did."

"We're all human and vulnerable—you're no different from your father. Tell me now, when there is no one to hear us, how did my son allow the village to be raided? What was his mistake?"

"Mistake?" Katerina said, puzzled.

"Yes, your father did something that permitted the raid to take place. An error in judgment perhaps, just as you say you made on the ice. There isn't a person on this earth who at one time or another doesn't make a mistake. Unfortunately, this time it cost Katlof his life and his people's. Now, tell me what he did."

"The men were drinking the night before leaving for the fortress. On several occasions I noticed Father wasn't able to consume the vast amounts of vodka he used to. He would reel drunkenly and sometimes fall asleep. If the men saw their hetman so, they naturally assumed they could do the same. Only two guards were posted along the camp. I haven't any other explanation for you, Zedda."

"It's not for me that you must provide the answer. It's for yourself. Your father was not perfect, and neither are you or

I. It is to be hoped that we learn from our mistakes. Remember your father as he was and how he loved you."

"He hated me in the end, Zedda. I can't forget his words to me. I tried to tell him, but he wouldn't listen."

"Your words were heard, and they ate at his heart every hour and every minute of the day. I say this to you in truth, little one. You must believe me! Your father loved you with all his soul, no matter what you did or didn't do. He was hurt and bewildered by what he didn't understand. In time he would have come to his senses and made things right between you. Believe that."

Katerina laid her head on the old man's knees, tears trickling down her cheeks. "I want to believe it, but he's gone. He never had reason to doubt me. I never lied to him, Zedda, just as I have never lied to you!"

"We'll talk more later. My eyes grow heavy, child," he said drowsily.

Katerina reached out her arms as her grandfather gathered her close to him, stroking the rich, coppery hair. "You must believe," he said sadly. "Always believe in what you do." The paper-thin eyelids closed as his bony hand dropped into his lap.

Quietly she got to her feet and walked back to her room, feeling better for having talked with him. Not once did he say a word about his grief over the loss of his son, she marveled. "His only concern was for me and my feelings," she said out loud. Her step lightened as she entered her room and crawled beneath the downy comforter on the bed. For a little while she could sleep; maybe this time her dreams would be pleasant.

An hour before dawn, Katerina climbed from her warm nest in the high bed. As she scurried to the fire to dress she looked longingly at the heavy pedina that had covered her. She couldn't afford to sleep another second, she had to dress and have her morning meal before the others were wakened. It would be a long, tiring day, the first of many in the coming winter months.

Katerina quickly donned a thick black body garment. Throwing the ermine cape around her shoulders, she descended the wide stone steps that led below.

Inside the cozy kitchen, she looked for her grandfather. She found him in the same position he was when she had left him during the night, only this time the big yellow cat purred contentedly in his lap. She smiled a greeting and immediately began to flex her arms and legs, the way Cossacks do when warming up for a saber drill.

"Have you spoken to Mikhailo, Zedda?" she asked.

"He and Stepan just left to see to the men and give them their morning meal. Mikhailo said you made wise choices of which he approved. For him to make a comment like that he must have been truly impressed. My old friend mentioned that there were a few among them who might give you trouble, but he felt sure you and the prince could handle it. Tell me, little one, how many men did you lose coming through the Urals?" He leaned back, the words costing him dearly. When he had his breathing under control he opened his eyes, waiting for her answer.

Katerina, alarmed at his ragged breathing, trembled and fought the urge to run to him and cradle the shaking white head to her breast. She knew how he hated open displays of emotion, so she remained seated, her breakfast untouched.

"I lost thirty-five of the prisoners and ten of the soldiers. It was my fault. I tried to rescue them, but it was a foolish thing to do—an impossible task. We worked doggedly to try to split the ice and rescue them, but they were already dead and washed away by the strong current. We lost two days because of the accident, that's why we were late coming through the pass. I'm to blame, Zedda! Not Banyen."

"Why do you dislike the prince?" the old man asked sharply, aware of her hostility at the mention of his name.

Katerina's mind raced. "Because he's arrogant and selfish. He mocks me every chance he gets with words, and with his eyes. My mistake on the ice convinced him I will fail. He hates me as much as I hate him."

The old man sighed and shifted so the cat could snuggle deeper into the crook of his arm. Fire and ice, he thought, and they'll be together for the entire winter.

"I'm the Kat now, Grandfather, and I won't let him forget it, not for a moment, for a day, or a month. Never!"

The aged Cossack leaned forward, jostling the yellow cat from her comfortable position. "Such hatred for a man who is arrogant and selfish! You lie to me, Granddaughter, there's more to it than you're telling me."

"I don't wish to discuss it, Grandfather. For now, those are my reasons."

"Be wary, child. If what Mikhailo tells me is true, this is a man who will bring you to your knees."

"Not to my knees, Zedda, my back!" Katerina muttered quietly. "I'll remember what you said."

"Why weren't you born a boy?" he grumbled. "Things would be so simple if you—"

The honey-colored eyes sparked, and Katerina's full, sensual mouth tightened into a grim, hard line. "You haven't said that to me in many long years. I've made one mistake, but I've done nothing wrong. I've trained as well as the men in Volin. I've managed to bring one hundred and fifty-five men through the Urals during winter, and you tell me he's a man that can bring me to my knees! Hear me well, Grandfather, the day will never come when any man can conquer me." Her voice was so quiet, so deadly, that the old man shuddered in his warm, cozy chair near the fire.

Katmon's tone was petulant. "When are you going to start thinking about taking a man? I think you need someone to warm your bed at night. I wanted to see grandchildren before I die."

"Then you'd better plan on living many long years," Katerina said bitterly.

Whatever retort the old man was tempted to make went unsaid as he noted the narrowing of the catlike eyes. Whatever was bothering her wouldn't last forever. Katerina finished her breakfast in silence.

"Zedda, would you like to come with me to the arena and watch?"

"Bah! I've no desire to see grown men cry with your wicked ways. Mikhailo and Stepan will give you all the help you need. I wish you well."

Katerina advanced near the fire. "Your mouth tells me you wish me well, but your eyes say you hope I'll fail. Speak the truth, Zedda."

"Yes, that's what I wish. To see you fail just once."

The titian eyes were stormy as Katerina gazed at her grandfather. He was an old man; already he had lived more years than a man had a right to expect. She loved him dearly, and would gladly lay down her life for him if necessary, but he was wrong, and she wouldn't fail—she couldn't.

Chapter 12

Katerina wrapped herself in the white ermine and, with a last fond look at her aging grandfather, left the comfortable kitchen.

She shivered inside the enveloping warmth of the rich cape, not with cold but with dread. How would it go? How receptive and dedicated would the men be? And Banyen, what of the prince? Again she shuddered, remembering the feel of his lean, hard body next to hers. Her cheeks flushed as she remembered how she had responded to his mouth on hers and strained her body next to his. It wasn't the men Katerina dreaded meeting, it was the prince, she admitted to herself.

She descended the cold granite steps to the huge arena below the fortress, noting the beads of ice on the rough gray stone walls. Her breath whirled and eddied around her in the crisp, chill air. For one brief moment she wished she were back beneath the soft pedina on her bed, with the fire blazing and her sleep untroubled.

The moment her foot touched the last step Katerina heard the babble of voices and knew her recruits were finishing breakfast and soon would be ready to start the morning drill. Perhaps they would be relieved that their shackles had been removed and would work diligently. She hoped none of them would give her trouble that required strong measures be taken against them. In her gut she knew it was going to be the prisoners against the prince's men. Banyen would fight her every step of the way. He would give nothing, and she knew instinctively that he wouldn't compromise in any way. In the spring would come the day of reckoning. He was a man and she was a woman. Men were entitled to their thoughts about women, just as women were entitled to theirs about men. And men, in her opinion, were good for only one thing: to help women bear children. That was the one thing women couldn't do alone. Since she had no intention of having a baby, now or later, she had no use for Banyen or any other man. She laughed delightedly at the thought. Somehow she must manage to voice her opinion to the Mongol and see his reaction. He would be livid, she knew, sputtering with rage, his indigo eyes dark and full of murder: hers!

She thrust open the door to the great arena that ran the entire length of the House of the Kat. Even with the brightly lit sconces, she couldn't see to the end of the vast underground cavern. The plank tables had been cleared away by Mikhailo, and now all that remained were the prisoners and soldiers stamping their feet and wrapping their arms around their chests in an effort to keep warm. All were clad in heavy fur coats, hats, and high boots.

A monstrous fireplace with whole tree trunks blazing was the only heat the room offered. Katerina walked over to the blazing fire and stood with her back to the dancing flames. She looked around at the men with clinical interest. She noted that Banyen stood in front of his men, who were off to the side, separated from the prisoners.

Katerina pierced him with her gaze. "It's you against me, is that what you're trying to say? The prisoners are my men and the soldiers are yours. Is it to be a test?" When he didn't answer, Katerina smiled. "They're babies." She smiled again as she looked at the youthful faces. "When a general goes to war, he should have men fighting at his side, not infants that need a wet nurse." Guffaws of laughter erupted from the prisoners as the soldiers tried to kill her with their eyes. Banyen refused to be baited and remained quiet.

Katerina dropped the ermine and waited a moment for the shock to register in the men's eyes. She knew how she looked with the body garment, the one-piece uniform the Don Cossacks were noted for, cleaving to her slim body. Each curve, each limb cried out starkly. If I stood here naked in front of them I doubt I would get more of a reaction, she thought. Katerina heard the indrawn breaths and noticed the looks of approval in the eyes of the prisoners as well as the soldiers. Banyen's face was a study in nonchalance, appearing impervious to her lithe body. She shrugged as she called Mikhailo to her side.

"Issue each man a body garment, and see that they move briskly. You too, Prince! We all wear the same attire," she said coldly. "This attire has always been made expressly for and given to each youth the day he began his training for the Cossack army. This year, because there aren't any Dons, you men from Sibir will wear them."

The agate eyes were darkening at her words. "I refuse to wear that ridiculous clothing," Banyen said savagely.

"Either you put it on under your own power or someone will help you," Katerina said threateningly. "You do what I tell you, not the other way around. Make fast work of it, for we are already behind with our drilling." Katerina glided to the front of the clustered prisoners. "These are my men, those are yours. Either you do what I tell you or my men will help you. As you can see, you're greatly outnumbered. Move!"

The Mongol's eyes narrowed till they were mere slits. He looked around, and Kostya's face was the first thing that came into his line of vision. A sly smile was on Kostya's mouth. Damn woman, she was right, he was outnumbered, and a good soldier always knew when to retreat. For now, he would do as she said and don the crazy costume she wanted him to wear. Later, he would strangle her with it.

Katerina suppressed a laugh when Mikhailo led the men back into the cavernous room. All appeared self-conscious and were holding their hands over their male organs. She waited till they were in line before she moved. Lightly, a saber held loosely in her hand, she literally danced in front of the men. "Welcome to the House of Vaschenko, or"—she let her eyes wander down the straggly line of men— "the House of the Kat. That is the name you've been whispering among yourselves, isn't it? Yes," she said, answering the unspoken question, "I'm the Kat. It would appear that you respect the title but not the person who owns it. You will, in time. From this moment on we will be together for sixteen hours every day for the next six months. We will work with the saber from dawn till noon. From noon till twilight you will work with the horses that will be assigned you. At sundown you will have your evening meal. You may eat as much as you wish at that time, and be advised, after today it is the only time you will be fed. Is that understood? A good Cossack can go days without eating, and if he has food he gives it to his horse first. Remember that. You come second.

"After your meal we'll work with the lance and the horse till the moon is high in the sky. Then you will sleep. A good Cossack can go for days without sleep, also. That is another point I want you not to forget.

"If for some reason your performance is judged poor, you'll spend your sleeping hours practicing your weakness. I said I would train you to be Cossacks, and that's exactly what I'm going to do. I'm going to work you till you think you'll fall in your tracks. Every day for as long as you're here you will curse me and hate me with a passion you didn't know existed. You will think and plot my death a thousand times over, and when you believe you have picked the right time and place, I'll be behind you, not in front of you.

"There are a few of you who'll be tempted to escape this fortress. Don't! I'll come after you and I'll find you, and then you'll force me to make an example of you in front of the others. There is no escape from the House of the Kat. An hour outside and your ears will drop from your head. Your eyeballs will freeze in their sockets. I have no wish to see any of you die," she said, looking directly at Banyen, "but if you insist on leaving here, be warned—it can't be done.

"The only link to the world below the mountains is our trained falcons. We have two birds. One is kept here, and the other is quartered in Kisinev. If help is needed, or someone wants access to the mountains, one of the birds is sent. I'm telling you this so you'll know if you have any plans to leave here, it can't be done. No one save a Cossack can survive this weather. At January's end the blizzards come, and they last till March. You must believe me when I tell you that at such time even a Cossack can't survive. You've been warned, and more than that I can't do."

One of the young soldiers standing near Banyen, little more than a boy, spoke haltingly. "I'm cold and I didn't get enough to eat, I'm hungry."

Katerina laughed, the sound bouncing off the thick stone walls, and raising the hackles on the boy's neck.

"In the House of the Kat we don't complain . . . ever. We don't whine like newborn puppies. You are a babe; where do you fit into the Khan's armies? As a matter of fact," she said loftily as she walked in front of Banyen's men, "I've never seen a larger group of infants in my life." While she spoke to the young boys, she was looking at Banyen, the amber eyes mocking and scornful.

"I'm no baby," the youth said belligerently.

"Your name," Katerina said coldly.

"Igor."

"If I say you are, then you are," Katerina said dangerously. "Mikhailo, hand this . . . child a weapon. Now tell me you aren't a babe with a sword in your hand. When you make a statement, be prepared to defend it . . . to the death, if necessary. Now tell me, are you a baby or not?"

"I'm no babe," the young voice cried defiantly, the blade held awkwardly in his thin hand.

"And I say you are," Katerina said, slicing down the front of the heavy fur coat, and with catlike speed she had the sleeve in tatters with her quick, cutting motions. "When are you going to fight for your words?"

Igor's eyes sought out Banyen's and pleaded with him to interfere on his behalf. Kat correctly interpreted the look and spoke. "Each man stands alone in the House of the Kat. A Cossack never asks or accepts help from another. A Cossack stands alone except for his horse. His animal is the only friend and ally he has," she said coldly.

Tears of rage burned in the youth's eyes as he lashed out with his sword, his movements clumsy and uncoordinated.

"Bah, you're impossible! Resume your place in line. I have no more time to spend on these childish games. I'll find a wet nurse for you unless the prince can make a man of you.

"Mikhailo!" The one word was an iron command. "Lock their furs away."

The Kat stifled her laughter as the men continued to hold their hands over their groins. All of Banyen's men—or youths, as she preferred to call them—wore sullen, angry looks. The prisoners wore puzzled, questioning looks on their broad faces.

"We're ready to begin," the Kat said in a clear, high voice. "Mikhailo, the music, please. You're going to learn Russian dancing. Form two circles and dance like this," she said, leaping into the air, twisting her body in a whirling motion, landing gracefully on her feet. "On your toes, and pretend you are holding a basket of eggs on your head. On the count of three." The Kat turned her head to hide her grin as the men leaped and cavorted through the air, their arms and legs flying every which way. A soldier named Vladimir protested as his feet left the ground and he ended in a heap.

"I came to be trained as a Cossack, not to learn to dance. Dancing is for women," he said vehemently.

"You're right, you're no dancer. I assure you, this is necessary. I care nothing at all about what you think. It's what I think and what I do that's important! Every Cossack goes through this phase of training. It will limber your muscles and enable you to move quickly and effortlessly. Now try it again."

"No!"

"Very well." The Kat sighed. "Mikhailo, take him to his quarters. No blanket and no dinner tonight. Perhaps he will develop a craving for the dance by tomorrow. Why are all of you staring?" she asked coldly. "I thought I told you to dance."

"But there is no music," one called Igor complained.

"If there's no music and I tell you to dance, what should you do?" the Kat asked coldly.

"Pretend!" cried a young voice from behind Banyen as he leaped wildly in the air, coming down with a thud. Banyen grimaced at the look on the Kat's face, and at the looks his men were giving him.

"Eggs, remember the eggs!" the Kat shouted as she walked among the men, the tip of her saber tapping this one and that one to show he was doing something not to her liking.

Mikhailo returned, and within minutes his fiddle was active. Katerina leaned against the wall as she watched Banyen leap into the air, his long, muscular legs doing exactly what they should be doing. His performance was almost as good as her own. She felt smug as she watched him help his men. The youths smiled crookedly, their eyes fearfully on the Kat.

As the noon hour approached Katerina signaled for Mikhailo to stop the music. She motioned for the men to fall into columns and stand at attention. She spoke briskly as she walked up and down among the straggly lines of prisoners and soldiers.

"Today is not an indication of what is to come. Today I'm judging you on flexibility and coordination. Timing and exact movement are extremely important. You must learn this or you could die. A good Cossack has a seventh sense. When you leave here, it will be honed to a sharp point. Your life will depend, at one time or another, on this new sense you're going to develop, always remember that. Your dancing leaves much to be desired. In time, with practice, you will improve. Now, cross sabers. Mikhailo will issue each of you a weapon, and you'll practice with a partner. I'm going to divide you into groups of fifteen men each, and you will have a leader whom you'll obey. The prince will do the same." She signaled to Banyen to begin choosing his men.

Katerina looked over the men she had come to know a little better than the others. Her first choices were Kostya and Rokal, then two others. She debated before she made her fifth, and final, choice, finally deciding on a tall, dark-skinned Russian.

Katerina's eyes danced when she saw Banyen's choice was a youth named Gogol and his second choice the boy Igor.

"Saber tips in place," she called loudly. "I have no wish to see the lot of you bleed to death, not today. Tomorrow you will remove them and slice at each other to your hearts' content. If your skill as a dancer improves, you'll be able to make your feet do what your mind tells them to do. Tomorrow," she shouted to Banyen, "your man who has been sent to his quarters will cross sabers without the tips. Is that clear? If he bleeds to death for some clumsy movement, it is on your head, not mine."

Lithely Katerina danced out to the middle of the arena and motioned for Mikhailo to join her. "A brief demonstration," she said, removing the saber tips. Deftly she backed off and flexed her legs, her slim body a study of perfection in the brightly lit center of the room. She brought up the saber and touched the tip of his weapon and shouted, "Begin!" Metal clanked against metal as she danced and reached, always finding her mark. Her movements were well practiced as she fluidly moved out of Mikhailo's reach. Twice the point found its target, Mikhailo's heart. The Cossack laughed as he moved clumsily, trying to get out of her way. She would advance, bring up her weapon, and slice up and down, her wrists barely moving.

Banyen watched, mesmerized as she leaped and thrust. He told himself her slim body had something to do with it. No woman could handle a weapon as she did. He understood her theory of dancing and crossed sabers. Grudgingly he admitted she was right. A body in good condition could handle anything—he was the living proof. Now all he had to do was convince these babes, as she called them, that he approved of what she was doing, without losing their respect. Damn, why couldn't the Khan have assigned him men instead of these raw recruits?

Her exhibition at an end, the Kat told the men to pair off according to their leader's instructions. She sat down near the blazing fire next to Mikhailo and watched as the men struck out with their heavy weapons. "What do you think, Mikhailo, is there any hope?" she asked softly, her eyes on Banyen as he lunged out at one of his men. His movements were sure and flexible, his weapon finding its mark each time. Not so the boy he was fighting with, who thought the weapon was something to hold across his chest for protection.

* * *

"In time they'll be all right, Katerina. Miracles do not happen overnight, nor in a week. The prisoners seem agreeable. I've heard no grumbling from any of them. They take orders well, but I expect trouble in the next few days."

"It is sure to come. For now, the lot of them are biding their time, waiting to see what's going to happen. Wait till they get one meal a day and then have to give up their sleeping hours to practice mastering their imperfections."

"The one called Kostya, I see the way he looks at you. He also seems to be the spokesman for the others. I've noticed the way they listen to him and look to him for some sign that they should do what he wants. I saw him give a slight nod of his head when you told them all to dance. He approved, and that's why there was no grumbling among the others. I noticed this, and so did the Mongol prince. His eyes hold cold murder, but for whom I don't know."

"For me, Mikhailo. If there is murder to be done, it will be me that commits the act. And it will be his body that falls to the ground, not mine!"

At the end of the second hour Katerina called a halt to the saber drill, and Mikhailo gathered the weapons and stockpiled them in the dim recesses of the cavernous room.

While Mikhailo tended to his duties, the Kat informed the men that their leaders were to follow Mikhailo to the underground stables, where they would select the horses and bring them back to the arena. "The rest of you may now take a rest period."

Deliberately, the Kat waited till the men filed behind Mikhailo, and found herself walking next to Kostya. She sensed the stiffening of his shoulders as she brushed against him going out the wide stone archway. She quirked an eyebrow and looked up at him. His bright blue gaze pierced her, but his stride never faltered as he continued to hold her eyes with his own. She searched for an expression, some sort of indication of what he was feeling, but his features remained blank, unlike Banyen, whose face and eyes were an open book. She felt puzzled but said nothing. She liked the feeling being near him gave her. There was hidden strength in his strong, sinewy arms, and his broad chest looked just right for a woman to be cradled against. She blinked. Now why had she thought of something like that? She wanted to say something just to hear his voice, but she remained quiet, some instinct warning her that this was not the time to speak with the Russian. She made a mental note to find a spare minute as soon as the men were on a strict schedule. Yes, she would make the time and use it to her best advantage.

She looked up as Mikhailo indicated a halt and opened the doors to the underground stable. She found herself staring into indigo eyes that spoke of many things, one of which was her death. She smiled to let him know she correctly interpreted his thoughts, and spoke softly so her words would not echo in the stillness around her. "I'll always be behind you, Prince Banyen. It promises to be a long, cold winter, so it would be wise if you diverted your thoughts to some other form of torture."

Banyen's tone was just as soft when he replied. "You can only be behind me if I go to the front, and I have no intention of doing that. It would be wise if you remembered that." The indigo eyes lightened as he gave her a low, defiant bow to allow her to precede him. A slight nick with the tip of her saber into his broad back and he entered ahead of her, an arrogant smile on his lips. He told himself it amused him to allow her her little flights of fancy. If she thought she could win out against him, let her. When he ceased to be amused, he would change things. He was a patient man—at times.

The stable was warm and moist with the horses' deep, even breathing. The sweet, pungent smell of horseflesh was like a balm to Katerina as she walked among the animals, patting them gently on the muzzle or stroking their flanks. The horses whickered softly as she cooed tender words to them. Their ears recognized the soft words of the Kat. Immediately they calmed as the men walked among them.

"I'm going to allow you to choose the horses yourself. I do, however, want to remind you that the animal you choose will be with you for the balance of your stay here in the mountains. Your life could well depend on the animal you choose, so be selective. Choose it as though you were choosing a woman."

Her eyes were banked fires as she watched first Banyen and then Kostya walk among the animals. Both men seemed to know what they were looking for. Their selection was slow, methodical, and thorough. In the end Banyen chose a gelding and named him Vengeance. Kat smiled into his eyes and waited for Kostya to choose his horse. He picked a mare and said he would call her "Horse" until he could think of an apt name. For some reason, Banyen's eyes were furious, his mouth a grim, tight white line in his handsome face. Kostya grinned as he continued his selection for the men who were training in his group.

Why do the men rub each other the wrong way? the Kat wondered as she walked among the horses. Was it because of her? Or was there some other reason, a reason that had to do with the Mongol camp, when Kostya was a prisoner and Banyen his guard? They were like cat and mouse. She was unsure which was which. Sooner or later she would find out, she told herself. She leaned against a bale of hay, her long, slender legs planted firmly on the floor. They were both handsome men; both had lean, hard, muscular bodies. Both had keen intelligence, and while Banyen was the more verbal of the two, the Kat felt instinctively that Kostya's actions would speak louder.

The stable was too warm for her liking, and she wished they would hurry up with their selection. She wiped impatiently at a loose lock of coppery hair with a slender hand, her eyes on the two men. She looked around and was surprised to notice that she was the only one with beads of perspiration on her brow. Her amber eyes grew stormy as she continued her scrutiny of Kostya and the prince. They were both having an effect on her, and one she couldn't deny even to herself. Kostya with hair the color of wheat, and Banyen with hair the color of a raven's wings. Day and night. Did she want either of them?

The remainder of the time until dinner would be spent with each man acquainting himself with his horse. They mounted and dismounted, getting the feel of the steed that was assigned to them. The Kat watched carefully through the long hours for any sign of dissension between animal and man. As Mikhailo entered the stable to let them know the hour for supper was at hand, she relaxed. The first day seemed to be going well.

Mikhailo motioned her to come near him and informed her in a low whisper that her grandfather requested the company of the prince at his supper table. The Kat was shocked at the request.

"And he said that he was appalled at your lack of manners!"

"Royalty does not eat with the common soldier?" Katerina asked snidely.

"The words are those of your grandfather, not mine. He's insistent, Katerina, that your Mongol prince dine with us each day, and not in our work clothes. He had Hanna get out the best dishes, silver, and the linen napkins and cloth. He told Hanna to serve in the kitchen because he is not well enough to entertain in the dining hall. Perhaps it means he's feeling better. What do you think?"

Katerina's amber eyes smoldered hotly. "What it means is I'll be forced to eat next to him every day if Grandfather doesn't change his mind. The prince should remain with his men. I'll try to convince Grandfather he is making a mistake."

"Save your breath. He wants to hear strange voices. He wants to hear new things, see new people. How can you deprive him of this small pleasure?"

"Very well, you've made your point, Mikhailo. But don't expect me to help with the conversation. And," she said emphatically, "I have no time to dress for dinner. A quick wash is the best I can manage. If you can convince the prince, more power to you, Mikhailo. With Grandfather's failing eyesight, I doubt he'll notice. And if he does, tell him I'm exercising my womanly prerogative."

Mikhailo shrugged. "It's time for the men to eat. How long do you wish them to remain at the table?"

"An hour, or a few minutes longer if you think it is advisable. What did Hanna prepare for the men?"

"A thick potato soup with chunks of lamb slowly simmered for many hours, black bread with yellow butter, and rice custard with raisins for a sweet. There should be no complaints." He grinned. "And she followed your orders so that the men could eat as much as they want." Katerina nodded as she left him to go to her room and freshen up before her dinner with the prince and her grandfather.

She felt her eyes smart as she picked up her small hand mirror, a gift from her father on her fifteenth birthday. Her cheeks were flushed, and the amber eyes were bright and shiny. Carefully she brushed her coppery hair till it shone in the dim lamplight. She whisked the stray strands away from her brow and hoped they would stay in place. She bit into her full, ripe lips so they would appear rose-colored. Satisfied with her appearance, she blew out the candles and left her high-ceilinged room to make her way to the kitchen.

Large oval windows were cut in the solid stone wall that led to the bottom of the circular stairway. Katerina stopped once to look out. All she could see was thick, swirling snow. A drift that looked as sharp as a razor's edge reached as high as the third window. She wondered which of the men would be the first to try to escape through the deep, suffocating accumulation. She sighed. They would have to learn by their own mistakes. Katerina knew they didn't believe her when she told them what it was like outside. Her father had said if you tell a man the truth, sooner or later he will learn to know that what you say is correct. It takes time, he had explained, for one person to trust another. Once trust is established, then everything settles into place. He was right; only time would tell. And for now, all she had to do was get through a dinner sitting at the same table with Banyen.

When Katerina entered the large, warm kitchen, Banyen stood up and greeted her with a show of respect. Her grandfather remained seated at the huge table. Hanna stood nearby, waiting for Katerina to be seated. Her rosy cheeks and wide smile made Katerina grin. Already Hanna was matchmaking—she could tell by the bright, twinkling eyes. Hanna approved of the prince, and it was obvious in the way she served him the biggest bowl of soup and the largest slice of her hot bread. The bright yellow turnip was mashed to perfection, with a round mound of butter nestled into a hollow. She ladled out the turnip on Banyen's plate and gave him a toothy smile. Katerina grimaced and looked down at her own meager allotment. She watched disgustedly as Banyen fell to his food as though he had never eaten before. He smiled at Hanna and praised her cooking, saying it was the best he had ever tasted. Hanna, beside herself with happiness, added another thick slice of lamb to his plate and then retired to the stove.

"I'm honored to have you visit my house," Katmon said in a frail voice. "Allow me to apologize for entertaining you in the kitchen, but these old bones of mine demand heat, and the dining hall is full of drafts. Tell me of the Khan and of Sibir. Did my granddaughter tell you that her mother was a Siberian Mongol and that she and the Khan were brother and sister?"

"The Khan told me all of the facts," Banyen said quietly. "There is no need for you to apologize to me. I also prefer the warmth and closeness of a kitchen. Many times when I was a child I ate in the kitchen with my parents and the cook, in our fortress where two rivers came together. I'm not sure I remember it clearly, for I only knew my parents a short time. They were slain by Ivan and his Russians." He felt his blood begin to boil, so he looked around the room and commented on its size and its cleanliness. He smiled. "Your kitchen is one of the best I've sat in."

Katmon pushed his half-eaten food away and leaned back in his comfortable chair, the lap robe pulled tightly around him. His pet cat jumped onto his lap and snuggled deeply into the robe. "Do you think you can survive the winter here?" he asked in a reedy voice.

"Yes, I can survive in this house, as can my men. In the spring we'll all be here."

Was she mistaken, or did he stress the word "we"? Was he implying that if anyone tried to leave it would be the prisoners and not those directly under his command? Probably, for everything he said or did seemed to have a double meaning.

Her grandfather's next statement stunned Katerina.

"My granddaughter fancies herself the next savior of the Ukraine in that she can train these men and regain the Cosars. Do you think she can do it?"

Katerina seethed and fumed as she waited for his reply. When she heard his terse, cold "No" she wasn't surprised.

The old man chuckled, enjoying the prince more each time he spoke.

"Savior! Hardly," she protested to her grandfather. She fixed a steely eye on Banyen and said, "According to the Radziwill Chronicler, in 6453, by the old Russian calendar, there was a great Russian heroine named Olga. When her husband was killed, she used her wits ingeniously and avenged his death. She tricked his killers into a bathhouse, locked them in, and burnt it to the ground. There are some women," Katerina said coldly, "who will do whatever is necessary to survive and to avenge a wrongdoing. Do you remember the story, Grandfather?" she demanded, her eyes on the Mongol.

Her grandfather answered with a light nasal snore. Banyen's eyes mocked her as he continued to stare at her.

"Since you seem so well versed in the Radziwill Chronicler, perhaps you are familiar with this verse," Banyen said sotto voce. "In the winter, the Cumans came to Kiev and captured many villages beyond Kiev, returning with much booty to their land. Glebe, Prince of Kiev, was ill, so he sent his brothers Mikhailo and Vsevolod to pursue the Cumans. Mikhailo, obedient, went after them and overtook them. God helped Mikhailo and Vsevolod against the pagans. Some were killed and others taken prisoner. They took their own prisoners, who were four hundred in number, from the Cumans. They sent the prisoners back to their own lands, and they returned to Kiev praising God and the Holy Mother of God and the Holy Cross. Old Russian calendar 6679," he said arrogantly.

"Bah, all that means is that you can read or someone told you the story and you remembered it," the Kat snarled. "Dinner is finished. We have a long night ahead of us; let's get on with it," she said, getting up from the table. "You first, Mongol, remember what I said—I'll always be behind you." She followed him down the cold, dank tunnel that led to the underground arena.

The flickering candles lent themselves to eerie shadows that played on her nerves as she kept her distance, the cloak wrapped snugly around her. "To the left," she said, as Banyen came to a stop. Almost colliding with him, Katerina backed off, but not quickly enough. Suddenly she found herself imprisoned in hard, muscular arms. Her face was cupped in strong yet gentle hands as his head came down to meet hers. She struggled feebly as she tried to free herself from his grasp. The feel of his moist lips on hers sent her mind reeling, and she became limp in his arms, responding to him as she had on the day of their arrival.

His lips were hungry, demanding that he be satisfied by her. Slowly she strained toward him, willing him to demand more of her so that she could feed his insatiable appetite. Her lips parted, and she tasted his sweetness as she felt his hands explore her body beneath the ermine cape. Her hands found their way to his thick, cropped hair, and she ran her fingers through it, moaning at the desire that washed over her as she crushed her lips into his. Everything was forgotten, all the promises, all the dire threats she had made in silence against him. All she wanted now was to be near him, to have him be part of her. He whispered soft endearments that were barely audible as he blazed a searing trail from her mouth to her neck to her breasts. His hands were tender yet searching. Low animal sounds erupted from his throat. Nothing matters, she told herself as she sought the devouring lips and the delicious feel of his body next to hers. Wave after wave of desire rose in her as she felt him stiffen against her.

"Later," he whispered. "Later I'll come to your room," he breathed raggedly. "Later we'll be as one," he said, tearing his mouth from hers.

She stared at him with glazed, passion-filled eyes. In that moment she would have promised him the moon if he had asked for it. Shaking, she straightened herself and drew the ermine around her slim body. He wanted her, needed her. God help her, she also craved his total embrace—but she knew that when he came to her room she wouldn't open the door. Not to this Mongol! Never this Mongol!

Banyen positioned his men with their assigned horses and lances and put them through their paces. While they were slow and inexperienced, he was satisfied with each man's performance. Not so with the Kat as she singled out man after man with the tip of her lance. Once Banyen ground his teeth together when she drew blood from a sharp-tongued soldier. Her rejoinders were just as caustic as his epithets.

Kostya wasn't having any trouble with his small column of men. They did his bidding, their movements were sure and precise. Banyen's eyes narrowed as he watched Katerina look at Kostya with approval. She smiled and said something that sounded like congratulations. Kostya nodded, his bright eyes appraising and full of . . .

Banyen shook his head to clear his thoughts. He berated one of his men for a senseless mistake.

The prince's gaze traveled back to Katerina as she slouched against the wall next to Mikhailo. What was there about the Cossack girl that could stir him as she did? Why did his senses get the better of him when he was near her? Why did he want *her*? A woman was a woman. He liked the sweet, heady fragrance that she exuded, and he liked the feel of her slim body, covered though it was by her heavy clothing. And her incredible eyes—he had never seen any like hers. One moment they were like ripe, golden apricots, and the next they were raging volcanoes. He had to have her, and he meant to have her, and the sooner the better. But even though he had told her he would come to her room this night, he knew he wouldn't. He would make her wait, wait till she craved his body, till the desire rose in her eyes for all to see.

A wild thought stormed its way into his mind, and he stiffened. What if the bastard Kostya got to her first? Even from this distance he could see that there was only one emotion exuding from the Russian. He bristled with anger at the Russian's fitness. Stronger, better men had broken in the Mongol stockade. What had kept him alive and in condition? He had seen men beg and cry to be freed from their shackles, but not Kostya.

It was true, Katerina had a keen eye for a man's worth,

but he knew in his gut she had made a mistake with Kostya. A sly look settled over Banyen's face. Let her learn from her errors; he owed her nothing except the promise he had made to her, that he would have her one way or another.

Kostya could feel the Mongol's eyes on him and knew the prince was filled with rage at his ability to carry out his orders so well. He smiled to himself. There was a lot to be said for hearty peasant stock. It was to be a contest between himself and the Mongol, but not for the obvious reasons. Who would get the Kat, the Mongol or himself? He was no fool, even if the Mongol thought otherwise. Hadn't he seen the approval reflected in the girl's face? Hadn't he felt her tremble at his nearness when they came through the archway? Time was his answer. Let the Mongol plow ahead like a bull and antagonize her every chance he got. It would be he, Kostya, who would win out. All he had to do was wait and bide his time. All things came to those who were patient. The Mongol was not a patient man; this he knew from his months in the stockade. He was tense, taut, as if ready to spring at a moment's notice. True, a formidable enemy and one who would give a good accounting of himself, but with a few weeks of the Kat's rigorous training Kostya would also be someone to seriously contend with. It would be interesting to see which of them won.

Katerina continued with her nonchalant pose against the wall as she whispered to Mikhailo, "A wise choice, don't you agree? Look at their eyes—they're like two fighting cocks. One won't let the other get ahead of him. Which do you put your kopecks on, Mikhailo?"

"The Mongol," Mikhailo said curtly.

"The Mongol!" Katerina exclaimed in surprise. "Why?"

"Several reasons," Mikhailo said harshly. "He's a man, the Russian is but a boy compared to him. True, they both have strength to their bodies, and both have a certain arrogance about them, but it's the years of experience the prince has behind him in the ways of the world that will drive him to be the victor. The question is, what will he win, Katerina? Observe his eyes and you'll see that I'm right. I see things in him I saw in your father and in your grandfather. Heed my words, Katerina, for I speak the truth."

Katerina was stunned at his words. "How can you say a thing like that? He's nothing like my father. And my father is dead because he made a mistake and thought he was infallible. No man is above that," she said gruffly.

"Not this man, Katerina."

Her honeyed eyes glinted angrily as she listened to the Cossack. She wouldn't, she couldn't admit that his words shook her to the core. How could he be so confident? She hated to admit it, but she knew the old man was right; she sensed it, felt it, every time she was near Banyen. "He's an animal," she seethed under her breath. And she would treat him as such. Kostya, on the other hand, was a . . . Yes, she asked herself, what is Kostya? She felt drawn to him for reasons she couldn't explain. Yet he showed nothing when he was near her, just that piercing gaze that was completely devoid of any meaning. Banyen's eyes spoke of many things . . . things she had no wish to see.

Shortly before midnight Katerina called a halt to the drill and ordered Mikhailo to collect the weapons and take the men to their quarters. "And," she said harshly, "I have no wish to hear that the Mongol is to be quartered in the big house. He stays here with his men, and you'll place a guard on the door and bolt it from the outside. Royal blood means nothing in this house; please tell him that for me."

Katerina neither spoke to nor looked at the men again as she left the vast arena. She had no desire to look into piercing blue eyes or smoldering, angry, dark ones that plotted against her.

She stopped in the kitchen before retiring to her room, and was surprised to see her grandfather still awake near the blazing fire, the cat clutched tightly in his bony hands. His eyes were bright with questions, but he waited for her to speak.

Katerina poured herself a cup of strong tea and sat down on the hearth. "It went well. Tomorrow, when their bones and muscles ache, we'll see how proficient they are. They all made wise decisions on the horses. I anticipate no great trouble, at least nothing that I cannot handle with Mikhailo's help."

"When are you going to tell them why they're here?" the old man demanded. "A man has a right to know what's in store for him. Withholding your reasons could well be your undoing. What will you do if, after you've trained them, they refuse to fight for you? What will you do then? These are not weak-kneed people but strong, virile men. Think on that while you sleep tonight. A man has a right to know what's in store for him," he repeated in his frail voice. "What you're doing is a magnificent thing, but what good will it do you if the men don't choose to fight with you when the time comes? You must be fair, your father taught you well. How can you be so shortsighted? Don't let it all be for nothing." The paper-thin eyelids closed, ending the argument. He was asleep.

Zedda is right, Katerina thought wearily as she rubbed at her temples. Tomorrow she would explain to the prisoners her reasons for bringing them to the mountains and what she expected of them. Tomorrow was another day. If only she had the Cosars, none of this would be necessary. Who had them? And what would become of them? Would they be scattered and sold to the highest bidder?

Katerina poured herself another cup of the scalding tea and carried it with her down the long corridor and up the steep curving stairway to her room. She set the cup on the hearth and added several logs to the already blazing fire. The high bed, with its thick, downy pedina, looked inviting. What would it be like to roll and move around in the big bed with a man she loved? Katerina blinked as she realized where she was, and quickly raced to the door and threw the bolt. The sound was comforting in the quiet room—a balm to her tightly strung nerves. Did she really want the Mongol to come to her room? Did she want to lie with him?

She sat down near the hearth and drew her legs up to her chin, her arms clasped around them, a red-fox blanket covering her like a waterfall. How could she respond to Banyen and still feel such dislike toward him for what he had done to her on the steppe? Tears gathered in the titian eyes as she remembered the time she had spent in the barn watching the young lovers. And then a picture of Yuri flashed before her. Even the embraces with Yuri hadn't been right. She hadn't felt the way the couple obviously had. What she had had with Yuri was passion; there had been no love. She knew that now. A meeting of the bodies for release was all it had been. If he had returned, would she have gone with him? No, she answered herself. There was no point in thinking about Yuri. Yuri was dead, killed by her own hand. She had put him to death to ease his suffering, just as she would put to death a wounded animal that had no hope of living.

Tomorrow was another day. Dawn would come before she was ready for it. She had to sleep. God, if it were only so simple, just get into the bed, close her lids, and sleep. She raised her eyes to look at the icon on the wall over her bed. She bowed her head and prayed silently. She prayed to God to free her mind of her torturous thoughts; she prayed for peace of spirit and soul; prayed for the resentment to leave her; and she prayed for love somehow to find its way to her heart. So many things to ask for; surely He would answer at least one of her pleas.

Katerina let the fur lie carelessly across the bench that stood near the hearth and shed the thick body stocking. She stood naked for a moment in the chilly air and again wondered what it would be like to lie next to a naked man who loved her as she would love him. She shook her head, freeing the coppery hair from its pins, and donned a woolen nightgown. Sliding beneath the thickness of the pedina, her eyes closing . . . No sooner was she asleep than she was racing Bluefire across the steppe, his hooves crushing the white earth with his long-legged gallop. Strong, sinewy arms reached for her as she tore over the snowy fields, her breathing coming ragged and harsh. Would he catch her. Ride . . . ride . . . ride . . . faster . . . faster.

Katerina sprang out of bed in the morning, anxious to get the ordeal of informing the prisoners over with. After a quick breakfast she summoned Mikhailo and told him to get all the men assembled in the training arena immediately. Shortly thereafter, the Kat stood before the prisoners, legs astride, hands on hips, waiting for them to line up in formation.

"Men, I have ordered you here a little earlier this morning because I want to tell you why you're here and why you're training so hard. My village was raided, and my father and all the people were slaughtered. The raiders got what they came for, the sought-after Cosar horses. I can't bring my father or the people of my village back, but I can get back the horses. That is why you're here, and that is what you're going to do," she told them with a vengeance. A loud moan of dissatisfaction was heard from the multitude. "Save the moans for your sore muscles. Like it or not, the horses will be found by us and brought back to the Don Cossacks. Now, go have your food and be back here ready to practice hard and long. Eat hearty," she called to them as they filed out of the arena.

Chapter 13

The white carpet of snow across the vast, endless steppe continued its relentless path into the fir-covered breast of the Carpathians. The massive fortress loomed like an intruder on the crystalline accumulation, trapped by the dense, mammoth evergreens. Winter had come in all its intensity to the House of the Kat.

Winter months in the Carpathians were well-waged wars between the harsh, ferocious winds that swept through everything and everyone and the cold, insidious, sparkling crystals that fell gently and constantly from the skies.

The snowdrifts hugged the walls of the fortress tenaciously, pushing and climbing their way to the second-story windows of the structure. All garrisoned within its cold walls shivered as the wind howled its song and shook the mighty walls with its breath. The monolithic trunks and branches of the giant firs accompanied the savage winds, hitting and striking against the thick gray stone of the dwelling, filling the interior with ghoulish, eerie sounds that chilled the dwellers to the bone.

The House of the Kat was no match for the clutching, all-consuming white giant that ruled the winter. The King of the North held fast its inhabitants, closing them off, making movements into or out of the fortress impossible. They were isolated and locked in for the winter. The smothering whiteness would take its toil on each of the hostages within the House of the Kat, but in a different way for each.

The tiny, shiny brass bells strung in the green, snow-ladened branches of the firs dared to sing out their merry melody to the stark, endless void. The whipping winds urged their constant activity, sending out their cheerful sounds to fall on the deaf ears of space. No human or animal moved to hear or applaud the mellow-sounding courage of the bells. During the reign of the King of the North, no man made the journey through the pass to the cavernous underground arena and stables that housed the Mongol prince and the prisoners from Afstar's Khanate of Sibir.

The training of the recruits and Banyen's men was long and seemingly endless. The prisoners worked diligently with something close to vengeance. Not so with Banyen's force. It was a contest of wills, and Kostya drove his men with quiet looks and a grim, tight line around his mouth when they did something he disliked. It was evident to Katerina and Mikhailo that the men respected him and even liked him. Banyen, on the other hand, drove his men unmercifully as he followed Katerina's orders. The young men serving under him resented Katerina and at times openly refused to follow her orders, which Banyen issued through clenched teeth. One night in the cold, bare room with no blanket and no dinner was all they needed to renew their hatred of her. She watched them through catlike eyes as they murdered her time and time again in their minds and hearts. Banyen remained aloof, and often openly ridiculed her with some snide remark or blatant show of contempt. Still, she admitted to herself, he didn't defy her; he did as she ordered even though he didn't like it. She felt in her bones that he was playing a game with her—a game that he intended to win. And Kostya, what was he planning?

She felt drawn to the tall, quiet man with the piercing blue eyes and found herself making excuses to talk to him, complimenting him on his skill or just standing near him, feeling the power his body exuded. And when she found herself standing next to him, she would feel Banyen's eyes on her, arrogant and mocking. She, in turn, would give him her sleepy Kat gaze and toss the heavy, burnished hair till it fell winsomely over her high cheekbones. Banyen would then shout at his men, and a look of cold, deadly hatred would settle over his handsome features. It was a game they played, and Katerina knew instinctively that if she wasn't careful the stakes would be something she was not prepared to lose. Kostya would watch the little byplay with an amused expression and smile down at Katerina, his white teeth gleaming in the dimness of the cavern. The three of them were playing a game, and each knew the unspoken rules. The only question in their minds was: what was the prize at the end of the game? Was it the Cosars, or was it Katerina?

Katerina led her horse to the water trough and watched him drink thirstily. Her back stiffened as she felt Banyen bring his stallion up next to her. Her eyes were quiet and languid when she looked up at him. Why hadn't he come to her room last night, as he promised? She would not have opened the door, but this way, she felt humiliated and embarrassed. He had said he would come and there were no footsteps in the great hall that night. Another game, cat and mouse. Well, she was no mouse, she was the Kat. This was the first time today that she found herself so close to him, close enough to smell his heady body scent, to feel the heat his lithe, muscular body gave off. Her hand trembled slightly as she grasped the reins of her horse and led him away from the trough.

Kostya waited a moment before he too brought his mount forward. His movements were slow, almost calculating, as he swaggered slightly, his bright gaze searching and alert. He nodded briefly to Banyen and let his gaze drift to the Kat, who was staring at him openly. She liked the way he carried himself, almost effortlessly, as though he moved to music. Banyen stalked and prowled, his eyes those of the hunter, his actions those of a killer bent on getting his prey. With Kostya present at the water trough, there was no way Banyen could talk to the Kat, even if it was only to needle her. His dark eyes smoldered with rage as he led the stallion back to his perspiring men.

Kostya grinned as he led his horse away and settled himself next to Rokal. "A small breathing spell," Kostya said, a smile in his voice.

"Best be careful, my friend," Rokal said quietly. "The Mongol knows how to kill. Read his eyes and don't say you weren't warned."

"I was warned back in Sibir, Rokal. If it comes to a personal battle between the two of us, I can give a good accounting of myself, have no fear. Those days in the stockade were not meant to be forgotten."

"He obeyed orders, Kostya, remember that. Back in the stockade, he had no stomach for what he was forced to do. Here it's another story. He wants the woman. You want the woman. Somebody's blood will flow, and, my friend, I feel it will be yours."

Kostya laughed, a sound that reached Katerina and Banyen. Both of them looked up to see the man's shoulders convulsing.

Katerina looked at Mikhailo and realized she liked the sound of the rich laughter the prisoner exuded. The stocky Cossack's face wore a strange look as he watched Katerina, a feeling of dread settling over him. He, too, knew trouble would come soon. Which of the men would be the one to bring matters to a head? And was it just Katerina that was at the bottom of whatever it was that was bothering the two men? The old man's gut told him there was more to it than a woman. Katmon was forever telling him stories of how men made fools of themselves over women and lost not only their manhood to them but their dignity and their wealth. All for a woman. Never having had one of his own, Mikhailo found it hard to accept the elder's words. A woman was a woman! But Katerina was different. He didn't want to see her a pawn between these two, didn't want to see her hurt.

"You're too young for all this responsibility and too innocent to be wounded in the heart and soul. Why must it always come down to survival? Which of you will be the survivor?" he asked.

"Is there doubt in your mind, Mikhailo? I will, and so will the others. Life is a matter of strategy and endurance, and there are none among us who wish to die."

Mikhailo shuddered uncontrollably at the determined look in the Kat's eyes, the same expression she had had when she announced a new breed of Cossack was soon to be born. "But, Katerina, hatred will cloud your thinking. When you hate, you cannot love," he said shortly.

"Love!" she cried. "I have no time for love."

Fear crawled into Mikhailo's chest as he blinked his heavy-lidded eyes. "Someday you will want it," he said softly.

"Perhaps, Mikhailo. Do you suppose there is a man somewhere who will understand me? Will he look into my eyes and see my love reflected in his? Is there a man who will smile at me with humor and hold me close in the darkest hours and tell me nothing matters but me?"

Mikhailo frowned. "Somewhere, Katerina, there is such a man, and you will search each other out." He patted Katerina fondly and walked toward Banyen.

Banyen watched the short, stocky Cossack approach him. His hand went instinctively to his right cheek, where he fingered the hateful scar. As always when he was angry, the damnable thick red welt throbbed. If he ever came across the bitch that did this to him, he would wring her neck without a moment's hesitation.

Mikhailo's voice was thick and guttural when he addressed the Mongol. "Your man, Igor, needs much preparation. Neither Katerina nor myself care for his insolent attitude. You'll bring him into line or he will be spending many long, cold nights alone. It could be the death of him."

Banyen's fingers continued to caress the swollen scar as his eyes raged at the Cossack. He knew the old man spoke the truth. His only defense was that they were boys. It took awhile for a boy to become a man. However, he said nothing to the Cossack, but nodded his head to show that he was in agreement. Igor needed a tongue-lashing, and perhaps a swift kick from his boot. His surly, untamed mouth could be the end of all the youths if he didn't shape up quickly. Another night or two without dinner and the thick woolen blanket just might do the trick.

Banyen motioned his men to fall into formation behind him as Kostya and the men assigned to him mounted their horses and took to the center of the arena. The Russian divided his men into groups of seven, and lightly touched his horse's flanks for the animal to move backward. Banyen watched carefully as the men settled themselves on top of the horses and then spurred their mounts forward, their lances thrust in front of them. He was shocked when no one was unseated, all weapons clasped firmly in hand. Grudgingly he admitted that Kostya would have made a good general. He had the ability to make men do what he wished just by speaking. As yet, the prince had seen no man give him an argument. How, Banyen wondered, was he delegated to be the leader of the prisoners? Did they have some sort of unspoken agreement between them? What was there about the fair-haired Russian that gave the prisoners such confidence? Was it, could it be, that he was their friend? If so, that might account for their seemingly implicit trust in the blue-eyed man. His face contorted in rage as he saw Katerina walk over to congratulate Kostya.

Now it was his turn with his men. He felt a coldness settle over him as he signaled his men to take to the center of the arena. He knew in his gut that he couldn't hope to do as well. They would try, and that was all he could hope for.

He was right. They were clumsy and awkward, their movements unsure, their weapons held loosely in lax fingers.

"Enough!" yelled Katerina. "We have no time to waste with this childish foolishness. Prince Banyen, you will assign all of your men to their quarters for two nights. If they wish, they can practice throughout the night. When I set eyes on them again, they had better be prepared to meet with the prisoners in the center of this arena, and there will be no safety tips on the weapons. If they get wounded and die, it will be their own fault. One more mistake and your men will be turned out into the snow. It makes little or no difference to me if they die of cold or not!" The titian eyes spewed sparks as she stared at Banyen. "And," she said emphatically, "if they go into the snow, so do you." Turning on her heel, she left the arena.

That's what she should do, pray that they failed so she could send them all into the frozen landscape. How would the Mongol fare? He had left her to freeze in the tent, and she could do the same if she had to. Soon it would be her turn to wreak vengeance on him. All good things came to those who waited. And she would wait and wait and wait! Soon it would be her turn.

Katerina had just folded the blanket from her horse and laid it on a tack box when she felt a presence near her. She whirled, thinking it was Banyen stalking her again. "Kostya!" she said breathlessly. "What are you doing here?"

"Mikhailo sent me for additional blankets. Where are they kept?" he asked as he deliberately brushed near her. His bright blue eyes were expressionless as he stared at her, waiting for a reply.

Katerina pointed to a chest in the corner and moistened her dry lips with her tongue.

The silence between them seemed more eloquent than words could ever be. When Kostya held out his hand, she reached out her own delicate one and felt him draw her to him. They walked hand in hand to the dimmest corner of the stable. Katerina drew in her breath and felt the man next to her tense at her intake. He, too, seemed to have trouble with his breathing. She was conscious of his height, of his nearness, and of his maleness. His arm around her shoulders made her tingle with the contact of his flesh. In the murky light they stopped their initial, tentative gestures. She felt her body move into the circle of his arms. His mouth became a part of hers, and her heart beat in a wild, untamed, broken rhythm. In their yearning they strained together as they mounted obstacles of the flesh and worked to join blood, flesh, and spirit.

In the quiet of the stable they devoured each other with searching, hungry lips.

His touch was gentle as he tore his mouth from hers, his breathing ragged and harsh. It was Katerina whose sensibilities returned first, and she stepped back from him, her eyes sleepy and almost content. Her passion-bruised mouth tasted sweet to her tongue as she licked at her lips in an effort to calm herself. She was alive! Her response to Kostya was what she had needed to prove that her body could respond to someone other than Banyen.

Kostya's touch was barely noticeable as he pulled her to him again in a hard embrace. Katerina, in control of the situation, demurred and moved farther away from his touch and his sinewy arms.

"You're right, this isn't the time and the place," Kostya whispered. "There'll be other times, other places. The winter will be long and cold, and one we'll endure together. It's been a long time since anyone stirred my blood as you just did," he said huskily. With a last lingering look deep into her eyes, he backed off, but not before he tenderly ran his finger down the length of her satiny cheek. The feel of his lean finger on her flesh was more shocking than the touch of his lips upon hers. She felt desire wash over her as he left the large, dim confines of the stable. Did she want him or did she need him? She admitted to herself that there was a difference. Sooner or later she would explore this feeling that was engulfing her.

Banyen stepped out of the shadows and watched through hooded eyes as Katerina stared after Kostya's retreating back. His tall frame was concealed by the heavy stone columns in the stable and by the stalls covered with brilliant blankets. What was the girl thinking; what was she feeling? Did she compare Kostya to him? Would she remember the kiss they shared in the sleigh? He didn't know why, but it was suddenly important to him to find out. He wanted to know—no, he *needed* to know which of them she preferred.

The angry, crimson welt on his cheek began to throb as he watched Katerina lay her cheek against a horse's head. Even from where he stood in the shadowy light, he could see the dreamy look on her face. Damnation, what and who was she thinking about? His loins took on an ache that threatened to erupt into full-blown pain. His strong hands gripped into fists at his sides, and he clenched his teeth in frustration.

Hunter and stalker that he was, he moved lightly to the heavy wooden doors and closed them quietly. He slid the bolt with barely a sound. Slowly, insidiously, he crept up on Katerina and stood behind her. His hands reached for her thick, coppery hair, but before he could touch the gleaming strands, she turned, her eyes wide and staring. What was it that he read in their flaming pools? He said nothing as he twined his hands in her rich wealth of hair. Gently, he drew her to him, then forced his parted lips upon hers in a savage, demanding kiss that she returned in kind. Unseen stars exploded overhead, falling, falling, until they settled like a cloak over Banyen. "Tell me," he said huskily, "that I don't stir your blood. Tell me and I'll leave you here and never seek you out again."

He kissed her eyes, her mouth, her cheeks, the hollow of her throat, and she felt a raging fire engulf her as she burrowed her head against his chest. It made no difference that he was the Mongol from the steppe. She wanted him. She needed him. She moaned softly as his mouth crashed down on hers in a savage, blazing kiss of passion. The banked fires began to smolder and burst into flame as she felt his searching hands explore her body through the thick clothing. His touch was scorching, searing, as her own hands ceased to tremble, and she caressed his high cheeks and ran her hands through his lustrous raven hair. Moan after moan escaped her as she strained against him, her mouth mingling with his, her tongue searching, darting to conquer his.

Within moments their clothing lay in a heap on the rough granite floor. Banyen spread his burnoose on the sweet-scented straw and gently lowered Katerina onto the lushness of the warm sable.

A thin streak of moonlight filtered through the high, narrow window that was not covered by the drifting snow. Banyen drew in his breath in a ragged gasp as Katerina's body was bathed in silvery radiance. His face was inscrutable in the faint rays, but his gaze was almost tangible; she felt it reach her, touch her, and was aware of the all-consuming fire that raged through her.

Katerina's response was unwavering as she stared deep into his oblique eyes. She was hypnotized by them as she felt his mouth crush hers. Her body took on a will of its own as Banyen caressed and explored every inch of her bare limbs. She moved to the rhythm he initiated and felt him respond to her in a way she had never dreamed possible. Searing flames licked at her body as she sought to quench the blazing inferno that engulfed her. He kissed her small ears, her eyes, her moistened mouth as he murmured tender words of love, as his hands traveled down the length of her, arousing, teasing her till her breath came in short gasps and her body turned beneath his touch.

His lips clung to hers as he pressed her down onto the softness of the rich fur. He buried his hands in the sparkling coppery hair, twining the thickness, holding her head still as he kissed her savagely. Katerina strained against him, her nude, rounded breasts flattening against his hard, muscular chest as she responded to his passion with an urgency that demanded release. He caressed her again and again, cherishing her, desiring her, imprisoning her body with his hard, muscular strength.

He felt the softness of her flesh grow warm and taut beneath him; his hungry mouth worshipped her, tracing moist patterns on her creamy skin. His dark head moved lower, grazing the firmness of her belly and down to the silky smoothness between her thighs. He parted her legs with his knees and felt her respond to him, arching her back to receive him. Her parted lips were a flame that met his raging, tumultuous mouth. She welcomed him, accepted him, his hardness, his leanness, his very maleness, as he drove into her. The unquenchable heat that was soaring through her beat in her veins, threatening to crescendo into a raging inferno of flames.

He lay upon her, commanding her response, and she offered it, writhing beneath him, exulting in her own femininity as she caressed his broad back and crushed her lips to his. The sound of her own heart thundered in her ears, or was it Banyen's that beat and roared about them?

Her breathing ragged and gasping, she opened herself like the petals of a flower. The searing, scorching aching erupted within her, consuming her in an explosion that matched his.

Banyen opened one azure eye and gazed longingly down at Katerina. Her long-lashed lids remained closed, her breathing slow and regular. Sensing his inspection of her, she opened her eyes and stared deeply into his dark, oblique eyes. Words at the moment weren't necessary. Banyen slept then, his dark head cradled against her breast. Katerina lay quiet, body and mind at peace for the moment. How vulnerable he looks in sleep, she thought. Defenseless, almost like a child. What was it her uncle said? Yes, that he was a compassionate man and perhaps one day he would allow her to see that side of him. She raised her eyes and looked at the bright shaft of moonlight. Were the stars out? Was there a brief respite from the heavy, suffocating snows? She stirred slightly on the sable burnoose, the sweet scent of the straw teasing her nostrils. The slight stirring of her body made Banyen tighten his hold on her, and he sighed contentedly in his sleep.

How had she allowed herself to forget what he had done to her? Was it because she wanted to see if he . . . It didn't matter now. She had lain in his arms; she had matched his ardor and his flaming passions and had been satisfied. The brief interlude with Yuri had been nothing compared to this wild, savage lovemaking. Katerina did not believe she could ever look at Banyen again after this. Her hand reached up to stroke the still-discolored welt on his cheek. Even after all these months it had not completely healed. She dug her teeth into her lips till she felt the salty taste of her own blood. Yet she didn't have the will or the power to take her hand away. Instead, she smoothed the ebony hair from his high forehead. She loved the shape of his eyes, and slowly bent over and lightly brushed her lips against the lids, feeling him stir against her with her touch. Gently she let her long, tapered finger trace the shape of his eye. Again her lips delicately caressed his lids, and she suddenly found herself pinned in a hard embrace.

Katerina pushed Banyen away from her, completely unashamed by her nudity. "No! This is not to happen again. We're both to look upon this as a moment in time between two people caught up in something they had no control over, Banyen. There'll be no more times. A meeting of the flesh, isn't that what men call it? Nothing more and nothing less."

Banyen nodded. He would agree to anything right now. Fully satiated, he boldly watched her as she dressed in front of him, not caring to avert his attention.

Once fully clothed, she stared down at him. "Remember, a meeting of the flesh, nothing more." Her eyes lightened till they were the color of taffy. To Banyen, they were the most beautiful eyes he had ever seen.

The moment Katerina walked through the door, he felt more alone than he had ever been in his entire life. He knew that if the stable were suddenly invaded by every recruit and every man under his command, he would still be isolated among the babble of voices. There was only one body that could communicate with his, and she was gone. What did a promise mean? Promises were made and broken. He owed her nothing. Well, Banyen conceded, maybe his body; she had seemed to like it well enough. He laughed, a deep, full, rich sound in the quietness. The laughter, however, was hollow to his own ears, and he sobered.

He lay back on the sweet straw and remembered the feel of her lips on his eyelids. Now why had she done that? And why had she let her fingers caress the damnable scar on his cheek? Evidently she had thought him asleep when she touched him so gently. No one had ever stirred him in quite that way. He was confused by the meaning of it. He told himself he had bedded enough women to know the answer, but he didn't. No woman had ever moved his heart in that way before. The action was tender, the way a mother would caress her infant. He sneered as he got to his feet and dressed. He was no child, and the Kat was hardly maternal. The fleeting instant puzzled him; it was something else for him to think about.

When Banyen left the warm, fresh-smelling stable, the

first person he saw was Kostya, returning with a pile of blankets. He gave the Russian an ear-to-ear grin and saluted him with a mocking finger to his forehead. He had won! The blue eyes were unreadable as the prisoner stared after the strutting Mongol.

Chapter 14

"The witches are out, the witches are out," Ivan chanted gleefully as he ran up and down the marble hall outside his quarters. "A banquet, we must have a banquet to celebrate!" he shouted as he began to shred a drapery with the tip of his staff. "Ready a banquet, now!"

"My Czar, are you aware of the time? It's past midnight, and the ovens are banked for the night. There isn't any food prepared," a guard bleated fearfully.

"Roast swan, roast peacock and sturgeon. Prepare enough for three hundred of my favorite guests!" Ivan continued to shout, ignoring the fearful guard. "We'll have the bears and entertainment fit for a Czar. See to it, my good man, within the hour. Ring the bells, wake everyone and tell them I wish their presence in the banquet hall. Tell the nobles and boyars to dress in their finest, and have the women arrive nude."

"My Czar, at this hour . . ."

Ivan wrenched his staff from the tattered drapery and with one swing of his arm thrust it into the guard's throat. "The hour doesn't matter," he said. "A celebration is what I want, and I have decided to prepare it myself. Now that you're dead, you won't be able to attend. A pity, you would have enjoyed the bears," he said, leaning over the body and dipping his bare toe in the man's blood. Languidly he traced a picture of a bear, and stood back to observe his handiwork. "Marvelous!" he shouted shrilly. "It looks just like my pet bear!"

Banging his staff against the stone walls, he made his way to the kitchen, walking drunkenly on his heels so the remaining blood would not drip on the floor. From time to time he stopped and squinted at the red substance congealing on his toes, and laughed delightedly.

Inside the cavernous kitchen, he poked and prodded everything in sight with the tip of his staff. "Roast swan!" he shouted at the top of his lungs. "I want roast swan for my celebration!" He yelled again. When the game did not materialize, he lashed out at the fire in the oven, by pitching his staff into its depths. Angrily he sat down in the middle of the floor and crossed his bony legs, chanting of witches and traitors.

A startled cook and two servants, who jutted their heads fearfully into the archway, were stunned at the sight. Ivan rolled over, banging his head on the hard stone. "I want swan and pheasant and sturgeon for my celebration."

"My Czar, when is the celebration to take place?" the cook asked uneasily.

"You ask when! How dare you ask me when! Now! The celebration is now! Wake everyone and tell them to assemble in the hall. Be sure to tell the boyars and their women they must arrive in a cart. It will be pulled onto the main floor by my bears. See to it!" he shouted as he staggered to his feet.

The two servants ran from the room, their faces masks of fear, to do his bidding.

"My Czar, your head is bleeding," the cook said hesitantly.

"Bleeding, bleeding, you say? I have no blood, how can

I bleed? What manner of fool are you?" he demanded, his eyes wild and staring.

"A mistake, my Czar, it must be the firelight," the cook said as she hurried into the storeroom.

When the cook returned, Ivan was again sitting cross-legged in the middle of the floor. He craned his neck to watch the cook as she began to pluck the feathers. "No, no, don't you know anything?" he grumbled as he again got to his feet. He reached an emaciated hand toward the cook and clutched at the bird. Without a moment's hesitation, he flung it into the oven. "That's how you roast a swan, my good woman, don't you know anything? Can't you see the feathers will burn right off? Then the meat will get done. Why must I do everything?" he pouted childishly. "Fetch me the pheasant and I'll show you how to roast it also."

The stench from the smoldering feathers sent the cook gasping from the room, her hand to her mouth. She returned in a moment, handing the freshly killed pheasant to the Czar, and stood back respectfully to await his further orders.

"Wrap this bird in a wet cloth and let it steam in the oven."

"Be . . . before or . . . or after removing the feathers?" the cook asked, her face blank and unreadable.

Ivan sighed wearily. "Good woman, how did you become chef in this palace? With the feathers, of course. I happen to like wet, juicy feathers. Everyone does. Order my throne to be taken to the banquet hall, and see to it that the Princess Halya is present. The pheasant is for her, a special tribute before she leaves the palace. This celebration is in honor of her departure." Suddenly he brought his hand up to his mouth and laughed wickedly. "No, no that isn't why I'm having the celebration, it's for the arrival of the witches."

He shrugged. "It makes no matter. Halya is a witch, too. Tend to the matter," he said regally as he hopped from the room on one foot, his skinny arms stretched straight out in front of him.

Tearfully the cook ran from the room to do as instructed, the pheasant clutched to her bosom.

Petrified with fear, Halya entered the banquet hall and took her place next to Ivan. She remained quiet, her body trembling at the insane expression on his face.

"Halya, my love, how nice of you to attend your going-away celebration. This party is especially for you. I want you always to remember how generous I have been to you. Tonight you will see my trained bears lead a cart of naked women around this room. The boyars and nobles will be dressed in their finest in your honor. I do hope you appreciate all the trouble I've gone through on your behalf. Why," he said, wide-eyed, "I even roasted the meat myself. Kiss my ear, darling Halya, to show your thanks."

Halya swallowed hard and bent over, her lips brushing against his ear. "This is a great . . . great honor, Ivan. May I ask where you are sending me?" she said fearfully.

"Never ask me anything, for if you do I shall tell you a lie. I feel like sending you away, so that is what I'm doing, but I want you to have this party before you leave. Later, if I have a mind to, I'll tell you why. Sit quietly now, for the bears will arrive shortly, and noise disturbs them."

Halya clenched her teeth so hard she thought her jaw would crack. God in heaven, what was he going to do?

Ivan stood up as a steady stream of boyars and nobles entered the room dressed in their regal attire. At a wave of his bejeweled finger in the air, the nobles and boyars sat, their eyes anxious and fearful. When all was quiet Ivan rose to his feet and shrugged his skeletal shoulders.

"We are now going to have a parade, which I will lead. Princess Halya will judge who is the finest. Following me will be the bears with the cart of women. After the cart, you'll all fall into place and we'll circle the hall. I will sing." He clapped his hands loudly as he jumped from the dais and landed with a thump on the marble floor.

"Bring on the bears," he cackled gleefully.

Halya sat rigidly in her chair as the bears, led by a trainer, entered the room. Merciful God, she prayed, whatever he plans to do, let him do it quickly before I collapse. Ashamed and humiliated for the naked women, she lowered her eyes and stared at the floor.

"Enough!" Ivan shouted. "The parade is now over." Waving his arms wildly, and hopping about on one foot, then the other, he made his way to the cart. He eyed one woman lustfully and, reaching out, pinched a rosy-tipped breast till the woman screamed in pain. His eyes widened, and before she knew what was happening, he lifted her bodily from the cart and flung her in the face of the closest bear.

Halya retched as the bear clawed at the woman's flesh, chewing into her shoulder, mutilating the pinkish-white skin.

When the woman's screams had faded, Ivan pursed his mouth and looked around at the seated nobles and boyars. "You may each pick a woman and fornicate here, where I can watch you. This must be a memorable evening for the princess. I want her to leave with happy memories. When I am seated, you will commence with your lustful ways."

Silence rang in Halya's ears, as no man made a move to leave the table. The women cowered, their arms crossed over their naked breasts. She knew that the moment Ivan sat down the men would do as he said, and the women would gladly surrender themselves, fearful lest their end be the same as the dead woman's. Her stomach heaved as first one man and then another got to his feet, eyes downcast.

Ivan squirmed in his chair, his eyes dancing in glee as he watched. Harsh guttural sounds escaped his drooling mouth as he stood up for a better look at something that pleased him. He clapped his hands and shouted his approval of the orgy going on beneath the dais.

"Tell me, Halya, have you ever been so stimulated? I must plan more celebrations like this. I've outdone myself this time, don't you agree?"

"But of course, Ivan, but then, you always arrange everything so perfectly. You must be very proud of yourself," she managed to say quietly, her stomach heaving at the words.

"That's very generous of you, Halya. And for being so gracious, I'm going to tell you where you are going when you leave here tomorrow. You are going to Volin, the village I sent Yuri to, to finish his mission. My darling Halya, did I neglect to tell you your brother is dead? No, no, I told you. Well"—he shook his head—"I can't be expected to remember everything. No weeping, Halya, you must be strong about our parting. Remember, your brother died for me." He sighed wearily at the tears in Halya's eyes. "You must uncover the secret of the Cosars. I will give you one month to do what he couldn't do. Yuri had a mission to fulfill, and he failed. You may redeem him in my eyes. If you succeed, I'll give you a medal. I decided to give you an award instead of taking you for my wife. Thank me now, Halya," he said childishly.

"Th . . . thank you, Ivan."

"I want the secret of the Cosars. Remember to find out how they breed the horses, I must know! Now, do you understand your mission?"

So that's what it is all about, those damnable Cosars of the Cossacks. Yuri is dead, and this is no time for grief. I've been through that already, the first time he told me of Yuri's death. For now I'll smile—anything until tomorrow, when I leave this godforsaken place. Once gone, she told herself, I won't return. Never! No matter how many men he sends after me, I'll run till I drop in my tracks, or I'll kill myself first. I will never return!

"Well," the Czar demanded, "do you understand?"

"But of course, Ivan, I understand perfectly. I have never failed you before, and I won't now," she said in a choked voice.

"Who is that man with the ugly face?" he demanded.

"Kubitsky," came a soft reply.

"Give him to the bears to play with. His ugliness upsets me," Ivan muttered as he tossed his rings into the center of the circling bears. "Now bring on the feast!" he roared in a deep-pitched voice.

Halya watched with horrified eyes as a servant set a platter before her. "I prepared it myself, especially for you," Ivan said happily. "Remove the cloth and eat all you want, dear Halya."

Gingerly, her hand trembling, she inched the cloth away from the mound on the platter. She drew back in horror at the smell and sight of the baked pheasant. Unable to restrain herself, she ran from the room, sobs tearing at her throat.

Ivan stood and stretched his scrawny neck till he could see all of the assembled boyars and nobles. "The princess was overcome with happiness," he babbled. "Women are like that at times. All four of my wives acted the same way. Now we'll share her special dinner," he said, pointing to the wild game. "The servants will serve you as much as you want, and eat heartily," he cackled, wagging a bony finger in the air. "I'll leave you to your merrymaking. With me gone, you may do as you please. Enjoy yourselves. I'll leave the bears for you to play with, so they won't become lonely."

"God help me!" Halya screamed as she ran down one hall, and then another, till she came to her room and quickly threw the bolt. She grabbed the pillow sack, still filled with her jewels and clothing, which she had hidden away in a cupboard. This time, even if Ivan had already posted a guard at her door, she would escape. He had stopped her the last time, but this time he couldn't. She was on a mission for him, had been told to leave. Nothing could stop her.

With the help of a young guard she had befriended, she made her way to the stable. The soldier kept watch as Halya saddled a sorrel horse. Mounted, she thanked the man and disappeared into the night.

Halya felt safe now that she rode freely, her security in the sack tied to the saddlebags. She had the next thing to a king's ransom riding with her. Jewels could buy anything. Could they buy a life? She wondered.

Halya rode steadily, stopping only to eat and to feed and rest her horse. She rode for many days before she arrived at a small village. She reined in her horse and wiped the snow from her forehead with the back of her hand. She knew she looked terrible. Carefully she smoothed the golden hair back from her brow and tucked in the stray tendrils, and then smoothed the gown beneath the lush cape she wore, trying to free it of the wrinkles that clung to it. More than that she couldn't do. Perhaps the peasants would allow her a bowl of water to wash with. They might even have knowledge of Yuri.

She knew instinctively that the men advancing on her were Don Cossacks, and just possibly they would help her. If not . . .

Halya waited patiently atop the horse for the two men to approach her. She knew that if she made a move to dismount she would be pinned from behind and dragged God only knows where. The men stopped some distance from her and waited for her to speak. Halya leaned over and raised her hand to show that she was a friend.

"I'm on my way to Volin in search of my brother, Yuri Zhuk. Could you tell me how much farther it is and if you have news of him? He traveled here in late spring to purchase horses and has not been seen since."

The Cossacks looked at Halya and her fine clothes and

the sleek animal she rode. They exchanged blank looks and said nothing.

"I mean you no harm. My parents are old and they want news of their only son. I myself come from a village no bigger than this, and I know that news travels from one village to the other. I want nothing more than information. Please help me," she pleaded.

The taller of the two Cossacks advanced another step and looked up at Halya. She was indeed a beautiful woman. What harm could talking with her do? he thought.

"The village of which you speak is no more. Marauding Tereks killed the villagers and burned it to the ground. I've heard that the man you speak of rode from Volin with no horses, and the contract he desired canceled by the Kat. None from my village saw the man you speak of, but if he has not returned since late spring, then there is little hope. A lone man is not safe on foot when the Tereks take to the road. And you, my fine lady, should also be warned."

"Are you telling me that the man known as the Kat is dead?" Halya asked in a shocked voice.

"That's exactly what I'm telling you. The Kat and all his people. The only person to escape the slaughter was his daughter, who was not in the village at the time."

"Where can I find the Kat's daughter? Perhaps she'll know something of my brother if she lived in the village when he arrived to negotiate the sale of the horses."

The two men looked at each other again. The spokesman debated a moment before he spoke. "She's in the mountains at the House of the Kat." He held up a large, beefy, dirty hand and motioned for Halya to remain quiet. "In truth, I don't know if she is there now or not, but it was the custom for the Kat to take his people and horses back to the mountains at the end of the summer. We haven't seen her since she rode from here after the slaughter. There is nothing we can do to help you."

Halya shivered inside the silver-fox cape and wanted to

cry. To have come so far only to find nothing . . . She bit into her full lower lip. She wasn't beaten yet!

"Tell me, how can I get to this House of the Kat you speak of? Is there a sleigh or a wagon I could buy to make the journey? It's not for myself, you understand, it is for my old parents, who love their son." Tears gathered in the sea-green eyes and trickled down her cheeks. She reached out a slim hand in entreaty and knew she made an appealing picture. Stronger men than these two had been captivated by her winsome ways; they would be no different.

The younger of the two Cossacks spoke hastily. He, too, had a mother who fussed and fretted over him when no one was around. "We might be able to send a message and . . ."

The first Cossack was also smitten by the sparkling tears. "Dismount and come with us. There is a way for us to let the people in the Carpathians know that someone wishes to travel to the mountains. It may take a couple days for a message to get back to us, but it is the best we can do for now. Snow will come shortly, look overhead," he said, waving his arm upward.

"Oh, thank you!" Halya said gratefully as she slid from her mount.

"See to it, Basil," the first Cossack said quietly. "I'll take the lady into my hut and make her comfortable."

Halya blanched but followed him. She knew what was in store for her, but she also knew she had no other choice. She would do whatever was necessary to find news of her brother. She wondered if Ivan knew the Kat was dead. Did his death mean there were no more horses? Please let Yuri be alive, she prayed silently as the Cossack motioned her to sit at a worn bench. He generously poured her a steaming cup of tea and placed a chunk of dark bread in front of her. Halya smiled gratefully as she nibbled, and wondered how long it would be before he told her to remove her clothing.

Basil trudged through the snow to the barns at the end of the village. There he opened the door to a small makeshift aviary and reached out for one of the falcons. His thick fingers were cold and numb, but he managed to scribble a message and attach it to the bird's leg. With luck the bird would cover the distance by sundown. By noon tomorrow he would have an answer. He felt envy and lust rise in him for his friend Kusma's good fortune. He wondered if his good friend would share her. A good Cossack did not keep his wealth to himself. Basil could only hope that Kusma would feel charitable toward him. It had been many long days since he had seen anyone as pleasing to the eye as this lady. He knew her skin would be like a flower petal, and her lips would cling to his as she whispered sweet words of love and passion. He groaned in desire as he removed the hood from the falcon's head and set the bird free.

All he could do now was wait for several hours, and then he would bravely stroll over to Kusma's hut and demand that they share what should be shared. He wouldn't take no for an answer.

Mikhailo deftly placed the falcon on a perch and covered his head before he removed the capsule from its leg. Unable to read the scrawled words, he set out in search of Katerina.

Banyen and Kostya both watched as she reached for the paper and scanned its contents. She frowned, her amber eyes turning the color of cinnamon as she stared at Mikhailo. Biting her lip nervously, she reread the message. She carefully folded the tiny piece of paper and stuffed it into the pocket of her trousers. With a puzzled look on her face, she left the arena and strode back to the kitchen. She poured herself tea from the samovar and marveled at the thick, syrupy consistency of the liquid. Hanna must have made it days ago, she told herself.

Katerina withdrew the note and scanned the contents again. What should she do? Should she allow the girl to come to the mountains; and if she did, who was to fetch her? If only Oles hadn't died in the slaughter. She would have to send Mikhailo or Stepan, or go herself. She could ignore the message and forget about it. It would be best to send another message with the falcon denying the young woman permission to come to the mountains, saying there was no one to fetch her. What could she possibly want? Did it have something to do with the horses? Didn't Yuri mention something about having a sister? It could be a lie, a trap of some sort. She would have to go herself.

Quickly she negated the idea. Stepan would have to go; Mikhailo was needed here. She didn't dare leave the men for the journey. Twice now she had sensed Banyen's presence when she went to Whitefire's stables. No matter where she went, no matter what she did, his eyes were always on her. Stepan would have to take two of the stallions, because none of the other horses would stand the trip. Only the stallions could maneuver in the deep snow, which they loved.

What would happen if she did allow the woman to come to the mountains? Would it cause a problem with the men? She admitted that that, more than anything else, was what was bothering her. How would the others react to another woman? A woman who, as Yuri's sister, would undoubtedly be beautiful and wear fine clothes. Envy ate at Katerina as she stared at the message. *I could just send word saying Yuri is dead and let it go at that. It would be a cruel, hard blow to the woman, but then, why should I care? I don't know her, and I owe her nothing. But if she really is Yuri's sister, I owe her an explanation of his death. It was by my hand that he died. She deserves to know how and why. I, likewise, am seeking answers to my father's death,* her niggling inner voice urged. *I won't be satisfied till I have the answers I want. Perhaps the woman feels the same way.*

Katerina shuddered as she gulped at the bitter substance in her cup. She knew that if her father had lived he would have denied permission for the woman to come to the mountains. But he was dead, and it was her decision. Right or wrong, she would tell her the circumstances of Yuri's death. Perhaps it would ease some of the guilt she carried within her. Yuri's pleading eyes flashed before her, and she cringed. Would the woman understand and forgive her for what she had done?

When Mikhailo and Stepan entered the kitchen, they found Katerina staring into her empty cup, the small piece of paper clutched in her hand. Katerina raised her eyes and nodded. "You will go, Stepan. You'll ride Wildfire, and Darkfire will be saddled for the woman to ride on the return trip. Send the message and dress yourself warmly. Tell the Dons to take the woman as far as Volin and have her wait for you. Under no circumstances are you to go to their village. Volin, that is as far as you go, do you understand? If you sense a trap or a trick of some sort, send the horses back alone. I'll come for you in the sleigh. You'll need eyes in the back of your head, my good friend. I hope you can do it with no harm to yourself."

"What you mean is, can Wildfire do it?" interjected Mikhailo. "Of course he can, and Stepan can make the trip as well."

At the confidence expressed in him by his friends, Stepan gained a new aura of dignity. He had no doubts about himself either. After all, he had made a similar trip with Wildflower some months before.

"What does she want? Why would anyone come here in the dead of winter?" asked Mikhailo.

Katerina shrugged. "We'll know as soon as Stepan returns with her and not a moment before," she said quietly, her eyes sober and reflective. Although no one mentioned it, Katerina knew that Stepan could easily be caught in a blinding blizzard. She pushed the thought away. Stepan was an excellent horseman, with a superb, specially trained mount. Despite the rapidly approaching period of horrible storms, her childhood friend would be fine and would return with Yuri's sister, though it would likely take much more time than usual.

"Dress warmly, Stepan," Katerina said with a fond pat on his arm. "I'll get the horses ready and food ready. And remember, do not attempt the trek back to the mountains unless the weather permits."

Katerina made sure Banyen was occupied in the center of the arena when she went for the stallions. If he saw them on her return, it would be all right, but she didn't want him following her and watching her press the secret catch. If he hasn't seen me already, she thought grimly. Bastard, he had eyes in the back of his head.

At the last minute Katerina negated the idea of saddles. Wildfire would make better time without the heavy leather on his back. Darkfire, on the other hand, needed the extra weight, and she chose a saddle with care, testing it before she placed it on his back. The stallion nuzzled her, and she laughed. "You know, don't you. A trek through the snow and you'll show us all who can survive out there in that vast white world, but remember, my friend, it's Wildfire that you follow. On your return you shall carry a beautiful lady. I'm trusting you to give her a comfortable ride, and no playful tricks, do you hear?" she said, stroking the horse's sleek flanks. It was Wildfire who gently pushed her away from Darkfire and waited patiently for the girl to respond to him. "You're to take Stepan safely to Volin, and no antics in the snow. This is business, Wildfire, and we have no time for playing. You'll ride like the wind and bring my guest safely to the House of the Kat and," she gurgled, "don't lose Stepan. He's not used to your spirited ways. No saddle, just a blanket for you." The stallion reared back and shook his great head at her words. Katerina knew he understood every word she said and would do as she instructed.

Katerina led the stallions down the long stone passageway and out to the main stable, where she waited for Stepan. Banyen strolled nonchalantly up to her and ran a hand lovingly over Wildfire's back. His voice was sincere when he spoke.

"Never have I seen more magnificent animals. You have every right to be proud of them, and I can understand your obsession with getting your Cosars back."

Katerina stared at him, expecting his arrogant, mocking eyes to belie his words. Instead, she read only respect and open admiration in their depths.

"I would give my life for these animals."

Banyen nodded. "I believe you would. I understand what you're saying. Perhaps it won't be necessary to give your life for them. You have others inside the arena who will do that for you." The old scoffing look was back as he stroked Darkfire.

"No one will give his life for me. Why do you think I'm training these men? Certainly not for myself. I have no wish to see any of them die. I see that you don't believe what I'm saying. And I care even less what you think."

Mikhailo and Stepan watched their friend and the prince a moment before joining them. "Good, you didn't give him a saddle. This animal," Mikhailo said, assisting Stepan onto his horse, "detests anything save a human being on his back. We bow to his wishes." He laughed into Banyen's face.

Banyen nodded curtly and walked away, his back stiff and straight.

"Did you make a mistake, little one? Do you think it wise for the Mongol to know of the stallions?"

"Mistake? Hardly, Mikhailo. I'm sure he knew they were stabled here before today. Those damnable eyes of his see everything." Smiling at Stepan, she said, "A safe journey to you, my friend," then flung open the wide oak doors.

Wildfire reared back and preened before Katerina, then thundered through the portal, Darkfire on his heels. Katerina laughed. They were like children, waiting for a romp in the snow.

When the heavy doors closed against the snow and cold, Katerina walked slowly back to the arena in search of Banyen. A confrontation. She would ask him what he intended to do with his knowledge. Why skirt the problem? She would ask and he would lie, and she would tell him that he lied. Whatever happened, she would let him know she didn't trust him.

Taking her position in the arena, Katerina watched the men go through their drills and exercises. The longer they kept at the rigorous training, the more proficient they became. Afstar would have no complaints when Banyen returned in the spring with his band of soldiers. No complaints at all, she thought smugly. She waited patiently for the drill to be over before she sauntered over to where the prince stood and motioned him to follow her out of earshot of his men.

"I want to settle something with you, clarify it for your ears," she said shortly. "Now that you know the stallions are here, and I suspect you have known for some time, I want it understood that if you ever go near them or try to take them from here, I'll kill you. No one takes what is mine. I told you once before, I give only one warning."

"Those stallions are your whole life, aren't they," Banyen said softly. "There are other things in life besides horses. When this is all—"

"When this is all over, I'll be the same. Yes, the Cosars are my life. It's a life I chose, not a life that was forced upon me. If you think for one moment you could get the stallions from here, forget it. They would kill you if somehow you managed to get by me. They know where they belong."

"A horse is a horse," Banyen said curtly.

"Just as a man is a man," Katerina snapped.

"Let us not forget that a woman is a woman," he retaliated.

Katerina laughed, the shrill sound bouncing off the thick granite walls and raising the hackles on Banyen's neck. "This woman says those horses will kill you if you try to take them from the stable. Once you didn't heed my words. You would be wise to listen to me now, before you make elaborate plans to take them from this fortress."

"Why would I want to take your horses? You did promise the Khan that you would give him a colt and a filly. Are you telling me now that you are not a woman of your word?"

Katerina flinched at his mocking words. How true they were. Bastard, she seethed. He knew she had no intention of giving Afstar anything.

The catlike eyes narrowed and flamed at his words. "Only time will tell if I keep my word," she said insolently, leaning back against the wall, her long legs thrust in front of her. Completely aware of the picture she made, she thrust out her chest, and watched one of the buttons slip and then open on her coarse shirt. She made no move to close it, and laughed again when she saw Banyen's eyes become clouded. "Thoughts such as you're having now will one day be your undoing." Katerina straightened and slowly buttoned her shirt, her eyes glittering. "No more Mongol." She let her eyes travel across the room to where Kostya was standing. "Suddenly I find that I prefer Western eyes and hair the color of summer sun." She laughed again as Banyen murdered her with his dark gaze.

Chapter 15

Days later, shortly before dawn, while the great fortress slept, a thrashing, tormented Katerina was wakened by the howl of the wind and the icy snow that pelted the windows. She wiped her perspiring brow and then shivered as she curled herself into a tight ball for greater comfort. She knew she would never be able to get back to sleep with the raging blizzard that beat at the fortress. She shivered again. The Mongol had invaded her once more, chasing her like a wild animal. She had been so sure, so confident, that after their hours of lovemaking he would cease to stalk her. She shouldn't have allowed it to happen. Katerina tried to tell herself it was because Kostya had kissed her, setting her body in motion and then leaving her. She chided herself for being so vulnerable; for responding willingly as soon as she felt a man's body. How had she let him touch her, caress her naked flesh, and then answered his urgings in a way that she had never thought possible? God, she cried silently as she buried her head in the downiness of the quilt. She wouldn't let it happen again. She couldn't let it happen with Banyen, and she couldn't permit it with Kostya, either. All she had to do was avoid looking into those sapphire eyes and she would be safe. Concentration on the matters at hand would solve the problem. Thinking only of the horses and training the men was to be her life for the next few months. When it was over she could ponder about herself and what she was going to do. For now, she would have to be strong and not give in to these strange, wonderful feelings that were happening to her.

Katerina withdrew her finely boned hands from the comforting warmth and rubbed her temples. Her face felt hot, flushed, and she knew that the room was chilly, for she could see the misty vapor from her mouth. If her grandfather was awake, she could talk with him the way she had as a child when she was troubled.

Katerina jumped from the bed and quickly dressed. She splashed cold water, which had a film of ice over it, on her face and drew her breath in with the shock of the freezing wetness on her steaming face. Quickly she brushed out her coppery hair and pinned it haphazardly atop her head. Reaching for the ermine cape, she flung it over her shoulders and tied it in place. Katerina rubbed a cheek against the rich fur, and for a moment her cinnamon eyes glazed over, reminding her of another gentle touch. Clenching her teeth, she ran from the room, along the long, icy corridor, and down the steep, curving stairwell. She continued to run till she came to the vast kitchen.

Only a pale lamp burned, and she could see without straining her eyes that her grandfather slept peacefully on his cot near the blazing hearth. His affectionate cat purred contentedly as Katerina prepared herself a cup of dark tea. There would be no talking after all, she mused as she sipped at the fragrant brew.

Katerina stroked the saffron ball of fur and listened to her purr her happiness at having attention paid to her. Her eyes raked the high ceiling of the kitchen, with its fragrant herbs and spices hanging in ropes from the rafters. Huge copper pots and skillets hung next to the dancing flames and gave off a subdued sparkle as the flickering light cast its eerie shadows. Large balls of cheese were strung from heavy, knotted ropes next to cooking utensils and gave off a tantalizing smell. How carefree she had been in this big old kitchen when she was a child. Her eyes went to the tall, thin windows that stretched from the low beams to the base of the wall. Her favorite window seat was still there. She remembered the day her father had built it and said that it was just for her and had a chest to keep treasures in when she wanted to play near the great fire. Her eyes took on a faraway look as she continued to look around the enormous room. Long, heavy wooden shelves dotted the sides and were stacked with dishes and everyday tools. Here and there a green plant rested, thanks to Hanna's tender nurturing. It had always been a happy, comfortable place to be. Now, she thought sadly as she glanced about, it held approaching death, secrets, and hostility. Now it was just a place to get warm and a place to eat. It would never be anything more. When had she outgrown this favorite hideaway? She had to stop thinking about things like this. She had to do something active.

The horses! Of course—she would go to the stallions' quarters and see how they fared. There was no one up to see her at this hour, and anyway, an observer would have no idea where she was going. Gaily Katerina set her heavy mug on the worn table and left the coziness of the kitchen. She needed to see all that was left of the Cosar bloodline. Perhaps when she looked at Whitefire and Snowfire she would regain her perspective. Dejectedly she shook her coppery head. What good were the stallions if the mares were gone?

Stealthily Katerina crept through endless corridors and passages till she came to the underground stable. Cautiously she looked over her shoulder and listened carefully for some sound, anything that would alert her to another's presence. Hearing and seeing nothing to alarm her, she inched her way over to the thick, heavy cupboards that housed the blankets and utensils for the animals. She stood on her toes and reached into the farthest corner of the top shelf. Her long, slender fingers fumbled for the catch that would release the monstrous shelf. Standing back, she waited for it to move on its well-oiled hinges. Quickly she stepped through the secret entrance and pressed another catch for the opening to close. Her lamp from the kitchen held high, she made her way down another long, narrow passageway, barely wide enough for a person to lead a horse. Gradually the tunnel sloped, and the Kat knew she was within sight of Whitefire's special stable.

The purebreds sensed her presence, and a low whicker reached her ears. She knew the noise wouldn't carry beyond where she stood; the walls and ceilings were thick and soundproof.

Her hands trembled as she slid the heavy wooden bolt on the stockade grill that separated the lengthy tunnel from the stallions' quarters. She would find peace and quiet for her troubled feelings here in this remote cavern. Just the feel of the horse beneath her hands was all she needed to make her aware of who and what she was. Quietly she prayed that the same feeling would come over her again today.

"Mikhailo," she called softly, "it is I, Katerina. I've come to see the stallions. This is the first chance I've had to come down here since I got back from the Urals. Tell me, how are the animals?"

Mikhailo's gentle hands stroked Snowfire's sleek hide. "All is well, Katerina," he said quietly as he peered at her in the dim light. "These magnificent animals, what good are they without the mares? I think they sense something is wrong. Snowfire has been especially skittish the past several days," he remarked, rubbing the back of his neck.

"How is Whitefire?" Katerina asked anxiously.

"Calm, and that's what worries me. The other stallions always sense his moods and act accordingly. He's quiet, almost placid, and Snowfire is the skittish one."

"Did you change their feed? Are the fires kept regulated? Perhaps it's the hay, or the fact that Wildfire and Darkfire haven't come back yet with Stepan."

"None of those things, Katerina. Even down here in the bowels of the fortress they know there is a fierce storm blowing outside. Maybe that's what is bothering them," he said, in a tone that conveyed his doubt.

Katerina sensed the agitation the old man was trying to keep hidden from her, and a small flurry of panic settled itself in the pit of her stomach. "They aren't ill, there isn't any sign of something being wrong, is there?"

The Cossack stroked his chin, his eyes thoughtful. "No, nothing visible. I've stayed with them as much as I could and had Stepan or Hanna sleep with them when I had my other duties to tend to. But it's hard, Katerina. I tend your grandfather, the men, and the horses. The others help a great deal, but it's much work. Stay with the horses, I must tend the fires," he said, giving Snowfire a gentle pat on his head.

Katerina watched him walk away with a frown on her face. She sensed that something was wrong with the stallions. Dear God, don't let anything happen to them, she prayed silently. Gently she walked between the animals, crooning soothing words to their ears. Whitefire whickered softly and tossed his great head as he reared back on his hind legs. He came down gracefully and nudged her shoulder playfully with his head, his silky mane swishing across her face. Katerina laughed. "You want to play, is that it? Don't they have time to play with you? They're busy, you know, keeping this place just right for you. All of you," she said sternly, "are upsetting him. You have to treat Mikhailo the way you treat me." Katerina smiled as she fondly petted Whitefire, to Snowfire's chagrin. The stallion tried to nudge

Whitefire away from the slim girl so he too could rub his face against her shoulder. "You're jealous," she giggled.

Katerina continued to comfort the noble horses, touching this one and that one, talking softly as she laughed openly at their display of affection. "I'm the guilty one; I've neglected you and I'm sorry," she said, clasping Whitefire, her favorite, around his thick neck. "I, too, have my problems, that's why I'm here. I knew if I came to see all of you I would get my wits back. Listen to me," she cried in a tormented voice. "I swore if he came near me I would kill him. Then my body betrayed me, and I allowed the Mongol to make love to me." Tears welled in the amber eyes, and a sob caught in her throat as she clung to the stallion. "I don't know what to do. He has a hold over me that I cannot explain. When I'm near him I feel calm, and at the same time so full of . . . of. . . It's like when I come to you and talk to you and you become calm. That's what Banyen does to me. I want him to stroke my head, as I stroke yours. I want to hear the soft words of love and yearning. I want . . . I want him near me, and yet . . . yet it can't be."

Whitefire picked up his foreleg and gently tapped on the floor as he tried to free his head from her tight grasp. He advanced a step and pushed her backward until she toppled onto a pile of yellowed hay. He continued to nudge her till she saw that he wanted her to lie down. Katerina laughed, the tears glistening in her eyes. "Sleep won't make it go away. I know, you want me to stay here, but I can't. I have things to do, and I must get the mares back. I know you understand what I'm saying. I'm doing it for you and the others. I'll retrieve them, you have my promise. I'll come back tomorrow and every day after that.

"Mikhailo, are you here? There's nothing wrong," she called. "They missed me, that's all. I've been so busy with the men and worrying about Grandfather, I neglected the most important thing of all. I'll come back each morning around this time. You're not to worry, Mikhailo, everything is fine. Look, see for yourself," she said, getting up and pointing to the animals.

Mikhailo's old eyes danced with glee when he saw that she was right. The stallions were quiet, all signs of skittishness gone. The touch of the Kat, he marveled. Who would have believed it, and yet he had seen the same thing hundreds of times. Yet each time he saw it he marveled at the way the girl had with the stallions.

Katerina brushed the hay from her clothing and, with a last caress to each of the stallions, left the hidden stable and made her way back to the underground cavern that housed the other horses. She stood a moment and listened for some sound on the other side of the wall. Satisfied, she pressed the catch and waited for the heavy shelf to swing back. She walked through the opening into the darkness of the stable and again closed the hidden door.

She remained still, checking the area as her eyesight adjusted to the darkness. This was her life. How could she, even for a second, have forgotten? She couldn't, she wouldn't, let Banyen into her life again; and as for Kostya, he had no place there either. Only the horses mattered! Always the stallions, never Mongol princes or blond, blue-eyed Russians.

Day by day the tension and hostility increased in the training arena. The recruits worked tirelessly, mastering all that Katerina set before them. The Mongols, under Banyen's command, came into their own. It seemed to Katerina that overnight they lost their youthful looks and childish, willful ways. They were now strong, muscular young men with keen eyes and coordinated movements. Their chests broadened, and the sinewy muscles in the calves of their legs gripped the horses' middles as if soldier and animal were one. Another few weeks and they will be an even match for Kostya and his men, Katerina thought. She watched Igor take to the middle of the arena. Without a second of wasted time, he charged at Rokal and unseated him with no wasted motion. Katerina watched as Banyen nodded approvingly. Grudgingly Katerina complimented Igor with a slight inclination of her head.

So far she had been able to successfully avoid staring into the Mongol's oblique eyes. She made sure that she was never near him or alone with him at any time. Always Mikhailo was at her side. During the dinner hour she was forced to share with Banyen, she sat by the hearth and gulped down her food and immediately returned to the arena, leaving him to converse with her grandfather. She wondered what they spoke of at such length.

Kostya looked for and found ways to be close by, and at these times she would force herself to be cool and aloof, to show that he was of no concern to her. Since the day in the stable, he had lost his appeal for her. She found that standing next to him was like standing next to one of the other prisoners or next to Mikhailo. One full, rich taste of the prince was all she needed, and nothing else would satisfy her.

Mikhailo, too, nodded approvingly at the Mongol's men. Everything seemed to be working well, just as Katerina had said. The only thing that worried him was Katmon, who had taken to his bed and was slowly dying. Katerina wore a haunted look in her eyes each time she sat near his bed. He knew without asking what was bothering her. She didn't want her grandfather to die until she proved to him that she could regain the Cosars. The old man knew in his heart that she would be successful, but the Cossack also knew he would never convince the girl. In her own way she was blaming herself, and nothing short of regaining the animals would satisfy her.

Then there was the prince, who also sat at the feeble man's bedside. They had long conversations about Russia and the

Czar. Katmon listened while Banyen did the talking. The relationship bothered Mikhailo, and it annoyed Katerina. More than once Mikhailo had seen Katerina stalk from the room, her eyes spewing flames, to the amusement of the prince. Why did it always have to be a contest between them? A contest where there would be no victory for the winner. His bent shoulders shook as he made his way back to his position against the damp stone wall.

The ensuing days were nerve-wracking for Katerina. While everything regarding the prince and the recruits seemed to be going well, the dread of her aging Zedda dying alone in his room made her pace the arena, her long, supple legs tense and straight. The bright amber eyes were cloudy and sad as she let her mind drift from time to time to happier days when she was a child and her grandfather held her on his knee and told her stories of the brave and fierce Cossacks of his day. She couldn't let him die without telling him what was bothering her! Was his mind lucid enough to understand? Could she convince him that she would get the Cosars or die trying? Should she tell him about the time on the steppe with the Mongol? What would he say? Her trim body shuddered with the thought as she lifted her eyes to meet Banyen's stare. His gaze was deep, penetrating, willing her to . . . No, she wouldn't look at him. She had no desire to be devoured by the indigo eyes that belonged to him as he wanted her to belong to him. Not just for now, for this short time here in the mountains, where the cold seeped into one's bones and virtually froze the blood in one's veins. She didn't know how, but she knew that he wanted more than she had to give. She was part of his overall plan. It had to be the horses, the stallions. Afstar must have made some sort of bargain with him. The wily, foxy Khan would leave no pebble unturned if he thought he could get the stallions. And if Banyen could manage to get them for him, so much the better. Blood meant nothing to Afstar; family meant nothing. Only owning the Cosars would satisfy him. Over her dead body, and, if necessary, over Banyen's.

When the evening meal was over, Katerina sat back in her grandfather's chair near the fire and sipped at her steaming tea. She refused to meet Banyen's eyes or to talk to him. They had eaten in a silence she had insisted on. Once she had raised her eyes and been aware of the angry red scar on his right cheek. She could almost feel the pain in his lean cheek; and for a split second she fought the urge to reach up and touch it, to make the throbbing cease. Instead, she lowered her lids and finished her dinner without comment.

The yellow cat, at a loss without her master, jumped up on Katerina's lap and began to purr. Absentmindedly Katerina stroked the soft fur, her thoughts on the man seated at the table. Three more long, arduous months to be gotten through. Could she do it? She had to do it; she had no other choice.

Katerina finished her drink and set the heavy cup on the hearth. Gently she put the cat on the floor and got up. Banyen watched her through narrowed eyes as she adjusted the black-tipped cape. She was going to go to her grandfather, as she did every night after the evening meal. She would sit near his bed and whisper soft words that held no meaning. Three times Banyen had stood outside the door and tried to hear what she was saying. The words were indistinguishable, but his ear picked up the torment in her voice. What was it about the girl that . . . ?

"I'll wait here for your return. I promised your grandfather that I would read to him from a book I brought with me. That is, if you have no objections," he said quietly.

Katerina shrugged and left the room. At this point if Zedda wanted the Mongol to read to him, who was she to object? One always acquiesced to the dying.

The thin, frail body beneath the thick pile of bedding shocked Katerina, as always. He had been a strong, robust man; a man of strength and character. Now all that was alive to her eye were the faded, pale eyes of the man in the great bed. The paper-thin lids fluttered at her approach, and he smiled weakly. She bent over the bed and kissed his dry, wrinkled cheek. "We must talk, Zedda. There is much I want to say to you. Listen to me and don't try to talk." The old man fluttered his lashes to show he understood, and Katerina began to speak. "I want you to die with the knowledge that I'll get the horses back. I won't just try, I'll do it—that's a promise I make to you!" She bent closer to the bed. "I have never given my word to you or Father and gone back on it. I will regain them and bring them here, where they belong." The sparse lashes fluttered again, and there was a question in the faded eyes that Katerina understood. "All is going well in the arena. The Mongols have come into their own, as I knew they would. The prince is a mighty leader and will one day be victorious, this too I know. I realize that the short time he has been here you have grown fond of him and enjoyed his company, and yet at the same time you have felt guilty because of the way I feel about him. You can't understand my hatred of him. The day I returned from Volin with the men, I wanted to tell you, but I couldn't. I don't know if you can really understand me now, but I have to talk about it. I have to say the words."

The old man's lashes fluttered madly, and he tried to withdraw his arm from beneath the covers. The faded eyes wavered and settled near the doorway, where a shadow loomed. He had to stop her from what she was going to say. He thrashed about feebly on the bed.

Katerina's strong arms lowered him gently back against the thick softness of the bed. She spoke softly, the way a mother would speak to a sick child. "You must not move about like this; it isn't good for you. Just listen to me, Zedda."

Resigned to the inevitable, Katmon Vaschenko closed his eyelids and waited for the words that he didn't want to hear, the words that he knew in his heart would change the life of the Mongol standing close by.

"Do you recall the day Stepan took the mare back to Volin?" Not waiting for a reply, she continued, "I set out after him to bring them back. I knew the boy would make it back to Volin safely with the mare, because he loved the horses as you and I both do. I could have stayed here, but Father was so angry, and in his own way he blamed me for allowing Stepan to take the horse. I told myself that I had to bring them back or at least make sure they were safe and sound. It's the only defense I had. On the way, once I got to the steppe and I was so cold and so hungry, I allowed myself to become trapped. I rode into a Mongol camp, and when I tried to ride out, there was this . . . this Mongol that followed me . . . and . . . he followed me and I tried to get away . . . The Mongol is Prince Banyen, and he doesn't even realize that I am the one. He looks at me with blank eyes and with lust, but he doesn't remember. Tell me, Zedda, how does a man fight a woman and then not remember who she is? You're a man, tell me so that I can understand," she pleaded.

Katmon lay still, willing her to think he had fallen asleep. She would rest easier if she thought she spoke to an empty silence. He forced his lids to remain still until he felt her move and leave the room.

Banyen stepped into the dark shadows outside Katmon's door and watched as Katerina left, the tears streaming down her cheeks. He wanted to run after her to tell her he was sorry, that if it took him the rest of his life he would make it right for her. He wanted to tell her all those things, and other things too, things a man only told a woman he . . .

A low gurgling sound drew him into the room, forcing the thoughts from his mind. He looked down at the elderly man with the tortured eyes and nodded slightly.

"Tell me how this happened. I want to know before I die, Banyen," Katmon gasped.

Banyen's eyes locked with those of the old man. "A man is bound at one time or another in his life to make a mistake. Hurting your granddaughter was mine, and one I will have to live with for the rest of my life. Would it make your death any easier if I told you I love Katerina?"

"If you speak the truth, then yes," Katmon whispered.

Banyen's hand caressed the scar on his cheek, his eyes still held by those of the dying man. "There is no need for me to lie to you. I knew the moment I saw your granddaughter that somehow, some way, we would meet again."

Banyen laid a gentle hand on Katmon's shoulder, forcing him back against the mound of pillows. "Don't speak, save your strength," he said softly.

"Bah, save my strength—for what? My time is near, we both know it, so there is no need to pretend. I want your promise, Banyen, that you will take care of Katerina and make it right with her. Women don't understand . . ."

"You have my word. Listen to me, Katmon. We have spoken many times after the evening meal, and I have come to treasure those talks. Never once in all that time did I lie to you. I understand that those times we spoke of Russia and the Czar are different. I could have made up stories just to please you, but it is not my way. Even now I could try to defend my actions that night, but there is nothing to defend. I was wrong."

"Will you tell her that you know she is . . ."

"Is that what you want? For if it is, then yes, I will tell her. If you will, I would prefer to do it my own way when the time is right, if ever there is such a chance. Trust me, Katmon, I will make it right, but in my own way."

Katmon nodded weakly, his eyes closing wearily.

"She's like no other woman I ever met. She has spirit and courage, more than some men. I find myself admiring these traits in her, which somehow amazes me. I never thought of a woman in this way. To me a woman was someone . . ." The words stuck in his throat, and Katmon felt a smile tug at the corners of his mouth at the Mongol's discomfort.

"You'll do, Banyen. When a man can admit that a woman has a special place in his mind as well as his heart, they belong together. I can go to my grave knowing you will do what is good. When . . . when I am gone . . . you must . . . comfort Katerina."

"If I can, I will," Banyen said quietly.

Long after the old man's breathing had stopped Banyen continued to read aloud from his book, his tone soft and full of emotion and regret. Emotion because a life was gone, and regret that he didn't know the old man in happier times, when he was full of life and living. It was a strange feeling that engulfed him, a feeling that was alien to him. He had to seek out Katerina and tell her and the bandy-legged Cossack, Mikhailo. But first he had to sort out his thoughts. The confusion he had heard in Katerina's voice, the turmoil in her eyes—how was he going to live with that? She disliked him, and yet she had given herself to him—and probably resented every minute of it, he thought bitterly. Still, he hadn't forced her that day in the barn, and her passion was as fiery as his own. She disliked him for his treatment of her on the steppe and for the fact that he didn't even remember who she was. Women are like that, he told himself; they would hold resentment and bitterness for as long as they lived. If he was any judge of women, she now believed she had him where she wanted him. That was it, she only gave herself to him so that he could see what . . . A chill washed over him. She would kill him and do it cheerfully. The vision of her crouched low, her teeth bared in a snarl, ready to spring at him with the long knife clutched in her hand, swam before his eyes. How could he make it right with her? Why had he given the dying Cossack his promise? Only Katerina herself could absolve him. And in his gut he knew she would never again come to him—willingly or unwillingly.

Banyen closed his book quietly and laid it on the table

next to the high, old-fashioned bedstead. He looked down at the peaceful face and felt saddened. He hated death and dying. In that moment he found out something about himself. If he could have breathed his own life into the old man, he would have done it without hesitation. He would have given anything not to have to see the look in Katerina's eyes when he would tell her Katmon was dead. And the look she always carried in her eyes when she stared at him, remembering, remembering, always remembering that he was the one, the one who . . . This was no time to think on matters such as these. It was over and done with. All he could do was go on from here and try to do what he promised.

"Damnation!" he cursed as he lashed out with his booted foot at the wooden frame of the bed. Pain, hot and searing, ripped up his ankle as he thrust his fist into the heavy text, sending it flying across the room. Satisfied with the aching in his foot and in his tightly clenched hand, he gritted his teeth and strode from the room.

He refused to allow the shooting sensations to slow his progress along the endless corridors and passages that led to the underground arena, where he knew he would find Katerina and Mikhailo. The pain was a scorching reminder of what he had done and what he had to do. "Pain be damned," Banyen snarled as he forced open the heavy oak doors that opened into the cavernous arena. His eyes sought Katerina's, and he motioned her to come to him. For a bare moment she hesitated, and then she ran to him, correctly interpreting what she read in his face. Quickly she raced past him down the hall, her feet barely touching the hard, earth-packed ground. On and on she ran till she came to her grandfather's room.

Seeing his peaceful face, his arms folded across his chest, she dropped her head to the covers, and great sobs wracked her body.

Banyen and Mikhailo stood in the open doorway and listened to the heartfelt wailing that shook the girl's shoulders.

Banyen twisted his hands and shifted from one foot to the other while Mikhailo let silent shudders course through his body. Both of them wanted to go to the bereaved girl, but something held them back. This was her own private grief, and nothing either of them could do would help her.

Katerina lifted her head from the bed and slowly got up. She stood a moment looking down at the face of her grandfather and then she turned and saw the two figures outlined in the doorway. "Leave me with what is mine. He was all I had left. Now there's nothing. I'll see to the preparations myself," she said, tears streaming down her cheeks.

Banyen slowly entered the room and stood towering over her, his dark eyes staring into her tear-filled gaze. His heart thundered in his chest as he made a move to reach out for her. Sensing his intention, Katerina moved backward, her full, ripe lips trembling, the gold-flecked eyes sparkling with her tears. "Leave me with what is mine," she whispered.

Banyen stared at her another moment, the wicked scar pulsating in his cheek. Then he turned and, with a motion to Mikhailo to follow him, made his way back to the arena.

Katerina removed her ermine and set to work. Tenderly she removed the old man's nightdress and set about washing his body in preparation for his simple funeral. The tears were now dry on her tawny cheeks as she cleaned and dried his thin body. At least she had this; with her father and the others she had just . . . dumped their bodies into a pit. Surely God would forgive her for what she did that day. Every man, no matter what, deserved a decent burial. Slowly she dressed the limp body in his Cossack uniform and buttoned the rows of shiny gold buttons with shaking hands. She set the pointed fur cap on his head and felt tears prick at her eyelids. It was an effort, but she managed to pull the shiny, soft leather boots up his legs and tucked the black trousers into them with no wasted motion. Every Cossack went to his Maker with his boots and cap. Frantically she searched the room till she found his saber, and with a quick swipe of a cloth from the chest she laid the weapon next to him. His cap, his boots, and his saber. All she had left to do was light the candle and kneel down to say her prayer. Her hand was steady now as she lit the long, tapered candle in its ruby container. She dropped to her knees, and in a hushed voice she said her prayer and asked God to help her. How peaceful her Zedda looked. His spirit was probably riding through the heavens at this moment, his and those of a thousand other Cossacks just like him. She knew in his first charge through the skies he would meet her father and they would be happy.

Katerina sat quietly, her mind blank, as she waited for the others to come and make their pilgrimage past the bed. At dawn the body would be taken to the vault under the fortress, where her grandfather would rest till the snows had gone. Then he would be interred in the great stone building that rested under the fir trees, where her mother and hundreds of other Vaschenkos rested.

All through the night she sat as the few remaining elderly Cossacks filed past the body, their eyes deep and sad. Each patted her shoulder in passing, their only show of grief. This was the last of the Vaschenkos. Only Katerina remained, and she was a woman. No son would bear the name of Vaschenko ever again. It was over, their eyes said, the old leader was dead and the horses were gone. There was nothing left save the fortress, the four stallions, and Katerina. It was the end for all of them. What good were the magnificent horses without the mares, and what could Katerina possibly do? Still, they stayed drinking their vodka, as was the custom when a Cossack died. Time and again they toasted his death and his ascent into the heavens.

The moment the taper gave out its last sputter the men stood, carefully lifted the body from the bed, hoisted it high above their shoulders, and carried the former hetman to his resting place in the fortress.

The procession was solemn, and Katerina made it with dry eyes. Once she closed them to ward off fresh tears, when they placed the body on the high marble table and then covered it with a sable blanket. Here he would rest till spring, when he would be lowered to his final resting place near his wife and Katerina's mother. Is it the end, can it be possible? she thought wildly. No, never—she had given her word to succeed, and she would. Now more than ever, she couldn't fail! She wouldn't allow herself to, not while there was a breath left in her body. She prayed to God and thanked Him as she made her way back to her room for the impulse that had led her to tell her grandfather what she wanted to do before he died. If nothing else, she was thankful for that one small favor.

Back in her bedchamber, she built up the dwindling fire till the logs snapped and crackled, their flames dancing and licking at the sides of the great oven. She sat huddled near it, the plush fur securely wrapped about her. She stared into the fire for hours, until her eyes began to smart from the smoke and the flying minuscule embers.

Now she was alone, more alone than she had ever been in her entire life. She was the last of the Vaschenkos. There would be no one to carry on except her; even if she should marry someday, the children she bore would not carry the name of Vaschenko. In one way it was the end, she told herself, but in another it was a new beginning for all of them. She had to do it for herself now that she was the only one left. And she would survive. The Kat always survived.

Chapter 16

As the days passed, Katerina's grief lessened a little. She kept herself busy with her training program. The men performed with skill she never thought imaginable in so short a time. It was almost as if they were trying to prove something. But to whom? she questioned. To her or to themselves? Whatever, the strict, structured routine she had laid out for them was finally paying off. There wasn't one among them whom she would be afraid to have at her side. Even Banyen's men were now on par with the prisoners. Each time they met for a practice battle, the match was a draw.

Katerina felt unnerved as she watched the men go through the paces Mikhailo laid out for them. Something was bothering her, and she didn't know what it was. Banyen seemed to be respecting her period of mourning, and not by look or action had he done anything to unnerve her. Kostya was intent only on perfecting his skill. While he looked at her longingly, he made no overt moves in her direction. Were they all biding their time? Were they waiting for something to happen . . . to her? What was it? Her stomach churned as she let her eyes sweep the arena and finally come to rest on the boy named Valerian. No, he was no longer a youth, but a man. A man with cold, hate-filled eyes. If eyes could kill, I would drop on the spot, she told herself as she stared at him. He hated her almost as much as she hated Banyen. He was acting like a wounded wild animal, as her grandfather used to say, which meant he was up to something. She continued to watch him as he, in turn, tracked the men, his eyes circling the room and always coming to rest on the door frame. Surely he wouldn't be so foolish as to try to escape. He could go nowhere in the freezing cold. Her glance strayed to Banyen, who was leaning nonchalantly against the wall, his eyes on the center of the arena, finally flicking to Valerian. He, too, sensed the young man's intent. The lynxlike eyes narrowed as she watched him. A vision of a trapped animal in a snare came to her mind when she watched his movements, jerky and uncoordinated. She was jarred from her thoughts as a shout went up from the center of the arena. One of the Mongols' spears had found its mark in the shoulder of the prisoner named Chedvor. Katerina raced to the man's side and sucked in her breath at the sight of the spurting blood. Mikhailo was on his knees, trying to stop the flow.

Katerina bent over the injured man and spoke softly. "You'll live! Another inch and the point of the weapon would be resting in your heart. It was a careless mistake on your part, one you already regret. Your opponent was younger by ten years, leaner and faster; remember that the next time you take to the ring. Never assume, never prejudge. Your wound will be taken care of, and then you'll return here and work with your horse. A very poor performance on your part," she said coolly.

The fallen man tightened his lips against the pain, his eyes full of shame. She was right. His opponent was younger, less experienced, and . . . What does it matter? he told himself. He carried the wound; he would make doubly sure it never happened again. Hurt by a damn Mongol, he thought bitterly. If it was the last thing he did, he would get revenge. He lay back while the men carried him on a litter to Mikhailo's small room, where he would be cared for. A glass of vodka to bolster his strength and he was back in the arena, leading his horse through her paces, his eyes angry and belligerent.

Banyen called Valerian's name and waited for him to work his way to the front of the line. Katerina frowned when she heard his name called a second and a third time. Suddenly it was quiet; even the horses had stopped snorting and pawing the ground at the sound of Banyen's harsh voice.

Katerina walked over to the prince, her eyes cold and hard. In her gut she knew he was gone. "If one of you doesn't speak up within the next few moments, you'll remain in your quarters for a full ten days. On the count of three someone had better speak and in a clear, loud voice. One, two, three!"

"He left," Igor stated simply. Too well he remembered the lonely, cold nights in his room, and he had no wish to repeat the experience for even one night, much less several. A man could die in that barracks with no blanket and no food, only water that turned to ice.

"Where did he go?"

"He said he was leaving this damnable fortress, and he said he would take his chances on the outside."

"Fool!" Katerina spat. "Now, I'll have to go after him and bring him back. This is your fault, Banyen," she snarled, "he was your man, you're responsible for him. I should make you go out in the storm and fetch him back, but then I would only end up going after both of you. When I bring him back, he gets ten lashes and three days in his quarters, understood?"

Banyen nodded. What else could he do? She was right, as usual.

He would have left the moment Chedvor was wounded and all ran to the center of the ring. A thirty-minute head start as of this moment. She needed time to get Whitefire and . . . She met Mikhailo's gaze and held up her index finger to show she meant the number one stallion. He frowned and tightened his lips, but he left to do her bidding.

When Mikhailo returned and nodded to Katerina, she secured the fur cape and left the arena, the others staring after her. Someone should stop her, Banyen thought, and it should be me, but she surely wouldn't thank me for interfering in what she calls her business. He motioned for the others to continue with their drilling while Mikhailo took Katerina's work.

A few moments later, standing in the open doorway, he backed off as a wild thundering shook the thick stone walls. A blur of white raced past him and down the long, endless corridor. It was Katerina on an ivory stallion, her cloak flying out behind her. Never had he seen such speed in an animal. It could only be Whitefire! He gasped. What an exquisite animal! So he too was kept here after all, like the other white stallions he'd seen. The question now was where they were stabled and how he could get to them. He shrugged; all he had to do was wait for her to return . . . if she did . . . and watch where Mikhailo took the horse. After that he could . . . He smiled to himself as he sauntered back into the arena to watch the next match.

Outside the great fortress, Katerina gave Whitefire his head and let him go. If there was another horse within ten miles, Whitefire would find it. This was what he liked best, the thick, swirling snow that made him and the whiteness one.

With both hands clutching the horse's thick mane, Katerina felt the great stallion swerve to avoid a thick clump of something and then hurtle down a steep grade. The snow-robed trees stood sentinel as she let Whitefire take to his stride. She should have brought something to cover her face; already the snow spray the horse kicked up was caking on her face.

The force of the cold, freezing air was making it difficult for her to breathe. She crouched lower, burying her head in the horse's ice-crusted mane.

The stallion moved effortlessly through the large drifts for what seemed like forever to Katerina. He knew where he was going, to the grove of firs; that was where another horse would shelter until its rider could get his bearings. The moment the copse came into sight was when she heard the sound—a horse's soft whicker, which was pure delight to the numb girl. The cold was having its effect on her now as Whitefire cantered into the darkness the firs afforded. Katerina sat up, her breathing ragged, as she watched the horse look around. A light tug on the mane and he was off, sure-footed as a dancer.

Deftly Whitefire trotted around a huge tree and worked his way through what looked like a narrow tunnel. In another few moments the animal would be out of the grove. Where was that stupid man? She called out, but her voice was harsh and sounded like a croak to her own ears. "Find him, boy, he's got to be here somewhere. I heard his horse. You can do it, Whitefire," she crooned. The stallion reared up his head at her words and snorted, his great hooves thumping the ground.

Suddenly Whitefire bolted forward, and Katerina felt her neck snap backward. Recovering, she crouched low and let the stallion have his way. He headed straight for the opening at the end of the aperture and was again in the open. He was going so fast it was impossible for her to see if there was a shape ahead of her or not. The horse swerved to the right, throwing her off balance as he again picked up his long-legged race to catch whatever it was that was eluding him and causing the woman on his back such anguish. Katerina was completely blinded by the spray from the horse's hooves. She gasped as the animal skirted another evergreen, this one so close she felt the branch brush against her head, knocking off the hood of her cape.

Whitefire snorted and slowed, rearing back on his hind legs. Katerina lifted her head, and there was the sorrel, with Valerian struggling to climb into the saddle. Whitefire brought his front legs down with a thump on Valerian's shoulder, sending him sprawling into the deep snow.

Katerina shook her head to clear it and slipped from the stallion's back. Valerian was all right, shaken and fearful but able to stand.

"You'll ride the stallion and I'll ride the sorrel. One false move on your part and Whitefire will send you to your death. Understand?" Katerina demanded in a harsh voice. "I warned you that if you tried to leave I would fetch you back; still, you had to try. At best you could have gone another mile and then you could have frozen to death. Look at the sky, you fool, more snow is already on the way. Now get on my horse and make quick work of it." The moment the man climbed on the stallion, Katerina slapped his flank and yelled, "Go, boy, straight to the stable!" She climbed onto the sorrel and followed the racing steed in front of her.

The moment the fortress came into view Whitefire slowed his breakneck speed and trotted along daintily as he waited for his mistress to catch up.

Katerina slid from the stallion and pounded on the great doors that opened into the underground stable. Whitefire pranced inside, snorting and throwing his head back to show he had done what was expected of him. The long white plume of his tail swished as Mikhailo pulled Valerian from his back. The old Cossack's eyes were wide and angry at the man's condition.

Katerina nodded. "There is no way he can live. Place him on a litter and take him to the kitchens; it's the best we can do for him. Have the men take the litter through the arena so the others can see what happened to him. Perhaps now they'll believe me. Do it now, Mikhailo," she said firmly, her voice cold and hard, her amber eyes points of flame. "It was so unnecessary, so needless. He is so young to

die, he hasn't even lived. Men can be such fools," she spat
as she climbed onto Whitefire's back to lead him to his private stall.

Banyen stood looking down at the man in the warm
kitchen. Valerian's eyes were glazed and unseeing, his lips
purplish, his skin a faint bluish white. He is the next thing to
dead, the Mongol thought bitterly. A stupid mistake and one
he is paying for with his life.

Banyen looked up at a sound he heard and turned to see
Katerina. Her face was unreadable.

"It would be wise if you informed your men that escape
is impossible. He'll be dead shortly. A low price for a life,
wouldn't you say? I warned you in the beginning. His death
is to rest on your conscience, not mine."

"It pleases you, doesn't it? It pleases you that you were
right and now you can walk into the arena and know that
the others will look at you and fear you as some . . . paragon
who is never wrong," he said harshly.

"You're free to have your own thoughts, whatever they
may be. I can live with what I've done and . . . and have no
regrets. I could have left him out there to die, but then, I'm
not a man and I couldn't leave an animal to die if it was in
my power to help him. His death is his own doing."

"A pity he can't appreciate your words," Banyen said
bitterly.

"Yes, a great shame he didn't heed my words, the words
of a woman who has lived here all her life and only tried to
warn him and the others by giving them the benefit of her
knowledge. Now he'll never know the truth. Sometimes an
example has to be made for others to learn," she said ex-
pressionlessly as she turned on her heel and left the room.

Valerian struggled for his last breath just before dawn,
and Banyen covered his face with a coarse blanket and
bowed his head. Another life was gone—would there be

others? Three more long months to go through. Who among the others would die?

Rage coursed through him at his inability to do anything to stave off what he considered to be the inevitable. He hated this helpless feeling!

Valerian's death did nothing to enhance Katerina in the eyes of the Mongols. It was obvious they blamed her for his death, and it was also obvious that it was Banyen to whom they now looked for direction, totally ignoring any and all orders from Katerina. Mikhailo told her it was a wise person who knew how to retreat. She made no threats against them and bowed to their demands. She wouldn't admit that the young man's death had shaken her. She hated the look in the Mongol's eyes, and she dreaded the indigo scrutiny of Banyen. Most of all, his words haunted her. Was he right? Did she want to be some kind of savior?

The close confines of the fortress were beginning to bother her, and whenever that happened she went to the stallions. Here in the warm, steamy, sweet-smelling stable she could pour out her heart to the animals and forget for a time where and who she was. She owed Whitefire the biggest carrot she could find and . . . and what else did she need, her mind questioned. She shook her rich, coppery curls till they were free of the knot on top of her head and sat down in Whitefire's stall and waited for the horse to come to her. He nuzzled her head and shoulder gently, showing her he understood she was troubled. Daintily he backed off and looked at her with huge chocolate eyes. His well-shaped head tilted to the side as if he were waiting patiently for her words. When they came, he shook his head and advanced a step and again nuzzled her.

Katerina's tone was soft, almost heartrending in its simplicity. "What else could I have done? I warned him, I warned all of them, and because I am a woman they ignored me. There is no other answer. The man is dead and they blame me. The prince blames me; he says I'm now happy that I proved myself right in the eyes of the men and that it took the senseless death of Valerian to make this so. How can I take the blame for something that isn't my fault? We rode out, you and I, and we brought him back; there was nothing else to do. And now he lays next to Grandfather, waiting for the snow to melt for a decent burial. I've already done something I swore I wouldn't do, and I hate myself for it. I compromised myself and didn't punish the others when they refused to follow my orders. The Mongols will listen only to Banyen now. I don't know if it was the right or wrong decision; I only know that I could not bear to see the look of blame they held in their eyes for me. They *all* think it's my fault." A lone tear dropped to her tightly clenched hand, and she looked at it in surprise. Tears were for children and frail, sickly women. She was neither, she told herself. She was the Kat.

Gregory marveled at the Cosars' slim-legged beauty. "Each of you," he muttered, "is worth his weight in gold, and if I can't figure out what to do with you, all my dreams will be nothing but clouds drifting in the wind." His mind raced with the gruesome thoughts of Ivan and the scenes he had witnessed in Moscow.

He squared his strong, muscular shoulders as he stroked one of the white geldings. "You may be a pleasure to look upon, but I would much prefer to look at gold and ko-pecks," he said harshly as he left the animal's pen.

As Gregory walked along the snow-covered road, he no-ticed that the Terek village was settling down for the night. The full moon was low in the east, casting shadows on the earth, multiplying the Cosars to twice their number. Fury ate at him as he lumbered along, anger at his circumstances, hatred for Ivan and his mental condition. The Czar was obviously insane—a lunatic, as the people said. He feared Ivan would remember how he had tricked him. If he did, he would probably send men after him and his band. He flinched as though from a wound and continued his walk. The Czar would conveniently forget the bargain they had made. Could Ivan even remember the original plans, conceived nearly a year ago, when he was lucid? Gregory recalled there had been a fanatical light to his eyes even then, when he made his proposal. He had been blunt to the point of insult.

Gregory could still hear the Czar's words: "I'm fully aware of your love of vodka, women, and parties. For this you need many kopecks, and your village is poor. I can promise you more gold than you ever dreamed possible. And all you have to do is secure the breeding secrets of the Whitefire bloodline. Failing that, I'll settle for the horses themselves." They agreed and the bargain was sealed within moments.

"He thought me a fool," Gregory muttered. "He came to me because no other Cossack would give him the time of day when the sun was high overhead." Gregory knew his reputation as a ruthless, vicious fighter must be well known if it had made its way to the Czar's ears.

Gregory's mind continued to race. There were other people who would pay handsomely for the Cosars. Afstar, Khan of Sibir, was busily buying men and horses. There would be no haggling with the old Khan; he would agree, as would many others, to deplete his treasury for the Cosars.

Satisfied that the cold, starless night held no surprises, he settled himself on a fallen tree trunk and lit his pipe. When he had it going to his satisfaction, he puffed contentedly. He needed time to ponder and decide which choice would be the wisest. His decision made, he watched as the spirals of smoke circled overhead. It would be the Khan versus Ivan.

The quiet night, his short walk, and the comfort of his

pipe helped settle his speeding thoughts. Now all he needed was a woman and a jug of vodka and he would be completely at peace. A vision of a long-legged beauty in the next village floated before his eyes. He could almost feel the softness of her proud, high breasts and her sensuous lips on his.

Stuffing the smoking pipe into his shirt pocket, he made his way to the stable and led his horse out into the snow-covered compound. He looked around the village and waved to one of the guards. "There are other things in life besides gold and horses." He laughed as he took off down the long, winding road.

Chapter 17

The moment the last of the vicious storms abated, Kusma readied the sleigh and personally escorted Halya to Volin to meet the guide from the mountains. Halya shivered inside the luxurious silver-fox robe she wore as she strolled among the gutted huts in Volin. She turned to look at Kusma and demanded to know what had happened to the village. Kusma himself looked around and felt saddened.

"So many of our people died here for the horses. It's always the Cosars. The Kat and his horses were a living legend, a legend that now ends. Perhaps one day this village will be rebuilt and it will live again."

"How will this happen? Who will come here to live, and if there are no horses, how can they live?" Halya asked as she drew the rich fur closer about her.

"Other Don Cossacks will leave their villages. Wanderers will settle here, and if Katerina Vaschenko makes up her mind, she will bring the elder Cossacks from the Carpathians and they will make this village live. As to the horses, I have no answers for you. Perhaps there are more of the magnificent whites in the mountains." He shrugged as his eyes took in the vast terrain around him. "We Cossacks live one day at a time. In our own way, we are fatalists."

Halya smiled. "I can understand what you say, for I, too, am a fatalist. What will be will be. One can move in one direction, but if it's not preordained, it will not happen." Quickly she changed the subject and smiled again at the muscular Cossack with the dark eyes. "You have my thanks for arranging this meeting. I don't know what will happen or if I will hear good news or bad news when I meet this woman you call Katerina, but I want to thank you from the bottom of my heart. It means everything to me."

Kusma grinned. "You've thanked me adequately already. I shall not forget. Mount up, your guide approaches. Can you hear the horse?"

Halya narrowed her eyes and squinted against the brightness of the blazing snow. She shook her head.

Kusma laughed. "From boyhood the sound of a pounding horse is one of the things a Cossack listens for. We do it unconsciously. One would think there is nothing to hear in deep snow, but the ground gives off its sounds. Many dispute this, but within minutes you will see a rider approach. Turn your eyes to the end of the village and you will see that I'm right. It appears that Stepan is eager to leave my brother's shelter to take you back to the mountains."

Halya laughed outright when she shaded her eyes with her hand to see a streak of ivory whip down the road and come to a roaring halt bare inches from her mount.

Stepan drew in his breath at the sight of the beautiful fair-haired woman atop the sorrel. His eyes sought Kusma's. The man shrugged elaborately, a shrug that clearly stated the woman was now Stepan's problem. Mine and Katerina's, he thought sourly.

"I will stable the sorrel in my village and you can claim him on your return," Kusma said to Halya.

He motioned Halya to slide from her horse and mount the white stallion called Darkfire. With a long, lingering look around the gutted, snowcapped village, Stepan patted Wildfire on his neck, and the horse reared back and took off, his hooves sending the thick snow backward. Darkfire, in his wake, thundered and pounded after the lead stallion. Halya hung on to the reins, positive her neck would be jarred from her shoulders.

For two days they rode, stopping only to feed the animals and for a brief rest. No words could be spoken between Stepan and the woman, and Halya felt uneasy at his strange silence. Stepan felt nonplussed. While he was not experienced in the ways of women, he knew she was going to be a problem for Katerina and the prince. And the one with the flower-blue eyes. Poor Katerina. Just as the Mongol and Katerina were fire and ice, this woman would be nothing but trouble compared to the Kat. Already he could see Prince Banyen taking her to his bed and ravaging her, the way men like him did. She looks so delicate and so pretty, he thought. One would want to cradle her fair head to his chest and whisper sweet, soft words in her ear. Poor Katerina. Would she come out second best with this woman? It was a mistake. He grimaced as he remounted and waited for Halya to do the same.

An hour before they cleared the pass, snow began to fall and the sky was black and ominous. Wildfire kicked up his heels and snorted in delight. It was impossible, but Stepan swore that the animal's stride increased with the swirling snow. Halya, petrified, clung to Darkfire's mane for dear life, trying desperately to understand how the animal beneath her could travel at such an ungodly speed in the deep accumulation.

Wildfire reared up and brought his hooves crashing against the stout doors of the underground stable. Daintily he backed off and waited patiently. When the doors swung open, he rose again on his hind legs and snorted long and loud, the conqueror returned with his bounty.

Katerina raced into the stable and immediately threw her

arms around Wildfire's neck. "You did it! I knew I could depend on you. It took a long time, but you succeeded. Good boy!" she crooned as she tightened her hold on the horse's neck. "And you, Darkfire, I see that you didn't unseat your rider." She rubbed her cheek against the horse's head and whispered soft words. The stallion whickered in delight as the woman slid from his back. Stepan led the animals away with a last fond pat from Katerina, who then turned to Halya. "Welcome to the House of the Kat. Come with me and I'll give you some hot tea."

Halya nodded. She was so cold. She wondered if she'd ever be warm again.

In the large, cozy kitchen, she let the fox cape slide off. Katerina drew in her breath. How beautiful she was, with her golden hair awry, stray curls clinging to cheeks flushed rosy red. Emerald eyes sparkled as she looked around before sitting down on the bench. Her voice, when she spoke, was soft and melodious.

"I'm Halya Zhuk. Princess Halya Zhuk," she corrected herself. "I want to thank you for allowing me to come to this fortress. I seek information about my brother, Prince Yuri Zhuk, who was sent to your village of Volin the spring of last year. I know he is dead, but I wish to find out how he died, and why, and who killed him," she said sadly.

Katerina's hand trembled as she poured tea into a mug for the princess. She heard the words and she understood them. A princess. A beautiful princess like in the stories her mother used to tell her. Banyen was a prince. A handsome prince in the same fairy tales. And according to the ageless fables, they would live happily ever after. Now she understood the look in Stepan's eyes. He pitied her and felt sorry for her. I must be ugly, she thought, if Stepan is worried for me. She forced her hand to be steady as she set the cup in front of Halya and then sat down to still the shaking in her legs. How beautiful her hair was, all bright and shiny like golden summer wheat. And her dress—never in her life had

Katerina seen anything so pretty. Katerina's long, slender hands stroked her coarse, tight-fitting pants, and she suddenly wanted to cry.

"Will you help me? Do you have information about his death? Was anything said to you about his killers? I must know," Halya pleaded, tears glistening in the bottle-green eyes.

Katerina swallowed hard. She would have to tell her. Tell her that her brother was dead by her hand. She cleared her throat and spoke quietly. "You must realize now that you're here you will have to stay until spring. The snows, the worst of them, have already started and last till March. Until now the snow has been intermittent, but this is the blizzard time. There is no way I can send you back, for to do so would only endanger the animals. We'll make you comfortable and do our best by you."

"I understand, and I cannot ask for more. I am truly grateful that you allowed me to come here. I mean you no harm and will do nothing to make or cause you trouble. But you must tell me what you know of my brother. I sense that you know and that you don't wish to speak of it. Please, I implore you."

Katerina decided she liked the princess even though she envied her rich clothing and beautiful face. How she felt about her brother was love, the same kind of love Katerina had felt for her father. She nodded slightly. "Your brother came to our village in the late spring, as you said, and bought many horses for the Czar. My father, in a fit of anger, canceled the contract. I cannot lie to you and make up some excuse about why he canceled it. He found . . . he saw your brother and me . . . what I'm saying is that your brother and I made love and my father came upon us. He misunderstood. Yuri tried, as did I, to explain to him that what he thought he heard was not . . ." Katerina raised her hands helplessly. "He canceled the contract, and I was brought before the Cossack council and ostracized. Yuri left to return to Moscow with the intention of returning for me at the end of the summer. He never came. I waited and waited. The night before we were to leave for the mountains I was away from the village, and it was raided, all of our people killed and the horses stolen. There are those who say your brother was at fault and there are those that blame me. It was not your brother's fault. Nor was it mine. I don't know who did it, but I plan to find out. Your brother did nothing wrong except to make love to me, if that's wrong. Sometimes I no longer know what is right and what is wrong."

"But Yuri never returned to Moscow. Where did he go, what happened to him?" Halya asked anxiously.

Katerina moistened her dry lips and reached her hand across the table and touched Halya gently. "Listen to me. After our village was gutted I left for Sibir. I was watering my horse when I heard a noise in a clump of shrubbery. When I investigated, I saw your . . . your brother. He was without a tongue and without fingers. He was near death. I don't know who it was that . . . I asked him if it was my father or my people and he shook his head no, but he couldn't tell me who did it. His eyes pleaded with me to kill him. I did. I'm sorry, but I could not let him lie there and suffer and die such a wretched death. I couldn't let the vultures circle overhead for him to see. If I had to do it again, I would." Tears streamed down her cheeks as she waited for Halya to comment.

"Thank you for telling me. No, you couldn't do less. Did my brother love you?" she asked huskily.

"He said he did, he said he would return for me and we would go to Kiev to live," Katerina said simply.

"Then you are as much my sister as if he married you," Halya said, getting up from the table and coming to put her arms around Katerina's neck.

Silent tears coursed down both their cheeks, and it was Katerina who smiled tremulously and said, "I never told anyone. I couldn't. I never killed anyone before. I don't know how I managed to. . ."

"Don't speak of it anymore. It was what Yuri wanted. I don't blame you, and therefore you must not fault yourself. It's over, and hopefully one day we'll find the person responsible and then it will be righted. Let us speak of other things. Tell me of this giant fortress surrounded by monolithic trees as far as the eye can see. Tell me of those beautiful animals we rode here. Allow me," she said, pouring Katerina tea and more for herself. "Drink this and we'll both feel better." Katerina nodded gratefully as she sipped at the scalding liquid.

It was Banyen who found them laughing and giggling like two schoolgirls when he arrived for the evening meal. Katerina watched as his eyes traveled over the princess approvingly.

There was no mocking look in his eyes and no sneer on his full, sensual mouth as he stared at the princess. Katerina watched as his eyes traveled the length of her and came to rest on her full breasts, which jutted from her lavender gown. It was obvious that he liked what he saw, and it was just as clear that the princess liked him also. She smiled warmly and introduced herself, to Katerina's discomfort. The green eyes sparkled and her moist lips parted, showing perfect white teeth. Banyen bowed low over her hand and then brought it to his lips. Bastard! Katerina seethed. He could charm the skin off a snake.

Dinner was a miserable, torturous affair for Katerina. She felt out of her depth as the princess charmed Banyen with amusing stories of her life in Moldavia and of the great Terem Palace in the Kremlin. Banyen sat like a lovesick boy, drinking in every word she spoke. Even to Katerina's untrained ear it was evident that they had much in common. It bothered her and she didn't know why. Lost in her own miserable thoughts, she was jarred from them when she heard Halya ask how Banyen got the scar on his cheek. She smiled coyly and said she was sure it was a fierce war wound. Banyen smiled sickeningly and said yes, that was how he got it, from a fierce soldier bent on cutting him down. Katerina almost gagged at the blatant lie and rose from the table. Banyen's eyes laughed at her as she tucked the coarse shirt into the band of her trousers, her breasts jutting forth with her tense, muscular movement. She matched his look and said coolly, "Another time you can regale our guest with tales of your . . . heroics. For now, you are to take the center ring with one of the recruits." Furious with herself, she continued, "It would be interesting to know how the fierce . . . soldier came out during the battle."

"Second best, of course. I won, I always win." He laughed as he reached out a firm hand to help Halya to her feet. "If you have no objection, we can have the princess observe my expertise."

Having Halya in the arena was the last thing Katerina wanted, but she gave in and nodded. Halya smiled as Katerina strode ahead, she and Banyen following in her wake. Damn! Why did he always manage to get the best of her? She prayed that it would be Kostya who met him in the middle of the ring, and she prayed that he would run the bastard through till his blood ran like a river.

The great cavern rang with sounds of laughter and hoarse shouts. This was the drill they had all been waiting for, the Mongols versus the prisoners. The men themselves were to pick the contestants, based on skill and expertise with both horse and weapon. Katerina drew in her breath when she noted that it *was* Kostya who had been chosen. She knew without a doubt that it would be Banyen that the Mongols selected.

With great care and a solicitous attitude, Banyen fetched a low barrel for Halya to sit on. He gave her a low bow and marched away to ready his horse.

Katerina positioned herself near Mikhailo to show she had no favorites.

Rokal stepped to the center of the ring and spoke in a loud voice. "We have chosen Kostya to represent us in the drill. Presenting," he shouted, waving his arms in the air, "Kostya, drill captain of our group." The men cheered his speech, and he withdrew as a Mongol stepped forward and in the same words introduced Banyen. While Banyen's men cheered, their enthusiasm was muted.

Her eyes on Halya, Katerina was puzzled when she saw the young woman's hand go to her throat, and all color drain from her face. Surely she wasn't one of those squeamish females who fainted at the show of a little excitement. Katerina watched intently to see where her gaze traveled. Kostya! Why would the sight of the blue-eyed Russian bring such a look of dismay to her face? Katerina swiveled to pay closer attention to the blond atop his mount, and watched as his eyes traveled the length of the arena and came to rest on the princess. Katerina frowned when he tensed in the saddle and jerked the reins.

Banyen, impervious to what was going on, smiled confidently to all who looked on. There was no doubt in his mind who the winner would be. Things were definitely improving in the fortress. A beautiful woman and a chance to show the steely-eyed prisoner that he was a fighting man despite his royal title.

Mikhailo also watched the byplay between the princess and Kostya. "I knew she would be trouble the minute I laid eyes on her," he said harshly.

Katerina nibbled on her lip as she watched Kostya's horse back off daintily and then wait patiently for his rider to give his first order. Her amber eyes grew wary as she saw his hand tremble slightly when he maneuvered the lance in his hand. What did it mean? Was she so beautiful that men . . . And that stupid Banyen, he was still smiling in the princess's direction, his seat lofty, his bearing regal in the saddle. Jealousy ate at Katerina as she watched both men stare at the princess. Damn! she seethed. Mikhailo was right. When you make a mistake, Katerina, you make a good one, she told herself.

Banyen's steed made his way to the center of the ring. The muscles trembled beneath the animal's hide, a sign that he was impatient to begin. On Mikhailo's count of three, Banyen, who had resumed his place at the far end of the room, charged forward. At what should have been the moment of impact, Banyen transferred the lance from his right hand to his left, Kostya rode straight as if to take the lance full in his chest, but instinctively swerved out of the way at the last split second. A wide grin spread across his face as he reined in the horse in preparation for a second charge. Again Kostya rode straight toward Banyen, but this time the Mongol anticipated his move and kept the lance poised in his right hand. Kostya, intent on his maneuver, slid sideways just as a scream ripped through the arena. The princess toppled from her barrel into a heap on the floor. Both men wore stunned expressions as they stared deeply into each other's eyes. Neither moved or said a word. Katerina walked over to the fallen woman and stood looking down at her, her eyes turning the color of cinnamon as she pondered what to do.

"She fainted," Mikhailo said gruffly as he bent to pick her up in his powerful arms. His gait with his wooden leg was uneven as he carried the woman from the arena.

Katerina resumed her position and motioned with her hand for the drill to continue. Kostya's mouth was a grim, tight line and Banyen's dark eyes were hooded as they charged at each other time and time again, neither man unseating the other. "A draw!" Katerina shouted. She swaggered over to the two men and looked up at them, her hands on her hips. "It's fortunate for all of us that this was a drill. If you had been in battle and the scream of a woman could divert you, then your life would be gone. Both of you are fools. I thought you were men. Boys! Babies! Infants! We're talking about your life and you stare at me as if I were some species of fly. Am I right or am I wrong?" she demanded loudly. "Answer me, for I want your men to know what manner of fearless leader they train under. Ask them," she said, pointing a finger, "who among them would agree to ride with you knowing a female shriek could divert you?"

Kostya and Banyen both looked to their men and were not surprised to see all of them lower their heads, refusing to meet their eyes.

"A Cossack has no time for thoughts such as both of you are having. For a faint you would have lost your lives. All these months wiped out for one careless, stupid mistake."

Katerina forced herself to stare into the Mongol's eyes, her own bitter and hate-filled. Kostya gazed at her shame-faced as he slid from his horse and walked to his men, who avoided him by moving away in small clusters, their voices subdued and quiet. Banyen's men moved to the end of the arena and busied themselves with their weapons.

Angry at herself, angry at Kostya and Banyen, Katerina stalked from the room. She would get to the bottom of whatever it was that had startled the princess and put an end to it. Why had she allowed the woman to come to the mountains? What a fool she had been.

The deep, ridged scar on Banyen's cheek throbbed painfully as he reached up to remove the saddle from his horse. Damn her soul, she was right! Why did she always have to be right, and why did he always have to be the recipient of her wrath? If she were within a hair's-breadth of him now, he would choke the life from her body. It was that damnable Kostya who was at fault. He should have killed him when he had the chance, the opportunity, but he held back. He told himself wanton killing was not his nature. Yet that shriek had startled him also. Fair was fair. How could he kill when he was as much at fault as the Russian? Sometimes it paid to be truthful with oneself. Like now, he thought bitterly.

Christ, she made so few mistakes! Was she human or

was she some kind of devil? He reached up to still the pain in his cheek and remembered who it was that was responsible. A feeling of shame settled over him as his rough kneading of the wound relaxed its throbbing. The Khan would be furious if he knew what was going on. Outclassed and outsmarted by a woman. A woman who hated him . . . totally. He knew one day she would kill him if he weren't careful. True, she had allowed him to make love to her, allowed him to hold her in his arms, but now that he thought about it, it was not quite right. She had done it for a reason. Well, this time she had made an error. Why had she allowed the princess to come to the fortress? She was a beautiful woman, pleasing to the eye with her softness and her voluptuous body, but there was something about her, the look in her eyes . . . it was as old as time itself. A look she could never rid herself of. She had been careful to skirt around the edges of what sort of life she had while living in the palace. Was she Ivan's mistress? Of course she was, he answered himself. He had seen women like her before, and while they performed well in bed, that was all they did. They were dull-witted, placid, content only when their favors were repaid with gems and money. Nothing had any meaning to women like her, everything they did was calculated and planned. No, he didn't need a woman like her. But, on the other hand, if she had news of Ivan that could help him, then he just might have to . . . He shrugged as he left the arena, Mikhailo staring after him.

Katerina stood looking down at the supine woman on the hearth, her head resting on a large goose-down pillow. She was awake and staring into the fire.

"I made a mistake in allowing you to come here," Katerina said matter-of-factly. "Your actions almost got the two best men killed. It was a senseless thing to do. It was a drill and both men were evenly matched. From now on you will only be allowed in this kitchen and in the room next to mine, where you will sleep. Do you understand what I'm telling you? From this moment on you are to have no contact with any of the men. I can't afford any mistakes. Why did you shriek like that? Tell me, so that I'll understand. Are you so naive that you didn't think, weren't aware that a disturbance like that was harmful to the men participating in the drill? If the prince hadn't held back at the last moment, Kostya would be dead."

At the sound of Kostya's name, Halya moved her head and stared up at Katerina. "I'm sorry," she said, struggling to a sitting position. "I owe you an explanation for my behavior. I was startled when I saw Kostya. We played together as children in my home in Moldavia. While I was of royal birth, he was a peasant, so our playful years were forced to end with my father sending him away. I was sixteen and he was seventeen. I was sent to Moscow with my brother so that . . . it isn't important why I was sent. When I learned that my father was sending Kostya away, I ran to him one night and we made love. It was the most beautiful thing in the world to us. We swore that one day we would be reunited and live happily ever after. Children say things like that, only we meant it, and after that night we were no longer children. I loved him then and I love him now. While I lived in the Terem Palace and was Czar Ivan's mistress, I had only one thought and that was to marry the Czar, thinking that somehow Kostya would hear of my marriage and come for me. I've done many things in my life that I'm not proud of, but with only one thought in mind—that somehow Kostya and I would be reunited. If it required the use of my body, then so be it. One only gives that which one wants to give, no more and no less. I've lost Yuri and I've found Kostya. My life is complete."

Katerina looked at the wide-eyed woman in front of her and felt a chill wash over her. If only life were so simple. In her own way she was glad that it was Kostya Halya loved and not Banyen. Banyen was a part of her whether she liked it or not.

Halya stared at Katerina, a strange look on her face. "Please tell me that you don't . . . that Kostya . . . please tell me . . . I have to know," she pleaded, the grass-green eyes moist with unshed tears.

"I have no feelings for Kostya, and he has none for me. Another time we'll speak of him and the reasons why he is here. I have much thinking to do. I want your promise that you'll not seek him out or do anything foolish."

"You have my promise," Halya said happily. "I'll do and say whatever you want as long as I know that he is here. I was going to go back to Moldavia and inform my parents of Yuri's death and make a new life for myself. At first I had many plans, each more difficult than the last. There is one other thing you must know. I left the Terem Palace with the Czar's permission, but a day early. A young soldier helped me escape. I'm sure as I sit here that he planned my death and was due to execute it shortly. He's a madman and I could no longer live under the same roof. If I were to tell you the things I was forced to do, you would die of shame. But I'm alive, and that is all behind me now. Now I have Kostya. There really is a God." She smiled. "Every day from the day we were parted I prayed, and He has finally answered my prayers. Now I must pray anew that Kostya feels the same way I do."

"Come, I'll show you where you are to sleep and let you turn in for the night. You look tired, and this has been a day of days for you. I think that you'll sleep happily and have dreams that only young, foolish girls have," Katerina said, her voice hard and bitter.

Halya regarded her uncertainly, was unable to fathom her tone or the look in her eyes. What was eating at the girl? Surely she spoke the truth when she said she had no feeling for Kostya. It must be the Mongol. Did she love him or did she hate him? Whatever, who was she to judge or assume anything?

While the two women talked, Kostya settled himself in the cot that was his and sighed deeply. It was impossible, Halya here in the fortress! How? Why? Feelings long submerged surged through him till he had to gasp for breath. He buried his face in the bedding and let his mind race. He had thought he would never see her again. God, how he had searched, day after day, month after month, year after year. And she was finally here, so close he could almost touch her if he wanted to. How did she feel? Did she still love him? Only thoughts of finding her had kept him alive in the stockade.

Katerina paced her room, a deep frown on her face. She was tired but knew she would never sleep. How was she to keep the princess locked up or, barring that, out of sight? What in the name of God was she to do with her for six weeks? What would Kostya do if at the end of the winter Halya . . . She would have to talk to Kostya and see if his promise still held. What will I say to him? she thought nervously. She knew in her heart that she couldn't force him to help her at the beginning of spring. Idea after idea raced through her mind, only to be rejected. Perhaps tomorrow she would be able to think more clearly.

The fire crackled as flames leaped up the hollow chimney, sending tiny sparks out onto the hearth. Katerina sat down and drew her legs up to her chin. Every problem had a solution. If she appealed to the princess, it would help. What if Kostya really did leave? If he did, the others would go with him, and there was nothing she could do about it. The promise of gold and dignity would not go far when he left. She had to talk to him, and plead and beg if necessary for his help. "It can't all be for nothing," she whimpered as she hugged her knees, a lone tear trickling down her cheek. Tomorrow she would talk with Kostya and promise him anything so long as he agreed to her terms.

Curling herself into a tight ball, she cradled her head in the crook of her arm atop the red-fox throw and was instantly asleep. From time to time she moaned softly as she raced across the snows, the Mongol in her wake.

When Katerina woke in the morning, she was exhausted as thoughts of what she had to do plagued her.

Her simple but hearty breakfast over, she ordered Stepan to fetch Kostya to the kitchen. While she waited, she paced the flagstone floor, her thoughts whirling. God, what was she going to say and do when he stood before her? By now all the men knew something was wrong and were no doubt speculating wildly as to what it was all about. And what was the bastard Banyen thinking? No doubt he has it all figured out, she thought bitterly.

Stepan escorted a perplexed Kostya into the vast room and discreetly withdrew as Katerina held out a mug of hot tea and told him to sit down. "I must talk with you, and there's no other place where we would not be overheard. I want you to listen to me carefully, because you are the only one who can help me. Back in the Khanate when I chose you to come here to the Carpathians, I did so for one reason. I sensed in you an honesty. And when you said only savages and animals rape . . . What I'm trying to say is your words rang true, and I knew that whatever your best was, you would give it to me in exchange for freedom. Was I right, was my judgment of you accurate?"

"You judged me correctly."

"Now that the princess is here, what does this do to my judgment? Will you stay with me after the winter is over? Will you keep your end of our bargain? Wait," she said quietly, sensing he wanted to speak. "If you leave here with Princess Halya in the spring, the others will go with you. I need you to help me regain the Cosars. Without you and the men, I'll never see them again. Tell me, are you a man of your word? That and that alone is what I want to know."

"Yes, I am. I'll do what I can to help you. I promised to keep my end of the bargain and I will. So will the others."

Katerina nodded, her eyes lightening to ripe apricot, as she listened to him talk.

"I've searched for Halya for years, and finding her last evening was so unexpected that I was shaken to the core. I love her and I always will. Suddenly it was too much for me. I was free from the damn stockade, my life more or less back on an even stride, and there is Halya to add the final meaning to my life." He looked around, almost expecting to see her sitting in the kitchen. "I understand that it's not good that she's here. I must see her and speak with her. That you can't deny me. If you do, then our bargain is over. After I talk with her and I explain, I'll do what you say. I also understand that you want no more meetings between us. I agree. It wouldn't look good for the men, and I have no wish to disturb them. What is good for one is good for all."

Katerina nodded. "There are those here in the fortress who think I have no heart, that I'm not compassionate. Today is your day. Yours and the princess's. Come, I'll take you to her. Just remember that a bargain is a bargain. If you should default, you'll leave me no other choice. I'll have to kill you and make it look like an accident so the men will not revolt. I want that understood, Kostya."

"I understand. If this were another time and another place, perhaps we could . . ."

"No, your princess would always stand between us. Rarely does one find true love, and when one does, it's not wise to tamper with the . . ."

Kostya smiled. "There is great understanding in you. I sensed it the first time you ever spoke to me. I have you to thank for my life and for my . . . love. I'll not abuse your generosity, you have my word."

"It grows light. Let your face be the first thing the princess sees upon awakening. Remember, only this one day, no more."

"You have my word."

Chapter 18

The Trotsnik tavern on the outskirts of the Terek camp shook with raucous laughter as the Terek Cossacks danced and drank late into the night.

They raised their mugs of kvass, first to one servant girl, and then to another. When they tired of toasting the women, they toasted their own fierceness and virility, laughing wildly and stamping their booted feet.

Gregory Bohacky, in a near stupor, climbed on top of one of the tables and began to dance, a bottle of wine balancing precariously on his forehead as he crouched low, his arms crossed over his broad chest. The music played wildly as the drunken Cossack thrust out one leg and then the other, finally falling off the table to land in a bevy of servant girls who were laughing as loudly as the men. Gregory lay on the floor, a wide grin splitting his face, his knees drawn up, feet flat on the floor. Two women perched themselves on his knees. The woman who could maintain her balance would be the fortunate one who would make the short ride back to Khortitsa and his bed for the night. The girls laughed and squealed as Gregory stamped his booted feet, trying to unseat each woman who clasped her arms around his muscular leg.

Gregory lifted his haunches and gave his right leg a mighty thump on the floor. One woman fell, amid loud shouts from the Cossacks. The other, Sonia, remained atop his knee, shouting that she and she alone was the victor. Gregory was pleased, for of all the women in the tavern, Sonia was his favorite. She could drink, dance, and make wild, passionate love better than any other woman he knew, and when the night of lovemaking was over she didn't cling and weep like the others. She dressed, kissed him soundly, borrowed a mount, and rode back to the tavern to wait for another time when Gregory would seek her out.

At the height of the din, Gregory gathered her close and whispered in her ear. She laughed as she waved to the other Cossacks and winked lewdly at the woman who had toppled from his leg.

Sonia giggled as Gregory tried to mount his horse. On his third try he seated himself, and reached down for the laughing Sonia and pulled her up next to him.

Back in his hut in Khortitsa, they tore off their clothes and tumbled·into Gregory's rancid, filthy bed. Their lovemaking was wild and fierce, with Gregory shouting lewd endearments to the grinning Sonia.

Later, relaxing in the aftermath of his proven masculinity, the woman draped across his chest, he became aware of a loud clamoring outside his home. Angrily he stalked to the window. Who would dare to disturb him at this hour? A small group of villagers were wildly gesturing and shouting. He peered into the darkness, seeing nothing to warrant the excitement the men were making. He dressed quickly and stormed outside, shouting to be heard over the excited men.

Holding up both hands, he demanded silence. "You, old man," he said, pointing to a half-dressed Cossack, "what is it, what's going on?"

"It's the Russians from Czar Ivan, they are here for the Cosars. Look, Gregory," he babbled excitedly, "at the end of the road, do you see the coach?"

"Of course I see it, you fool, do you think I'm blind? Did they say why they arrived so early? They weren't due for another month. It's a trick of some sort. Post guards and surround this coach, and at the first sign of a trick, kill them!" he said harshly, striding toward the waiting coach.

"Explain yourself!" he bellowed to a soldier standing guard at the doors of the coach.

"Basil Makoviy, representative to Czar Ivan. I've come for the Cosars. Your gold is in the coach, full payment as agreed."

"Bah! I made no agreement. I told the Czar I would give him my decision in one month. I didn't say I agreed to sell him the Cosars . . . You made your journey for nothing."

The soldier was unimpressed with Gregory's words. He opened the door of the coach and pointed to six chests that rested on the floor. He nodded slightly, and one of his men opened a chest. Gregory blinked at the gold coins that sparkled in the glowing torchlight. Another nod from Makoviy and all the chests were opened. "My orders were to deliver the money to you and return with the herd. Those are my orders," he repeated.

"And what will you do if I order my men to take this gold and kill you? I'm the leader of this camp, and I give the orders. Your Czar be damned! I made no bargain with him," Gregory said harshly.

"The Czar has given us a certain number of days to reach here and return with the Cosars. Men were positioned along the route we followed and they are reporting our progress to Moscow. The last messenger was sent back to the Czar the moment we rode into this camp. If we don't return on schedule, this village will be nothing more than a memory. Do you understand me?"

Gregory's heart pounded in his chest, and sweat dripped from his forehead. He knew he had to make a decision, and he knew that if he didn't strike a bargain with the Russian his own men would kill him and take the gold for themselves. What good were horses when there were six chests of gold? "Agreed!" Gregory shouted, to the approval and wild stamping of his men.

The Russian nodded and spoke quietly. "The Czar was sure you would agree. We'll make camp here for the balance of the night and start our journey back at dawn. See that the herd is ready at sunup," he said briskly as he ordered his men to unload the chests of coins. "A wise decision on your part. If you had refused, as I said, this village and all your people would be nothing more than a memory. A very wise decision."

Gregory strode into a circle of his men and laughed loudly. "I said the Cosars were worth their weight in gold, and now we have the gold to prove it."

The men added logs to the campfire in the circle and brought out containers of vodka to celebrate. "To Gregory!" they chorused.

Chapter 19

As the endless back-breaking days dragged on, Banyen became hostile and intense, his dark eyes brooding and hate-filled, while Kostya drove his men to a near frenzy, his own bright gaze smiling and alert. They were like oil and water. Banyen would sneer, one large fist pounding into the other, when one of his men fell short of the mark. Kostya would laugh and make his man do it over to his satisfaction, his mind on other things. Anger was a waste of time, and for now there was none in him. He could, at this time, even be charitable and forgive Banyen his rough treatment of him in the stockade. Rokal was right, he merely followed orders, and a good soldier always followed orders and gave the best that was in him. He owed Katerina the best that was in him, and he would keep his promise. Halya understood and promised to wait for him back at her home in Moldavia at winter's end. For once fortune smiled upon him, and he had no desire to tamper with God's work. He would do as he had promised and be happy doing it so long as he knew Halya and he would be together.

The days were just as endless for Katerina. She watched the men for hours on end, finding no fault with their performance. They were as near to being Cossacks as was humanly possible. Even the Mongols gave an excellent accounting of themselves. The Ķhan would find no fault with her training. Banyen, she admitted, bothered her. His indigo gaze was angry and hostile each time he looked at her. Did he think that the princess had been brought here for his personal enjoyment? Katerina smiled.

Banyen was unable to fathom why Halya was secluded from the others. He ate alone with Mikhailo while Katerina dined with the princess in her room. He wondered if she had something to do with the horses. It was possible Ivan had sent her here. How was he to gather news of the Czar if he couldn't talk to Halya? It disturbed him that some manner of conspiracy was going on and he had no clue as to what it was. Sooner or later he would have to make a decision about the stallions. Now that he knew they were in the fortress, all he had to do was follow Katerina on one of her early-morning jaunts and find out exactly where they were sequestered and then decide what to do. How many more days was he going to wait before he made any of his decisions? Not long, he promised himself; winter was slowly coming to an end and before long the perpetual snows would cease, and he could think about the vast outdoors and the chances he would have to take if he decided to take the stallions.

Christ, he ached with wanting a woman. Not just any woman, he told himself, but the Kat. He wanted her, desired her more than he had ever wanted anything in his life. He rubbed at his throbbing cheek and felt his fingers go to his eyes. She said she preferred Western eyes. She said she preferred hair the color of winter wheat. No, he told himself, Katerina had only one reason, and he doubted he could ever make it right with her. His dark eyes became hooded as he watched her throw back her head and laugh at something Kostya said. Rage surged through him as he thrust out his booted foot to kick at the low oak bench where saddles were piled. The pain in his foot made his eyes smart with the pain. "Bitch," he seethed. Skinny, scrawny, bitch, how could she have such an effect on him? He stormed from the arena to the corridor, where he saw Katerina walk each morning before the others were awake. He would search the stable till he found what he wanted, and the first person who tried to stop him would find his hands around their neck. After that, they would be dead.

Banyen investigated methodically, the way he did everything. "Somewhere there must be an entrance to another room. I won't give up till I find it even if it takes all night." Already he had spent hours, and still he was no wiser. "It has to be this room. She went in two hours ago and still hasn't come out," he muttered in frustration. "The only thing I haven't done is tap the walls to see if they're hollow. And what will I do if I manage to find a secret opening?" he asked himself, shrugging his shoulders. If I just knew where to enter the room, that would be sufficient for now, he tried to convince himself.

This area, what was so special about it? Katerina had said it was off limits to any and all people in the fortress. Later he would decide what he would do. For now he wanted to see if what she said was true, that the animals responded only to her. If there wasn't any way he could handle them, then there would be no point in doing anything or making any sort of plans. One step at a time, he told himself as he began tapping the thick stone walls.

While Banyen hunted his way around the underground chamber, Katerina stirred restlessly and finally woke, her amber eyes smarting from the smoke that was whirling about the room. She struggled to her feet and added another log to the fire and sat down, shivering from the cold. Tears gathered in her eyes as she leaned back against the large fireplace, the ermine cape wrapped tightly about her. She admitted to herself that she hated her circumstances, the position she was in, the beautiful princess and the damn Mongol. She hated everything and everyone. All she wanted to do was lie down and sleep forever; she was tired, very tired. Somehow, somewhere, her hatred had waned and been replaced by strange, unfamiliar feelings. She needed to talk, and decided to seek out Mikhailo. By now he would be up preparing tea for himself. She dressed quickly and ran to the kitchen.

"Katerina, what is it?" he said gruffly as she threw herself into his arms.

"Help me, Mikhailo!" she pleaded. "I have so many peculiar feelings that my mind cannot deal with." Tears formed in the gold-flecked eyes and trickled down her smooth cheeks.

"Is it Banyen or Kostya?" Mikhailo asked, seating her near the fire.

"I don't know. I haven't any experience in the ways of the world, like the princess."

"What do you feel for Kostya?"

Katerina answered honestly, "I have no feelings for him."

"Then it's the prince that's making you unhappy. Do you feel drawn to him?"

"Yes, Mikhailo," she said unhappily. "Soon it will be spring and he'll leave. What will I do, how will I feel when that happens?"

"I have no answers for you, Katerina, you must search and find your own answers."

Kat wiped her tears with the back of her hand. She couldn't allow any man to come into her life, consuming her to the point where there was no room for anything else. That couldn't be love. Love was understanding and forgiveness.

"What is it, Katerina? What is tormenting you?"

"Can a person love and forget something . . . something bad? No," she answered for the old man. "It's possible to forgive, but one never forgets. Never!" she exclaimed, jumping to her feet. "Never!"

"What is it, tell me!" the Cossack said, drawing her to him.

"Nothing, Mikhailo. Don't concern yourself. I'll go and visit with Stepan and the stallions."

Mikhailo nodded. The stallions would work their magic and comfort her as he couldn't.

The moment she stepped into the stable, she heard a sound. Standing in the darkness, she watched Banyen rapping on the walls, an iron bar in one hand and a lantern in the other. She remained quiet as he slowly worked one side of the chamber and then another. From time to time he cursed softly in the dimness and moved on, the iron bar clanking and grazing off the rough stone. Her eyes narrowed as she watched. What would he do if he found the latch that opened the door? Would he walk through, or would he wait for another time, a time when the snows had gone, and would he try to lead the stallions from their home? Her heart felt heavy as a deep sadness settled over her. It was always the horses; it always ended with the horses.

Katerina stepped forward boldly, her boots making no sound on the hay-strewn floor. Banyen, intent on his search, did not see her or hear her till she reached up a slender arm and pressed the latch at the top of the shelf. "Is this what you're looking for?" she asked quietly.

Stunned, Banyen dropped the bar he was holding and stared at her. "Yes. I would never have thought of looking there. Why is it that the walls give off no echo?" he asked, hoping to wipe the look of defeat from her face. She shrugged as the shelf moved, and motioned him to precede her down the narrow tunnel.

Banyen drew back, hating the expression he saw on her face. "There's no need for you to take me. I would never have found it on my own."

"Eventually you would have, or watched me, and sooner or later you would have discovered their stalls. This way,

I'll give you a tour of the stallions' quarters and you'll tell me what you plan to do. Note, I said 'plan,' not 'do.' There's no way you'll ever take these stallions from their home. I have no intention of parting with them. What do you think you could do? They are worthless to you without the mares. Is it possible that you believe that I'll regain the Cosars and that way you'll have the breeding secret? Fool!" she said softly. "I'm the only one who has the secret, and I would die before I gave it to you. A stallion is a stallion, a gelding is a gelding, and a mare is a mare. There's no way you could succeed. And another thing, as long as we're discussing the horses, let me tell you that I lied to my uncle. I am not going to give him a colt and a filly. The only way he could get the animals is to kill me, and even then I would fight and kick to the death."

"Yes, I know of your intention. The Khan himself was aware that you lied to him. It amused him to watch you barter the one thing you held dearest for his help. He would have given you assistance for nothing, he has no need of the horses."

"You lie. If what you say is true, then why are you seeking out the stallions? Do men ever tell the truth?" she asked in a tormented voice.

"About as often as a woman tells the truth," Banyen said coolly.

"Why should women be any different from men?" Katerina asked, just as coolly.

"It takes a strong, honorable person to tell the truth. I need you," he said simply.

Katerina's heart leaped in her throat at his words. She stopped and stared into his eyes.

"Even from here I can smell the fragrance of your desire." He made no move to touch her, but stood still, returning her deep gaze.

"No," Katerina whispered huskily.

Banyen's voice was deep and sensuous when he answered, "Lie to me, but don't lie to yourself. You want me, desire me as much as I want and desire you."

"No," Katerina whispered again, backing off a step.

"Look at me!" Banyen ordered. "Tell me what you see in my eyes. Put a name to it. Do it," he said, advancing until he was mesmerizing her with his nearness. Still he made no attempt to touch her.

Katerina swallowed as she gazed at him. "I don't know what it is," she moaned.

"It's the same thing that is mirrored in your eyes. You must be the one to give it a name." Unexpectedly, the red welt on his cheek began to throb, and he fought the urge to reach up to still the pain.

Katerina saw the muscle in his cheek begin to twitch and, without meaning to, reached up and laid a gentle finger on the angry, throbbing welt. The words tumbled out.

"I did that to you, but I'm not sorry. What you did to me that night on the steppe was wrong. I can forgive you, but I'll never forget."

"If I say I'm sorry, will that help? If I grovel at your feet, will that make any difference? I can do anything but undo what has been done. I'll devote the rest of my life to helping you forget," he said, reaching out to gather her in his arms. He took her in the damp, clammy tunnel, and afterward he stared deeply into her eyes. "What we just did was savage and animalistic. Now I'll make love to you the way a man makes love to a woman. Come!"

If Mikhailo had stood in front of her and said the Cosars were standing at the doors of the fortress, she couldn't have cared less. All she knew was she had to follow him, she needed to follow him as surely as she needed to breathe. She nodded, moistening her lips as he wrapped his arms around her. "The stallions," she whispered inanely.

"I don't care if I never see the stallions. You're the only thing that matters to me." Suddenly he stopped and spun her around by the shoulders. "You want to hear the words, is that it?" He shook his dark head, an amused light in his eyes. "I can't undo the time on the steppe. What I did was bad. I ask your forgiveness. You belong to me now and forever, so that might ease your feelings about what I did to you." His face took on a dejected look as he stared at her, hoping against hope that his words were meaningful to her.

She felt a slight trembling in his arm as he drew her to him. Not trusting herself to speak, Katerina laid her head against his broad chest and sighed deeply.

He led her gently from the tunnel.

The blazing fire snapped and crackled, sending sparks shooting out of the cavernous depths of the enclosure.

Naked flesh met naked flesh. Savagely, beneath the gossamer tent of her cascading hair, his lips met hers in a searing, burning kiss that sent a dancing line of white fire coursing through her body. He allowed his touch to become gentle, stroking her skin with tender, teasing touches, stirring her to heights of passion she had only dreamed of. Katerina stirred as he smothered her with kisses, pulling her to him, closer, always closer. Her passion heightened, she was totally aware of his maleness, his lean, hard, muscular body next to hers. Husky murmurings filtered throughout her being as he stroked and caressed her breasts with his gentle touch. Moaning in ecstasy, Katerina strained toward him as desire rose in a tide, threatening to engulf her.

Strong arms encircled her more tightly as she felt the rippling muscles beneath the broad expanse of his back. Her tone was low and throaty as she called his name over and over, bringing her lips to meet his, searing and scorching his very being with her nearness.

Banyen released her for a mere moment, looking deeply into her eyes. A low moan of passion escaped his mouth as he tore at her, his lips searching and hungry for her sweetness. His hold became tighter and tighter; Katerina clung to him, reveling in the feel of him, cherishing this moment of time, remembering it, burning it into her very soul. She knew without a doubt that this Mongol would love her and cherish her for all eternity.

She stirred slightly, moving her head from the hollow in his neck, and reached up a slender finger to trace the outline of his oblique eye, her own eyes moist and full of love. Gently she traced the deep-ridged scar before she brought her lips to meet his, her long, slender body straining toward him.

Katerina knew in that one sweet kiss that she could never belong to anyone save Banyen. Without doubt, without reservation, she gave herself to him.

Spent, they lay in each other's arms. Quiet, rapturous words were whispered, words that only lovers use.

Banyen lay studying her beneath hooded eyes. She was beautiful, more beautiful than he could ever have imagined.

Katerina moaned, delighting in his touch, feeling him against her, aware of the comforting weight of him. He twined his fingers through her hair and lifted it off her neck and shoulders as she suddenly realized the stroking she felt were kisses, warm and moist across her shoulders and the nape of her neck. A barely audible groan escaped his lips as he brought his head to the curve of her throat.

Drawing in her breath, Katerina turned, encircling him in her arms, offering her mouth. She felt his powerful hands in her hair, his lips burning hers. She drew his head gently into the cradle of her hands and lowered it to her breasts, her body arched beneath him. She needed him, wanted him, as she was sure no woman had ever wanted a man.

When he pulled away from her, she clung to him, forcing him back with her passion-filled lips, gentling away his reserve and hers with bold, intuitive caresses of her tongue.

Banyen's mouth was on her throat, her breasts, drawing moans from somewhere deep within her soul. Her senses soared, making her lightheaded with passion, bringing her to the borders of lust, as she answered his caresses with her endearing embraces, responding to his kisses with animal passion she had never dreamed she possessed. She sought for and found the most rapturous caress, reveling in the pleasure she gave him.

Banyen rejoiced to find his passion matched by hers, delighting in her moans of exquisite joy as her body welcomed his.

White flames of passion raced through her veins as she sought to extinguish the scorching fire engulfing her.

"Have me, have me now!" she urged.

Banyen moved his head slightly to stare down into her eyes. Her words were softer than the muted sounds of the sparks in the fire, echoing in the fullness of his heart, filling him with fierce protectiveness toward her that left him gasping for breath. He had never heard the words spoken before. An ever-surging tide of ecstasy swept over him as he once again crushed her to him, mouthing the words aloud that she wanted to hear, needed to hear. She was his, now and forever more.

As the heavy snow continued to fall, word came by falcon from the village of Kisinev that Ivan's madness had worsened. The word spreading throughout Russia told of Ivan wandering through the palace howling so loudly his cries were audible to people outside.

Several weeks later, a second message arrived that read:

Czar Ivan forsakes Christianity, seeking comfort in the prophesies of witches and magicians who were brought to Moscow from the far north where paganism still flourishes.

The last message received in the fortress read:

The peoples of Russia say each day Czar Ivan commands his servants to carry him, sitting in a chair, to his treasury. While his attendants stand and watch, he plucks jewels from their coffers and puts them against his skin. Ivan fancies the jewels change color, proving that he was "poisoned with disease."

Katerina turned to Mikhailo. "I understand the Czar still has moments of rational thinking. If he were completely insane, the boyars would have taken over his rule."

"You're right, Katerina, the man is mad, but still strong enough to rule. We all know his days are numbered," Mikhailo said dourly.

Chapter 20

The days that followed were happy days for Katerina. The men were honed as sharp as a razor's edge. They were indeed Cossacks to be proud of. Happiness radiated from her whole being. Just being in the same room with Banyen, meeting his warm gaze, was all she needed to complete her joy. Passion-filled nights were sweet at the end of a long, hard-working day. She cherished the warm, tousled look of the man next to her on awakening. There was no one in the whole world that was more exultant than she was unless it was Banyen, she told herself. He, too, took on a fine-honed look. His mocking arrogance was gone, in its place a fierce protectiveness to Katerina and all in general.

Banyen watched his men, a smile on his face. He was proud of them. Totally untrained when they arrived at the fortress less than six months ago, now they were efficient soldiers he would be proud to fight with and serve with. He told himself he was a happy man. There was nothing he lacked. His eyes swiveled to where Katerina stood next to Mikhailo. His deep scrutiny made Katerina aware of him, and she looked up and smiled sweetly. How he loved her! Six months ago he would have laughed if someone had told him he would love a Cossack woman, a woman who wore men's clothes and looked like an angel. He blinked and turned from her silent gaze, his loins taking on an ache only she could quell. Was it only hours ago he had felt her next to him, her head cradled against his bare chest? It seemed like an eternity. He wished it were night so he could gather her close to him near the fire and make love to her. A love that she returned with every fiber in her body.

Another week and he would leave this vast fortress. The feeling saddened him, and a light film settled over the agate eyes. What would he do without her? How would he get through the days, and what was he going to tell the Khan? The truth, of course. She would wait for him, she promised. She said there were things they both had to do, and until their lives were straightened out they must make the best of it. A vision of her lying dead on some endless plain rose to haunt him. What she intended was for men, not women; not his woman. He understood and knew there was nothing he could do to stop her. She had to do what she had to do, just as he did. She said she understood, and he could do no less. Would he ever see her again once he left? What would life be like without her? His stomach lurched, and he forced himself into a false calmness. It would work out, it had to. Rarely did one find happiness such as his, and when one did, one treasured it.

A week. Seven days.

His thoughts suddenly turned to the princess and his intention of seeking her out and talking with her about Ivan. Somehow he had become lax, his thoughts only of Katerina. He would do it the first chance he got. He needed all the information he could get on Czar Ivan. The princess was the only one he knew who had left Moscow recently. Her information, whatever it was, would be the most recent. Katerina had told him of Halya's search and her love for Kostya. He was happy for the prisoner. Now he could understand what had kept him alive.

With two days to go till Banyen's departure, Katerina's eyes took on a haunted look, and her body trembled and tears burned at her eyes. What was she to do without him? She wanted to run, seek him out, throw herself into his arms and tell him the horses didn't matter, nothing mattered except being with him. She did nothing but look at him longingly and cry in his arms at what their parting would mean.

Over and over Banyen promised his return and a full, happy life, telling her he wanted a dozen female children, all to look like her.

On the eve of the departure of Banyen and his Mongols, Katerina instructed Hanna, the cook, to prepare a feast to be served in the arena. Mikhailo was to see to the tables and the music. She would be generous and allow the princess to attend and sit next to Kostya. They deserved this special occasion. Not once had either one of them complained of their separation, abiding by the bargain they had made.

As the hour of the feast approached, Katerina raced to the kitchen, imploring Hanna to help her with her dress. "It hangs here and there," she cried frantically. "You know I am all thumbs with a needle, you must do it for me now. The meat can cook itself."

Deftly Hanna pinned, tucked, and sewed, and an hour later she had the bronze-colored gown fitted on Katerina's slim body. She shook her old head and wished she were fifty years younger. The girl was beautiful, and would turn more than one head. The old cook pursed her mouth and told Katerina she was more lovely than the princess would ever be.

Katerina laughed delightedly as she poked her head into her wardrobe and withdrew the soft silken slippers that matched the gown. Was it only a year since she last wore the garments and shoes that rested in the depths of the cupboard? Momentarily tears glistened in her eyes as she remembered the formal evening meals in the great dining hall, where her father and grandfather dressed in traditional

Cossack uniforms. What would Banyen think? He had never seen her in a gown before. Would he like her? She surveyed herself in the long mirror, turning slowly to see how the gown swirled around her feet. She knew she looked well, the low cut of the bodice showing off her tawny shoulders and the swell of her full, round breasts. The long, full sleeves, gathered together at mid-arm, fell in soft graceful folds at her wrists, accentuating her long, slender hands.

"My hair, what should I do with my hair?" Katerina squealed. "I can't let it just . . . hang. Hanna," she pleaded, "do something."

Hanna sighed and worked industriously with the long-handled brush, swirling and pinning until she had the effect she wanted. Wispy fringes of the coppery hair framed Katerina's face becomingly, while the wealth of her hair was set into deep curls, one cluster draped over her bare shoulder.

"Pinch your cheeks for color," Hanna gurgled, "and you will stir every man into a frenzy." Katerina hugged the old cook, making her laugh as she struggled from the girl's tight grip. Her iron-gray hair, pulled back into a tight knot, freed itself from its pins and tumbled down to her waist. Her bright gaze was merry as her round body shook with happiness for Katerina. She had never seen her so happy or so beautiful.

"Wait, wait, tell me, what are you serving for our feast?" Katerina called excitedly.

Hanna pretended forgetfulness. "Black bread and jam. Silly girl, I'm preparing just what you told me to prepare. Roast lamb and duck, three vegetables from the winter cellar, and fresh popovers with honey and jam. Boiled potatoes in butter with herbs and spices, seasoned the way you like it, and a soup—barley with carrots and cabbage. Rice pudding with raisins for a sweet. Wine and vodka till the jugs are empty. Does it meet with your approval?" She laughed.

"But of course. Did you cook enough? Will there be

enough for the men to eat as much as they want? Training is over, and this is a day I want them to remember."

"They can eat until the moon is high and still there will be food left for another feast. There is no cause for worry. Mikhailo tells me the men are bathing and dressing in their best, which was laundered by me days ago."

"Do I need a jewel?" Katerina shrugged. "What if I did, I have none," she said, her eyes dancing. "I can barely contain myself, Hanna."

"I noticed," the old woman said tartly. "Rest now, so that you are not tired when the feast begins. A little sleep," she coaxed, "like when you were a child."

"Very well." Katerina acquiesced for the old woman's benefit, but she knew she would never be able to sleep. All she could think of was Banyen and the look in his eyes when he saw her in the bronze gown.

The raucous shouts and the sounds of merrymaking ceased when Katerina and Halya made their entrance. For the first time in her life Katerina felt beautiful, and the men's looks of approval proved it to her. Her eyes immediately sought out Banyen's, and she felt a warm glow spread through her as his dark blue eyes softened and a smile tugged at the corners of his mouth. She wanted to run to him and throw herself into his arms, but instead she seated herself next to Mikhailo and Halya.

"Katerina," Halya whispered, "what is the matter with Kostya? He looks ill to me. Is something wrong, is there something you aren't telling me? Even from here I can see the flush on his face, and it isn't because I'm in the same room. He looks ill to me," she said fearfully.

Katerina stared across the room and felt frightened at Kostya's reddened complexion. "Perhaps a small fever, he could have become chilled. I'll have Mikhailo see to it," she said. She beckoned Mikhailo and whispered in his ear, cautioning him to be discreet when he spoke with Kostya.

"Do you have medicines here in this fortress?" Halya demanded harshly, her lips trembling, her eyes fearful.

"Of course we have medicines here in the fortress. Mikhailo is as good as any physician. He can even pull teeth with little pain to the patient," Katerina said confidently. "You must not show your alarm to the others. I'm sure it's nothing more than a small temperature that will abate by morning. Kostya has been working hard, and I'm sure the reason is that with his strenuous work he could put you from his thoughts. It's his way of making the days go faster. Nothing is going to happen to him, I give you my word."

The princess nodded, but the look of worry did not leave her face. She nibbled at her food and refused to take her eyes from Kostya.

Mikhailo returned to the table and bent over to whisper in Katerina's ear. "The man is ill. Not only does he have a raging fever, but chills also rack his body. He refuses to leave until the meal is over. He agreed to bed down in the kitchen, where it is warm. I told him I would tend him and that it was best he remove himself from the others so he does not infect them with his illness. A day or two and he'll be on the mend," he said, a ring of confidence in his voice.

"The best time for you to take him to the kitchen will be when Stepan begins playing his fiddle. By then the men will have much vodka in them and they won't notice his departure. Tell Kostya that later the princess will come to sit by his side."

Halya nodded her thanks when Katerina explained what Mikhailo had said.

Katerina pushed thoughts of Kostya and his illness from her mind. Nothing could spoil this last evening with Banyen. God alone knew when she would see him again. Impatiently she waited for the meal to be over with so she could sit next to Banyen when Stepan began to play. Her eyes sought out Banyen's, and she smiled, her whole face alight with happiness at just knowing he was in the same room. Don't let anything spoil this night, she prayed silently.

As soon as Hanna and several of the elderly Cossacks who lived in the fortress cleared the table, Stepan, resplendent in his full Cossack uniform, walked to the center of the arena and brought his fiddle to his chin and began to play a rousing Cossack song. The men stomped and stamped their feet, their hands clapping wildly. Out of the corner of her eye Katerina watched Mikhailo and Kostya leave the room. A sigh of relief escaped her as she noticed that no one paid any attention to the two men's departure, everyone busy singing and dancing in accompaniment with the music.

Banyen excused himself to his men, who paid him no heed, and worked his way among the laughing, shouting men, who were demanding that Stepan play louder. He stood looking down at Katerina, who smiled into his eyes. He seated himself in Mikhailo's chair and immediately searched for Katerina's hand beneath the tablecloth. He leaned over slightly and spoke softly. "This night is ours. In all of Russia there is none more beautiful than you."

Katerina forced her voice to remain calm, but there was nothing she could do to still the trembling in her body. "You'll be gone from here and from me by sun-up tomorrow. I don't know when I'll see you again." Impulsively she tightened her grip on his hand and stared into his eyes. "Don't go, Banyen. Please don't go."

Banyen's heart pounded in his chest. "I have to go to Sibir, you know that. There is nothing on this earth that could keep me from returning to you. I'll come back to you, you have my promise. I couldn't live without you," he said tenderly.

Tears misted in Katerina's eyes. She had heard those same words once before, a long time ago. Yuri spoke them to her when he left Volin, and now he was dead. Dead by her hand. A deep shudder ripped through her body at the thought, and Banyen felt saddened. How he loved her. What else could he say to her? How could he prove to her that he would return? It always came down to words. Words he did not know how to string together. Surely she understood his feelings. Didn't actions speak louder than words? "I love you, for now, for forever more," he said huskily.

Katerina's amber eyes glistened with tears. "I know, I understand; it's just that I'm acting like a female. You are my life," she whispered.

"If you don't stop looking at me like that, I'll drag you by the hair from this arena and then what will the men think?" he teased.

Katerina shrugged. "Who cares? I only care about you. Tonight I don't even care about the Cosars, just you."

"We must talk of other things or I'll carry you from here. Tell me, what is wrong with Kostya? He looked sick to me when we entered the arena this evening. Where did your man take him?"

Katerina frowned. "Mikhailo said he has a raging fever and his body is racked with chills. Mikhailo is ministering to him in the kitchen, where the heat from the fire is constant. We couldn't take a chance of him infecting the others. Especially your men, as you leave tomorrow. You have a long ride ahead of you, and nothing must go wrong."

Banyen and Katerina sat watching Stepan as he fiddled away, his eyes merry and his fingers flying with the bow. Banyen leaned back on the rough chair and let his eyes travel to Halya. He *had* to talk with her before he left. What was wrong with him? For days he had promised himself that he would seek her out, but there hadn't been time. He had to do it tonight, before he left, or he would never do it.

Mikhailo walked back into the cavern and, with a nod to Katerina to show that Kostya was resting, strode to the center and took the fiddle from Stepan and began playing. The young Cossack raised his arms and started to dance. The faster Mikhailo played, the faster Stepan's feet flew, up and down, up and down, his feet shooting out in front of him precariously. The men shouted encouragement as he continued with his wild dance.

Katerina felt Halya rise rather than saw her move to make her way to join Kostya. Her eyes were on the dancing Stepan and Rokal, who suddenly entered the middle of the ring. Mikhailo's fiddle stopped, and Stepan stood up and bowed low, a wild grin on his face.

Rokal shouted to be heard over the wild clamors of "More, more!" "My mother used to call me a dancing fool!" He laughed. "What this Stepan can do, I can do. Play, Mikhailo!" he shouted imperiously. Full of vodka and good food, Rokal steadied himself and began to imitate Stepan's movements, to the amusement of his comrades. Seeing that his legs were going in different directions, Rokal sat down in the middle of the floor, a look of defeat on his face. Suddenly he grinned and jumped up and raced to the table where Katerina sat. He pulled her to her feet. "You promised, back in the Urals, that you would dance for us again. Now is your chance. Music, loud music," he ordered Mikhailo.

Banyen grinned at the look on Katerina's face. She had promised, and now she had to dance. Good. This was the perfect time for him to seek out Halya. She would be with Kostya. Katerina wouldn't miss him, and he would be back by the time she was finished with her dancing.

No one paid any heed to his leave-taking; all eyes were on Katerina and Mikhailo.

Banyen crouched down in the kitchen and looked at Kostya's flushed face. The man was lying on a sable carpet and covered to his chin by another length of fur. The princess sat next to him, tears streaming down her cheeks.

She looked up at Banyen, despair written on her beautiful face. She stood up and brushed her hair from her forehead. "One moment he is lucid and the next he's . . . he . . . It's been so long, and now when I've found him, he . . . It's so unjust. What if he dies?" she wailed.

"He won't," Banyen said, quietly. "He's survived worse than this. Mikhailo says the fever will abate by morning. Believe the old man. Katerina says he is well versed in herbs and medicines. You must believe and have hope. If you don't, you can't survive. Katerina told me of his search for you and you for him. He will survive."

"If I could only believe that," Halya whimpered. "It can't all be for nothing. I don't want to live if he dies. I couldn't bear to go through endless days knowing I would never see his face again. I just couldn't." Suddenly she threw herself into Banyen's arms and sobbed brokenheartedly. Banyen was jolted backward as she flung herself at him. He reached out to grasp her waist in order to break his momentum, and Halya came to rest against his chest, his arms around her to still her shaking and trembling.

Awkwardly he mouthed soothing words of comfort, and gradually felt her relax against him. His arms still around her, he gently pushed her a little away from him and looked down at her. "It will be all right. Nothing is going to happen to Kostya. He's young and strong and if he could survive the winter here in the fortress, he can survive this illness. I've seen fevers such as his many times in the Mongol camps, and it's a temporary illness. Believe me, he'll survive," he said, patting her on the cheek the way an indulgent father would pat a child.

Halya smiled tremulously and reached up and kissed him lightly on the mouth.

Banyen blushed and turned to see Katerina standing in the doorway. He blinked at the look on her face. She didn't think, she couldn't think . . . To his tortured eyes she resembled a tapered candle flame ready to spring to life. He watched as she swallowed hard and ran from the room.

"Oh, God! Oh, God! Oh, God!" Katerina whimpered as she ran down first one corridor and then another till she came to her room. Panting, she raced inside, slamming the door behind her. Quickly she threw the heavy bolt and leaned against the stout door, her hands to her cheeks. Oh, God, he didn't, he couldn't. It was all a lie, a trick. A dirty, sneaky Mongol trick. Fool! her mind shrieked. Stupid, foolish Cossack woman! She had believed all his lies. "I knew I should never have trusted his damn eyes," she moaned as she slid to the floor, her back never leaving the door. She sat huddled there for what seemed like hours.

Some time later, a knock sounded on the door. Katerina's eyes flew open but she said nothing, her body stiff and rigid.

"Katerina! It's not what you think. Open the door so I can talk to you. I can't leave you thinking what you're thinking. I love you," Banyen said harshly.

"Liar!" Katerina whispered.

"It's not what you think. I'll not apologize for something I didn't do," he called through the door in an agonized voice.

"Bastard!" Katerina hissed between clenched teeth.

"I'm asking you to let me in so that we can talk. We must clear this up before I leave. I won't ask you again."

"Dirty, sneaky Mongol, I should have known better than to believe your lies. All men lie," she muttered to herself, the tears streaming down her cheeks. "I believed you and you lied to me," she whimpered as she crawled to a warm place near the fire. "It was the horses, it was always the Cosars. I saw the way you looked at the princess and I . . . I still thought, I still believed that you could love me. Liar!"

Banyen, standing outside, refused to believe the silence that roared in his ears.

"Katerina, I meant every word I said to you. I love you, I'll love you for the rest of my life. You didn't see me do anything except comfort the princess. Ask her yourself. It's you that I love. Let me prove it to you."

"You would lie to it and the princess would swear to it," Katerina whispered. "Oh no, Mongol, this is the last time you make a fool out of me. I believed you, I loved you!" she cried.

"If you loved me, you would open this door!" Banyen shouted gruffly.

"Well, I don't love you anymore. Go! Take the stallions, I no longer care. You know where they are. Take them. All of them," she shrieked, long and loud. "That's all you ever wanted. You lied to me. You tricked me. Take the stallions, that's what you wanted all the time. They're my gift to you on leaving!" She continued to shriek.

Stunned, Banyen could only stare at the door. His shoulders slumped as he lashed out with his booted foot to kick at the door. Damnable woman, if she thought he was going to stand here and beg her, she had another thought coming! He rubbed at his temples as a film swept over his eyes. He shook his dark head and was jolted from his angry thoughts by the sound of Katerina's heartrending sobs. They tore at him, ate at him, as he walked away, his head lowered, his shoulders shaking. He knew he would never see her again.

When all the sound ceased outside the door, Katerina jumped to her feet and threw back the bolt. He was gone! A few moments of pleading and he was gone! That was all the time he could allot her, a few seconds. He would leave and she would never see him again. What did it matter if he took the stallions? Her life was over. In a few hours he would be gone and she would never see him again.

Throughout the endless night Katerina sat like a sick animal and licked her wounds. Her mood alternated between searing anger and devastating despair. It was over, there was no point now to anything. All her magnificent plans to regain the Cosars would never come to fruition. It always came back to the horses. She told herself she was a fool. A foolish, lovesick woman who couldn't see what was in front of her eyes. Banyen must be beside himself with glee, she thought bitterly. Another conquest to add to his credit. Fool! Fool! her mind shrieked.

An hour before dawn she stood up to ease her cramped

legs, and was about to crawl into bed when she heard banging.

"Katerina, I have to speak with you," Mikhailo called through the thick door.

"Go away. There is nothing to talk about," Katerina answered.

"Open the door, there is much to be said. We have to talk."

"It's over, finished. There is nothing to discuss. Go away."

"I stand here alone, no one is with me."

"I don't believe you. The Mongol put you up to this. I wouldn't open the door to him, and now he thinks he'll use you to get to me. I thought you were my friend, Mikhailo. From the first you liked him, all he has to do is ask you to intervene and you do it. Go away."

"Have I ever lied to you? You know I haven't," he continued to plead. "Open the door, and you can lock it again as soon as I am inside. I tell you, I'm alone."

"If you're lying to me, I swear I'll kill you, Mikhailo. I'm in no mood for tricks. Swear to me on the icon."

"I swear to you on the icon. Now open the door."

Katerina slid the bolt and quickly looked right and left. Mikhailo was alone. Her mouth tightened into a grim line as she stood aside for him to enter. Damn sneaky Mongol, he couldn't even have Mikhailo plead his cause, she thought unreasonably.

Mikhailo was shocked at Katerina's appearance. Her eyes seemed as cold and dead as the ashes that lay in the grate. The deep purplish smudges on her tawny cheeks frightened him. Quickly he threw logs on the fire and poked at the ashes with tongs, his mind racing with the words he wanted to say. He had never thought he would live to see the day when she could be cowed like a cornered animal. Where was her spirit, the sense of fairness that she was known for? Females were stubborn, he knew, but he had never thought stubbornness was one of Katerina's traits.

"What is it? What did you want to talk about? Whatever it is, I'm not interested in hearing it. I only allowed you in this room to show you that I care for you."

"The Mongols are preparing to leave. If you look outside the window you'll see them. Banyen is leaving," he said distinctly, making sure she heard him. "He was in the kitchen talking to Kostya for a few moments before he left to see to his men. Kostya, in case you're interested, is no better. I haven't been able to make the fever abate. He's been in a delirium since midnight. Once or twice he has had lucid moments, but then he lapses into his ramblings again. I am concerned, and I tell you this because I know you are worried about him."

"Was worried. I'm no longer worried," Katerina said in a flat voice. "I've changed my mind since last night. When he recovers, if he recovers, they can leave. You'll take them to Volin and give them the gold I promised. I don't care what they do, I don't care where they go. Harness the stallions together and give them to the Mongol. All of them, even Whitefire. I never want to see those animals again. Tell him . . . tell him they are . . . Just give them to him," she said bitterly. "Leave me now, Mikhailo, and no tricks. The stallions are mine to do with as I see fit, and I want that bastard to have them. Every day for the rest of his life I want him to remember where he got them and why. Do it, Mikhailo, and no questions."

The Cossack stood, dismay covering his face. She couldn't be serious. Not the stallions! His mouth worked convulsively as he waited for her to throw the bolt on the door so he could leave.

"No tricks, Mikhailo. I'll watch from the window to be sure the horses are outside. If you harness and ready them, they'll not kick up a fuss. They'll follow him docilely. Do it!"

The ring of iron in her voice startled him, but he said nothing. What could he do? He was an old man.

Banyen's face wore a look of controlled anger when he entered the kitchen. Kostya looked up from his cocoon near the fire, and Banyen was relieved to see that though his face was heated and his hands trembled, his mind was clear. Banyen dropped to one knee and spoke in a hushed tone so that Halya wouldn't hear him.

Kostya frowned, but listened intently to the prince. Weakly he nodded his head, agreeing to look after Katerina during Banyen's absence, and tried to wipe at the perspiration on his brow.

Banyen placed a hand on Kostya's shoulder. "Each of us must do what he must do; I know that you understand this and hold no animosity toward me. That is the only reason I'm here now. You have many qualities that I admire, and I wish you well. Perhaps we'll meet again someday. If not, this is our last farewell." He was saddened as he watched Kostya's eyes cloud. He was no longer lucid but mumbling strange, incoherent words that Banyen didn't understand.

Even though Halya's green eyes were fearful, her tone was tight and confident. "I know he will recover. I pray constantly that it is not his time to join his Maker. Surely God will answer my prayers. Good-bye, Prince Banyen. I wish you a safe journey back to your camp. One day our paths may cross again."

Banyen nodded farewell and strode from the room.

Outside, in the damp, cold corridor, he hesitated a moment. Should he try to see Katerina one more time? His heart thundered in his chest. What did she want from him? To crawl on his knees, to beg her to believe him? Why was it that you could lie to a woman and she would believe you, but if you told her the truth it was suspect? It made no sense. Real men didn't beg; men didn't grovel. He had spoken the truth to her. He had pleaded with her to open the door so that he could explain that she didn't see what she thought she saw. Women! Rage whipped through him at the injustice of his position as he stomped from the corridor to take his place with his followers.

Busy with the wagons and his men, he didn't see the stallions at first. When he looked to the end of the small caravan, he almost lost his footing. Holy Mother of God, she meant what she said! The four stallions were harnessed together and standing docilely, waiting for the order to move. Panic gripped him, a feeling he had never experienced before. Even in the face of death he had never weakened. If he wanted to he could step out and touch the horses and . . . The scar on his cheek began to ache as he walked over to the waiting animals. A month ago he would have asked no questions; he would have taken the animals and been ecstatic. Now he hated them for their sleek beauty, and he hated the fact that they stood in front of him, waiting for him to take them wherever he wanted to go. There was no question in his mind as he loosened the harness and led the animals back into the fortress. They weren't his. They didn't belong to anyone except Katerina, the beautiful woman with the amazing eyes. The stallions could never be his. They could never belong to anyone but her.

Mikhailo's mouth dropped open when Banyen led the snorting Cosars to the oak doors.

"Tell Katerina that I have no need for so priceless a gift. These stallions belong to her for now, forever more, just as I thought she belonged to me. Tell her that for me, will you, Mikhailo?"

"I'll tell her, but she won't listen. I tried to talk with her this morning, and while she heard my words, they made no impression. She's like a wounded animal—not responsible for her actions. A person does what he has to do to survive or he dies. It is as simple as that," the old Cossack said quietly.

Banyen touched the old man's shoulder and then abruptly moved away. He mounted his horse and spurred it forward. He didn't look back as he led his soldiers from the House of the Kat. Banyen was going home to the Khan, the only home he had ever truly known. Returning without the breeding secrets of the Cosars, and leaving behind four white stallions and the only love he had ever known.

From her window Katerina watched as Banyen led the stallions out of sight. She frowned and tried to see what was going on below. She saw him return to his horse and ride away. He didn't look back, but rode straight ahead. She blinked her eyes to clear her vision. Whitefire and the others weren't with the caravan. He wasn't taking them! What did it mean? A clever trick, that's what it meant, she told herself.

For five days Katerina remained in her room, almost hoping as each hour dragged by that Banyen would return. At the end of the fifth day she emerged from her room, her face gaunt, dark smudges ringing her vacant doe eyes. She made her way to the kitchen and stood impatiently waiting for the princess or Mikhailo to notice her. It was Halya who walked over to her and tried to take her in her arms. Katerina brought up her arm and swung out, striking her full across the face. "Send the falcon to Kusma," she directed Mikhailo. "Saddle a horse for her, she leaves within the hour. Have one of the men take her as far as Volin, and from there Kusma can see to her well-being, whatever it is."

Tears welled in Halya's eyes. "You can't send me away. Kostya has not recovered. Mikhailo says that by morning he thinks his fever will break. I want him to see me when he awakes. Please," she pleaded, "you can't be so cruel."

"Think again," Katerina snarled. "Within the hour, Mikhailo. If you have to, tie her to the horse."

Halya's eyes were bitter. "You're wrong. I'm ashamed to call you a woman. You act like a thoughtless child. There was nothing between your prince and myself. He comforted me. He belongs to you, no one could ever take him from you. Are you so foolish that you didn't know that? If you truly loved him, there would have been no doubt in your mind. Yes, you have the right to send me from this fortress. And, yes, I'll go. I have no other choice. But you can never separate me from Kostya. I love him and he loves me. I've seen cruel, heartless men, many of them, but never have I seen one as cold and as unforgiving as you, and that's what makes you a disgrace to all women. It's no wonder men have a low opinion of women."

Katerina reached up and gave her a second resounding slap on the side of her head.

Halya took the blow full force, her head reeling. "He'll never come back here for you. Is this how you acted with my brother, my brother that you killed? He's well rid of you even if he had to die to do it. If it will pleasure you, strike me again, it doesn't matter. I'll leave, and I wish you misery for every hour, every minute that you breathe for the rest of your life."

Katerina hated her, hated the words that spewed from her mouth. Her own lips trembled at what she was hearing and at the look on the princess's face. Was it possible that she spoke the truth? No, Mikhailo was right, the Mongol was a son of a bitch.

"Save your breath and do not concern yourself with my well-being. If I live, I live; if I die, I die. It is no concern of yours. I allowed you in my house and I confided in you and you betrayed me."

"You betrayed yourself," Halya said softly. "You played a game and lost. Now you have nothing. Live with that for the rest of your life," Halya said bitterly as she gathered up her silver-fox cloak. "I'll fetch my belongings and be gone from your sight."

Katerina's eyes shot sparks as Mikhailo watched her, speechless at her tirade. She defied him to say a word, anything to chastise her. The old man resumed bathing Kostya's flushed face, his heart heavy in his chest.

"I thought I told you to loose the falcon!"

Mikhailo didn't bother to look up. "I have a sick man that needs my attention. I want no deaths on my conscience. Since you're as perfect as Almighty God, do it yourself."

"And just exactly what is that supposed to mean?"

"It means whatever you want it to mean," Mikhailo said, just as harshly. "Leave me, I can't bear to look upon your face. I never thought I would live to see the day that I would hate the sight of your beautiful face, but that day has come. Go, send your falcon to Kusma."

Katerina was stunned at the old man's words. How could he talk to her thus? Who did he think he was? He had never spoken to her before with anything except kindness and understanding.

"You were the one who said no Mongol was to be trusted. Tell me now you didn't say that."

"Yes, I said that, and at the time I meant it. Foolish words from a foolish old man. Your prince is not like that, nor are his soldiers. They're all men to be proud of, and I am truly sorry I ever uttered those words. The princess's words were just words also. You hurt her and she retaliated in the only way she knew how. You yourself are guilty of the same thing. You've just left girlhood behind and become a woman, a difficult transition."

He looks rather like a fat, precocious squirrel, Katerina thought as she saw him tilt his head to the side as if his own speech surprised him.

"You still don't know what you've done, do you?"

Katerina frowned, not sure she knew of what he was speaking.

"You are guilty of the very thing your father was guilty of. How does it feel, my dear? You assumed, you judged, and you found the prince guilty just as Katlof found you guilty. Now tell me, how will you live with that? Your father is dead and you're alive."

"Oh my God, you're right!" she exclaimed, a stunned look on her face. "Banyen!"

"He tried to explain to you that you were mistaken, and you wouldn't listen. You didn't even give him the chance to defend himself. Your father at least gave you that chance before the council. True, they found you guilty, but you had your say. Which is more than you allowed Banyen. He *loved* you. I don't know what he feels for you now. Possibly disgust, probably hatred. You ridiculed him, denied him the chance to defend himself. It would be a rare man who could still care after all of that."

"He never loved me, all he wanted was the horses," Katerina spat, stunned at the Cossack's words.

"Then why didn't he take the stallions with him? He told me to give you a message."

A spark lit up Katerina's large eyes as she waited for his words.

"He said the stallions belonged to you for now, for forever more, just as he thought you belonged to him."

"He said that?" Katerina whispered. "If you're lying to me, Mikhailo, I'll cut your tongue from your throat."

"I'll say no more. You must be the one to decide what is true and what is false. And," he said snidely, "you still have the falcon to turn loose. Or have you changed your mind?" Where am I finding all these words? he wondered as he again dipped the cloth into the pan of water to sponge Kostya's feverish face.

"Did Banyen really say that?" she asked huskily. "Tell me, Mikhailo," she pleaded with moist eyes.

"Where would an old man like myself hear such fancy

words? Only men in love say things like that. I never heard such words before he uttered them," he snapped, a crafty look on his face.

"You can be a sly fox when you want to be." Katerina grinned. "I'll apologize to the princess and send her down the mountain. It's time for her to leave anyway. Kostya will recover."

Halya strode into the kitchen, her belongings tied up in a canvas sack. "There's no need for you to apologize to me. I understand, for I love Kostya the way you love the prince. One day you'll make amends, I know you will. When Kostya recovers, tell him that I'll be waiting for him in Moldavia. I could never hold bitterness for you in my heart, for if it wasn't for you, I would never have found Kostya."

Katerina floundered for words. "I'm sorry that I lashed out at you. I have never, in all my life, felt so hurt. I had to hurt something, and unfortunately it was you that I hurt. Forgive me."

"It's not my forgiveness you need, it's Banyen's."

"Yes, I know. One day perhaps he'll forgive me, if I can find him," Katerina said sadly, "and if it isn't too late."

"It's never too late," Halya said, clasping Katerina to her breast. "Remember that. Take care of Kostya for me, will you? I wish you well, and I wish you success in finding your Cosars. Just send Kostya to me when it's over. Promise me that and I can leave here with a light heart."

"You have my vow. Come, I must release the falcon and see that you have an escort down the mountain."

Mikhailo smiled to himself as he rocked back on his heels. Love! Women! Foolish men with their fancy words! Bah!

True to Mikhailo's word, Kostya's fever abated by dawn of the following morning. He was weak and shaky, but managed a few spoonfuls of broth from time to time. He apologized for his illness, saying he knew it delayed her descent down the mountain.

"A few days longer makes no difference. Another three days and you'll be fit as Stepan's fiddle," Katerina said. "The Mongols left a week ago, and Halya yesterday. She waits for you in Moldavia. She made me promise that I would return you to her safely. I told you that many times, but you were feverish, and I want to be sure that you understand what I'm saying."

"Then our plan is still the same, nothing has changed?"

Katerina grinned. "If you had asked me that a week ago, my answer might have surprised you. Nothing has changed—myself possibly, but that is all."

Kostya lay back exhausted, his mind wandering. Something teased at his mind, but he couldn't grasp it. Did he forget something, was he supposed to do something? What was it Banyen had asked? He sighed. He needed sleep. Later he would remember whatever it was that nagged at him.

Each day found Kostya's strength returning twofold. He was like the stallions, champing at the bit to move, to get it over with so he could begin what he said was the rest of his life.

Ten days from the time Kostya's illness broke, the Cossacks assembled outside the great fortress known as the House of the Kat and waited for Katerina's signal to move.

Astride Whitefire, she leaned over to speak to Mikhailo. "Another week and you can see to the burial of Grandfather and Valerian. Say the same words over the Mongol that you say for my Zedda. After that, go to Volin with the others and see to the rebuilding. The process is slow with so few men. Leave this fortress unmanned. There is nothing for us here now. It's possible that I may never return—you understand that, don't you, Mikhailo?"

Tears burned in the old Cossack's eyes at her words. He knew what she meant. "You must let me know if the wildflowers have sprouted when you get to the Dnieper. If you don't return, I'll never know. Take your new Cossacks and go. I'll wait for you in Volin."

Kostya mounted Darkfire, while Rokal leaped onto Snowfire's sleek back. "We leave you Wildfire to ride to Volin," Katerina said softly. "Take care of him." With a jaunty salute, she dug her heels into Whitefire's flanks, and the stallion burst from the enclosed compound, clumps of sod and bits of snow flying in his wake.

Mikhailo shielded his eyes from the glare and thought he had never seen such a magnificent sight. They were Cossacks, and she had done the very thing she had promised she would do. There was not one among the lot of them who had betrayed her or tried to undo the bargain she made with them. This new breed of Cossack will serve her well, he thought smugly. He had known all along she could do it. Not once did he have a moment's doubt. His conscience pricked him slightly at the thought. Perhaps a dozen or so times, he consoled himself, but no more than that. The only thing that mattered was that she was successful. He knew she would return. But when she did return, would the Mongol be with her or would she be alone?

Chapter 21

Banyen and his men made the journey to the Khanate with few utterances. Banyen trotted ahead of the others, his thoughts on Katerina and their time in the House of the Kat. On the long ride he alternated between fits of rage and melancholy at his circumstances. *She's just another woman*, he told himself over and over. At night his empty arms proved the thought a lie. She was part of him, a part of him he needed to live. Without trust, what would happen to their love and the life he planned for them? He told himself that women were foolish in the ways of love and men were strong and forceful.

Would he ever see her again? His recurring nightmare of her lying broken and battered in some raid swam before his tired eyes. All for those damnable horses. Why couldn't she be like other women, who thought only of lovemaking and babies? He admitted to himself that if she were like that he wouldn't want her. Katerina was like no other. She was his. When all his affairs were in order he would go back for her and to make her understand. Women liked men to say sweet words and hold them close. There were worse things in life, he told himself. But he wouldn't beg; he would never beg.

His mood lightened somewhat as he let his gaze take in his surroundings. An hour more and he would be at the Khanate. He would soon be home. Home meant Afstar and telling him he didn't have the secret and that he had given back the stallions. No more lies or half truths.

Banyen rode his mount fast and hard, and brought him to a skidding halt outside Afstar's yurt.

"My ears are delicate, Banyen. A little respect, please," Afstar said smoothly, his eyes taking in Banyen's appearance and dark look. He didn't fail to see the deep scar pulsating and twitching. Something was wrong. "Come, I've missed you. Join me in some wine and some real food. I'm most anxious to hear all about the winter. And tell me, did you beat the snows?" he questioned affably, holding the flap of the yurt aside for Banyen to enter.

His hand to his cheek, Banyen strode through the yurt. "No, I didn't beat the snows, and yes, we had problems, your detestable wagons for one. That girl is smarter than both of us put together. The long months worked their magic, and I fell in love with her. I'm returning to you without the breeding secret, and I rejected her offer of the four white stallions. We had a misunderstanding, rather your niece misunderstood something she saw, and I left with hatred between us. One day I'll go back for her and explain fully, if that's possible. That, Afstar, is the beginning and the end of it," he said, bringing the wine to his lips and drinking greedily. "Your men are as good as any Cossack. They'll serve you well. There will be no complaints."

The Khan was outraged. "Is this how you repay my generosity? I send you on a mission and you return and dare to tell me you had the stallions in your grasp and gave them up for love of my niece! I never expected Katerina to keep her promise, but I did expect more of you.

"You failed me, but you won't a second time. I have another mission for you, Banyen. You will go to Moscow and seek out those who can aid us when we attack. All the necessary preparations must be made. I will not and cannot tolerate failure this time."

The Khan's anger cooled. "You failed, and that is the end of the matter. Tell me, did my niece say she was withdrawing her offer of the filly and the colt?"

"Not withdrawing it," Banyen said, coldly, "not fulfilling it. We both know she had no intention of ever giving you the animals. She would lie through her teeth for those animals, and that's exactly what she did. They're hers and no one else's. They belong to her, not you and not me," he said, bringing the goatskin to his mouth a second time.

The Khan sighed. "I hoped," he said pathetically. "It wasn't too much to ask, one little colt and one little filly."

"It was too much. If you had asked her for her life, she would have given it to you. She'll never part with those horses."

"And I thought you were the man that could turn the trick," Afstar said sourly. He shook his head and leaned back in his comfortable nest of cushions. "Is there more?"

"No," Banyen said curtly. "Arrange for a bath and a woman in my yurt. Any woman will do as long as she has two arms and two legs," he said, emptying the wineskin and reaching for another.

"I never thought of it in quite those terms." Afstar grinned. "I myself require a few other . . . It makes no mind. Go, you're smelling up my yurt with your unclean body. Your request will be taken care of. We'll talk tomorrow."

Banyen staggered from the tentlike dwelling and entered his own, his head reeling from alcohol. So what if he was drunk? Who was there to care, and what difference did it make? He would live each day as it came. What more could he do?

Banyen stripped off his clothing, muttering to himself as he drank yet more wine. Even in this condition, he had seen the new men at the end of the camp. Things looked different. Afstar must be rebuilding slowly. Well, the hell with him.

The moment the sun rose in the east, a resplendent Tatar chief rode into the Khanate, his men trailing respectfully behind.

Khan Afstar stood outside his yurt, his dark eyes speculative and wary. He motioned with his pudgy hand for the chief to dismount, and stood aside for him to enter his yurt. They seated themselves on the colorful cushions and watched the brazier as the coals flicked to life, neither of them saying a word. It was understood that they waited for one other confidant, Prince Banyen.

The Tatar chief looked around the dwelling and nodded his round head appreciatively. He pursed his mouth as he caressed the sable carpet that rested at his feet. While he preferred bear rugs himself, he acknowledged that each man had his own tastes. The eyes moved slightly as the flap parted and a tall man stood outlined in the bright sun. Now it would be business.

Batu, the Tatar, motioned for Banyen to sit and join the discussion. Crossing his arms over his massive chest, he looked at Afstar and Banyen, then spoke carefully, his voice deep and guttural. "Word reached me at the beginning of the new year that you search for, and are in the process of buying, an army. I have such a force, and my warriors number two hundred thousand. I know that it has been your dearest wish for many years to avenge Kazan and Astrakhan. With my soldiers and the army you're building we can accomplish that which you desire. You'll help me and I'll help you," he said matter-of-factly.

Banyen regarded Afstar and Batu with amusement. You pat my back and I'll pat yours, he thought.

"My plan is to attack Moscow at the onset of winter, if you feel that your fighters will be ready. By my figures your army should number one hundred thousand. With this amount of men we can't fail."

"What is it that you want?" Banyen asked coolly. "I haven't heard why you seek out this Khanate. The Khan and I know why we're preparing to go into battle. I wish to hear your reasons."

Batu twirled the ends of his long, drooping mustache as he stared at Banyen. "I need women for my slave trade."

Afstar, seeing the look of stunned surprise on Banyen's face, quickly spoke. "Your business is your own, but I want it understood that I do not approve. In no way will we help you in this endeavor. My army will join strength with yours, but it will be every man for himself. Let us understand each other, Batu."

The chief nodded his bulbous head slowly. "It is understood. We will rendezvous on the outskirts of Smolensk. Agreed?"

Afstar nodded and stood up. The meeting was ended.

Banyen followed the Tatar chief outside. With one long, steady look in Afstar's direction, he headed for the military compound, where his men waited for him. Now it would be drill and prepare, prepare and drill, until a messenger arrived from Batu.

Chapter 22

Katerina rode the Cossacks fast and hard down the mountainous terrain. Whitefire was in his element, racing across and pounding the earth as though the devils of hell rode his heels. The other horses, trained to perfection, followed quickly behind.

They stopped once to feed the animals and for a quick meal themselves, then remounted, the earth spewing behind them like a giant swell of water from the sea.

When they arrived at Volin, Katerina dismounted and looked around the village that had been her home for so many years. She sought out several of the elder Cossacks who were already busy rebuilding the village. Rapidly she told them that Mikhailo and the rest of the men from the fortress would arrive within days to help with the new construction.

"We camp here for the night and then we ride north. A light meal and a good night's sleep, and we'll depart at dawn."

Katerina and her followers left with the first sun and began their trek across the steppe in their search for the Cosars. No village went unnoticed. As was their plan, Kostya rode ahead with a two-man patrol. Each settlement was inspected, and long, lengthy discussions with the Cossacks who inhabited the towns ensued.

One month followed the other, the Cossacks unsuccessful in their attempts to learn the whereabouts of the famed horse herd. One evening, weary to the point of exhaustion, Katerina sat near the campfire and complained bitterly to Rokal and Kostya. "One would think by now that somebody, somewhere, would have seen or heard something. Especially the Don Cossacks, my own people."

"Is it possible that your people are lying to you?" Kostya asked cautiously. "You told me they branded you a traitor, and that you are in disgrace."

"I, too, thought that in the beginning, but no, I don't think that now. These are my people. They understand what I'm doing, and for that reason they wouldn't lie. What belongs to a Cossack belongs to a Cossack. We kill to regain what belongs to us. I am no different from any other Don."

"Another month and summer will be at an end," Rokal said, stirring the fire with a long stick.

"Yes, I know. And we still have a two-week ride till we reach the Terek territory. It'll be another month before we can cover all their camps on the grasslands. By that time the snows will have started and God alone will be able to help us. I can tell you now that the Terek is a bloodthirsty Cossack. They kill for sport. A life to them means nothing. When we ride into their camps they will tell us nothing. One Terek will lie and another will swear that he speaks the truth. We have to be prepared to search, and we must have eyes in the back of our heads. I want you to add more men to your patrol, Kostya. My gut tells me that our search is almost at an end. I can think of no one who would have the manpower to have raided Volin, save them. The Don would never steal from their own. But a long time ago I learned that you don't trust your instincts one hundred percent, and that is why we rode through every Don village. I'm tired and I need to think. Give me the map of the steppe, Kostya, I want to look it over one more time before we leave tomorrow."

True to her word, the next weeks found the Tereks hostile and closemouthed. Katerina knew instinctively that each and every village they rode through was bringing them closer and closer to the Cosars.

It was Kostya's idea to free the horses from their pens in each town they rode through. "We need no advance warning of our coming," he said shortly to Katerina as a herd of horses galloped across the plains. "It will take the men weeks to gather them together. We have the advantage now, and I want to keep it that way. Every day becomes more important to us.

"In the last village before Khortitsa a mealy-mouthed Terek said he knew where the white horses were being kept. Then he laughed and said it was a joke, the Cosars have been in Moscow for many months. He boasted that it was his brother Gregory Bohacky who was responsible. His brother is now a hero and a saint to his people. A rich hero and saint," he amended. "No amount of persuading could make him change his story."

Katerina nodded to Kostya and watched as the horses ran free.

Gregory Bohacky! Could it be the same Gregory who came to Volin with Yuri? Was it possible that that was what Yuri was trying to tell her? It was the Tereks who killed him, and not the Dons! If that was true, then it was they who raided the village. Her mind raced. Bohacky, he's the man responsible for my father's death!

The days were never-ending so far as Banyen was concerned. Spring passed into summer as he drilled and trained the new men who came in droves to the Khanate. Day after weary day passed with him doing nothing more than working out with the latest arrivals, eating, and sleeping. Summer was fast ending when the Khan called him into his yurt and told Banyen it was time for them to make their move. The agate eyes narrowed and Banyen nodded curtly when the Khan informed him that a messenger would ride at dusk with a message for Katerina, advising her of his plans.

The Mongol courier had been riding for days, following the trail of Katerina and her Cossacks. Finally his perseverance was rewarded as he caught sight of the band leaving a village on the outskirts of Azov. Carefully he followed them and watched until they camped for the night. As the skies blackened he approached the campsite, making as much noise as possible. Immediately he was stopped by a Cossack guard posted in the tall grass a hundred feet from the main camp. The Mongol identified himself to the guard as one of the men who had trained in the Carpathians with the Kat, and spoke of Prince Banyen and the Khan of Sibir. Reassured, the guard felt it was safe to deliver the messenger to Katerina. When her tired amber eyes looked upon the face of the young man, Katerina recognized him immediately as one of Banyen's soldiers.

"Come, Igor, sit by the fire and tell me what brings you this far from Sibir. Join us in a drink and a bite to eat."

He took a long swallow of vodka, chewed on a piece of bread, and said, "Your uncle sent me to find you and tell you that he and the Crimean Tatars have joined forces. Their plan is to attack Moscow."

"Why are they doing this?" she asked Igor before he could go on.

"You know your uncle and Banyen wish to avenge Ivan's raids on the Khanates of Kazan and Astrakhan, where family and friends were killed. When Afstar heard that the Crimean Tatars numbered two hundred thousand strong and were making plans to attack Moscow, he and

Banyen set out to meet with them. The Tatars are seeking women for their thriving slave business. Certainly the Tatars don't need your uncle's men, but after listening to your uncle's story of avenging his people, along with Prince Banyen's tale, the Tatars agreed to unite. Khan Afstar's army has grown somewhat larger since your visit. Many men have come, and his riches have brought him many more horses. He feels confident now that Moscow can be taken. The Mongols and Tatars stand thousands strong. Now he awaits word from you if you wish to join him. He also asked me to find out if you have found the Cosars."

"And what of Prince Banyen?" she asked coolly. "Has he whipped the Khan's men into a fighting unit with the help of the boys I shaped?"

"The prince is still very hard at work with the newer men. He puts them through a rough training, similar to yours. When he is finished, they can compete with any man and be proud of how they handle themselves."

"That's good news," she went on, hoping he might mention a word from Banyen for her. When it didn't come, she continued. "We haven't found the Cosars yet, but we have one village left to raid. I saved it until last, until my Cossacks had proven themselves. I'm proud of them; they fight as if they were born to the saber. We have lost only two men in all our raids, and that was in one village where the people fought us. Most of the towns we pillaged were small, and the people harmless. We didn't fight with them; in fact, in most of them we rode in and asked if they heard or saw anything of the Cosars. After a search convinced us the horses weren't there, we left peacefully. The larger villages, where people resisted, we fought. We haven't raided the smaller Don Cossack villages because I know they are our friends and wouldn't steal from us. We have one place left to visit, and that is the Tereks, across the river on the Island of Khortitsa. The Cosars are there or have disappeared, I'm sure of it. Tomorrow before dawn will be our true test, when we commence our raid on the island. These Tereks are known to be the most savage of the Cossack tribes. They will work for anyone or do anything for gold. If we win a victory tomorrow, my men will truly be men of stature. They'll be able to hold their heads high and proud, for they will have beaten their toughest enemy. Then they'll be known as the Cossacks to be feared. If you wish to ride with us you may, but if you want to wait for us, do so. Tomorrow, after our visit with the Tereks, you will have my answer for my uncle. Will you join us?"

The man shook his head. "No, Katerina, I can't. I'm too weary. I've been traveling for days searching for you. I'll wait in a safe place where I'll be able to watch you and your men, and I'll meet you afterward. In the meantime I'll rest, for as soon as you give me your answer I must leave and return to Sibir."

"You're right, you must stay alive to bring Uncle Afstar his answer. Let's all get some sleep now, for in a few hours we'll move toward the Tereks' village."

In the tall grass on the east bank of the Dnieper River, after the guards were posted, Katerina and her men bedded down under the stars on the sweeping steppe.

Across the river, on the west bank, was the island of Khortitsa, the outskirts of the Terek village. One by one, on foot, several of her men would cross the water and scatter, seeking out the guards and killing them. Quickly and without a sound, horses and men would then also cross and storm Khortitsa.

Katerina was still awake, her mind not allowing her to sleep. The Cosars had to be there; they had searched everywhere else. She knew her men would find them. Her men—she liked the phrase. They *were* hers, for she no longer worried about them killing her in her sleep or deserting her. They were all one now: the Cossacks of Volin. Volin . . . By now Mikhailo and some of the elders from the fortress would be rebuilding the village. She had told Mikhailo that she at least wanted an enclosure put up, so that if they found the horses they would have a place to quarter them, if all was done before the winter came. Knowing Mikhailo, Katerina was sure he was busy chopping trees. Once more her mind insisted that the horses have to be in the Terek village. Secure in the knowledge that her plan would work, she closed her tired eyes and slept.

She heard her name called, and she thought she was dreaming. Then she heard it again, and someone was shaking her shoulder. She opened her eyes to find Kostya kneeling beside her.

"It's time."

Katerina leaped to her feet and ordered the group of Cossacks to seek out the Terek guards. Within the hour, one man returned, announcing the sentries were no longer a problem.

Katerina mounted Whitefire and signaled her men to cross the river quickly and quietly. When they reached the west bank they rode silently to the gateway of the village. With a forward motion of her arm, Katerina gave the signal to attack. The raid was on.

Whitefire needed no second urging. He snorted loudly and galloped down the road, Darkfire and Snowfire in his wake. At the end of the settlement Katerina reined in the stallion and, with a quick look right and left, saw that the entire encampment was surrounded by her Cossacks. Her voice was shrill in the quiet night.

"Send Gregory to me or every man in this village will die! On the count of three, bring him to me."

Silence met her ears as doors opened and a few old women walked out to the road and stood huddled together.

"He was here at sundown, but I have not set eyes on him since then," one woman said in a reedy voice.

Rokal dismounted and dragged a protesting man to the middle of the road. "Count, Katerina." He laughed loudly. "On three I'll slice his ugly head from his neck!"

"One! Two! . . ."

Rokal brought up his saber with a quick slicing motion, his hand steady, a grin on his face.

"Three!" Katerina shouted.

"In the barn, in the barn!" the Terek squealed in a high, thin voice.

It was Kostya who sprinted to the building, just as the door opened and a giant of a man walked out. Two Cossacks pinned him by the arms, and Kostya dragged him to stand before Katerina as he fought his captors with all his strength.

"Are you the one they call Gregory?" she asked him hatefully, recognizing him instantly. "You! You're the buyer who came to Volin with Yuri Zhuk. Now I understand. You weren't there to purchase horses. You came to spy on us and steal the Cosars, you bastard!"

Gregory was belligerent, a sneer on his mouth. His eyes widened at the sight of the white stallions.

Katerina noticed the surprised look and laughed. "A mare is a mare, right, Terek? Without the stallions a mare is just another horse." She leaned over and whispered, so that Gregory had to strain to hear her words. "Where are they?"

Gregory shrugged. "What are you talking about?" he blustered.

Katerina remained silent atop Whitefire. The Cossacks closed in, forming a circle around the sweating Terek.

"Since the beginning of spring I've been searching for the mares and haven't found them anywhere. I know they're not in any other Cossack village. Where are they? I won't ask you again! For now, all I seek is the horses, but later you'll pay for what you did to my father and the people of my village. You can't escape me."

The hackles rose on Gregory's neck, and his stomach

turned over at what he knew she meant to do. His mind shrieked for him to lie. Lie to her and she'll let you go. He had a long, rich life ahead of him, with more gold than he could ever spend. "They were stolen from me when the village was asleep."

"That's very amusing. It's almost as sad a tale as the night Volin was plundered. I don't believe a word of it." She laughed, the only sound in the quiet night, with the exception of the horses' deep breathing. "Do I have to count again? How much were you paid for the Cosars? Who did you sell them to?"

A sharp jab with Rokal's saber and the man lurched closer to Katerina, who was leaning over, her position relaxed and nonchalant. "Whatever you were paid, you were cheated. I'll kill you if you don't answer me. I want those animals back in their rightful pens by the time the first winds of winter come. Either you tell me now or I'll slice your tongue from your mouth. Then I'll castrate you in front of everyone, and I'll laugh while I'm doing it. The same thing will happen to every man in this village. Your death will be slow and painful, and the road will turn to a river of blood. Now where are my horses?"

She was bluffing, she was a woman, she wouldn't cut out his tongue or . . .

Free of the imprisoning hands, Gregory backed off a step and licked at his dry lips. Faster than the blink of the eye, he had Rokal's saber free of its sheath and in his hand. "Now tell me what you're going to do if I don't answer you," he sneered. "Yes, I stole your horses and I raided your village. Yuri and I were under orders from Ivan. Crazy Czar Ivan is the buyer. But now I have a weapon, and it makes us evenly matched. I can take a woman in my stride seven days out of the week. I'll fight you, but I want none of your men to interfere."

Katerina nodded and stepped closer to the sweating Gregory. "I find it strange that you should say what you just did.

Every Cossack stands and fights alone. My soldiers will not interfere."

The men's eyes were glued to Katerina as she advanced a step and then stopped before the fearful Terek. Before Gregory knew what she was about, she had brought up her saber and flexed her knees simultaneously. She slashed out at his weapon, jarring his arm, causing it to jolt backward with the force of her blow. Gregory, stunned for a second, retaliated quickly and thrust his saber at Katerina's midsection. Nimbly, like a dancer, she sidestepped him as her weapon again struck out, this time whacking his shoulder. The sound of his shattering bone was loud in the quiet night.

Katerina laughed at the look of pain on Gregory's face. "With little effort I can do the same to your other shoulder. Tell me where the Cosars are! I can smell your fear from where I stand."

Gregory spat for an answer, bringing his weapon up clumsily to strike out at the woman in front of him.

"So you pay no heed to my words. Then you shall suffer, and if you die, then it will be your own fault." She laughed as she feinted to the left, the saber finding its mark across the man's other shoulder.

The crack of the splintering bone brought shouts of approval from the Cossacks. Before Gregory could recover, Katerina danced out of the way and then crouched low in a sprint, lashing out at the Terek's leg. Blood splattered in the dusty road. Gregory looked with disbelieving eyes at his injured leg. The saber dropped from his numb hand.

"Now tell me, where are my Cosars? If you don't speak, then your tongue will lie in the dirt with your blood."

Gregory reeled uncontrollably, falling in a puddle of his own blood. He fell face down, the blood and dust settling over his face, making a hideous mask.

Kostya stretched out his foot and forced the Terek to roll over. "Answer the lady when she speaks to you."

"In Moscow. The Czar has the Cosars," Gregory gasped. "You're too late. By now they're scattered all over Russia. You'll never get them back," he said shrilly.

"I'll get them back, no thanks to you. If I could find you, I'll find the Cosars. Where is the gold you were paid for the animals? Make fast work of your answer."

"He can't hear you," Kostya said. "He's out of his mind with pain. Ask one of these other . . . puppets."

Katerina lifted her saber and looked around. She waited, saying nothing.

"In the barn," came a babble of voices. "In the chests beneath the saddles."

"Take it all," Katerina ordered Rokal. "It's yours to divide among the men. When we get to Moscow you can thank Ivan for his generosity personally."

"What do we do with these . . . this scum?" Kostya questioned.

"Put them in their own stockade. Shackle them together and move the poles in the way the Mongols do."

"They'll die," Kostya said softly. "Is that what you want? Do you want men's deaths on your conscience for horses? If so, you'll have to find someone else to obey this particular order. The stockade, yes, but no shackles, and the poles stay where they are."

"You're right. I'm sorry, I wasn't thinking. For a moment I was blinded by my own hatred. Place them in the stockade, and when the men are finished in the barn we ride out."

Katerina and a patrol of five men made camp for the night in Kharkov on the outskirts of Smolensk. Patiently she waited for the rest of her force, traveling in small groups so as not to draw attention to themselves. She was exhausted, more so than she ever remembered being, and now she was faced with a week's wait until it was time for her rendezvous with the Tatars and her uncle, Afstar.

As the men trickled in she was not surprised that those

whose loyalty she had once doubted were now steadfast and committed to her cause. She wondered if the loot from Gregory's barn had anything to do with their decision to stay with her. All were now as determined as she to regain the Cosars.

Never one to remain idle, Katerina found the endless days a living torture. As always when she had nothing to do, thoughts of Banyen filtered through her mind. Where was he; what was he doing? Did he think of her? Would he forgive her? When the amber eyes filled with tears, she would get up and have the men practice. When she tired of watching their expertise with their weapons, she had them brush and groom the animals. At sundown they ate their evening meal and sat around the fire, their voices pitched low in serious conversation.

Shortly before sunrise on the sixth day the Khan cantered into her camp. Briskly he ordered his men to dismount and set up tents. Katerina's eyes widened at the sight of the thousands of men who rode with him. All seemed fit and hearty. Banyen did well, she thought.

"You look well, my child," the Khan said, dismounting. "Tell me, have you any news for me?"

"Everything is well, Uncle, but this waiting is beginning to play on my nerves. How many more days?" Unable to contain herself, she blurted, "Where is Banyen?"

"In Moscow," Afstar said, watching Katerina carefully.

"Moscow! Why? But I thought . . . I expected . . ."

"He arrives tomorrow," Afstar said, sparing her the need to ask further questions. "He's been in Moscow for a week. The Tatars are also due to arrive tomorrow, sometime after dusk. Our plan is to camp for one day and go over our plans. However, in order to do that we must wait for Banyen and the information he is bringing us. Our plan is to attack at night, and it was left to Banyen to arrange our entry for us. Does that answer all your questions? The one-day delay is necessary, but any longer would only harm us. By now the peoples of the steppe are no doubt wondering where this massive army is heading. There is bound to be one among them that has sent word to Ivan by now."

"Are you telling me that Banyen is spying in Moscow?" Katerina asked, her eyes reflecting fright. "It can't be safe, and his life could be in danger."

"He is the only man who has allies there, and that is why the decision to send him was made. He agreed," Afstar said gruffly. "No harm will come to Prince Banyen. I'm tired, my young niece, and I wish to bed down for the night," he said, walking over to join his men, leaving Katerina staring at his retreating back.

As the sky darkened, the multitude of bonfires glowed like fireflies on the edge of the grasslands. Guards were posted as the Mongols and Cossacks ate and then bedded down for the night.

Settling herself beneath the stars, Katerina anxiously waited for sleep to overcome her. Please, she prayed, let nothing happen to him, keep him safe.

Chapter 23

With a sharp tug on the reins, Banyen brought his black Arabian to a halt. Moscow stood before him, a little less than a mile off. Never having been in this metropolis before, he wanted to observe it from a distance. Prior to this visit, all his dealings with the boyars had been on a pre-arranged no-man's-land or by messenger. Now he needed to know the city and its secrets. A week in Moscow, shown around by the boyars, and he should be able to lead the attack through it without any problems. He knew he had to be careful, because as much as the boyars hated Ivan and constantly undermined him, they were a lot not to be trusted by anyone. What was it the boyar had said? Banyen ran it through his mind again: "Take the main road into Moscow, through the Wooden City, then travel the White City, which will bring you into Kitai Gorod. You will know Kitai Gorod from the other cities by the fence built around it. Once in Kitai Gorod you'll see an inn, a large log building, and you'll recognize it by the wine pitcher which hangs over the entrance. We'll meet at the inn after dark, but before you enter Moscow you must dress yourself in the clothes of a rich merchant."

Banyen, dressed in the appropriate attire, spurred the horse in the flanks and headed for the way into Moscow.

He rode his stallion slowly through the Wooden City, choked with log houses and a maze of streets lined with poor artisans and laborers. Weavers, gardeners, sheep skinners, and coach drivers were busy working at their trades. He trotted on into the White City, where he noticed a difference in the buildings, many made of ivory-colored stone. The filth and wooden buildings in the Wooden City were here, too, but here also stood ornate stone churches and palatial homes. Pungent markets along the main roadway, selling foodstuffs and objects of all descriptions, dotted the sides of the street. He was amazed at the unfamiliar sights and the number of people who milled and thronged the crowded, narrow roads. He knew that the masses of people would pose no problem when it came to the actual attack. To his discerning eye, the streets revealed only women, children, and merchants. Seeing no sentries to alarm him, he rode on, his eyes constantly on the alert.

Momentarily wrapped up in his thoughts, he almost lost sight of the wall that stood before him as the sun, blotted out by the cover of the archway he passed under, awakened him to the fact that he was now in Kitai Gorod, or Basket Town. As his agate eyes raked the city he knew the boyar had spoken the truth, for in front of him were the kitais filled with earth, piled one on top of the other, reaching as high as the top of the wall. Banyen smiled to himself. The dirt-filled baskets would not deter the attack, only add fuel to the fire when the time came to burn the city. His eyes darkened and were sharp and alert for anything that looked the least suspicious as he continued toward the meeting place.

Noticing a busy crossroads ahead, he approached, seeing a log building to his right. As his Arabian minced his way closer, he saw the wine pitcher hanging in front of the building. Nudging his horse to the side of the inn, he dis-

mounted. Unsure as to what he should do with the animal,
he tied it to a projecting log near the back of the building.
Once he had spoken with the boyars and knew his way
around, he would stable the animal.

Entering the inn, Banyen was amazed to see the interior
was large and bare. Except for the massive wooden tables
and benches scattered about, a counter where the food and
drinks were served, and a huge fireplace, nothing else was
in the room. The starkness took Banyen by surprise, for
Mongols always had drapings, rugs, pillows, and clutter
around them. He walked to a simple table and sat down. He
leaned back on his rickety chair and knew that he would
draw no attention in his gray caftan.

Banyen eyed a Russian serving girl and motioned for her
to take his order. The oblique eyes narrowed as he watched
her approach, her long chestnut hair billowing out behind
her, her heavy breasts bobbing. Her bright, green eyes were
bold and speculative as she leaned over to take his order,
her breasts touching his shoulder. When she made no effort
to change her position, Banyen reached out his hand and
gently stroked the outside of her thigh. Still she didn't
move. "Soup, meat, and bread," he said coolly as he continued to touch her leg. The girl smiled as she straightened and
reached down to remove his hand. He matched her bold
look and nodded slightly. Later he would investigate her
charms. For now, he was impatient, knowing that darkness
was fast approaching. And soon the boyars would arrive.
He cautioned himself to watch for men who wore gold
medallions around their necks. He knew that the attire of
the boyars was to be tall black sheepskin hats, black caftans, and black robelike capes decorated with golden tas-
sels.

When the girl brought his food, he ate heartily. The soup
was so thick it was almost a stew; the roast lamb was succulent; the black bread was warm and tasty. Again he motioned to her, ordering a tall glass of kvass. A smile tugged

at the corners of Banyen's mouth as the girl pressed herself to him again, this time more heavily. When she reached over to pick up the kopecks, her gown fell away, revealing large, creamy orbs. Banyen drew in his breath, wanting to reach out and fondle them. He grinned as he watched her eye him languorously. His loins began to ache as he watched her sway back to the kitchen regions. Later, he told himself, there's always later. For now, he would sip at the kvass and wait for the boyars.

He was finishing his third glass when the inn became crowded with the supper patrons as twilight gave way to total darkness. Still Banyen waited, enjoying the bold glances the serving girl was bestowing on him. His own gaze became sleepy as he watched her swaying buttocks when she walked around the inn, serving the patrons. The moment the ache in his nether regions became a pain, two men walked through the door, dressed exactly as the boyar had described them. Banyen recognized one of them.

Banyen watched them closely as their eyes scanned the room, coming to rest on him. Bright gold medallions hung around their necks. The men fingered the medals and slowly maneuvered their way to his side of the crowded room. As they approached the table where he sat, Banyen stood and spoke.

"I beg your pardon, my boyars, might I have a quiet word with you?"

Both pairs of eyes took in Banyen's merchant attire and the oblique eyes. They nodded. "Of course, how can we be of assistance?" they asked, seating themselves at the table.

Holding up his hand, Banyen ordered kvass for his guests.

The older of the two boyars spoke first. "This inn is not the place to discuss details. Tomorrow, during the day, we must do the Czar's bidding, but in the evening we'll meet in my home in the White City. When we finish our kvass we'll ride through Moscow so you can become familiar with the sites and the names of the places of which we speak. As we ride, I'll tell you of the many details you'll need to know. We'll also ride past my home so you'll know where to meet me tomorrow evening. Might I say, Prince Banyen, you look well. It has been many years since I last saw you. Fortune has been good to you. Soon you'll be able to avenge your family." His voice was sad and solemn as he stared into Banyen's eyes. "How long ago it was that we played together as children. I'm happy that I can now be of some help to you."

Banyen nodded, saying nothing.

"I suggest you take a room here at the inn, as it would be the obvious thing for a stranger to do. Most newcomers to Moscow stay at this particular inn. It would be best if you booked your room now. We'll wait here for your return. Where did you secure your animal?"

"I tied him to a log at the side of the inn. Is there some place I can stable the animal?" Banyen inquired with concern.

"There's a stable in back of the inn. When you secure your lodging tell them you wish your horse to be taken care of, and they will tend to the rest. Just pray your horse is still where you left him, for it isn't uncommon for horses to be stolen."

Alarmed that his black stallion could be missing, Banyen first checked his steed. He was relieved when he found the animal still tied. Rushing back into the inn, he took a room and asked that his horse be tended to. The owner called out, and a moment later a stable boy appeared, listened, nodded his head, and was off in the direction of Banyen's horse.

"What name did you give?"

"Ivan Toborschev."

"That's good. What did you say for business?"

"I said that I was a merchant from Kiev."

"Good."

Growing impatient with all the chatter, the elder boyar

suggested they finish their drinks and leave for their ride around Moscow.

"How did you gain entry to the city?"

"Exactly as you instructed me. I came in on the main road through the Wooden City to Kitai Gorod."

The two nobles looked at each other, frowns on their faces. "Perhaps we should take him farther on and show him Red Square and the Kremlin. This will give him a working knowledge of the city and the way the roads are laid out."

"A commendable idea," the other agreed as they walked toward the stable and his waiting coach.

The men boarded and drove through Red Square and the Kremlin. The two boyars pointed out the palace and surrounding buildings, which were heavily guarded and closed to the public. As the coach turned and headed back to Kitai Gorod, the driver was ordered to go through the other cities.

"Even in the darkness you'll be able to see parts of the cities you did not see on your ride in. Tomorrow, during the day, become familiar with as much as you can. If necessary, ride through more than once, and pay attention to the things you think will be important to you. Tomorrow evening, when we make our plans, sites we speak of may be recognizable to you." Their drive at an end, the two men bade Banyen good night and were off, their coach lumbering down the road.

Exhausted, Banyen lay down on the soft bed, mulling over the activities of the day. His thoughts turned to the plans for the attack due to take place in less than a week. Satisfied that he hadn't overlooked anything, he let his thoughts drift, and he remembered the wanton smile and the firm, hard breasts that had pressed against his shoulder. A warm glow swept over him, and Katerina's face swam before him. He ached for her touch. Warmed by his memories, he fell into a deep sleep.

Refreshed and rested, Banyen dressed and descended the

stairs for breakfast. He was relieved to note that the Russian girl was not in evidence. He knew that if she continued to flaunt herself, desire would take hold of him, and he would bed her like an animal. The girl's absence and the work at hand drove passion to the back of his mind. He finished his meal and left the inn. Done saddling his horse, he began his ride through the streets of Moscow. As he trotted he made mental notes concerning the various roads, bridges, rivers, and sights which he felt might be of importance to him. At the end of the day he made his way back to the inn, had his supper, freshened up, then walked to the house of the elder boyar.

The finery of the home impressed Banyen to a degree. The wealth of the noble and his trappings were different from those of a Mongol. The overstuffed chairs with their beautiful carvings and the small highly carved tables which sat around the large rooms, holding ornate lamps and art objects, drew his attention, but seemed utterly useless. A Mongol liked the best of things, but they were things that had a practical purpose, not merely for display. He complimented the boyar on his home, however, as they made their way to his private business chamber, where the others waited.

Quickly the boyar closed the doors behind him. "These are some of the other men who will aid us. They too would like to see Ivan fall from power. We have been together for many years, and I give you my word that they can be trusted."

The nobles and Banyen sat around a big table in a corner of the room as the elder boyar unfolded a map of Moscow and placed it in the center of the group. "Banyen, study this map carefully and pay special attention to the places that are marked in red. The marks represent the weak spots in the chain of Ivan's defense. There are many entrances into the cities through the main roadways, but when you reach Kitai Gorod, Red Square, and the Kremlin you will see they are surrounded by walls, the highest of which is around the Kremlin. The plan is for you to have your people surround all of Moscow. You will not have any trouble with the Wooden City or the White City, as they are open to raid. Have your main thrust come through the main roads of each city. Push straight on until you see the walls of Kitai Gorod. In the meantime you can have the rest of your army surround the entire outside walls of the Kremlin, Red Square, and Kitai Gorod. My men will be stationed at the unguarded places to open the gates to your men. As your army storms through the main road of Basket Town and keeps Ivan's soldiers at bay, the rest of your men can pour through the gates. Moscow will be yours! We must now set the exact time of attack, and it must happen at exactly that moment, as seconds may spell the death of my comrades at Ivan's mad hands!"

"Understood," acknowledged Banyen. "The supper hour will be the time. The moment the church bell chimes."

"Yes, an excellent idea. It should be dark by then, when most people eat, including the Czar and the soldiers. It will take them at least an hour to get back to the garrison where the main bulk of the weapons and ammunition is kept. Are you all in agreement with the plan and time for the attack?"

"We agree," said one voice, representing all.

"Banyen, you will spend three more days in Moscow with my men, a different one each night, showing you the exact gates which will be opened to you. On the fourth night the attack will take place. Are your armies ready and together, waiting for you?"

"It has been planned. When I ride out on the fourth day, all will be ready," Banyen said, choosing his words carefully. As much as he trusted these men, he had no intention of giving them the exact location of the rendezvous point of the Mongol army. He did not regret his decision not to divulge exactly how large the force was, or that it would be joined with Crimean Tatars numbering in the hundreds of thousands.

Motioning to one of the nobles, the boyar spoke, "Tomorrow you'll go with this man and be shown the locations where my men will be stationed. Do this in the evening. I suggest you make yourself unavailable during the day. This way you will not draw attention to your actions. The hour is late, so let us leave one by one, quickly and quietly, so as not to arouse suspicion. Banyen, if I don't see you again before you leave, good fortune."

"What do you gain by helping me? Is overthrowing Ivan enough? I offered you and your men gold for your help, but you refused. I don't understand."

"If Ivan is overthrown or killed, we can place a man of our own in power and be the guiding force behind him, perhaps even one of our boyars. We'll have control of the Russian people and want for nothing. If we lose, then it will be all over for us. What good would the money you offered do us then?"

Banyen held out his hand. "I hope we both succeed. Good fortune to you too, old friend."

Following the boyar's instructions, Banyen rode along the walls of Moscow for the next two nights. During the day be kept to his room except for his meals, which he took in the dining hall. At the end of the second day he waited for the serving girl to lean over him, her smile wanton and her breasts pressing against him each time she served him. Each time he thought of the Russian girl, Katerina would intrude into his mind, forcing the smiling, chestnut-haired girl into the background.

The third and last day of his stay in Moscow began. Normally he did not stay in bed past dawn, but this day he made himself remain beneath the covers and rest. The forced inactivity drove him into a near frenzy as he dressed and went downstairs for his breakfast. His meal finished, he headed for the stables to make sure his stallion was properly fed and watered. The animal had to take him to Smolensk and back to Moscow, and he prayed the stable boy had followed his instructions.

Banyen nodded to the young boy tending the animals and praised his care.

Carefully, his eyes alert, he walked around Kitai Gorod. A vague feeling of unease seemed to be settling over him. Several times he glanced over his shoulder and thought he saw someone following him. Each time, the street was empty. Still, the feeling persisted as he walked back to the inn. Bolting the door of his room, he lay down on the coarse bedding to think. As always, his thoughts drifted to Katerina and their time in the mountains. Each day was bringing him closer to when he would see her again. Somehow he would make it right with her, convince her he had done nothing wrong, that it was her he loved for all eternity. Tomorrow he would ride to Smolensk, and even that ride would bring him nearer to Katerina.

He shook his head to clear the thoughts of Katerina from his mind. He had to think of other things. The Russian servant girl—there was something about her that bothered him. Each time she stared at him, her eyes would drift to the kitchen, as if she were working with someone. He admitted that he wanted her, desired her flesh next to his, but not at the expense of his life. Tonight he would take her and see if his theory was right.

Seating himself at a table in the dining room, he watched through slitted eyes as the girl walked languorously toward him to take his order. As before, she leaned over him, her breasts pressing against his shoulders. She gazed at him with the same bold scrutiny, saying nothing, almost daring him with her sleepy gaze. This time Banyen let his hand trail up the inside of her tunic. She shivered slightly, but made no move to stir from his side. "Come to my room after you finish work tonight." She nodded, and Banyen was not surprised that she didn't bother to ask him which room was his. His mouth tightened when he saw her eyes go furtively to the kitchen, where a figure stood outlined in the doorway.

Banyen ate leisurely, knowing the girl had a full hour of

work ahead of her. When he left the table to go to his room he could feel her eyes boring into his back.

She walked back into the kitchen and held out her hand to the man slouched against the door. "Pay me now!"

"I'll pay you half now and the other half when the merchant you claim is a spy proves to be so. As an Oprichnik I can't afford a mistake."

"My cousin, the cook in the boyar's house, listened outside the doors and overheard the merchant called Ivan Toborschev from Kiev and the others making plans to attack Moscow. Pay me the full sum we agreed on."

"I followed him on several occasions. With what you just told me and his furtive attitude, I'm convinced. He can only mean trouble for the Czar." The Oprichnik placed a small pouch of gold in her outstretched hand. "The hour grows late, make fast work of your seduction."

Banyen waited, and the door opened slowly. He motioned for her to enter, neither saying a word. When he made a move to throw the bolt on the door, the girl threw her arms around his neck, kissing him soundly. He let his hand drop, then cradled her head in his hands, kissing her passionately. All desire left him as he felt her lick at his ear, her hand moving down the side of his body. He forced himself to play her game, and again he kissed her, his hand busy removing her shirt and slipping the peasant skirt down over her hips. When she stood naked before him, her eyes full of lust, he sent her reeling against a chest in the corner of the room.

"If you make so much as a sound, I'll slit your throat," Banyen said quietly. "This way you have a chance to live, unless the man who is coming here kills you. Not a sound, do you understand?" he said, bending over the cowering girl.

He waited, his eyes going from the fearful girl to the door.

Suddenly the door was flung open with such force that it crashed against the wall and came to rest drunkenly against the door frame. "Where is he, you had enough time?" bellowed a voice. "The man is a spy and is to be taken to the Czar!"

Banyen stepped from behind the armoire and grinned. "You're wrong, my friend, she did not have enough time to play your game with me. Did you think I would fall for such an age-old trick?"

Banyen's eyes quickly took in the size of the man charging into the room. He was built like an ox and obviously was just as strong, if his bellow was any indication. Banyen would need his wits about him to deal with the burly man, who had hands the size of a newborn colt's head.

The girl remained mute as the husky peasant charged across the room, the floor shaking beneath his weight. The moment he was abreast of the armoire, Banyen sent it crashing down upon him. A roar of rage filled the room, but Banyen was up and racing out into the corridor, taking the plank steps two at a time in his wild descent.

Outside he ran in the crisp, cold air, skirting the buildings and staying in the shadows and hoping and praying he had enough time to get to his horse before the man called the guards.

Staying in the shadows, he cautiously made his way to the stable and stallion. He saw that a guard was posted at the wide double doors. Banyen circled, came up behind the sentry, and flung his arm around the man's neck. The guard jerked free, yanking out his saber and slicing at the air, missing Banyen. Again the guard lunged and missed. Desperate, Banyen knew he needed a weapon. Somehow he had to get into the stable, where he could grasp something, anything, to defend himself. He couldn't be caught now, not after all he had gone through.

"Dance as if you have eggs on your head." Katerina's words roared in his ears. He laughed, never taking his eyes from the advancing guard. Nimbly, as good as any dancer, Banyen leaped and cavorted and backed himself into the barn. The guard, his eyes wide and full of shock at the insane man in front of him cavorting and laughing, blinked and momentarily lost his advantage in the darkness. As Banyen continued to leap and twist, his hands struck out at the wall, trying to reach for something that would help him defend himself. In one of his jumps he fell backward into a pile of straw. As he flung out his arms to break his fall, his hands found an upended pitchfork that rested in the dry stalks. His hands reached for it as he got to his feet, the fork thrust in front of him. The sentry thrust outward and upward, slicing the handle of the fork in two as he drove Banyen back against the wall. Banyen held on to the fork end, and as the guard lunged at him a second time, Banyen leaped into the air, coming down gracefully as the guard raised his eyes to take in his spectacular jump. Banyen struck out, the tines of the fork finding their mark in the center of the guard's chest.

Quickly Banyen picked up the saber and tossed it across the length of the stable. He saddled his horse, keeping a sharp eye on the door for any further intrusion.

In the cold, bracing air, his mind clear, he realized he couldn't go to the boyar for help; the Oprichniks would be watching, and he couldn't expose his friend to danger. He was alone.

Through the rest of the night he and his horse, who walked behind him, moved under the cover of darkness from one place to another. He watched for a shadow, a move or a noise indicating the soldiers were still on his trail. He felt them, smelled them around him, and although he couldn't see them, he knew they were there. Slowly he made his way toward a doorway in the wall so he could be near an exit. Crouching low, his ears alert, he waited.

As the first rays of dawn lightened the area, exposing the hidden crevices and flushing out all that hid in the night, Banyen made his move and tried the handle of the door nearest him. Slowly he turned the knob and pushed the door with his foot. There before him stood four of Ivan's soldiers. Quickly he slammed the portal and turned to run, grabbing for the reins of the stallion. As he did so, two Oprichniks seized the animal and led him away. Taking a deep breath at his narrow escape, Banyen raced for cover.

The morning hours passed quickly as Banyen and the Oprichniks played a cat-and-mouse game. He had to be free and ready to ride by the noon hour; he had to do something, and he had to do it now. Slowly he inched his way between some barrels, and was surprised by the four soldiers once again. As they lunged for the kill, one by one, Katerina's training rose to the fore. He parried a thrust, a lunge. Steel met steel as he leaped and nimbly danced his way among the startled Oprichniks. His face grim, he looked down at the dead bodies and felt no remorse.

Seeing his stallion being led from the city, he climbed onto the wall and slithered along the top on his belly, praying no one would notice his movements. He lay still as two soldiers reached the gateway, leading his horse. Banyen jumped from the wall, his arms outstretched, knocking the Oprichniks to the ground. Like a streak of lightning, he leaped onto the stallion and headed toward the main road, leaving Red Square, Kitai Gorod, and the White City behind him.

Two hours outside of Moscow, he dismounted and concealed himself in some dense brush, watching to see if he was being followed. He saw and heard nothing to alarm him, so he mounted the Arabian with relief. He sighed wearily as he spurred the horse, urging him to a full canter. The closer he rode to the rendezvous, the more erratically he rode the stallion. He knew he couldn't travel straight toward the waiting armies, for word was out that an attack was imminent. At the last moment he deliberately rode through Smolensk. When he was sure he was not being followed, he continued on to the meeting point. Silently he prayed that the armies were still waiting.

* * *

Katerina was beside herself with anger and concern. "Uncle, where is he?" she snapped. "We stand ready to ride and can't make a move without him." Suddenly her anger gave way to concern. "Uncle, what if something happened to him? What if he never arrives?"

"Banyen will be here. Where is your faith, your courage? You can't allow your men to see you in a fit of tears. He will be here," he said firmly. "Any man who wants to taste Ivan's blood as badly as he does will not let us down. Compose yourself. Check your men and see if all is in readiness."

"I've checked them five times. I can't stand this endless waiting. We've been waiting for five days and now we must wait again. I don't know how those Tatars can sit so placidly. Nothing seems to bother them."

"When you number in the hundreds of thousands, why would you worry? They can overrun anything in their path. I'm happy they're on our side." The Khan grinned. "Their leader rides toward us. Perhaps he, too, is becoming concerned."

A tall man rode majestically on a sleek brown horse, the animal strutting its pedigree. The deep eyes of the rider bored into the Khan. His body looked immense in the quilted vest which covered him to his elbows, knees, and up the back of his neck to the bottom of his hat. The heavy padding would stop the blow of a saber, Katerina knew, just as the heavy sheepskin vests and coats protected her men and herself.

"Where is the man we wait for? Time is growing short, and we have a four-hour ride to the city of Moscow," his deep voice boomed.

"He will arrive within the hour," the Khan said reassuringly to the chief.

The Tatar leader was impatient and in no mood for further delays. "My men are ready to ride now. Our slave trade works on arrangements also, and promises have been made to deliver girls to ships that wait on the Black Sea. You see the baskets my men have placed on each side of their horses? Those baskets will each hold a young girl. When we attack Moscow, we steal the girls, and then we ride back to our village by the sea, where the ships wait. It will take us three days of hard riding to get back to Crimea, but my men will ride straight through, stopping only to rest their horses. My arrangements with the captains of the vessels and other slave traders were for the arrival of the girls three days from now. If your man doesn't arrive within the hour, we'll ride ahead and storm Moscow alone." Angrily he jerked the reins of the horse, turned his back on the Khan, and rode to wait at the head of his army.

The Khan's eyes were furious. Why hadn't Banyen arrived? Something must have happened to him.

Suddenly a guard shouted from a distance, "Prince Banyen is coming! That cloud of dust you see in the distance is the prince!"

Katerina's heart raced madly, her anger forgotten. Thank God he was safe! Once again she would see her love. Her eyes never left the speck of dust. She watched, her heart pounding, as the speck grew larger and larger, until Banyen and his black stallion stood before them.

Time was crucial. There wasn't a moment for anything but the discussion of the plan. Banyen drew a map in the dirt, representing the wall around Kitai Gorod and the Kremlin, as the Khan, the Tatar chief, and Katerina watched and listened. He explained that the boyars would be stationed at the points he circled, ready to open the gates at the first chime of the bells at sunset. He explained about dividing up the army to surround the walled cities and the charge down the main road through the Wooden and White Cities. When he finished, he looked up and smiled at Katerina. With that smile, all was right between them once more. There was no need for words. The Khan and the Tatar chief decided on the disposition of the men who would surround the walls and those who would lead the charge down the main road. Katerina asked if she and her men could join those who would ride through on the main road. The Khan and the Tatar agreed. It was decided that Banyen and a division of the Khan's men would make up part of the same contingent.

Plans finished, each leader aware of his part, they assumed their places at the head of their armies. All was in readiness. The signal was given, and the earth shook under the thousands of hooves that pounded it, carrying death and destruction toward Moscow, just as the first snowfall of winter began.

The soldier trembled as he reported to Ivan the news of a spy in the city. He waited, a feeling of dread settling over him, hoping, wishing the Czar would dismiss him. Instead, Ivan's face closed in rage.

"Spy? Spy? Possible attack? What are you talking about? You must be mad! No one can spy on me! No one can attack me! My Oprichniks see to my safety." He wrung his hands, and his eyes rolled wildly in his head as saliva with bits of chewed food dribbled from his mouth. "Spy! Begone, soldier, before I have you beheaded before me for such a stupid story. Take him out of here. Get him out!" the Czar shouted insanely. Ivan pounded his gold staff on the floor in a frenzy as the soldier ran for his life.

The boyars and nobles whispered among themselves with the news. Could it be so? Tales of a spy in Moscow were an everyday happening. What could one man do? Their bellies full of breakfast, and in a rush to escape from Ivan, they paid their homage to the Czar and left the room, deciding Moscow and the Kremlin were not in any peril.

Several boyars among them smiled knowingly to themselves as they left the room and continued with their affairs of court.

Chapter 24

The population of Moscow's five cities were relaxing around their evening meal as the sun set in the west. Without warning, thousands of men on horseback stormed through the City of Wood. Everything and anything that stood in the path of this well-honed machine of destruction was slaughtered. The city became a tinderbox blazing across the night skies as the Mongols, Tatars, and Cossacks rode into the White City. Within an hour, it too was leveled, all killed and the buildings set aflame. While the city crumpled, the second segment of the massive army reached Kitai Gorod. The boyars, at their appointed spots, opened the gates for the thousands of Tatars and Mongols who poured into the Kremlin and Red Square. The battle raged as they fought on the streets, on the walls, and in the palace.

The citizenry died by the thousands in a vain effort to flee the horde. Many sought safety near the Kremlin, hoping to take refuge behind the gates, not knowing they had been opened to the enemy.

As the battle waned, the Tatars began their search for slaves. Moscow burned like a torch in the night. The Moscow River became so choked with the bodies of people that the course of the river was diverted, the waters crimson for miles downstream.

Katerina worked her way through the city, searching for Banyen and Khan Afstar. She galloped in the direction of Red Square, still without any sight of the two men. As she approached St. Basil's, she looked up. There, for all to see, was her uncle on the execution block where Ivan performed his mass murders and tortures, his body sliced and cut to pieces. She turned away, fighting back the tears, hoping with all her heart that she would find Banyen alive. She rode Whitefire into the Kremlin, looking, searching, weaving the animal between broken, lifeless bodies. She found Banyen sprawled on the steps of the Terem Palace. When she saw how motionless he was, she panicked and screamed. "Banyen!" tore from her mouth, from her heart, as she slid from the horse and ran to him. "Let him live! He can't be dead!" she cried out.

Bending over the still body, she turned him over, searching for a wound. There was a deep gash across the left side of his head, oozing blood. She put her head to his chest and listened. He was alive but unconscious. Quickly she removed her outer garments and ripped off a sleeve from her shirt. Wrapping it around his head, she covered the wound. She donned her outer garments once again as the snow began to cover the bloodstained streets. Before it got too cold, she knew, she would have to move Banyen. Slipping one arm beneath his back, she lifted him to a sitting position. The weight of his body proved too much for her. Gently she lowered him to the steps and called for help.

A low moan escaped Banyen as he tried to move his head, his eyes glazed and full of pain.

"You're injured, Banyen, you must lie still. You must remain quiet until help comes. I'm with you now. It's over, Banyen, it's finished."

"What happened? Ivan, where is he? I must keep my

promise and put my saber through his heart," he said, trying to struggle to his feet. "Katerina, where is Ivan, you must tell me, it can't all have been for nothing. Where is he? Is he alive?"

"If you lie still, I'll tell you. You're still weak from your head wound, and the gash on your leg needs tending. You must forget the Czar."

Before she could utter another word, Banyen shouted, "Katerina, where is Ivan? Will you tell me or must I seek him out myself?"

"He's gone, Banyen."

"Gone! What do you mean, gone? Gone where?" he demanded harshly.

"When we captured the Terem Palace, the boyars and nobles were trapped inside. They were the ones that told us Ivan and his family escaped with the Kremlin treasury. The boyars informed us that the Czar headed toward the north of Russia. Your saber will not draw Ivan's blood this day, Banyen. The Czar is a tormented, insane man. What pleasure would you gain in killing a madman? Tell me I'm right, Banyen. There would be no revenge in killing a diseased dog, so why persist in your desire? There has been enough death. The Khan . . . he's . . . he's dead."

Banyen's eyes closed. What she said was true. It was over.

"As usual, you're right," Banyen said, trying to force a smile. "It no longer seems important to me. If I set out after him, I would be as insane as he is. One day he will reap his just rewards. Tell me of Afstar."

"My uncle . . . the Khan . . . your friend . . . The Russians strung him up on Ivan's torture rack in Red Square. I couldn't take him down. I had to look for you."

"Katerina, where is my stallion?"

"I haven't seen him."

"My black is never far from me." He whistled two short

bursts, and the stallion appeared. Banyen grinned. "See, he's never far from his master. Horses, horses, I almost forgot—have you found the Cosars?"

"No, not yet. My men have been searching, but when I could no longer see you or my uncle after the battle, I came looking for you both."

"Let us go to Red Square so the men can take Afstar back to Sibir and give him a chief's burial. Then I'll help you find the herd."

"Are you sure you're all right?" Katerina asked, not convinced he was ready to ride.

"My head throbs and I'm a little weak, not just from the cut but from last night's escape, this morning's battle, and the ride from Moscow and back again. I need rest and food, but first the Cosars. Katerina," he whispered huskily, "there is so much I want to say."

"Later, later we'll talk," she said, kissing him lightly on the mouth.

Together they rode into Red Square to the rack where her uncle was tied. They cut the ropes and gently lifted his battered body. Banyen tied the lifeless Khan to his horse and mounted behind Afstar.

"Now for the Cosars, Katerina."

Their progress was slow, as the streets were strewn with the bodies of men, women, and children. "It's a sad sight to see, but innocent people are always the victims of war," Banyen said sadly. As they proceeded around the cities, soldiers and Mongols still skirmished here and there. A Russian, hidden away, would try to make his escape and chase would be given.

"I think we'll find the horses somewhere around the palace. We'll ride in that direction," Banyen said with assurance.

They rode toward the Terem Palace, inside the Kremlin. Searching on foot and on horseback, they found nothing.

Kostya, with a small patrol, also reported no success in finding the Cosars.

Angry and frustrated, Katerina lashed out. "The raid on the Tereks placed the horses in Moscow. Gregory sold them to Ivan. What did he do with them? Did he sell them off before we stormed Moscow?" She turned to Banyen. "Do you think the Czar sold them to someone else?"

"No. If Ivan bought them, he wanted them for himself and his bodyguards, the Oprichniks. Ivan would never sell something that was one of a kind. Has anyone checked outside the wall behind the palace?"

Kostya's men looked at each other and shook their heads.

"It's possible Ivan had them taken out of the city when he heard it was being attacked. If he fled with the Kremlin's treasury, he wouldn't waste time on the Cosars. They must be somewhere outside the walls of the city." Calling two of the Mongols to him, he ordered them to remove the Khan's body from the stallion. "Secure a litter to the back of a horse with a stout rope and pull his body home," he ordered gruffly.

Beyond the Kremlin walls, a quarter mile away, a hill rose up out of the flatness. Narrowing his oblique gaze, Banyen was aware that the attack now came from the west. The outlying section was remote, and he was sure no man was near. As they rode closer, noises could be heard coming from behind the hill. When they reached the top, there stood the mighty herd of Cosars, in the middle of snow-covered brush and dense fir trees. Katerina was beside herself with happiness. She leaped from Whitefire, and was about to run into the herd of horses when Banyen shouted for her to stop.

"Why should I?"

Without warning, a small band of the Oprichniks emerged from within the herd. They had hidden themselves among the horses, hoping to escape with a Cosar or two. As they charged toward Katerina, Banyen, Kostya, and the patrol swooped down, killing them in the first rush.

"The next time wait until your men are sure there aren't any Russians lurking about," Banyen said harshly.

"Yes, my master." Katerina grinned as she ran into the herd and seemingly smothered herself in them. Now, she had everything. Now, she had avenged her village, its people, and her father. She had fulfilled the promise she made to herself and Mikhailo: the Cosars once again, and forever this time, belonged to the Don Cossacks. The secret and the horses were still theirs. At last she could rest. It was finished.

The Mongols avenged the raids on Kazan and Astrakhan, but had lost their leader. But now Prince Banyen could lead them, and he would have a Khanate to rule. She had her Cosars, and the old men would soon have a hut or two ready in Volin. By now there would be a compound fenced in for the horses which she would bring back. Lastly, the Tatars had their baskets filled with young women for their slave trade. Everyone had been successful, save Banyen. He would have to settle for victory without the blood of Ivan on his sword. But his people and the village of Kazan were avenged, so it should be enough. Katerina prayed it would be enough.

Banyen sat atop his black Arabian, his bloody sword in his hand, watching Katerina running through the horses in the white snow. He knew he loved her deeply.

"It's time to take your Cosars where they belong."

Katerina ran to Whitefire, who whinnied in delight at the scent of the mares. She leaped onto his back and laughed aloud. "Kostya, we ride for home. Inform your men. The Mongols will drive the herd to Volin."

"Banyen, can you make the ride, or should we prepare a litter for you?" she asked, her face full of concern.

"There's no cause for worry, Katerina. The wound on my leg is a mere scratch. The bleeding has stopped, and my head is clear. We have much to say to each other," he said huskily. "Many decisions have to be made. And," he said softly, "you must be the one to make them."

Slowly the animals followed the Mongols and the Cossacks to the road that would lead them to Volin. Katerina's eyes were misty as she saw Kostya raise his hand, the Cossacks shouting in victory as they thundered down the snow-covered road.

They rode in silence, intent on their own thoughts, the Cossacks and Kostya long gone from their sight. The moment Whitefire's hooves set down on the plain, he threw back his head and snorted, rearing up on his hind legs and almost unseating Katerina. She laughed as she gave him his head, and the white stallion pounded his way across the familiar ground. He galloped like the wind, the girl on his back laughing and shrieking in delight. Once she turned her head and saw Banyen hard pressed to keep pace with Whitefire. She knew he would catch her, and what better place than here, on the steppe where it all began? Only this time, atop Whitefire, she knew she could elude him if she wanted to. Now the dream was behind her and she welcomed the reality. "Easy, boy, he has to catch us."

Imperceptibly, the stallion slowed, and Banyen gained on the racing woman. The moment he was abreast of her, he reached out and pulled her from the animal's back onto his own racing mount. Katerina giggled in delight as her legs flailed the air, her arms clutching Banyen, whose own seat was unsteady on the racing, snorting steed. Suddenly he, too, laughed, and they both slid from the horse into the deep snow. In their tumble, Banyen's pack slid from the horse's rump and came to rest at their feet.

"All the comforts of the mountains," Banyen said, reaching for the sable carpet.

"Love me," Katerina whispered throatily.

"Forever," Banyen said huskily, his mouth finding hers. "For now, forever more."

"Banyen, where will we go, what will we do?"

"It has to be your decision, Katerina."

"While I waited in Smolensk for you and the others, I made my decision. My plan is to give Kostya and Princess Halya a filly and a colt, and, of course, some of the other Cosars. I can't take a chance of this ever happening again. I would never feel secure if I and I alone kept the secret. I'll set aside certain conditions, but he will be in charge of his own breeding in Moldavia. I can either go back to Volin with my horses or I can go with you to the Khanate that is yours now to rule. I want you to help me make the right choice. When I am with you, my judgment is faulty. Where will you be happy?" she asked, gently tracing the outline around his oblique eyes.

Banyen laughed. "The day you make a faulty decision will be the day I'll take to my bed, never to stand on my legs again. You could never be happy separated from the Cosars. I have no desire to rule the Khanate; there are others far better suited than I. I vote to go with you to Volin, where we will work with the Cosars together. Has it been decided that Kostya's men will stay in Volin?"

"I offered them their freedom and they chose to stay." Katerina smiled. "Tell me, are they Cossacks or not? I left none dead in Moscow, and only two men carry flesh wounds. They're Cossacks, and what better place for them to live than Volin, the Don village? One day there will be none left that remembers they were not Cossacks by birth.

"Love me, Banyen."

"Always, for all eternity," he said huskily as he crushed her lips to his.